LIVING LEGEND

BOOK ONE

ALLIE SHANTE

"The dark and the light, they exist side by side."

*To my thirteen-year-old self who thought writing and publishing a book
was merely a dream...
Time to do your happy dance sweet girl.
We did it.*

*Also, to my mom and husband, thank you for being...you. I would never
have done this without you. And frankly, thank you for not giving up on
me or letting me give up on myself.*

CHAPTER ONE

DANI

Blood.

It was the only dramatically consistent smell down there; that and sweat. They were so incredibly strong, I hardly registered them anymore. There were a few other, less potent odors that lingered for short periods of time, but nothing like the pungent scent of sweat and blood.

Helplessness was a common one, fear another. The newest souls were steeped in fear, but eventually, it started to mold into something else. It contorted itself into something I could never place, a mix of agony and soul-crushing longing for death that never comes. I was their jailer, their torturer, their *misery*. I provided the constant pain for others to gawk at, like animals on display, and I thrived off it.

Purgatory. That's where I resided, where I was beloved and envied by so many. I had the occasional memories, tiny snippets of a time before Purgatory, but nothing to deeply hold onto, nothing I could piece together to make anything close to a concrete past.

A high-pitched shriek brought me out of my thoughts, enough to make me press my hand against the red stone wall. I was still here, in this *place*.

The place with blood-stained walls and floors, with creaks and moans that came from nowhere and everywhere at once.

The place I called home.

A weathered, gray stone door between two towering columns stood in front of me. Handles shaped like serpents hissed as I approached. It was a soothing sound; one I'd grown accustomed to throughout time. Another shriek followed by a whimper hit my ears again. It was pure music – no, pure *magic*. My blood boiled as I inched closer to the door, wrapping my hand around the snakehead to pull it open.

The humidity hit me first, hot and molten. The scuffling of feet and excited shrieks caught my attention next. I knew the noise came from the risers along the back of the torture chamber. Torture arena was probably a better name. Demons got there early to get as close as possible, sometimes leaning over the dividers just to possibly catch a drop of blood. The risers practically spat dust when anyone touched them, but they held up, even with all the commotion. Brimstone shards and what looked like sand littered the floor. I felt sweat start to prickle on the back of my neck from the fires burning in their holders along the walls. I could taste the thick heat, but even more, I could smell the pain. I could *taste* it, the unbridled desire to surrender to death but never getting the chance. I let my nose guide me to where the feelings felt strongest.

My prey looked older than middle aged. His eyes were covered with thick black cotton, tied over thin blonde hair peppered with gray. His skin was ashen, almost ghost-like. *Typical*. He was nothing special. I didn't ask many questions about the dead brought down for me to poke and prod; it seemed pointless when I only wanted to hear pleas for mercy riddled with agony. Blood trickled down his arms, his knees, his temples, even his belly button. His clothes were torn, soiled with sweat and something brown I was sure to all Hell wasn't dirt. I lifted an eyebrow, surveying the scene when the sound of steel-toed boots stopped next to me.

"We loosened him up for you," Elise smirked.

I let my eyes slide to her gray ones. "Seems like you did more than that."

She let out a sharp, echoing laugh, her silky black hair swaying around her neck. "I only made one small cut with a dull blade. The other little shits wanted their fun; blame them." Elise motioned towards the lesser demons.

Lesser demons came in various shapes and sizes, some with the stereotypical horns and tails, some with skin that perpetually bled, others with hoofed feet. Most were demons forged in Hell by Lucifer himself, sent here for Lilith's amusement.

Lilith owned this realm, hers to do with as she pleased. She'd filled me with power and a blood lust that wouldn't quit when I arrived. She hardly ever looked at me anymore, but I was still the favorite.

The bloody thirsty looks on their faces proved they weren't satisfied. Elise shrugged. "They wanted to impress you, the attention seeking little fucks."

Elise had been my friend since I first woke up here. Well, friend may be a loose term, on her end at least. I'd used the phrase 'friendship' one time and had gotten a disgruntled sound back, so I'd buried the need for a friendly tether and settled for a benevolent alliance. We'd made an art form out of continuous torture, always with an audience to marvel at our masterpieces. Throughout the years, I'd become smoother with a blade, more demanding with a dagger, more in control of my power to create the loudest crack of bone, the hardest crunch of a nose. At some point, Elise had gifted me her respect and her allegiance. I became, as she reminded me, a 'lethal idol for the lowly fucking demons in this god-forsaken place'.

I turned to face her, but she knew what I wanted before I could ask. Her long fingers intertwined around the leather hilt of a small blade -- small, about the length of my forearm, but sharp, gleaming in the firelight. The weapon had razor-like slits in the middle and a tip that curved up to a precise point, making it easier to yank souls and innards out of bodies. I'd learned small cuts, minuscule slices, could bleed for hours, but those cuts wouldn't kill. Time and pure patience were the sick enemy of anyone in my chair.

"Be a fucking boss." Elise let the blade slip from her fingers and fall gracefully into mine. It carried a weight only someone bonded with it would be able to comprehend. It was the weapon I always started with and the weapon I always ended with.

My name was engraved on one side of the blade—DANI. I ran my fingers over the deep grooves of the letters, feeling my skin warm. I could feel passion filtering through my veins. My fingers gripped the hilt, each digit snapping into place next to another.

I made the soul of my prey rage and boil before using the curved tip of my dagger to pull it out and tear it to shreds. Souls weren't pure mist or clouds; they were living and breathing. As much as angels hated to admit it, demons had souls too, some deep inside and covered in shadows, others with purpose, with discipline and strength. I was told I had a mixture of both, but I leaned towards the latter. The extraction of souls, the mutilation of them, had grown to be my salvation.

Elise moved to the man in the middle of the room, bound to a leather chair. She circled behind him, leaning her head on his shoulder. I turned to give her a terse nod, and she untied the knot at the back of his head, whispering something in his ear as she went.

He was terrified.

I was more than ready to proceed. He was already so pale, but as he assessed the room, he turned ash white. "Please, let me go!"

I could feel the crowd, the lesser demons around the perimeter, watching to see what I'd do next. I smiled, licking my lips, and took my time, letting the seconds tick by with every slow stride forward. Once in front of him, I bent down, resting my hands on the arms of the chair, wet with what I assumed was his sweat. I let my blade pierce the material, digging in with a harsh rip. I smirked, watching him shake his head, pleading with widened eyes. He was no different from all the others I'd played with. He reminded me of my first ever victim. Every new soul made the oldest one fade away; to give them a second thought would be to show weakness. *Weakness* was something I couldn't afford.

Still, you never forget your first.

"You don't have to do this. I'll go back to my cell. I can do hard labor! An eternity of work I could endure, I swear," he begged, his voice cracking with fear.

"Back to your cell?" I stopped him before he could ask again.

He nodded so vigorously, blood flung from his hair to the floor. Elise toed it with her boot, smearing it onto the stones.

"You think you've had enough?" I questioned, letting my eyes drift over him from head to toe. I lifted my blade and drew small circles on his thigh with the point, letting it caress his flesh. I was careful not to press too hard, lest I make a premature slice. He flinched, trying to scramble back, but to no avail. The restraints on his wrists pulled tighter the more he resisted.

I stopped circling, his silence palpable. "I asked you a question." I pulled my eyebrows together. "What's your name?"

His Adam's apple bobbed as he swallowed hard. "Luke."

I nodded, biting my lip. "I asked you a question, Luke. Do you think you've had enough?" I brought the blade to his throat, letting the tip push into that beautiful carotid artery, just enough to scare him without drawing blood. The demons around us growled impatiently, craving their fill of blood and anguish.

"I do. I promise, I've had enough." His eyes were a shade of blue I'd never seen before, the kind of blue the sky would be -- if I remembered it correctly. I didn't remember much of life before. Those gorgeous eyes tried to plead his case.

They tried. Boy, did they try.

I shrugged my shoulders and took a step back. I could see him physically relax, thinking his prayers were answered, that I would be merciful. My eyes narrowed; I could feel the predatory nature rising inside of me at his assumption. I spoke slowly as I said, "I'm the one who says when you've had enough, Luke." A large smile spread across my face as his eyes widened.

He was not winning this battle.

I took the blade by the hilt and held it over his thigh again, inches away from an area of untouched skin. I needed to do what I did best, what so many demons came to watch and marvel in. "Luckily for me, we are just beginning." I slammed the blade into his thigh, watching as he screamed in agony. Before he could take another breath, I pulled it out swiftly. Blood sprayed in all directions, spouting out and pouring over his knee onto the floor.

The crowd roared.

Luke choked out a cry when I plunged the blade back into the same spot, this time moving it around on the inside, see-sawing it into the wound, making it bigger, breaking the skin so much, I could start to see muscle. Blood flooded out, but it wasn't enough. Heat filled my cheeks and neck, blood splattered onto my hand as I drove the sharp tip into his chest, not piercing his heart just yet. Trickles of blood dribbled from his chest, drop, drop, drop.

I leaned forward to his ear, licking his lobe, and asking, "have you had enough yet, Luke?" I pulled back, looking at his face, hoping to see more crying and sobbing, but all I saw was Luke looking past me. I didn't hear the crowd anymore, and I glanced over at Elise, also looking behind me, intrigue masking her normal glare.

I let out a low growl at whatever had gotten in the way of my performance, holding my blade so tightly, I felt my hand cramp. My eyes were met with a light, not bright enough to blind me, but bright enough to know it didn't belong. Purgatory was no place for that kind of illumination. I started to inch closer to it when Elise pushed me back a few steps. She shook her head, a sign to wait. The demons around us whispered in hushed tones but made no move closer.

A figure appeared, rimmed in light, the silhouette of man. The sound he made as he walked onto the stone was light, as if he were floating, only his toes meeting stone floor.

Average height. Shoulder length red hair. Not a bright, obnoxious red, but the color of red wine. I noticed his green eyes and chiseled jaw, but what I couldn't pull my eyes from were his wings.

Angel wings. Large, commanding, angelic wings.

Delicate, intricate thin feathers sprouted through each wing. They were pulled in towards his back, not hard to miss. Each feather had a gold tint that sparkled in the light. I knew they didn't walk around with those things out all the time, so he was doing it just for show. It was laughable.

Most demons had wings; I possessed them and so did Elise. We really didn't have much of a use for them, but they were there, all the same. They weren't as beautiful and voluminous, but they had a rare beauty that stunned when we actually showed them off.

Elise seemed highly uninterested in any of it. "Fuck's sake. For people with manners, you sure know how to make a fucking scene. Ever heard of knocking, or are you just too good for that?" She rolled her eyes, stepping in front of me, before he could get any closer.

Two other angels walked out with the red head, their wings just as white, but the gold tint sparingly dim in comparison. They each had two swords strapped behind their backs, no smiles on their faces. They were sentries, if I had to guess, but the red headed man held up his hand for them to stop.

"We mean no harm," he finally spoke in a deep, commanding voice

Elise scoffed. "I find that hard—"

I interrupted her thought, stepping in front of her. "Why are you here? The only time your kind comes here is to blame us for something." I placed my hands on my hips, waiting for his excuse. He looked a bit stunned at my demand, but I couldn't have cared less.

He raised an eyebrow. "Who here is the Soul Seether?" He looked around, seeming to make eye contact with each demon patron, like he were counting every being, weighing the numbers in his head.

I snorted. "Right in front of you. Who are you?"

He peered down at me as realization glazed over his eyes. He looked over his shoulder at the other men, but they just shook their heads and continued to stare into the distance.

"You're the Soul Seether?" he asked in disbelief.

I sneered and rolled my eyes. "That's what I said. I'm not really a fan of repeating myself."

His eyes widened as he searched for an answer, I could see he didn't know the question to. "I'm sorry, I thought you would be a..." He pressed his lips together before blowing out a breath. "I thought you would be a man."

I rolled my eyes again. Angels and their way with words. "Pity for you, I'm sure. Now, who the fuck are you, and why are you looking *specifically* for me?"

He ran a hand through his hair and let out a long sigh, mumbling something about being in for a surprise. "I'm Ariel, and your presence is requested."

I clasped my hand on my chest in feign delight, as if I'd just been asked to a royal party, blinking rapidly. Elise mimicked me before we both leaned over in a fit of laughter. "I would love to accompany you, but I'm a little busy right now." I pointed my blade towards the bloodied man still strapped to the chair, wiping blood from my face with my free hand. His head was dipped down, his hair falling around his motionless body. He had either passed out or died from the intense blood loss. I severely hoped it was the former.

Ariel looked between us, as if he was trying to figure out the joke. "You can either come with me willingly, or we can do this forcefully."

A threat. I wanted to laugh so hard, my stomach would hurt for days after.

I could see the steam from Elise's nose at his threat, no laughter to be found. Her fingers pulled together into fists at her sides. I let a simmering growl leave my lips, warning her to calm down before we had bigger issues than a bold angel with a death wish.

"Where exactly am I being summoned? Limbo? The place is a bore, but I'll go," I countered, hoping it wasn't Limbo, seeing as it was just an open void where the lost souls went. It's truly a valley of unforgiving boredom. Some get trapped in limbo forever, eternally roaming, never knowing any kind of peace.

"Not quite. You are being summoned to Heaven's Gate," Ariel replied.

I blinked. My mouth opened, but nothing came out. It was as if the breath had left my body.

Elise spoke for me. "Heaven's Gate? That pretentious place? I honestly think it's worse than Heaven."

One of the two sentry angels came up to Ariel's side, holding a pair of golden handcuffs. He lingered close enough to me that I could see the sweat on his temples. Both my eyebrows raised as I assessed the cuffs. Magic dampening handcuffs.

"If you wanted to play, all you had to do was ask." I stuck my tongue between my teeth and reached my hand out to smooth down his cheek. He brushed it off, muttering something about demon females, but there was a spark in his eye that went away just as quickly as it appeared.

"What is this all about?" I questioned, curiosity creeping up as I looked past the sentry and locked eyes with Ariel.

"I cannot discuss that here," he said with striking authority. Ah, so he was someone of influence back in angel land.

I eyed the handcuffs again. "I have to wear those?"

"For protection," he answered sternly.

Elise whipped her head towards him so quickly, her chin length hair swished from side to side. "We all know the only thing those cuffs do is protect you pricks from our *dangerous* magic."

The tension grew thick, so suffocatingly thick that I had to break it before more blood spilled. My curiosity was peaked at seeing how the other half lived. I was a moth to a flame -- something inside me was pushing me to go, so I went with my gut, but not without a contingency plan. "I'll wear the cuffs and go with you, but I have one request."

"I'm not at liberty to grant requests for...demons." He had to chew on the word a minute before he spit it out.

I pretended to ponder his response for a moment, flipping my weapon to tap the pommel on my chin before I responded. "You either honor my request, or I remain here. We both know what will happen if you try to take me." I gestured to in the demons in the stands above, hungry for the bloodshed Ariel stole from them. "I don't think they appreciated you dropping in unannounced."

Ariel pretended to fix his stark teal suit collar with a shaky hand, letting out an exasperated sigh. "What is your request?"

"Elise comes with me. Take it or leave it." I nodded towards her.

His eyes narrowed. "That's your request? To bring your ill-mannered friend?"

"Fuck off," Elise spat back, lifting her middle finger. I nodded as an answer. Ariel looked back to quickly confer with his comrades, granting me the opportunity to flip my blade silently and swiftly into a more compact size, sliding it into the pocket of my shorts. The cuffs had no jurisdiction on magic that had already been done.

The third angel remained in the back shadows, and now rounded to Ariel's side with another set of handcuffs. Elise and I laid out our wrists, about to be trapped in angelic magic. I felt myself settle the moment they locked into place; there were no longer a million whispers in my mind.

I turned around towards the crowd, hunger and waiting still clear on their faces. "He can be your reward for your patience." I motioned towards Luke's limp body and watched as the demons descended to his chair and encircled him in a massive swarm.

"I fucking hate you for this," Elise stated as we walked behind the angels towards the light, which I now recognized as a portal.

"Aren't you the least bit curious about how the other half lives?"

Elise turned around right in front of the portal. Ariel crossed his arms, clearly irritated with us already. "No, Dani, I'm really fucking not."

"You could have told me to eat shit and go by myself," I pointed out.

She let out a loud groan before turning back to the portal, disappearing into the winding tunnel.

Ariel gestured forward. "Go on."

The closer I got to the light, the more I realized it was actually quite blinding. There were portals to get to every realm, but unless you resided there, finding those portals or even getting someone to open one up for you wasn't easy. Even I hadn't seen a portal up close and personal. I stepped into the winding white wisps. Another step, another, then another.

I felt my body shift forward and a bit to the side. I felt off balance, but I was upright.

I blinked.

Suddenly, I saw blue skies and white clouds, grass, flowers, *fruit*. Angels soared above me, drifting, letting the wind take them up as far as their wings would take them. The trees seemed to disappear into the clouds above, giving the illusion that they went on forever.

I felt a small shove to my shoulder, forcing me to move forward to where Ariel and Elise moved down a gravel paved pathway.

"This way." Ariel stalked toward a gate of thick marble. Behind it sat a building of multicolored stones: red, beige, and gray in various clusters around the exterior. It was a *castle*. The tops of each peak had symmetrical, curved, burgundy rafters, the tops built high into the clouds, much like the trees. The gates seemed to tower over all of us, and instead of serpents as the handles, wings took their place. Two bored looking angels opened the gates, letting us pass. If they had any knowledge as to why I was here, their faces revealed nothing.

"We will hold you in a room on the ground floor until we're ready. I'm sure you know how to be on your best behavior." Ariel glared at us with skeptical eyes.

"I think we have different ideas of best behaviors." I winked at him, and he scowled. He shook his head, grumbling something under his breath.

Heaven's Gate: its own world from the actual Heaven above it. Two demons roaming around, handcuffs or not, was a risk. Good thing I happened to love a little risk.

CHAPTER TWO

NICK

I raised my sword and swung upward, meeting Reese's sword in the middle. The clashing sound reverberated through the entire training room. I pushed forward, barreling my weight towards him as beads of sweat flung from my forehead. He bucked forward, forcing me to release my stance and fall back. I felt the cool air from the fan above through my drenched shirt, sleeves sticking to my biceps. Reese thrusted his sword towards me, assuming, as he always did, that he had the upper hand. I darted to the left, the silver tinge of the blade sliding past my abdomen.

The look of pure confusion on Reese's face was priceless and a little daunting, as we'd practiced this sparring set up dozens of times in the last two and a half hours. Reese had complained the entire time, even though he knew that you had to make a request to even be able to use a training room on the weekends.

The walls in the training room were gray, one with a long rectangular mirror, another with a one-way window, and yet another covered in training weapons. The Skies had six training rooms, one for each floor. The Skies was a sort of general hub for all the top positions in Heaven's Gate. It was shaped like a castle, but no royalty resided there. Reese would have opted for a lower floor with less stairs to climb, but I personally enjoyed the sixth floor, with its spectacular view of the grounds and all the messenger angels who flew above them.

I caught his right ankle with my right foot, hooking my ankle around it and lifting it off the ground, causing him to tumble forward before he could steady himself. I grabbed his sword as it flew out of his grasp. His slim body made a less than graceful thud onto the scuffed mat.

"At least you used your hands this time to brace your fall," I laughed, "instead of your face."

Reese only grunted in response; his face still squashed on the mat. His tumbles of blonde hair splayed out wildly around his head.

I rolled my eyes. "This is your own doing, you know."

He pushed off the mat, bending to stretch out his back. He clasped his hands together, pulling down to stretch out his long arms. "I did everything you told me to. You must have changed something halfway, sneaky bastard."

"No, you just don't listen." I tossed his sword back to him. "You, sir, have tunnel vision."

"Tunnel what?"

I walked behind him, pointing my sword so that it was perfectly aligned and parallel to him, forcing him to lift his own sword and follow suit. "Tunnel vision. As in, you only see what's in front of you and never look at the perimeter."

I patted his shoulder, coming around to stand in front of him again. "Your eyes have to be everywhere, or else, you know, you could die." I backed up, tapping the tip of my blade to his. "One more time." I could feel the heat in my cheeks; I already knew the color of my neck matched Reese's flushed skin. I could feel the ticking of my pulse without having to lay a finger at my neck.

Reese nodded, taking his position again.

"Fuck." Reese slid his hands over his face as he laid on his back on the mat. I peered down at him, shaking my head, my sword inches from his throat.

"Reese, your only problem—" I started before he interrupted.

"I swear if you say tunnel vision one more God forsaking time, I'm going to strangle you in your sleep."

I chuckled, placing the sword over my shoulder and stretching my hand out to help him up. Once he was up on his feet, we moved to re-rack our weapons.

Reese placed his sword on the rack with a heave. "I don't know how many times I've told you, Nick, I'm not a swordsman. Never have been, never will be," Reese stated between breaths, rolling his shoulders back.

"You aren't going to get very far with just one weapon skill," I countered, grabbing a towel before throwing one at Reese and grabbing a water bottle.

"Not necessarily," he argued. "You're the sword guy and I'm the one with the bow and arrow. Perfect team." He lifted his hand for a high five, but I ignored it and swung open the door, propping it open.

Reese was a prodigal marksman with a bow, something we'd noticed as children. He'd had the highest scores throughout our training and had been given many handmade bows when we were teens, but he'd acquired a taste for sleeker and shiner ones as we grew.

As we walked down a hallway towards the showers, I heard my name called by a familiar voice. I peered over my shoulder to confirm my thoughts.

"Nicholas!" Markus Seraph, a short, gray-haired angel, shouted again. He wore a teal suit with velvet lapels, the various rings on his fingers sparkling in the mid-day light. "Nicholas!"

Reese muttered under his breath near my ear. "What did you do?"

I smacked him across the back of the head, and a swift *fuck* left his lips. I smirked, moving my attention back to Markus, now only a few feet away.

He paused as he caught his breath, placing a hand on his chest and another one his knee. He smiled at me and then at Reese. "Nicholas Cassial, I am—" he began, but I cut him off.

"I'm aware of who you are, Markus. We all are."

Reese's hazel eyes scanned Markus from his pointed shoes to his thinning hair. He was clearly contemplating whether he could leave the situation without any backlash.

Markus nodded and continued. "Mr. Cassial, you are wanted in the briefing room."

I furrowed by brows in confusion. "Briefing room? What for?"

Markus searched around the hallway quickly before speaking in a whisper. "I am not at liberty to say." His round eyes almost pleaded for my cooperation.

"Am I in some type of trouble?" I questioned. I'd only been summoned to a briefing room twice before. The first time, I was a child, accompanied by my father and scolded for swordplay on the grounds without supervision, and the second time was to offer me my sentry angel position.

The Skies lived and breathed hierarchy and balance among the people. Knowing your place but understanding how you fit into the bigger picture were huge. There were entire classes on how the system worked, and I'd been to every single one of them. Executive angels thrived at the top, where they made and oversaw all the rules. Sentry and guardian angels resided somewhere in the middle, and messenger angels fell right below. We got paid accordingly in celestial coins, which I made sure I monitored like a good, adult angel, unlike Reese.

Markus' round eyes grew larger as he answered. "No, no, of course not. I honestly cannot say anything more."

Reese spoke before anyone else could. "Have fun with that, man. I'll go take a shower."

"You as well, Mr. Diniel."

Reese narrowed his eyes at Markus. "Excuse me?"

Markus sized him up just the same, eyes narrowed. "You must come as well. None of this is up for discussion, I assure you." He turned on his heels. As much as I hated it, Markus, as an executive angel, ranked higher than both of us. "Briefing room 3!" he yelled before disappearing around a pillar.

"What in the hell just happened?" I asked, dumbfounded at the encounter.

"We just got treated like someone's bitch, that's what. Somehow, *you* did something and got me dragged into your mess." Reese swiveled towards the shower room door at the end of the hall. "You really are a bad influence."

I opened my mouth to protest that *he* was the bad influence, but he just winked as he went.

OUR FOOTSTEPS SOUNDED IN RHYTHM AS WE MADE OUR WAY TO THE BRIEFING room. My shower had been less than pleasant, my thoughts running rampant. I thought back to the last few weeks, all my training days and sentry posts, but couldn't find any issue. I had a slight moment where I reveled in the idea that I could be up for some type of promotion, but I was pulled out of my outlandish ideals when I remembered Reese would be there as well. The only thing Reese could be admired for is how to offend someone in ten words or less.

What would they need with two sentry angels who had only been appointed to The Skies six years ago? There were plenty of other angels who could do what I do, could do what *we* do.

"I can literally hear you thinking from all the way over there," Reese said, shaking his head as he took one long stride after another. I wore a white t-shirt and navy jacket, while Reese decided a sleeveless gray tank top was appropriate, his hair in a messy high bun.

"You have to admit, this is odd."

He shrugged, turning a corner and nodding to another sentry angel we had trained with. "Odd? Maybe. Intriguing? Hell yeah."

My face twisted in confusion. "You're excited about this? I'm afraid to ask why."

Reese stopped midway down the hall, turning to me. "Every day, we do pretty much the same damn thing. What if this is something *different*, Nick?"

I rolled my eyes slowly and deeply, knowing it intensely aggravated him. "Or, it's just a meeting to tell us they are desperately in need of trainers for the incoming angelic class."

Reese pressed his lips together and shuddered at my words. We had only been temporary trainers once, and it was the last time. New angels, not yet granted a title or job, were assessed in all skills until they were deemed worthy of a place in The Skies, if they are to have a place at all. It seemed easy at the meeting, but angels with no discipline and no home training was the first time I'd ever had to bite my tongue quite so much.

We'd both politely asked Markus to never volunteer us for that again. *Ever.*

Reese set his hand on my shoulder, squeezing hard before responding. "Don't ever say that again, unless you want me to revert to calling you Nick the Dick."

I slapped his hand away, groaning at the distasteful nickname. We laughed as we walked down the hall, halting at the entrance to the briefing room. Usually, the doors aren't guarded by any angels, but today was a rare exception. The angel in front of us was tall, taller than my 6'2 frame. His shoulders were wide, and his biceps pulsed outwards with quite a few tattoos.

"State your business." His voice was deep, and it put me on edge.

I could feel Reese's eyes on me, waiting for me to answer. I swallowed hard, pushing back my shoulders and straightening my back. "Nick Cassial and Reese Diniel, summoned by Markus Seraph."

The sentry angel glared, seemingly swallowing us whole. He analyzed every inch of us before turning slightly and sliding his hand over the doorknob. The Skies' security measures relied almost exclusively on angelic magic.

Gold flecks and white wisps danced over the knob until we heard a click. The door creaked open, but we remained on the other side. The angel stepped to the side, allowing us a view into the room. Markus and another angel, Ariel Fortes, turned towards us, the side of Markus' mouth lifting into a small smile. He raised his hand, motioning for us to come in.

All the briefing rooms were generally the same: a long table of stained-glass, cream-colored carpet, dozens of windows, pearl marble walls. The only thing that set them apart were the ceilings. Each one was decorated in clouds, but that there was an angel sitting on a different one in each room.

Reese nudged my shoulder, using his index finger to push me forward. I stepped inside, trying to disguise my anxious curiosity with confidence. Reese shuffled in behind me just as the door shut with an intense snap. I heard someone clear their throat from the table in the middle of the room, and Markus moved aside to expose them.

"Mr. Cassial, I am delighted you could join us," Jonah Zuriel, highest executive angel in The Skies, welcomed us. His voice was smooth as butter, but so commanding, it made me want to straighten my spine even more.

"Please, have a seat." His skin was beige with a golden undertone, and he wore a teal suit trimmed in black. That black trim told a quiet story: Jonah ascended to his position through his father, his birthright, not through promotions. As all high executives normally do. I didn't honestly care how Jonah got his powers; I respected him regardless.

He pointed his hand towards two chairs at the table, kicking out his middle and index finger in a quick motion so the chairs pulled back from the table on their own.

I sat in the one closest to him, while Reese settled into the other, Markus and

Ariel taking the seats across from us. They'd decided not to display their wings, tucking them into their backs. It was a painless process that required simple magic, the kind of magic every angel learns from childhood. Reese claimed it came in handy when in bed with a female; I was inclined to agree, but *sometimes* the wings could be just as handy.

"You're probably wondering why we called you here," Jonah

finally spoke. The last time I'd seen him was a few weeks ago. He seemed stress free and happier then, but now, something was off.

"That would be a good place to start," I answered.

Jonah leaned into the back of the tall leather chair, letting his arms run down the armrests. "How much do you know about our dealings with the ones below, Nicholas?"

I shrugged. "I know we try to keep them quick, with as little hostility as possible."

Jonah nodded - I had given him the answer he wanted. "Do you know the *specifics* of those dealings?"

"I don't understand, sir." I responded honestly. "I have no idea. It's not really my place to know that kind of information."

"Not that anyone would tell us in the first place," Reese chimed in, crossing his arms over his chest.

Jonah chuckled as Ariel and Markus went rigid at Reese's snark. "I suppose you're right Mr. Diniel, but that's why I called you here."

Reese leaned forward, elbows on the table. "You brought us here to gossip?"

I kicked him in the ankle under the table, satisfied at the low grunt that left his lips.

"What do we have to do with the demons?" I questioned, hoping he would ignore Reese and his big mouth.

Thankfully, he did. "We have a....security problem, of sorts." He placed his hands flat on the table, his palms down. "Years ago, we had a one-way portal system to other realms put into place. With our portal keys, only angels and designated guests can use them, making them impenetrable to demons." Jonah took a breath, leaning to the side and pressing his index finger to his temple. "There was a...mishap."

"Mishap?" I asked.

"We caught a demon on the grounds," Markus answered. When Jonah made no move to reprimand his interruption, he continued. "We placed him in the Ethereal Bastille—"

Jonah raised a hand to silence him. "He won't speak to anyone, but ideally, the plan is to send him back where he belongs. We just need to know how he got here."

I digested the information in pieces, collecting my thoughts. The Ethereal Bastille was my posting a few times a week, watching over the lowlifes and miscreants, a hell hole within itself. "Don't the portals have alarms?" It was one of the few things I knew about when it came to our magical transportation system.

"They do, but when we checked them, the portals were secure, without failures."

I scratched my chin, feeling the small stubble I'd missed. "I guess I'm just not understanding what any of this has to do with us." I nodded towards Reese, his face twisted in skepticism.

Jonah let out a small smile and laugh. "Well, Nicholas, I guess I'll get to the point. You both have the highest in your respective skill sets, and I've been told you both did quite well with the trainees last year." I had to stop myself from rolling my eyes and settled for an internal grumble.

Reese pushed his seat back and perched at the edge. "We appreciate the compliments, but personally, I'm not seeing the connection between our resume and your problem."

Jonah clasped his hands on the table. "We are assigning you this mission."

I blinked. "You want us to figure out how the demon got through?"

Jonah nodded, tapping his fingers. "Yes. Start at Oculus, where the portals were first conceived."

"Oculus! No fuck—" Reese started.

I quickly cut him off. "Sir, we appreciate the opportunity, but that seems a bit out of our reach."

Oculus wasn't a part of Heaven's Gate; it was off to the side, in the forest region. The history of Oculus was complicated. It had once been a promising land, filled with beauty, but now overflowed with ivy, ruined weaving, and winding gravel roads. Its inhabitants were called Enchanters. I'd been told they were beautiful, magical beings, but there were also people who claimed they looked like old hags in dark cloaks.

"I'm quite aware of the stories of Oculus, Nicholas, but I wouldn't send you there without some sort of plan, much less with a threat of violence." Jonah reached out and squeezed my shoulder, watching as I settled at his words. Oculus was old magic, something I had no interest in understanding. Its people had magic we didn't comprehend. I wasn't one to automatically judge, but our history hadn't been a pleasant one.

Ariel slapped his palm on the table, catching everyone's attention. "I think it's time, sir." He looked over at Jonah, hoping he'd agree. Jonah gestured towards the door, Ariel made a beeline to it. "We don't plan to leave you two to your own devices." Ariel rapped his knuckles on the door four times and stepped back.

The door opened slowly, two wide shouldered sentry angels stepping inside. They moved away from each other, allowing me to see the glow of golden handcuffs. I looked down at the ground, noticing a pair of black, knee-high boots, then raised my eyes to a pair of thighs, shorts, and a face.

Her face.

Her eyes were a deep rich brown, staring right at me, as if she knew I'd been eyeing her. Her lips melted into a smirk, like she knew something I didn't. Her skin was a warm brown, and it looked so smooth, like the finest silk. Dark brown hair flowed down to her shoulders, loose and tight curls interspersed throughout. Even though I was sitting, I could tell she was significantly shorter than me, even with the slight heel of her boots.

Fuck, she was pretty.

I had to physically force myself to look away and stare down at the floor. My cock started to twitch – fuck, it'd been too long since I'd last gotten laid.

"*Demons*? Aren't they the problem?" Reese quipped, staring at Ariel. "I'm not seeing the logic."

Ariel looked over our heads at Jonah, who looked taken aback. I followed his gaze to the two female demons in front of us, the one I'd marveled over now joined by one with the most severely annoyed smirk. She had the palest skin I'd ever seen, two crossing switchblades tattooed on her neck. Her blunt bangs sat right over her defined eyebrows, but I could clearly make out the way she pulled them together in disgruntled distaste.

"Ariel, what is the meaning of this?" Jonah sputtered.

Ariel swallowed hard before responding. "Sir, I brought you what you asked for." His pale cheeks turned tomato red, and it looked like he was starting to sweat.

Jonah got out of his chair and moved around the table, unbuttoning the silver buttons holding his teal jacket closed. I looked over to Reese, who made eye contact with me, a million unspoken questions darting between us.

"I *know* what I asked you to do, but it clearly seems you didn't do it."

"There was one—" Ariel started, voice cracking. He cleared his throat, running a shaky hand through his hair. "I assure you, I provided what was asked."

Markus knocked on the table, commanding our attention. "Maybe we shouldn't squabble with two young angels at the table, hmm?"

I tried to sneak a glance around Jonah to the female from before, noticing a small glint of light from her back pocket. I blinked, thinking the light was playing tricks on me.

There it was again. A small glimmer.

She'd brought something with her, hoping no one would notice. The handcuffs shut down most, if not all, magic, but they don't make magical objects undetectable. She was smart for hiding it, but not smart enough not to get caught.

"Explain yourself," Jonah ordered.

Ariel took a deep breath. "I went to retrieve the Soul Seether. I absolutely despise going to that abhorrent place run by *that* woman, but I did what you asked. This is the Soul Seether."

"Isn't the Soul Seether a guy?" Reese asked, causing Jonah to raise an eyebrow at Ariel.

"Yes, Ariel isn't the Soul Seether a male?" Jonah repeated.

Out of the corner of my eye, I saw the female give a tight-lipped smile, as if she was holding in a laugh.

"Sir, you sent me to exactly where they would be and all I found was her." He pointed to the female with the high boots and curls.

Jonah balled his hands into fists at his side, flexing his fingers as he slowly turned his head. "You are the Soul Seether?"

I saw her lift her eyes to him. I couldn't make out her body language, but she looked him dead in the eyes, as if she was prepared to make him wait, *squirm.*

"At your service," she finally answered. She sounded powerful, but she didn't have a deep voice. It was airy, as if the words floated on a cloud as they left her lips, but as if every word held thunder among the clouds.

She spoke again, this time with more sass. "Although, I've never liked being called Soul Seether. First impressions, am I right?" She looked over Jonah's shoulder and winked at me.

I shifted in my chair.

Without looking away from her, Jonah pointed to a chair. "Sit, Soul Seether. We have much to discuss."

The sentry angels grabbed them by their elbows and lead them to the other end of the table. They placed their arms on the colorful tabletop, the handcuffs sparkling in the refracted light. Jonah sat again, followed by Ariel, who I could've sworn was about to shit his pants.

"Misconceptions aside, I only requested one demon, Ariel," Jonah began, leaning back against his chair again.

"Of course, sir, but the Soul Seether requested she come. I assumed it wouldn't do any harm."

I finally opened my mouth. "You took a request from a demon? Just like that?"

Ariel side-eyed me with a look that was supposed to ground me - it seemed I'd spoken out of turn. "Anything to get her here."

"Remember your place, Nicholas," Jonah ordered, turning his focus to the demons at the table. "Now, I know the Soul Seether, but may I ask who *you* are?"

The female with the short black hair had her head tilted back against the seat, almost as if she was bored. "You can ask, but I probably won't tell you."

"What if we added a please and a cherry on top, would that suffice?" Reese countered, sarcasm oozing from his voice.

The female turned her head to the side, challenging his stare. Her eyes were a gray I'd never seen before. "Blondie, I pop cherries, I don't eat them, so I'd say hard pass."

Reese slowly turned his head to catch my eye and mouth a *wow* at me before shaking his head.

"It's Elise. Her name, I mean," the Soul Seether answered. She perched in the chair with her back straight, but her shoulders were rounded. "Soul Seether is honestly a fucking stupid name, so call me Dani or take me back. Better yet, tell me why the *hell* I'm here."

Jonah placed his hands under his chin, intertwining his fingers, as if in deep thought. "One of your kind has passed through a portal. They are detained, but it is quite troubling."

"So, what, you think we had something to do with it? *Typical,*" Elise countered.

"Not quite," Markus snarked back.

Jonah cleared his throat. "We can only do so much. We aren't privy to the inner workings of demons and your realm."

"So, you want us to solve your problem for you? I don't know anything about your rogue demon. You aren't really selling yourself here, especially since a few minutes ago, you thought I had a dick." Dani shrugged, stretching her neck out. I kept having to force myself *not* to look at her. "I'm getting bored."

"I'd watch my mouth if I were you," I stated, not glancing in her direction, though I could feel her eyes penetrating the side of my head.

"Shove it up your ethereal hole," Elise shot back so quickly, it caught everyone's attention.

Reese sharply turned his head, two seconds from pouncing, when I pressed my foot on top of his, hard. He looked at me and then Jonah, who seemed to be waiting for us to either continue or let him speak. Reese nodded and settled back in his chair.

Jonah explained everything to them: the portals and how Oculus was the first place to find answers. They took in the information but said nothing. For a short while, we sat in silence, waiting for some type of response.

We finally got one.

"You got an Oculus Enchanter to create your portals?" Dani asked. "They actually helped you build a portal?"

"Yes."

Elise burst out laughing, bouncing up and down in her seat. Once she settled down, it looked like a few tears had left her eyes. "That was your first mistake, you *fucking* idiots."

"Oculus Enchanters are serious old magic. They don't take kindly to men in obnoxious suits asking them for favors," Dani added. "The ones I've met don't speak highly of your kind."

I jumped in, on the defensive. "Oculus is truly the only magic that can create that kind of portal." I'd heard rumors angels used to be able to create their own portals, but that was before my time. It was a forbidden art, mostly used by messengers and guardians, one no one really spoke about. Portal keys had been implemented by Jonah when he came into power, and I wasn't one to question it. There had been no issues until now.

Dani shifted her eyes to me. "You would be correct, but putting that much faith in them? Oh, come on. You're too pretty to be so deluded."

Reese stifled a laugh.

Markus let out an exhausted sigh. "Regardless, that's in the past. We need to go back to the source. Jonah would go himself, but there matters here to attend to."

Reese clapped his hands onto his knees. "If no one is going to ask, I will. You want us to go to Oculus, alright. So, why are *they* here?"

Elise answered before Jonah could open his mouth. "Correct me if I'm wrong, but I'm pretty sure we're here to make sure nothing goes wrong, or I don't know, be your scapegoats?"

Reese wasn't about to take that. "I can handle myself just fine around a bunch of Enchanters."

Elise snorted. "I bet you've never met an Enchanter in your entire existence. You'd piss yourself the moment one even came within ten feet of you, Blondie." Elise stuck her tongue between her teeth and smiled. She wasn't wrong. We'd never actually met one before.

Reese's shoulders tensed as he seethed. I broke the tension with a question. "Is that the plan, sir?"

Jonah waved his hand through the air nonchalantly. "More or less."

"Don't worry, *Nicholas*, I'll take good care of you." Dani raised an eyebrow and settled back in her seat. She bit her lower lip, causing me to look away quickly before I blushed.

"You leave tomorrow. As for your stay—" Jonah fixated on Dani and Elise. "The guards will show you to your room. The South Wing, second floor, where we've blocked off access. Same floor as Nick and Reese."

Elise scoffed. "Reese, huh? I think I'll stick with Blondie for now."

Reese scoffed right back. "You're actually letting them stay here?"

"I can't just let them go back and then send someone to find them again, can I?" Jonah challenged, catching Reese off guard.

"No need to make Daddy mad," Dani snarked, earning a genuine smile from Elise. Her brown eyes caught Jonah's amber ones. "What happens when this is all over, huh?"

Jonah placed his hands in his lap. "We'll send you home, no questions asked."

I asked a much-needed follow-up question. "How do we make sure they don't make any moves?"

Jonah smirked. "The South Wing is heavily guarded, and I have little doubt they will do anything. You are a sentry yourself, Nicholas, You can protect yourself."

"A sentry?" Dani asked, a hint of intrigue in her voice. "Do you plan to sleep with one eye open tonight?"

"I might."

"Such a good little soldier."

I rolled my eyes, hard.

"Either of you try anything, and you'll see the other end of my fucking bow," Reese threatened, pushing back the chair and standing.

Elise looked up at him, in no way intimidated. Pure curiosity was there instead. "I can't tell if this is just some big dick energy, or if you're just overcompensating for a small one."

Reese gripped the back of the chair, his knuckles turning white. I clapped my hand on his shoulder, bringing him back, reminding him we weren't the only ones there. He nodded, face now completely red. Jonah motioned for the sentries at the door to collect the demons, and they stood, hands in front of them with the golden handcuffs. They shuffled towards the door when I stopped them, silently letting the sentries know everything was alright.

I walked over to Dani, who showed no signs of confusion or worry, Jonah and the others distracted in their own conversation. She simply looked at me and smirked. Her lips were pink, her bottom lip full and pouty. I was close enough her to know she smelled like pure, raw cinnamon.

"If you are going to hide something—" I whispered, reaching down around her waist. I eased my index and thumb into her back pocket, her eyes popping wide at the intrusion. I felt the small hilt of the weapon before anything else, easing it out of her pocket and dangling it in front of her. It was small and compact, clearly not its original size, but it had weight for something so tiny. "Make sure you do a better job next time." I dropped the weapon into my jacket.

She only continued to smirk, leaning in to whisper back. "I think you just enjoyed feeling me up, Nicholas. I know *I* did."

The sentries pulled her towards the door and out into the hallway. Ariel and Markus nodded their goodbyes, exiting the room, while Jonah stayed back with us.

"We're counting on you. This could look very good for you both if you succeed."

I quirked an eyebrow. "And if we don't?"

Jonah narrowed his eyes, the corners crinkling. "You'll succeed."

27

CHAPTER THREE

DANI

"You really believe they're going to just send us back once they're done with us?" Elise asked, the condescending tone in her voice loud and clear.

They'd removed our handcuffs once they'd locked us in. I guess they assumed their threats were enough. Neither of us had any reason to use our powers here anyways -- well, at least I didn't.

"I never said I believed it. I also think you are a huge pessimist."

Elise grumbled over to the large armchair in the corner. The space was massive, although anything was big compared to Purgatory. Four delicate light fixtures dangled from the ceiling, dispersing light all around the room. Navy blue covered the walls, sterling silver covering the trimmings. The floors were vinyl, no creaking sounds as I walked. A gray loveseat sat next to the entrance door, a six-foot mahogany dresser against the adjacent wall. It had two, full sized beds on opposite ends of the room, one near the window facing the loveseat and one perpendicular to the door.

The sentries had to push me inside, since I'd stopped to take the whole room in at the threshold. Elise had walked in as if none of it phased her, which I'm sure it didn't. She didn't like the idea of being here, and the mention of staying overnight almost sent her over the edge.

"Just being here is making my skin crawl, and that right there is saying something," she stated, huffing as she fell into the chair.

I raised my eyes to the ceiling, considering my words. "Like I said, you didn't have to come."

She waved her hand, shushing me. I let myself relax as I sunk into the most comfortable mattress I had ever laid on, closing my eyes to replay the last hour.

A demon got through an "impenetrable" portal. A team of two demons and two angels are meant to fix it. We had to work with angels.

Angels.

I saw the uppity attitudes Elise always grumbled over. I got wind of the distaste of having to even be near us, even if it *was* to save their own kind. The pungent smell of frustration seeped out of the blonde one Elise toyed with. Still, I did catch a whiff of something else.

Intrigue. It was a light scent, so light, I might have missed it, but it was there.

Nicholas.

"Dani!" I shot my eyes open to see Elise standing over me, her hands around my shoulders. "Wake the fuck up. You aren't going to get any sleep until we talk about this."

"About what?" I asked, pushing against the bed and pulling myself up against the headboard. Elise sat at the edge, giving me a knowing look.

"You know what."

"I don't want to talk about *that.*"

"Tough nuts."

I kneaded the heels of my hands into my eyes. "Lilith isn't going to care."

They'd mentioned Lilith at that meeting, and it didn't sit well with me now, just like it didn't then. Lilith was the Queen of Purgatory; she created a blood bath of pain and depression long before I arrived down there. She was one of the main reasons demons had such a horrendous reputation. I understood each and every demon's feelings towards her. Some hated her, some loved her, but most of them feared her. I didn't fit into any of those categories. She just existed in my eyes. Lilith had given me my dagger and all the power that comes with it. She taught me how weapons weren't always needed when you had dark power to rely on: the black smoke I can command to come out and play.

She'd been the one to dub me the "Soul Seether," and it stuck. I'd learned how to enjoy provoking pain from the most deluded victim, how to soak up the joy it brought to those around me. All from her.

That feeling of praise and those bloodthirsty cries leaked into my mind, and I could feel my skin going hot. I blinked a few times, tearing my hands from my face, breathing in and out.

In and out.

Elise let out a loud "ha" before responding. "You're delusional if you think she won't care, and even more insane if you think she won't notice."

I shrugged. "It's not like she can come scoop me up." That was the truth.

Elise's gray eyes darkened. "You have no idea what she's capable of."

It was my turn to let out a laugh. "I'm not scared of Lilith, and you shouldn't be either. Every other demon in Purgatory goes running for the hills when they see her—"

"For good reason." Elise caught my eyes. "Look, I'm not saying go running scared like a little bitch. I'm just saying, make sure you're prepared when the time comes to explain yourself."

I smirked. "She isn't my mother."

"She's everyone's mother, or at least she likes to think so. Whether you like it or not, you wouldn't be here without her," Elise countered, punching my ankle and getting off the bed.

That comment cut me the most. Souls meant for Purgatory and Hell don't need help finding their way, but Lilith gets to decide who she keeps. If she doesn't see you fitting her standards, then off you go to the fiery pits of Hell, where Lucifer makes Lilith look like a fucking cake walk. With the souls she does keep, she plucks just a few for her inner circle.

I didn't have time to mull over my feelings for Lilith or what would happen when she found out we were gone. She favored me in a way that makes you feel special, but also makes you wonder *why*, though she always found a way to skate around the question. I'd deal with her and her wrath back in Purgatory.

"Also, don't think I didn't notice," Elise teased.

I raised one of my eyebrows at her, dropping my head back against the headboard.

"The pretty one with the dark hair. The one who just so happens to be playing keep away with your dagger." She was scary with how much she paid attention to everything.

"No idea what you're talking about." I side-glanced over at her as she untied her boots on the edge of her bed. "I'll get the dagger back; that's a non-starter."

She threw her shoe at me, which I caught seconds before it hit my face. "Fucking around with angels is not the plan."

"No one is fucking around. A bit of fun and flirting never hurt anyone," I shrugged.

Elise swiped her tongue over her bottom lip before unlacing her other shoe. "Good, but I wouldn't stop you if you did. I'm sure Blondie would hate that his pretty friend got up close and personal with the *enemy*."

I moaned in annoyance. "Elise, no. As much as you would love to blow up their lives, I would like to make it out of Oculus in one piece. I'll stick to shameless flirting."

"Ha, *they* should be worried about Oculus. Not us."

I tapped my index finger on my chin. "Um, I'm sorry, but I'm pretty sure demons are obnoxiously low on the friendship meter, last time I checked."

Elise stripped off her shirt, throwing it on the ground. In only her bra and shorts, she sauntered over to the dresser. "We're higher than those ethereal asshats on their nice list, so that's all that matters. I can already tell you those angels think weapons are gonna save them. What a fucking joke."

"We're there to make sure they don't die. Remember that."

She turned around before reaching for the handles to the dresser, giving me a pointed look. "Actually, *you* are. *I'm* here because *you* requested it. Therefore, *I* have no obligation."

"A lifetime in Purgatory and still have a heart of ice, I see," I responded, laughing.

She stuck out her tongue and pulled the dresser open. "Is this a joke?"

"What?" I questioned, trying to look around her at the array of clothes.

Elise looked at me wide eyed, stepping to the side so I could see for myself.

The clothes were a mix of white, yellows, and various colors of the rainbow -- nothing either of us would be caught dead in on a regular basis.

"Holy Hell."

Elise stomped her feet as she made her way to the entrance. "I would rather an Enchanter strike me fucking dead than wear that shit."

She forcefully grabbed the handle and ripped open the door, letting it slam against the wall. The two sentries guarding the door looked at her skeptically, a bit in shock -- she still had only her bra and shorts on. Elise placed her palms on either side of the frame and leaned in towards the sentries. "If either of you thinks I'm wearing anything in there, you are out of your damn mind. I suggest you go find your leader and find me something in black."

I knew her eyes had turned black, just as I knew her voice was reverberating through their skulls. The sentries tried to hold their positions, but their shoulders shook, their bodies wavering.

Elise shut the door and shook her whole body, as if to regain control after using some dark power, her tattoo pulsing on her neck. She was so good at being the boss of her own power. Lilith may have been the one to teach me, but Elise was the one who taught me how to regain my sense of self when it was all said and done.

"Was that really necessary?" I asked.

"Yes."

THE SENTRIES GUARDING OUR DOOR GAVE US NO REAL WARNING WHEN WE
needed to be awake. A courteous wakeup call with a side of breakfast
in bed? No. Elise and I woke up to a stark bright light from the wide,
three panel window and a pounding at our door. Elise had flung a
series of curse words towards whoever was on the other side, but
eventually made her way out of bed. I had no idea if she'd fallen
asleep last night, but I hadn't been able to relax the whole night.
We'd woken to an entirely different closet, which suited both of our
styles. Fewer rainbows and more neutrals. A point to the angels on
that one.

I opened the door to two different guards, who seemed a little
more prepared for the job of wrangling two demons than the last
two. We both raised our wrists with the intention of being hand-
cuffed again; they obliged and grabbed our shoulders, pushing us
along. Instead of walking back the way we came, they had us
walking towards the end of the hall, where a singular wooden door
greeted us. It had a handle shaped like a wing, just like the gates
outside. The originality in this place was *astonishing*. We were shuffled down two flights of stairs and through another door, where a
silver brick interior met my eyes. It smelled like food, and I could
hear chattering. If I remembered our room assignment correctly, we
were on the ground floor of The Skies.

"Do you guys ever get lost in this place?" I questioned, looking up
at the sentry to my left. He didn't even acknowledge me. He didn't
even flinch.

The sentries yanked us through another door that immediately
led us outside. The sunlight was almost blinding in Heaven's Gate,
almost artificial with how bright it was. The smell of roses and
honeysuckle filled my nostrils. I looked around, trying to determine
where exactly we were. I leaned forward a bit, tilting my head to
both sides, when I zeroed in on the gravel landing and stepping-

stones. I turned my head up and over the castle-like structure of The Skies and saw the arching gates of the entrance.

I didn't know much about Heaven's Gate, but I did know that everything centered around The Skies. It was the epicenter, while everything else simply existed. The Skies and the surrounding villages were the main spots, and places like Oculus were overlooked, almost erased entirely from the atlas. Angels wanted to *use* Enchanters, but they'd rather not be so closely associated with them.

It was pathetic.

"How much fucking longer are we waiting on these pricks?" Elise huffed, agitated.

I felt the gust of wind first, causing my hair to pull away from my face and towards my back. The wind sent a cool breeze towards us, and the grass at my feet bristled back and forth. A perfectly carved shadow moved over me, another one over Elise. We glanced upwards to see two sets of decently hefty wings. The harsh wind settled and slowed, but the breeze seemed swifter as the flapping wings descended, growing closer. One more jolting blast of air hit us before everything went still, the shadows now in the shape of a person.

Two people.

I only noticed the wings at first, white like Ariel's, soft looking and structured. The feathers were long and broad, their tips were rounded and delicate. The blonde one, Reese, halted in front of Elise, Nicholas in front of me. He had his wings pulled in now, the tops of them sitting above his shoulders.

"Did you really have to make an obnoxious entrance?" Elise asked, the annoyance in her voice obvious.

Reese scoffed. "You can just admit you're impressed and feel inadequate."

"Impressed by what exactly?

Reese jutted his wings out to their full extension. The shadow he created covered both Elise and I, plus the sentries who held us.

Elise's gaze went from one wing tip all the way to the other. She pursed her lips and swished her cheeks from side to side, then let out a small laugh that morphed into an even louder chuckle. "Oh, come on, Blondie. There are better ways to try to prove you have a big dick. The only thing I'm impressed by is your failed attempt."

I pressed my lips together to try not to laugh. I peeked up at Nicholas to see him trying to hide a laugh as well. He ran a hand through his thick head of dark hair, and I noticed he had a small scar below his eye. I started to wonder how he got it. In the heat of the sun, I noticed his cheeks flushing pink.

"Reese, put them away. We won't be needing them anyway," he commanded, his own wings shrinking and vanishing all together. Reese followed suit with a grumble.

I was curious. "How do we get to Oculus from here? I assumed we could just fly there."

"Ha, like we're gonna let you use your wings!" Reese exclaimed.

"Scared they're bigger than yours?" Elise countered.

Nicholas put a hand on his friend's chest. "We can't risk you wandering around on your own, and flying will make more of a commotion than we want. We don't want to alarm anyone. Besides, no one has flown to Oculus in years."

"So, what's your plan then, Nicholas?" I asked, trying to catch his attention. For a moment, his eyes latched onto mine, but he looked up at the sky after a minute.

"We use a portal," he responded.

I pulled my eyebrows together. "How do you have access?"

Nicholas reached his hand into the front of his shirt, pulling out a necklace with an amethyst gem at the end. "Jonah gave me access to one of his, but only for this trip. I'll have to return it when we come back."

"Didn't portals get you into this mess in the first place?" I tilted my head to the side and bit my bottom lip.

Nicholas shook his head. "That demon got in without anyone's notice or prior access. Jonah already knows you're coming with us, just like how Ariel brought you through before."

Reese cleared his throat. "Nick, I'm bored as shit over here. Let's go." He pointed at the open space in front of us. He had his back to us now, and I noticed his bow and arrows strapped to his back, strikingly different from Nicholas' sword. "Do the magic thing."

35

Nicholas unhooked the necklace and pointed it in front of him. He started from the top and began to draw a circle, white light pushing through with every inch. Once he finished, the middle turned white, wisps of light and gold sparks pulsing out, spinning like a whirlpool.

The sentries finally stepped in front of us, unlocking our handcuffs before silently making their way back inside. "Ladies first," Reese said, motioning for us to go in front of him.

"Then I suggest *you* go," I found myself saying.

Elise shot a strong smile my way before turning back to Reese. "You heard her."

Reese narrowed his eyes at her, his hair pushed back from his face with a slim headband. "I said *go*, so go, demons."

I met his hazel eyes with my brown ones and walked past him. Nicholas, securely fastening the necklace back around his neck, watched as I quickly walked into the portal.

THOSE WHITE WISPS CARESSED MY LEGS AND ARMS, AND I COULD FEEL THE electric warmth even through my leather leggings. It didn't burn, but it made my spine shiver. I continued forward, trying to keep my mind straight as I felt that back and forth, off balance sensation. I took another step and blinked.

I was here.

The sky was no longer bright. The air didn't smell of flowers or freshly cut grass. The trees didn't stand tall and proud. There were no sounds of wings flapping gracefully above me. It felt as if time stood still here, as if time were preserved.

Oculus was just as I had always imagined it would be, although I'd never given it much thought. The Enchanters in Purgatory had never spoken much about it, not that I ever asked.

I heard feet behind me, and I turned around to see Nicholas pull out the necklace and turn the gem counterclockwise. The portal quickly closed in on itself and disappeared.

"Jonah placed a timer on the portal, so we only have about two hours to figure something out before we have to be out of here."

I pulled on one of the branches of the weeping willows to my right. "You aren't afraid of being stuck here, are you, Nicholas?"

"Of course not, but that's not the plan."

Elise stepped in front of me, trekking forward. "Can we get going? We won't figure out anything just standing around." She made sure to step over thick puddles of mud, which seemed to be most of the pathway. It was quiet – almost deathly so.

Big stones shot from the ground in random patterns and ivy wrapped around the tilted pillars of the rundown buildings and shops. The slight breeze that touched my skin almost felt like a song whispered in my ear. It smelled like rain and wet grass.

"Shouldn't *we* lead the way?" Reese asked, taking a few long strides to catch up to her.

"Aren't *we* supposed to be the ones who keep your asses alive?" Elise countered.

"Believe me, you aren't needed."

I walked in between them, placing my hand on Reese's bow. It was made of ash gray wood and the bowstring had the gloss of silk. "You think your weapons will save you here?"

Before he could answer, Elise commented. "You're bringing swords and bows to a mind fight, you idiot. Enchanters don't need weapons to drop-kick you."

Reese let out a long sigh of frustration but moved on ahead of us. I slowed my pace so Nicholas and I were walking in sync. He didn't look at me, just ahead, his face unreadable.

"Is your friend always this easy to rile up?" I asked, smirking.

He shrugged. "Sometimes. He's just not used to someone talking back at every turn."

"Someone or us?" I inquired, peering up at him. He was much taller than me, so my head came in just above his elbow. The vein in his neck pushed out a tiny bit at my question.

When he didn't answer, I asked another. "Do you know what happened here? Why it's so... abandoned?"

Nicholas pulled on the strap over his chest. "I don't know much, but it dates to when Enchanters were more common. The magic they used was never malicious, but then something changed. There's always been separation of our kinds, but I don't think the line was heavily drawn. There was a war or a big fight, I don't know, and Enchanters were caught in the middle of it. I guess they sided with demons and got the short end of the stick. I know sentries sieged this land and had no mercy, hence why this was a delicate matter. That's where my knowledge ends."

I mulled over this new information, not quite understanding. "So, you assume Enchanters just said fuck angels, chose demons, and then what? They get practically slaughtered, no questions asked? Sounds like you're missing big chunks of information."

"I'm only telling you what I know. Take it or leave it."

"Who told you all this? Other angels? Tell me, Nicholas, have you ever met an Enchanter?"

He stuck his tongue out and licked his lips. "No, but—"

"Then I suggest you do before making assumptions," I spat, starting to say something else when I ran into Elise's back. "What the—"

"Shut the fuck up," she whispered forcefully. Reese walked backwards away from us, looking around at the trees above.

"We heard something just now. Stay alert." Reese reached behind him, grabbing his bow and arrow.

Elise rolled her eyes as she whispered. "That thing won't help you."

"How about you let me handle my business the way I want to handle it," he threw back.

Nicholas reached for the hilt of his sword, the black hilt duller in this place, but he didn't unsheathe it. He stood his ground, motioning with his hand for me to move, likely to cover more ground. The song-like whispers I'd heard before had stopped.

Everything was still.

The willows had stopped moving and all I could hear was our

breathing. Reese backed into a pillar, notching his arrow and pulling back, scanning the perimeter.

"What did you hear?" I lowered my voice, speaking to Elise.

Before a reply could leave her lips, she shouted, "there!"

Elise pointed over Reese's shoulders, and I followed her arm to see the long, slender arm pushing itself out of the pillar and reaching for Reese. He looked over his shoulder and quickly shifted away from the clawing hand and its long fingernails, but instead fell into its extended hand on the other side. Fingers wrapped tightly around his arm, pulling him back against the pillar, its' other hand creeping its way around his neck. Reese held onto his bow and tried to pull away, turning his head vigorously, trying to get as far away as he could.

Nicholas pulled out his sword, sweeping it out in front of him. He began to run towards his friend when I shouted, "No!" He looked in my direction, his eyes frantic and confused.

I stretched out my fingers and closed my eyes for what felt like minutes, but I knew it was merely seconds.

Then, I opened them wide.

I knew my eyes had turned into sunken black holes when the world changed from various colors to a more muted color palette. I could still see faces and features, but they were outlined in black. I could make out the people I knew, but I could also fixate on the enemy.

I knew black smoke was seeping out of me: my fingertips, my hair, every pore and fiber of my being, circling around me, trusting me.

I focused on the hands pressing Reese to the pillar, on the pillar itself and whatever was using it as a hiding spot. I lifted my hand, watching as thick smoke cascaded off my palm and towards the pillar.

The smoke struck right above Reese's shoulder, barreling into the stone. A loud groan sounded around us as the smoke morphed into a person, its hands releasing Reese. He scurried away, watching as a male, holding his bleeding shoulder, peeled away from the pillar and fell forward. I made to shoot my shadows again when a cry sounded above us. Elise let out a sharp yelp as an electric blue dart of magic sliced her arm. I shot another dark wave in the direction it came from, the dark matter leaving my hands with ease, seeking a soul to torment.

A string of blue magic shot out again, breaking us apart in different directions. I peeked up from my crouch to see them standing on roofs of buildings and the nearest hilltops: Enchanters. Elise shot her own stream of darkness their way, making a few duck and lose balance. Reese angled his bow and shot an arrow at one just as it released a flaming cerulean cloud in our direction, and we all ducked closer to the ground to avoid it. A female Enchanter took the arrow to the leg, falling backwards. I looked up to see Nicholas climbing the vines on the side of one of the shops, sword in hand, barely reaching the top before grabbing an Enchanter's ankle and yanking them down out of his way.

I shot two more streams in separate directions as I watched him hop onto the roof and slice the heels of another Enchanter. A blue dart sailed across a hilltop towards him, but instead of moving out of the way, he held up his sword and let it ricochet off the blade. The dart rebounded towards the sky, creating an umbrella of magic as it hit just above the treetops.

Odd.

Elise shouted my name as I watched the blue sparks dissolve into nothing. Before I could realize what was happening, a blazing cobalt rope slithered around my ankle and yanked me to the ground. I felt the cold mud hit my back as I was pulled forward. I was able to lift my head up slightly to see a beautiful girl with long, wavy, hair the color of midnight standing on top of a flat roof. Her fuchsia dress swung around her ankles. She had no expression on her dark-skinned face but nodded to two men beside her. They let out their own magic, spewing it from their palms.

I tried to grab onto anything as the magic dragged me along the ground, my hands scraping along grass and crumbled rocks. I looked to my left to Elise clapping her hands together, sending a wave of black over a small crowd of Enchanters barreling towards her. Those hands were suddenly bound by a teal rope; she frantically pulled and tugged at it, eventually being hurled to the ground.

Reese shot another arrow, striking two Enchanters in one shot. Another arrow flew towards the female who had me in her grasp. She turned her hand towards the arrow and in seconds, it turned to dust. The male Enchanter next to her whipped out a yellow rope that bound Reese's ankles, and he fell, only to be covered in ropes of magic.

Nicholas looked down at me as we locked eyes, and I could feel the rope heating through my leggings into my skin. This female wanted me to feel pain from beginning to end. I saw the ivy from the side of the building snake itself around Nicholas's ankles and tighten as it pulled them together, throwing him face down. Branches wrapped around his wrists, making him lose hold of his sword, which tumbled off the roof onto the dirt below.

Weapons to a mind fight, indeed.

I had to stop this.

I dug my heels into the ground hard, making solid impact into the muddy ground. I closed my eyes, letting the black veil wash over me, collecting my feelings.

Discomfort. Anger. Rage.

I slid my hand to the ground, small rocks and shards of wood slicing through my hand. I felt the ground begin to shake, black smoke seeping out from small holes. The smoke grew thick, and I turned my hand towards those who wanted us dead. Each smoke stream coiled around itself, tightening into a thick cord, bobbing and weaving out of the dirt. I splayed my fingers, commanding the cords forward.

They found their way to each Enchanter, constricting and squeezing like a snake. I motioned for one cord to slice the blue rope at my ankle, releasing me. I did the same for the others, cutting their binds with ease. I jumped up from the ground, watching my magic at work, until I caught sight of my captor, her once emotionless face one of confusion and relentlessness. She brought her palm face up, a ball of infernal power in her hand aimed at me. The flames were a light blue, the center clear and growing larger, but I was one step ahead.

A smoking black ribbon snuck up behind her, wrapping around

her shoulders, another grabbing her thighs, and yet another around her neck, slowly squeezing. The Enchanters struggled and writhed against my restraints, but I didn't let up. Others tried to free them, but I yanked them back.

I motioned my magic to bring the woman towards me, carrying her from the roof to only a few feet in front of me. Her face shimmered with patches of glitter, her ears decorated in jewelry. I let the cord around her neck stiffen more, and she let out a guttural noise from her closing windpipe. I brought up my right hand again, a ball of a black flame in my palm, my fingers stretching around its smoking surface.

I knew her heart was racing, her hair stuck to her face as she sweat profusely in panic and defeat. I pressed the flame into her chest, little by little, until she started to grunt and moan, sweat beading on her forehead—

"Dani, stop!" I looked over my shoulder to see Nicholas standing a few inches away from me, yielding his sword again. He placed a hand on my elbow, delicately, his wrist marred by bruises. If the blackness of my eyes frightened him, he showed no indication of fear. "We need answers, remember?"

I turned back to my captive - she was clearly their leader.

I stood my ground, though, shaking my head. "They tried to *kill* us." I felt Elise step to my other side, defending me. "I say slaughter them all."

"You trespassed...on...our...land," the Enchanter choked out in response.

"Dani, let her go," Nicholas commanded, staring at me like I was the only one there. "Now."

I brought my hand down, dissolving the black smoke, but the ribbons around her remained. I tilted my head to the side, letting the rage subside, but holding the power steady.

I stared into her round, honey eyes. "Either I tighten my shadows around you and your friends' necks until they snap, or you tell us what we want to know."

The whispering breeze started again, the willows moving along with it, and she nodded vigorously. I eased the ribbon around her neck, allowing her to speak more clearly. "Fine. You leave us alive and I will answer whatever you ask, Soul Seether."

She certainly knew who I was.

I removed the ribbon completely, followed by the ones at her shoulders and thighs, leaving a smaller black cord to entrap her wrists. I surveyed her companions massaging their wrists and necks as the cords were released, disappearing into nothing. The woman in front of me turned her head to look at them, and most of them nodded, a silent understanding.

Nicholas and Reese took her shoulders, walking her over to a decaying shop door. I overheard Reese ask, "so, how long do we have?"

Nicholas sighed. "We have an hour until we have to be back through that portal."

"Let's hope she knows something, then."

REESE FETCHED A CHAIR AND SAT THE ENCHANTER DOWN WHILE I REMOVED my smoke from her wrists, securing her arms and chest to the chair instead, holding her in place. She said nothing as we circled her, a few other Enchanters with her but at a distance. Elise tapped her foot on the wood floor impatiently, leaning against the doorframe as she waited.

Nicholas twirled the hilt of his sword in his hand, making an indention in the floor as it landed. "What do you know about the portals?"

She said nothing, her lips pressed closed.

"Are you the one who made them?" Nicholas asked, this time leaning closer to her face. Reese clucked his tongue, his hands in his pockets.

She only looked straight ahead, undeterred by the situation. I was getting annoyed. This trip would be pointless if she didn't tell us something.

I lifted my hand and closed it into a fist. Her breaths came heavier as the cords pushed into her chest. "Speak."

"Yes." One word.

"Yes?" Reese repeated.

She nodded, looking at me in a silent plea to stop the pressure. I unclenched my fist, watching the cords relax but still keep their hold. She adjusted herself in the chair, her hair falling against her chest . "Yes, I made your portals."

"Impenetrable?" Nicholas questioned.

She nodded again. "Yes, that's what Jonah asked of me."

"Impenetrable means nothing can get in or out. Are you sure that's what you did?" Elise asked from the doorway, casually picking at her nails.

"I will not be questioned about the strength of my power."

"Then explain how a fucking demon got through one, huh?" Reese exclaimed, squeezing his bow in his hand.

The Enchanter opened her mouth, but closed it without speaking. Her eyes moved back and forth, as if replaying something in her head. "A demon? Through the portal?"

"Just showed up out of the blue," Reese confirmed.

"I don't understand how that could have happened." She sounded sincerely confused.

"You're telling me you didn't happen to leave a door open for something like this to happen?" Reese pressed, waiting for her to say exactly what he wanted to hear.

"I would never betray Jonah like that. He has been nothing but kind to us, to me. Years after the attack, he has been a good soul." She let out a long breath.

"This is truly shocking to you, isn't it?" Nicholas asked, his voice quiet, an eyebrow quirked. The female bit her bottom lip, looking down at her feet.

"Attack?" I inquired. "Attacked by who?"

She leaned back in the chair as best as she could. "Years ago, Enchanters befriended angels and demons, and we worked together in harmony. They called on us for the magic they could not produce. Somewhere along the way, that friendship was lost, and the war for power ensued. My mother, Moira, fought in those wars, tried to keep the peace between both sides.

"Then, that she-devil got involved and led our kind into the darkness. Angels, the allies we once had, began to call us heretics and traitors. Oculus was once a land of peace and prosperity, much like your Heaven's Gate, but sentries came, hoping to eliminate us from existence, wanted us to relinquish the powers they deemed dangerous, the powers they once sought us for." Her voice broke, her eyes glassy, but she carried on. "When Jonah was appointed High Executive, he made it a point to come speak to my mother. When she was no longer of this world, he spoke to me. He faced skepticism and backlash, but he earned our respect. I would not have developed a mediocre portal for him."

I stepped forward, watching as she squared her shoulders. "How do you know who I am?"

"Everyone knows who you are, Soul Seether. I wasn't sure when I first saw you, but your power speaks volumes. The she-devils' little pet." She pressed her lips into a hard line.

"I am no one's pet," I spat, clenching my fist again, the cords tightening around her chest. Her eyes widened at the force against her chest.

"Dani, simmer down," Nicholas ordered.

I released her, but I didn't remove myself from my position in front of her.

"She-devil? You mean Lilith?" Reese asked. Elise looked up from her spot, her ears perked up.

"We do not speak her name here." The Enchanter looked into my eyes, challenging me. "She must be quite upset you aren't where you belong."

Nicholas spoke before the tension could get any worse. "Your mother's name was Moira? As in High Priestess Moira?"

She nodded a yes.

I'd overheard a few Enchanters Lilith kept speak about Moira, their words always ones of respect. High Priestesses were practically equal to Lilith, which I knew she hated. Their power ranged from shifting their appearance, to being in two places at once, to shaping reality. The list went on. If the timeline was correct, Moira would have been one of the last ever seen.

"Well, well, well, looks like we're in the presence of royalty." Elise clapped loudly, walking into the room. "Royalty with no hold on her powers if a demon can just walk through one of her portals. Good job fucking that one up. I'm sure you made your mother very proud."

The female tugged at her restraints, practically hissing at Elise. Elise stood her ground, feigning alarm and fear before doubling over in a laugh.

Nicholas cut her laughing short. "If not you, then who? How could this happen?"

She opened and closed her hands over the armrests. "Magic always has loopholes. Someone who is desperate enough to find one, will. The most powerful of Enchanters can't stop that. Even Jonah knew that."

I stayed quiet as I mulled over a question of my own.

"You said Jonah let you stay in your lands, in your...rubble?" I questioned, stepping around the chair to circle her.

"Yes, that's what I said."

"After the attack, you didn't try to rebuild, regrow your numbers? If your mother was so beguiling, she would have made this land better for you and your people. I doubt she would have let you live your life in this empty shell of a place." I squatted near her ear and whispered, "It doesn't add up."

I could see her biting the inside of her cheek, and her throat moved as she swallowed. I could taste the nervous energy radiating from her. "I have no idea what you're talking about."

"When Nicholas propelled your magic into the sky, it didn't disappear into nothing towards the clouds -- it dispersed like a rain shower, which could only mean one thing."

Nicholas said my thoughts out loud before I got the chance.

"Your mother glamoured the real Oculus, didn't she?" he asked, his eyebrows furrowing.

"You are standing in Oculus. This is it," she stammered, clearly a poor attempt at a lie.

Elise crossed her arms over her chest, stepping to the other side of the chair. "This may be Oculus, but this isn't what it looks like."

"Your mother rebuilt your land, then covered it in the shadow of its brutalized state." I wanted her to give me some type of answer, anything to finalize my thoughts.

My words had the desired effect. "Yes! Is that what you want to hear? I was just a girl when it all happened. She did it to protect us, so anyone who could harm us would think we were meek, haunted and forbidden in their history books. Jonah knew, along with a few others my mother chose to let in. I tried to keep things up, maintain as much normalcy as possible with Jonah's help, and he received my help in return. Hence the portals and the keys."

"You don't want demons crossing portals unannounced any more than we do. You just want your people safe." Nicholas softened his tone.

Her eyes went soft, glassy. "It's what I've always wanted."

Reese let out a loud huff. "No wonder you wanted us dead on sight."

Before she could retort, Nicholas asked a question. "What's your name?"

Surprisingly, she didn't argue. "Natalia."

"Well, Natalia, do you have any idea how these loopholes were discovered? Books, maps, word of mouth?"

"As I've said, you have to want it enough to break apart that much magic. What I *can* tell you is that Enchanters wield a special brand of magic. I used much of my strength to build those portals. One can create the magic, but it will take more than one to destroy it."

Reese wiped a hand down his face. "What the fuck does that even mean?"

Elise rolled her eyes, ripping his bow from his hands to point it at him. "It means you have *two* possible problems now."

"Why bring the Soul Seether?" Natalia asked suddenly, interrupting their argument.

"Why does it matter?" I argued back.

"That's the question, isn't it? What makes you so special? I'm sure there are plenty of demons who could have taken your place." She cocked her head to the side, intrigued. I didn't have an answer. She knew her question was rhetorical; she just wanted it to remain in my head.

But it seemed as though our time here was running out.

Nicholas pulled out the amethyst stone, which pulsed slightly. "We have to go." He looked to me and then to Natalia. "Let her go – and be nice about it. I can't guarantee we won't be back."

She raised both her eyebrows but nodded.

I flicked my wrist as I freed her from darkness, but not without whipping at her exposed arms a bit, leaving small red marks. She rubbed her arms, moving them around a bit. The Enchanters came to her aide immediately, looking her up and down.

"Tell Jonah I'll fix the portals. It's the least I can do," she said with surprising sincerity.

Nicholas gave her one quick nod as he made his way towards the door. Elise looked from him to the Enchanter. "So that's it? We aren't gonna kill anybody?"

I smirked, placing my hand on her shoulder as I shook my head. She shrugged away from me, muttering something I couldn't hear. We'd started to follow Nicholas towards the door when Natalia asked a sudden question back.

"And your name?"

He turned on his heels. "Nicholas?"

She cocked her head. "Your last name doesn't happen to be Cassial, does it?"

He arched an eyebrow. "It is. What's it to you?"

"Our mothers knew one another back when the lines weren't so thick. I think I remember seeing her here. I could be wrong, but you share the same eyes."

Nicholas paused, as if his heart stopped beating. He looked at Natalia, almost through her, as he absorbed her words. I wanted to shake him, but he resumed his stoic face quickly. "My mother left my family when I was a boy, so I'm not sure what to tell you." He slapped his hand against the doorframe and rushed out. The unshakeable angel wasn't so put together after all.

Reese slid his bow behind his back and followed, Elise stomping out after him, directing her words at him. "Are you gonna admit I was the slightest bit right about your shitty weapons?"

I went to follow, and I ducked my head down as I made my way to the door. I stopped dead in my tracks, though, when I heard a strong, booming voice outside. My companions were frozen with me as I watched a large man with broad shoulders, muscles pulsing down his arms, tattoos scattered along his skin, long, shiny hair in a braid down his back. He was intimidatingly tall and had a look of utter confusion and complete rage on his face.

"What the hell happened? Where is she?" he shouted, pushing Enchanters out of the way and barreling towards us. He stalked over to Nicholas and shoved a finger in his face. "You have no business here! What have you done to–."

"They were just leaving," Natalia interrupted, her voice completely calm and maybe a slight bit irritated. "I have it under control."

"Under control? Look around, this is not under–." She cut him off as she raised her hand. "We've talked about this; I am not a damsel in distress."

Maybe I could learn to like her.

Natalia looked over and motioned for us to go ahead. The man just heaved a frustrated sigh and swiped a hand down his face. We shuffled around him, watching as other Enchanters gave him a wide berth. Natalia eyed me before I got too far out of sight.

"Don't worry, Soul Seether. We'll meet again."

49

CHAPTER FOUR

NICK

I had to wait a whole day to speak to Jonah when we got back from Oculus. I assumed he'd have wanted to see me immediately, but Ariel shooed me away from his office and told me the high executive would see me the next day. I honestly didn't want to be alone with my thoughts; the last words out of Natalia's mouth remained front and center.

My mother.

I had no interest in entertaining the idea of her, let alone talking about her with someone who'd hog tied me with a tree vine. I had no quarrel with Natalia, but what she said ate at me, like a worm slithering its way through an apple core. Dani and Elise had taken to being by themselves, and Reese had decided he'd nap away the exhaustion.

The Skies offered its sentries rooms if they decided to remain permanently. Flying home while your eyes fluttered closed from lack of sleep wasn't always the safest bet so they had decided to give us rooms here instead. Unlike my best friend, I'd opted to go home. I hadn't seen my father, Maurice, in weeks, so a visit was much needed.

The flight to the North Village was filled with breathtaking scenery. I let the wind hit my wings as I relaxed into it. The leaves on the trees tickled the tips of my feathers, and the breeze sent different aromas through my nose: fresh bread, running streams, even a slow burning fire. Everything seemed so small up here; I was so high, I could touch a cloud if I wanted.

The North Village came into view quickly enough. All the villages were distinct. The South was in the countryside, and when it rained, it poured. East was secluded in the mountains with some of the best hiking trails. The West, on the same side of the map as Oculus, faced the water. The summers there were the best, with a few monstrous beaches I'd only been to a handful of times. The streets in the North were flooded with cobblestone, each house constructed with the sturdiest wood with brick chimneys. The houses were connected to each other by small gates with a narrow grass patch in between. The weather varied from village to village, but the North was usually a constant autumn. The leaves were no longer green, but various colors from orange to red to deep brown.

I started my landing, weaving a bit so I wouldn't hit any tree branches. Stone crunched beneath my sneakers as I planted my feet on the ground, a breeze rustling my hair, surrounded by my home. I realized I'd landed behind the village, a short walk from my house, so I began to walk. I could see one of the two large fountains that proudly remained no matter how expansive this place became. I heard children laughing, old creaking doors opening and closing, the faint chime of bells in the distance. It made my heart hurt being back here, realizing I hadn't been home in quite some time.

I noticed the two-story building and large green lawn my father and I used to spar on first. Once Reese and I became close, it became the three of us clashing fake swords and ending up in a wrestling match of fists and slaps. Then we got older, and I got a better sword with actual weight, Reese got his first bow made of cedar, and my father set up targets for us to practice with. I felt my chest swell with pride at the nostalgia, and I walked a few steps up to the back door and knocked. I heard him grumble something from inside, then nothing but silence. I looked around awkwardly, my fingers tapping my thighs. I was about to knock again when the door swung open and my father's tired but youthful face stared back at me. His bored expression melted into a happy one as he took me in. Despite his age, he still looked spry.

"Nicholas! It's been too long!" he yelled, embracing me in a tight hug.

"How are you, dad?" I muffled into his shoulder.

He didn't say anything for a minute as he held me. Eventually, he grabbed my arms and held me out in front of him, looking me over.

"I'm alright. Same old, same old." He said that every time I visited. "You look well."

"I'm doing okay I suppose." I shrugged, not wanting to give away too much. His mustache had grown since the last time I was here, now down past his lips. It had specks of gray in it, the same as his hair and beard. We shared the same dark hair, but his was longer, meeting the bottom of his earlobes, curling outwards. "Smells amazing in there, dad." I nodded inside.

He squeezed my arms and let go, motioning for me to follow him inside. "I was just about to have some lunch, if you're hungry."

"Is that even a question?" I teased, settling down in a wicker chair at the table. The house was small, but nice for a small family. The kitchen and living room were consolidated into one space, a bear skin rug in the middle of the room. There was a small closet in the far corner next to the fireplace with extra blankets and pillows. I remember lounging on the loveseat and never having to wonder if dinner was ready, because I could just look over my shoulder and see it.

The light outside was still bright, coming in through the square windows, but I looked up at the string lights my father had strung up for when evening came. I could see down the hallway leading to my bedroom and one of the bathrooms, to the staircase leading upstairs. The sound of taps and stirring pulled me out of my thoughts.

"I know it's just soup, but I have bread from the baker that I think you'll like," he called from the corner, pulling some bowls down from the cabinet.

I chuckled. "You know I'll eat whatever you make." He was such a good cook.

I couldn't hear his laugh, but I noticed the way his shoulders shook, confirming he approved. My father walked the bowls to the table, setting them down gently and going back for the bread. I got my height from him, so reaching tall things around the house was never an issue for us; it made me smirk to see his long arm effortlessly reach the top shelf before closing the cabinet door. He took the seat adjacent to mine and looked over his meal.

"I'm sorry I couldn't bring your *actual* favorite this time," I joked, referring to Reese. He usually accompanied me on my visits home, even though he avoided his own family a few houses down. He had issues with his parents, and it was a rabbit hole he refused to dive down.

My father dunked some bread into his soup and popped it into his mouth. "Shame. How is the troublemaker?"

"Just as you'd expect." Reese really hadn't changed. He was just as loud and arrogant as ever, just taller. "As obnoxious as ever."

"Is he still handling that bow like it's his first-born son?"

I shifted forward in my seat, laughing. "He cradles that thing like a damn baby."

I scooped up some of the soup, blowing on it to cool it down. The garlic hit me instantly before the soup even touched my lips, but it was heaven, spicy but subtle. I peered up and noticed him staring at me.

"Could you be any weirder right now?"

"I'm just happy you're home, that's all," he stated. I pressed my lips together and let out a breath. "Your company is always appreciated."

I reached out to rip off a piece of bread. "I'm happy to be home, but you know I can't *stay* right?" Each visit came with small talk, an update on my life, and the endless speech about how I could do better. "I love visiting you, but I'll have to go back to my job."

"Thank you for the reminder, Nicholas." He shoveled more food into his mouth. We had just started eating and we were already at this point, the one where Reese would leave and wander into another room.

I rolled my eyes. "I don't want to fight, but you can't keep trying to convince me to not go back." I got my persistence from him, but I also got his stubborn nature.

"I've never once told you to not go back; don't put words in my mouth." He wagged his index finger at me, his eyebrows furrowing.

"Dad, you literally said *you shouldn't go back there, Nicholas* last time I was here." I mimicked his words, taking another spoonful of my soup.

He dropped his spoon into his bowl and sat back in his chair. "I said you shouldn't go back there if you plan to live the same lifestyle. Those were my exact words."

"What does that even mean?"

My father let out an exasperated sigh. "I mean you're so much more than they're letting you be. You can't really tell me you're happy guarding posts and seeking souls." I pushed my bowl away from me and placed my hands on the table at his mention of our weekly duties. Animus Seeking was what he meant -- soul seeking. Sentries were expected to fly around human lands and guide souls to Heaven, and I truly enjoyed it.

"It's more than that and you know it," I argued.

"I brought you to The Skies because you wanted to go so badly, and yeah, maybe I wanted to show you everything you could be. You're a great sentry, but that's not all you *can* be. They said they wanted you there because of your skills, but you've hardly used them. I've seen you with a sword, the way it calls to you. I bet you haven't had any real chance to wield one."

"It's not my fault a war of bloodshed and death isn't happening right now, like it happened to you." He didn't flinch at my reminder of his past as a sentry and revered angel.

My father ran a hand through his hair. "Then aim higher. You have always been a leader, my boy, so lead. I can have a talk with Jonah, if that's what it takes."

I groaned, hating the direction this had taken yet again. "You want me to be an executive? You think it just works like that? Like I can go to Jonah and ask to be promoted? When he asks me why, I'll just say my father would really fucking *appreciate* it," I spat back, crossing my arms over my chest.

My father reached across the table, his palm up. He wanted me to take his hand, and after a minute, I did. "I'm aware of how promotions work, and I know you've made yourself scarce when it comes up. Hell, when I was your age, I probably would have done the same. You deserve more, you and I both know that. Jonah's coddling you too much."

"Just because you left doesn't mean I plan too. Maybe I just so happen to like what I'm doing." He raised an eyebrow, nodding and looking at the ground. He never spoke much about his time at The Skies, but I did know he left on his accord. When he lifted his head, a ghost of a smile graced his lips.

"They are clueless asses, the lot of them."

I scoffed. "You sound like Reese."

"I always liked that kid." He squeezed my hand.

He looked down at my wrist poking out from under my jean jacket. The bruise from the vines at Oculus was still there, the purple still dark, the line thick. "What the hell is that?"

"Battle scars, for lack of better words."

He traced his thumb over the line. I knew he could feel the indent it left in my skin.

"You and Reese get into a rope fight?" A valid question.

I pulled my arm away, shoving my sleeve down. "It wasn't with Reese."

His eyebrows raised. "Who was this fight with then? You've never been the type to get into a random scuffle."

"We just ran into a little bit of trouble at Oculus, that's all," I said nonchalantly, picking a piece of imaginary lint from my pants.

"Oculus! Nicholas, what—" He stopped mid-sentence, collecting himself. "Why didn't you tell me?"

I let out a small laugh he didn't seem to appreciate. "It happened a lot faster than you think, Dad. It isn't as bad as you think, believe me. You just told me to use my skills more."

"You went by yourself?"

I shook my head, biting my cheek. "No, I went with Reese and some others." I'd almost told him about Dani and Elise but telling him would mean explaining. That was valuable information I couldn't divulge. "We got caught up in a situation, but it was fine."

"Jonah sent you on this mission?" He said each word slowly, as if testing them out on his tongue.

I nodded my response.

"Well, as long as you're alright." The corners of his mouth began to climb. "I don't quite approve of an Oculus trip, but maybe those prissy pants are realizing your potential."

I wanted to say something witty, but there was something else on my mind now. I got up from my chair, walking further to the wood burning fireplace surrounded by brick. "There *is* one thing I need to tell you." I bit my lower lip so hard, I could almost taste blood. "We spoke to an Enchanter while we were there." I let out a breath. "She mentioned Mom."

The heat of the fire evaporated as the words left my lips. The room felt smaller and slightly colder. I only had a few valid memories of her, vague and blurry.

"What did this Enchanter say about her?" my father asked, his voice cautious. I could tell he wasn't sitting down anymore, but he was keeping his distance from me.

"Nothing of real merit. She just said her mother spoke well of her." I clasped my hands into fists at my side. "I mean, how would she even know her?"

My father let out a long, slow breath, coming up behind me to lay a hand on my shoulder. "Your mother was a kind woman. I don't doubt Enchanters remember her. She had her secrets, but I don't blame her for them. We are all entitled to a few."

I met his eyes, remembering a time when I had to tilt my head back to meet those same eyes. "That may be true, but she left both of us so she could keep them."

My father placed his calloused hand on my cheek, almost as if he was searching for something to say. Instead, he led me to the loveseat and patted the spot next to him as he sat. I fell into the cushions, almost forgetting how uncomfortable it was. I tried repositioning, but it was no use. "How about you tell me about training in The Skies? I promise I won't butt in."

I DECIDED TO SLEEP THERE AT MY FATHER'S REQUEST. I'D SAID FINE AFTER HIS never-ending nagging ceased. I flew back earlier than he'd antici- pated, but I told him I had business to attend to. He was a smart enough man to know that pushing me any further on any subject would just make matters worse. We hadn't spoken any more of my mother -- not that there would have been much to say. I had made my position clear. I was back at The Skies. All previous conversations were a moot point for now.

The light was starting to creep through my window, one that gave me a perfect view from the second floor. I knew at any moment, I could be summoned to meet with Jonah, so there was no point to going back to sleep. I sat on the edge of my bed and reached for the handle of my desk drawer. Sliding it open, I pulled out a beautifully crafted piece of metal.

Dani's dagger.

I let it sit in my palm, letting my fingers slide over the edge of the blade, lightly so as not to cut myself. It had weight, but it wasn't too heavy. I narrowed my eyes at the engraving of her name, perfectly etched into the metal. I couldn't believe I was admiring this weapon. I gazed at the hilt, how the leather seemed to have a glossy texture, how the tip curved to a seamless point.

I should have given this to someone, but I didn't. *Shit.*

She brought it with her for protection, no doubt. I would have done the same, if I was being honest. She hadn't asked about it and I'd forgotten about it until now. It didn't feel evil or dark. It felt like a normal weapon, but I knew it was forged in darkness.

It was *made* for her.

The closer I looked at it, the more I kept it in my palm. It released puffs of dark smoke, disappearing around my hand. I could have sworn I heard it whisper something, and I tilted my head down, trying to hear.

Three quick knocks on my door had me dropping the dagger with a clang. I rapidly picked it up and threw it back into my drawer, slamming it shut.

"Yeah?" I answered, realizing I was out of breath. *Shit. Shit. Shit.*

"You are wanted on the tenth floor." Whoever it was spoke quickly, and I heard their footsteps retreat almost immediately. The tenth floor was Jonah's floor.

The elevator ticked up as I leaned against the wall. Our rooms were on the second floor, so I'd crowded into the elevator with other angels and waited. A few of them noticed the tenth was illuminated, but they didn't say anything. It wasn't something you saw every day. Eventually, I was alone with my thoughts, one floor to go and my nerves setting in.

I didn't know what he wanted. Did he want answers? Would he approve of my information? I was startled out of my self-doubt by the elevator chime.

The doors slid open, revealing a dimly lit hallway. I stepped out to see marble walls, and the smell of forest trees filled my nostrils. A narrow gold carpet with emerald leaves extended down the hall. Everyone knew his office doors were tall, oak behemoths in the very middle of the hall, so I began walking. I passed open doors, each with name plates. Ariel and Markus' offices were here as well, nowhere near as large as Jonah's. I made it a point to observe a few of the paintings on the walls. Executives that came before him stood proudly in a few portraits, while others were classic moments in our history.

I knew it was coming up on my right. I could fucking feel it. Jonah suppressed the power he had when in meetings, but I could feel it now. This was his domain. As much as he shared this floor with the others, all you could feel was him.

I swallowed hard, a knot going down my throat.

I stopped my hand from shaking so I could wrap my fingers around the winged door knocker. I slammed it against the door, a loud knocking sound echoing through the hall as I stepped back.

The creaking came before the sound of a lock. I let my eyes dart around the door, trying to pinpoint where the sounds were coming from. The door slowly opened inward, a small crack in the middle, growing wider and wider with every moment. I felt my feet move as I walked towards the opening doors, revealing a large room with a man with a smile on his face.

Jonah.

"Please, Nicholas, do come in." He motioned with his hand for me to step into the room, one silver ring on each finger.

I nodded tightly and made my way past the doors, instantly feeling the temperature change. The hallway had a cool breeze to it, but here it felt warm, like the perfect summer day. Jonah flicked his wrist towards him, closing the doors behind me. He didn't wear the traditional executive attire today, no variation of teal or blue. Instead, he wore a simple, long sleeve button down, crisp and white, with long black pants, the amethyst gem that I used to portal us to Oculus around his neck. He turned away from me to one of the bookshelves that encompassed the room.

The shelves weren't high, but they were wide, one wall nothing but red oak. I spun around slowly to take in the white stone walls and chandeliers forming a triangle on the ceiling. A square rug with feathered tassels covered the middle of the room, a large fireplace and a bar cart decorating it. Jonah's desk was near the back, covered in papers and manuscripts.

"Have a seat, please. You don't have to stand," Jonah insisted, patting one of the armchairs across from his desk. I ran the tips of my fingers along the velvet before I took a seat.

Jonah placed his hands under his chin as he sat down. "You have news to report?"

I shifted in my seat, suddenly uncomfortable. "I'm afraid we may not have gotten the answers you were hoping to find."

One side of his lip pulled up in a half smile. "So, you met Natalia?"

"Yes. She told us you knew of each other."

Jonah leaned back in his chair, letting his power simmer. "I knew her mother. When she died, I made a visit to the new leader."

"If you know them so well, why didn't you go yourself?" I was putting myself on thin ice with my tone.

"I couldn't. I have duties here. I may have good ties with Oculus, but they are still on our lands in our realm, as much as they would like to remain in the shadows. Therefore, they are still in my jurisdiction. I have to show I have the means to get my questions answered."

"So, you already knew Natalia had nothing to do with it? The escaping demon, I mean."

Jonah lifted his eyes and tilted his head, mulling over my question. "Yes and no. I have good reason to assume she did not betray me, but you must always be prepared for surprises." He gave me an inquisitive look. "You seemed to have made it back in one piece. I presume our guests were helpful?"

I nodded tersely. "Dani...well, she's a lot to take in."

Jonah's eyes seemed to widen. "Purgatory is no joke, Nicholas. It becomes a mindset to those who remain there too long."

I finally settled back into my chair, casually resting my arms. "She did discover something you apparently were already aware of." Jonah raised his manicured eyebrows. "The Oculus glamor."

He let out a low laugh. "Ah yes, that. I discovered it during my initial meeting with Natalia. Beautiful craftsmanship. Her mother really was a wonder. I promised Natalia and her mother it would remain a harmless secret."

"You could also tell them to remove it. They can go back to living their lives as normal without having to hide."

Jonah shook his head, casually tapping a pen on the desk. "If it were that easy, I would agree. The Enchanters have been ravaged -- they would rather remain the way they are, just to have peace of mind. I won't force them. It isn't my place. You know, once upon a time, you could travel to Oculus and were greeted with a smiling face and a hug."

I smirked. "Things have changed, I assure you."

"So it seems." He nodded at the bruise on my wrist. "None of this concerns the issue at hand, though. What have you brought me?"

I cleared my throat. "Natalia didn't give much, but I get the feeling none of her people want anything to do with this or would have the power to pull apart a portal. She did say she created it, but it would take more than one to destroy it."

Jonah rubbed his thumb and index finger over his stubbled chin. "More to destroy it."

"Yes, sir."

He pushed back from his chair, walking to the fireplace. A lit candle sat in the center, the flame small but releasing that intense forest scent. "So, we have more enemies than I thought."

I remained in my chair. "It would seem that way."

I waited for a response, but he said nothing. He stayed with his back to me, facing a fireplace with no raging fire. "She knew Dani; not like a friend, but almost in a curious way. She asked why Dani was there instead of another demon. I've been wondering that myself."

Jonah turned over to his bar. "Do you know why Dani is called the Soul Seether?" I shook my head as he poured an amber liquid into a glass, raising it to his lips and taking a long drink. "I only know Lilith gave her that name for her ability to rapidly and violently mutilate the soul. Not just the body it lives in, but the very nature of your being. That kind of power... people either gravitate towards it or cower in fear."

I got to my feet. "If you fear her, then why bring her here?"

Jonah downed the rest of his drink, placing the glass gently on the bar. "I don't fear her, Nicholas. Lilith covets her, but the Soul Seether isn't tethered to that place. Having her on our side could give us an advantage for what's to come, however dangerous it may be."

"What's to come?" I asked.

"You think one demon coming through the portal was the beginning and end? He was likely an experiment for something I assure you will cause bigger problems."

"Shouldn't we be preparing for that?" I questioned, confusion heavy in my voice.

"We will never be truly prepared for what may come. Unfortunately, I am no oracle."

I tapped my fingers on the bar. "What if Lilith decides to come looking for them? The portals are already weak."

"We will fight as we have always done, but Lilith coming through is quite impossible. Do not concern yourself with that -- I have

Natalia working on the portals as we speak. For now though, I have restricted access to portal keys for the time being."

I walked back over to my chair, laying my hands on the back. "You make this sound like the calm before the storm."

"Exactly," he replied. "I will summon you again soon with your next task. You handled yourself quite well."

I squeezed the chair in annoyance at my dismissal. I wasn't annoyed with Jonah, but with the situation. I felt like someone's errand boy, like exactly what my father warned of. The doors creaked open as I headed towards them.

I stopped, turning slightly. "You aren't planning on sending them home, are you?" He acted as if Dani was a demonic calling card. Maybe she was.

Jonah peered at me, his gray eyes sparkling. "Not quite yet."

"How long do you plan on napping for?" I asked, shaking my best friend. I had taken the elevator back down to the second floor and strolled down the hall to Reese's bedroom. The lights were off, but I could hear his faint snores.

"Go away."

I rolled my eyes, shaking him again. "Wake up! You slept all day yesterday, you ass." I lightly punched right between his legs as he was turning over, receiving a loud groan in return.

"Fuck off."

I snickered, walking to the window and pulling up the blinds. Light flooded the room. To anyone else, it would seem like a beautiful morning, but to Reese, it was pure venom. He shoved his face further into his pillow, muffling what I could only imagine were a slew of curse words.

"Let's get up. Sometime today, please."

"What time is it?" Reese asked, his voice raspy and sleep filled.

I looked at his clock. "Nine in the morning."

"My fucking god. You know I'm allergic to any time before noon."

I grabbed a chair and pulled it up to the bed. I plopped down, placing my elbows on my knees. "Oh really?"

Reese pulled a pillow from behind his head and pressed it onto his face, shielding himself from the sunlight. "Yeah, it's somewhere in my medical profile."

I pretended to ponder his words. "You didn't seem too allergic to early mornings when I saw you sprinting out of Tessa Yeal's room naked at eight in the morning."

Reese threw the pillow off his face and gave me a hard look. "Her boyfriend came back earlier than expected. Don't act like you haven't fucked around and been a little shit before."

I shrugged, lifting my feet and resting them on the bed. "Yeah, well, I don't go around fucking girls with boyfriends. I'll leave that to you and your low standard dick."

As the last words left my mouth, I saw more of the ceiling and then the other side of the room when Reese grabbed my ankles and tipped me over. I landed with a hard thud and a groan. He laughed, pushing the covers off his legs.

At least he had on boxers this time. Seeing Reese's dick unannounced for the hundredth time was not what I had signed up for. He padded to the bathroom as I got up from the floor, rubbing my neck.

"I saw my father yesterday."

"How is old Maurice?" Reese inquired from the bathroom.

"Doing alright. Almost had a fight. Spent all night telling him about training."

Reese peeked out from around the open door. "Did you tell him I'm getting close to your level with a sword?"

"Yeah, I don't like to lie to my dad." I bite my bottom lip, watching as he scrunched his face with irritation. "I did have to omit some things to him."

"Such as?" he asked, leaning against the door frame.

"Dani and Elise..."

His eyes widened. "They're still here? What the hell?"

"I guess Jonah wants to keep them around."

He ran an exasperated hand through his hair. "Can't we put it to a vote?"

"You're the only one with a problem," I said, crossing my arms over my chest.

Reese shook his head. "My problem is not with *both*, it's with *one*."

"She seems...harmless."

He took two long strides over to me and smacked my forehead. "Do you just stop listening when she speaks? Harmless is not the word I'd use. She's like a damn piranha. If she could, I'm pretty sure she would have poofed me out of existence by now."

"I guarantee plenty of angels would poof you out of existence if they could."

Reese stuck his tongue behind his teeth and nodded. "Okay, Nick the Dick, valid point."

"Can you please go take a shower, so we can get out of here?"

Reese pointed to the bruises on his body. "Can I get my bearings please? You should be happy I'm not traumatized from yesterday's events."

I bite my tongue, suppressing my laugh. "We weren't going to let you die. Let's not forget Dani saved your ass." I gave him a pointed look.

He ignored my comment, walking over to his dresser and pulling out clean clothes. Instead, he said, "is it weird to say Natalia was kind of hot, or is that too soon?"

I waved my hands out in front of me. "Wait, wait, wait. Elise wants to kill you and you can't stand her, but Natalia actually tried to hurt you and you think she's hot? I don't follow."

Reese tucked his clothes underneath his arm. "Natalia did it to, you know, protect her people. Elise just wants to annoy the living fuck out of me until the day I die, which would undoubtedly be her fault anyway."

I looked up at the ceiling and fell back onto his bed. "Shower, please."

"Okay, mom." He walked back into the bathroom, and I shut my eyes, mentally checking off all the things I planned to do today.

"Hey, so what are we doing this early anyway?" Reese asked.

"I set up an impromptu training session with Dani," I started, opening my eyes and pushing up on my elbows, only to be faced with a completely naked Reese casually standing in front of me. "Fucking shit, Reese, a little warning would be great."

He smirked, turning away towards the bathroom again, giving me a prime view of his ass before slamming the door behind him. "Ain't nothing little about it."

CHAPTER FIVE

DANI

"Punctuality must not be part of being an angel," Elise said. Once the sentries had led us to this training room, removed the handcuffs, and promptly left thirty minutes ago, she had made herself comfortable on the glossy floor. She propped herself against the wall and tilted her head back. "I don't like being woken up early for no fucking reason."

"At least you get to release some of the anger you've been harboring today," I answered, my hands on my hips.

"Very true. I know just who I can release it on." She tapped each of her black-polished fingernails on her chin dramatically.

I rolled my eyes. "Give him a break."

"He can have a break when he dies," she quipped, pressing her lips together. "Of completely natural causes and not by my hand, of course."

I raised an eyebrow at her and opened my mouth to respond when the door opened. I turned to see Nicholas and Reese walking over the threshold, expressionless. We had been told to dress for training, which to angels meant comfortable, breathable attire. They were no exception, both sporting sweatpants and worn t-shirts. Elise had opted for a baggy shirt and shorts, while I decided on just a sports bra and dark red leggings. I had braided my hair to keep it out of my face, but small, wispy curls had escaped around my forehead and temples.

"Look who decided to grace us with their presence this glorious morning," Elise sneered.

Reese gave a tight smile and walked to the weapons rack near the door. He pulled a sword out and lightly tossed it to his friend, who smoothly caught it.

"Bit of a late start this morning." Nicholas nodded behind him just as Reese let out a disgruntled sound of agreement as he wrapped his hair in a messy bun.

"Aw, did Blondie not get his beauty sleep last night?" Elise placed her hands on either side of her legs, palms to the ground.

Reese pulled out a sword for himself and twirled it in his hand. "Fuck you."

Elise pushed out her bottom lip. "You wish."

I decided to cut in before any more shots were fired. "You want us to train?"

Nick laid the sword over his shoulder, letting the blade rest on his clavicle. I noticed the prompt tick at his neck, his pulse strong but relaxed. His skin was smooth, but there were imperfections that broke the porcelain mold: small shaving cuts at his chin, a scar under his right eye, the bruises still heavily purple on his wrists from our trip to Oculus.

I hadn't realized he was a few feet in front of me until he spoke again, those brown eyes looking right at me. "I made sure to block off this training room so we wouldn't be interrupted. We wanna see your skill sets."

I gave him a small smile. "You'll have to be a bit more specific, Nicholas. I'm *skilled* in a lot of things."

"Skills with a sword."

I kept my smile but traced my eyes down his body. "I assure you my sword skills come *highly* recommended." I raised my hand and let my finger trace down his forearm.

His eyes never left my face, but I could feel the hairs on his arm rise, goosebumps making a welcomed appearance. His attempt to disregard my innuendo was cute. He let his eyes drop for a minute to my chest until he cleared his throat and backed off, turning towards Reese, who stood there with his eyes narrowed.

"Are you sure you have no intention of a piece of that?" Elise asked from behind me, her voice low enough for only me to hear.

I glanced over my shoulder. "No, just to tease. Passes the time." I admired the way he looked in his sweatpants. No one should look that good in loungewear.

She whispered, "you're boring."

Reese stalked over to us, two swords in hand. "Here." He motioned for us to take them.

Elise looked down at the weapons but made no move to touch them. "You don't really mean for us to use those, right? Like actually fight with them?"

Reese's nostrils flared in annoyance, his jaw tensing. "No, I just brought them for you to *look* at."

I grabbed one of the swords and twisted it slightly in my hand. The hilt was wrapped in leather, shining from base to tip. It wasn't anything special, but I assumed training swords were meant to be simple. "We understand, Reese, but that's not where our value lies."

"I didn't ask about your values, did I?" His voice was deep but monotone.

Elise pushed his hand away, clapping her hands together. "I'm going to have to happily decline your ridiculous offer. Thanks, but no thanks."

He shoved the sword towards her again, his bicep flexing. "It wasn't a suggestion."

Nicholas put his hand over the hilt and forced Reese to lower it, pushing him back behind him. "It's just simple sparring -- that's all, Elise. Nothing more."

"I understand that, but I'm pretty sure I can handle myself without lugging around one of those gnarly things." She made a disgusted face at the sword.

Nicholas stuck out his tongue and licked his lower lip. "You can't always rely on magic to solve your problems."

Elise smirked. "I don't; I just highly prefer it."

"Magic seems to be solving our problems just fine, like I'm sure your good looks and charm solve yours," I said, coming to Elise's defense. "Magic is what saved that one's ass in Oculus." I cocked my head towards Reese, who lifted his eyes to the ceiling.

Nicholas ran a hand through his hair, pieces of it still standing after he was done. "Regardless, we'll be sparring today and you'll both be active participants." His voice wasn't harsh, but there was a slight command in it that made my stomach flip.

Elise let out a loud, harsh laugh. "We can spar just fine. I'll show you." She flicked her fingers, dark smoke shooting out to smack Reese in the chest, flinging him into the wall. The sword he held flew towards the window, landing on the ground. I glared over at Elise, who looked pleased with herself. Nicholas bolted over to his friend, who pushed himself off the wall, rubbing the back of his head.

"What in the fuck?" Reese shouted, pulling out of Nicholas's grasp and stalking towards Elise. She stood her ground, tapping her foot on the floor patiently.

"I thought we were sparring?" she said innocently.

"With *weapons*, you *fucking* demon!"

She shrugged. "Well, magic is my weapon, so technically the same thing, right?"

"I could send your ass back to Purgatory so fucking fast.." Reese started, trying to break through Nicholas, who was holding his arm in front of his chest, pushing him back.

"Please do, Blondie!" Elise snapped, lifting her hand as red tendrils sparked from her fingertips. I grabbed her, silencing the magic, squeezing so hard, she flinched.

I could see the way Reese's tan face flushed red with pure rage. His hands shook and his breathing became ragged and rough. Nicholas grabbed his shoulders and stood beside him. "First rule for everyone is that you don't use magic on anyone on your team."

"Yeah, I'm not much of a team player." Elise countered.

69

"Nicholas, you forget we don't live in the world of holding hands and working together. Purgatory was survival of the fittest, so the all for one and one for all bullshit really isn't going to work," I said, hoping to be the reasonable voice in the chaos.

He looked down, and I followed his gaze to my hand. My fingers were still wrapped around the hilt of the sword. He leaned in towards me. "I know you know how to handle some type of weapon, or did I not pull a dagger out of your pocket?"

"Ah yes, I've been wondering where you've been hiding it. I'll be wanting that back."

Nicholas stepped back, taking a still-seething Reese with him, pushing his friend to the side. "How about you fight me for it?" He looked at his sword and back over to mine. The sly smile that crossed his face *almost* made me clench my thighs together. He was attractive, I'll give him that.

Reese's face started to slowly retreat from its bright shade of red, his breathing starting to return to a normal pace. "No magic. Just weapons." He shot a look over at Elise, who blew him a kiss. "Keep that one on a leash."

"Now you're speaking my language," Elise said, placing a hand on her hip.

I took a few steps back and slowly sliced the sword in the air. "Can I ask one question?"

Nicholas looked at me expectedly.

"Is there a reason the ceiling is so high?"

Reese and Nicholas side glanced over to each other and let out similar soft laughs. "So we can get a feel for aerial fights as well."

"I've always wondered what demon wings looked like," Reese said to no one in particular.

"The tips are sharp enough to slice through that sweet little neck of yours," Elise answered, sliding her middle finger across her neck. Reese flicked both his middle fingers at her in response as he backed up towards one of the walls to watch.

Nicholas looked over to me, lifting his sword. "What do you say? You spar with me and win, you can get your dagger back. Deal?"

"Deal," I answered, the challenge thrumming in my veins.

Elise pulled on one of my curls. "Make him bleed just a little, for me."

Nicholas twirled his sword in one swift motion, twisting his wrist with the kind of confidence that didn't come from good looks and charm. That kind of confidence came from the sheer knowledge that you're just *that* good.

I knew that feeling all too well.

I held the sword so tight, I could feel my palm starting to sweat, so I raised the blade and raced towards him, bringing it down in front of me. I was met with the clashing of our swords connecting as he blocked me, using his weight to shove me away. I preceded to rush him again, aiming my sword lower, thinking our height difference may provide an advantage. Nicholas pivoted to the right, his foot-work flawless as he escaped my attack. I felt the tip of a blade at my back, just a light press, and I knew he was taunting me with it.

"Soul Seether, don't tell me there is something you *can't* do?" he teased with a smirk.

I turned to face him, using my sword to move his to the side. "Are you mocking me?"

He turned his lips down in an innocent frown. "I would never."

I moved my sword up, then slashed down towards his shoulder. Nicholas met it with his own sword and tried to push me back again, but I gathered my own weight and met his resistance. He put one foot behind the other and pressed his weapon up to mine, the metal screeching. He moved us, walking a circle, and I felt my wrist twist, beginning to lose my grip on the hilt. I released our stance and backed up, my breath no longer at a normal pace.

I was prepared to take a moment to relax when Nicholas barreled towards me, cutting his sword upward, light bouncing off the sharp edge. I raised my sword and blocked him, causing him to move his blade to the right, creating a horizontal slash as he swiped his sword towards the ground. He came back up, hoping to attack my exposed right side with a clean cut, when I brought my sword down and forced him to a halt.

He looked up at me, an impressed look on his face. The sun beat down on us, the humidity and heat beaming in from the windows.

Beads of sweat formed across his hairline, and I could practically count each one, his hair beginning to stick to his forehead. I started to release my hold, thinking we would start from the beginning, but Nicholas took my relaxation as a window of opportunity. He forced his sword up against mine, breaking free of my block. He flipped the hilt in his palm with a bit of flourish and sliced my left calf. It wasn't deep enough to do any real damage, but enough to make me look down in pure astonishment.

"I told you to make *him* bleed, you fucking idiot!" Elise yelled from the wall.

Nicholas stayed stone still. I watched the blood seep down towards my ankle. I didn't think he'd attempt to draw blood, but apparently, I was mistaken. His confidence never wavered as a drop of blood dripped from his sword.

"Never release until you know you've won." He looked up at me, those eyes so desperately determined.

I didn't want words.

I grasped my sword and quickly brought it down, catching his shoulder with the sharp tip almost as fast as a paper cut. He looked stunned, but glanced over at his shoulder as one, two, three blood droplets ran down his arm. Nicholas slowly turned to me, eyes narrowed and keen. He ran a finger over the cut, wiping away the blood.

I thought he was going to tell us to start again, critique me more, dismiss this whole sparring altogether, *something*.

Instead, he held the hilt of his sword with vigor as he sliced at me, causing me to jump back. He propelled his sword downward, the silver blade almost connecting with my collarbone. Pieces of my hair floated to the ground, causing me to realize that my braid had flung to the front of my chest -- he had cut a piece of the end with one swing.

He wasn't holding back. I don't know why I thought he would.

I collided my sword with his as he moved up. Holding my sword with two hands, I pushed him back, my blood starting to boil. I wanted to win just as much as he did. A jolt of energy caused my simple push to transform into launching him at the window. Right before what should have been his back smacking into the glass, he shot out his wings and flew upwards. He flapped them hard, sending a gust of air towards me, and I shielded my face with my arm.

Nicholas circled me, sailing toward me, swinging his blade as he went. I curved my sword left and right, swinging up to block a move, then dragging my sword across to slice his other shoulder. He fluttered his wings back, effectively moving away from my potential blows.

He had too much of an advantage. I settled that quickly by freeing my own wings.

They were narrower than his and dark as the midnight sky, with slight hues of red, like bat wings. The edges jutted out into points with a razored talon, sharp points that could shred skin if I made the right moves. Nicholas looked at me in awe, but he was still as relentless as ever. He soared above me, sword in front of him, ready to force me to the ground, but I dipped down low and watched as he flew over me. He tried again, his feathers rustling with irritation when that ended the same way.

"Nick, just finish this already, for fuck's sake," Reese bristled.

I thrashed my wings back and sped towards him, taking advantage of his momentary distraction. He intercepted my hit, his sword high enough to graze my cheek. He ripped his sword away suddenly, just to swing underneath mine, creating that grating sound of connecting metal and sliding hard along my sword, flipping the tip of his own blade up to sever my blade from my hand. I watched as the sword clattered to the ground, useless. Nicholas grabbed my arm and pulled me to him, his face mere inches from my own. His breath smelled like mint as he took a few breaths in and out, slowly and methodically.

"I wouldn't try to get that now," he noted of my abandoned sword.

I retracted my wings, but before I was completely dead weight, he turned me around so my back was to his front, holding his sword up to my throat. This time, the metal wasn't so close to my flesh -- he was just trying to prove a point. We descended slowly, but he didn't let me go.

He moved his lips to my ear. "Color me impressed."

I dipped my head back enough so his face was in my view. "I told you I had some skills—" I pressed my back flush against him and let my ass rub against his pelvis. My hand wandered over his hip, fingers tiptoeing around the low waistband of his sweatpants. I let my finger dip slightly inside and fiddle with the elastic band. "Just sucks that this is the only skill you're interested in." I felt his heartbeat thump frantically and the muscles of his stomach tighten. I felt something else make an appearance as well, hardening against me. I was satisfied I still won in *some* way.

I wrapped my hand around the angelic blade in front of me and shoved it to the side, not looking back at him as I removed myself from his grasp. I pressed on my cheek, pulling my hand back and seeing blood, thick and deep red. I turned around at the sound of clapping.

"You guys are a real treat, making us all look like shit down here," Reese said, punching Nicholas in the shoulder.

Nicholas handed Reese his sword. "Don't worry, you still have a chance to make me look bad." Reese rolled his eyes as he pressed the tip of the sword into the floor.

"Well, I'm ready for another round," I claimed, making my way over to my sword.

Nicholas chuckled and shook his head. "Oh no, you're done for now."

I gave him a confused look. "Then who is he—" I stopped myself before pressing my lips together and shutting up.

Elise appeared at my side, my sword in her hand. She examined the blade, letting her hand caress the sharp edge. Reese's eyes went wide with what I assumed was both shock and probably a little bit of fear.

"You can't be serious, Nick."

"It's only fair."

"No, it's not fair. You're trying to get me killed. She didn't even want to do this in the first place!"

Elise swung the sword from side to side. "Their little show intrigued me, what can I say?"

Nicholas looked over at Elise, a serious expression on his face. "No funny business, okay?"

Elise gave him a thumbs up and a forced smile. "Of course."

"See?" Nicholas motioned towards Elise as he locked eyes with his friend. "She isn't going to kill you. Don't be a fucking baby." He gave Reese two strong pats on the shoulder and moved out of the way. I followed him to the back wall as he leaned against it.

"I guess this means you'll be keeping my dagger a bit longer?" I asked, curious. I could hear Reese taunting Elise, a terribly bad move on his part.

"Do you really want it back that badly?" His eyes slid over to me, curiosity in his voice.

I shrugged. "It seems to be in your good and *capable* hands." I watched his Adam's apple bob sharply as he swallowed. "As long as I get it back before we leave."

He coughed as he stretched out his neck, moving from side to side. "About that..."

"I assume that won't be anytime soon, since we're here, *training*," I cut him off, knowing that if they were planning on sending us back, they would have done it already.

"I don't know what Jonah has in store, but you might want to make yourselves comfortable," Nicholas suggested with a shrug.

"The handcuffs are just the greatest form of hospitality." My sarcasm was evident in every word. The sound of clanging swords and curse words filled the room; there were no screams of agonizing pain, so I didn't bother to acknowledge it.

He laughed, a smooth, deep one that matched his voice. "If Elise wasn't...*herself*, I'm sure I could get them to do away with the cuffs, but she's a bit of a loose cannon."

"Understandable."

"You underestimate yourself, you know," he noted, slightly under his breath. "I'll give credit where it's due." I glanced over at him, my eyes skeptical. "You hold your sword with hesitation but given the right motivation, you could be a force."

I smiled. "I'm *already* a force, Nicholas. I don't need swords to prove that."

I didn't say anything after that, but I knew he'd looked over at me. He'd realized he was looking too long and ducked his head down to look at his shoes.

"I'm literally going to fucking kill you!" I heard Reese shout from above. I looked up to see them circling each other, Elise trying to find a good angle to attack, while Reese stabbed towards her as he weaved around her sword.

"Reese, I told you to stop with the whole stabbing motion! That's not how this works!" Nicholas shouted.

"Tell her that!" Reese spat back, continuing his sparring match.

Nicholas extracted his wings and pushed upwards into the air. He flew between them, dodging Elise's blows and yanking the sword from her hand. I stifled a giggle as I looked out the window. Messenger angels were flying around, doing twirls and free fall drops at the tree lines just to soar upwards with silken ease.

Oh, now I have an idea.

"You said you had an idea? What is it?" Nicholas asked, leaning against the wall of the briefing room. I had pulled him to the side after Reese and Elise landed in one piece and showed no signs of lunging for each other. I told him I wanted a more secure place to speak about it; training rooms aside, I thought our companions had been confined to this room for longer than necessary. He had looked skeptical at my request, but he'd decided to hear me out.

"Someone would have to know how the portals operated to be able to destroy them, right?" I asked, casting my eyes on each of them. Nicholas crossed his arms over his chest and sighed, nodding his answer.

"Natalia knows all about them, but she had nothing to do with this. That's information we are already aware of," Nicholas answered, exhaustion lacing his voice.

I shook my head. "No, not Natalia. She may have created these new and improved portals, but she doesn't use them. She doesn't need to with the magic she has."

"Your point?" Elise turned a chair around and sat down, leaning back.

"Maybe the issue isn't making them, but who can use them. It at least could be a clue."

Nicholas scratched his chin. "You think someone who has access to the portals knows who is threatening to destroy them? Who is sending demons through them?"

I tilted my head from left to right. "Maybe. At the very least, it might be a lead to the bigger picture. Natalia did say it was more than one being trying to wear the portal down."

"Who do you suggest we interrogate for this information, huh?" Reese questioned.

I bit my lip, knowing they weren't going to be thrilled. "There are only a few angels who have access to portals, and even fewer who have access to Purgatory or Hell." I looked at both Nicholas and Reese, watching as their eyebrows began to draw up in realization. "Being down there means a higher chance of running into demons and...*her*, making them more susceptible to pretty much the unimaginable." I made my voice low and sharp when I spoke of Lilith. "The only angels I know who can go in and out without supervision are messengers, right?"

Reese laughed, holding his stomach. "Sure, but you honestly think a messenger has something to do with this?"

"It's just an observation."

"It sounds like you're trying to suggest angels have *anything* to do with this."

I stood my ground, unintimidated. "That's not what I said. I don't appreciate the twisting of my words."

"It sounds like you're insinuating demons have *everything* to do with this, Blondie," Elise said nonchalantly from her chair.

Reese rolled his eyes. "Isn't that obvious?"

"Just like an angel to assume they aren't at fault," Elise argued, shaking her head and pouncing up. "You all think you walk on fucking water. It's pathetic how righteous you can be."

"I'm sorry for assuming your kind would have anything to do with the fact that one of your own just walked through a fucking portal into Heaven's Gate like it's normal," Reese argued, not even looking at her.

Elise pulled her fingers tightly into a fist at her side. "Would you like for me to blast you into a wall again? I seem to remember enjoying it an hour ago." Reese blew steam out of his nose at her words.

"Everybody shut the fuck up, please, for the love of all that's ethereal!" Nicholas shouted, holding his hands up at them. He turned to me, his eyes focused. "It does make sense for messengers to be your first thought, but there are a few flaws in your idea." The sweat from our sparring match was completely gone from his face, but his skin still looked dewy. "Messengers don't have the authority to bring demons through portals. Only executives and a select few sentries have the privilege." He placed his hands on the back of one of the chairs.

Reese pointed at his friend, wiggling his index finger. "Makes perfect sense to me."

"Doesn't mean they couldn't have some type of role in all this, malicious or not," I retorted, causing Reese to narrow his hazel eyes at me.

Nicholas spoke again. "True, but there's another flaw. Where you're going and where you've been is always noted. If you have a portal key, it's reported. Jonah would have seen some sort of discrepancy and dealt with it by now." He shrugged his wide shoulders.

"Or not," Elise said nonchalantly, and we all turned to her.

"What's that supposed to mean?" Nicholas asked.

Elise let out a small breath of a laugh laced with impending sarcasm. "I don't know, pretty boy. Maybe start looking at everyone as a suspect and not just the obvious."

"You think Jonah has something to do with this?" he asked.

I stepped between them, using my body to eliminate Elise from his gaze. "I think what she's saying is no one is innocent here." I turned slightly, giving her a look that said *cool it for at least the next five minutes.* "You do give me an interesting idea though, Nicholas."

He smirked, waiting to hear what I had to say, his body language cautious but patient.

"You said that all of the ins and outs were documented, right?"

He nodded.

"So there's physical documentation on who went in and out of Purgatory? Probably organized by dates or times?"

Reese let out a loud and exhausted sigh, his annoyance on full display. "We've been over this. The portal keys are connected to a book, and whoever uses one gets logged and reported."

I rolled my eyes, ignoring him. "A book. I assume Jonah has this book?"

"The answer is obviously yes," Elise piped in from behind me. "If you are thinking what I think you're thinking, I would much rather just torture the information out of every messenger than try to narrow it down. Where's the fun in that?" Her voice was almost pleading, dying for some type of normalcy here.

Nicholas stepped closer, leaning slightly around me to Elise. "What is she thinking?"

Elise stepped out from behind me, a mischievous look on her face. "What she's thinking is that we need to see that book."

"Good fucking luck with that," Reese huffed, walking over to the door and leaning into it. "You can't just go asking for it."

I mulled this over. "I'm sure Jonah would let us see it, since it pertains to our mission."

"It's not that, exactly. It's just that..." Nicholas spoke carefully, his mouth opening and closing, trying to find the right words. "If we ask for the book, Jonah will want to know the reason. All the details. If we tell him why, it'll look as if we blame our own people for this." He blew out a breath when he finished.

"No one is accusing anyone, Nicholas," I countered, looking up at him. My breath almost caught the minute I remembered how tall he actually was.

"I know, but that's how it will look."

Elise let out the harshest laugh I've ever heard from her. "Of course, the perfect angel duo is worried about their reputations."

I never let my eyes leave his. "You would give up getting closer to the answer for the sake of your undying loyalty. It's commendable but it's idiotic. *Hypocritical.* You claim to be loyal, so you take on this task of figuring out the broken portals, like the good little soldiers you are. The moment the road gets a little hard, you back off because of that same loyalty. How does your loyalty even work? You can't just pick and choose what kind you want on display."

Nicholas pulled his strained eyes from mine. I knew he was thinking it all over. He knew it made sense.

"I know a way everyone can get what they want, without rocking the boat," Elise offered.

"Any time before I'm dead would be fantastic," Reese spat at her as he pulled his hair out of its tie, letting it fall to his shoulders.

Elise let out a groan and answered. "You and the pretty one can steal it."

"Steal it?" Nicholas pressed his fingers to his temples.

Elise leaned back against the table, pressing her thighs into the glass. "Simple and easy."

"No, not so simple. Stealing is probably even more stupid," Reese said.

Elise waved her hand in the air, as if she was swatting his words away. "Fine, don't call it stealing. You don't even have to leave the room with it. We just need to know the messengers who used the portal that day." She swiped her palms together twice. "Easy."

"I think *borrow* is the word she's looking for," I corrected, eyeing my fellow demon.

"That's kind of impossible. There's no way into Jonah's office when he isn't there," Nicholas pointed out. "Plus, I have no idea what the book looks like."

I turned away from Elise and smiled at him. "I think it's called a distraction, Nicholas. Buy yourself enough time to find it and get the information. Jonah seems smart, but ideally, something like that is kept in plain sight, where anyone and no one can find it, or it's kept somewhere remotely close to him." I shrugged a shoulder and looked up at him through my long lashes before winking. "I think you're underestimating your sleuthing skills."

"A distract—" Nicholas started but was cut off by the door opening. I could feel the room tense with the angel's uneasy feelings. We shouldn't be in here; well, Elise and I shouldn't be in here. A briefing room was not on our certified list of places to go today. Nicholas stood a little straighter, his hands clasped behind him, and Reese removed himself from the wall, his arms over his broad chest.

I leaned back against the table next to Elise, no tension to be found from either of us. I saw gray hair and the confused expression first. I recognized him from the meeting a few days ago, the one who saw the demon in the first place. His name was right on the tip of my tongue.

"Markus," Nicholas greeted.

"What is the meaning of this?" the executive angel responded, looking around the room.

Reese cleared his throat. "We took them to the training room this morning for some sparring—" he began, but Markus cut him off.

"Correct me if I'm wrong, Mr. Diniel, but is this the training room?"

I peered over at Elise, who had her lips pulled tightly together, holding in a laugh.

"No, I guess it's not," Reese answered, looking down at Markus. The angel was only a few inches taller than myself, and I thought Nicholas and Reese were giants. Markus looked back with the same fierceness, causing Reese to eventually look to the floor.

"No, it's not. So, I will ask again, what is the meaning of this?"

None of us said anything. There really wasn't a good explanation for it and we knew it.

"Strategizing," Nicholas said at last. I noticed his shoulders were pulled back and his back was straight.

"Strategizing?" Markus repeated as he walked towards Nicholas, giving Reese a chance to roll his eyes.

Nicholas nodded. "About the issue at hand. The training room didn't seem like a good place for strategic planning, so I thought it would be a good idea to voice our thoughts here."

Markus had his back turned to me, but I knew he was sizing him up as best as he could from his height. I saw Nicholas's Adam's apple bob when he swallowed hard with nerves.

"I appreciate your thinking, Mr. Cassial, but you can't gallivant off with these two as you wish. We're working with a delicate matter, and anyone could have walked in on you. You're quite lucky it was me." He placed a hand on Nicholas' shoulder and gave it a firm pat. "I'm meeting a few others here shortly, so I suggest you get them to their room before you cause unwanted trouble. If you would, Mr. Diniel."

"Me?" Reese asked, stunned.

"Yes, you. I'd like to speak to Nicholas in private." I saw the moment Nicholas' deep brown eyes went wide. He looked over to Reese, who was staring back with the same bewildered look on his face. Whatever silent conversation they were having was cut off when Markus motioned for Nicholas to sit. He seemed to forget Elise and I were there, but Elise was already making her way out the door. Reese tilted his head towards her, wordlessly telling me to follow.

I had the urge to fight to stay. I wanted to hear this conversation. I had only known Nicholas Cassial for a short period of time, but I knew meetings with high executives didn't present themselves like this often. I had one foot out the door and one hand on the door frame when I turned my head and saw him staring back at me. He gave me a short smile, as if acknowledging my thoughts, before returning to his meeting with Markus.

WE GOT BACK TO OUR ROOM THROUGH A SHORT SERIES OF HALLWAYS AND staircases Reese claimed no one used. The staircases were cold, but not freezing. Elise had hopped up on one of the railings and slid down, getting an aggravating grunt from Reese.

"Come on," Reese had said, opening the door to the second floor and peeking out.

"Don't get your panties in a twist, Blondie. If anyone sees us, I'll just compel them to forget," Elise taunted.

"What?" Reese asked, stopping her before she could get through the door. "Compel?"

"Yeah, like making people do and say what you want."

Reese continued to block the door. "You don't have that kind of magic. You can't. Compulsion was outlawed years ago."

Elise grabbed his chin and shook it. "All that hair is blocking your brain cells from operating properly. Outlawed means it doesn't exist in plain sight. No one is stupid enough to use it in front of beings like you." She shoved his arm down and away from the doorway. "It was a joke, if that makes you feel any better. I can't compel anyone." Reese watched her as she strolled into the hallway. "But she can." She nodded towards me and disappeared down the hall.

He hadn't said anything the short walk to our living quarters. I knew she'd caught him off guard. Elise liked using action to get her points across, but there were many times when her words could do just as much damage, if not more. I grabbed the handle to the door, but Reese caught my arm before I could make a move.

"Have you ever used it?" he asked me.

I tilted my chin up at him, letting my eyes wash over him as I realized what he was asking. "Yes."

"But you know you technically shouldn't. I don't love rules, but that's one I support."

I looked up at the ceiling, licking my upper lip. "You're aware the rules you follow up here don't apply down there, right?"

"Do you need it?"

"For what I do? Yes, it can come in handy on occasion."

Reese looked around us, making sure no one was coming. "You and I both know Lilith is the only one capable of giving you those powers when she made you. Having you here is about as good as having *her* here." He wasn't wrong. Lilith's compulsion powers were flawed, contrary to what everyone believed. She could only compel those who lived in Hell, those who graced us with their presence in

Purgatory and stayed there forever. How she managed to keep that power after the war was a question I'd never gotten around to asking, although I assumed it had to do with the Enchanters she kept close and a lack of angelic supervision. My compulsion powers, though, resided in my dagger, and it only came out to play whenever I wielded and summoned it.

"That's a big judge of character."

He ignored my comment. "How many times have you used it?"

"I don't know. I don't keep a record of all the poor souls I got to do humiliating things to. I haven't used it in a long time, if that's what you are really asking. I found I don't like using it as much as I thought." I placed my hands on my hips.

He narrowed his piercing eyes at me. "A demon with a conscience?"

"Not quite. I just find you can get anyone to do anything with the right motivation, and I can be very persuasive." I cocked my head to the side, raising an eyebrow.

He was unamused, his face like stone. "I'm sure. I don't know much about what you do down there, but you're here now, so I suggest you start realizing it and..."

"And what?" I stopped him. "Comply? What if we don't? You gonna throw us in the Ethereal Bastille with the other demon?" I challenged him, standing my ground. "I was brought here to do a job and frankly, I've been doing it. If you don't like it, take it up with your boss."

His face started to blotch red, and I could tell his breathing had changed. "I don't understand why they need you here. Nick and I could do this all on our own."

I pushed my lips out in a pout and nodded in fake understanding. "Yeah of course, like when you almost got attacked by an Enchanter and I saved your ass. Good times."

He bared his teeth. "You want me to thank you for that, is that it?"

"Not at all, but a little respect would do. Some friendly hospitality, maybe."

84

Reese let out a low, swift laugh. "You'll be waiting a long fucking time for that."

"I figured." I slid to the door and leaned back against it. "Is there some deep reason as to why you resent us so much, or is that just something you learn in angel primary school?"

He started to tie his hair up again as he spoke. "No reason. I just don't see anything good coming from your presence. This demon through the portal ordeal is just one step in a bad direction, and now *you're* here. It's almost laughable how fucked up this is."

"Maybe you should stop looking at the glass half full and start realizing we want the same thing."

He nodded, almost in annoyance and hostility, turning to walk towards down the hallway. "Your plan sounded like you had a different idea of how you think this story will end."

"So single minded, huh? I'm not saying I know anything. Why does everything have to be so black and white with you? I'm just saying I came here to help figure something out and I'm doing just that." I let out an exasperated sigh. "You can't tell me you aren't dying to sneak around Jonah's office?" I rocked back and forth on my heels, waiting for the expected answer.

I could see him biting the inside of his cheek, considering my words. I surveyed him from head to toe and said one final thing I knew would end this. "You really can't let Nicholas do this all alone, can you? We both know he'll see things through with or without you."

He pulled his head back a bit, taking me in. I knew their friendship was something he valued, that was obvious. He wouldn't let his best friend complete this mission alone. He ran a hand down his face, a frustrated sigh tearing from his throat. "Fine, we'll go with your stupid plan, but if nothing comes of it, you shut your mouth."

I pulled my braid over my shoulder. "Of course. See? I don't need compulsion."

He raised a thick eyebrow at me.

I let a smile form on my face and unlocked the door behind my back. "You just agreed to do exactly what I wanted of your own free will." I opened the door and backed up into the room.

"You really didn't give me any other option."

My head gently hit the side of the door, my fingers fiddling with the lock. "I didn't have to. You and I both know Nicholas is going to see this plan through no matter what he thinks. You being the good friend that you are, you just can't let him go it alone." I smirked. "How's that motivation tasting right about now?"

His mouth popped open to speak, but, wanting the last word, I slammed the door.

CHAPTER SIX

NICK

"Ihonestly can't believe you agreed to this plan at all. You seemed pretty set in your ways about it before," I said to my best friend as I sprawled out on the grass. I raised my hand behind my head, resting it on a slanted rock. Reese had taken me aside and told me that he would help in Elise and Dani's plan. He never let me respond; all questions were halted when he walked into his room and closed the door.

"Things change. I'm allowed to change my damn mind," Reese stated, flexing his fingers in his leather gloves. Two large wooden circles with colorful red targets stood in the distance. He looked at them and then towards the trees that hit just the tip of the clouds above. The sun was beating down with intense rage, and I plucked my sunglasses from my pocket.

I scoffed. "You don't change your mind that quickly. That has never changed."

Reese unhooked his bow and slapped the side of my thigh with it. "I'm a complex individual, what can I say?"

He had told me he wanted to do some target practice, to which I jokingly said that releasing some of his pent-up frustration would do him some good. What I didn't say was that I would be happy to join him outside and watch him hit a bullseye every time to uplift his ego. That was how it always went. I couldn't speak much either way, seeing as every time I handed him a sword, he always ended up on his ass. Fair is fair.

"You couldn't have picked a hotter day to do this." I could feel the sweat forming at my brow. "I actually envy the demons right now in their room."

Reese started to get into position but paused, looking down at me. "I wouldn't envy them in any regard."

"I just meant we're out here in the heat, and they're in the air conditioning, that's all. Not everything has to turn into a brawl." I rolled my eyes at his annoyance. It seemed like normal angelic logic to loathe them, but I found myself neutral for the moment. They hadn't given me any reason to doubt them. Reese saw doubt in almost every breath they took. He was all action and no thought.

Reese muttered *whatever* under his breath before turning back to the targets. He picked out an arrow from the quiver at his feet. Standing sideways, he pulled the bow up, aligning the arrow along with it. He pressed his feet to the ground, shoulder width apart. His back flattened and he bent his knees as he clasped the arrow and his bow string, pulling back.

This was one thing that Reese did stop to think about.

The sound of the released arrow was sharp as it pulled the wind with it. The arrow flew forward, unrelenting. The target made a small cracking sound as the head of the arrow pierced it right in the middle. Reese pulled another arrow out and proceeded to position himself again. He angled his elbow out behind him, perfectly still. He released the second arrow after a few moments, and I watched as it sailed towards the target, hitting the red middle.

"There's something you should know about her," Reese said, taking out another arrow and moving so he could aim for the other target.

I readjusted myself against the rock. "What would that be?"

He placed his arrow against the bow, pointing it towards the ground. He paused, as if wanting to find the right words. "She has compulsion, Nick."

"Who?"

"The more tolerable one, if that's a good description," Reese answered, raising his bow.

I opened my mouth to speak, but no words came out. Compulsion was outlawed in Heaven's Gate and all the other realms since before I could remember. My father had always told me it was one of those things you used in the most necessary of times -- it was tempting, too much for one person to handle. The idea of making someone do your bidding, to have them at your mercy... the magic was just too much to resist.

"How do you know this?" I questioned, tipping my sunglasses down my nose.

"She fucking told me, that's how. The only way she got those powers was from the Queen of Darkness herself." He released the arrow straight to the bullseye.

"It's alarming, something we should keep an eye on, but I don't think she has any reason to use it," I said, pushing myself up and cross my legs, resting my hands on my knees.

Reese let out a barking laugh that nearly echoed through the trees. "Alarming? Nick, please don't tell me you're that stupid."

I stared at him blankly. I knew he couldn't see my eyes, but I narrowed them from behind my sunglasses. He picked up another arrow, this time with more force than the others.

"You don't think she has any intention of using it? You think her little psychopath friend doesn't plan to murder us all? You think she isn't going to screw us over in the end?" His voice was like fire, crackling and full of venom.

My heart started to beat harder in my chest at his anger. "I never said any of that. You're overthinking this entirely, Reese, and you know it."

"Don't tell me what I know," he spat back, raising his bow with enough tension in his body that I'm surprised it didn't snap in half.

I scoffed. "I won't, since it doesn't seem like you know much at all."

He released the arrow suddenly, and I watched it fly forward, connecting with the back of the first one. The tip thinly cut through his initial arrow, splitting it, taking its place at the bullseye. He threw the bow down and turned around to face me, stomping over with so much frustration that I stood up as he got closer, the wind whipping his blonde hair around his face.

"I tell you a piece of vital information and you tell me I don't know anything?" Reese huffed, his neck growing red in a way that had nothing to do with the sun.

"Vital information yes, but have you really given any real thought to it?" I stated, the back of my t-shirt sticking to my back. Reese crossed his arms over his chest, waiting. "What's she waiting for, hmm? She's had ample opportunity to use it, more than enough time to use it on Markus when he walked in on us. She didn't. What's she been doing the whole time, Reese? She's been trying to help us figure this shit out!" I took my sunglasses off; Reese and I were around the same height, so I looked him dead in his hazel eyes as I spoke. He never flinched as every word left my lips.

"You have it all figured out don't you, Nick? Defending the demons. You spend like two fucking days with them and now what? They're the good guys now?" he pushed, mocking me.

I pressed my lips together, swallowing hard, trying to keep it together. "Not in the slightest. That's not what I'm saying at *all*, Reese. You're just so fixated on them and what you think of them, and it's not going to help us in any way."

"So this is my fault now?"

I let out an exasperated sigh, so deep that it took the wind out of my chest. "No! My God, can you stop being so fucking dramatic? This isn't your fault—" I began, watching as he opened his mouth in what I knew would be a rebuttal. I continued before he could get his words out. "This isn't their fault either. We *all* were asked to find out about the portals and that's exactly what we are going to do. Then, they can be sent on their way. You harping on this is only going to prolong it, and you know what? More demons are going to come through and we'll be in more shit and then it really will be all your fucking fault! I don't know what changed your mind about their plan, but you agreed, so stop complaining, get your bow out of your ass, and focus on what we were asked to do. Do it for me."

My chest felt heavy as I finished, my throat a bit rough; I hadn't realized I'd been shouting. I ran a stiff hand through my hair, not realizing I'd balled it into a tight fist.

Reese looked back at me with an unreadable expression on his face. The only sound between us was the sound of wings ripping through the sky above us. He raised an eyebrow at me, his lips curling into a smirk.

"The last time you yelled at me like that, we were still living in the North Village and I wanted to give up the bow. You went ballistic on me."

I released a small smile, the moment replaying itself in my head. "I didn't yell at you."

"Yeah, you did. Your dad had to come out and pop us both on the ass for being so loud that late at night. I hated both of you for all of three minutes."

"So sensitive, even then," I teased, punching him in the arm. He rolled his head up towards the sky, the tension leaving his body almost instantly.

"You seem to always know when I need a kick in the ass," Reese said, pressing his palm to my forehead and shoving me slightly backwards. I swatted him away, setting myself upright again. He brought his index finger to his chin and tapped it a few times. "I'll attempt to keep myself in check, although that in itself is asking a lot."

I jogged over to the bow and pulled an arrow out of the quiver. "Oh, I'm well aware." I aligned myself with a target and placed the arrow in the notch. I didn't dare look back at Reese, most likely critiquing my every move. I would do the exact same thing, so I couldn't comment.

"Do you have a plan on how to get us into Jonah's office? And by that, I mean, do you have a plan that gets us into Jonah's office when he isn't there?" Reese asked from behind me, pure curiosity spiking in his voice.

I took two slow breaths as I tightened my fingers around the back of the arrow and bowstring. I eyed my target with determined purpose. I knew I could never slice another arrow like Reese, but I could likely hit any of the target's rings. I waited a beat before I released, watching as the arrow sailed into the air, faster and further...

It darted past the target. It flew past the trunks of the trees that lined the woods, into what lay beyond them.

"Hmph," I grunted, pressing the bow to my temple.

Reese's muffled laugh filled my ears as he came up behind me and yanked the bow out of my grasp. "Leave it to the professionals, swordsman."

I let out a fake laugh, shoving him away. "To answer your question, I do have a plan."

"And you didn't think to tell me?" he asked.

"Up until yesterday, I didn't think you were coming, so forgive me for keeping you in the dark."

He grabbed another arrow and started positioning himself again. "Care to share with the class?"

I shrugged, waiting as he set himself into his full archery stance. "You might have to dust off your acting skills for this one."

Reese pulled back the bowstring and then stopped, whipping his head back at me, a confused expression all over his face. "Nick, what the f—"

Fluttering wings above us interrupted him, shadowing the green lawn. A female with long, fiery red hair gently descended onto the lush greenery. A messenger angel.

"Nicholas Cassial?" She looked to me, her eyes round and the color of dark green moss.

"Yes?" I answered. Reese looked at me over her shoulder, his eyes wide with interest.

"Jonah regrets to inform you he cannot see you, but says Ariel will see you in his place." She spoke distinctively, as if she memorized the words exactly as they were spoken to her.

"Of course. I will see Ariel this afternoon," I replied, meeting her gaze.

A sharp nod and blink later, she was in the sky and out of my sight. I raised my hand to block the sunlight as I watched the blue above me after she was gone. Reese cleared his throat.

"So, is that part of the plan? A meeting with Jonah? Well, Ariel now."

"You catch on quick," I answered sarcastically.

Reese repositioned his footing as he turned to the targets again. "Ha, ha. Won't that be a problem, since we're trying to get the office empty before we raid it?"

"That's where you come in."

I MADE THE TRIP TO JONAH'S OFFICE, BUT THIS TIME, I KNEW MY INTENT. I knew the outcome of this meeting. At least, I knew the outcome I was hoping for. Whether it be Ariel or Jonah, it didn't matter; they just needed to be distracted long enough for us to do some digging. The thought of getting caught, of having to explain myself, was the only thing that made me shudder. I could handle being scolded by Ariel, but Jonah made me cringe.

Three raps of my knuckles on the doors were enough for them to slowly start to open. The smell of cedar wood and citrus hit my nostrils immediately. Ariel was a strong believer in heightened senses, especially scent. He could differentiate between particular poisons and could even tell whether you've come through the southeast forest or the west. He looked especially exhausted as he sat in Jonah's grand chair, slumped over his desk. He looked so small compared to the towers of books stacked around him.

When he didn't look up after a beat, I cleared my throat. I had to get the conversation moving; I only had a few minutes before my plan revealed itself. Startled, he looked up at me, the emerald green in his eyes dimmer, his eyelids hooded. He had tied his red hair in a tight low bun against the back of his neck. The wood from the fireplace crackled, echoing around us.

"Ah, Nicholas. You wanted to speak, yes?" He blinked a few times, collecting himself.

I nodded, walking further into the room. I had this conversation all planned out. "I was hoping to possibly sit out of the Animus Seeking tonight?" I knew this was a lost cause. Animus Seeking was something all sentries did once a month, removing souls from the human realm and bringing them to their new home, Heaven. Getting out of the task was impossible.

The executive angel's eyebrows shot towards his hairline in surprise. "Sit out of the Animus Seeking?"

"Yes, sir."

"You and I both know that is quite impossible."

"I would do it another time, just not tonight," I added, knowing this would get me a heavy sigh followed by an incredulous laugh.

Ariel leaned into the desk, watching me from across the room. I had no intention of sitting down, so I stood my ground. I could see, even from a distance, that small lines pulled at the corners of his eyes. I noticed them every time he smiled, which wasn't often, but when it happened, they caught my eye. "We set up the duty schedules in advance. Sitting out is unacceptable; there is no replacement for you."

I quickly glanced up at the gold metal clock above his head. The minute hand ticked away, and I counted with it. Just a few more seconds.

"Jonah's tasks have been taking a toll. I was just hoping to get a night of rest." I shrugged, fiddling with the hem of my shirt.

"Out of all the sentries, you are the last I would expect to want a day of rest," he pointed out. "You and that overzealous friend of yours."

He was right, on all accounts. My eyes peeked up at the clock again, my heart thudding hard in my chest. "All I'm asking for is one night, Ariel. I'm sure if Jonah were here, he wouldn't mind." I knew I was overstepping a bit, but not enough that I would regret it later.

Ariel pinched the bridge of his nose, taking a deep breath. "Nicholas, I will not tell you again, the answer is—" I heard the door slam before he could finish, followed by the sound of running, footsteps pressing hard against the stone floor. Voices carried from the hallway into the room, rushed and speaking all at once.

At least he was on time.

Ariel looked behind me, waiting for the reason behind the commotion.

Two sentries opened the doors, a panting and sweaty Reese pushing past them. His face was flushed, his hair sticking to his neck. It was a decent number of stairs to get here, but not enough to make him sweat puddles. He had an exasperated and crazed look on his face.

"Sir, we have a problem near the southeast woods!" he started, not glancing over at me, but standing beside me. Each word came out harshly as he tried to catch his breath.

"What kind of problem?" Ariel prompted, his face dissolving into concern.

"Two of the trainees got into it with another sentry and a guardian. I didn't catch the reason, but it didn't look good. There were more getting involved before I came here." His voice was loud, but not loud enough to rattle the walls. He had enough strain in his voice to sound stressed and concerned, but not enough to draw any suspicion.

Ariel pushed back his chair and stood, placing his hands on the edge of the desk. "And there were no other sentries to help control the situation?"

Reese shook his head. "I'm not sure. I tried to diffuse it, but I think it would best be dealt by someone high up." I'd told Reese to stroke Ariel's ego, make him feel needed.

Ariel pressed a hand down the front of his velvet blue jacket, looking around the room. "Southeast woods?"

"They're starting the new open terrain training today." That was the only thing that wasn't a lie.

Ariel walked quickly past us to the sentries dutifully guarding the door. He spoke to them in hushed tones before finally turning to us. "I will clear this matter immediately." The sentries followed him out the door and through the hallway. I waited until I heard their footsteps soften and a door close, telling me they weren't within earshot.

Reese's heavy breathing and the ticking of the clock swam in my head. He let out an unnecessarily loud sigh, placing a hand on his chest. "I don't think that could've gone better."

I circled around Jonah's desk to the shelves stacked with books the size of my head, examining the collection, while Reese headed to the ones on the far back wall. "I would have to agree with you, except you had to say the southeast woods?"

"What's wrong with that?" he asked, picking through a few of the books.

"That only gives us maybe ten minutes to search for the book, find what we need, and make sure everything is back in place," I explained in a frustrated voice.

"Ten minutes is plenty of time. Don't be such a worrywart," Reese teased, moving to another bookshelf.

I knew the book was of decent size. It was old, so the spine and edges were frayed, and the leather had significant creases. It may have shown wear and tear, but the book was never going to disintegrate; the pages were never going to tear apart. It was bound to Heaven's Gate by magic. Gold and silver thread decorated the spine, forming wings that spread from top to bottom. The front and back had an outline of a hand with the palm facing outward in gold stitching. The book wasn't meant to look like anything special, since what was necessary and most important was inside. It made this search more frustrating, since I knew what I was looking for but then again, I didn't.

"I feel like I've looked at every one of these books twice, Nick. I don't think it's here."

"It has to be. There isn't any other place it could be. This is the most logical place," I answered, checking the last shelf on another bookcase. The clock's never-ending ticks and the heat from the fireplace almost made my skin crawl, made my hands start to fidget more than they already were. I was afraid to touch anything else, afraid the shakiness of my hands might cause me to drop something and fuck us entirely.

Reese looked up at the clock, slapping a hand against the solid wood of the bookcase. "You know we aren't going to get another chance at this, right?"

"You aren't helping," I grit out as I leaned against the desk. If I was a book of coveted information, where would I be? Time wasn't on my side. I felt Reese next to me, hand on my shoulder. I instinctively shrugged him off, knowing he was about to say it was time to call it.

Reese lifted both his arms in a surrender. "Fine, I'll keep looking for the sake of fucking looking." He turned around, not realizing a stack of books was right next to his elbow as he collided with them. The books tumbled down, thudding as they connected with the ground. We tried to collect as many as we could as they fell, but our efforts weren't enough.

"Shit!" I yelled, covering my mouth. We didn't have time for this.

"I'm sorry, I should have looked," Reese apologized, getting on his knees to start picking up the fallen books.

I waved him off, getting on the ground with him. They were going to be back in a matter of minutes.

"Umm, Nick..."

I blinked a few times and looked up at Reese, who was waving his hand back and forth, trying to gather my attention. He peered down at a large book in front of him. It sat open with no pages inside. It was hollow, a fake book.

Reese put his hand inside, grabbing a hold of something, a smile plastered on his face. A smile started to form on my own when he pulled out the impossible. The leather was worn. The gold and silver traced wings on the binding were exactly like I imagined. He turned it around for me to see the gold hand on the front, confirming our thoughts.

"Is this what we're looking for?" he teased, pushing off the ground and placing the book on the desk. I gave the clock above us one last glance, realizing we had less time than I wanted to find what we were looking for, and hoped it was worth it.

"Grab the rest of the books off the ground and I'll start looking through this."

Reese nodded, scooping up the rest of the scattered books. I needed to find the days leading up to the invading demon, so I flipped through it, passing anything earlier than this month; I needed the last few weeks at least. When I'd found what I was looking for, I scanned down the pages, noticing names and the portals they used next to them. Portals were used for each of the villages, Limbo, and even Heaven itself, but those were all normal, regulated, and didn't really need to be accounted for. I let a few pages flip through my fingers, and I noticed Ariel's name and Purgatory written next to it, from the time he'd scooped up Dani.

I thumbed two pages back and let my eyes glaze over the names. My finger stopped.

Keegan Finley— Purgatory

His name was the only one that fit in the timeline. It was a few weeks before Markus found the demon, so it was spot on. I flipped through each page, looking for his name again, but didn't find it. I was slightly glad he hadn't made any more Purgatory trips, but not making any trips at all was odd. His name didn't show up anywhere and for a messenger, it was weird.

"Does Keegan Finley ring a bell?"

Reese leaned against the desk, tapping his finger on the solid wood. "Yeah, from what I've been told, he's kind of a shitty messenger, but I mean, it's not really a hard job."

"He can't be that shitty if they let him go to Purgatory."

Reese's eyes widened. "No way. You're telling me he has something to do with this?"

I shrugged, pointing to his name in the book. Reese blew out a low whistle. "I don't know how involved in this he is, but I *can* tell you he's completely disappeared."

"Disappeared? Like gone, gone?"

"I mean gone as in, his name hasn't shown up in the book since that trip to Purgatory. That seem odd to you?"

Reese looked up at the clock, tapping on the desk again before circling it. "It does, Nick, but we don't have time to look any more suspicious than we already do. By we, I mean me."

I nodded, closing the book and finding the hollow wooden box it sat in. I gently placed it inside and closed the lid. I had no idea where it was before, so I put it between two books from the fallen stack. I started to walk around the desk and position myself next to Reese, but something else caught my eye: a picture frame near the corner of the desk, glass with rounded edges. I reached my hand out and picked it up, slowly bringing it closer.

"Nick, let's go!"

I could hear the flutter of wings and knew our time was up. My eyes were still fixated on the photo of a much younger Jonah. His hair was a thick, rich black, long enough to meet his ear lobes, curled at the ends. It was slicked back away from his face. He was with a woman, who I assumed was his late wife, Amelia. She was Asian just like Jonah, her hair long and wavy, matching his with its inky black color. Her face was narrow and small, and she looked so tiny next to him. Her eyes were round and seemed kind.

They were next to two other people, and I caught my breath when I saw my father. It was like looking in a mirror. People in the village had always told me I favored him in so many ways, but I hadn't understood how right they were.

"Nick, come on, get over here!"

I heard feet on stone. I had to move, but something held me in place.

A face.

Standing there next to my father, arm wrapped around his middle in a loving, playful embrace, was the face of someone I recognized, but didn't, almost as if I didn't want to.

My mother.

I had vague memories of her, but nothing that ever quite sustained a full idea. Regardless of what I thought of her, I'd seen enough pictures to pick her out of a crowd. Her face was creamy, cheeks a blushing pink. Her hair was short, about shoulder length, the sunlight in the photo enhancing the strawberry blonde color. I had her eyes. I started to feel something in my heart pull and tug in different directions, but I didn't understand why. My head started to throb the more I looked at it.

How did Jonah know my mother? I knew he and my father were sentries together in their younger days, but this seemed so much like a pure friendship, my mind couldn't fully understand it. I never asked questions about her because she left us -- that's all I ever needed to know. Maybe I'd spoken too soon. Maybe I hadn't asked enough questions.

The photo vanished from my hand and was back on the table before I could take another look. Reese grabbed my arm and dragged me around the desk, back to my original spot in the room right as Ariel and the others made their entrance. I took one weak glance at the room and confirmed everything was as it was meant to be, not that it would matter now. Ariel looked us over as he took his place behind the desk.

"I wanted to stay to make sure everything was resolved," Reese said, clasping his hands together behind him.

Ariel straightened the lapels on his jacket and nodded. "Yes, it has. It has been dealt with accordingly, Mr. Diniel. Thank you for bringing it to my attention."

I glanced over at Reese, confused by Ariel's response. Reese only winked at me before looking down at the ground.

"You both may go. Mr. Diniel, I sent some of the recruits to the north woods. See what you can do with them," Ariel commanded.

Reese opened his mouth to protest, but I let out a low cough. He hated training new blood, but if I knew anything about Reese, he would take advantage of the woods and intentionally get them lost, making the goal of finding their way back home into a training exercise. He simply answered with a 'yes, sir' before turning and heading out the door.

"Mr. Cassial, prepare yourself for duties tonight. Accommodations cannot be made for every angel who says they are tired, despite their workload." He gave me a once over and then swiped his hand towards the door, letting me know the conversation was over.

Unlike Reese, I didn't try to respond when I headed out the door. My mind was too busy. Reese was waiting for me, leaning against the wall. The doors slammed closed behind me, and I looked around, wondering where the sentries had gone.

"If you're looking for Ariel's little bitch hounds, they went back to their posts. When I came up here, they busted out of fucking nowhere," Reese explained as we walked.

We stepped into the elevator, both of us leaning against the wall railing. "So, there really was a fight in the woods?" I asked.

"Well yeah, how else was I supposed to keep him out long enough?"

I ran my hand through my hair. "Like an actual fight? Or did you tell them to fake it?" Reese looked from side to side, trying to figure out what to say. "I mean, yeah. A fake fight wouldn't look authentic." I shook my head with a smile.

We walked out of the elevator, greeting a few angels as we passed them until we arrived at Reese's room and closed the door behind us.

I finally let my voice relay my thoughts. "What do we do about Keegan Finley?"

"I'll admit it's fishy that he hasn't been accounted for since that trip, but if he's somehow gone missing, where's his portal key? Did that just disappear too?" Reese pointed out, sitting down on his bed.

"Exactly. Let's say, God forbid, one of them dies -- where does the portal key go? Does it magically transport itself back to Jonah or does it just eliminate itself from existence?"

Reese shrugged. I lifted myself on top of his desk, setting my feet on his rolling chair. "You know this means that the demons were right."

Reese rolled his eyes, rubbing the back of his neck. He looked up at me skeptically, pushing himself all the way back onto his bed until he was propped up against the wall. "What was with you back there, by the way?"

"What do you mean?"

"Right before Ariel came in. You seemed really into whatever was in that photo. It's like you were in your own world, deep enough to almost fuck up the entire plan."

I bit my tongue, the decision whether to let Reese in on my family drama or not looming. He'd been there shortly after my mom left and he was the friend I'd needed at the time. He'd never met her, so he only knew the things I'd told him. Surprisingly, Reese was always the one who wanted to look more into it, but I'd always halted him. I'd always told him I didn't care.

"It was a photo of Jonah and Amelia, with my dad." I swallowed hard. "And my mom."

"Your mom!" Reese shouted, right before I jumped up to cover his mouth. We didn't need attention, especially for this.

"Yes. I don't know anything else but that. They looked like they were friends, which is odd because my father never mentioned having any sort of friendship with Amelia. From the stories of my mom, they weren't close enough to take photos like that."

"Are you going to ask him about it? Or at least your dad?"

"No, not now. The woman has been a mystery to me pretty much my whole life; she can stay that way a little bit longer," I answered, sitting back in my spot.

Reese rubbed his chin, blonde stubble poking out along his jawline. "So, Jonah was best pals with your mom and a messenger who went to Purgatory before the demon invader arrived has gone missing. Could this day get any more interesting?"

Another idea I had been mulling over found its way out of my mouth. "Maybe?"

Reese slithered down the wall, lying flat on his comforter. "Lay it on me."

"For now, the stuff with my mom is going to have to take a backseat, because Keegan Finley could be a major key. Completely disappearing is something else, along with our questions about the portal keys. We can't ask anyone about it; it'll just lead back to all the messenger angel shit," I began, trying to ease him into the notion running around in my head.

"Okay, that makes sense."

"When I was looking through the book, I noticed Keegan did go to one place out of the ordinary before the Purgatory trip."

Reese pushed himself up onto his elbows, getting a better look at me. I fiddled with a loose thread on my jeans as I continued. "I'm thinking we can go there, get some answers to our questions, or at least try to."

Reese nodded. "Okay sweet. Where are we going?"

I sat my elbow on my thigh and tilted my head into my hand. "Oculus."

He narrowed his eyes at me, pressing his lips tightly together. I knew it was taking everything inside him not to grab me by the shoulders and tackle me to the ground for suggesting another Oculus trip at all. "Why do I feel like you are constantly trying to get me killed?"

"I'm not, I promise. I want to figure this out as much as you do. The quicker we do, the faster the demons go home. If Keegan went to Oculus, that meant Jonah trusted him. It also means he spoke to Natalia, so she's our next best bet. She seemed like she wanted to help." I knew the main thing Reese heard was that the demons could go home sooner rather than later. The minute Dani told Elise they weren't going back as soon as they'd hoped, Elise lost her mind. If Natalia could bring us closer to what we needed, than we had to try.

"Riddle me this Nick: we don't have a portal key anymore, so how the hell do you expect us to get to Oculus?" he asked, raising an eyebrow at me expectedly.

I jumped off the desk and paced across the room. I kept stopping at his bed, opening my mouth, then turning around to walk away again. I knew he wasn't going to like it, but he had to keep sucking it up. Once I'd made my sixth circle, I crossed my arms over my chest.

"We're going to fly."

Reese put his hand out, motioning towards the bathroom and back to me. "What's with all the back-and-forth pacing? Flying is fine."

"We're taking Dani and Elise. I plan on telling them all this tomorrow morning."

Reese looked around his bed, then his room, then the walls and ceiling, as if he was contemplating everything I said, like he was breaking down every word, every syllable.

"But they can't fly. The minute someone sees those wings, we're fucked."

I covered my mouth and just hummed in response.

"You don't expect us to carry them *and* fly, do you?" Reese laughed. He dropped his elbows, flopping back down to the bed. I cleared my throat to try to fill the awkward silence, since I didn't know how to respond. After a few moments, he sprung up, his eyes boring into mine. "You expect us to carry them *and* fly?"

"It's not that far of a flight."

"That's not the point! We both know you're going to carry the normal one and I'll be stuck with *her*, so I'll just say it now: this is bullshit." He shoved past me to the bathroom.

"So does that mean you'll do it?" I winced, even though I knew he was nowhere near me.

"Of course, I'm going to do it. I'm obligated to see how this shit plays out. Now, though, I have to go train some little shits in the woods." He shut the bathroom door, leaving me relieved. This conversation went much better than I'd imagined.

"You're a dick, you know that?" he yelled from behind the door. "Nick the Dick."

I chuckled, my laughter only lasting so long until I closed his door behind me, alone in the hallway, left to my own mind. I'd said my mother would have to take a back seat to the issue at hand, but that wasn't exactly the truth. I wouldn't let it cloud my judgement or deter me from my goal, but that didn't mean that it would completely fade from my thoughts. I could solve one mystery, while deep diving into another. I could multitask.

I had to.

CHAPTER SEVEN

DANI

It didn't surprise me that the plan had been fruitful. A place like Heaven's Gate can't be all lush lawns and clear blue skies all the time. The outside had a posh exterior, but I had an inkling the inside had a dimmer disposition. I watched from the window as angels frolicked in the grass, how their wings were almost one with the wind, like it was always meant to be that way. It almost made me smile to think there was a place to be truly happy, to want for nothing, but then my smile faltered. I thought about what Natalia had said about angels destroying Oculus for the sole purpose of proving a point: that they could do as they pleased.

Ask any angel and I'm sure the answer would be a resounding *"we did it for the good of everyone."* Angels were all about justification for their actions, even when no one else agreed with the logic. I understood the idea, except where I came from, no one cared or questioned you about what you'd done. Lilith had left me with a small shred of humanity, but I never understood why. Was it to make me feel empathy for my terrorized victims, so I could hurt with them as some type of fucked up torture? Elise could feel sad or anxious or ruthless, but it wasn't the same. She felt them as an instinct, while I felt them deeper in my soul.

I'd felt a small twist in my heart when Natalia told us of her mother and their reasoning for glamour their land. Natalia had pieces to the story that Nicholas didn't, but it still felt incomplete.

Our plan had been successful, but none of us were all too eager to head back to Oculus. On the outside, I was calm and collected, but inside, I was bouncing around in my skin. They had woken us early in the morning, and Elise grumbled past all of us into the thick trees of the woods while Reese followed her, trying to keep up with her quick pace. Nick stayed next to me and whispered in a low voice so only I would hear. "Thanks for the suggestion. It actually paid off."

I side-smiled and waved him off. I didn't need a thanks. I wanted this little adventure of ours to end soon. I didn't want to go back to Purgatory because it felt right, or because it was a home I *wanted* to go back to. I wanted to go back simply because at this very moment, Lilith was probably trying to find any and every way to drag me back. tearing everyone and everything apart along with her, like the fucking tornado she was.

We passed a line of large trees shaped to a point when the angels stopped, taking one solid look around before giving each other a solid nod.

"Okay, this should be a good spot," Nicholas announced, cracking his neck before pushing his wings out from his back, rattling the sword he strapped to his shoulder. I'd almost forgotten how large they were, how white they were. I looked around as his wings propelled a shadow around us, making it look as if he had swallowed the sunlight.

"I almost didn't think you were serious," I laughed, completely baffled at the plan he'd told me a few hours ago. Elise and I had just stood there while he ranted about some messenger disappearing and going to Oculus. What made our ears perk up was his way of getting there.

He tucked his wings inward, letting the light back in. "It's the only way, unless *you* want to ask Jonah for a portal key?"

I pulled my eyebrows together and shook my head. "I'll pass, thanks." I walked the few feet it took to get to him, the leaves cracking under my boots. His expression remained the same when I stood only inches in front of him. "Besides, I can't pass on such an intimate bonding moment." I let my hand slide from his wrist to his bicep, squeezing a bit to feel the hard muscle underneath.

The only sentries I'd ever interacted with were silent, stoic. These angels weren't like that at all. Reese was an easy read, all talk and quick at the whip when needed. As much as he'd hate it, he was turning out to be one of my favorite people.

Nicholas was a harder read. His eyes were soft, as if he could listen to your problems all day. Being this close to him, feeling his muscles and listening to how steady and calculated his breathing had become, I knew he was the kind to push it all down, exude pure confidence on the outside. He wasn't the obvious flirt, but I could flirt enough for the both of us. He didn't react to my forwardness at our training session, so I took that as a good sign. His sex appeal went up dramatically when I watched his abilities with a sword.

Nicholas looked down at my hand and let his hazelnut eyes peer into mine. He stepped back a bit, letting my hand fall, rolling his eyes. I let a smile creep across my face, confirming my initial assumption. He didn't mind my flirting.

Noted.

"Nick, can we fucking go?" Reese whined, looking up at the sky. The wood on his bow seemed to glisten on his back. "I really want to get this—" he motioned between him and Elise, "over with."

Elise kicked him in the shin and Reese bent down, holding his leg, letting out a few choice words under his breath. "Yeah, let's see if your flying skills are better than your sword skills, Blondie."

"Knock it off, you two. Oculus isn't *that* far, but if you keep going like this, it will take us hours to get there." Nicholas gave them a knowing look and stretched out his arms in front of him. I grabbed a hold of his left arm and swung my legs up so that he held me bridal style. He cradled me, adjusting so my placement was more comfortable for him.

"You drop me, and I will fucking cut your dick off, got it?" Elise threatened, hopping up into his arms. She gave him a subtle slap to the cheek before settling back.

Reese released his wings from his back and hovered above the ground. "If I drop you, you'll die, so that sounds great to me." He shot into the sky and quickly vanished out of sight.

I felt Nicholas rise from the ground, his wings flapping softly, gaining momentum with every inch we rose from the ground. He bounded upwards, the wind hitting my face in a slap. I saw trees go by, their leaves blurry messes of green and reddish brown. I looked down, the ground becoming smaller every time I blinked. I almost felt tears at my eyes from the speed we were moving. At times, I felt like I would fall from his grasp, but Nicholas held his grip on me effortlessly. We started to slow, but I realized it was because he was turning.

Nicholas flapped his wings, each beat more powerful than the last. I could see Reese and Elise ahead of us, having slowed their pace a bit. I let my free hand glide across the clouds near us, like silk on my fingertips. I caught a glimpse of Nicholas' face; he looked so serene up here, as if he could do this all day. The wind was less harsh up here, so I could get a better look at his face, at all those features that made him one of the most pleasant sights I had ever seen.

He had a perfectly sculpted face that I almost wanted to chisel away to find some type of flaw, knowing I would never find one. Even the scar below his eye wasn't a flaw in my eyes. It only made me want to reach my hand out and touch it. His hair was short and tousled, as if he just woke up . It was thick and dark, the kind that made you want to pull on it. I wondered if he liked that, having his hair pulled. I didn't know much about angels and how they liked to fuck, but I always assumed it was different, depending on the angel and how sheltered their upbringing was. I had only known him for a few days, but I had a feeling the determined look he had during our training was the same energy he brought to bed. I bit my lip at the thought.

I started to deepen my thoughts about his bedroom habits when he snapped me out of them with his voice. "He told me, you know."

I blinked in confusion. "Told you what?"

Nicholas only looked ahead, his eyes focused. "Your special gift."

I swatted the clouds as they passed, trying to figure out what he was talking about. A special gift? Any gift I would be given would be nothing special. *Oh shit.*

"My compulsion, you mean?" I wriggled my shoulders around, sinking into his arms so my legs hung off a bit more. "What about it?"

He scoffed. "You didn't think to tell us?"

"Why would I need to? It's not really something I need to disclose," I pointed out, tilting my head back to view the open sky. The peacefulness of it was something I envied.

"You're aware that it's outlawed, right? A literal crime." I knew he was trying to scold me, but all I heard was an angel with a deep, dominant voice. *Shiver.*

"Oh, I think everyone is aware, Nicholas."

"But you still use it."

I brought my head back up, letting my nails casually graze the side of his neck, feeling tiny goosebumps raise in his skin. "I'm going to tell you what I told your friend. The way you operate here is the least of my fucking concern. What you outlaw and what you don't are more like suggestions where I'm from. We both know angels aren't coming down to check on us. It's not high on the to-do list for your kind. As long as days go on as normal, a blind eye is turned."

He swallowed, his Adam's apple bobbing. "Have you ever thought of using it while you're here?"

"Not really. I mean, you angels are pretty easily motivated as it is."

His face scrunched up in a perplexed look. He quickly looked down at me and then back towards the sky. "What's that supposed to mean?

I looked over at where Reese was flying with Elise, highly annoyed in his arms, and smirked. "No reason."

"I'm going to be honest and tell you I don't really care that you have it, but only that you don't use it. If you do and you get caught, I won't help you," he explained, expanding his wings so we were gliding instead of pure flying.

"Duly noted, sir," I answered, saluting him. I decided to let him in on a secret, just to ease his mind. "If it makes you feel any better, I can't compel anyone even if I wanted to right now."

He was silent, as if waiting for my answer. I traced my fingers around his neck into the collar of his t-shirt, feeling the skin above his collarbone. I adjusted myself a bit so I was somewhat level with his face. "You have something I need."

"Ah, your dagger, you mean," he quipped, interest peaking in his voice.

"Ah yes, you actually hold the key to my compulsion, Mr. Cassial." I tapped my finger on his collar bone, letting my hand rest there. He made no moves to brush my fingers away, no slight shift of his shoulder to completely remove my fingers from his body.

"I assume you got that fun gift from Lilith?" he asked.

"The dagger or the compulsion?"

He adjusted his arm so that his hand now wrapped around my thigh. "Both."

"They came as a package deal, although I didn't know about the compulsion until later. She decided to keep that fun fact to herself. The dagger was forged for me and me alone. She infused it with additions like the compulsion."

His fingers tightened around my thigh. "So, you only use it when you're torturing people?"

I nodded. "It tends to make what I do a little bit more fun. I can make people do and feel whatever I'd like."

"Isn't that a little cruel?"

I giggled a little, causing him to malfunction a bit in flight, as if the sound made him stutter for a moment. "You're adorable when you're naïve."

I placed my hand on his chest, feeling his heartbeat in a steady rhythm. "Nicholas, you say it's a little cruel, but we're talking about torture in Purgatory. It's nothing but cruelty."

I could see he was biting the inside of his cheek, thinking on his words.

"I don't always use it to be cruel, if it's any consolation. Sometimes, I tell them to think about their favorite place in the world, or that they are in a deep sleep. It just depends. Sometimes, demons want screams and sometimes, they just want buckets of blood. You kind of have to be there to get what I mean." I tapped my fingers one by one on his chest. It would be awkward to try to feel for the abs I knew he had, so I forced that thought out of my mind.

"I think I understand. I guess I can't really fault you, at least for now." He glanced down at me as I started to look up at him. He had a look I couldn't read, like he was expressionless on purpose. "There is something that's been on my mind, though."

I smiled softly. "Let it out, Nicholas."

"How come you aren't shaken by the idea that Lilith could find you?" He genuinely wanted to know.

I answered with the only response I had. "Because she can't. Not on her own, at least." I didn't admit that her attempt to find me had been on my mind, but it wasn't eating away at me.

"What?" He continued to look at me, one of his eyebrows raised in suspicion.

I let out a long breath that made my stomach collapse. "I guess a long time ago, during the war that Lilith caused, angels locked her in Purgatory. It wasn't so easy for her regardless, but now she has no way of getting here by herself. They chained her up in her own cage.

"I don't look over my shoulder constantly because I know she can't be here. That doesn't mean she won't try. Who knows, maybe we're both wrong and she doesn't care about me at all."

"Could she possibly be the one who started all this?" He was talking about the portals.

I brought my fingers from his collarbone back to his neck and grazed the skin again. The hilt of his sword, the cool metal of it, created cool pressure when it slightly bumped my hand. I felt his heartbeat thrum off beat for a minute with my other hand. "I wouldn't doubt it, but I'm not running to your master with the information because that part is obvious. Lilith would need someone to help her, so until we find that someone, it doesn't really matter. She can't do much on her own, no matter how powerful she is."

"How do you know? I doubt she would just decide to tell you that information."

I wrapped one of my tight curls around my finger. "Demons talk, you know. Even if she didn't tell me, she told someone who told another and so on. I learned about it at some point, but all the history behind it is beyond me."

He veered right to bypass some clustered clouds before responding. "You don't seem as scared of her as I assumed you would be."

"That's because I'm not, but I know she scares you. She scares all of you."

He narrowed his eyes but didn't say anything in return. It was like I'd just told him a secret when really, it's known to everyone. I decided to lighten up the mood from the darkness of the conversation. Eventually, I would speak to him about Lilith, let him in on my time there, but right now, I *really* didn't want to.

"Purgatory really isn't *that* bad, in the grand scheme of things," I confirmed, pressing some of my weight to the arm around his neck and lifting myself up to his ear. "I have a really nice room with the biggest fucking bed." I let my words travel through him, his expression never changing as his shoulders stiffened a little and his heartbeat seemed to miss the beat it wanted. "You should see it sometime and test it out for yourself, Mr. Cassial."

He looked down at me, the corners of his mouth starting to pull up, as if he wanted to laugh. "I think I'll stick with my bed here. I wouldn't want to ruin your precious beauty sleep."

"Ruin my beauty sleep? Hmm, does that mean you're the kind to keep me up all night? I can appreciate that kind of stamina." I let my teeth graze his earlobe slightly before I satisfyingly slid back down into his arms, letting my fingers playfully tickle his neck.

I felt goosebumps again, but this time, they didn't go away -- they lingered a while. His heart thumped against my hand on his chest. I let my eyes climb from his chest to his slender neck to his perfect face, up to his eyes that always looked at me when I wanted to look at him.

When he'd caught my attention, he let those eyes creep down to my chest. The tank top I wore pushed up my breasts in a way that from this angle would be the downfall of any male.

Nicholas was no exception. He let his gaze stay on my chest one more minute before he looked away, back to our destination. He made a slow but steady descent towards the ground. I couldn't see much of the trees yet, but I assumed he wanted us to have an easy landing.

"Have you ever spent the night with a demon before?" I asked casually.

"I can't say I have."

"Have you spent the night with *anyone* before?"

Nicholas let the tips of his wings curl upward as we continued our descent. "I really don't see how that is any of your business."

"If we're going to work together, I'm going to need to know more about you. If you're a virgin, I wouldn't judge you." I smirked.

He raised an eyebrow at me. "I hardly think knowing my sex life will help this situation."

I ruffled my hair, letting my curls tumble and hang down his arm. "Maybe not, but I promise I'll annoy you until you answer."

He let out a deep breath, rolling his eyes. "No, I am not a virgin."

I let out a sly smile, letting my hand slide under his chin and caress his cheek. "Angelic females, I presume? That's no fun. I bet they never told you you can use that precious sword of yours for something other than fighting."

He swallowed hard, his cheeks starting to flush. I hadn't met many angels, but the ones I had come across didn't seem like the adventurous types. To them, hair pulling was likely a capital crime. I couldn't tell if the flushed cheeks came from embarrassing nerves or from shameful curiosity, but either way, I was enjoying the show.

Nicholas was about to say something when we heard two familiar voices slightly below us, traveling towards the ground.

"I swear, I will fucking drop you right now if you don't stop licking my face!" Reese shouted, swerving a bit.

"I'm just seeing how you do under pressure, Blondie, that's all. A little distraction never hurt anyone," Elise laughed.

I let out an exasperated sigh. "Oh, for fuck's sake."

We were no longer up in the clouds. Trees surrounded us, and Nicholas had to do a lot more maneuvering to avoid them. The weeping willows were the first things I noticed as the grounds of Oculus grew closer. The dirt wasn't as muddy; it looked like it had hardened into scattered clumps. The small number of buildings were still in disarray: roofs smashed, windows and doors shattered with glass littering the ground.

Nicholas steadied to a stop once we were inches above the ground before completely setting his feet on the dirt. He set me down gently, but not before allowing his hand and fingers to linger on my back and shoulders. It almost felt like a swipe of heat as he skimmed over my body. If he'd felt anything, he showed nothing on his face. I looked past him to see Reese practically throwing Elise out of his arms, shaking his arms as if to get her scent off him.

"I'm never doing that again," he said, irritation showing on every inch of his face.

"We both know you loved every minute of it," Elise teased, shoving him.

Reese pointed over at his best friend. "You owe me big time for this."

"I'm going to assume you all aren't trying to sneak around this time," a familiar voice said from the trees in front of us.

"Holy fuck!" Reese snatched his bow and notched an arrow, readying his position.

Natalia leaned against a thick trunk of a cypress tree. Her sandals crushed dead leaves cluttered on the dirt. She didn't move from her spot, unbothered by Reese. He lowered his bow, placing a hand on his chest.

"You couldn't have given me a warning?" he said, his breathing starting to return to normal.

The breeze that whipped by blew her long hair around her shoulders. "I saw you from one of the hills. I was going to let you find me, but all your shouting would have been disturbing and we don't need another scuffle like last time." Her honey-colored eyes seemed to look right through me, as if those last words were meant just for me.

Nicholas stepped up closer to her. "We don't. We need your help."

"Are you planning to strap me to a chair again and interrogate me?"

Elise clucked her tongue. "Are we going to have to?"

Natalia looked over at her and gave her a smug smile. "Not if I can help it."

"We think we have a lead on the portals. It's a small lead, but a lead nonetheless." Nicholas crossed his arms over his chest.

Natalia raised one of her dark eyebrows. "Ah, well then, I'm intrigued to hear this. Come with me." She turned around, walking towards the run-down buildings.

Her long purple dress flowed around her ankles with every step. She had a tight silver bangle around her arm and I noticed a small, five-pointed crown tattooed on her shoulder blade.

Natalia led us past the initial buildings we'd noticed on our first visit and further into the unknown land. She was soon joined by two other Enchanters who I recognized from the fight. They flanked her, never quite looking us in the eyes. They wore tunics that matched her dress, but their purple was lighter, more pastel. Nicholas looked as if he was focused straight ahead, but I knew he was scanning the perimeter every chance he got. I noticed Reese doing the same.

We stopped in front of a larger building, watching as the two Enchanters stepped aside to let us inside after Natalia. The roof was rounded and made of wood, old and slightly moldy. When the breeze picked up, it seemed like pieces would fall off and fly away. Nicholas pushed against my arm with his own, motioning for me to go inside, with him on my heels. It was much bigger on the inside; rows of pews and a narrow carpet runner decorated the space. The pews were full of dust, but Natalia sat on the closest one and crossed her legs. Elise wiped the dust off, watching as it floated down onto the creaking wooden floors.

"How can I be of assistance?" Natalia asked, a hand on her knee. The sun that came through one of the windows danced across her dark skin.

"The portal keys you made and gave to Jonah, are they meant for certain people, or did you just give them to Jonah to disperse how he saw fit?" Nicholas started, deciding to forgo the pews and prop his back against one of the stone statues.

"Jonah simply wanted me to create portal keys. I had no indica-tion who he wanted me to create them for. I created ones for all the executives. It was up to Jonah to decide who they were for and where they could use them," Natalia explained, propping her other hand onto the back of the pew. "To my knowledge, I suppose messengers and guardians would need them most."

"Did you ever meet any of the messengers who were sent here?" Nicholas questioned.

"A few, but they didn't stay for long. Jonah would usually come himself."

"Does the name Keegan Finley ring any bells?"

Natalia shook her head. "I never really caught their names. I mean, you must know most messengers have one job, and a conversation isn't included in the job description."

"If we described him, do you think you could remember him?" Reese asked.

"Probably. We see so few that I'm sure I could."

Reese nodded. "About five foot ten, dirty blonde hair, glasses, freckles around his nose and below his eyes?"

"You would have seen him right around a week ago," Nicholas added.

Natalia's eyes gleamed with remembrance. "Ah, yes, the nervous one."

"Nervous?" I asked, my voice echoing softly against the walls.

"Yes, quite nervous. I don't know whether it was being here or if it was his first day on the job, but it took him five minutes to get two words out." She chuckled, as if that moment was replaying right in front of her.

"How long had Keegan been a messenger for?" I directed my question to Reese, who didn't look at me when he answered.

"A few months. From what I'd been told, he wasn't the best at it. He would forget what he was supposed to say, or he would relay the message to the wrong person, but I guess I can see how being here can scramble someone's brain."

"What exactly did he say?" Nicholas turned back to Natalia.

Natalia pressed her lips together and closed her eyes for a few seconds. "He wanted to know the details of the portal constructed for Purgatory, the one my mother created."

"The Purgatory portal?" Elise and I asked at the same time.

Natalia nodded. "He was afraid to ask at first, but soon enough, he was speaking quite clearly. I didn't create it, so I couldn't tell him much. My mother's magic and mine are both strong, yet different. Her magic was strong enough to create a one-way prison for people like Lilith. It was much more sustainable than mine, I can admit that."

Moira created Lilith's prison. *Holy fuck.*

Natalia continued. "I explained only one angel can ever open a portal into Purgatory. There can't be two portals open at the same time. Less room for error. The portal is constructed with a block and forces to push out the unwanted and keep in what it needs. You need permission to go in, unlike if you were to portal to any of the villages. You could do that all day long with no issues whatsoever."

Reese scrubbed a hand down his face. "Why would he want to know any of this?"

Natalia shrugged. "He said Jonah wanted to know the exact precautions and blocks used. He wanted to know the types of wards put up, the intricate details that went along with them. Our magic isn't meant to be hard to understand, just difficult to remove and destroy."

"You didn't think it was weird Keegan was asking and not Jonah himself?" Nicholas pressed, moving from the statue.

"Questioning angels didn't really get my people far before, so why rock the boat?" Reese looked down at the ground, and Nicholas pushed a mound of dirt around with the toe of his shoe. "My mother created that iron gate on the portal for Lilith personally. When the war was over, Jonah's father asked her to make a force so strong, Lilith couldn't escape. For the good of everyone, my mother agreed, trapping our people who decided to remain with her. She hoped they would forgive her one day." Natalia tucked a piece of her hair behind her ear slowly. "My mother told me she had to do three hard things in her entire existence and that was one of them."

"Did Keegan mention anything about going to Purgatory?" I pushed.

Natalia combed through her hair with her long fingernails. "Not that I remember. Why?"

"Because the last time he flew anywhere was to Purgatory, and then he just vanished. He came here before the portal breach, and then took a trip to Purgatory, then nothing. He isn't logged to have gone anywhere since," Nicholas explained, taking a seat beside her.

"I assume that's odd for a messenger?" Natalia asked.

"Very," Reese answered.

"Wouldn't Jonah have noticed some type of discrepancy in his messengers? I know he has a lot of angels to look after, but it seems weird he wouldn't notice when one just stopped showing up for work," Natalia posited, looking out the only stable window in the building.

Elise let out a small noise, a mix between a laugh and a cough. "Now you're asking the right questions. Jonah's missing a lot of key information, isn't he? Pretty convenient."

"There has to be an explanation for it," Reese insisted, turning his head towards Elise behind him.

"Oh *okay*, when you're ready to get your head out of your leaders' asshole, come talk to me." She leaned back in the pew, bending her right leg, placing her ankle on her left knee.

"There is the question of portal keys," I mentioned, leaning so my elbows were on my knees to get a better look at Natalia.

"What about them?" She sounded curious.

"If Jonah gave keys to certain people, would their keys automatically return to Jonah if something happened, or would they disintegrate? How does the magic you've developed work?"

Natalia ran her hand along her arm, as if inspecting something I knew wasn't there. "The keys aren't made to remove themselves from existence. Executives are, for a lack of better words, almost like the master keys to the keys themselves. I created the book to better help Jonah keep track, almost like a master logbook. If they noticed something happened and the key isn't back, they retrieve it. They can't change the magic I've already put in place, but they can change minor things about it, like permission to a certain place or for a certain amount of time. Keegan's key could be stolen, but it would only give them the access he was allowed at the time."

"Doesn't seem like we need to be worried then. I highly doubt Keegan had access to much," Reese noted, stretching his arms above his head.

"That still doesn't explain why he would go to Purgatory in the first place. Usually, the messengers who go there have been doing their job for years. That would be something Jonah would do himself," Nicholas expounded, sliding his hand through his hair.

"My thoughts exactly. It isn't a coincidence when someone doesn't make it back from Purgatory. They didn't come back because someone or something there didn't want them to go." Elise commented, swiping her bangs out of her eyes before letting them fall back into place.

I continued with her thought. "Keegan either found out something he shouldn't, or he was sent there for a reason. Maybe it's both. Either way, the key must still be with him."

Nicholas rubbed his temples. "Could you locate it?"

Natalia stuck out her tongue and licked her lower lip. "Perhaps. If it happens to still be in Purgatory, do you plan to seek out this angel? I fear you may end up just like him if you do."

"I don't know what we'll do, but we at least have to try."

She let out a long and draining breath. "I'll seek out the key, but I would unfortunately assume your friend is long gone by now."

I got up from where I sat. "I hate to say it, but she's probably right."

Natalia looked up at me, fascination in her eyes. The moment was gone when she spoke again. "For me to locate it, there are a few things I need, but I will let you know tomorrow."

"I thought you guys just did some simple one, two, three point and shoot type magic," Reese said, pointing out his fingers in multiple directions, mimicking his words.

"Not everything is that simple. Locating something like that takes a bit more effort on my part." Natalia gave him a soft smile before getting up from the pew. The two Enchanters opened the doors, revealing a group. Natalia wiggled her fingers in a small wave.

"I have some other matters I must attend to before then," she stated, making her way to the open doors.

I grabbed her elbow before she retreated. The Enchanters immediately flanked her, blue and lilac hues surfacing from their hands. She made no move towards me, but simply turned around and gave a small shake of her head towards her guards. They extinguished their magic, but never moved from their position.

"Do you expect us to just hope you find an answer?" I asked, letting go of her arm.

She placed her hand on my arm. "I'll seek you out. I've been meaning to go back to Heaven's Gate anyway. I did tell you we would meet again, Soul Seether, and here we are."

"Last time, you asked why I was here. You said it like you knew something we didn't," I pressed. She spoke like she was hiding something, and I didn't trust that.

"I honestly have no idea why you were pulled from your dark home, but I like to think everything has a purpose. I suppose that doesn't always have to mean the purpose is for the better or the worse." She cocked her head to the side, pressing her glossed lips together. "What I meant is why would they want someone beloved for untethering souls from the dead? Someone like that must be meant for something bigger if you're wanted here."

She had a way of saying things and letting them linger in the air, as if it had no place to go but right in front of me. I had to accept them, figure out what to do with them. She made no sense, but then made perfect sense in the next minute. She had a satisfied look on her beautiful face that made me want to ask more questions, but that would have to wait. Frankly, I didn't even know what my questions were.

Natalia swiftly turned on her heels and sauntered out the door. The Enchanters followed her while the rest of her people watched. They seemed in utter awe of her, but they weren't afraid. I noticed as we walked out behind her that they looked on with adoration and pride. She lifted her hand and moved her wrist in a large circle. The space in front of her made a concave motion and turned hollow and purple. She had created a portal for us.

"You seemed to have an interesting time getting here. I thought I'd make it easier." She let out a soft laugh to herself.

"Oh, fuck yeah." Reese pushed past us to get closer. Elise shrugged, following him, but remained close enough to lean out and trip him. He almost landed face first in the dirt before catching himself. I shook my head and looked over at Nicholas, who was sluggishly following behind. He stopped next to Natalia, looking as if he was mustering up the courage to speak.

Natalia spoke first. "I know the last time we spoke I mentioned your mother. If that was a sore subject, I apologize."

He blinked a few times but waved her off. "No need. I completely forgot about it. I'd rather *someone* have a good opinion of her."

I cleared my throat, needing to know one more thing before we left. "There's something I wanted to ask before we leave."

She dipped her head down, waiting.

"Your mother had to do three hard things in her life. You mentioned one, but was another glamorizing your land?"

Natalia nodded. "She knew it was the right thing to do."

I looked around, as if hoping to see what she saw, but I couldn't. In her eyes, the glamor didn't exist, and she saw this place how it was meant to be seen. I was conditioned to see death and carnage as pure beauty and something about it was entertaining and marvelous, but I knew she saw beauty that made you feel something in the deepest part of your heart.

"What was her third?"

"I don't know. She never told me. I think that was the one that hurt the most." Her voice was steady and composed, but there was a sadness to it, as if she could feel her mothers' pain. I felt for her, and it was the strangest feeling I'd ever felt. "I'll see you soon, Soul Seether."

CHAPTER EIGHT

NICK

It was near the middle of the day when Jonah summoned me. It wasn't to his office, like it would normally be. He summoned me to the Divine Library. The library was so unfathomably large, it needed its own stone exterior away from the main building. It was walking distance from The Skies, but I'd been told there was an underground passage inside. That was a rumor that had been floating around forever, so I never paid it any mind, nor did I really need to consider it.

I hadn't slept much last night, especially not with Reese constantly in my ear telling me how horrible yesterday was, how he will never let me put him through that type of torture ever again. He would 'rather take ten arrows to the dick' than have Elise that close to him. Despite the hours of whining, he finally left my room, and I was alone with my wandering mind. I had settled into my bed and like every other night, assumed I would fall asleep with ease, but I found that an insufferable task.

I kept thinking about Jonah and my mother; I pondered over Keegan and whether we would ever find his body or his key; and to my utter surprise, I found myself thinking about Dani. I was simply thinking about her, nothing promiscuous or filthy. Reese looked at them, at demons, like they were a disease, that every word from their mouths was to be overthought and torn apart. I was nowhere near that end of the spectrum, but I didn't quite trust them either. Dani wasn't the kind of demon, outside of her realm, to genuinely be afraid of. If I was being brutally honest, I wanted to speak to her more. She seemed so willing to give up information to me, almost as if she wanted to tell someone everything weighing on her chest.

I was willing to listen.

Halfway through the night, I rubbed my eyes raw with every attempt I took at going back to sleep. I stared at the darkness of my room and tried to run through everything Natalia had said, but every now and then, Dani came back into the forefront. I was good at holding in my emotions, but she'd tried hard to get me to crack, and I almost had. *Almost.*

Did I think she was attractive? Sure. Could I hear my blood thrumming in my ears every time she grazed her hand across my skin? Perhaps. Did I practically almost drop her when she mentioned swordplay in bed? Yup.

Whether or not I could imagine us in bed together, if I even wanted that at all, wasn't the main concern. I wasn't Reese; I didn't do things without thinking them through. We had a job to do, and some forward flirting from a pretty demon wasn't going to skew my priorities.

The Divine Library was built minimal on the outside, but on the inside, it was a grand masterpiece. I'd read they wanted it to be a place of peace and learning, the mystery and beauty on the inside, not the outside. I stepped up to the doors. Any angel was allowed in with the right magic. I grabbed the handle and let out a breath as gold wisps encircled my hand. I heard a click and satisfyingly opened the door.

A small puff of dust greeted me as I stepped inside, the door shutting behind me. Orbs of light hung from the ceiling, casting a soft white glow throughout the room. Rows and rows of books surrounded me. There were a few desks and tables scattered around for the diligent angel who wanted to study there. The stained-glass windows brought in natural light, colors dancing along the shelves, almost erasing any trace of dust, making each book look new and inviting.

"Nicholas," Jonah called from above me. I tilted my head up to see him leaning over the metal railing. "Please come join me."

I palmed my hair down, hoping it wasn't a total mess from the wind outside. Unlike The Skies, there was no elevator here, so the stairs were the one way to get from floor to floor. The Divine Library only had two floors, but they were wide. If you didn't know much about what you were looking for, you could get lost. I took the stairs two at a time, feeling the cold metal of the railing against my hand, even though the room itself was warm. The lights followed from the bottom floor to the second, instantly casting brighter light as I went. Tapestries hung on the walls, beautifully designed with angels in flight. I spotted Jonah at one of the tables. I walked past a tapestry that caught my eye before I reached him.

The image was of someone in long, flowing clothing, stars around their head and blue wisps were firing out of their hands. The other character had wings, large and pronounced. Gold wisps circled them, which caused my eyebrows to raise. Why would a tapestry of an Enchanter and an angel be hanging in the Divine Library?

"Nicholas, have a seat," Jonah said with more authority than I'd like.

I pulled myself away from the tapestry and sat down across from him. The orbs above us bowed back and forth, leaving shadows on the floor. I let my fingers travel to the collar of my t-shirt and fiddled with it. I knew he was going to bring up the snooping in his office. On the walk over, I mentally prepared myself for an ass chewing worse than any I had ever gotten.

Jonah sighed, placing his hands on the table, clasping them together. "I know you made an unauthorized trip to Oculus."

I opened my mouth to spew out the excuses I had meticulously formulated in my head, but I paused. So, he wasn't aware of the poking around Reese and I had done.

"That's correct." There was no point in lying.

"Whatever for?"

"There was information only Natalia could assist with, that's all,"

I answered, trying to appear as nonchalant as I could. I had only myself to blame for not developing a story. I wasn't like Reese; I couldn't construct a full-blown story in one go.

Jonah shook his head. "Information? Involving the portals?"

"Of course. She gave us some valuable information last time, and I assumed she could be of assistance again."

"And was she?"

"She...well...I..." I didn't know how to answer. If I said yes, this conversation would be even more difficult to execute and I'd likely have to explain the office invasion. If I said no, he would most likely leave it alone, but I would be more closely watched. I decided to meet him somewhere in the middle.

"I wanted to go back to speak to her without all the tension and hostility. I've found that people are much more accommodating if you aren't interrogating them. I took the others along for support and insight, like you asked the first time we went. She mentioned something about a...messenger angel," I responded, deciding that having the idea not be ours at all would be the best plan of action. Jonah and Natalia already got along, so he would assume nothing of her mentioning something like this to us.

"A messenger angel? That's a bit odd." Jonah mulled over my words. He brought his finger to his temple and pressed, as if trying to make sense of it. He almost looked perplexed.

Natalia said that Keegan came to Oculus to question her because Jonah told him to. Jonah shouldn't be shocked by the mention of a messenger angel. He should be instantly telling me what I already knew, unless sending Keegan was meant to be a secret. Elise and her theories were starting to get in my head, but this time, I couldn't even begin to remotely ignore it.

"I suppose it is." That was all I could say as I tried to manage my own thoughts.

"Did she say anything about this angel that could be helpful in any way? Did she give you a name?" Jonah looked into my eyes, and I was afraid to even try to look away.

I did what I thought was best for the situation, at least until I had more substantial evidence. "She couldn't remember much. All she really gave us was that it was a messenger and he had asked some questions about the magic holding Lilith at bay and the portal into Purgatory. Nothing full of details, just the protocols on it."

"Hmm, that's a wondrous thing to ask about. I'm the only one who knows about the bells and whistles of that portal, besides Natalia. Oculus does require permission to portal there, so he would have had permission from another executive."

I dipped my head to the side, raising an eyebrow. "Precisely. If this angel had anything to do with it, which I'm not saying he did, he seems to be succeeding, since a demon is in the Bastille." A demon chained beneath The Skies, underground in the hollows of confinement.

"You make a solid point, Nicholas. I just can't wrap my head around one of our own being a part of this. It seems highly unlikely and quite absurd."

"Unlikely, sure, but impossible... I don't know. Look, sir, I don't like the idea of that any more than you do, but as much as I hate to admit it, we might have to look at everyone as a potential suspect for the moment." I wanted to sound clear and concise, to seem put together and driven, even though my hands were shaking. I pressed my palms to my thighs, forcing them still. I could have mentioned Keegan going missing, but I needed to handle this delicately.

Jonah nodded. "Yes, of course. We cannot be biased given the circumstances. I will speak around and see who may have given our mystery angel the go ahead to travel to Oculus. I don't want it getting out that one of our own may be involved."

Was Keegan mistaken in saying Jonah sent him? Fuck, my brain hurt. I let my feet drag along the rug, kicking my feet before planting them flat. "Sir, may I ask you a question?"

He tilted his chin down, motioning for me to continue.

I turned my head to the tapestry on the wall. "This is a purely angelic building, but there is a tapestry of an Enchanter here. Why?"

Jonah's eyes followed where I looked. I looked back at him to see the way his lips seemed to pull upwards, then retreat downward into a straight line, as if he was seeing a fond memory play out in front of him. "Enchanters and angels used to be united, you must know that."

I didn't say anything, but I nodded.

"That was the last tapestry hung here after the war. Enchanters used to roam Heaven's Gate in freedom. Now, they remain in Oculus where they feel safer, I presume."

"Couldn't you just explain to them that everything isn't what it was back then anymore? They can be free to roam once again," I asked, needing to understand.

Jonah got up from his chair and walked to the tapestry on the wall. He ran his hand, decorated with golden rings, down the sides, his fingers gliding over the design, his nails tracing the stars and precise points. "If only things were that simple. Forgiveness isn't as simple as throwing up your hands and saying I'm sorry."

His eyes closed and he stood still for a moment. I knew this wasn't all about the Enchanters – it was something more personal. I looked down at my hands, not knowing what else to say or do. Jonah had lived through the war, and he had seen things I only heard about.

"Is there anything else I need to know about your Oculus expedition?" Jonah finally asked, facing me with kind eyes.

I wanted to trust him, but trust was going to have to take a back-seat right now. "No sir."

He walked over to me and placed a hand on my shoulder, squeezing. "I know you'll figure this out, Nicholas. I have the utmost faith in you."

"Thank you, sir, really."

"I have some young angels to attend to. Stay here as long as you like." He gave me a solid nod and began to make his way towards the winding staircase.

"Sir?" I heard myself say. Jonah turned around, his ears perking up. "I won't let you down."

"I have no doubt."

I watched him leave and heard the door close before I buried my face in my hands. I'd gone into this blindly, but just when things start to reveal themselves, I'm given the sight to see something I didn't want to see. Elise may have the world's worst attitude, but she went into things with her dark gray eyes wide open. He had faith in me when my faith in him was starting to falter. He was hiding something. I always had every intention of seeing this through, but now, I wasn't only doing it for Jonah or my ambition. I was doing it for the truth.

NATALIA SHOWED NO SIGNS OF APPEARING AS THE AFTERNOON WENT ON AND when the sky turned a deep indigo growing darker by the hour. I presumed she had either forgotten, or she was coming later. She had no obligation to us. She had her own people to attend to. I headed up to the fourth-floor training room, where I'd told Reese to meet me with Dani and Elise. If Natalia wasn't going to show up, I wasn't going to sit around and do nothing. My brain was still trying to reconstruct itself after the conversation with Jonah. The best thing I knew to do in this situation was hit something repeatedly with a sword.

I swung open the door, surprised to only see Dani there, leaning against the back wall. She had tied her bundle of curls into a loose bun on top of her head, little wisps of escaped hair falling along the sides of her face.

"Where's Reese?" I asked.

"Elise was taking her time in the bathroom, so he *kindly* escorted me down here, told me to *wait* in what I assumed he thought was a harsh tone, then left again." She shrugged, twirling around on her heels to face me again.

"How long ago was that?"

She bit her lower lip. "Like ten minutes ago. Don't get your balls in a twist, alright?"

"My balls are just fine, thanks."

Dani laughed, a sound I could've listened to on repeat. There was almost no darkness in it. It wasn't high pitched, but it wasn't a mani-acal laugh. It had a softness to it that created dimples in her cheeks. "Good to know, though I think it's only fair I figure that out for myself."

I rolled my eyes at her abruptness, but I felt my stomach knotting with nerves.

"Have you heard from Natalia today?" she inquired.

"Not yet. The day is coming to an end, so I doubt she'll show up."

"You don't know that," Dani said, walking over to the weapons rack.

I followed her, trying not to let my eyes take in her entire body from behind. "If I was her and had the information, I would have given it by now."

She placed a hand on the hilt of a training sword and pivoted around to face me, causing me to snap my eyes up to her face rather than somewhere between her waist and the curve of her ass. "Well, what if she doesn't have the information yet? She did say her locator magic takes time. 24 hours is a bit of a quick turnaround time. Are all angels so annoyingly fucking needy?"

"Excuse me?"

She tapped a finger on her chin. "I don't believe I stuttered."

"Needy is not the word I'd use. We like to get things done in a timely manner, that's all."

"Now that I don't believe. You have met your best friend, right? I don't think he's ever done anything in a timely manner." She grabbed the sword and weighed it in her hand.

I circled her and walked down the line of swords, surveying them. "Fair point. Well, I personally like to get things done in a timely manner."

"Ahh, so you don't like to *take...your...time*, Nicholas?" She paused, enunciating every word. She lifted the sword, pointing it at me as her eyes glared down the silver blade.

I plucked a sword, raising it to swat her sword from my vision. "It's situational."

"Situational, huh?" She slashed the sword in one direction, then the other.

"You know, if you didn't have your compulsion dagger and your endless torture skills, I'm sure you could really mind fuck someone with that flirting of yours." I stopped her sword, pushing it and causing her to step a few paces back.

"I save that for the ones who really deserve it." She winked at me and swung her sword downward toward my legs. I jumped back and met her silver blade with my own.

"I assume I should feel special then." I pushed my sword against hers, her wrist twisting in an uncomfortable way. Her weapon hit the ground with a clang, rattling until it stilled.

Why did it sound like I was flirting back?

"Speaking of special—what did Markus want to talk to you about the other day?" She placed her hands on her hips. Her voice was low, but soft like her laugh, warm and inviting. It was something I hadn't noticed until now.

"That was nothing," I answered sharply.

She bent down to pick up her fallen sword. "So, we're going to play this game?"

"I have no idea what you're talking about."

"Shit, alright Nicholas, alright. I'll play along and pretend like you didn't have a semi-serious conversation with an executive angel other than Jonah," she joked sarcastically.

I looked towards the door, wondering what was taking Reese so long. "Glad you understand the rules of the game."

"Too bad I've never been a fucking fan of rules." Dani took a quick start towards me and swung her sword. The clash of metal echoed throughout the room.

Our swords met in every direction as she tilted one way, and I met her going the other. I had her backing up at each strike. "What's too bad is that you're starting to rub off on me."

She met one of my hits and shoved her sword towards mine, pressing her weight into it she looked at me from between them. "I could rub off on you in a different way if you'd prefer."

Her voice got deeper, sending a small shock wave through my body. She was so blatantly forward that I didn't know what to make of her verbiage sometimes. After tonight, I knew she would show up more in my thoughts, more in my head than she already was. I fucking hated myself for it. I fucking hated myself for looking down at her chest. I couldn't cross that line.

I felt her leg hook behind my ankle. She gave her sword one good thrust forward, causing me to spring backwards. She shifted to the right and rammed the hilt into my shoulder. I held onto my sword as I landed on my side on the hard floor. She walked around me, squatting down when she got to my head. She let her fingers glide over the side of my head and down my cheek. "Maybe you're right. Maybe my flirtatious energy can win me some fights. Since we're on the same team, I could give you some pointers."

She was doing the same thing as when we were flying to Oculus, letting her nails graze my skin. "I think you just like me in this position."

"I think I would like you in *various* positions." She licked her top lip and pressed her fingers to my mouth, tracing my lips.

Fuck.

I reached out and grabbed her ankle, pulling her so she was went flying backwards towards the ground. Her sword flew towards one side of the room, hitting the window and bouncing to the floor. I jumped up, sword still in hand, tilting it down towards her neck. I pressed the cold metal to her throat, letting her feel it just a tiny bit. "Now what did I say about letting your guard down? Tsk, tsk."

She lifted her arm and flicked the metal. "Has anyone ever told you you're kind of hot when you get all bossy?" She pulled her hair tie and sat up, shaking out her hair as it wildly tumbled down her shoulders. Each curl had a mind of their own. Some of them went right back and remained in place, while others recklessly did what they wanted.

I brought my hand out to help her up and in return, she ended up so close to me, I could smell her breath: raw cinnamon, just like the rest of her. "Thank you for the compliment."

"You still won't tell me what Markus talked to you about, will you?"

"You're still on that, I see?"

"Oh, for fuck's sake Nicholas, you think that some sparring and sexy banter is going to just cause me to forget? You don't know me at all." She kicked my sword out of my hand.

"I really *don't* know you at all, so that's a fair point. As for Markus, it really wasn't anything of any importance."

"How do *you* know what I find important? I could find your conversation interesting, and you would never know because you're being a secretive little bitch who won't tell me," she argued, shoving her hair out of her face. "Fine, keep it to yourself, but know I'll ask you again."

"I don't doubt it. You're a persistent demon, but I'm stubborn. We're at an impasse."

"Or I can just figure out where you have my dagger and make you tell me." She narrowed her eyes at me, her thick lashes almost hitting underneath her eyes.

"Why do I get the feeling you wouldn't *actually* do that?" I pressed, reaching down to pick up my sword.

I felt her eyes follow me as I moved, as if calculating every second I was in motion. "Maybe you *are* starting to know me, Nicholas. Though I do kind of like being without it for a while; it gives me a clear head. I'd advise you to not hold it for too long, though. It can mess with your head if you aren't the wielder." She let that notion sit in the air; I didn't bring up how the minute it hit my hands, I started to hear whispers and feel cold. I looked back at her to see her brown eyes dancing around with amusement, as if what she said was just a fleeting thought. "You and Reese are fighting for the spot of my favorite angel, you know."

"Oh really?" I answered, smirking. "I'm surprised I'm not already at the top."

"Nicholas, I promise, you can be on top anytime you'd like." Dani grabbed my arm and slid her hand down until she skated over my fingers.

I pulled away; the ghost of her fingers felt like the sting of a burn, a phantom whisper of where they had been. I was starting to get too warm in a room that was meant to be kept a constant cool temperature. I wanted to be close to her, but I also wanted to stay as far away as possible. I lifted the bottom of my shirt to wipe my forehead, hoping some of the cool air would reduce the heat I felt on my skin. It was almost instinctual, the way Dani's eyes moved to my stomach. She cocked her head to the side as she pulled her lip between her teeth.

"If this is your way of telling me to back off, you're fucking terrible at it. I think you're a flirt without trying, Nicholas," she teased, turning her head at the sound of the door opening.

"You don't happen to have any of the magic dampening hand-cuffs, do you?" Reese asked, exasperated.

Elise walked in behind him, a sly smile on her face. "Stop whining. I didn't do anything."

"The fact that you could have is the point!" Reese shouted.

"Well, I'd advise you to calmly wait instead of banging on the bathroom door every five seconds while a girl is getting ready. I wouldn't have to threaten you with violence!"

Reese looked around the room incredulously. "What could you possibly need to do that takes twenty fucking minutes?"

"A lot of things! Wash my face, brush my hair, and oh! I know, take a massive shit in your honor!" Elise laughed, striding over to me.

I stood in front of Reese as the windows in the room started to shutter. Not loudly, but they shook and moved as if it was an illusion. Slowly and meticulously, a circle was carved in front of us. A light wind blew as the circle closed and caved inward. Electric sparks flung off the sides and bounced around the rounded edges of the portal.

A small foot stepped out, then another. My eyes traveled from the foot to the waist and then to the face of the person before us. Natalia had her hair in two buns on each side of her head, held in place by thick silver bands. The portal closed behind her, telling me she had come unaccompanied, but I knew if needed, her guards would come. The dress she wore flowed down to her ankles just like her previous one, but this one was royal blue and pleated.

"Better late than never, I guess," Elise huffed, crossing her arms over her chest. She'd braided one small piece of hair so that it swung back and forth as she moved.

"I did tell you locator magic would take a minute, but I can assure you I did come upon a discovery," Natalia replied.

"A discovery? Did you find Keegan?" I asked, taking a few steps in her direction.

She walked backwards and then turned around, heading towards the window. "It's not as you hoped, I'm afraid." We all stayed silent, waiting for her to explain. "I was not able to locate your friend. I tried the name and even his description, but I could see nothing about him. I did feel something, something faint, but it was there." Natalia pressed her hand against the glass softly, as if the window would shatter from just her fingers against it.

"You felt something?" I asked, stepping up behind her, but not so close that she would think I was intruding on her personal space.

"Yes. I felt scared, I felt cold, I felt sadness." She shuddered.

"But no real sign of him?" Reese wondered.

Natalia shook her head. "I couldn't feel any *life* there, just those feelings, potent even if they were fleeting. I am sorry to say, I fear your friend is no longer alive, and those feelings were the last remnants of him. It felt as if..."

"His soul had been taken from him," Dani finished, staying behind all of us. I saw the moment her eyes glazed over, as if seeing what happened to Keegan without having been there.

"Exactly," Natalia confirmed. "It's a different type of feeling than a death by—" she gestured to the sword I held, "stab wounds. Those can be quite quick if done right but having your soul removed is like having nothing else to live for."

"Especially for an angel," I added. "I've read it can be excruciatingly painful."

"Lilith sure knows how to ruin a mood," Elise muffled.

"Lilith?" Reese asked.

Elise scoffed. "You can't fucking tell me you don't think that she is behind this? I *know* she is behind it, but who she's getting to do all the work she can't is another issue entirely. She's one of two demons who can remove a soul, and the other is standing right here." She looked over at Dani, who pressed her lips together in the awkwardness of the moment.

She glanced over at Reese. "I know what you're thinking, and I only pull souls at a certain time. I don't go doing it for fun. I've never met this Keegan person."

Reese glared at her, but said nothing. I saw the way he swallowed hard and rolled his shoulders. He replanted his feet, as if regaining the composure he so desperately needed.

"What about the portal key?" I asked, pulling back everyone's attention.

"Ah, now I do have some less upsetting news for you," Natalia responded, turning to face me. "Your portal key has been located, in a way."

"In a way?"

"Yes. I traced it to Purgatory. It remained there for some time before being relocated."

"So, someone else has it?" I mentally kicked myself for instantly thinking about Jonah, how he seemed to be so unaware of what I was talking about this afternoon. I wasn't prepared to learn that the man I'd looked up to was the villain. I was hoping that eventually, I could bring up the photo of my mom. I could finally understand. I wasn't ready to quite let that go.

Natalia adjusted one of the bangles around her wrist. "The interesting part is that it's here, in Heaven's Gate. The locator turned dark and smoky, as if hiding its knowledge from me. Whoever this person is has put up a smoke screen to hide its whereabouts."

"Who has magic to even do something like that?" Dani questioned.

"Angelic magic is strong, but not that strong. That kind of discipline would take years to master. Most demons know nothing of that kind of magic to begin with, Lilith included. There are many Enchanters in Purgatory that chose Lilith's side during the war that could have tainted the key with darkness. Their magic would only be elevated by Lilith's power and influence, a loophole of sorts I didn't think possible." Natalia wrapped a lock of hair around her ear.

"Even if that's the case, the key is here, right under our noses," Reese said.

"What would someone want with a messenger angel's key?" I asked no one in particular.

"That's the question I've been reeling with myself. I don't like relaying bad news, so I was afraid of your reaction to my findings on your friend. This hunt of yours is coming too close to my home and people, so I'll give you my help whenever needed." Natalia sounded genuine.

"You said that the first time we came to Oculus," I noted.

Natalia gave a small, short shake of her head. "I said that if Jonah needed my help, I would help. I am telling *you* that if *you* need my help, I'll help, with or without Jonah. You are welcome in Oculus if you find yourself needing me again."

I gave her a smile, but I knew the corners of my mouth didn't pull up all the way. *With or without Jonah.*

"I can try to remove the haze as best I can, but whoever placed it has been perfecting their magical holds. I can almost taste the smoke hiding everything, almost feel it wrapping around my lungs and seeping into my eyes."

"Okay, okay we get it. Your magic is way too realistic and creepy," Reese interrupted.

"Nicholas, there is something I wanted to give you before I see myself out." Natalia took hold of my empty hand and gently placed something in my palm. Just the touch of her hand exuded a lightness I didn't know I needed until that moment. She closed my fingers and took a step back. "I feel like you've been quite limited on this mission of yours, and I thought this could be my first contribution in your success, regardless of how all this pans out, good or bad."

Natalia reached out behind her and flicked her fingers, creating blue specks of light, her portal creating itself. I tightened my fingers around the object, feeling it dig into my skin.

"What did Jonah say about you coming here?" Reese asked the question that had slipped all our minds.

Natalia's face was illuminated with the light of her portal. "Due to the nature of our last meeting, I thought it best if I came to you and only you with my findings. I have a feeling Jonah has not been informed of recent events, and I'm happy to seal my lips for the sake of more answers." It was only a second, but her eyes flickered over to me, as if knowing I had chosen to omit most, if not all, the information from the last time we spoke. Before we could say anything else, she was gone.

I lifted my hand and opened my fingers, revealing Natalia's gift to me. It was a tiger's eye crystal, wrapped in gold wiring. She had given me a portal key.

"Is that what I think it is?" Reese looked at me wide eyed.

I took the chain and hooked it around my neck, tucking the crystal into my shirt. "Yeah."

"I'd say it's a step in the right direction. Having an Enchanter on our side could come in handy." He picked up the sword Dani had let fly out of her hands, moving it out of Elise's reach.

"So, when do we take that thing for a spin?" Elise asked, rubbing her hands together.

"We aren't going anywhere. If what Natalia said is true, there's a lot more going on here than we thought. I also don't want to use my key while Jonah has them under restriction."

"So, what you're saying is that I was right and this isn't just a demon issue?" Elise said obnoxiously. "Funny how things work out, huh?"

"Shut the fuck up. You say random shit all the time; it's just a coincidence," Reese shot back, walking towards the other side of the room. Elise yanked the sword from my hand and slowly stalked behind him, sword at the ready.

"You have that look on your face," Dani noted, tilting her chin up to look at me. "Utter contemplation. Your eyebrows come inward, and your nostrils tend to flare. Your shoulders tense, but your breathing is steady. It would be cute if the situation wasn't so damn alarming."

"It's not alarming; I just don't know where to go from here. It's stalemate after stalemate. Maybe I should give you your dagger so you can just find out the ending of all of this bullshit for us." I heard myself saying the words, but I couldn't believe they'd come out of my mouth.

Dani raised one of her eyebrows and poked my shoulder. "We

both know you would do it and then instantly regret it. You'd probably throw *yourself* in the fucking Ethereal Bastille. You think too much, Nicholas. You have a few pieces of information, so retain it and figure out how to use it. You know the key is here and I highly doubt it's going to move anytime soon. Lilith has learned about striking too hard and too fast. She'll bide her time, but be prepared for when she does strike. Once she does, the one helping her will strike as well."

"Are you guys going to clash swords or just sit there talking like a bunch of little bitches?" Elise yelled from across the room.

I gave Dani one last, long look before walking past her. She grabbed my forearm, keeping me in place beside her. "You signed up for this, so you have to see it through." She let go of my arm and shrugged past me towards the others.

She sounded like me if I was talking to someone in my position. She wasn't pushy, but she was persistent. Underneath all her attractive physical qualities and the fact that she kept me laughing, she seemed to want this just as much as I did. I wasn't afraid to fight. I was afraid I would have to confront one of my own.

"Nick! Get your ass over here. It's two versus one," Reese called, pulling me from my thoughts.

The portal key felt like molten lava against my chest as it bounced against my sternum with every move I made. I needed to tell someone who wasn't in this room how I felt. I wanted to honor the idea that I could keep Dani and Elise a secret, but if I was going to explain myself, they had to be a part of the story.

I needed to talk to my father.

CHAPTER NINE

DANI

A few days had gone by after our enlightening meeting with Natalia. Nothing she said surprised me, not one bit. What I didn't quite understand was who would work with Lilith. A plan like this would have to take time and patience, be meticulously sorted, manipulated to be exactly what they wanted. They had to have time on their hands but be full of malicious intent to have one of their own kind killed. This place was supposed to represent solidarity and loyalty, the one place elevated above all others, yet it was falling short every time we turned around.

"Your little boy toy looked pretty disappointed in that witch's findings," Elise snarked, inspecting her split ends. She lounged on her bed, propping her feet up with one of her pillows.

"It's understandable if you think about it," I countered.

"I mean I guess but come on. He couldn't really think this entire realm was all honor and allegiance. Someone was bound to go rogue."

"*We* know that, but we're talking about two sentries who've pretty much pledged their lives to this place."

"Teaches them not to be so quick to judge us. They should be looking in the damn mirror," she stated, no empathy in her voice.

I got off my bed and walked to the window. Today was quiet. I couldn't hear any noise from passing conversations. Even the wind had settled, the leaves on the trees dormant.

"Why would Lilith kill a messenger angel?" I asked, the question burning my tongue.

"What makes you think *she* killed him? She took the soul; it doesn't mean she finished him off." She propped up an eyebrow, her eyes still fixated on the ends of her hair.

Taking a soul was like death, but it wasn't a complete one. Without a soul, there's just an empty shell, probably *wishing* for death.

"You don't think so?"

She pushed her hair away. "I mean I don't know, but what would she gain from grabbing the soul *and* murdering him? It's one or the other."

"She does like to do those kinds of things for fun, you know."

Elise leaned back against the headboard. "Ok, sure. She always had some motivation, though. This would just seem messy. She isn't the type to do the dirty work. She physically doesn't draw the blood. She took the soul because it was torture to the unwilling party. She gets someone else to do all the hard stuff, which would include killing this Finley person."

"Valid point. An angel killing another angel would be a satisfying show to her."

She continued. "Why this messenger angel, though? There are a million of them here."

I tilted my hip towards the windowsill, propping it against the white trimming. "They did mention Keegan was fresh on the job. They likely needed someone who wouldn't ask questions, someone who wanted to prove themself. I think Keegan was just the first one they came across. He served whatever purpose he was needed for, then removed from the situation."

"The question still remains. Why take his stupid portal key thing?" Elise looked at me with expectant dark eyes.

"It still holds magic, so it *could* be used for something else, now that I think about it..." I let my words fall away, my eyes hitting the floor. I had a thought, peering up at her. "Natalia said that regard-less, Keegan's key would remain. It's not attached to him, so it's not like the object would show any indication he was dead, right?"

Elise slowly shook her head. "Yeah, I was half listening, so I'm just going to say yes."

"I think whoever killed him had an inkling Natalia or another Enchanter could locate the key, so they created a smoke screen. They covered all their tracks." I pulled my hair into a high ponytail, feeling the hairs tickle my back as it swung back and forth. "The key is still enchanted by someone who has likely been highly influenced by dark magic. Mix that with the magic that an Enchanter already wields, and you've got a bit of a disaster."

"So, Lilith has just been sitting on her ass, grooming this myste-rious helper of hers for years until the right time to strike on a messenger? Lilith is smart, but she's not that smart. She couldn't have predicted Keegan would just come walking in all dumb-like," Elise pointed out.

I pressed my hand against the window. "I don't think she had to. I think someone else decided on Keegan for her, I mean they very well couldn't use their own key. Now that person is gate-keeping Keegan's key. He was just a means to an end. The Enchanter was just one of the things she brought to the table." It was a solid recipe for disaster. Each party involved brought an ingredient in preparation for a meal we were on the edge of our seats waiting for.

Elise made a humming sound, making me slide my eyes over to her. She fiddled with the collar of her black jean jacket. "I might know a few Enchanters close to Lilith's ear."

"Enchanters with the kind of magic to cloud Natalia's?"

"I don't know about that, but we never went into deep conversa-tions about it. We were busy doing other things that were way more important at the time." She shrugged.

I rolled my eyes. "Other things?"

Elise waved her hand at me. "Fuck off, you know I put my sex life above most things. It's right there next to the cries of grown men and sleep."

"How could I forget," I laughed. "Do you know anything that could be of use?"

Elise tapped her teeth together, thinking. "One of them mentioned that they wanted out just as much as Lilith did. She kept saying how they didn't deserve to be detained there, that Lilith would make it right someday."

Elise swiped her hair over her ear. "I don't know if she's the exact Enchanter involved, but she wasn't the only one who felt that way. They were all adamant on improving their magic and proving to her how much they wanted out."

"So, an Enchanter in Purgatory would've been ready and willing to cultivate their skills with Lilith's influence and taint the key for the sake of leaving Purgatory."

"I promise you, people have been motivated by worse things," Elise noted, walking backwards to the bathroom.

"So one Enchanter was able to overpower Natalia's magic? That doesn't make sense. She's the daughter of a High Priestess, for fuck's sake." I was exasperatingly tired of this thought process. I sympathized with Nicholas' frustrations. "We need a reference book for all this shit."

Elise stepped inside the bathroom, her feet making softs thuds on the tiled floor. "Your obscenely large brain isn't going to solve this in one damn day, you know."

"The faster we solve this shit, the sooner we can go back, and you and I both know you are counting the days."

"I have to admit, I'll enjoy not playing demonic liaison to those angelic shits anymore." She left the bathroom door cracked enough for me to see her turn the sink on. "I think you'll miss it here more than I will."

"Yeah?" I prompted.

"Oh, come on, you're practically begging pretty boy to rail you with every blink of your eyes." She pulled open the door and leaned against the doorframe.

"It's harmless. It passes the time and gives me a good laugh."

"That resistance is crumbling. Honestly I feel it in my cold, dark bones that he has a big cock." She clucked her tongue and took a few steps to her bed.

My mind instantly slithered down, to when I was in his arms flying to Oculus. I started to wonder about his shaky resistance. I lightly touched my thigh where he had wrapped his hands and pressed his fingers into my skin. I remembered the way his goosebumps had teased my skin when I said things I don't think he was prepared for. I was honest when I said it was all in good fun, but there was a small, tiny part of me that wanted to know what he was like unleashed and wanting, what it would be like to have him over me, panting and urgent, untethered from the confinements of what this realm has made him believe he had to be.

"Oh, my fucking god, you're thinking about what it would be like to fuck him right now, aren't you?" Elise's usually raspy voice took on a slightly high-pitched tone and pulled me out of my thoughts.

"Grow the fuck up, would you? It's your fault anyway. You brought it up."

She threw her hands up in surrender. "I just spoke the truth, that's all. If you don't like it, I suggest you stop making 'fuck me' eyes at him and focus."

I snorted. "Wow, you actually sound like you care how this whole mission goes."

"Like you said, I would like to leave and go home, *in peace*. I don't want all this bullshit to follow me. It's been exhausting enough trying to be the smart one."

Home. It was a word she used easily for that place. Every time I called it that, it came out dry and brittle, foreign on my tongue. To everyone around me, it was where I belonged, so I accepted it for what it was.

I caught a flash of something gliding across the front of my face and back again. It looked like a hand. I blinked rapidly for a second to focus on Elise standing in front of me, waving her hand back and forth. I swatted her away and walked around her.

"You zone out like that again, I swear I'll slap you," she claimed, returning to her bed.

I sat on the edge of my own bed, letting the events of the past week run through me. We'd been secluded in this room since Natalia's visit, and I was starting to get a bit antsy. I had seen so much of this place, and I couldn't help but want to see more of it while I had the chance. I found myself staring at the window again, but this time, my intentions were caught.

"I know what you're thinking," Elise said.

"Oh yeah? What's that?" I challenged.

"You want to go exploring, and now you're a depressed bitch. So, since I don't want to sit here and feel your sad ass energy, we can keep blurting out ideas for the portal key until I fall asleep. I only offer this one time, though, so take it or leave it."

I placed a hand over my heart. "I'm honored you're choosing me over taking a nap."

The doorknob started to turn suddenly, causing both of us to jump. Elise stood up from her bed, her shoulders tense, with a stance that meant she was *not* in the mood for anyone's bullshit. The door creaked open, letting our new besties inside. They said something to the guards outside before closing the door behind them.

Reese casually sauntered over to the loveseat behind the door, resting his arm over the back. Nicholas sat on the arm, looking uncomfortable.

"Are either of you going to tell us why you're here?" Elise asked, relaxing her shoulders a bit, the annoyed look on her face never evolving.

"We've been thinking—" Reese started.

"That's never a good sign," Elise interrupted, tilting her head up to the ceiling.

Reese bared his teeth, pulling the sleeve of his shirt up to his elbows. Nicholas continued for him. "At the moment, we might need a little bit more help than Natalia can give us."

"What do you suggest? Seeking out one of your executives to help? Because from the looks of it, they haven't been very honest," I said, leaning back on my bed.

He gave me a look as if I had just said everything he'd been trying to avoid. It was like the words he'd been trying to stuff down a hole had just been blurted out. All the evidence pointed to the people in charge. That was something I wasn't going to say out loud, though.

"That's not an option at the moment."

Elise pushed out her bottom lip in a pout. "Why is that? Did you finally come to your senses and realize that maybe not everyone here shits rainbows?"

Nicholas rolled his shoulders, taking a deep breath. I noticed the chain from the portal key Natalia had given him rattling slightly and the muscle in his neck tick before he spoke again. "That's beside the point. I know somewhere we can hopefully get information."

"I'm going to just put this out there and say I think this idea is terrible and risky as hell, but that makes me want to do it all the more," Reese chimed in.

"What are we doing?" I asked.

He looked at the door and spoke in a lower voice. His voice was already deep as it was, but this low whisper sent a feeling into my stomach that made me press my thighs together. "It's not what we are doing, it's where we're going."

"The anticipation is killing me," Elise deadpanned.

"Tonight, we're going to the Divine Library."

THE ANGELS HAD GRABBED US FROM OUR ROOM WHEN THE SKY TURNED midnight. Nicholas led us down the hallway we always took, opening the door to the stairway to the first floor. Elise shot me a confused look over her shoulder as she shuffled down the stairs. We exited to the ground floor, following Nicholas hurriedly past a small group of sentries. We passed a door marked Grand Hall and a few rooms with desks and large whiteboards. He eventually stopped in front of a narrow wooden door that didn't look like much at all.

"Nick, it's a cleaning closet," Reese whispered, putting a hand on the door frame as his best friend opened the door, looking inside.

"So, this is your Divine Library?" I taunted, poking the back of his shoulder.

The hallway was dark, save for the sconces that held flickers of light. I almost didn't realize he'd looked back at me. I knew his face was near mine when I could feel his breath, prominent against my cheek and smelling of mint as before. "Not quite."

He turned away, taking his scented breath with him, and stepped inside the room. A few seconds went by before I heard a click. A single bulb doused the room in light, revealing cleaning supplies and a few sets of blankets and sheets. The room was plain, dusty. *What.*

"You told me you knew a better way to get to the library. I told you to just use your fancy new portal key to get us there," Reese said, looking around the room.

"Is this where the room magically turns into a library and we feign shock and awe or some shit?" Elise asked, pushing past Reese and pressing her hands against the stones.

"Nicholas, care to offer an explanation?" I questioned, staring at his back.

He didn't turn around. "A portal would have been ideal, but as I said, I'm not risking it." He grazed his fingers along a supply shelf. "Help me move this."

Reese and Nicholas grabbed both sides of the shelf and lifted it off the floor, shifting it over. The shelf had a wooden backing that concealed the entire part of the wall it covered. Once they'd moved it into the corner, I saw what Nicholas had wanted to find. Nicholas wiped his hands together, dust floating off his skin towards the ground.

"Well fuck me," Elise said.

"I stand fucking corrected," Reese affirmed.

A small wooden door, no taller than me, stood before us. It was square, with dark metal hinges that matched the handle, small stains smattering it. Nicholas raised an eyebrow at me in a devious way, as if he was thrilled at the idea of figuring out something behind all our backs. I watched as he wrapped his hand around the handle and pulled the door open. It made a creaking noise as it slid across the floor. He stopped abruptly, waiting for any notion we'd been figured out. When there was no sign of anyone coming for us, he continued. What lay beyond was darker than any midnight sky. It looked like an endless tunnel towards absolute nothingness.

"Alright, I'm going first. You two will follow, then Reese will cut the light and shut the door," Nicholas directed before crouching down and taking a step inside, no hesitation to be found. His confidence thrilled my entire body.

I stepped in behind him, Elise at my heels. It smelt wet and muggy down here. Reese reached to grab the dangling ceiling light string and yanked it down, leaving us in pure darkness. I heard Reese close the door behind him. I felt like I could hear the walls breathing, blowing the dust and debris towards us while extracting the oxygen from the passageway.

I wasn't afraid. Purgatory was the darkest of realms next to Hell itself. I wasn't afraid at all. I was simply not used to what it was to be in pure darkness. I always had some glimmer of light, even if that light was through fire or magic. Purgatory could envelop your dark thoughts and see to your every dark deed, but it didn't put you in true darkness. You had to be void of your entire purpose and soul for that to happen. Those in Limbo had no purpose, but they had their souls to hold onto. Right now, in the pitch black of the passageway, where my vision was blackened and my other senses heightened, I knew I never wanted to be in that place of vulnerability, to have my soul and purpose removed so I was void of everything I knew.

My thoughts started to descend further when a flicker of glowing light caught my attention. Nicholas peered down from in front of me, his hand extended between us. A small ball of light hovered over his palm. It wasn't bright enough to cast light all over the walls, but it was enough to lead our way, enough to make breathing a little easier.

"You alright?" he asked, the light casting a soft glow on his face. His eyes were caring as they investigated mine.

"Just peachy," I said, letting my hand move over the light. It was warm against my skin, tickling my palm. "Neat trick."

"It comes in handy," he teased, the corners of his eyes crinkling a bit before he progressed forward. Reese moved past me as he followed his friend.

I walked quickly to catch up with them, as their long legs made their strides harder to match. Nicholas was determined to get to his destination, as if he was blindly following the path ahead. There were no diverging pathways, no hidden doorways, no sounds except for our breathing and footsteps. The pathway eventually turned into a steep slope downward and curved. I realized we were now underneath The Skies.

"I thought this was a myth," Reese said, looking right and left at the stone walls.

"So did I," Nicholas confessed, letting the light in his hand guide him onward.

"Wait, is this tunnel a myth?" Elise asked.

"For the most part. Reese and I heard about it years ago, but it wasn't really something in the curriculum. It was just a rumor passed around."

"And no one has been able to find it," Reese added. "Until now."

"How did you find it, Nicholas?" I saw the way his back tensed. He tried to casually keep walking, but I knew the answer was something he wasn't prepared to give. I wanted to press further, push his limits, but I was halted when he stopped walking. Reese ran into his back, causing them to topple forward into the door in front of us. They collected themselves, muttering a few curse words, before brushing off their clothes.

Nicholas opened the door with his free hand and our eyes were met with a staircase made of glossy gray stones. Dim light sprouted out, and Nicholas closed his hand. Two wall torches of angelic light, soft and soothing, adorned both sides of the staircase. The first step inside was about an inch above the ground, so he stepped into the open space and ascended the stairs. We followed closely behind, Reese closing the door behind us. It wasn't long before I was met with a warm feeling, like a roaring fire caressing my chilly bones, that smelled like pine.

I heard hands against wood as Nicholas pushed against two wood doors above his head. The doors tented open, slowly, eventually coming apart completely, revealing an open space above us. That pinewood smell completely overwhelmed my senses and relaxed every part of me. Four more wall torches were fastened into the stone, and a tall wooden door lay before us. I knew by the way Nicholas sighed with relief that we had arrived. He pulled on the winged handle and opened the door, letting the warmth rain over us. Thick curtains lay in front of the doors, but when they were pushed apart, a stunning space was revealed.

The first thing I noticed were the lights hanging from the ceiling, orbs that set a comforting tone, bobbing back and forth. I looked around, a shelf of books catching my eye at every turn and angle. All the darkness that settled itself in my soul relaxed and lay dormant.

"I didn't think the secret passage was real," Reese admitted, spinning in a slow circle as he looked around. "I haven't been here in years." Nicholas raised an eyebrow at him expectedly. "I'm not much of a reader," he shrugged.

"I had no idea you *could* read," Elise taunted, patting his shoulder as she passed him.

"What exactly do you think this place will do for us? There's no way we'll have time to go through all these books just to find some small piece of information," I said, moving closer.

"The library is divided into floors and sections within those floors. The first floor, where we're at now, has all the books on training, architecture, and maps of the land over the years."

Elise laughed. "You guys have this many fucking books dedicated to training? You all take this shit *way* too seriously."

"Sentries and guardians have the bulk of it," he explained, plucking a book off a shelf.

I grabbed it from his hand, reading the title out loud. "*Arsenals of the Guard: A History of Weapons Used Throughout the Years.* Wow, sounds like a fun read."

"What does this have to do with anything? I did not trek through an underground tunnel for this," Elise complained, leaning on a table.

Nicholas tilted his chin towards the metal railing above us. "The second floor. It holds books on the history of Heaven's Gate, The Skies, and anything else in this realm."

"Why would knowing the history of your land help us? We aren't trying to learn more about your realm's historical properties," I question.

"True, but there's a tapestry up there of an Enchanter and an angel. Their past is intertwined with ours, so there must be *something* here."

"Fair enough. Second floor, here we come." I made my way over to the staircase winding up to the second level. The orbs were dim but brightened a bit as we got closer. Decorative rugs were placed under the tables and desks, tapestries littering the walls. I stood in front of the one Nicholas had mentioned, no doubt an Enchanter and an angel, their magic clashing. The stars above the Enchanter's head reminded me of Natalia's marking. Her story of the way the fallout erupted had me pondering on how Lilith could have brought the two together.

"Luckily, this floor doesn't have as many bookshelves as below, but I say we split up and look for a book, any book, related to what we're searching for. Reese, don't get distracted," Nicholas delegated, breaking from the group towards one of the further bookshelves.

I tried to keep my attention on the task in front of me, but it was hard to move at a decent pace when I had to climb up each bookshelf to truly see the spines. My short stature frustrated me profusely. I heard Elise huff loudly, clearly not finding her mark. I hadn't heard a peep out of Reese, which meant Elise had finally killed him, or he was being serious about this for once.

"Fuck!" a male voice exclaimed in a low shout. Books crashing onto the floor had me whipping my head around as I hung from one of the wooden shelves. I saw Reese's mop of blonde hair peek out from behind a shelf and lift one of his hands. "My bad, guys."

I shook my head with a snort. I jumped down, my calves tight from all the climbing. I retreated to the floor, scooting back so my spine was against the railing. I stared at the last bookcase and blew out a breath. I ran my hand through my long hair, brushing off the dust that had settled on it. If something was here, I highly doubted it would be on these shelves. This library already had a secret entrance; why not have a few more secrets as well?

I moved towards my last shelf when something made me turn to the wall in the middle of the room where the tapestry with the Enchanter and angel hung. I tilted my head from side to side, wondering why I felt so drawn to it. I had no magic, especially not the kind this place welcomed or that would unlock anything. I let out another sigh of exhaustion and frustration.

The sun would be up in a few hours, and we'd have nothing to show for it. I touched the pointed end of the tapestry and bit my bottom lip. I casually lifted it up, hoping I would find a hidden door or something behind it, only to be greeted by uneven, multicolored stone. Light bobbled back and forth over my shoulder, illuminating a crack on the side of a stone. It made my eyes narrow in curiosity. I slid a finger into the crack, biting into my lip harder with concentration. I removed my hand and moved it to the opposite side of the stone, pressing my fingers into where I hoped would be another crack.

I heard the grinding sound of stone against stone as it moved slightly when I pushed. I knew my face was flushed with excitement at my discovery. I pulled the tapestry up and around the pole it hung from, wrapping it around until it wasn't in my way. I reached out and tucked my fingers into the sides of the stone, shimmying it out of its slot. The ear-piercing slide of stone was awful and my fingers burned from my tight grip, but with each motion, the stone loosened.

"What the hell are you doing?" Nicholas called from behind me. I didn't let him stop me from my extraction.

"One second," I answered, watching as the stone released from its spot, a rectangular hole left in its place. I placed the stone on a table behind me as Nicholas caught my arm.

"I'd like an explanation," he demanded, not releasing his hold.

"I think I might have found what we're looking for, so you can thank me later," I teased, using my free hand to caress his cheek with the back of my hand. He grabbed my hand and pulled it away, letting his fingers linger a moment on mine. I yanked my arm out of his hold and watched him walk over to the wall.

"That's impossible," he murmured, leaning in to get a better look inside.

"There's a secret passage to this place. I hardly think a hidden book is something to fawn over." I stood next to him, bumping his hip before reaching into the dark space, feeling around.

"Anything?" he asked. The hope in his voice almost lightened my heart.

I flattened my palm and patted the space. I felt small bits of destroyed stone and dirt, but nothing of interest until...cloth. I felt cloth. I felt a spine. I traced along the edge and engraved stars greeted my fingertips. I grabbed as much as I could and pulled it out. Delicately, I brought it into our sights, noticing its front cover was plain, a simple, iridescent blue.

Nicholas lightly took it from my hands and motioned for us to take a seat. I pulled out a chair, sitting down next to him. Elise walked over, dust covering her cheeks, and Reese came around from the other direction.

"What's that?" Reese asked, pointing to the book in his best friend's hand.

"The book we've been looking for."

Elise looked behind us at the wall and let out a laugh. "I'm not fucking surprised."

"It's getting closer to morning, Nick. I'll keep an eye out from the first floor but take a page out of my book and skim over the unimportant shit and get to key points. That's how I passed all my classes." Reese made his way to the stairs.

"No, you made it through your classes cheating off me," Nicholas threw over his shoulder as Reese descended the stairs with a hardy laugh.

"Call me over when you're done. I saw a book about *civilized* torture, and it's been a few hours since I've had a good laugh." Elise winked at me, nodding over to Nicholas, who'd already begun to devour the pages.

Nicholas flipped over it all, skimming through lines of texts that clearly held no meaning to him. I placed my hand on his wrist, stilling him.

"Nicholas, it's odd an Enchanter was able to overpower Natalia's hold on a portal key."

He didn't remove his hand from my hold, but instead pressed his palm on a page, smoothing it out. "Believe me, I'm well aware of that."

"Does the book explain that?"

"Dani, I'm not an idiot. That's what I'm looking for. For now, it's just the history of their people and a log of their ancestors." He sounded stern and annoyed, but his hand remained firmly underneath mine. I shifted my chair closer to him so I could read over his shoulder.

I heard his breath start to hitch with the proximity. I saw the slight red of the back of his neck, thanks to the lights above us. I slid my arm around so it hung across the back of his chair.

"You know, reading over someone's shoulder its actually really annoying," he said, flipping another page.

"I think you rather enjoy my level of annoyance. I think it excites you a little."

"I get my daily level of annoyance from Reese; I don't need it from you."

I laughed. "Fine, you can get your annoyance from Reese, but there are plenty of other things I can give you that Reese can't." I pressed my lips together. "Well, I mean he *could*, but I feel like he's not your type."

"You think you're my type?" he asked in the most nonchalant way possible, even though I knew he'd read the same sentence twice.

"That's yet to be determined. Although, I think I might be," I said in his ear as he straightened. His face contorted like I had just slapped him in the face.

I slid the book over to me to start where he left off. He reached over to grab the book back, but I slid it further away. He started to open his mouth to protest, but I cut him off. "So, does your magic just consist of concealing your wings and being a night light?"

He looked confused and a bit insulted at my question. "Yes, it's more than that. It depends on the angel. If I really wanted to, I could use it to fight. I've seen angels practically blind someone."

"Then why don't you? Use it to fight, I mean."

"I don't like relying on it. Sometimes, being an angelic night light is enough, I suppose," he joked, catching my eye when I looked up. The way his lips pulled into a smirk let me know he was making my joke his own. I kicked him from under the table, letting my foot remain near his.

"I knew I liked you for a reason."

He looked at me, but this time, he looked into my eyes as if was searching for something. I could almost feel his heart start to thud in his chest. His eyes traveled from my eyes to my mouth. His lips parted a bit as his breathing slowed. He made no move to get closer to me; he just looked at my mouth as if he were contemplating his very existence in the curves of my lips.

I broke away from his gaze as I began to look over the book again. "I wasn't completely alright in the tunnel, by the way."

"What do you mean?"

"When we had just gotten into the passage, and you asked if I was alright. I'll admit, I wasn't, but only for a moment. Purgatory is deemed this place of debauchery. Yes, the inhabitants are dark and mystifying, but you aren't fully void of light down there. You have a mind, you have a soul, but when *that* is lost, that is the real darkness."

"You still believe in the light?" He sounded cautious, almost as if I'd stunned him.

"I don't know if believing in it is the right way to phrase it, but every time I take a soul, I think it will be the last time I'm able to think for myself, that this soul removal will be the one that voids me of everything." As much as it was supposed to increase the darkness, sometimes, it felt like it was devouring me little by little.

"I didn't know demons thought like that."

I kept my eyes on the book. "I don't think they do."

"Dani—" he started to say, but I held my hand up, my palm covering his mouth.

"It's right here." I pointed to a paragraph in the middle of the page. "*Between equals, magic was a battle fought fairly and just. Battles of an unequal pairing of magic may have been amplified from tethers relinquished willingly from Enchanters of all magical families."*

Nicholas leaned back in his chair. "So that's how they did it. Enough Enchanters from Purgatory relinquished their powers to the Enchanter Lilith chose. With the help of her magic, it was enough to break Natalia's strength over the key."

"That would likely take most of the Enchanters who reside in Purgatory. Who knows if their magic would even be restored after that?" I remembered Elise's words, how they wanted out, that they didn't deserve to be detained there. They would have done anything to prove themselves worthy, maybe even giving up their own magic for the sake of freedom.

Nicholas stood up from his chair and began pacing the floor. "So, let's say that happened and Keegan gets to Purgatory on Jonah's orders. He's killed, and then his key is stripped from his neck, tainted by an elevated Enchanter and ends up in Heaven's Gate in the hands of a traitorous angel? My main question is why?"

"You know you are asking the question all of us would like to know, right? Whoever this is has been hiding for a long while and I don't know, maybe it's time you started to face the truth. It's almost like you're trying to find a reason not to believe it at every fucking turn."

Nicholas opened his eyes wide. "What does that mean?"

"Jonah is the one who told Keegan to go to Purgatory. Keegan winds up dead and no one is suspicious about it. One of the main angels who looks in that logbook doesn't seem to notice one of his messengers hasn't come around lately. It's all pretty cut and dry."

"I can't believe that. That just sounds way too obvious. Sometimes, not everything is what it seems." He looked disheartened at my suggestion.

"Some things are actually just obvious. Maybe it's time you realized—" I stopped as I felt something down my spine, like ice cold water thrown directly onto me. It was a familiar feeling I didn't think I would feel here.

"Dani?" Nicholas said, but I ignored him. Instead, I went to the railing and looked over to the stained-glass window. Only the lights moved, which had me letting out a sigh of relief. I started to turn when a shadow flashed across the window. I caught sight of it -- it wasn't an angelic shadow I could shrug off. I caught a glimpse of shadowed horns before it disappeared.

I wasn't afraid of my own kind, but I was becoming increasingly more frustrated that Nicholas had so much pride in his authority, he wouldn't see what was right in front of his cute, naïve face. One of my own was already in the Ethereal Bastille, and now there was another one. I didn't know how many more had ripped through the supposedly re-secured portals.

"We have to go," I said frantically, picking up the book and placing it back in the slot before covering it with the stone. I started to make my way to the stairs when I hit Reese's chest right as he grabbed my arms and pushed me back the way I came.

"Someone's coming."

Elise creeped out from around a bookshelf as we hit the floor. We made enough room so we would be out of sight but could still somewhat see and hear who and what was going on.

"I knew we had been in here too long," Elise hissed.

"You didn't say anything!" I argued, trying to keep my voice low.

"I didn't think I had to, for fuck's sake."

Nicholas lifted his palm from the floor and shot a few golden sparks. The orbs from the second-floor ceiling dimmed again, removing any evidence anyone had been up there.

The door creaked open, and I heard two sets of footsteps. I couldn't extend too far towards the railing or I would be seen, so I inched as far as I could and noticed Markus' distinctive grey hair. The other was right underneath us. One of them eventually spoke.

"Nicholas is doing well. I suspect we will have this matter sorted soon." *Jonah.*

"He's a smart boy. I wouldn't put it past him," I heard Markus say, his voice hesitant.

"You have more to say than that. Speak your mind." I looked to Nicholas as Jonah spoke.

"I don't understand your favoritism. There are plenty of sentries who could do this job."

Jonah sighed. "It isn't favoritism."

Markus huffed. "You've kept an eye on him ever since he got here." I pushed my head up a little and saw Markus wave his hands in Jonah's direction.

"I don't have to explain myself to you. The only person who will ever need an explanation is him. All in due time." Jonah sounded tired. "Ariel and the others will be arriving shortly." They shuffled around the room, the sound of moving chairs filling my ears.

Reese pressed his forehead to the floor, whispering, "Ariel and the others? We're stuck here until they leave."

Elise slid her hands under her cheek, attempting to sleep. I slid my eyes over to Nicholas, who faced forward, expressionless. He seemed content to wait until it was safe to leave.

I only had one thing to say to him. "Maybe it's time to reevaluate your loyalties."

CHAPTER TEN

NICK

Earlier

The sky was a deathly black as I soared through it, the lack of wind making me push forward with more effort. I was not eager to feel the tops of the trees on my hands or savor every bit of glow the stars showed. I had only one thought as I saw the buildings of my village appear. I used that thought alone to block out all the others wanting to make a home inside my already crowded mind. Information and ill spoken words were at the tip of my tongue, and I had to release them to someone.

My father would still be up, even as the hour grew late. He was always nocturnal, always reading old books by the fireplace or sitting in a chair outside to look at the stars. I wished I could simply sit back and enjoy the things around me, but the moment I decide to release the tension from my bones, something else comes out of the shadows to rile them up again. I needed a sounding board who wouldn't think less of me but would also give unbiased advice.

I saw the flickering light of the fire from the window as I set my feet on the ground. The night had turned chilly, and I clutched my jacket around me. I rapped my knuckles on the door, sucking in a breath as I waited. I heard the shuffling footsteps before the door swung open and my father smiled up at me. His brow furrowed, but he smiled and motioned me inside quickly. I was pulled into a tight and warm hug before I could make my way to the couch, but my arms gripped just as tightly around him.

We settled back onto the couch after a few minutes of my father asking me without fail if I was hungry and not backing down until I agreed. I couldn't lie and say the smell of his chili wasn't enticing, so I nodded in agreement, knowing I would have lost this fight regardless. My food steamed in front of me as I watched the flames in the fireplace dancing around the logs.

"I have never questioned a visit before. The hour is late and if I know that look, you must have something on your mind," He said, turning to face me while crossing his legs. "Would you care to share, or do you just intend to stay silent the entire night?"

I sighed, leaning over to grab the bowl. I gripped the spoon and stuffed chili in my mouth, letting the warmth consume me. I swallowed before responding. "I need you to promise me something first."

Without looking, I knew he was thinking it over. My father was someone who wanted all the facts before deciding; he never promised something without knowing the other's intentions. "Promise you what?"

"That you won't ask questions or throw fatherly judgment until I'm done."

He pressed his thin lips together. "Fatherly judgment?"

"You know what I mean. You, trying to impose your fatherly wisdom before you've heard the whole story. You've been known to do it—frequently."

He let out a small laugh. "Alright then, for you, I promise."

I swallowed another spoonful before setting it down on the table. I let my elbows rest on my thighs as I roughly ran my hands through my hair. I stared down at my legs as I said, "It wasn't just Reese and me in Oculus." I peeked to the side and noticed my father rubbing his mustache with the tip of his finger. He made no move to say anything.

"We went with two demons from Purgatory," I continued. I assumed letting out the information piece by piece would be an easier pill to swallow. "They were summoned by Jonah to aid us in our mission." I saw my father nod, but his face was unreadable. "We were to uncover how a demon slipped into Heaven's Gate undetected and unaccompanied through a portal. That demon now lies in the Ethereal Bastille, awaiting whatever may come to it." I sucked in a breath, holding it for longer than I had intended, letting it out in a long-winded exhale.

I opened my mouth again and everything came flooding out. Keegan and his disappearance, how Jonah gave the order for him to venture out to Oculus and Purgatory. My mouth moved nonstop as the words just kept coming.

I felt my father's hand on my shoulder as I prattled on. "I spoke to Jonah in the Divine Library about everything, but I found myself omitting everything because my trust in him is dying. The demons are wanting me to act against him. How could he have missed so much?"

I felt my heart thud in my chest at the release of everything I harbored. The silence that surrounded us could have echoed back if it wanted to and I wouldn't have believed them. The story sounded completely insane, and it wasn't even finished. It hadn't even reached its peak.

I noticed my father's hand still on my shoulder. I felt him squeeze a small bit, a gesture I knew from growing up that meant I should give him my attention. I turned my head, raising my eyes to see a mix of sympathy and a bit of shock. I didn't see the things I feared the most; no signs of distaste or disdain. I saw no hint of disbelief in his eyes.

"Can I speak now?" he asked softly. I tilted my chin, letting him know it was alright. He patted my shoulder and removed his hand. "You can no longer trust Jonah?"

"That's the thing. I don't *know* if I can. Maybe I'm overthinking things."

"A demon slipping through a portal without anyone's knowledge is a big deal, son."

I let out a huff. "I'm aware. I just feel like I'm being disloyal in the harshest form."

"Disloyal? You're doing exactly as you're told."

I stood up as he finished, feeling my cheeks heat, displaying my utter frustration at the way this conversation was going. "Is it *loyal* to lie to your authority's face and claim allegiance? Is it *loyal* to want to keep valuable information from someone who entrusted you with seeing this through? Tell me, is it *loyal* to want to side with those I've been told to hate?" I let the words out of my mouth before I was able to assess them. I was angry at myself, and I didn't know what to do with the sudden rush of emotion.

My father grazed my hand with his own and nudged me back down to the couch. His face appeared the same, a content expression of worry and sympathy. A flicker of understanding seemed to follow, which made my beating heart change course and start to slow its rhythm.

"First off, I have never told you to hate demons. I have never taught you to hate anyone." He rubbed his mustache. "Secondly, I think you misunderstand loyalty. That was something I was afraid would happen when you joined. I knew your skills would be sought after, but I also knew you would fall to the thin line between unbridled loyalty and blind following. You would blur the two, think you were wrong in something you had no reason to be wrong in. You don't owe loyalty to someone just because they're your higher-up; they have to deserve it, earn it."

A corner of his mouth turned up at my confused expression. "Loyalty is a fiery support of someone or something you believe in. If you think in your heart that something is amiss, who's to call it disloyalty? Asking questions and seeking out answers is neither disloyal nor cowardly. As your father, I would think less of you for not seeking the truth. If you were to do everything by the book, I would not think you were my son at all." He smiled to himself as he said this, almost like it brought up a memory.

I leaned back at his words. "You want me to make up my own rules?"

He shook his head, bringing his feet to rest on the coffee table.

"No and yes. I want you to do the right thing, but the right thing isn't always what everyone else thinks it is, especially if something is not as it seems. You'd be doing a dishonor not bringing the truth to light."

"You sound like you had the same thoughts when you were a sentry," I asked, reaching for my food.

"Things were different then. I also wasn't alone in my thoughts, and I shared my fears with others."

"You mean Jonah?" I questioned, not knowing if I was moving into sensitive territory. He'd told me about his time with Jonah, his time at The Skies, some of the adventures they'd gotten into, but those stories were when I was younger, before I got entangled in it all.

My father went quiet, rubbing his hands on his thighs. "Jonah and I go far back. He was always set on rising high above the station we shared. I always knew his father, the high executive at the time, would pass that down to him. At the time, he was my brother; we fought together, ate meals together. He was one of the first to hold you as a baby, but people change, Nicholas. They grow apart, and that's alright. There are some things we can't change."

As a baby? It baffled me that he'd never mentioned it. I had never been one to need the hand of favoritism thrown in my direction, but to not show any interest in our shared past struck me as odd.

"I know you aren't exactly happy with me not telling you any of this," I muttered.

My father shrugged. "Don't get me wrong, I'm concerned, but I know why you kept it to yourself. As I said, when things weighed on me, I had people to talk to and it seems you do too."

My father started to laugh at the astounded look on my face. "I raised you to know who you are and stick by that. You will always be an angel and they will always be demons, but that doesn't mean everything surrounding us is plain and simple. You can always find common ground. You trust Reese and we both know that boy has gotten you into some serious trouble. Somehow, you would lay down your life for him and from what you say, this Dani and Elise have their own bond. Maybe it's time you forged a bigger one altogether.

Lilith will have less to lose and more to gain this time around, so a stronger alliance may be worth it."

"I would think after all the fighting you've done, you would be highly against demons, especially where Lilith is concerned. I'd think you would want them out as much as Reese does."

He lifted his hand and laid it on my head, stroking my hair before resting it at the nape of my neck. "Reese is young and only sees what's right in front of him. He hasn't seen the world for what it is. Demons aren't the only ones who can cause harm and destruction, they are just easier to blame." He looked at me with eyes that held a story, one I hadn't read.

"What if I'm wrong? Trusting them completely, I mean." It was one of the many things I was afraid to say.

"We've all made mistakes and trusted people we shouldn't. That doesn't make us stupid and naïve. It just means that next time, we're more vigilant. It also doesn't mean that we shut off help when it is so clearly in front of us." He removed his hand from my neck and gently tapped his hand against my forehead. "How did you and Reese get to look in that portal book anyway?"

I narrowed my eyes, tilting my head from side to side. "Let's just say you have to bend the rules to get to the truth. Plus, Reese has a niche for active storytelling."

My father laughed loudly, placing his hand over his face. A welcomed laugh came from my mouth as well. I set my hand on my chest, feeling the key around my neck. I forgot it was there for a moment. I let my fingers feel the stone underneath my shirt, all the ridges and points.

"What's that?" my father asked, pointing at where my fingers now froze. I realized that was something I hadn't mentioned.

"Natalia, the Enchanter we met, she gave me a portal key. I haven't used it, but she wanted me to have one so I could go anywhere I desired if needed."

"That is an awesome gift to hold. This Natalia has aided you quite a bit."

"She has. Her mother was the High Priestess Moira. Natalia's the one who spoke about mom."

For a moment, something like a memory flashed over my father's face. It was quick and gone before I had time to blink, but it was there. "Ah, well, has she spoken of her anymore since?" he asked without hesitation.

I shook my head. "I did see a picture of mom on Jonah's desk, of you, Jonah, his wife, and mom. I wasn't aware you were *all* so close."

"As I've said, we fought together. We both got married relatively young and he was there when you were a baby, of course our families were aligned in some way. That's no secret. Just because we went in different directions does not mean he isn't allowed to remember a happy past." He said the last word with such finality, I knew the discussion was over for now. I was no closer to understanding my family tree than when I started. The fire had started to burn a little less bright, but the light still reflected on my fathers' gray hairs, turning them silver.

"What's your plan now, Nicholas?" he asked me, changing the subject.

"Personally, I'd like to figure out how a portal key got enchanted enough to break through Natalia's magic. I saw a tapestry of who I assume was Moira and an angel in the Divine Library. Jonah spoke a bit about it, but I feel like that's where I would find what we're looking for. That's the only place that seems to have a small piece of Enchanter left."

My father picked up my bowl and walked it over to the sink. He pulled out a plastic container from the cabinet above him and starting spooning chili into it. "So, you need to go to the Divine Library to find your answers? With two demons in tow across the lawn, hoping no one will see you? Son, it's different if you are maneuvering within the building or heading out into the woods. The Divine Library is in open land. You would be spotted."

"Yeah," I admitted, walking over to him. I leaned against the refrigerator. "I might just have to risk it."

"Or not," he said, spooning the last bit of chili into the container then throwing the spoon in the sink. He reached his hand inside the cabinet for a lid.

"What do you mean or not?" I pressed.

"I mean, you might not have to risk being discovered, at least not as easily."

"How? I suppose I could use my portal, but I don't want to raise any suspicions."

My father abandoned the food and patted my shoulder, raising a scheming eyebrow at me. "I'll tell you, but you have to promise me something, just like I promised you earlier."

I nodded, eager for the knowledge he was withholding.

"You have to promise that you won't ask how I know this information or even why it exists. Just take it and find what you need." His voice was stern, almost like a warning.

"I promise."

He let out a breath and crossed his arms over his chest. His eyes had a twinkle of mischief behind them. "You've heard the tales about the secret entrance, haven't you?" My eyes widened, but I nodded yes. "It's all true." My father's voice went low as he spoke again. "You're aware of the hall near the dining hall, yes?" I nodded, a map of The Skies forming in my head as he continued. "Start there." I listened as he weaved the pathway I'd always thought was a rumor.

My father's past in the world of sentries is only something I knew on a basic level, and I needed more. He grabbed my chin, lifting it up. "I always wanted you to perhaps be an executive one day, to invoke change and forge a path different than those before you, but I don't know why I thought you needed a title to do it."

I wanted to be proud of those words, I wanted to honor them. My trust was fleeting and needed a place to land. Maurice Cassial, the man who showed me how to hold a sword, who taught me how to propel my wings out without knocking over everything around me, who always told me that trusting your gut is something to never turn away from, was also the man who wanted me to place that same trust in demons.

I was finding it hard to not be close to one demon in particular. I couldn't deny it *didn't* feel unsettling or uncomfortable when she was next to me, or when she smiled at me after one of her flirtatious comments. She was slowly starting to become a distraction, and she didn't even know it. With my luck, she did, and she was laying in her bed laughing about how my mind drifted to her, my hand so close to stroking my cock. Every single time, I stopped myself. I wasn't an animal who only thought about my base needs, and I already seemed to have debilitating trust issues, so I needed to prioritize the important things.

The idea that we could work as an actual team was something that needed to be addressed before anything else. I couldn't turn my trust away from Jonah, even when we had settled back on the couch and my father began to really push me about my first visit to Oculus. If I was going to trust Dani, she was going to have to trust me . My gut was telling me something didn't make sense. I had to prove myself right by finding this secret entrance.

Present

I ROCKED BACK AND FORTH ON MY HEELS, MOVING MY WEIGHT FROM LEG TO leg as Reese and I waited on the lawn. Hundreds of other sentries gathered around, talking amongst themselves. I saw Reese yawn and I found myself mimicking his actions. We were both exhausted from the night before, which turned into us heading to bed around five in the morning. We had laid down on the floors of the Divine Library and listened to executives have a meeting on some development with the new recruits, portal reconstructions, and a whole lot about morale boosting for a few hours before they decided to leave.

We ended up retracing our steps through the tunnel, placing the shelf in front of the doorway before heading back to our rooms. Unlike Reese, I wasn't the type to sleep in or attempt to make up for the sleep I missed. My mind was too full of everything we'd discovered. Enchanters were willing to give up their powers for the sake of getting out, not knowing if they would ever regain their abilities.

Jonah's mysterious words hadn't left me, either. He was hiding something, and last night proved it. I wasn't surprised, but it was hard when it was so blatant in front of me. I couldn't make it seem like a misunderstanding when the words were so clear. I couldn't wrap my head around why he would want to work with Lilith or bring demons among us when he had fought so hard to keep them out. Dani and Elise wanted to make things so black and white, but I didn't see it that way. My trust was thinning, but it wasn't completely lost. I could place my trust in them, while also saving a small piece for Jonah.

I felt a shove on my shoulder. Reese pointed ahead as Ariel came walking towards us. The sun had gone down, and the sky was turning a misty purple. A small fog drifted over the trees, making it hard for me to make out the stars.

"Remember to use your light to signal me if anything goes wrong or if you encounter something out of the ordinary. There is guardian training going on, so don't engage if you notice them. They have a duty, just like you," Ariel instructed. He looked us in the eyes, as if he was trying to pull something out of us without words.

He shook his head and moved on to the next set of sentries. The Animus Seeking was always something I enjoyed. We'd be whisked away to the human world, dropped in different regions, and then pick out the souls to be taken to Heaven. Those meant to be taken had an aura - a soft white glow. They wanted no mistakes, no soul unspoken for, so we always went in pairs.

"Why do I feel like every time we do this, it's a competition?" Reese said, wrapping his hair into a messy bun at the top of his head.

"Um, because *you* make it into one."

"I do no such thing. I do have a bet going with Ollie over there." Reese nodded to a tall sentry who nodded back, flinging out is middle finger.

Reese replied the same way before laughing. I shook my head and zipped up my jacket. "How do you know the truth? That you aren't lying about how many souls you guided back?"

He let out a hum before responding. "I don't know. I guess we just trust we'll be honest with each other. Also, Ollie is a terrible fucking liar, so I'd know."

Ariel blew a whistle that echoed even in the large open space. He pulled his portal key from around his neck and gripped it tight, twisting and swaying his hand until bright lights appeared. The lights grew until they were wide enough for us to walk through. I lifted my watch - it was 8pm.

"Eight hours until I can go the fuck back to sleep," Reese said, rushing into the light. I followed him, letting the light wash over me. We weren't home anymore and everything in me told me we were in the human world. I looked down to see that the soles of my shoes were pressed against asphalt. The transition between worlds never ceased to amaze me. The sky looked like the same sky, the trees swayed and carried a breeze just the same, but there was always something off, something that let me know I wasn't home.

"Over there." Reese brushed past me towards a white glow ahead of us. Before I could move, a police car rushed past me with blue flashing lights, followed by an ambulance, its sharp sound blazing through my ears.

We pushed off the ground, expelling our wings and following the flurry of lights, slowly descending close to the site. The whole area was congested with men in blue uniforms and a few people with panicked expressions, tears flowing down their faces. I blinked a few times, adjusting to bright lights, trying to find the source of the only one I cared about. I searched until it caught my eye. There wasn't just one, but two: one in the totaled car that looked like an accordion in the front, and another a few feet away near a tree. A few people pulled open the driver side door, attempting to extract them from the car, while two others went towards the one at the tree. My stomach dropped knowing it was already too late.

"Which one do you want?" I asked Reese, who was leaning up against a tree trunk, watching.

"I was already planning on the one in the car, so you can take the one by the tree." He gave me a small smile that didn't meet his eyes. This was always fucking depressing. I headed to the tree, trying to peer around the people wanting to help. It was a useless feat, but I appreciated the effort.

"She's gone. Get a stretcher," one of the humans said, pointing towards the ambulance.

The sound of heavy breathing made my ears perk up. I looked up from where I stood and saw a girl, her arms wrapped around her middle, panting. The light below threw a faint glare on her face, now pale and filled with shock and disbelief. I peeked down at the body slumped against the tree - it was her. She gazed down at her body, starting to hyperventilate.

"What's happening? That's not me, is it?" She was yelling, but she was out of breath.

I took a step towards her, and she took a step back. I circled around the humans, keeping space between me and the girl, but moving us away from the commotion. I lifted my hands a bit, letting my palms face her, showing I didn't mean any harm.

"What's your name?" I asked, calmly and slowly.

She sniffed a few times, taking small breaths. Her arms closed in tighter around herself as she retreated further into the forest. "Meredith."

"Okay, Meredith. I'm Nick," I said, "I'm here to help you."

"Help me? I don't need your help! I need to go home!" she yelled, looking around to see if anyone noticed her. They all ignored her. A stretcher came towards us, and we watched as they hoisted her body up. The white hue started to dim as they rolled her body away.

"I'm taking you home." I took a step towards her as the light dispersed around her feet. I motioned to a spot further away from the ambulance. She hesitated a moment, but then started to follow me. The wind was starting to pick up a bit, causing a chill to run down my spine. Meredith tucked a piece of her long hair behind her ear.

"Meredith, I'm so sorry to tell you this but..." I looked past her to where the stretcher was being lifted into the ambulance. "You're dead. I know it's scary and confusing but know that you are going somewhere amazing now with my help."

"Dead? I can't be dead. I'm right here, I'm right...." She looked over her shoulder as they placed another stretcher into the vehicle, closing the doors behind them.

I bit my bottom lip, trying to find the right words. I'd done this a million times, but this part never got easier, trying to convince someone of the impossible and then the inevitable. The past few years I had started to get used to it, but right now, that confidence was failing.

"Do you remember anything?" I asked, placing my arms at my side.

I could hear her breathing begin to slow. "The last thing I remember was being in the car with my boyfriend and changing the radio station. I saw a bright light out the window and I ended up here. Then you showed up." She let out a breath when she finished, sniffling a few times.

"Alright, that's a start. Did you feel any pain?"

"No. I mean, for maybe a minute, but everything kind of just went away."

"You felt at peace?"

"Yeah, I guess, until I saw myself. I was just lying there...dead. Now I don't know how to feel. Does this mean I'm a ghost?"

I let out a small laugh. "No, you aren't a ghost, Meredith. We're angels."

"Angels? I'm an angel?" Her voice pitched higher as her breath hitched. She walked to a tree and placed her hand against it, leveling herself.

"I'm here, which means yes, you're an angel." I squatted down, pointing at the light around her feet. "That's also a giveaway as well. It's the light your soul is producing. It helped me find you."

"That's freaky," she said, squatting down and touching the light with her fingertips. It danced in-between her fingers as she brought them closer to her face. In the light, I could see her hair was auburn, freckles across her cheeks. She looked so young.

"How old are you, Meredith?"

She looked up at me, her eyes an emerald color. "Sixteen."

I was sad for her at that moment. She wasn't the youngest I'd taken up, but it didn't make this moment any easier. "You won't be alone on your next journey. I can promise you that."

I looked on to where the ambulance was leaving, and the police lights followed it. I caught a glimpse of the other white light across the street near a bundle of bushes. I knew Reese was starting to wrap things up. I lifted my chin.

"Is that...?" Meredith asked, skepticism in her voice.

"Your boyfriend, I'm pretty sure. My friend is talking to him right now, just like I'm talking to you. It's time to go home." I put my hands on my thighs and pushed to stand.

Meredith hesitated a bit. "You're taking us to Heaven, aren't you?"

"Yes, I am. I know it's not an ideal end to your night, but you can be together forever now." I reached my hand down towards her. "You just have to take my hand."

She rubbed her palms on her knees, looking around as if searching for something, before shakily reaching her hand out and touching mine. She didn't fully grab my hand immediately; she simply touched it, as if trying to figure out if I was real or not. "Are you dead, too?"

"Um, not quite." Things like this were hard to explain. Angels to humans were already dead, come to protect them. They didn't ask them many questions or hesitate when guardians came around. I had to work harder to state my case. "You're an angel by way of dying. I'm an angel by birth."

I watched as her eyes grew bigger when I pushed out my wings, extending to their full length. I let some of my power drift to the feathers on my wings, letting angelic light line each one. Her eyes were shining with awe, with disbelief. A tear rolled down her cheek as she pushed herself up and squared her shoulders. She used the back of her hand to wipe away the tear.

"Just breathe," Meredith said to herself, nodding.

"Exactly." I reached my hand out towards her again and she took it, wrapping all her fingers around my hand. Her grip was tight; I could feel her nerves as if they were my own. I hoisted her up, letting her wrap her arms around my neck,

"What about my parents? I'll never see them again, will I?" she asked softly, quietly.

"You won't," I answered solemnly. "They'll have to learn to move on. Eventually, you will see them again, just not in this life." I pressed my lips together, not knowing what else to say. She didn't push for anything more.

"Take me home." She looked up at the sky, her eyes twinkling in the light of my wings.

"Nick, I'm tired as hell and Ollie won our bet. I'm not in the mood," Reese groaned, walking down the hall towards his room. I followed behind him, wrapping my palm around the back of my neck, pulling at the hair.

"I really do need to talk to you," I pleaded. We'd returned from the Animus Seeking an hour ago and were just now heading back to our rooms for much needed sleep. Reese was the first one off the lawn and into the building, heading straight for his bed.

Reese whirled around, my sneakers screeching on the ground from my abrupt stop. "Speak. Just know I am too tired for anything heavy right now, so *please* tell me it's got to do with you getting laid or one of the executives falling down a flight of stairs or something."

I rolled my eyes. "Sorry, but no to either one."

"Cool, well, fuck off and I'll talk to you in a few hours." He turned away, walking the few feet towards his room. I grabbed his arm before he could reach for the doorknob.

"It can't wait." Before he could say anything else, I tightened my hold and started dragging him down the hall to my room. He begrudgingly let me yank him the whole way there with only minor curse words to fill the silence.

I closed the door behind me as he settled into my desk chair. His green eyes looked heavy from lack of sleep, but what I needed to tell him was more important. I touched my fingertips together, thinking of how to begin.

"If I wanted to sit in silence, I would go home, so open your fucking mouth."

I shuffled over to my desk, Reese watching my every move. I slid open the top drawer and reached inside, wrapping my hand around the hilt of the familiar weapon. I pulled it out slowly, letting him rake his eyes over every inch.

"What the hell is that?" he asked.

"It's a dagger, clearly."

"We both know you don't fuck with daggers, so unless you've decided to become a master of yet another pointy silver weapon..."

I raised my eyebrow at his thought process and knew he wasn't wrong. "It's Dani's."

"Excuse me? Dani's? Dani has a dagger?" He pushed out question after question.

"I took it from her when she first got here. I've had it ever since."

Reese reached up to take it from my hands, weighing it in his palm. "I mean it's pretty gnarly she got this past Ariel. What did Jonah have to say about it?"

I swallowed and turned around to face my bed, letting out a sigh. I let his question dangle in the air. Without having to turn around, I knew he was counting to ten before exploding on me.

3...2...1...

"What the fuck, Nick? You haven't told anyone about this? You've just been harboring a demonic weapon in your room this whole fucking time? I don't understand how people think you're the smart one. This thing is like a beacon for bad news and we both know it." I heard the clang of the dagger on my desk. I turned around to see him on his feet, rubbing his hands on the front of his jeans.

"Calm down; nothing's happened."

"That you know of."

"It's a weapon made specifically for Dani, and *she* told me to keep a hold on it, so clearly she doesn't plan to do any harm." I explained, hoping to simmer him down.

Reese smacked his hand against his forehead and shook his head. "You dragged me to your room to basically prove you're an idiot."

"No, I brought you here to tell you something, so sit your ass down." I pointed to my desk chair and watched him let out a huff before sitting down.

I sat on the edge of my bed so I could face him. I glanced over to where the dagger sat lifeless on my desk. There were no dark sounds, no whispers in my head like before. It just remained on the desk, a simple weapon.

"You remember my talk with Markus? The one he made me stay behind for?" Reese nodded. "He asked if I'd gotten anything off Dani or Elise when they arrived, if I had anything in my possession. He told me they wouldn't be upset, but they needed it handed over."

"Makes sense. That's normally what happens, Nick."

"It was weird, though, like he was looking for a particular answer. I asked him what they were looking for, and he shrugged it off, to let him know if anything comes up."

Reese rolled his eyes. "Let me guess, you said you knew nothing, had nothing?"

"Pretty much. It's like Dani was taken out of Purgatory for more than just the portals, like her dagger is somehow a part of it. They knew she would bring it with her."

"Nick, come on—" Reese started to say, but I cut him off.

"Things have been so fucking weird ever since we found out about Keegan, so you can't honestly tell me you're one hundred percent decided about this."

"Now you're siding with the demons? You think Jonah and the other executives are behind this now? All because you've been paranoid by them wanting a prohibited item?" Reese released his hair from his top bun and his blonde hair tumbled down to his shoulders.

"It's not about sides, Reese." I let out an exasperated sigh. "It's about what's right and what's the truth. Dani told me her dagger was forged for her, that no one else could use it. Dark objects like that only end up destroying someone who isn't the wielder. She hasn't wanted it since she arrived, and she's always known where it is; stop making her the enemy."

"Who's the enemy then, Nick? Enlighten me."

I put my head in my hands, letting my frustration wash over me.

"I don't know, but I know we aren't going to figure it out by playing sides."

Reese looked over at the dagger. "What do you suggest, then? We just settle our differences, say fuck Jonah and everyone we've ever known, and sing a proud fight song with our two demon companions, one of whom can compel you to do whatever she wants?"

"I'm just saying, we're never going to finish this unless we stop looking at each other like *others* and start being equals, as equal as we can get."

"You're asking a lot of me; you are aware of that, right? You want me to compromise my beliefs on your word alone."

I snorted. "I think you can handle it. Besides, I've never steered you wrong."

Reese rubbed his eyes with his palms. "You haven't."

I laughed a little, narrowing my eyes at him. "You know she can't compel you, right?"

"She literally told me she can. Come on, Nick, I know I can be a shit listener sometimes, but I do pay attention on occasion."

I waved my hand. "She has compulsion, yes, but she needs her dagger to conjure it. It's a whole thing with Lilith, so you've been worried over nothing. As long as it's in my possession, she can't hurt you. Well, not with compulsion, at least." I patted his knee.

"I haven't been worried; I just don't like being blindsided by all this demon nonsense. How do you know she isn't lying?"

I narrowed my eyes and thought about it. Dani had given up the information willingly and I had accepted it as truth. It was like she wanted me to know things so I'd start to trust her, and I was leaning towards doing just that, but I didn't want to make that leap alone.

"I just do. It may be hard for you to accept, but I don't think they're the bad guys here. Maybe Jonah and Markus aren't the bad guys either, but for right now, I just don't know."

"So, you want my full support or something?"

"I already have my father's, so yeah, yours would be appreciated. I would feel weird if you and I were on opposite sides of the issue."

Reese got up from my desk chair and stalked over to my window. The sun was slowly starting to set. "You spoke to your father?"

"I did. How in the hell did you think I knew about the secret passage? I may be the smart one, but I'm not that smart."

"Huh. Maurice Cassial, keeper of epically cool secrets," Reese noted. He side-eyed me. "He wants you to put your faith in them?"

"I mean, he knows it's my choice, but he does think I should stop holding back."

Reese pressed his back against the window and smirked. "I swear, if you fuck us up, I will bury you where no one will ever find you and call you Nick the Dick in your eulogy." He reached his hand out to me, bending his elbow. "The fact you ever thought I wasn't going to side with you hurts my feelings. I may not like it, but I've always got your back."

I pushed off my bed and grabbed his hand, bumping his right shoulder with my left one. Reese walked over to my desk, picking up the dagger and examining the blade.

"What do you plan to do about this?"

"For now, it's staying right where I've had it."

"That sounds like..." Reese began, but a knock on the door startled us both. Reese let go of the dagger, letting it drop from his hand. I swiped my hand underneath him, grabbing it before it fell to the ground. I dragged open the drawer and shoved it inside. Reese winced, as if to say sorry as I passed him towards the door. A messenger angel greeted me with a blank expression.

"It's a little early for messages," I said plainly.

"Jonah wishes to speak to you."

I looked over my shoulder at Reese, who shrugged. "About what?" I asked.

"I'm not sure. Make your way to his office this afternoon." The angel gave me a small smile and then made his way down the hall. I stuck my head out and watched as he sauntered down the dim hallway. They normally did us a favor by allowing the lights to not be so bright when the night shift came back in.

"Well, maybe this little talk will bear more information for your anti-Jonah campaign," Reese stated sarcastically, crossing his arms.

I leaned my forehead against the door. "Maybe, but it's time to start demanding more answers."

CHAPTER ELEVEN

DANI

Time went by extremely slowly when you had absolutely nothing to do with your time except wait. We hadn't seen or spoken to the guys since that night in the Divine Library, and my entire mind and body was getting antsy. I was starting to enjoy the excursions they brought us on and I had to admit, that I was beginning to understand the appeal of being in a place like this for all eternity. I'd gotten used to the dimly lit Purgatory, the constant changing of temperatures, and I'd even gotten accustomed to just lying in my bed, alone, awaiting my next hedonistic moment.

I didn't have free reign here like I did in Purgatory. Even if I did, the reactions would be close to the same. Only a few in Purgatory considered us friends; most cowered at my presence or just kept their head down and ignored me. Elise was the first one to come up to me and introduce herself. She wasn't afraid of anything and she made it known, straight to my face, that she wasn't afraid of me. It almost made me smile. *Almost*.

I'd noticed formations of angels headed out towards a larger field that I couldn't quite see. I knew a line had formed between my eyebrows as I tried to figure out a reason for their gathering. A soft snort came from the other side of the room. I moved my head from where it was propped against my pillow and looked over to Elise. Her arms were splayed out at her sides, one of her legs hanging off the bed. Her mouth hung open a little and she snorted again.

I covered my mouth before a laugh could escape into the otherwise quiet room. I looked out the window and noticed the sun was rising. I stared up at the ceiling and I let my mind wander. Elise had a valid point when it came to Lilith: she never really got blood on her hands, had always let others do terrible deeds for her. I thought I had seen one of her demons outside of the Divine Library, but I had no proof. I hadn't spoken of it since then, not even to Elise.

My mind kept leaning to one idea above all else. Lilith had her reasons for wanting to ruin Heaven's Gate, but why would an angel want to destroy their home? Why would an angel partner with the Queen of Darkness in the first place? What did *I* have to do with it? Natalia's words came back so eloquently from the first time we met.

"What makes you so special?"

Lilith had given a lot of demons powers, but theirs had always been minuscule, and she sometimes even took those powers back when she deemed them unworthy. Compulsion was one not often given, the power of pulling souls even more unlikely. I had been given both. I guess that made me quite special, in retrospect. I decided that something less challenging might let me drift back off to sleep. I let thoughts of Nicholas flood their way in, settling themselves nicely into every inch of my brain. I think about his eyes, how they had a way of settling my mind; how his thick dark hair made me want to rake my hands through it; how his mouth angled upward every time he wanted to laugh or smirk at my comments but tried so hard not to.

I enjoyed peeling back his resolve. We were so close in the Divine Library; he had looked at my mouth as if he considered kissing me. Nicholas gave the impression that he was upstanding in the eyes of his authority figures, but my gut told me when no one was watching, in the dark confines of his bedroom, he was something else entirely. I would be lying if I said those thoughts didn't make me want to drop to my knees and take his cock in my mouth.

If he had been a demon, I likely would have done just that, but

Nicholas was an angel and my intentions didn't really matter. I would tease him endlessly until he combusted, but that was all. Fucking him would be something I would leave to my imagination.

Another snort came from the other side of the room and I shook my head, deciding that throwing a pillow at Elise would be a bad idea. Turning on a lamp would cause her to throw multiple pillows at *me*, so I was forced to wait until the sun had risen. I leaned forward, placing my elbows on my knees still covered by the comforter. I tousled my hair with my fingers, closing my eyes, massaging my temples with my fingertips. I peeked over at Elise when I heard her turn over, pulling her pillow over her face.

I rolled my eyes, before seeing the light from underneath the bathroom door. It was faint and easily missed if you weren't staring directly at it. There was no window in the bathroom, so it couldn't be the sun, and I'd turned off the light last night, unless Elise forgot. The light flickered and grew brighter, eventually disappearing all together.

I pulled the covers off my legs, letting my feet feel the cold floor. I heard a small sound come from the bathroom, if someone was trying to hide. I heard a hand on the knob and the soft, slow turn of it. I reached next to me and grabbed my pillow, throwing it at Elise. Her arms flailed and she chucked the pillow to the ground, sitting straight up, frowning.

She opened her mouth to start ranting, but she saw my hand point to the bathroom. Elise pressed her lips into a hard line, looking towards the bathroom door right as it began to creak open. She swung her legs over and stood to join me. Black smoke with red tendrils started to form in her hands and her eyes turned molten black. I was ready to defend myself as well, letting my power start to flow out, but I held it back just a little.

For good reason, it seemed. The bathroom door opened more, and a sandaled foot and bright gold anklet appeared. A lilac dress came into full view as Natalia stepped into our room. I let myself relax, but Elise thrust her hand out, black and red threatening to pierce the Enchanter's neck. Natalia raised her hand and grabbed the ball of darkness that hurdled towards her, snuffing it out. She opened her hand and we watched as dust fell from her palm.

"What in the fuck?" Elise looked Natalia up and down.

"Well, hello to you as well," Natalia greeted, nodding towards her. She looked over at me, giving me a small smile.

"The bathroom?" Elise questioned, looking around Natalia towards the bathroom.

"It was convenient. I couldn't very well portal right into your room."

"A heads up would have been *convenient*." Elise crossed her arms over her chest.

Natalia squinted. "How would I have done that?"

Elise opened her mouth and closed it again. She let out a frustrated sigh and mumbled a whatever before making her way into the bathroom and closing the door behind her.

"What *are* you here for?" I asked, skeptical. "The boys aren't here."

"I know. I'm here for you. Both of you." She looked towards the closed bathroom door, biting her cheek. "I would like to bring you to Oculus."

I tilted my head to the side. "You what?"

"You can stay here if you'd like."

"No! I mean, I don't know. Wouldn't you rather wait until you have all four of us here?"

Natalia made her way over to me, leaving only a few inches of space between us. "I wouldn't be here right now if I wanted all four of you. The angels aren't who I seek." She tapped her finger on her chin. "I can offer you food, if that at all piques your interest."

"Isn't it a bad idea to accept food from strangers?" I joked, letting my brown eyes meet her honey-colored ones.

"I wouldn't call us strangers, Soul-Seether."

"I wouldn't call us friends either," I said, retorted my eyebrows.

"Maybe, but I'd like to rectify that."

Elise yanked the bathroom door open. "I don't care, I'm starving. Let's go."

"Elise..." I started.

She lifted her hand at me, palm in my direction. "Stop. You woke me up, so the least you can do is make up for it. I vote for free food." She walked over to our armoire, opening the doors and examining her outfit choices.

"It looks like you are without a choice," Natalia said, turning away from me, the crown tattoo on her shoulder glittering as sunlight filtered through the window.

"I could always choose not to go."

Natalia looked over her shoulder. "You could, but we both know you won't."

I opened my mouth to challenge her but was stopped by clothing flying at me. I caught the shirt and bra but had to let the leggings fall to the ground. Natalia perched herself on top of Elise's bed, pretending to be interested in her fingernails.

"What if someone comes in and finds we're gone?" I asked, gathering my clothes and heading towards the bathroom to shower.

"Has anyone besides Nicholas come to check on you?" Her face was expressionless as I shook my head. "I think you'll be fine. Besides, if we are to be friends, I think getting you into trouble would be a poor choice."

I narrowed my eyes but said nothing. We changed quickly and watched as Natalia herded us into the decently large bathroom and flicked her hand, creating a portal. She stepped through, Elise and I following closely behind. The portals from the keys she made always had me feeling off balance and wobbly, but this one, an authentic portal from her own organic power, yielded none of those effects. The colors began to evaporate; trees came into my sight and I looked around at my surroundings. The smell of pastries filled my nose, making my mouth water.

"Take me to wherever that smell is coming from," Elise demanded.

Natalia just laughed and led us forward. We'd landed in a completely different part of Oculus. The landscape and buildings were the same, but I smelled fresh water nearby, my ears perking up at the sound of it. Natalia led us to the village, the smell of the sugary food growing more intense. The buildings were large and stretched out along most of the area. I took a few steps inside one, noticing it was some type of banquet hall. The ceiling was rounded, and colors ran from along the walls and into the ceiling. Tables littered the room, laden with platters of every pastry imaginable. Enchanters watched as we arrived, some whispering and giving us intense stares, while others simply nodded and moved along with their plates of food.

"We like to celebrate how far we've come every now and then. This place used to hold grand parties when my mother was around. I thought you might enjoy something other than Heaven's Gate," Natalia offered, her voice genuine.

It was odd to me that these people had lost so much but acted like they still had it all. This building didn't seem so run down like the others; large tree trunks decorated it like columns. Fairy lights wrapped around the trunks as leaves fell to the floor, crunching under our feet. I moved towards one, letting my eyes roam around the bark. It looked like any other tree until I saw it, small and pink, then another. I reached out my hand to touch it, lightly running my fingers over the tiny petals.

It was a flower. It was budding and there would be more, but right now, it was all I needed to see. I started to turn around when I ran right into Natalia. She eyed me knowingly, looking over my shoulder. I thought she would say something, but she didn't. She was waiting for me to speak. "This place isn't glamoured is it?"

"No."

"But everywhere else is?"

Natalia nodded. "Yes."

"Why?"

"I get the feeling you don't trust me, Soul Seether." She touched the tiny flower buds, and I didn't say anything. I just watched her. "Maybe I wanted you to see a bit behind the illusion. You're the one who noticed it in the first place."

"You brought me here to prove I was right? That's hardly a reason."

Natalia's dark skin seemed to glow. "We met under imperfect circumstances. As you can tell, my people remember that, even though I have insisted you and your friends pose no threat. I like to acknowledge the past for what it is and move on. It hurts everyone to dwell on it. I'm aware I have the trust of your angels, but I'm also aware that I lack yours."

"And my trust is so important?" I tapped my foot on the ground.

She tucked a piece of her dark hair behind her ear, revealing a hoop on the shell of her ear. "If I'm to be of any help, I'll need everyone on the same page. Divided trust won't help anyone. The information I provide will always be questioned. You've made it clear that my people are a part of this. Therefore, I'm part of it as well."

"Your people—the ones who chose to side with Lilith?"

She nodded again. "Regardless of their decision, they are still my people."

I glanced over at the tables of food. Elise had two plates in her hands almost filled to the brim, and I had a feeling neither of them were for me. "You think bringing us here for free food will somehow make me like you more?"

Natalia looked down at her hands, a nervous gesture. "I haven't interacted with demons much and you are quite a conundrum."

"I don't dislike you," I confessed. "I don't exactly know you, but you have been a necessary resource for us, so I guess this—" I motioned around us, "is a good start."

Natalia clasped her hands in front of her, smiling. "Wonderful. Please enjoy the food—"

"I'm not hungry, actually," I admitted. The food smelled good, and my stomach would have thanked me for it, but there were other things on my mind.

"Not hungry?" I heard Elise say behind me. I turned around just as she was stuffing a piece of toast into her mouth. "You can't look at this and say you aren't hungry. Fuck off."

I laughed. "You enjoy it. I'll be outside."

Elise rolled her eyes. "I guess I can bring my food with me."

I waved her off. "No, you stay here and eat. Come find me when you're done."

Her gray eyes searched my face for a moment, but eventually, she shrugged. "Fine. I'll just stuff my face by myself then."

I shook my head, heading towards the doorway and bumping shoulders with a few Enchanters who gave me confused looks as I passed. I felt my shoes sink into the soft dirt as I walked towards some rocks farther from the building. I decided to follow my ears towards where the running water flowed. The sharp sound of it against my eardrums told me that it wasn't too far away. I grazed my hand along trees as I passed and took tentative steps when the path got a bit steep, but eventually, I found the stream. The water was clear and rippled where it hit rocks. Plants cascaded over the water, glistening from the morning dew. I bent down and wiggled my fingers in the water, watching my reflection as it looked back at me.

"It's pleasant, isn't it?" Natalia said from behind me. "I used to come here and watch myself in the water when my mother would have meetings in the hall."

"She didn't worry you'd gone missing?" I asked, drawing circles in the water.

"She always knew where to find me. I was a predictable child," she laughed.

I stood and wiped my hands on my leggings. "Do you remember much about her?"

She moved her mouth around, poking her lips out. "A lot and not much. I remember all the things that made her a great mother and I know much about her leadership. You can ask anyone, especially the older generations, but I suppose I never really knew her as a person."

"Doesn't that bother you?" I asked, genuine curiosity in my voice.

"Sometimes, but I trust she was the person everyone claims she was. That's all I can do."

I noticed a layer of rocks near the stream and perched myself on top of one of the larger ones. Natalia watched me silently. "Were you around when she did all of this?" I whipped my hand around, indicating I meant all the glamouring.

"I was. I don't remember much, but of course for us, nothing changed. She explained everything to me later. She knew what it would mean for me as the next leader." Natalia took a few steps closer and leaned against a tree. A small breeze picked up the ends of her dress.

"Have you ever thought about taking it down?"

She shrugged. "There was talk a few years ago, but it was shot down. I may think that our worlds are at a different point now, but not everyone feels so comfortable just yet."

I nodded in understanding. I rubbed the front of my legs, not really knowing what else to say. I rummaged inside my head for something. "How much can you tell me about your mother's relationship with Jonah?"

"They were friends before anything else, before the war, but after she placed the glamour, he visited less and less. He stopped coming for a long time; I suppose that was around the time his father was prepping him to become the next high executive. My mother threw herself into fixing the mess the angels had caused in Oculus. Years later, when she got sick, she asked for him and me to start communicating more. Oddly enough, he quickly obliged."

"I bet Jonah was thrilled to be working alongside a child."

Natalia barked out a laugh. "Probably. I was eighteen at the time, so I definitely felt naïve. He treated me like an equal, though, as he did my mother."

The silence between us was heavy, even though the tone of the conversation had swayed towards slightly light-hearted. Natalia broke that silence. "You are dead set on Jonah being the culprit, aren't you?"

"I'd say so. It doesn't look good for him."

"Nicholas and his friend feel this way too?"

"That's still up for debate."

She pushed her hair over her shoulder. "I thought you'd have convinced them by now."

"So, you think he's guilty as well?" I placed my hands under my chin.

"Perhaps. There's a loyal place in my heart for Jonah, but it doesn't mean I'm blind. Just because my mother trusted him doesn't mean I have to, given the evidence."

"What makes you think I can convince anyone, especially

Nicholas? Pretty sure his head is way too high up Jonah's ass." I caught myself laughing at my comment.

Natalia placed a hand over her mouth, stifling her giggle. "It just seems you two had an understanding, vastly better than your friends, unless their understanding is pure distaste."

"We have a common goal, that's all. Elise isn't my friend, just so you're aware."

Natalia looked behind us, a surprised look on her face. "That girl isn't your friend?"

"Nope. If you ask her, she'll tell you the same damn thing, but my advice is not to ask."

"Hm, I've never known anyone to tag along to Heaven's Gate. That seems like something a *friend* would do. Maybe I've just misunderstood friendship this entire time." She scratched the back of her head. "Although it does make sense, seeing that showing any sort of friendly emotion where you're from might end terribly. Regardless, I may be wrong about your friendship with her, but I'm not wrong about your relationship with Nicholas."

"Relationship?" My voice cracked, startled at the word.

"I meant like a working relationship, Soul Seether, not romantic. Unless..." She let her words trail off, looking down at the leaves around her.

I bit my lower lip, shaking my head. "Thanks, but no thanks. He's adorable, but you have a better chance of a relationship with him than I do.

Natalia walked over to me, moving her dress around so that she could sit comfortably. "Interesting idea, but I don't think he's my type."

"Maybe blondes are more your speed, but just know Reese might be a little leery about coming back here by himself. Given the right motivation, though, he could be persuaded."

Natalia fiddled with the rings on her fingers. "Blondes aren't the issue, believe me."

I eyed her expectantly, not quite understanding her meaning. She peered up at me and smiled, one of her eyebrows perking upwards. That's when it clicked: *women*. "Well, Reese would've been a terrible choice for a boyfriend anyway. I'm sorry for even considering him." We both let out a laugh. "I feel like dating a literal queen would be intimidating as hell."

"It is and it isn't. I luckily found Isabel early on and it's been blissful ever since. She's the one who told me to play nice."

"Thank the realms for Isabel, then." I looked at the stream, at how the water lapped over itself with no means of stopping. I asked my next question while staring directly into the stream. "Have you ever been to the Divine Library?"

She widened her eyes at my question. "Once, about a few months after my mother's death. Why do you ask?"

"Did you know there's a secret tunnel to get there from The Skies? That there's a book with your people's history inside the wall?"

"Wait, slow down. A secret tunnel? Inside the wall?"

I took a breath and shot up from my place on the rock, nodding. "It's underground, and there's a book, one on your people that explains everything." Natalia remained on the rock, her eyes following me as I paced. "We read there's a way to overpower your magic, but it takes a lot of power. It seems a hefty number of Enchanters gave their magic to one single Enchanter to disarm Keegan's key."

"Like a catalyst," Natalia said under her breath. She caught my stare and blinked. "Trying to remove my magic is difficult; it must be done a certain way. It would have to be simultaneous, in perfect formation. It would take skill I'm sure most in Purgatory don't have. Giving their powers to one Enchanter would make it easier. It's a perfect plan." She paused for a moment, almost hesitant. "Can I ask you something?" Natalia placed her hands delicately on her lap.

I raised my eyebrows, waiting.

"I know you have evidence, but have you thought about *why* Jonah would do this?"

"What do you mean?"

"No one does something like this without a motive. This is a thorough plan with a lot of factors involved. If Jonah has something to do with this, there must be a reason. With everything he's been through with Lilith, it would have to be a really good one. Why would he *want* demons in Heaven's Gate?" Natalia explained, mimicking my earlier thoughts.

I placed my hands on my hips, shifting my weight from side to side. "I guess I'm not used to looking at things from all sides."

She shifted off the rock and walked towards me. She was maybe a few inches taller than me, but not so much that she towered over me like Nicholas. "I don't see how someone like you could possibly be a demon."

I smirked, shrugging my shoulders. "Anyone can be anything, if we're being honest. I mean look at Reese. I can't believe that shit is an angel, but I don't make the rules."

Natalia cracked a smile, but it quickly disappeared. "I guess what I mean is that yes you have a demonic soul, but that doesn't make you deserving of it."

I let my lips part, kind of in shock.

"Do you remember anything about your life, before Lilith found you?"

I thought back to when I first woke up in Purgatory. It was a cell with solid stone walls, a door with a small opening to peek out of. I was there for days or weeks, I couldn't remember.

"I don't. None of the demons do." I'd never thought about my life beforehand, had never wanted to. It seemed silly to ponder something that wouldn't benefit my future.

Natalia chewed on her bottom lip. "I have never been this curious in all my life, Soul Seether. You are quite the conundrum."

"I'll take that as a compliment."

She smirked. "I admit, I may have judged you harshly at our first meeting. I was flustered and I wasn't expecting you of all people. All I saw when I looked at you was Lilith. The way people spoke about you, you may as well have been her. Quite the conundrum." She said this quietly, loud enough for just me to hear. A few Enchanters were making their way down towards us, likely to spend time laughing by the stream. It was such a relaxing place to be, I had almost forgotten where I was.

Natalia seemed to have the same revelation as me. "We should probably get back up there. I need to show my face a bit more." She turned away, letting me catch a glimpse of her shoulder tattoo again.

"Did your mother have the same one?" I asked, nodding towards the crown.

She peeked over her shoulder and smiled at it fondly. "She did. It's magicked onto the skin. It never fades, never gets old. Every High Priestess has had it."

"It suits you, being the wise leader and all that," I said, hoping I sounded sincere.

"That means a lot coming from the demon who tried to kill me." She turned on her heels and took a few steps from me, then turned back. She was closer to me now, her voice hushed. "Jonah may be your answer, but I would look closely at everyone. Jonah may be the head of them all, but I wouldn't count anyone out." She squinted her eyes, grabbing my hand and squeezing.

I wanted to blurt out that I thought I saw another demon on the grounds of the Divine Library. I wanted to say I felt a dark presence was so familiar, I knew down to my core that something was off, but I was stopped by a high-pitched voice.

"I was wondering when I'd find you." A woman looked Natalia over with striking blue eyes. "Who's this?" She didn't sound jealous or alarmed, just curious.

Natalia looked over and raised her eyebrows, silently communicating. The female raised her eyebrows in return, laying a hand on Natalia's shoulder. Her golden hair swished back and forth around her chin.

"It is nice to finally meet you, Soul Seether. I'm Isabel." She brought her hand out, which I grasped with my own.

"It's nice to meet you as well." Her hand was warm and inviting. She enclosed her other around our joined fingers before glancing back at Natalia. "See, I told you all you had to do was talk to her and you'd get along."

Natalia moved her dress around her feet and rolled her eyes. Isabel released my hand and dipped her head down to whisper, "I know she can be a handful, but she really does want to help. If she gives you any problems, come talk to me." She winked, turning around, and reaching her hand out to Natalia. They started to walk up the hill towards the party when Natalia turned back. "You should find your friend. Come find me when you are ready to go back."

"She's not my friend."

"We'll agree to disagree, Soul Seether."

I ran my hand through my hair, my finger getting caught on a few tangles. "Dani."

Natalia gave me a quick nod. "Dani, it is then."

It took me a full thirty minutes to find Elise in the crowds of Enchanters. When I did find her, she was tipsy off some cherry wine Natalia had told me was meant for taking sips of and not chugging. Elise had, thankfully, started to sober up a bit when we got back to the room.

"You get out for five minutes and you get drunk."

"I'm not drunk," she argued, scowling at me. "Tipsy. Not drunk."

Elise started to undress herself, letting her clothes scatter the floor as she walked in circles. I let my eyes follow her, but she started to make me dizzy. She finally sat on her bed and let her head hit the pillow, her eyes wide open. "What did you and the Queen talk about?"

"Nothing of importance. I'll fill you in when you're sober."

"Fuck you, I am perfectly cohear-hat," Elise muttered, trying hard to shove my knee, but I moved out of her grasp.

I shook my head, but tucked her in, watching as her eyes fluttered close. She was nice when she was quiet and exhausted, too much alcohol in her system. It would wear off quickly and she would be back to her old self, but for now, I let myself sit in the quiet. I would speak to Elise when she was coherent, but in the meantime, I settled on thinking about Natalia's words.

"Jonah may be your answer, but I would look closely at everyone. Jonah may be the head of them all, but I wouldn't count anyone out."

Nicholas had been trying to say the same thing, but I just wasn't getting it. He was accepting of Jonah looking like the enemy, but to him, it didn't make sense. Maybe I wasn't opening myself up to all the options. Maybe I wanted the guilty party to be the leader of them all. It didn't have to be that black and white. I knew it could be any of one of them or even all of them, but I was dead focused on Jonah. Had I blinded myself? I inherently knew that Lilith was a bad person, so there was truly nothing to defend her with, but with Jonah, there were pros and cons that made decision making difficult.

If I stopped staring at Nicholas's biceps or his mouth for two seconds, I could focus. If only he had a horrendous face, my mind wouldn't wander so much. I listened, but clearly not hard enough. It wasn't something I said or took lightly, being wrong. At least, being *this* wrong.

I needed to talk to him and explain what I now understood. I thought I could potentially have one of the guards get him for me. They always came to get us, so it seemed like a logical move to ask to speak to him in return. I glanced over at Elise, softly snoring in her sleep. I walked over to the door and turned the knob, preparing to address the sentries, when I was met with a familiar chest, biceps, and when I looked up higher, a familiar mouth. Nicholas peered down at me, and a nervous smile escaped his lips.

Fuck. That mouth would seriously be the death of me.

The sentries made no move to look at him. He tried to let himself inside, but I placed a hand on his chest, stopping him. He glanced down at my hand, and I moved it away.

"She's sleeping," I said, pointing to Elise.

Nicholas looked over my shoulder and I could see him press his tongue to the inside of his cheek. He swallowed hard. "We need to talk."

"You can come back in a few hours. I'm sure she won't be ready to talk, but she'll be awake." I wanted it to sound like a joke, but his face was unmoved.

"No, I need to talk to *you*."

"Me?"

He nodded, his dark hair swishing at his movement. It looked as if he had been running his hands through it repeatedly.

"Okay, talk." I leaned against the doorframe to make myself more comfortable.

Nicholas looked at both the sentries and shook his head. "Not here. Come with me." I stepped out, closing the door behind me. Nicholas was already a few steps in front of me, moving towards one of the side doors we normally took.

"Where's your partner in crime?"

"Sleeping." Figures.

We circled down the stairs before we made our way out the door. He didn't speak to me the entire time. I was trying to put together the words I wanted to say, but it was proving difficult. I followed him as he opened the door to a training room.

"What did you need to talk to me about that you had to take me here to tell me?"

He wrapped his hand around the back of his neck. "I went to speak to Jonah today."

"Jonah, right. Well, speaking of Jonah, Nicholas, there's something I need to tell you—."

He didn't let me finish. "He wants you to talk to the demon in the Ethereal Bastille."

"I might have been...wait, what?" I asked, confusion in my voice.

"They found another demon, and they want you to speak to the original one Markus discovered, the one locked in the Ethereal Bastille. They think it will provide some answers, get a lead." He sounded nervous, like he knew this was something I didn't want to hear.

I shook my head, not understanding. "Another demon?" I should have said something.

"Last night. It was already dead when they found it. Look, they wouldn't tell me much more than that, but they wanted me to tell you your skills are needed. The sentries have tried, but they can't seem to get anything out of it."

"My skills?" Of course, they needed my skills. "You don't want me to *talk* to it. You want me to *torture* it."

Nicholas stood there, silent, confirming what I already knew. I could feel my blood boiling. "You want me for the one thing I'm known for, but want to reprimand me for it later, calling me a monster, saying Soul Seether like it's a fucking disease."

"Dani, this is what you do. Just do it and get it over with. Don't make this a big deal. Leave the dramatics to Elise."

They didn't know what they were doing. Torturing a demon wasn't like scolding your child. You give demons two options: a bad option and an even worse one, or you give them no options at all. They could hold out for hours and die with the truth hanging on their tongues. After this, I would be useless if I didn't provide information they wanted.

I slowly walked over to him. His shoulders were tense as he waited for me to make a move. I didn't. I just perched on the tips of my toes, just reaching his mouth and speaking against his lips. "No."

CHAPTER TWELVE

NICK

Earlier

Reese had already gone to bed when the messenger came to tell me I was being summoned. I had tried to sleep, but that proved harder than I anticipated. I had placed my covers over my face, wrapping myself in complete darkness, but my mind still ran a mile a minute.

Eventually, I pushed the covers off and placed a hand to my forehead. I kept trying to make excuses that the reason for Jonah needing to see me was to go over something small, or that they had figured out who had manipulated the portals, and everything could go back to normal. I almost laughed at my own wishful thinking. I knew whatever he wanted to say, or ask, it was something I wasn't going to be prepared for. I knew myself though, and since sleep evaded me, I spent the rest of my night doing what I do best: spiraling.

I WALKED SLOWLY TOWARDS JONAH'S OFFICE, MY HEART THRUMMING IN MY ears the entire way. I leaned against the back wall of the elevator as I watched the numbers go up and took a minute when the doors opened. Maybe he found out about our trip to the Divine Library and wanted to speak to me about yet another unauthorized excursion. That was something I didn't have the energy to explain.

I almost felt a wave of vertigo wash over me as I stood in front of the doors. I couldn't hear any sound from the other side, but who could with how thick the doors were? I knocked and stood back, swallowing the lump that had developed in my throat. I heard a click and then the sound of the door shifting open. The smell of cinnamon and burning wood entered my nose immediately. I cautiously stepped forward to see Jonah at his desk, leaning back in his chair. He wasn't alone. As I stepped further into the room, I noticed Markus and Ariel.

"Ah, Nicholas, are you well rested?" Jonah asked, placing his hands on top of his desk.

I cleared my throat nervously. "Yes, I am."

"Wonderful to hear. Your Animus Seeking was successful?"

"As successful as they normally are. Nothing special," I said, tapping my foot.

Jonah waved his hand in my direction. "It really isn't meant to be all too exciting. Standard protocol, really. Anyways, you're probably wondering why I asked you here today."

I gave a quick nod, but never moved from my place in the room. Jonah seemed nervous.

"There is likely no easy way to say this --" Jonah started, but Markus finished for him.

"We found one on the grounds this morning. Well, a group of trainees did, which, let me tell you, was not easy to explain away."

I felt the indent form between my eyebrows in confusion. "You found one? One what?"

"A demon, Nicholas," Markus answered, his gray hair ruffled.

"Another one? But how?" I had prepared myself for many things, but that wasn't one.

"If we knew the answer, things would be much easier, wouldn't they?" Ariel sneered. "Natalia was supposed to have maintained the portals until we could figure something out."

"Someone has reopened it, at least enough for one to come through," Jonah explained. "I do not blame Natalia. This is much bigger than even her." The sympathy in his eyes when he said her name made me want to disregard every bad thought I ever conjured up about him.

"Is it locked in the Ethereal Bastille with the other one?" I asked, walking towards them.

They gave each other looks before returning their eyes to me, but it was Markus who spoke. "It's dead."

"So, one of the new trainees killed it? That's impressive."

Jonah let out a small laugh. "No, Nicholas, it was already dead when they discovered it."

I opened my mouth to ask another obvious question, which Ariel answered before it left my lips. "Clearly, someone killed it and hid it, which makes things even more difficult."

"Have a seat, Nicholas, please. You standing there is making me anxious." Jonah gestured towards the open seat in front of him. I sat down, but on the edge, my mind reeling.

Jonah rubbed his forehead. "We have been trying to keep this under wraps, but I think that plan is wearing thin. Someone has slain a demon and is clearly not making a big show about it. I have sentries monitoring the grounds. I've shut down the portals and already collected all the portal keys for the time being, but there is only so much I can do with the information I have."

I touched my fingertips to my chest, feeling the portal key hanging around my neck.

"I knew those demons had overstayed their welcome," Ariel stated.

"What do they have to do with any of this?" I thought to myself. By the way they were looking at me, I realized I'd said it out loud. When no one spoke, I continued. "You brought them here *after* the first demon, so it makes no sense for them to have anything to do with this."

"So, you've spent a few weeks with them and now you, what? Know what they are capable of?" Ariel mocked, rolling his eyes.

"That's not what I'm saying."

"Nicholas has a point, Ariel. Logically, it wouldn't make any sense." Jonah said.

"You of all people should know what demons can do, especially under Lilith's influence." Ariel wrapped his hands over the back of Markus's chair and gave Jonah a knowing look. "You have let them get too comfortable here."

Markus crossed his legs. "As much as we would love to send them back, we can't. You are aware of that, Ariel. Besides, *you* are the one who brought an extra demon along."

Ariel shook his head. "That's beside the point. We can just send them back and figure out another way to handle this."

"Yes, opening a portal to Purgatory is a good idea right now," I said under my breath, but, yet again, they heard me. Ariel scrunched up his nose but kept quiet. Markus scrubbed a hand down his face and turned to look at Jonah, who was tapping his index finger on his desk.

"We can't reopen anything to the demonic world right now, but Markus does bring up a good point." He let out a sigh and looked me in the eyes. "Which brings me to you." I sat up straighter, waiting. "I think it's time to introduce our guest to our prisoner."

"You want me to take Dani to the Ethereal Bastille?"

"It doesn't have to be you, Nicholas. It can be your troublesome friend with the bow, but we request the Soul Seether be escorted," Ariel spat.

Jonah got up from his chair and slowly circled his desk. "Our sentries have been working on the demon for a while and have nothing. It won't speak to them, no matter what they do. Maybe it will answer its own kind."

"Either way, she will play her part and help us," Markus chimed in.

I rubbed my chin. "You want her to torture an answer out of it? I don't think she'll be thrilled to be doing your bidding, no matter the activity."

"She doesn't really have much of a choice," Ariel huffed. "Besides, she did our bidding when she came here. She went to Oculus with you and that was a mild success."

I thought this over. "That's different, though. She was there as a buffer, to take some of the blow if things got too tense. You're asking her to do so much more right now." I could see Ariel holding himself back, probably trying not to throttle me. "What makes you think this demon will tell her anything? What if it's just a waste of time?"

Jonah placed a hand on my chair. "It *will* tell her something. The things she can do, our sentries would never be able to accomplish. There's a reason she's so feared, Nicholas."

"Why can't you just ask her yourself?" I could feel my heartbeat pick up pace at the thought of having to bring this to Dani's attention.

Markus answered. "You've spent more time with her; she seems to trust you. This request coming from your mouth instead of ours might go over better."

"I doubt that," I said honestly.

"You act as if she hasn't done something like this before. She tortures people where she's from, doesn't she? What is the difference? It's absurd to be picky about such a crude skill."

I rolled my eyes. "Yet, you want her to do something so crude at your own request. It's a little hypocritical." I tightened my lips together. It was pure back talk and completely out of character.

I felt a hand land on my shoulder and then a wave of soothing calm wash over me. I looked over my shoulder to find Jonah hovering over me, looking at his other executives.

"Gentlemen, this is a lot to hear at once, so I'm sure Nicholas didn't mean for that to come out so...assertively." He removed his hand, but the calming wave remained. "He takes after his father in that way."

My father? I would say Maurice Cassial was the last person to be condescending. The man cringes at every word that comes out of Reese's mouth.

"Nicholas, all we want is for her to get any information she can from this demon and then she can do what she wants with it," Markus said.

"Do what she wants?" I asked, confused.

"You know, whatever she does when she's done with them. Once she's done, it won't do much talking, so we might as well make room."

I shot up from my chair and backed away. "Let me get this straight: you want her to torture answers out of it and kill it? You said you would send it back once you got answers."

"We can't let it go back to Purgatory now, can we? Not with what has happened," Ariel answered, smugness in his voice.

I opened my mouth to protest, but he was right. I looked to Jonah, but he refused to look back at me. We couldn't risk creating an opening for more demons if we tried to send it back. I knew none of this would matter to Dani, no matter how logical anything sounded to *me*.

"Exactly," Ariel said with a satisfied grin when he saw I had nothing to say.

"She won't see it that way and we all know it," I said, crossing my arms.

"You will have to make her see it and try to make up for it later," Jonah said. "We need this, Nicholas. Do what's right."

"How are you so sure this is right?" I could hear my father's words echo in my head. I could feel myself wanting to be blinded by what they said. I didn't want to be led by the simple idea that I was lower than them so whatever they said had to be the only possible option. Although right now, I didn't see another path to take.

"Because right now, it's all we have," Jonah confessed, exhaustion in his voice.

"You have the charm, Nicholas. Use it," Markus added, winking. I narrowed my eyes at him but looked back at Jonah. There was something on the tip of my tongue that I wanted to say but couldn't. I had the one thing that would make this torture even possible, the one thing that could turn this meeting between two demons into an unfair playing ground.

I had her dagger.

Markus would have a field day learning that I'd lied. Yet, if she went down there without it and came back empty handed, they would know something was wrong. I knew she could retrieve the information they sought, but would she want to finish the job?

Dani wasn't an easy read, but I'd learned enough about her to know that she needed motivation. Markus and Ariel had other business to attend to but gave me pointed looks as they left the room. Jonah stood near the fireplace, not facing me.

"You honestly think this is a good idea?" I asked, stepping up behind him, far enough away so I wasn't crowding him.

"As I've said before, it's the only plan we have. I wasn't planning for another demon to appear, and I certainly wasn't planning on it being dead already." He sounded tired. "We're hoping it tells us who Lilith is working with."

"So, you know it's Lilith?"

"That's obvious. We all knew she would try to infiltrate Heaven's Gate. I just don't know who she would trust with this plan."

I mulled it over in my head. "You want this figured out just as much as the rest of us, don't you?"

Jonah turned around to face me, dumbfounded. "Of course, I do. I don't want to have to keep things from our people. I don't want messenger angels disappearing—."

"Disappearing?" My breath caught in my throat.

He nodded. "I did some digging -- Keegan Finley is missing. I've sent scouts out to find him, but nothing has come of it. Natalia doesn't know much about it, so I'm back to where I started. Perhaps he defected and Lilith got to him, or maybe this demon can tell us where he is." Jonah shook his head, his shoulders slumped down. "I should have paid more attention."

I looked down at my shoes, silently thanking Natalia for keeping her mouth shut. If Jonah just found out about Keegan, then how did he send him to Oculus in the first place? I was starting to understand their incentive for needing answers, yet I made no move to give more information. I knew I would regret my next words, but I had to do it. I needed to see how this played out. "I'll ask her."

"Nicholas, if it's something you don't feel comfortable with, I can do it myself," he offered, his sincerity speaking volumes.

I stuck my hands in my pockets. "It would probably be better coming from me. Maybe she'll be thrilled." I said this with as much enthusiasm as I could muster, which wasn't much.

Jonah nodded, taking in my words. "Just like your father, making the most of things." Jonah looked into my eyes this time. He looked at me and smiled so the corners of his mouth ticked upward the slightest bit. His eyes scanned my face as if he was seeing someone else, someone he was remembering fondly. "I always admired that about him."

Present

"No?" I repeated. She said it with such determination and malice, I almost took a step back. *Almost.* "What do you mean, no?"

"No means no. Do they not teach that in your angelic education?" she snarked.

I rolled my eyes, hating how she was so close to me that I could almost feel the hairs on her arms tickle mine. "Stubbornness isn't an attractive trait, so just stop."

She let out a one note bark of a laugh and crossed her arms over her chest. "Ah, not a fan of it when your backs' against the wall, huh?"

"That's not what's happening."

She tapped her index finger to her chin and looked up at the ceiling. "Really? From where I'm standing, you're being told to do something with no real choice, like the little servant bitch you are."

"Wow, a little aggressive, aren't you?"

"I'm just getting started. Unfortunately, that pretty face of yours won't get you very far this time." She pushed her bottom lip out in a fake pout. "I've given you my answer, Nicholas."

I gazed at her incredulously. "Did you not hear what I said?" She raised one of her dark eyebrows at me. "Demon. On the grounds. Found dead. None of that rings a bell?"

"It does. That sucks ass for you." She pushed her index finger into my chest. "Doesn't really fucking matter. Just send me and Elise back. Deal with this shit on your own."

"I can't."

"What do you mean you can't?"

I shrugged my shoulders. "Guess I forgot to mention Jonah shut down all the portals for now. Especially ones to Purgatory. So I'm sorry to say, your ass is stuck here, so you might as well make the most of it."

She stepped back from me and turned around. "Fuck! Of course, that's how it is. You trap me here without a leg to stand on so that I'll have to do what you want." As she spoke, I couldn't help my eyes from roaming down her body. I was frustrated with her, but that didn't mean I was blind. The way the leggings she wore fit just right, how her neck curved perfectly.

I ran my hand through my hair, clearing my thoughts. "You're being overdramatic." I lifted both my hands up in hopes of reclaiming control of the situation. "All of this is beside the point, Dani. You know you can do this, so just do it and get it over with. I'm sure we could be in and out in minutes."

Dani slowly turned and tilted her head to the side. "Aw, thank you for reminding me how good I am at my fucking job. That doesn't change the key fact that I need something to do the kind of damage Jonah wants. I don't think they would appreciate knowing I brought a party favor with me."

I looked around as if someone else was listening in on our conversation. "I'll make sure you have it, as long as you don't get out of hand."

She widened her eyes. "Oh, now there are stipulations? Torture the demon, but not too much. Only kill it a little bit. You guys are fucking ridiculous."

"I never said you have to kill it."

"You can't honestly look me in the eyes and tell me they want me to let it live? After I'm done, it won't have any reason to want to live."

I peeked over to meet her eyes. "Dani, come on."

"No, Nicholas, just no. I do those things because I have to. I'm good at it, yes, but I do it to survive, if you haven't figured it out. Lilith gave me that dagger and helped me become who I am to make me worthy, so that's what I became. I don't have a crowd cheering me on, I don't have the motivation to *want* to do this. All I know is that this demon broke through the portal. That doesn't call for ripping his soul out at the end." She stared right at me, eyes almost burning right through me. "All I have is a bunch of angels on my back telling me to be a good little demon and know my place. That's not how it fucking works."

"Okay, okay, I get that, but you can't just sit in your room and do nothing. This will get a lot worse before it gets better, you and I both know that."

"Believe me, I've seen worse, so I'll let you figure out how to survive on your own."

"For fuck's sake Dani, how are you this selfish?"

"*Selfish?!*" She sounded surprised.

"Yes! This is could be a huge turning point, but you won't do it because of your fucking pride!" I could hear myself yelling, but I didn't care.

"Have you ever taken a soul, Nicholas? No, you haven't. It's more painful than you could ever know. You just become a void, reckless, so easily contorted, because you aren't quite dead yet, nothing but an empty vessel that breathes and moves. Angels couldn't stand the thought of what I do weeks ago, but now angels are using me to get what they want? What do you plan to reward me with when everything gets resolved?" She started to stomp towards me. I opened my mouth to answer but she stopped me. "A fucking medal? A pat on the back? No, you will send me back to Purgatory until the next time I'm fucking useful, or better yet, you'll just get rid of me since a dead demon is better than a *selfish* one."

"You are out of your fucking mind if you think that's what's going to happen."

"Yeah, probably, but I'm pretty sure that's what Natalia's people thought before angels slaughtered half of them. Excuse me for expressing all of my options."

I watched as her chest rose and fell with each breath. She wrapped her hair around one side of her neck and tugged at the ends. She had ended her statement and I didn't know what to say. She had a point, but none of that mattered right now. Oddly enough, I knew I wouldn't let them hurt her if it came down to it. I had to find a way to turn this around, but without manipulation. She would sense that from a mile away. So, I used the one and only tactic I had.

"Alright, you have a point." I let out an exhaustive sigh. "That doesn't change the fact that there's a demon that needs to be broken down, so how about we do this fairly?"

Dani eyed me skeptically. "Explain."

"You didn't seem to mind the wager I made when it came to your dagger, so how about we do that again?"

"You want to fight me, in hopes that you'll win, and I'll be forced to help you?"

"There is no hoping. I will win. We both know that," I said, giving her a sly smile that I had a feeling she'd enjoy.

She looked away, but not before dropping her eyes to my mouth for a moment, then over at the rack of weapons. A smile ticked at the corners of her lips. "Possibly. How about we make it a little more interesting?"

"Go on."

"You have a way with a sword, I'll give you that, but what happens when the sword is taken away and all you have are these?" She lifted her hands and wiggled her fingers.

I held my stomach as I started to laugh. "You want to legitimately fight me?"

"No magic, no weapons." She had a glint in her eye, almost as if she was excited.

"For someone who *doesn't* want to torture someone, you sure do get excited for violence." I tilted my head, hearing my neck crack a bit.

"You're known for your sword skills, but that doesn't mean you'd want to use them on one of your own without any sort of pretense."

"It stepped into Heaven's Gate without permission, Dani. What more of a pretense do you want?"

Dani pressed her lips together hard before replying. "That, Nicholas, is where you and I differ." I started to chuckle, but that got cut short by her fist colliding with my jaw. It was bone against bone and the pain was quick, my jaw throbbing as she stepped back. I lifted my hand up to cover the likely bruise on my face, surprise written all over my face.

I staggered back a few paces. "Did you just punch me?"

Fake innocence appeared across over her face. "Oh, did I not mention we were starting? My bad." She shrugged.

"I'll disregard how completely unfair you are," I said, realizing the pressure in my jaw wasn't so bad, meaning she hadn't hit with all her power, just enough to make a point. I looked up at her to see her other fist in my periphery and felt her knuckles connect with the other side of my face. She chuckled when I almost tripped backwards.

"I'll disregard how annoying you are." She cracked her knuckles.

"I'm annoying? Have you met *you*?"

"I have, and if I do say so myself, I'm a fucking delight." She took a few steps towards me, bringing her fist up again, but this time, I wouldn't be caught off guard. I blocked her fist and grabbed her wrist, twisting.

Her body followed along with my slow but deliberate cranking of her wrist. She squinted her eyes at the pain, but I couldn't be in charge for long, because she wrapped a leg around the back of my knee, causing me to bend awkwardly enough to release her wrist. She spun around, lifting her leg and aiming for my side, but not before I regained my composure enough to grab her leg mid-swing.

Dani tried to yank her leg back, but I held on tighter, knowing she wouldn't be content hopping on one leg for long. She let out a huff that reminded me of the sound a disgruntled toddler would make. "How does this end, Dani?"

She brushed a piece of her hair from her eyes, almost losing her balance on the one leg. "I don't know, Nicholas. Since you're making all the shots, you tell me."

I finally yanked her leg towards me, watching as she lost her footing and fell onto the floor with a thud. I looked down at her, eyes shut, no doubt calculating her next move. I started to circle her. "You are making this insanely more difficult than it has to be. You think that you'll be betraying your own kind by doing this one thing for us, but it's for the good of everyone. You'll be doing a good thing."

She slapped the floor with both her palms and pushed herself up, jumping a bit as she landed upright. "You still don't understand, do you?"

"Understand what?"

"You think I'm worried about other demons!" Dani laughed out loud. "I don't care about other demons. I'm talking about myself. I don't want to do it for *me*, because, for once, I just don't fucking want to." She pushed forward and shoved my shoulders, hauling me back.

"So, this is a matter of you being a brat?" I reached for her wrists, and she tried to shove me again, but before I got ahold of her, she spun around and got her foot to connect with my stomach. I hunched over, clutching my middle, trying to catch my breath.

"Oh, I'm a brat, but why, after all this time, are you still acting like a little bitch?"

I tried reaching for her ankle, but she jumped back. She closed the distance to punch me in the jaw again. "I was starting to think you weren't like the others. You had a mind of your own, but you love playing both sides. You can't do that forever. Let me guess, you didn't want to even consider asking me and then they got into your head. Better yet, Jonah did. Jonah has his hand so far up your ass, he uses you like a damn puppet. They all do!"

I shot my legs out from under me and swiped her ankles with my feet. She fell backwards, but I caught her, shoving her towards one side of the room. She tried to refocus herself, but I'd had enough. Dani lifted her hands up and tried to strike, but I ducked down and elbowed her side. I watched as she reached for her ribs, but I didn't give her much time to recover. I turned and grabbed her shoulder, swinging her around against the wall. I hustled over to her as she lunged towards me, but I smacked my hand against her chest, shoving her back.

I bent my arm, placing my forearm at her throat and locked both her hands in mine, making her immobile. She squirmed and lifted her head up, gazing up at the ceiling. "You know what's hilarious?" She didn't wait for me to answer. "If they had sat you down and told you that the only way to save everyone was to kill me, you would have done it. You would have thought about it for a moment, but you would have done it and probably apologized the whole time. You would have told yourself that you did it for the greater good, while deep inside, you would hate yourself. I've felt it and it's shitty."

Dani leaned her face towards mine so I could smell the raw cinnamon of her skin. She was so close; I could practically count her eyelashes.

"You have no idea what you're talking about. That's crazy."

"Is it? You would do anything to make a name for yourself. Survive. Be seen as something other than what you are, just so what? You can move up the angelic power ladder? They would use you, your knack for a sword, and your loyalty for their purpose and you would let them. You want to do right by them, but you also *love* the recognition."

I blinked at her statement. "What are you talking about? You're making them out to be monsters when all they're trying to do is fix things."

"Don't act stupid." I felt her pull her hands against mine, but I held on tighter. Her legs brushed my own and before I realized it, I was leaning in. "You live to hear people cheer you on, tell you how great you are. You want to know that you're the best, that you can *fix* things, regardless of the kind of fixing you must do. We aren't so different. I just know when it's not *worth* it." She said the last part through gritted teeth as she continued to tug at my hands.

The laugh she let out was breathy, mocking. "Demons aren't the only monsters around here, Nicholas. They're just easier to blame."

"Don't try to tell me about myself." I pressed her back into the wall, feeling my heartbeat rapidly. "Nothing you say is going to change my mind and what you need to do," I stated, her eyes trying to search for something in mine, her words trying to get a rise out of me. A part of me wondered why she didn't jump at the chance to unleash herself on something in the Ethereal Bastille. She was getting the opportunity to be exactly what she was without consequences. Maybe she was right, and things weren't that simple, then again, Dani wasn't easily understandable.

"You have a choice, Nicholas, and you have to make it soon, because by the looks of things, shit isn't getting less complicated." She looked down at my mouth and then at my arm trapping her neck. "Do you want to stand behind people you can't even decide if you trust enough to be honest with, or do you want to go with your gut and make a decision for yourself, despite the consequences?"

I remained silent and looked at her. I could feel the ache in my stomach from her powerful kick, but I powered through it. I could feel the way she was trying to escape me, but without her powers, she couldn't free herself. I could feel my body wanting to lean completely against her and I fought hard against it. Her shirt rose from where I pressed her hands together and my fingers got a taste of her skin, sending a small shock through my body.

"What do you want, Nicholas?"

Her words ran into me like a punch to the gut. Her stare was intense, meaningful, as if she wanted her look to burn right through me. I felt her chest thump, her body tense against mine as I laid my weight on her. Her breathing was slightly uneven but strong, as if she could go at this with me for so much longer than I anticipated.

That's when I noticed her mouth.

I'd noticed it before, but never this close. I hadn't noticed the way her bottom lip pushed out whenever she was out of breath, or the pink hue of them. My eyes traveled from her mouth to her neck, to her shoulders down the rest of her. We were so close, I could feel her body heat.

My eyes shot back up to her face as she squirmed, trying to

release herself from my hold, but I pushed back, forcing her back to the wall, her shoulders slamming against it.

What did I want? *What did I want?* That was an extremely loaded question.

Her tongue snuck out and licked at her bottom lip, my eyes following the movement. I knew what I wanted. At least, what I wanted right now.

The last thing I saw was her eyes widening when my mouth collided with hers. Her lips were just as soft as I'd imagined. They slid over mine so quickly and were taken away just as fast. The kiss was surprising to both of us. I had never been shy about initiating anything, but this was *different.* Her eyes weren't laced with confusion or disgust when she met mine. They were perplexed. Intrigued, even.

My forearm still pressed to her chest, but she fell back onto the wall, not resisting anymore. My eyes darted along her face, waiting for her to say something, make some sort of move. I almost considered apologizing and could feel my hand start to lose their grip on her wrists. After a beat, she smirked.

Before I could take another breath, she had snaked her hands out of my hold and wrapped them around my arm, escaping me. She grabbed my shirt and pulled me to her, pressing her mouth to mine again. Dani held onto my shirt so tight, I felt the fabric strain against my shoulders. I walked forward, using my entire body to pin her against the wall again. My hands aimed for her waist, squeezing so hard, she groaned against my mouth. She wrapped her arms around my neck and started to lean her body against me, letting her hips push against mine. My hands found her ass, forcing her to press harder into me.

She unleashed her tongue, exploring my mouth while I grazed it slightly with my teeth. I moved my hands up into her hair, tugging it to get a better angle to her mouth. I shouldn't have felt the heat rise in my skin when she took her hand and rubbed it down the front of my pants, but it happened automatically. Chills crept along my spine from the sounds she made when my lips traveled from her pretty mouth to her perfect neck.

My hands skated over her waist again and towards the elastic of her leggings, letting my fingers tease the exposed skin of her stomach. I grabbed the ends of her shirt and lifted it up and over her head, her brown skin glowing in the light of the afternoon. Her skin felt soft and warm on my fingertips, but I wanted more. She let out a loud gasp as I grabbed the back of her thighs and lifted her, preening at the way she instantly wrapped her legs around my waist and grabbed my face to kiss me again.

I walked us backwards towards the middle of the room and dropped to my knees, laying her on her back. She lifted her arms and started to reach for me, but I leaned back out of her grasp. I hovered over her and pressed my lips on her collarbone and over the top of her breast, nipping and biting. She started to whimper, and I almost came at the sound of it. My mouth traveled down, licking over her stomach until I got to where her leggings began. I expected my hands to be shaky or for my subconscious to kick in and stop this, but my hands were steady. I pulled down her leggings, yanking them off her legs and chucking them away.

I scanned her body underneath me. Her eyes were glassy and filled with need, and I knew mine mirrored the same. I fell on top of her and kissed her, rougher this time. She kissed me back with an equal level of aggression. She ran her hands through my hair and pushed up, brushing her nearly naked body against mine. I felt her open her legs more, felt her grind that needy part of her into where my cock strained against my pants. I groaned into her mouth as she slid her hand down again and found me, wrapping her hand around it as best she could.

I let out a grunt before reaching for my own pants and removing them. I watched as she bit her lower lip as my cock sprang free from its confinement; she watched so intently, she started to come off the floor to grab it, but I took her ankles in my hands and pulled her forward. Her body descended back onto the ground as I spread her legs out further. I grabbed her panties and pushed them to the side, exposing the most mouthwatering sight I'd ever seen. Her pussy glistened from her arousal, and I had to force myself not to lean down and taste it. I slid my fingers between her legs and heard her release a sharp moan.

She was soaked, and I have never been more turned on in my entire life.

Dani looked down at every move I made, her breathing quick and harsh. Her cheeks were flushed and grew a deeper shade of red when I grabbed my cock. Without tenderness or warning, I pressed one of my hands to her thigh and pushed inside of her with one swift motion. She tilted her head back in a low, deep moan.

"Fuckk, you're so tight." I pulled out to the tip and then pushed back inside, leaning down to brace one of my hands next to her head. I brought her leg up, causing her to bend her knee, and wrapped my arm around her thigh.

She started to move against me as I pressed my hips forward, hitting her deeper, again, again, again, again. She wrapped her hands around my shoulders, digging her nails into my skin. I started a solid rhythm, my hips slapping against her the only sound that echoed through the room. I had to close my eyes to try to steady my breathing, but she felt too good.

"O-Oh my god, fuck," Dani moaned, the words vibrating with my thrusts. I squeezed her thigh so hard, I knew she would bruise. She leaned up and kissed me, taking my bottom lip between her teeth and pulling. "Fuck me harder," she begged when she released my lip.

I groaned at her request, increasing my pace. I could feel the sweat rolling down my face to my neck. Her body was slick with her own perspiration, but neither of us seemed to care. I took my hand off the cold floor beneath us and grazed it over her chest, wrapping my hand around her neck. I applied enough pressure to hold her in place but not enough to hurt her. My heart thudded at the sight of her slender neck underneath my hand, of her body so willing to take my punishing thrusts. My cock pounded in and out of her with ease, proving just how much she was enjoying this. I pushed her thigh towards her stomach, gaining better access and a deeper position, so deep it made me let out my own string of curse words. "Is this fucking hard enough for you?"

Dani let out some unintelligible words and sounds that would haunt my dreams. "Yes, don't stop. Don't stop." It was plagued with want, and the cracking in her voice had me pounding so hard, I thought I would crush her. I released her neck just as she started to let out a scream underneath me. I grazed my hand down her body and pressed my thumb against her clit, watching as she writhed beneath me. Her voice went hoarse from her sounds, and I felt her orgasm shoot through her. I felt her body shudder and her inner muscles pulse and pull, clenching around my cock.

"Fuck!" I shouted, feeling my own body began to tense. I pushed my hips against her a few more times before I came, the release a welcome feeling. I had to catch my breath. I had to focus my mind back on the situation. I had to remember why we were here in the first place.

Dani was still sprawled out on the ground, the movement of her chest the only thing telling me that she was alive. I surveyed her, trying to relay back to the beginning of this, how we started talking the Ethereal Bastille and ended up fucking on a training room floor.

I liked it. I had enjoyed it, to the point where I felt like I could want more of it.

I pulled out of her slowly and pulled up my pants. I rose from the floor, my movement causing her to peek out from under her lashes. The way she looked from where I stood, I admitted to myself she was beautiful. Even sated and exhausted, she was beautiful.

Fuck, she was *beautiful*.

I grabbed her clothes from around the room. When I returned, she was leaning back on her elbows, looking up at me. Dani didn't speak, but her mouth turned up in a small smile, a knowing smile. She knew I had enjoyed myself. That was evident.

I reached my hand down, offering her help. Her hand was so much smaller than mine and felt like soft and supple velvet. We stood in front of each other, our breathing almost even now. I handed her the clothes, watching as she placed her legs one at a time into her leggings.

I didn't want to look at her face again. I couldn't. I had to reevaluate and really try to understand what the fuck just happened. I let her finish getting dressed before I started to turn to the door. I couldn't say anything to her. I couldn't even begin to piece together what just happened. I felt like an asshole, but there was nothing I wanted to say now.

Except...

I was already at the threshold when I thought of one thing, even if she hated me for it.

"Ten in the morning," I said, turning slightly to look over my shoulder.

Dani narrowed her eyes. "Ten?"

"Ethereal Bastille. Reese will get you."

She let out a breath, knowing she'd lost. "You won't be escorting me?"

I shook my head towards the ground. "No, I'll be there when you arrive, but he'll walk you. I think that's a better idea."

She clucked her tongue. "My dagger?"

"I'll bring it, don't worry."

"I'm not worried." She walked over to me, resting her hand on my shoulder before she passed me. "Worried is the least of my feelings at the moment."

She was close to me again, letting her brown eyes shoot up at me. I started to realize that face would ruin me if I looked too long; I'd picture all the other positions I could have her in. I brushed her hand off my shoulder and turned back for the door. "I should get you back."

I stood at her door as she turned the knob. I rubbed the back of my neck, hoping my fidgeting wouldn't alert the sentries. Once she was inside, I started to walk down the hall, practically wanting to sprint to my room. I heard her say my name, which caused me to turn on my heels. I saw her half smile, more like a smirk, but only the kind she could pull off.

"At least you figured out what you want," she said, letting the words hit me like ice cold water. She narrowed her eyes before closing the door. This was way more than a lapse of judgment and even if it was, it was something I had to keep to myself.

CHAPTER THIRTEEN

DANI

I leaned against the back of our door, letting my spine become parallel with the solid wood. It felt cool against my thin shirt, refreshing my overheated body. I tried to piece everything together in my head, from beginning to end. I tried to recollect every detail I could conjure, but it was all one big fucking blur. The only parts I remembered were the ones where Nicholas was moving over me, and I had fucking egged him on. I wanted him to keep going and I had fucking liked it.

This fact didn't surprise me much; it more so solidified the fact that he was everything I already assumed he would be: demanding, frustrating, rough, *hot*. I had let him fuck me *hard* against that floor. I squeezed my eyes closed, not wanting the replay of what happened to make its appearance for the tenth time in my thoughts.

"Where the fuck have you been?"

It took me a minute to realize that it was close to early evening now. The sky was that orange-purple color that seemed to make everything feel calmer. Unfortunately, it wasn't helping. I looked across the dimly lit room to where Elise was propped up against her headboard, eyebrows raised. I opened my mouth to answer, but anything I could think would come out made me close my mouth again. I could feel my cheeks start to heat again.

"Dani, have you gone mute? I asked you a fucking question." This time, she swung her legs out from under her covers off the side of the bed. The drunk look in her eyes was gone, replaced by the Elise I had always known.

"I heard you," I answered, annoyed. I wanted to sleep and hope that my dreams didn't drag me back to the training room floor with a broad-shouldered angel balls deep inside of me.

"An answer would be fucking nice." Elise gave me a condescending smile.

"I was having a conversation with Nicholas, that's all." Simple answer.

"A conversation?"

"Yes, you know, that thing that two people do when they want to talk about something?" I started to explain.

"I know what a conversation is, you bitch. I mean, what would he want to have a conversation with you about? Was the blonde one there or something?"

I shook my head nonchalantly, trying to look uncaring. I realized I was still leaning against the door, so I walked over to my bed, pulling my sheets down.

"So, you guys were alone? With no supervision?"

I glared at her, giving her my middle finger. "We aren't children, Elise."

"Why couldn't you just talk in here? No need to whisk you away like a creep." She shrugged her shoulders, but the intrigue never left her eyes. Elise seemed to intimidate everyone she met with her blunt confidence and killer instinct, but she was a notorious gossip.

I waved over to her side of the room. "You were asleep in your drunken little haze, so it's no big deal. Can we please just leave it alone?"

She let out a sharp laugh. "No."

I rolled my eyes, choosing to ignore her instead. The silent treatment wasn't something that worked with Elise. We've never had to use those talents on each other, and I was mentally crossing my fingers she would assume it's not worth her time and shut up.

Luck was not on my side.

"What did he want to talk about?" she pressed on. At least this was something I could answer.

I pulled my hair around, facing her. "I'm torturing the demon in the Ethereal Bastille tomorrow morning."

Her eyes narrowed, as if she was trying to understand the words. She tapped her black fingernails on her knees, letting the seconds tick by. Eventually, she spoke. "Why? I can't say I'm surprised it's come to this, but why now?"

I scratched my cheek, trying to remember what Nicholas told me. "I guess matters are worse than they thought. Another demon breached the portal and now it's all hands-on deck. Get the demon to fix the demonic problem." I fiddled with my hair, watching as the curl I pulled straightened out then popped back into its spiral. "Fun fact, the demon was already dead when they found it."

Elise stood up abruptly, both hands on her hips. "What the hell? By them, you mean Jonah and his band of idiots?" She looked to me for confirmation, and I nodded. "Nicholas was sent to what? Charm you into torturing their prisoner?" Another look of confirmation.

This time, I didn't nod. I just looked at her and let out a heavy breath, trying to maintain eye contact. She let out a slow breath of her own, and I watched her inhale before her face contorted into something usually directed at Reese, but never me.

"I can't fucking believe you agreed so easily to do their bidding. I mean, I know I have bigger balls than all of you combined, but I at least thought you had a decent sized pair. I like to torture just as much as the next demon, but damn, put up a little fight. I literally would have gouged his eyes out for asking something like that and made him thank me for doing it."

I bunched my fists at my sides, feeling my nails dig into my palms. "You think I just stood there and let him just tell me what to do?" The room was starting to darken as the sun set. Elise turned away from me, unaffected by my tone, and clicked on the lamp on her end table.

"You haven't told me much, so I just work with what I'm given."

"He told me what happened and told me what they wanted me to do, but I said no. I. Said. No. Don't you for a fucking second think I didn't fight. It's not like *you* have any authority on what happens to me and the decisions I make!"

Elise smoothed a hand over her hair, nodding, unmoved by my tone. She pressed her lips together, then stuck out her tongue, wetting them. "Alright, simple enough, but how does saying no translate to doing the thing you said no so strongly to?" She tilted her head to the side, eyeing me "That's where I'm lost, Dani."

I felt myself losing my words again. My tongue felt like sandpaper. I wasn't nervous or ashamed about what happened, but I couldn't put my finger on what had me frazzled. Actually, I was well aware of that answer: I got manhandled by an angel ten minutes ago and can still feel the ghost of him between my legs.

This was my first time with an angel and maybe things were just *different* - and sex with Nicholas *had* been different - but I couldn't give that reason my mental stamp of approval. He fucked like someone with pent up, crumpled frustration. I paused in my silent processing; I kept going back to when he first kissed me.

His face looked like he was contemplating every unexplained anomaly the realms had to offer, but then, for just a small moment, he relaxed and then his lips were on mine. When he pulled back, he gave me a look of shock, and I had responded like a starved animal. Things had just escalated. He didn't have an air of hesitation the entire time, foreplay seemingly overrated. We only came back to reality when we'd both finished and could process our...thoughts? Emotions?

"Oh fuck," I heard Elise say in her raspy voice. I snapped my eyes closed and quickly opened them to see her staring back at me wide eyed. "Fucking...Dani. Oh, my fucking...*fuck*." Elise stated, just looking at me. Her gray eyes danced with amusement. It was slightly unnerving, but I remained quiet. She shook her head, gazing at the floor. She wasn't too far from me, but she leaned over a little so I could make out the shadows and strong, delicate curves of her neck tattoo. "You fucked him." She said it like it was a fact, like I wouldn't dare argue with it.

She wasn't a mind reader. Was she? Was this some skill she only decided to reveal to me now? There were about a million things I didn't know about Elise, so for all I knew, it could have been true.

Elise didn't say anything else; she just simply waited for my reply, one I couldn't conjure up. If I replied, it would come with a whole string of 'yeah I know it was stupid'. She just stood there, looking at me with those knowing eyes burning into my skin. I realized I hadn't moved. For the time being, I was immobile. I didn't know what else to do.

She finally let out a small smile and pursed her lips. "The answer is either yes or yes, so the choices are rather complicated." Her tone was sarcastic, accompanied by a knowing laugh.

I smacked my forehead, tilting my head back and closing my eyes, silently counting down from five. When I reached one, I let my eyes open and my head spring forward. I let out a loud, annoyed, but defeated breath. I nodded.

I almost took a few steps back when a closed mouth, gurgled, throat snort came out of her. She blinked, widening her eyes, and nodding her head a few times. She opened her mouth to show her teeth clamped together but poked her tongue out between them. "Well, that doesn't surprise me one fucking bit."

"Excuse me?" I blurted out, watching as she turned towards her bed to sit.

"Oh, come on, Dani, you've been dancing around this whole thing with Nicholas for days, even weeks now. It was positively sickening to watch, but I loved it. If I'm honest, I thought you were going to *literally* just tease him forever, but hey, a girl's got needs."

I squinted. "That's not what happened! I didn't just throw myself at him." Not completely anyway....

She lifted her hands up. "I'm not saying that because I know that's not how it went. I told you his restraint was shredding, and I was right, as per usual."

I walked over to the window and perched on the sill, staring at my feet. "Well, if you must know, it was terrible." The lie rolled out so easily. I looked up to meet her face, but I was met with a pillow launched directly at me. I swatted it away, watching as it landed with a soft sound.

"Fuck off with your shitty lies. I can practically *smell* the good sex on you." She did a few casual sniffs before nodding. "The guy gives you some good dick and you just do what he pleases? That manipulative little shit." She clucked her tongue. "Damn. It must have been phenomenal."

I shoved the heels of my hands into my eyes, hoping the pain of pressing into my eyes hard enough would somehow turn back time. "It wasn't...I...ugh, just fucking forget it. The sex and torturing a demon are mutually exclusive. The sex isn't even important."

"Well then, please give me the important part," Elise said.

I let out a disgruntled noise. "I told you already: another demon got through, but this one ended up being found dead, so it's pretty clear someone is aware of this problem, and they aren't keeping it as low key as they would like."

Elise slid her index finger over her bottom lip and nodded. "That means their only option now is to get the first demon to try to give them answers." She shook her head. "Don't they already have sentries doing that job, getting answers from this demon?"

I place my hands on my knees and let my shoulders slump. "Yeah, they do, but it's not doing anything. If that demon is working for Lilith, it's pretty much a lost cause."

"Do *you* think you can do it?" Elise asked, giving me a pointed glance. Her voice sounded like she really wanted to know, but also as if she already knew the answer.

"I *know* I *can* do it, but that doesn't mean I *want* to."

"I can't say I completely understand that mindset. I would give anything to curdle some blood without consequence right now. Are you going soft on me?"

I pushed off the windowsill and moved to my bed. "Not at all, but I don't want to be used and then thrown away by angels."

"Did Nicholas give you any indication on what this would mean for you afterwards? I mean, regardless of what happens with Lilith, Purgatory will always be there," she inquired.

"He claims I'll be fine, but his word is pretty shit until he can make a fucking choice on what side he wants to follow."

Elise slid back towards her headboard. "You think he's playing into their hands?"

I shrugged. "Perhaps."

"Nicholas does understand that your dagger will need to make an appearance?"

"Yeah."

"And he hasn't told anyone that he has it or that you brought it with you?"

"No."

"Well, I may not want to put my entire trust in him or his little blonde lap dog, but I commend him on that." Elise lifted her hands behind her head, pressing her head into her palms. "I'm jealous you at least got laid before shit hits the fan here." I let myself fall face first onto the mattress, laying prone against the bed, my sigh muffled. "I can't say whether or not you fought like you say you did, but I'll choose to believe you had some sort of push back, maybe a few swift punches at that sharp jaw of his."

I turned my face, my cheek pressed against the cool crisp sheets. Her eyes were closed, but she opened one when she felt me looking at her. "You're insufferable." I joked.

She shrugged her shoulder. "So, 8 to 10?"

I pulled my eyebrows together, pushing myself off the bed and climbing in the middle to sit. "8 to 10?"

Elise stretched her arm out between her legs and wiggled it. "Inches."

"Ugh, Elise I don't know. I didn't happen to have a ruler with me to get an accurate measurement."

"Damn. Well, bigger than you thought? Bigger than the number in my head?"

I pondered this for a moment. I hadn't really let my mind wander into that territory. I mean I had thought about it, but now, I *thought about it*. "I would say bigger, if you must know."

"It's not that I *must* know, it's that you *will* tell me. Simple."

"Is that how it works?" I answered, sarcastically.

She waved her hand dismissively. "Was it what you imagined?"

"Imagined?"

"Don't fucking pretend like you didn't fantasize about him fucking you until you couldn't move. You do it in your sleep, you do it when you're awake, and you literally do it when he's around so much, I wonder why you don't just orgasm at the sound of his voice."

I lifted my eyes to the ceiling. "That's fucking ridiculous. You make me sound like I'm a love-struck freak."

She started making gagging noises. "Love? Yeah no, but you *were* someone who needed to get some dick and you did, so for that, I should give him a high five."

"I don't think he wants anyone to know, which I'm not shocked about. He seemed almost surprised after it was over."

"Surprised that he made someone orgasm?" It was my turn to reach behind for a pillow to chuck at her. Elise pushed out her bottom lip in a pout "So, I can't tell Blondie about your naked encounter? The look on his stupid fucking face would really make my year. I could honestly die the happiest demon."

I shook my head and pushed my legs underneath the covers. I let my head softly hit my pillow and watched as the light from Elise's lamp clicked off. "Thanks for being a solid friend."

Suddenly, it was like the air had been sucked out of the room, the silence growing. The sky was pretty much completely dark, so I couldn't make out her silhouette in her bed. All I could hear was her steady and solid breathing.

One long inhale in.

One long inhale out.

In. Out. In. Out.

"Elise?" I started to call out, but she cut me off so quickly, it made me suck in a breath.

"We aren't friends Dani. I made that clear a long time ago. In a game of survival, if it ever came down to just you and me, I'll always pick myself and have no regrets about my choice. I wouldn't mourn your loss, nor would I hold onto your memory. Friends are for pathetic fuckwits who think that being together is better than being apart. I don't need you. Don't call me that again."

I was on the verge of saying something, but I bit my tongue. Why had she come with me to Heaven's Gate in the first place then? I knew if I asked, she would send a whole new wave of rage at me, so I remained silent, wrapping the covers tighter around my shoulders. There were things I didn't know about her and maybe never would.

A few moments passed before I heard the rustling of sheets. I heard creaking, as if to tell me she was repositioning herself. Her voice rang out, causing my slow drift to sleep to end.

"You are aware Lilith usually shows her face in her plans, one way or another? The fact she hasn't for this long, especially when her prized pupil leaves, means something."

"We already know someone is working with her, or *for* her."

"I know, but just keep your fucking head on straight, because someone is watching us. If Lilith can't do it, then someone else is."

I nodded even though she couldn't see it. "We know how you feel about Jonah, Elise. We get it."

"Jonah or no Jonah, I don't trust any of them. They have hardly given me reason to. Lilith is trying to destroy this place from the inside out and they're just too stupid to see it. I swear Dani, I won't be in the middle of it when it all goes to shit. Whatever you find out tomorrow could either fuck us or help us, remember that."

"Where is this all coming from?" I asked, staring up at the dark ceiling.

"Have fun with your angel all you want, but don't forget for a fucking second *who* you are...*what* you are," she said in a lower voice, ignoring my question.

"I couldn't if I tried," I replied, waiting for her response, but all that came was silence. I felt my eyes slowly close, letting my mind attempt to settle, but I knew it would never reach that level of rest. My head was never quiet enough for a night of blissful slumber. There was always a voice in my head that never quieted. There was a warmth to it I didn't understand, but it mumbled something to me. When I closed my eyes completely, whatever it was became brighter, as if it was trying to push to the surface, as if something was holding it back, but I never considered it too much to care. I didn't have time to care. So, I pushed it back further into my head and watched as it retreated to wherever it came. Just like I always did.

"YOU REALLY KNOW HOW TO MAKE A GIRL FEEL SPECIAL, DON'T YOU," I SAID, straining to move my wrists around in the golden handcuffs. Reese had all but grabbed my hands and shoved them into the metal contraptions this morning. I had asked him why I had to wear them, but I got no response, only an eyebrow raise and the jingle of the handcuffs in response.

His blonde hair fell in waves around his shoulders, and he had tucked part of it behind one of his ears. I couldn't help but notice the way his white shirt fit against his chest, how his arms filled out the quarter-length sleeves, his bow strapped to his back. He took a step back, looking down the hall and tilted his head for me to follow him out.

"Bring her back in one piece, Blondie, or I'll make sure you end up in many," Elise said, loud enough for Reese to stop and roll his tense shoulders.

We had made our way down an array of staircases and before I knew it, we were almost out back. Reese was about two steps ahead of me during the journey and I couldn't help but stare at the back of his head, knowing he could feel my stare like a slow burn.

"Can you not stare at me?"

"Where else would you like me to look?" I asked.

Reese shook his head. "Fuck if I know. Anywhere else."

"But the back of your head is so pretty," I said in the most girlish voice I could conjure.

I was just ignored. We passed sentries that nodded to Reese, going about their duties. There were a few who kept their eyes on me, and it took everything in me not to laugh at how ridiculous they were. We went down another flight of stairs, the hallway even darker this time.

Reese made a sharp right at the end of the hallway, and I had to hustle to keep up with him. The minute we turned, the air grew a bit colder, causing me to stop. Down the hall, I could see a large metal door, clearly steel, with two bronze handles. There was nothing remotely special about the door, but I knew what lay behind it was something entirely different. I stopped when I finally stood in front of it. The air around us chilled further, but not enough to make me shiver. Reese walked up next to me, completely unfazed by what I was feeling.

I looked down, noticing a tiny slit at the bottom of the door. Small puffs and whirls of smoke danced out of it. They encircled my ankles and then dissipated, leaving a phantom touch in their wake. He pressed on the handle, gold flecks wrapping themselves around his hand, white flecks close behind. I heard the crank and ticks of locks unhinging and bolts loosening.

I stared up at the side of his face, seeing the small bits of stubble that settled along his jawline and underneath. "Nicholas seems to be handling our presence here just fine. Why are you so unwilling to just trust we have absolutely nothing to do with this? It must be exhausting harboring all that resentment."

I heard a final pop, and he grabbed my arm, pulling me back as the door started to shift open and more smoke poured out in waves. Reese sucked in a large breath and blew it out through his nose. "Nick can do whatever he wants. He can think whatever he wants. I just don't trust you as far as I can throw you."

"I haven't done anything underhanded to make you second guess me."

"You haven't really told me where you stand in all this to begin with, nor do I really give a fuck, so the next best thing is to get you in there, let you do whatever it is you do, and hope that the whole realm doesn't come tumbling down in your wake." He looked down at me, lifting an eyebrow and waiting for me to say something back. I started to answer him, but he put up a hand to silence me as the door came to a halt.

"You aren't one to ask the hard questions, are you?" I said under my breath, as I looked examined the gold handcuffs decorating my wrists.

"Excuse me?" His hazel eyes stared down at me as I gave him my lazy attention.

"I don't know, you just seem to go with whatever is easiest, which, in my humble opinion, isn't always the best option. I would go as far as saying that *that* very nonchalant way of thinking could be your realm's impending downfall. *Not* me."

Reese pressed his lips together, hard enough for me to see his jaw clench. I stood my ground and waited for him to say another word. He clucked his tongue and clasped my arm, dragging me to the other side of the door. I heard the door starting to rumble as it closed us in. A thin fog surrounded our ankles, slowly making its way up our legs and spilling out around us. This place didn't have the wet, damp feeling the tunnel to the Divine Library—no, it felt worse. The air was stale, and I had to adjust my breathing as we settled. The walls were a dull gray stone, fixtures on the wall that would be lit to create a pathway for the sentries. Our footsteps echoed loudly, making me realize no one could ever escape this place on foot.

Ahead of us, I could see a smaller version of the first door, a small glass window at the center of it, two men on the other side. I couldn't make them out, but I could hear their muffled voices as we got closer. Reese stood in front of me, rapped his knuckles against the door, then looked through the window. I heard one of the men on the other side chuckle, but then the bolts and unlocking clicks rang in my ears. Reese pulled the door open and swung me to the other side. I blew my hair out of my face as I gave him an annoyed look.

A click sounded as he closed the door behind us. Reese and one of the men patted each other on the back and Reese said something quietly that I couldn't hear. The man subtlety nodded past my direction. I thoroughly hated the idea of being left out, so I turned around to see if I could get a glimpse of what he was gesturing to when I collided with a hard chest. A muscled, hard, familiar chest.

I looked up, tilting my head slightly at Nicholas's overtly awkward but unreadable expression. I had a feeling I had the same look all over my face. I dropped my eyes down his body, noticing he was wearing the same clothes from yesterday, aside from a black bomber jacket. His hair looked like he had run his hands through it repeatedly until his scalp hurt. I saw the small speckles of a bruise on his jaw from where I'd punched him. I saw the start of every sentence he wanted to say when he opened his mouth a little, but nothing came out. I didn't miss the way his eyes ran over me, as if scanning and remembering everything that happened.

"You are the biggest shit for making me do this," Reese growled, coming up behind me and breaking our eye contact. Nicholas blinked from me rapidly and focused on his best friend.

"I had other things to take care of. Besides, your part is over so you can stop whining."

"I don't whine," Reese argued, motioning for me to follow as they walked down the hall. "I'm not going anywhere, especially when you're letting her use that...thing."

I narrowed my eyes as they walked a few paces in front of me.

"How else do you expect this to work, huh? Did you want me to explain a demonic weapon got in and I knew about it this whole time? Also, you knew about it and didn't say anything when I told you." Nicholas shot question after question at his friend.

Reese let out a loud huff of irritated defeat. "I get it, okay, fuck. I'm just saying, I'm not leaving you alone with whatever is in that cell, our demon companion, and that *thing*."

"I never knew you cared so much," Nicholas joked, squeezing Reese's shoulder.

"I don't. I'm doing it for your dad, so he won't say I didn't try to save you from an untimely death." Reese pushed his palm against Nicholas's face, making him step to the side.

I almost—*almost*—smiled seeing them play around with each other. I tried to check out the situations behind each door we passed, but none of them had windows on them. Sentries passed us here and there, but no one else came into sight. There were name-plates on the doors, all labeled as holding rooms. As we passed one, a loud bang came from the other side, causing the wood to vibrate. My head shot towards the sound, but I made no move to retreat from it.

"The wood is fibered with strong magic from the inside out. Whatever it is, it isn't getting out," Nicholas noted as he kept walking. He had his head tilted so that he could talk to me without looking at me.

They stopped at yet another steel door with a brass handle, this one with a nameplate that read *Ethereal Bastille Cells: Authorized Personnel Only*. The plate was gold, but rusted. Nicholas began to cast his own magic to open the door, the handle glowing like it was burning.

"What happened to your face?" Reese asked, making room for the door to open.

Nicholas absently reached up to his jaw, letting his fingertips graze the bruise. "Nothing."

"Nothing? Train too hard or something?" Reese inquired, reaching behind him and grabbing me so I followed them through. "You don't usually walk away from training with any evidence. I can count on one hand how many times it's actually happened."

Nicholas cleared his throat and rubbed the back of his neck but didn't say anything.

I tried to hold in my chuckle. The best I could do was keep my mouth closed and let my shoulders move up and down at my internal laughter. That laughter ceased the moment I entered the room. The smoke from before didn't creep around my thighs, staying low to the floor. The room was a big open space with the same gray dull stones, but without an echo as we walked. It was utter silence, as if the prisoners deemed even a fraction of a breath worthy. I started to feel something I hadn't felt in a long while since being at Heaven's Gate.

That feeling was pain, so thick I could almost suffocate on it. Suffering followed close behind, and it soothed the heat the pain left along my skin. I knew my dagger was here, and my fingers ached to get to it.

"Is it much farther?" The cuffs started to bite at my wrists as I jostled them in my newfound need to do this job with all the power Reese feared I had.

Reese stopped in the middle of the room. "Nope. Your demonic little friend's room is right down that hall." He pointed to the path on my left. I looked past him, further into the area, noticing it went on like this for quite some time, a sentry at every open entrance.

They began to walk down the path, and I kept close behind. The closer we got to the prisoners' room, the more time seemed to slow down, and I had to bite the inside of my cheek to keep myself together. I knew a demon was close and I knew it was stubborn. It was in the air; no wonder they'd had a hard time with this one. This demon wasn't scared or confused or even forthcoming. It was posed and strong. It was a challenge, for lack of a better word. The door came into view, and it wasn't the same steel as the others. It was all gold, silver bolts around the trimmings, no handle. I cracked my neck, suddenly wanting this more than anything.

I hadn't heard what the two angels were speaking about before we got to the golden door, but my mind halted and my eyes flicked up to him when I heard Reese speak. "All I'm saying is I think you'd be a lot happier if you got laid."

I sucked in a sharp breath right as Nicholas let out a choked laugh. It was strained, but if Reese suspected anything, he didn't show it. Those few words had me tumbling back to that now-tainted training room. I remembered the look on his face with every thrust, the way he groaned in the deepest part of his throat right before he came.

"Yeah, let me just contain our demon problem and I'll get right on that."

Reese chuckled. "You should -- I know plenty of girls who would love to train you."

The light was dim all the way down this hall, but I could see Nicholas roll his eyes before turning to face me. He took a short step so he was right in front of me, his breathing even.

"We're going to be right outside. No one else will bother you," he explained, reaching inside his jacket.

My dark eyes followed his movement, and I fixated on the

weapon he pulled from his inner jacket pocket. It felt like decades since I'd last laid eyes on it. The curve of the metal, the sharp indentations along one side; I'd missed it. Only I could hear it sing a soft, compelling melody to me. It was a song we both knew and we were continuously writing together.

"Dani?" Nicholas regained my attention with my name on his lips. Reese removed the handcuffs, giving me a stern and pointed look that said any *funny business and I'll run an arrow through your chest.* I gave him my best tight-lipped smile before he moved back towards the corner, a few feet away from us, letting himself be shrouded in darkness.

I twirled my wrists before reaching my hand out to take what belonged to me. Nicholas held it just out of reach, hesitation in his eyes. I tilted my head to the side. "I know what I'm doing, Nicholas, I promise."

I let my hand ghost along his, ever so slightly touching his knuckles, fingers, then letting the tips touch my dagger. I felt my eyes flutter closed at the contact. I closed my hand around it, but he still refused to let go. He looked at me as if trying to decide if this was a good idea.

"It's way too late for a morality check," I stated, looking him up and down, letting my eyes linger a bit longer on his crotch. I felt my thighs squeeze together from the thought of it inside of me. "Far, far too late."

He followed my eyes, a vein in his neck pulsing. "It was a mistake." He said it in a low voice, so low I had to lean in to hear him. Our hands still barely touched on the hilt of my dagger, neither of us wanting to let go.

I mirrored his low tone. "Oh, of course it was." I shuffled my feet so I was closer to him, so close that I could smell him again, but this time, I focused in on every scent I could catch. The ends of my lips tilted upward. "Is that why you still smell like me?"

His eyes dilated right as he let the dagger slip from his hands and into mine. He watched as I rolled the hilt around in my palms and ran the pad of my index finger down the silver metal. He opened his mouth slightly to challenge my words, but I didn't let him.

I placed my hand against his chest and whispered, "I'm flattered you loved the scent of me so much, you couldn't bear to remove it, but you don't seem like the type to make the same mistake twice." I bit my bottom lip and watched as he stared directly at the movement, as if he was remembering the way my lips felt against his. "Or maybe you are."

He broke away after a moment and moved to the door, shaking his head as he placed his palm on the door. It moved open, the tension in the room beyond dispersing around us.

Reese let out a low whistle. "You've got thirty minutes, no more, no less."

"Thirty minutes?"

"From what I've heard, you should be able to do it in five, but Nick here decided you might be a little rusty."

Nicholas stopped the door from opening any more than necessary. "Get as much information as you can get, that's all we ask"

I nodded, placing the dagger in the side pocket of my leggings. "I got it, thanks." Inside the room, there was nothing but a chair and a demon tied to it.

"We'll come in when time's up. We'll be right outside," he said, a hint of caring in his voice.

"I got it," I repeated, not giving him another look before disappearing behind the door. I heard it slowly close behind me. I was finally alone...sort of. The room had the same stones as the rest of the prison. There was a cement bench protruding out of the left wall with cobwebs hanging from the corners.

I looked over at the demon tied to the chair. It sent a wave of déjà vu over my body as I remembered all those souls I had torn in Purgatory. I remembered all the blood and the screams; it almost made me smile now. There was a blindfold over its eyes, and if I listened closely, it was humming something softly.

I stepped closer to it. Closer, closer, and closer.

A familiar scent hit me, and I paused. It was notably familiar, but it wasn't at all what I expected. I smelled boredom; it floated in the air and through my nostrils as if this demon had physically just shrugged its shoulders. It was a man, by the looks of it.

"Finally. I was wondering when they would send you," he said, his voice smooth. I knew that voice.

I reached toward the blindfold and yanked it off. He tilted back at the motion and shook his head. A few of his inky black curls bounced as they settled back near the tops of his ears. His skin was tan and dusty from the cell's dirt. I narrowed my eyes at the face I had seen so many times during my early years in Purgatory, before Elise had made her entrance. He was the first teacher I'd had. At the command of Lilith, he'd happily stepped aside when Elise strutted in and told him to get lost. I had only seen him from time to time after that.

He looked up at me with those deep green eyes I knew so well. They never held any care or passion for me, but they did have a sense of chaos I used to adore.

"Cullen?" His name came from me laced with confusion and a hit of anger.

He smirked at me with amusement. "I'm surprised you remember me."

I held the crumpled blindfold in my hand and squeezed tightly, hoping the dirty cloth would somehow disintegrate. "You are quite unforgettable, if I remember correctly."

He laughed. "You seem upset."

I walked around the chair, letting my fingertips glide across the top of the back. "Me? Upset? No, why would you think that?" Cullen being here didn't surprise me. He was, after all, one of Lilith's right hands, always there and willing to do whatever she wished with no questions asked and no hesitation.

Cullen looked straight ahead. "I know you expected to find a demon less familiar to you, but I have to say, I'm so very happy to see your face again."

"Under these circumstances, I can't honestly believe that."

"You don't have to believe it; I say it as a fact. I am quite joyous at our current reunion."

I rolled my eyes, slipping my hand into my pocket. Leaning against the chair, I let the dagger dangle from my fingers near the side of his face. The feel of the weapon in my hands, knowing all the damage I could do with it, sent a rush of pure dark energy through my veins. Cullen was a tall demon, not quite as tall as Nicholas, but his head peeked over the top of the chair, allowing me to lean down and let my lips reach his ear. "How about you make this reunion joyous for both of us and tell me why you came through the portal? Tell me how?"

Cullen blew out a breath. "Oh, come on now, Dani. You think that it's going to work like that? I am shattered by your underestimation of my resilience."

"I was hoping you would just be forthcoming."

"Your mistake."

I pushed off the chair and made my way to one side, changing my hold on my dagger and letting my fingers wrap tightly around the hilt. I let the curved point hit his cheek, watching as the skin sunk in a bit at the pressure. I pushed the dagger harder into his skin and watched it pierce the flesh. Blood trickled down slowly, and my skin started to heat at the sight. He winced at the pain, but otherwise kept his same stance.

"Lilith sent you here, correct? She had the Enchanters help her."

Cullen tried to shift away from the dagger. "The Enchanters are no secret. None of what you say is knowledge unknown to you. I wasn't sent to do any harm, which may come as a surprise to you."

I pulled my dagger back, walking in front of him. I hovered over him and watched as he looked at me with attentive focus. Blood dripped down one side of his face. "So, you're telling me she sent you here with no malicious intent? What about the other demon?"

"That is what I'm saying. I did not harm a single little angelic figure. And let me tell you, it was hard to hold back. Lilith commanded I don't touch anyone." He shrugged as best he could while strapped to the chair. "As for this other demon, that's something else entirely."

I let my dagger rest on his other cheek, curving the hooked side near his skin. "Something else?"

His eyes sparkled with delight. "Oh yes, quite a mistake, that one."

I let the curve slice through his skin swiftly. It started leaking blood, but he showed no signs of discomfort. "Care to share?" I sliced another line under the previous one.

"Lilith is quiet in the way she works, you know, waiting for the right opportunity, even if that means waiting. Everything lined up so perfectly I almost can't believe it."

"What the fuck are you talking about?"

"I used to think she made a mistake with you, but it seems I was wrong."

"Staying on topic was never your strong suit, was it?" I held my dagger downward and slammed it into his thigh. Cullen let out a cry before regaining his composure and plastering a smile back on his face. I noticed the way dark smoke formed around my feet and legs, crawling up my arms from the dagger. I had to hold out for a little longer. "I'm trying to give you a chance to tell the truth before I have to make you. As much fun as that would be, I'm trying to be nice."

"We both know you were never your best when you were nice. It makes you weak. You are anything but weak, my dear. Lilith made sure of it."

"Lilith sent the other demon, but that one got killed. Did it not mean to do harm as well? Were you some kind of test to see if the portal would let you through?" I ignored his words and focused on my task. I kept my dagger in his thigh, applying a slow amount of pressure.

His breath was slightly ragged, but he maintained his composure. "The delightful angels have heard all this before. I am not without information, but there are things that need to play out. Telling you would ruin the fun of the reveal."

"Lack of information really won't do here." I ripped my dagger out from his thigh and slammed it into the other one, closer to his inner thigh this time. I lifted it out and ripped through his skin again near the outside of his thigh. The pressure I felt was growing, almost a delicious suffocation.

He smacked his lips together. "You think you scare me with your torture. I come from the same place you do, love. I take pleasure in watching you work."

"Tell me what I want to know, Cullen! Tell me who is helping her! Tell me why she's doing this! Tell me something!" In a swift movement, I took hold of my dagger and let the hooked end hang over his ear before I ripped it from his head. He let out a piercing scream as blood poured from his head. His ear dropped to the floor, and I watched it silently.

Through the pain I saw in his eyes, he started to chuckle through sharp breaths. "I didn't think you would be what she wanted, but I was *so* wrong."

I pinned my dagger to his throat, admitting to myself I was done with toying around. I let the darkness settle itself around his neck like a noose. I watched his Adam's apple bob as he swallowed against my blade. I wanted my answers, and I wanted them now.

"You will tell me what you know, and you will do it with a smile on that smug face of yours." I let my compelling power, the power my dagger provided me, surround him. I watched as it seeped into every wound. I waited for the words to spill out of his mouth, for all the truths we had been waiting for to expel themselves from his throat. I waited.

Waited.

Nothing.

The confusion on my face must have delighted him. Even though his face was bloody, Cullen still looked as if he could beam from ear to ear. "You don't know Lilith at all, it seems."

I pressed my dagger further into his throat, watching as the skin started to tear. "Tell me!" I could hear myself yelling. Why wasn't this working?

"That won't work on me, Soul Seether," Cullen taunted. "Lilith gave you that power, and she gave me the power to withstand it."

I pulled the dagger away from him, standing up straight, tapping the metal to my cheek. I knew his blood was now smeared on my skin, but I didn't care.

"That look of pure bewilderment does make these wounds worth it," Cullen sneered, making my chest heave.

"This was all worthless, wasn't it?" I asked, more to myself than to him.

"Perhaps. Perhaps not. At least we know you're as strong as ever."

"You understand you aren't going back to Purgatory, right?" I asked.

"I am fully aware of my fate. I would not have it any other way."

I could feel my anger start to boil up, anger mixed with a high concentration of irritation. "You would do all this to simply be a pawn? All the Enchanters in Purgatory are okay with being simple pawns in your game?"

He cackled a sickeningly evil laugh. "What do you think you are?"

"Excuse me?" I swiftly shoved my dagger into his shoulder and stepped back, leaving it lodged.

He spoke through gritted teeth. "You think you aren't a pawn to all sides?"

"You're talking about the angels."

Cullen let out a grunt and took a few deep breaths. "You have come to enjoy their company, haven't you?"

I didn't answer. I let my face remain neutral, even though my entire body was overheating. I no longer felt the weight of my dagger, but that didn't mean the darkness inside of me had left along with it.

"It's a shame you have no idea who to trust. You're stuck in the middle of everyone's shit and you don't even know if you're an asset or a liability? Maybe one of the angels isn't so...*angelic.* Right under your nose and you can't figure it out before it's too late."

I remained quiet, standing just a few steps in front of him, watching as the blood from his legs stained his pants and dripped onto the floor, pooling at his feet.

"It'll be a pity when a mess of shit and blood replaces them. That day will be glorious!" Cullen shouted, grabbing the arms of the chair as best he could.

I snatched the dagger, yanking it out of his shoulder and watching as thick, red blood spurted out. I grabbed a fistful of his hair and pulled it back, his head forced to look up at me. I was practically straddling him as I placed the hooked tip right at his throat. "Shut up, you insufferable fucking shit."

"You think that *they* won't toss you aside when this is all said and done? This place will never care about you as much as Lilith does. She is trying to make things even, make things better. Angels have always wanted for themselves," Cullen spat, looking past me towards the door where Nicholas and Reese stood. He knew they were here.

"And you're so much better? I'm aware of where I stand with them."

Cullen licked his thin lips. "I'm not so sure. You certainly smell like you're undecided."

I tugged his hair further, exposing his tan throat even more. Nicholas still had my scent on his body, but I didn't think his scent would still be on mine.

"Sleeping with one isn't going to change their fate or yours. Your fate was written the day you were brought to Purgatory. It's amazing how little you know about yourself."

I leaned down closer to his face. "You don't know what the fuck you are talking about."

I heard magic clicking behind me. My time was coming to an end.

"Their end is going to be the same either way! You need to be here for all the reasons you don't understand! They will end up just like their precious little messenger friend. Better yet, you'll be the one to do it. She will get what she wants, no matter how much you fight her!"

I felt my entire mind blank, and my vision was no longer full of ordinary color. I wasn't in control of myself, but I was. I could never find the correct way to describe the feeling of losing yourself but having a piece of it still there to watch the chaos from the inside. I moved my dagger to the left and sliced across his neck, hitting it deep and hearing the ripping of flesh. Blood tore through the opening, down his neck and onto my face, splattering all over my shoulders and chest.

I felt my rough breathing, saying to myself over and over that he deserved it. I said it to myself as if I needed reassurance. I should have taken his soul, made him suffer. He had implanted the image of me murdering Nicholas and Reese and everyone else...for what? Why was I the focus of Lilith's plan? If the angels were her targets, why was I so important?

I heard Nicholas and Reese come through the door, but I also felt them pause at the sight. I was still on top of Cullen, whose head was slumped back against the chair, the front of his shirt covered in dark blood. I looked over my shoulder, feeling my hand tighten around my dagger.

Reese's eyes widened as he looked at me. He moved his hand slowly towards his chest, prepared to unstrap his bow and make good on his promise. Nicholas crept toward me, one of his hands outstretched. "Dani?" he said cautiously.

I made no movement. I just stared at him, watching as he got closer. Eventually, he was stepping in the blood at the foot of the chair. "Dani?" he called again, still with the calm, cautious tone. He wrapped his hand around my fist. "Let it go. It's done."

The warmth of his hand and fingers rushed through me in a continuous wave. My tight shoulders started to melt and uncoil. I heard his voice again. "Dani, let it go."

The way he said my name made me blink. Blink. Blink until I saw everything for what it was. I saw the gray stones of the four walls. I saw my blood-stained hand. I saw Nicholas's brown eyes looking down at me with concern and just a small bit of unnerved fear.

I let go of my dagger, watching him quickly remove it from sight and back to the inside pocket of his jacket. I pulled back from Cullen's body and planted my feet on the ground, a shot of vertigo hitting me like it always did when I came down from one of my dagger's highs.

"You look like shit," Reese pointed out, walking over to Cullen and pushing his limp head forward so his chin now rested on his chest.

"We need to get you out of here and err...cleaned up," Nicholas said, reaching his hand out to me. I looked down, tilting my head to the side. My hand wanted to reach out, but I didn't know why. I let Nicholas pull me out of the room, each of our footsteps leaving bloody marks on the floor. I looked back over to Cullen and tried to make sense of his words, even after his body left my view. Nicholas held my hand the entire way while I kept my eyes trained on the floor.

Cullen said I was a pawn. That rubbed me the wrong way, since I had no idea what I was here for. Lilith was using me to achieve something. If Lilith was using me as a pawn, then I was the worst kind of pawn.

A dangerous one.

CHAPTER FOURTEEN

NICK

It was raining. Rain that splattered against the glass of my window. It was soft and delicate, the kind of rain you could let yourself fall asleep listening to. The wind picked up, but it was nothing that would hinder an angel from flying. I watched the drops of water hit my window as I sat on my bed, letting my elbows press against my knees. The sky was starting to darken as the rain continued and it was only mid-afternoon. I had a feeling the weather was about to get even worse as the hours went by.

I had remained in my room once we took Dani back, not missing the way Elise stared both of us down but said nothing. We had stopped in at a washroom to let her clean herself up, but small remnants of blood remained, as if tethered to her in some way. Reese had tried to start conversations with me when we headed back to our own rooms, but I wasn't in the mood. I didn't try to get anything out of her as I held her hand the entire way back to the more delightful part of The Skies, but I could feel the way her hand tightened around mine, the soft feel of her fingers and the way they'd hooked around my own, as if she would lose her grip at any moment. She didn't let my hand go immediately once I deposited her into her room. She had her back turned, my hand still in hers, and she squeezed. One quick squeeze. A squeeze that meant she would be fine, or maybe like a pinch— letting her know this was reality, that she was okay.

I was alright with either.

I had said my goodbyes to Reese, kicked off my shoes, and settled into my bed with my clothes on. I was exhausted. It had only been a short amount of time, but I honestly couldn't remember when life had been simple and all I had to worry about was my next training session or the Animus Seeking. I let my forearm drop over my eyes as I let my mind drift to that place I promised myself I wouldn't go. I was completely fucked.

I kept myself together when Reese brought her through that door, but I couldn't help looking at her. *Really* looking at her. I looked at her curls that flowed over her shoulders and remembered how they'd looked splayed around her head as she writhed underneath me. Her bottom lip had almost jutted out in a pout, making me want to take that lip between my teeth and pull her into me. I *knew* she knew I was looking, and that made it all the more embarrassing. It was a little unnerving, thinking she was remembering the same thing.

Reese and I had always been different when it came to girls and dating and sex; he was the promiscuous playboy whose longest relationship was with *me*, whereas I was the one who had monogamous sex, with just a few random hookups thrown in that I tried to forget about.

I wasn't the type to do something like this, but here I was— having done it. I had crossed that line I hadn't even known was a line I needed to be worried about. It had happened literally a day and a half ago and I had already jerked off twice to that memory. The way she kissed, the way the skin of her stomach and thighs felt against my hands, the little sounds she made every single time I pushed into her. The way she felt around my cock was...fuck. I didn't want to have to jerk off a third time, so I forced myself to sleep.

I woke to the sound of rain, the same continuous rain I looked at now, and a knock at my door, an obnoxious, repetitive knocking, almost as if whoever was on the other side was trying to create a beat with their knuckles. I knew exactly who it had been.

The same person was currently pacing the length of my room and talking about something. A loud clap startled me, causing my gaze to shift from the window and look directly at Reese. He had his hands together inches from my face, his lips pressed in a hard line.

"Nick, did you even hear a word I said?" he asked, annoyed. I pushed his hands out of my face and shook my head. "Well let me sum everything up. We have a meeting with Jonah today and we have no idea what our demonic princess is going to say."

"So?" I shrugged. "We don't really have a say in what comes out of their mouths."

He rolled his eyes. "This is different. What if she knows everything and it's worse than we thought? What if she knows nothing and we just risked our dicks with that dagger bullshit?"

"Reese, calm down. If what she had to say was serious, she would have told us."

He narrowed his eyes at me. "Are you sure? You saw her, right? Black eyes, dark smoke, another guy's blood all over her face with his throat open. Whatever he said triggered her, so I'm going to go with whatever he said wasn't good."

Reese had a point. I had seen her face when I walked into that cell. Through the black wispy smoke, I had seen the distant look on her face. The whites of her eyes were gone, and she was breathing so heavy, I thought she would pass out. She seemed to settle at the sound of my voice; she had snapped out of her madness and come back.

"Whatever it is, we'll deal with it. Jonah will deal with it. It will be dealt with." I sounded like a crazy person.

Reese leaned back against the wall opposite me, crossing his arms. "How much sleep did you get last night?"

I rubbed my fingers against my eyes. "Enough." The way my body felt, I would have said it felt like I had only just fallen asleep. I peeked up at him to see him regarding me carefully. He was taking in my day and half old clothes and distraught facial features.

"Take a shower."

"I'm fine."

"I didn't ask if you were fine. Take a shower." He had a serious tone to his voice.

I firmly rooted myself onto my bed, refusing to move. He stared back at me, equally ready to stand in front of me for hours. A small smile played at his lips.

"Reese."

"Nick."

I let out a defeated groan, but I knew he was right. A hot shower would do me good, as long as I removed any thoughts of a bratty, petite, curly-haired demon whose tight pussy gripped my cock like she owned it. No, nope. That thought *definitely* didn't help.

Reese walked over to me and laid a hand on my shoulder. "Do you remember when things were normal?"

I let out a laugh that was meant to be small but ended up being loud, and Reese let out one of his own. I glanced at him, noticing the way his eyebrows were so blonde, they almost disappeared into his face. There was no spoken rule about fucking demons, but it was a rule that never needed to be expressed fully— until now. If it was a rule, I'd already broken it and I...didn't regret it?

I might regret the way I went about it. I didn't mean to be as relentless as I was with her. She hadn't seemed to mind and there was a small part of me that knew she wouldn't. There was an even smaller part of me that wanted to take my time with her.

"Nick, can you give me an honest answer to what I'm about to ask?"

I blinked, bringing myself back into the conversation. He looked serious now. "I'll always give you an honest answer."

Reese chewed at his bottom lip for a moment before opening his mouth. "Are you still suspicious of Jonah?" The corners of his eyes crinkled as he narrowed his gaze at me.

I wasn't expecting that. I never really knew what would come from Reese's mouth, but that wasn't what I was expecting. Reese had never once shown doubt about Jonah. He, like all of us, was indifferent towards any other executive, but Jonah was different. I had placed all my faith in the man since I moved here. When my father came back to The Skies after being away, he had a meeting with Jonah. I had been twelve and overly curious. I remember having the most erratic heartbeat knowing I was going to the place I'd dreamed about since I was old enough to hold a sword. Granted, I could hardly hold the blade over my head, but my father would smile at me each time I tried.

My father told me he had a meeting with the high executive and if I could behave, I could come along. I didn't do anything wrong, but I didn't know non-members of The Skies were not allowed to be involved with weapons anywhere near the building. My father had gone inside, telling me to stay put and that he would be right back. He'd been gone a total of two minutes and I was already getting anxious. The sentries stared down at me with watchful eyes.

They didn't unnerve me exactly, but they still caused me to walk away from that area and over to the lush green of the front courtyard. I knew I shouldn't have done it. I knew I should have just turned back and waited patiently for my father. The swords against the stone fixtures surrounding the courtyard instantly caught my eye, and Reese's voice peeked into my thoughts. He would pick one of the weapons up with no hesitation, no questions asked. I looked around and didn't see an angel that could likely claim them or stop my steps over to the shiny blades. I wrapped my fingers around one of the silver hilts and tried to pick it up. It was cold against my palms as I tried to lift it, realizing it was heavy as fuck.

I finally lifted it and wobbled a bit as I tried to find a good stance. Once I was settled, I felt a smile creep along my face and started slashing. The movements were slow, a bit off beat due to my swaying. I spun around and made a "hiyah" sound as I slashed, then again, the other way. I was in my own world. I laughed at my imaginary opponent when I heard a familiar voice.

"Nicholas!" my father shouted from the other side of the courtyard. He had two sentries beside him, and one snatched the sword from my hand. My body instantly missed the weight and the feel of the metal. The other one grabbed me by the shoulder and almost dragged me to my father. "I told you to wait. What in the hell were you thinking?"

I opened my mouth a little and then closed it in a straight line. I didn't have an answer. So, I shrugged. My father let out a huff and pulled me to the gates, telling me everything I currently know about the rules of The Skies. Soon after, I had come face to face with Jonah, saying *I'm sorry, sir* in the smallest of voices. I didn't really think much of the tension I felt when they were in a room together.

Ever since I got accepted into The Skies, I thought it would be smooth sailing. Jonah had always smiled at me with fondness as I trained. He had even taken the time to teach me other techniques my father hadn't. How could I not place my trust in this man? My father did...well, he did once upon a time.

I cleared my throat, realizing I had replayed a whole memory while Reese waited for an answer. I looked over at my best friend, who waited patiently for my response. He had one of his legs bent sideways and placed over his other knee, tapping his finger on this thigh.

I needed to answer honestly. That memory had a special place in my head, but it was starting to get clouded by doubts. If Reese was asking me this, any special memories he had were starting to get overcrowded with his own doubts, too.

I took a long breath. "I have suspicions."

Reese didn't make any sort of weird face or surprised noises. "Me too." Those two words almost came out pained as he tried to keep his face neutral.

I narrowed my eyes. "You?"

"I've said it before, and I'll say it again: I'm allowed to change my damn mind."

"Alright, fair, but you have fought for this idea that Jonah and everyone around him is innocent. You don't flip switches without a good reason."

Reese chewed on his bottom lip for a moment. "It doesn't mean I won't flip back, but something is bothering me. Do you remember when we snuck into the Divine Library and almost got caught?" I nodded, wondering where he was going with this. "Do you remember what they said? Jonah and Markus?"

I racked my brain for the words. Before I could think any further, Reese continued. "Jonah talked about explaining something to you eventually. Markus mentioned his favoritism."

I remembered that. "And you finally have thoughts on it, now?" I asked.

"I've always had thoughts on it, just not ones I wanted to discuss. Executives don't need to tell us lowly angels anything, but he sounded like it was something specific."

"That's a large assumption."

"Let's not insult my intelligence. We both know Jonah has had his eye on you since we got here. I may have defended him, but that doesn't mean I can't put two and two together."

I lifted my hands up in defeat and ran a hand through my hair. I stared at my palm, surprised my hair hadn't started falling out from all the stress.

"Nick, what if everything is a set-up?"

I slowly moved my eyes over to him. "What?"

Reese shook his head, mustering up some courage. "What if Jonah planned this whole thing...like he wants you to figure it out for...I don't know...malicious intent?"

"So, you think Jonah fucked up the portals, murdered Keegan, brought another demon into the fold, got that demon killed, and now what? He wanted Dani to torture that demon for...her benefit? What do Dani and Elise have to do with any of this? What's the end goal?"

Reese let out a groan. "I know, okay. It sounds fucking stupid, but it's plausible. He could have brought the demons here for his own undetermined reasons, seeing as he did say he was going to let them go and now he can't. Jonah has been mute about his time during the war or after Lilith got trapped in Purgatory. Maybe there is more to that story than he's letting on."

I tried to process his ideas. His words ran through me like a sharp blade to my stomach. None of us really knew much about Jonah or his past. We just knew him as he was today and my father pretty much refused to really speak about him other than a few sentences here and there.

"Where would I come into all of this?"

Reese shrugged. "You told me he and Maurice don't really speak anymore. Maybe that's something to consider. Jonah has done a lot for us, but the past can really fuck people up."

I've tried to press my father for answers, and he's given me ones he finds suitable, ones that will appease me, but still leave me as if I never got a real answer at all. My father only held his friends in the highest regard, so for someone to fallout with him like that, it needed to be something bigger than just a petty squabble. "The executives only know what he's telling them."

"He is who he is; of course they do." *Blind loyalty*, as my father put it. Was I no better?

"This meeting shouldn't just be about Dani, then." I stood up, nodding.

Reese pushed himself further up my bed, looking skeptical. "It shouldn't?"

I turned around to face him completely. "No. This is one fucked up mess and if we are going to move ahead with anything, we deserve some information. This has been a give and take with a lot of taking and no giving on their part."

"Well, we both know I'm all about the giving," Reese said with a wink.

I rolled my eyes. "Jonah has to tell us something or I'm done."

Reese widened his eyes. "You are gonna tell the highest executive that if he doesn't tell you something solid right then and there, then he can fuck right off? What about the demons?"

"I don't know." I hadn't thought that far ahead.

Reese extended his hand out, and I lifted him off the bed. He stretched, saying, "I like my stories with a little bit of mystery so that's good enough for me, as long as they go somewhere far away when this is all over." He was quick to question my decisions, but, in the end, equally as quick to stand by my side.

I gave a small smile, but it vanished quickly. That little place in my chest when I thought about Dani started to thump and I took a few small breaths to relieve it. Reese motioned his hand towards the bathroom.

"Take a shower, Nick. You stink."

I PRACTICALLY COUNTED EVERY FOOTSTEP UNTIL WE WERE AT THE BRIEFING room, one that a while ago would have made me feel bad for all the angels that would never get to see it. Most angels would only get up to the floor before the level with Jonah's office. He had his own special briefing room, opulent and beautiful. Reese and I had knocked and been ushered inside by the sentries, the weapons strapped to our backs echoing throughout an otherwise quiet room. Reese had insisted we have them, *"just in case."*

Jonah sat in the plush emerald chair that headed the long table. He stood up and motioned his hand towards the empty seats nearest him. It may have been a different briefing room, but the cast of characters were all the same. Ariel and Markus sat opposite us and gave us each a stark nod. Ariel was clearly annoyed, while Markus kept side-eyeing the other end of the table.

"Mr. Cassial, Mr. Diniel, please sit. We have much to discuss." Jonah patted the table.

I gave a quick look to Reese, who raised his eyebrows slightly and made his way towards one of the chairs. I followed, both of us removing our weapons and setting them down. He took the seat closest to Jonah, which I didn't mind. I could still get all my points across regardless of proximity. I moved behind him to take the chair next to Reese when I saw who graced the chair at the other end of the table.

Natalia.

Her black hair fell in waves around her shoulders, shoulders that remained poised and proper as she rested her clasped hands in her lap. Her dark skin seemed to glow, even though the light outside had dimmed due to the rain. She gave me a small, closed smile, which I returned, more confused than ever. I settled into my chair and almost melted into the velvet cushion. "What is she doing here?" I looked to Jonah, who casually nodded towards Natalia.

"She has been a vital piece in all of this, so why not have her as part of the discussion?"

Ariel cut in. "You seemed to think she was helpful enough when you made that unauthorized trip to Oculus."

I cleared my throat and gripped the arms of the chair. "Dwelling on the past isn't a good look on anyone."

"The rules are for a reason -- just because you are given special assignments and certain instructions doesn't mean you can do as you please." The disdain in his voice was clear, but it wasn't completely directed at me, but at anyone who fit that category.

"Gentleman, I would love to sit here and listen to you bicker, but I was brought here to speak of the current situation," Natalia said, her voice as smooth as honey.

Jonah rubbed his hands together. "Of course, Natalia is right. Now is not the time."

Ariel shook his head, leaning back into his seat, running a hand through his hair. The doors opened once again; two sentries stepped inside with two females in tow. We all faced in their direction and watched as Dani and Elise stepped up, wrists decorated with golden handcuffs. Elise blew a kiss at the sentry who unlocked hers, causing his face to twist in an awkward expression. Dani just looked at Natalia, eyes narrowed. Natalia gave them both a small wave as they walked to the seats next to us. Of course, there were no seats next to Ariel or Markus; they wouldn't want them near them. I felt my heart start to beat out of rhythm as I watched Elise take the seat closest to Natalia, letting her mouth drop when she felt the comfort of the chair. It was like everything slowed down when Dani easily slipped into the chair next to me, not looking in my direction as she crossed her legs, which were bare thanks to her shorts, giving me a prime view of her thighs and down her legs.

I had changed into a fresh navy t-shirt when I had gotten out of the shower, but I could have sworn I felt myself starting to sweat. The skin on her thighs seemed to be an even deeper shade of brown against her red shorts. My fingers twitched with the need to touch her and see that perfect place between her legs again. The plain black shirt she had on was doing way too much for her chest; I had to close my eyes for a moment and will myself not to look directly at her breasts. I had left her bra on when I fucked her, and right now, that was a terrible mistake.

"Perfect. Now that everyone has arrived, we can begin," Jonah announced.

I practically jolted my attention back to him, but not without noticing Dani was laughing under her breath. I tried to give her my best nonchalant look, but she just gave me a raised eyebrow that told me that my thoughts were not as private as I wanted them to be. She smiled and placed her elbow on the table, resting her head against her hand. Her face was so different from the face I had seen in the Ethereal Bastille, the face of someone so lost in their own darkness, they were practically begging for someone to pull them out. I hoped I never saw that look again.

Jonah started by bringing everyone up to speed. Dani and Elise just looked hopelessly bored. "I had enlisted Natalia to try and find our missing angel, Keegan Finley, but she was not able to locate him. I fear he is lost to us." Jonah explained. I looked over at Natalia, whose expression never changed; she just simply nodded. "She has informed me that she does not think he defected to Lilith's side." He nodded his head towards her.

Natalia placed her hands on the table. "Yes, his presence would feel fuller and livelier if he had. All I felt was just a hint of his last moments and then nothing."

Markus tapped his finger to his jaw. "You believe Keegan is dead?"

"Sadly, I do," Natalia answered. This whole conversation felt like déjà vu. Natalia didn't seem to mind playing along. She looked serious, as if this was the first time she had ever searched for Keegan, that this information was new to everyone's ears. Reese kicked me under the table and pulled his eyebrows together, telling me that we were on the same page.

"Murdered would be the best word for it," Elise chimed in, investigating her nails.

Everyone looked in her direction as she blew out a loud breath of amusement. She looked up from her nail beds and stretched her palm out, lifting her arched eyebrows up in question.

"You are also confirming he was murdered?" Markus questioned.

Elise looked over to Dani, then back to Markus. "Is that honestly a huge revelation? You can't truly think he would have made it out of there alive, especially if he met with Lilith."

Markus answered. "She could have tried to possess him somehow, used him against us."

Elise snorted. "You may not be able to see a possession with your fragile old eyes, but I certainly can. If he was out here stumbling around with the dark queen inside him, I would know." She rolled her eyes. "Keegan was a small part of something bigger."

"She's right," Natalia chimed in, causing Elise to smirk over. "Keegan was minuscule, a means to an end for Lilith."

"And what is her end, hmm?" Ariel huffed.

"To get rid of you," Elise answered casually.

I eyed Dani, who remained quiet. Her brown eyes were piercing into the table in front her. She blinked every so often, and her eyes would roam around the table, but that's all. She seemed to be in internal contemplation, as if considering the words she would say soon.

I overheard words thrown back and forth across the table as I removed my gaze from Dani. Ariel was getting heated, whereas Elise seemed to enjoy the show.

Elise dug her nails into the table. "I know her better than anyone and let me tell you: this is more than boredom. Lilith has been planning this comeback of hers for as long as I've known her, but *she* wouldn't kill Keegan. She would have kept him as bait, tortured him."

Markus scratched his head. "You don't think Lilith is the one who killed him?"

"Awe, how sweet. It seems someone is paying attention." She gave Markus a sinister smile before leaning back in her seat.

"How do we know you aren't in this with her? You came here of your own volition. Not many demons would do that without an ulterior motive," Ariel shot back.

Elise licked her lips but kept them closed, as if she didn't want to say more. Reese blew out a long breath next to me, his knee lightly hitting underneath the table as he bounced his leg. He was anxious. I was too, seeing as half the things being said were part of a bigger truth we were already aware of.

Jonah cleared his throat. "The demon coming through the portal didn't happen until after Keegan went missing. How do you suppose that correlates?"

I knew what I wanted to say: Keegan's key had opened the portal, with the help of an Enchanter who had been given the magic of other Enchanters in Purgatory to overshadow Natalia's magic. I wanted to say that the portal key was here, shrouded in a cloud of darkness. I wanted to push out of my chair and ask why he and my father didn't speak anymore, what he has been keeping from me all this time.

No. I had to stay on topic. This wasn't about me. I had no idea what the right approach was, but it didn't matter. I didn't get to formulate any more sentences, because Dani's voice rang out through the silence.

"It was an experiment. A test," she said softly, but with enough force that it caused even Natalia to break her practiced facial expression for a moment.

"A test?" Markus asked.

"The portal. She wanted to test the portal, to see if she could send them through it."

"And you know how?" Reese questioned, but realization dawned on him within the next moment, when she looked directly into his eyes.

"That's what that demon told you?" I leaned closer to her, hit in the face with cinnamon again. It was heady but sweet, as if she shampooed her hair with it.

She nodded, the small curls near her forehead swinging back and forth.

"And is it still..." Ariel started, but Dani quickly cut him off.

"He's dead." Her shoulders were tense, and she looked like she was physically trying to keep her hands from shaking under the table.

Jonah looked to me, as if this was something I should have told him, but I shook my head. "It's already taken care of. The mess is cleaned up." He gave me a curt nod and settled back in his seat.

"He knew this was going to happen, that you would capture him, that I would be the one to question him. He was ready for it all."

Markus treaded lightly. "You sound as if you knew him."

"I did."

Ariel let out a small chuckle. "Of course, she did. You put too much faith in these demons, Jonah. What makes you think they didn't discuss things she isn't telling us?"

"She killed him, isn't that enough?" I heard myself saying. It felt good coming out.

"Killing him means nothing, since I expected that anyway. Her awareness of who he was and her killing him aren't parallel to one another, Nicholas. Demons have no boundaries."

"Speak for yourself, you obnoxious piece of shit!" Elise yelled, slamming her hand on the table. The power of it reverberated through the wood.

Natalia spoke next. "Everyone please. Dani, did he say anything else?"

Dani swallowed. "He kept saying how you were all dead anyway or that you would end up like your messenger." Jonah closed his eyes but said nothing. "He called me a—" She stopped and shook her head, meeting every eye in the room, but stopping right at Jonah, as if wanting him to feel her words.

"A what?" Reese said, as if the suspense was too much for him.

She let her tongue stick out, wetting her bottom lip, and I shifted in my seat, pretending like that didn't do something to me. "A pawn."

"A pawn?" Ariel repeated.

"As if you were basically planted here," Reese stated, his eyes darting back and forth, as if trying to keep his emotions in check.

"He told me Lilith set my fate the moment I was placed in Purgatory, that all this was part of a greater plan, a pawn on all sides." She spat her words out at Jonah, who she had yet to look away from.

Markus looked to his fellow executives. "I'm sorry, was he claiming someone in Heaven's Gate is a part of this supposed idea?"

"He didn't explain how or when my being here would show its true colors, just that she wants me here and it won't end well for you. That's why she hasn't made a move. She doesn't need to when she has someone on the inside." She was calling people out without saying too much at all. I was impressed and a bit unnerved at the same time.

Markus looked perplexed. "Lilith and an angel, working together? After everything that woman has done to us and—" He pointed at Natalia, who narrowed her eyes at him, "to her people during the war?" He ran a hand through his gray hair. "You speak nonsense."

"Is it though?" I said under my breath.

"Nick," I heard Reese whisper beside me, nudging my arm.

I had sworn my words were just for me, but that wasn't the case, I realized. Those three words had formed into a question now causing everyone to look in my direction.

Fuck.

"What did you say?" Ariel asked, annoyance lacing his words.

"Is it really that preposterous?"

Markus waved his hand around. "You believe an angel sold their soul to Lilith to bring down Heaven's Gate?"

"We also believe the angel you speak of killed Keegan," Elise chimed in, smiling. "Loyalty to Lilith can come in many forms. What better way than to kill one of your own?"

"You all are quite insane! What did Keegan bring to the table for her, for anyone?" Ariel exclaimed.

"His key!" Reese said swiftly, both words coming out like one. He let out a breath that sounded as if he was finally relaxing a bit. I heard Natalia take in a sharp breath, but when I looked at her, those honey eyes weren't pained and cautious; they were waiting for the other shoe to drop. Reese closed his eyes and then opened them again, watching the angels and demons all staring at him with curious but stunned faces. "Oh, fuck."

I felt Dani and Elise's eyes looking past me to Reese, who was now rubbing the back of his neck uncomfortably.

"Key?" Jonah looked confused. "His portal key?"

"Umm, well...yeah." Reese stuttered over his words; his bow landed with a loud clang on the ground when he tried to readjust his seat.

"Young man, that portal key wouldn't work in the hands of Lilith," Markus explained, looking towards Natalia for confirmation. "Correct?"

Natalia nodded her head. "You are correct." Markus nodded in satisfaction, until Natalia continued. "But in this situation, the key wouldn't be used by Lilith. It could be used by another angel. The key could be taken over if enough Enchanters got involved— and she has *enough* of those in Purgatory. We both know those Enchanters are not too happy with angels." Her words were shot back harshly at Markus.

"I beg your pardon?" Ariel seethed.

"Not everything is cut and dry, Ariel. I think it's time we all stopped thinking like that."

"Keegan would never have gone to Purgatory without being instructed to," I said, this time wanting the whole table to hear me. "He was new, he was fresh, he would do anything someone higher said."

"Nicholas, no one would have sent Keegan there without super-vision, knowing he was so new to The Skies," Jonah said calmly. He was trying to explain something I clearly already knew, but the words from his mouth just didn't make any fucking sense.

"But you did." I watched as he tried to unravel my words.

"What did you say?" Jonah asked.

"You. Did," I repeated. Each word pierced him as his face contorted into understanding.

Ariel opened his mouth before Jonah could grab his own explanation. "Mr. Cassial, you will not sit here and accuse Jonah of such ridiculousness…"

"It's true!" I practically combusted out of my chair. I looked directly into Jonah's eyes and was immediately unnerved when he didn't look upset, just taken aback. He was regal enough to want me to explain myself without jumping down my throat at the first opening.

"Nicholas, how have you come across such an idea?" Jonah asked calmly, having placed a hand on Ariel's forearm.

"I…" The words got choked up. I knew exactly how I obtained the information, but do I throw others into this already boiling pot with me? My lips pressed together and then opened, trying to find the best way to express my knowledge, when a voice broke through.

"He got it from me," Natalia announced.

Jonah looked over at Natalia and nodded, as if he was starting to understand. "Your unauthorized trip to Oculus." His amber eyes peered over at me, hoping to receive verification. "You told me Natalia simply told you an angel had gone to Oculus, but you knew much, much more than that, didn't you, Nicholas?"

"Yes. I…we've known all of it." This was the all or nothing moment that was either going to solidify my suspicions, nullify them, or make me more confused than when all of this started. I clenched and unclenched my fists underneath the table. "None of us would deny a request from you, let alone question it. Keegan was new, like you said. He would have been an idiot to say no, so you sent him there! You sent him to his death to prove yourself to Lilith."

"Young man, you are entirely out of line," Markus accused.

"Oh, shut up, you old fuck, and let him speak," Elise commanded.

"You didn't even think twice when I mentioned an angel had been sent to Purgatory. You were so calm. You didn't even…you didn't even know his name was gone from the book until a few days ago…"

"And you did, Mr. Cassial?" Ariel growled.

Reese's leg was bouncing under the table again in a more unhinged rhythm. I pressed my foot on top of his in hopes of stopping his knee from connecting with the table. I took a deep breath.

"We may have gone into Jonah's office and collected that information ourselves."

"You *what*!?" Ariel screamed, leaning over the table. His palms were braced firmly on the wood, his knuckles even a starker white than his already pale skin.

"You were watching Jonah's office that day, so it was under your watch that this happened, right? You left two angels, regardless of stature, alone in a high executive's office, did you not?" I could hear myself saying these things, and it felt good, but I could also feel my heartbeat start to drum harder. It was so bad, it started to hurt, but I pushed past it.

Ariel slammed both his fists into the table. "You will *not* speak to me like that!"

Reese matched Ariel's stance at the sound of his rumbling voice. I looked over to where he stood, my eyes following his torso to where a vein in the side of his neck pulsed. "I think we are well past that now! That key that I spoke about, Natalia told us that it was still here in Heaven's Gate. Keegan died for his key and now someone here is using it to open portals for demons. I don't like believing it, or even thinking about it, but this shit is too much!"

"An Enchanter has overwhelmed my magic to cloak the person using it," Natalia offered.

"Your magic is too powerful for something that simple," Markus said, trying to pull Ariel back into his seat and failing.

"It's not, actually," Dani said, breaking her own silence. "Given enough Enchanters willing to extend their powers to one. You have made many enemies in those you trapped down there, so I'm not the least bit surprised they were willing to help."

Ariel widened his eyes in disbelief. "Are you making this up? Has being here for so long made you delusional? You're also an issue, if you'd forgotten."

Dani smirked over at him. "Oh, I'm aware I'm an issue, but right now, this isn't about me. The real issue right now is why you have a book in the Divine Library about Enchanters when they are not even supposed to exist anymore."

"The Divine Library?" Jonah and Ariel both said in unison.

"This should be fucking good," Elise said under all the commotion.

"How?" Jonah questioned, but he was looking directly at me, as if he already knew I was the reason she had been there at all.

"Jonah, don't be daft. We know how. Your prized puppy took her, without any thought to the consequences," Ariel answered for him.

"Prized puppy?" I tilted my head to the side in question, feeling my heart beat faster.

"You don't think we all see how he treats you as if you are something special? You think you are so special because of your unique skills; well, I'll tell you something -- your father was just like you, coddled, too proud, and look where that got him!" Ariel huffed out, spitting his words as if they would sting me into submission.

I shoved back my chair so hard, it rattled. Elise and Dani shot their faces up to me and Natalia shifted her shoulders, trying to maintain her composure. "You will *not* talk about my father like that!" I breathed heavily, feeling the heat creep up my neck. "You have been so secretive about this from the moment it started, and you want us to just go along for the ride, no questions asked. I'm sorry, but I'm fucking done with that. An innocent angel is dead, a key is being used to let demons through, there is likely an angel roaming around trying to ruin all of us, and you are upset with the way I'm fucking talking to you?"

Jonah slowly got up, likely hoping to diffuse the situation. "Nicholas, just calm down..."

"I won't! From the beginning you've been hiding things from me. You've been lying." Jonah was silent. "You sent Keegan, you brought Dani here. I don't know why, but you created this whole problem and for what?"

Jonah shook his head. "You are wrong, Nicholas."

"Cullen said, the angel was right under our noses. Why not you?" Dani questioned.

Reese turned his face away from Ariel's. "You have kept your entire past a secret, Jonah. I will be the first one to say I was on your side, but nothing is adding up for you."

"Maybe all those years ago, you and Lilith settled some kind of pact," Elise offered, crossing her legs.

"I would never. I..." Jonah rubbed his forehead with his finger, flustered. "I have been honest. I will admit that I have been quite busy with other things, and I have not been as adamant with my checking on the book but seeing Keegan's name disappear after his trip was my first knowledge of it." He looked over at Natalia. "I did not send him to Purgatory." Then he looked at Reese. "I do not have his key." Lastly, he looked at me. "I brought the Soul Seether here to help, that's all. I would not bring her here with the knowledge she would harm us. I have been honest with you in those departments."

"All those departments but one, right?" I questioned, right at the edge of walking around the table and getting right in his face, but my legs wouldn't move so I decided staying put would have to do.

Markus cleared his throat. "Everyone we can just sit down and..." Jonah shot up his hand clearly telling Markus to shut up. He looked back at me and tilted his head in question.

"You want me to believe you. That you had nothing to do with any of this? Then tell me, why me? Tell me what you are hiding from me and maybe I can give you the benefit of being honest to my face about something."

"Nicholas, I have been nothing but honest about..." I waved him off and finished speaking.

"That's not what I asked you. I asked you to be honest with me. In the Divine Library, you told Markus you weren't playing favorites, but I'm the only one you would ever explain things to."

Realization dawned on his face when he understood what night we had been there. Jonah closed his eyes and nodded. "Nicholas, I can assure you, I am hiding nothing and have nothing to do with this mess we're in." It seemed like he was done, but he wasn't. "But there are some things I simply cannot say."

"Then I'm done helping you with this," I said, dropping my head.

Ariel started, "You will be finished with this when he says you are done."

Jonah placed a hand on Ariel's shoulder. "Ariel, enough. Nicholas, you have to understand..."

"I can't help someone I don't trust," I finally said, my heart starting to slow its rhythm after what I'd been harboring in the pit of my stomach was finally said.

"But you trust them?" Ariel said with as much disgust as he could muster. I didn't say anything to that. Ariel carried on without my answer. "You trust their judgements and their words. You value their opinions over Jonah's. You think that wise, Nicholas?"

"Do you think it wise I should trust someone who isn't telling the whole truth? It makes me believe that nothing is true." I bore my eyes into Jonah's. "You brought them here, which makes sense. You asked me to work alongside them, which I have, only to find out that they aren't the problem. I don't know what Lilith has promised you. I don't know why you would want to do all of this, go to these lengths, but give me something or that's all I will believe. That's all I'll go on." I was practically pleading with Jonah now and he knew it.

"I brought them here to help us, Nicholas. You must know that."

"I don't know anything!" I exclaimed, the words practically flying out of my mouth before I could stop them. It was too late for that. "You want her here for a reason; maybe you've kept that reason to yourself, or others are in on it with you to some degree." I looked over to Markus, thinking about when he asked me if Dani had brought anything with her, almost coaxing me say it was her dagger. I could point fingers at any one of them, but Jonah was their leader. He was our leader. If I couldn't fathom trusting him anymore, how in the hell could I trust any of them? "I won't let you use her for anything you've got planned. I won't let you ruin our home."

Reese eased himself away from the table and stood with his arms crossed over his chest beside me. Both demons sat calmly in their chairs, patiently assessing. Natalia had her index and middle fingers placed gently over her mouth as she leaned to one side of her chair.

Jonah let out a long breath and looked out the window to the rain. The storm was causing the wind to whip the trees violently, and it looked as if it was just the beginning. "Nicholas, I don't know what you need me to tell you. It seems as if you have already made up your mind about this, but you need to really look at me and see I am not your enemy. I have cared for you as if you were my own. I would not put your home, my own home, at risk."

"But I'm not yours. I'm not your own. I'm my father's son and he doesn't seem to think so much of you." Jonah was almost startled by my words. I was making this entire meeting about myself, and it was wrong, I knew it was wrong, but maybe everything connected.

Jonah sighed. "Your father and I have nothing to do with what's happening in Heaven's Gate right now. That should not factor into your feelings about this or about me."

"It does though! It factors into my entire life! It looks like you have spent some time planning this so meticulously, there has to be a reason. Why did you and my father stop speaking? Was it because you knew Lilith too closely? Why am I so important to you, why is Dani so important to you, because if you tell me it's because of this portal bullshit, I will literally put my sword to your throat!"

"Nicholas!" Markus shouted, but Jonah stopped him.

"Does Dani have something that you want? Is that it?" I taunted, hoping that he would tell me something about the dagger, that he would tell me anything at all. "Does Lilith have something over you? If she does, we could work on that together. Did she force you to kill Keegan? Does it have something to do with your own father all those years ago? Did he make you seek Lilith out because you had nowhere else to turn?"

Jonah licked his lips and pressed them together. His eyes looked almost sad, as if he knew that anything he said was useless. I needed to know. I had to.

"Does it have anything to do with my mother?"

Jonah didn't move, almost as if he stopped breathing. I was about to question him more when I heard a *thud*. Reese grabbed my forearm and looked past me to the door. I followed his gaze, noticing Dani and Elise doing the same. Natalia had risen from her chair, her back turned to us, listening for the noise again.

Thud, thud, thud.

They were quick but loud, as if someone had fallen onto the stone floor outside. No, not fallen, *thrown*. Yanked around and chucked in the opposite direction.

"What was that?" Markus asked, pushing back his chair.

"Nothing good," Reese said, confidence faltering.

I looked down at Dani who sat in her chair, but not with the ease I had seen a few seconds ago, her shoulders stiff. I could see goose-bumps prickling on her skin. Elise had the same tense way about her, but she cracked her neck and just seemed to wait.

Another thud, this one a bit closer.

Silence ensued, enveloped us and tightened its grip around my bones. I shook my head, thinking maybe it was all in my head when—

Thud.

A body hit the window. The rain made it hard to make out who it was, but the white wide wings with blood spatters on them made it clear *what* they were.

"What in the fuck?" Reese said, backing up a little and picking up his bow as he made his way to the opposite wall.

"What is going on *now* in your fucking realm?" Elise said, propelling herself out of her seat when a pounding noise came from the door and split it wide open.

I blinked once, twice, three times to take in what I was seeing. Small, dark waves tumbled into the room, small waves followed by larger ones and then smaller ones again. It covered the floor around us, like a sharp burn when it touched my skin. I grabbed my sword from where it leaned against my chair, steeling myself.

Dark shadows started to fill the room now. I could see flowing hair and arms, fingers. The shadows weren't so dark that they were completely shrouded, but it covered them as if part of them.

"Oh shit," Elise said. I saw that her right hand was cupped upward and a growing ebony ball of smoke there. Dark ropes of magic shot down Dani's arm as she got up from her chair and kicked it over to the waiting guests.

"You have no business here!" Jonah yelled, moving past me and Reese. "You must leave at once." His voice was unwavering.

They looked at Jonah as if they either didn't hear anything he said, or they didn't care.

"They have no interest in what you say or who you are," Dani explained, the ropes around her arms widening and pulsing, the shadowy magic dripping from her fingertips. "They don't even care who *they* are anymore."

One of them looked over to Dani, its eyes locking on her. Its eyes gradually became unclouded for a moment, letting me see a deep green. No matter the color, its eyes were blank, as if it was moving through motions. Dani didn't seem fazed by it, as if she knew what was happening but had no way to explain it now.

"Oh shit," Elise repeated. "I think this meeting is over."

"What have you brought here?" Ariel shouted, and I realized he was speaking to Dani.

Dani cocked her head toward him and squinted her eyes but said nothing. Ariel wasn't worth it; he never had been.

One of the shadow figures lunged towards Dani, who propelled one of her black ropes at it, wrapping around its neck and yanking back. The cracking sound it made had me cringing as one of them came in my direction. I held my sword tight, and I watched as a sword manifested itself from the shadowy creature's hands. My fears were affirmed when it slashed the sword and created a rip in the front of my shirt, nicking my skin the smallest amount.

The figures started to move in all directions. Gold magic pulsed out of Jonah's fingers as he shot streams towards two of the intruders, causing them to shield themselves but also shoot a few of their own streams, pushing him back a few feet.

Reese shot arrow after arrow, piercing them one by one, but where a few fell to the ground, turning to a shadowy dust, others seemed to pull the arrows out and move forward. He shot another when one of the figures caught it and pointed it towards him, seeming to pull back an invisible bow, and the arrow went flying. Reese shot out his wings, ascending towards the ceiling, avoiding his own arrow and shooting another, hitting the figure right in the head.

I fought back and forth with my sword, meeting my opponent at every turn. Our swords blocked one another, and I turned to see Markus and Ariel aiming white magic at a few of the clusters, watching them fall one by one. Natalia had rainbows coming out of her hands. Her back was turned to me, and I saw how her crown tattoo glowed as she propelled her own magic forward. Elise grabbed one of them by the neck with her bare hands and threw them up in the air while Natalia grabbed them with a stream of blue light and burned right through their chest. I buried my sword into my opponent and watched as they slumped to the ground.

"Nick!" I heard Reese above me as he shot an arrow that looked like it was in my direction but was made for the shadow lunging for my back. I turned around to see another one barreling at me, a shadowy sword in its hand with a sweeping motion, causing me to jump back. I pivoted to the right and moved forward, using the hilt of my sword to strike its back. It staggered forward but turned around, lunging for me again. It was as if it didn't even need to take a breath. I swung downward and caught its shoulder, then spun around when it tried to pierce me directly, ramming my blade into its side. I pulled my sword out as they descended to the floor.

"What the fuck are they?" I yelled.

"Hell if I know!" Reese shouted, having tucked away his wings and was now back on the ground. He plucked one of his arrows and used it to plunge into a neck.

"Why don't you ask your trusted friend?" Ariel shouted as he shot out his own wings and nearly missed a pitch-black wave of magic two figures shot in his direction.

Dani looked over to me as she laced two thick, pulsing ribbons of magic around one of the figures' legs and yanked them off their feet, hoisting them upside down and bringing them over to her. She shot out two more, plowing through two faces. I watched as the magic surges connected with their face but pushed past it and through the back of their skulls. The now upside-down creature was in front of her. She tilted her head to the side, almost examining them. "They're demons, Nicholas."

The answer didn't shock me, but the way she said it did. It was so casual, as if the answer was obvious and we should have known this would happen.

I bent backwards as a long, shadowy sword moved towards my face. I kicked the demon at its feet, causing it to fall backwards, piercing my sword through its chest as I stood over it.

"Did you know this would happen?" I wasn't asking Dani -- I was asking Jonah. He pulsed out magic that launched a demon towards the wall with a crack.

"Nicholas, I promise I had nothing to do with any of this!" His voice was breathless from fighting. Jonah looked as if he was trying to expel all the magic that came with his status and upbringing, the kind of magic that could likely end this. Puffs of golden light threaded through his fingers but were snuffed out in an instant, as if something was clogging his magic, letting him use only the bare minimum.

"She is sending you a message, you idiots. She has you right where she wants you. At any time. Anywhere," Elise pointed out, shooting one of the demons towards the ceiling and then clasping her red tinged ropes around it, lunging it over to collide with its friends. She quickly turned to face us. "From the looks of it, you'll ruin each other before she gets the chance."

An arrow flew by her head, causing her to blink a few times, but she didn't flinch. I heard flapping wings above my head as I slashed the neck of another demon. Reese relaxed his arm as he nodded towards Elise; she turned around, seeing a demon laid out on the ground.

"You're welcome," Reese said, descending to the ground.

Elise rolled her eyes but looked past me. Dani was surrounded. I knew she could take care of herself, but I didn't *want* her to. I didn't think she should have to. A sound came from outside the room, out in the hall: a scream and then another. They were all over The Skies. Natalia looked back, giving me a look as if she understood my concern.

I raced to Dani, thrusting my sword into anyone in my way. I watched as different demons were pushed back by magic, the way their bones would crack from whatever pressure she was laying on them. When I got through, she looked at me, but not with eyes of discontent. She looked at me as if she was stunned I had come to help her. These things seemed to want her, to be drawn to her, and in a fucked-up way, I couldn't blame them.

"We have to help the others!" Markus shouted as he made his way to the open doorway.

We had eliminated most of the demons in our room, but there were still enough to keep us here for another hour or so. I plunged my sword into the only other demon in my way when I felt a brutal pain at my side. I grabbed Dani's arm and yanked her away from the four or five that were left. Natalia turned around and flung what looked like indigo darts at the group, and they fell one by one. I pressed my hand to my side and watched as crimson liquid decorated my fingertips. The cut was deep enough that my shirt was quickly soaked. Dani looked down and noticed my fingers, her face contorted into concern.

"Nicholas..." Jonah called from the other side of the room, helping Ariel with his hoard of demons. He saw my blood-stained hand and shuddered.

"It's just a cut, I'm fine." I held my sword steady and was ready for more. I could patch myself up later. I could feel myself getting woozy, as if more blood was leaving my body than I had imagined. I looked down to see blood dripping on the floor. I felt Dani start to steady me.

Elise released a rush of deep red magic caught by one of the demons, who slashed it back to her, slapping her in the face and pushing her back towards the table. Reese shot an arrow, catching a demon in the leg and then another in the thigh. I watched as Natalia glanced over at Jonah and then at me, as if she was deciding something for herself.

"Get him out of here!" Jonah yelled to her. "We've got it from here."

Natalia waved her hand around, creating a portal that opened slowly, letting in light that pierced the darkness of the room. She looked over at me as I started to press my hand to my side. "Get out of here!" she shouted at me before she yanked both Reese and Elise through the portal before it closed. How did she want me to leave? In the condition I was in, I couldn't fly, let alone carry Dani. If Dani wanted to use her own wings, I didn't want *her* to have to carry *me*.

Then it dawned on me. I dipped my fingers into my shirt and

pulled out my portal key. Natalia's gift. Where did she want me to go? Where would I *want* to go?

The demons had dispersed to only a few around us, some following Markus and Ariel out of the room, but Jonah watched me as he hovered near the door. I wanted somewhere I could be safe, somewhere I knew Dani would be safe.

"Jonah, let's go!" I heard Markus yell from somewhere in the hallway.

The dark shadows on the ground remained, letting us know that their presence was still very much a fixture.

"Nicholas?" Dani asked hesitantly. She watched as I held the portal key in front of me. Somewhere safe? Somewhere...safe? I reached my hand out for Dani to take it. She looked down at my outstretched hand and took a small glance over to my blood-soaked shirt before taking it. Her skin was just as warm as I remembered. I didn't know where I was taking her, but it was going to be out of here and it was going to be right now.

I started making a circle with the key, watching as the space in front of us opened and light shot out, almost blinding me. I pulled her through without a second thought and hoped that I was thinking about somewhere plausible for her to be. I hoped we would end up far away from this shit, if only for a little while.

We had run through the portal so fast, we had no time to think about the in-between. We didn't need to keep our balance or be aware of the glowing colors creeping from every surface. I blinked and felt a sharp pain in my back. I heard a thud next to me, seeing Dani arch her back as if she'd landed roughly. I saw as she reached behind her head and rubbed the back of her skull.

I looked down at my shirt and saw that the blood was moving its way out of my wound and had trickled down to my pants. I was still holding her hand, her fingers still intertwined in mine. I let my head fall back against the floor and I sighed.

Wait.

I sniffed. Then I sniffed again. That smell was familiar. The smell of meat and onions and peppers. I shifted my head to the side and saw a familiar mantle, a familiar rug. Dani looked over at me and took in my confused expression. She looked above our heads as a shadow appeared over us. I slowly moved my eyes away from her and up at the figure above us. I closed my eyes the minute I met his face.

He had his hands on his hips and an eyebrow raised. "Nicholas?" my father said, no sign of a smile.

I was home.

CHAPTER FIFTEEN

DANI

The man standing over us had a mixture of amusement, concern, and confusion etched across his face. He had his hands on his hips and had given me a quick look before landing his pointed stare on Nicholas, who had his eyes closed as if he was pretending this wasn't happening. Then, the man said his name, as if they were close. I tilted my head as best I could to get a good look at the person above me, but that movement only made my head throb harder.

Where were we? It felt warm and cozy, probably someone's home. The rain still pattered against the windows, but inside, there was a fire roaring and the smell...fuck, the smell. It was amazing. I felt Nicholas remove his hand from my grasp, leaving my hand with an ache I didn't want to think about. He laid his hand over his wound, pressing down to staunch the bleeding.

"Jesus, Nicholas," the man said, leaning down to haul him up from the ground, careful not to injure him more. I managed to lift myself so I was sitting up, watching them. Nicholas proceeded to protest he was fine, while wincing at every slight movement. The man grunted and sat him down in one of the chairs at a wooden dining table.

I looked to my left, seeing the fire that made the room toasty and inviting, the couch with a blanket slung over the back, and a hallway that led to three doors, each one opened just a tiny bit. The lightning outside didn't seem so nerve-inducing with so much glowing energy in here. I heard a sharp hiss and then a groan, springing up from my place on the floor and looking over at Nicholas. He had his back turned to me in the chair, but his shirt was off, and I saw the way his back muscles tensed. Another hiss and the ropes of muscle around his arms pressed against his skin. I looked down around my feet and saw his sword not a few feet away from where we landed. I reached down to pick it up and placed it upright against the nearest wall.

"You have to stay still, Nicholas," I heard the man say as he had a bottle I couldn't make out and a tube of ointment. "What the hell happened?"

Nicholas remained quiet. I made my way over to them, wanting to get a good glimpse of the man. They had a first aid kit, the contents spread out. The man threw a bloody cloth towards the supplies and used another one to gently dab what I now realized was alcohol from the bottle onto the wound, not even flinching when Nicholas hissed out low curse words. He reached for some ointment to smear onto Nichola's gash and peered up at me. My breath caught when his eyes met mine. His eyes were a deep brown, simple but wise. The man's jaw was cut and defined and if the way his shirt hugged his arms and chest told me anything, it was that he kept himself in good shape. His hair was thick and dark, so, for an older man, he was fucking hot. I gave him a once over and he raised an eyebrow at me, as if waiting for me to speak first.

I looked from his face to Nicholas, who was now looking at me as well. He remained just as quiet as before, but now it looked as if his was trying to configure a story. I looked back to the man and then quickly back at Nicholas. The eyes, the jaw, the fucking muscular arms. Fuck, even their mouths had the same curve.

"Are you Nicholas' dad?" I asked tentatively.

The man furrowed his brow and looked to Nicholas, who was taking the gauze from the first aid kit and ignoring us. The older doppelgänger let out a little sigh and a laugh that almost made me want to smile. He nodded towards me and stuck out his hand.

"I'm Maurice Cassial, Nick's father." His smile was friendly and open. I grasped his hand and nearly watched my hand disappear with how small it was compared to his. "I assume you are one of the demons he's told me about?"

I widened my eyes at his son, who simply looked up at me and shrugged. Mr. Cassial waited patiently for my reply. "Yeah, I'm Dani. I didn't know he talked about me."

He chuckled. "Well, since you are here, would you so kindly do me the honor of telling me what the hell is going on and why my son has an open wound, bleeding all over my floor?" He was casual and easy about it, but I knew the tone was serious.

"Dad," Nicholas tested.

"*You.* You do not get to speak right now unless the next thing out of your mouth is an explanation." Mr. Cassial yanked the gauze from his son and pressed the material to the wound. Nicholas let out a grunt, which is father just huffed at. I pressed my tongue into my cheek, holding in my laugh.

"You really think you can just portal in here and think I'll just patch you up without asking questions?" his father said, securing the gauze onto his skin. "You may not want to tell me anything, but by the look on her face, she might just sell you out, son."

Nicholas peeked over at me as his father wiped his hands on a cloth. I crossed my arms over my chest and bit down another laugh. Nicholas let out an exhaustive groan. "Dad! Can I have a minute to, I don't know, pull myself together?"

"Alright. You have a minute," his father said pointedly. He grabbed the first aid kit and the clothes soaked with blood and walked towards the kitchen.

"Thank you," Nicholas replied, getting a *yeah, yeah* from his father in return.

I took Mr. Cassial's spot in front of Nicholas and placed my elbow on the table. "You brought me home?"

He squinted his eyes at me, but his shoulders slumped down in an exhaustive stance. "Looks that way."

"May I ask why?" I questioned.

He scrubbed one of his hands down his face. "I wish I knew. I just wanted somewhere I knew we would be safe. I'm not super familiar with how portal magic works."

I peered around the room, around the home that wrapped around you like a warm hug. "I can see that." I reached over and tilted his chin up to look at me directly. "You told your dad?"

He shrugged, removing my fingers from his face. His fingers seemed to glide off mine, like he wanted me to be severely burned by the heat I felt from them.

"Like everything? From the beginning everything?" I asked, shaking my hand.

"Pretty much. You'll find he is probably the most understanding yet annoying father in any realm."

"If you didn't pull stunts like this--" His father strutted over to us after he cut the water off at the kitchen sink, wiping his hands with a clean cloth, pointing to where blood still lay on the floor. "I wouldn't have to be so annoying."

Nicholas tilted his head back. "I get it, okay, I'm sorry. I didn't know what else to do. It was a shit show back there."

His dad arched an eyebrow.

"The Skies, it—" Nicholas started, fumbling over his words. I abruptly finished for him.

"We got ambushed, Mr. Cassial. Like your son said, it was a shit show."

His father pulled out a chair and sat down. "An ambush? Was it demons?"

"Sort of. I mean, I'm pretty sure they were." He chewed on his bottom lip. "They seemed dead set on killing all of us, like it was their mission." Nicholas looked down and pressed his fingertips to his gauze-covered wound.

Mr. Cassial looked between me and his son, doing a mental calculation that we were obviously missing the rest of the *us* his son was referring to. I eased his mind. "Natalia took Elise and Reese with her somewhere. I'm sure they are fine under her care. I trust her."

"Jonah and the others?" he pressed.

Nicholas rapped his knuckles on the table. "I don't know. All of this was meant to be kept severely under wraps and now..." He let the rest of the sentence hang in the air.

I knew what we had left behind and how it probably gutted him to have left without continuing to fight. I also knew he wouldn't have lasted in that fight.

"Jonah...always underestimating things. Did that man really think these girls were going to fix this problem? He put everyone's life at stake," his father spat out, muttering *typical* under his breath.

"Dad—"

"And look at you! I'm not saying that fighting doesn't lead to wounds and bloodshed, but dammit Nicholas, this was out of nowhere. I wanted you to ease into this stuff. I don't know, practice battles like we used to do, small missions that gave you experience. This... *this* was likely preventable and what does that man do? He throws you to the damn wolves!"

Nicholas lifted his hands up in a surrender. "I get it, alright! You wanted me to do more and so I did, I am. I didn't know that it would come back to fuck me over. I have a lot of issues with Jonah, but for right now, neither one of us can do a thing about it."

I blinked. "You want to lay low? Do nothing?" I could understand the gravity of the situation, but that didn't mean I wanted to just give up.

He slid his tongue across his top row of teeth. "It's the best option. Who knows what The Skies even looks like right now. Besides, we need to hear from Natalia first and foremost. We didn't exactly end on the best of terms with Jonah, so going back there now wouldn't do anyone any good, especially you."

I leaned back into the chair and gave one solid nod as a response. I was stuck in that room in The Skies, waiting for instructions, so to have to do it again was pinching at an annoyed nerve. I knew he was right, though. Ariel thought I was an issue, that I had something to do with those things that ambushed us. I didn't, but they had seemed to eye me like I was a calling card. He would want my head on a spike pronto, and I wouldn't let that happen until I figured out why I was Lilith's final piece in this web of confusion and lies.

Cullen had said I would be the one to ruin it all, but Lilith couldn't honestly believe I would be able to deconstruct Heaven's Gate? I was powerful, but I didn't possess that kind of power and she of all people knew that. I was Lilith's pawn, I understood that, but was I the kind where others could seek their glory while I shielded them or the type that showed no signs of disruption but then rattled everyone's world when they least expected it? If I knew anything about Lilith, I had an inclination that she would use me as both interchangeably. Nicholas wanted to know how I fit into all of this and unsurprisingly, I wanted to know how he fit as well.

"You and Jonah had a falling out?" his dad asked, laying his forearms over each other on top of the table. He had two small cuts on his throat, as if he had cut himself shaving, and there were a few faded scars next to them. They had a story behind them, but I could guess he probably wouldn't be up to sharing it.

"Something like that. It was nothing."

I rolled my eyes. "You are way too modest for your own good. Your son basically accused Jonah of orchestrating this whole thing and hiding a bunch of shit, basically calling out his shady ass. Jonah got his ass handed to him."

His father arched a thick eyebrow at his son as if to say, *is this true?*

"He didn't get his ass handed to him." Nicholas shook his head at me, but a small smile played along the corner of his lips.

"I was there for the whole thing. You handed him his ass on the shiniest plate you could find." I brought my shoulders up and did a little shimmy in my seat. "It was glorious."

"Flattery will get you nowhere," he said, tilting his head to the side and shifting one of his feet to knock against one of mine playfully. I scoffed but let my foot hit his back. Flattery gets me somewhere, by the looks of it.

His father let out a hmm, scratching his neck. "You think he sent these killer demons?"

"I think I'm done trying to rule anything out at this point," Nicholas stated. "Maybe I'm completely wrong, but he *is* hiding something. I'm just too exhausted to figure it out right now."

Mr. Cassial looked off to the side. His father's face was serene but there was a thin line that lay across his forehead, as if he was in thought. His eyes were fixated on the mantle, on the photos there, like he was remembering something. A crack of thunder made him blink out of it.

I leaned slightly closer to him. "What is Ariel's deal when it comes to you?" Nicholas's father gave me a confused look.

Nicholas cleared his throat. "Ariel may have said some things that I didn't take well."

Mr. Cassial's soothing dark eyes lit up with a childish delight. "That man has never liked me, ever since we entered The Skies together as trainees. I was wide-eyed and dead set on being a sentry and he didn't make the final cut. I think I always rubbed him the wrong way or something. He came from a decently high up family, like Jonah, but he always had his nose turned up at anything or anyone that was a little bit off key." He shook his head, as if he was thinking back to irritating the smirk right off Ariel's stupid face. "I'm not surprised he never changed. He's always been—"

"A little shit," I offered. I could have guessed Nicholas's father was a former sentry.

His father pressed his lips together to keep his laugh in. "More or less. I can't say I wasn't a little shit myself, but I made up for it."

"I think *he* thinks your son is a little shit."

"Well, Nick *can* be a little shit, believe me." He winked over at his son.

Nicholas let out a laugh, but immediately hissed and pressed a hand to his stomach. His muscles tightened, and I looked at his defined abs, watching as small wisps of dark hair trailed a line under his belly button and disappeared beneath his pants. His father jumped around the table to tend to him, but Nicholas waved him off, breathing through the sharp pain, the sound of his breathing catching my attention back again.

"I didn't know demons played with weapons like ours," his father said, concern etched all over his face.

"We don't. I mean, not real ones at least. We know how to use them, but they're not particularly necessary. We can simply make a replica, without the issue of weight in the way." I brought my hand up and let dark shadow strings rise from my palm and curl around each other. They twirled and braided together, slowly forming a small dagger, the shadowy hilt lying in my hand.

Mr. Cassial looked at me almost stunned, but then something that could be amazement dawned over his face. "And they can do physical damage?"

"They are as lethal as any silver blade." I tilted the black, wispy weapon downward and carved a small line into the table, watching as the wood split apart easily.

I cocked my head towards Nicholas' father. "You don't seem fazed by all this." I let the dagger disperse into the air.

"All this?" He looked genuinely confused.

I shrugged, swinging one of my arms over the back of the wooden chair. "Oh, I don't know, demons, for starters."

"You would be surprised by the things I've seen and can deal with. You aren't the first demon I've met."

My eyebrows shot up a bit. "Oh really? You can tolerate being in the same room as me?" I was more surprised he wasn't like Reese. His reaction was more like the ones I was used to, but this nonchalant attitude towards me was something that sent an unknowing heat creeping up my neck. That voice that always seemed to push its way into my head while I slept, the one that always seemed to be trying to tell me something, started to come to the surface, trying to expel the heat as I shoved them both down. I twisted one of my curls with my finger tight, so tight that I felt my finger starting to lose circulation.

Mr. Cassial slapped his hand on the table and looked at me with a stare that I swallowed nervously, letting my hair untwist from my finger. "My son claims he trusts you and it looks as if you are part of his team. I know what you are and who you are to Lilith. I'm not so old that I don't hear gossip and stories." He rubbed one of his fingers over his stubbled chin. "He wouldn't have brought you here if you weren't someone worth bringing, so if you are important enough for my son to want to keep you safe from Lilith or even from Jonah himself, then I don't ask questions." I opened my mouth to speak, but nothing came out. The way he spoke was so fervent and commanding. His words were laced with everything I knew made him a good father.

He continued. "I would love it if next time, you don't come tumbling in here on a shit night full of thunderstorms, bleeding all over my clean floor, but all I can say is—" He looked over at his son. "Did you make your father proud with that sword?"

Before Nicholas could answer, I spoke for him. "He did, Mr. Cassial," Sword skills ran in the family, it would seem.

His father nodded, slapping his hands together, rubbing his palms against one another and getting up from the table. "Big news around The Skies threads through the villages pretty fast, so either whatever is happening there isn't over, or they have sustained what they can and are laying low themselves." We both looked up at him, curious as to where this was leading. He nodded towards the kitchen. "While the calm before the storm is upon us, you can stay here for the night. I have a roast in the oven, so how about we eat, and you can tell me all about this shit show of yours?" He pointed his index finger at his son. "*Everything.*"

Nicholas caught my attention with his pretty brown eyes and rolled them.

"You threatened to kill him?" Nicholas' father said, taking his glass of water in his hand. Nicholas had recounted the whole meeting to his father, not leaving any details out. Mr. Cassial listened so intently, I knew he was absorbing every piece of information his son gave him. He never stopped eating, but never once looked uninterested or even threatened to interrupt.

Nicholas finished chewing his food and swallowed. "Sort of. It wasn't as dramatic as she's making it seem."

I lifted my fork and pointed at him. "So humble, this one. I didn't know your son could get so angry." I remembered being slightly turned on by his rage and determination.

Mr. Cassial shook his head as he drank from his glass, using his free hand to wipe his bottom lip. "You should have seen him and Reese as teenagers. The rage of hormonal teenage boys is astonishing."

I raised one of my eyebrows suspiciously at Nicholas, who looked at me from over his own glass of water. I knew a lot about his *hormones*. Something told me he knew exactly what I was thinking. I blinked away from him and focused on his father. "How do you stand him?"

"Who?"

"Reese."

He let out a hearty laugh at this. "He is a good kid. Don't get me wrong, I've wanted to smack him across the head more times than I can count, but he's a good soul, just a bit rough around the edges. Can't see the big picture unless it's convenient for him."

"That about sums it up," I said.

"But when it has really counted, he's stood by Nick's side, so I can't fault him on everything," he said. "I can only assume he wasn't the biggest fan of yours at the start, but he's still here, standing with you, so that says a lot."

I shrugged, his words ringing true.

"Did you know we were coming?" Nicholas said when his father had brought over his plate earlier.

His father had chuckled and shook his head. "No, some days I like to cook a big meal I can keep for a few days, that's all."

Nicholas had swatted his hand away when his father tried to ruffle his hair and I let out a small giggle at their exchange. No matter how any of this ended, whatever lay waiting for us at The Skies, this moment would be lodged in my memory and probably ingrained in whatever was left of my heart, if I even had one. Lilith always told me the thing I heard thumping in my chest, that rhythmic beat that I felt, was merely something that told me I could keep going, keep torturing, keep killing, killing, killing. It wasn't meant for things like emotions to make you weak and feelings to keep you from what you were meant to do.

But right now, right here, I wanted to feel...something. The pull at my chest was proof that it wasn't just meant for the darkness I'd grown so accustomed to.

"You alright?" Nicholas said, pulling me from my thoughts. I saw they were both looking at me with concerned faces. I looked down, noticing my hands were still in the position to cut my piece of roast. I continued as if nothing had happened. I had something on my mind that I wanted to ask that would change the subject immediately, leading me away from my thoughts.

"Did your son tell you he practically forced me to torture a prisoner?" I stuffed a piece of meat into my mouth casually.

Mr. Cassial raised an eyebrow. "He did?"

"I had to; it was what the executives wanted," Nicholas explained.

"We both know that they can always rely on their good little soldier to do their bidding," I said, rolling my eyes.

Mr. Cassial tapped his index finger on his water glass. "Alright, stop that. Was this the demon that got into The Skies originally?" He looked over at me.

"Yes. We used to know each other, so it made the torturing much more personal and demeaning." Just like Lilith would have wanted.

"From what Nick has said, this demon said Lilith had them bring you here as a means to an end or something of the sort?"

I brushed a curl out of my eye, but it swayed right back into my line of sight. "Something like that. I don't know if Ariel is in on it, or Markus, or hell, even Jonah. There is way too much finger pointing going on and Lilith is just laughing at the way her plan is worming its way through."

"Lilith always had a way of sealing her plan's fate right under everyone's noses," his father said.

"I mean, a whole other demon ended up at The Skies and no one seems to give a fuck about how it wound up dead. It's ridiculous. How could they not assume a damn ambush would be the next step?"

"Another demon?" Mr. Cassial put down his fork and looked over at his son, who pressed a finger to his temple.

"Dad, they said they handled it. They found it; Markus took care to make sure the trainees were dealt with and that's when I got the task of convincing her to come to the Ethereal Bastille."

"Convincing...right," I muttered, remembering the way I had kicked him in the stomach and the way my knuckles felt connecting with his jaw. The bruises had all but faded by now. I crossed my legs, thinking about the way his body heat radiated over me when he had me pinned against the wall, the moment his resolve had cracked to small pieces that neither of us were willing to find and put together again. I remembered how *good* his convincing had been.

Nicholas, clearly having heard me, let out a cough and started picking at his food more.

He wanted to play the pretend game, the *it was a mistake* game, so fine. I could give his father something else to worry about than his son sticking his dick in me and getting cut up by a shadowy demon.

"He had to be sneaky about it though, since he had to give me my dagger to perform my soul seething duties," I admitted nonchalantly, grabbing my water glass and taking a nice, long drink.

"Dagger?" Mr. Cassial looked stunned. "What dagger?"

"It's nothing—" Nicholas started, but I cut him off.

"The one I brought with me to Heaven's Gate when Ariel plucked me from Purgatory." I looked between father and son, watching how his father blinked a few times and Nicholas again went back to rubbing his temple with his index finger. "Oh gosh, did you not tell your father about how you are harboring a demonic weapon without your higher ups knowing? That you let me have it to torture Cullen and then walked in right after I slit his throat with it? I didn't even get to pull his soul out, but it is likely all part of Lilith's plan, because why the hell not? Weirder shit has happened. I honestly wonder what you did with it after that." I pressed the tips of my fingers to my lips, as if I had mistakenly let something slip.

Nicholas narrowed those brown eyes at me, his breathing slow and methodical. He was annoyed, that was for sure. I, on the other hand, was sensationally satisfied with my words.

His father tapped his fork against his plate, the echoing noise playing against the loud rumbling rain outside. "You didn't tell anyone she brought it here?"

"Your first question isn't to ask her why she brought it in the first place?" Nicholas asked, a little shocked.

"Son, if I'm going to a place that sees me as the enemy, I would surely bring a weapon along. So, no, that part does not surprise me."

I swiveled my head over to Nicholas, who gave a slight shake of his head at my shit-eating grin. "No, I haven't told anyone about it, except Reese. I don't know why. I just didn't think about telling anyone. It was just a feeling."

"I bet he was thrilled," I laughed.

"Oh yeah, he was just over the fucking moon about me having it."

"You *are* allowed to make your own judgment calls, but if I'm just clarifying here. You just told Reese. That's it?" his father asked again.

"Yeah. I mean, Markus did ask me if she brought anything with her, like contraband, but that's just strictly protocol type stuff." He waved his hand dismissively at the thought, but by the look on his face, it felt as if he had so much more to say about that interaction.

Mr. Cassial just seemed to nod, as if he too agreed that it was simply an executive's duty to ask those types of questions. It made sense, but with everything going on, nothing just seemed simple anymore. I honestly didn't like any of them, Jonah, Markus, or Ariel... especially Ariel, but maybe my position in all this made me more cynical. There was silence around us broken when a large crack of thunder practically vibrated the room, followed by strikes of lightning.

"Where is it now?" his father asked.

"I left it in my room, like I always do."

I scoffed. "Well, there is a huge reason to go back to The Skies."

"You are not flying in this weather, and I don't want to think about what could happen if you tried to portal into that mess right now. You will stay here, like I said. We can figure everything out in the morning, with a good night's sleep and fresh eyes," Mr. Cassial said in a way that had us both quiet and submissive. I bet he used that tone on Nicholas all the time.

"I do like it when you get all authoritative, Mr. Cassial," I said, winking at him as I took my last bite of food, throwing my napkin onto the plate.

He smirked at me. "When I was a younger man, that kind of talk worked wonders."

Nicholas practically choked on his water, setting it down with an obnoxious slam. "Oh, my god. Stop."

"Is that how you pulled Nicholas' mother? Your big bad authority?" I asked, laughing at my words, but soon realizing no one else was laughing with me. Nicholas' father had started to clear the plates and bring them to the kitchen but stopped mid step, facing away from us. Nicholas was looking at his father with a steady gaze that wasn't reciprocated. "Did I say something wrong?

Mr. Cassial continued to walk to the counter. He turned around, facing the mantle and looking over at the pictures I had yet to really see, before letting out a huff. "No. She wasn't impressed by me much."

I didn't know anything about Nicholas' family, how far his family tree branches extended, but I did know *some* things. Those things were vague and not really pieced together at all, but it was something. I was there when Natalia had mentioned his mother and his reaction wasn't at all what I had expected. I was there this afternoon when he had let his mother slip from his lips again in an accusatory tone with Jonah, as if he had something to do with her lack of presence in his life. His words to Jonah were something I had a feeling he didn't want to let his father in on, and I would let him have that one. His father gave nothing away when it came to where his mother was. He just let a small smile leave his lips when he spoke those few words about her to me.

Nicholas tapped his foot on the ground, causing his right knee to bob nervously. He was biting the inside of his cheek, as if he didn't want to talk about this topic at all. I let my hand drift to his knee and squeezed. He stiffened under my touch and moved his eyes away from his father, down to where my hand sat. He peeked up at me through his long eyelashes and one corner of his mouth lifted, giving me a good look at the scar underneath his eye that I kept meaning to ask about.

"She was a special lady, but that's enough. It's getting late and you'll probably want to change," Mr. Cassial said, pulling us both out of our short-lived moment.

"I don't think you have anything in my size, Mr. Cassial," I joked.

"I have some sweatshirts you can wear. It's not a big deal. You can change in the bathroom," Nicholas offered.

"Sounds cozy," I mocked. Nicholas rolled his eyes and got up from his chair. He walked past me, holding onto his side, and retreated down the hall to the room on the left.

His father turned back towards the sink and pulled out a sponge, drizzling dish detergent. "Go on now."

BEFORE MR. CASSIAL SAUNTERED OFF TO BED, HE TOLD US THAT NICHOLAS would happily let me sleep in his bed while he slept on the couch. I watched as Nicholas narrowed his eyes at his father for casually giving away his room, but held down any back talk that might come up if he opened his mouth. I had laughed and said I didn't need a bed, but he had insisted, so I didn't fight too hard for it. His father told us goodnight with a wave of his hand over his shoulder and retreated upstairs to his room.

Then we were alone. I stood in front of Nicholas, who had already changed into another t-shirt and sweatpants, crossing my arms over my chest.

Nicholas handed me the clothes—a sweatshirt and a pair of sweatpants, telling me that obviously the sweatpants would be too big, but they had a pretty lengthy drawstring, so I could make it work. I gave him a nod before making my way to the bathroom. Shutting the door behind me, I leaned my back against the solid wood and could almost feel the whole door vibrate from the crack-ling thunder. The thunder isn't what got me, but the rain, ah, the rain soothed me. The sound of the pattering liquid against the roof allowed me to clear my head whenever I needed it.

The bathroom was small, but not so small that I didn't have room to move around. I couldn't see myself doing a full cartwheel in here, but it was spacey enough. I set the clothes on the toilet lid and pulled my shirt over my head and scuffled out of my shorts, looking at myself in the mirror. I brought my hair over my shoulders, watching as it settled right in front of my breasts, each curl twirling whichever way it wanted and springing up the minute I wrapped a finger around it and let it go. I leaned against the sink, sucked in one long breath, and let it out, in, out, in, out. I looked down at the clothes and a surge of trouble ran through my veins and heated my skin. I unclasped my bra and let it fall to the ground, collapsing on top of the pile of my other clothes.

I reached for the sweatshirt, which was solid black, but when I turned it around, I noticed that two white wings decorated the back. I rolled my eyes but stuck to the plan. I pulled the sweatshirt over my head, pulled my hair out, and let it settle in its large mess around my shoulders again. My eyes traveled to the sweatpants still laying gracefully on the toilet lid, willing me to put them on, but I just blinked and opened the door to leave.

I took off my shoes as I left the bathroom, reaching down and picking them up, placing them right outside Nicholas' room. I could hear rummaging in the kitchen and made my way over. The couch had a set of sheets on the arm and the throw pillows were arranged in a way that told me those were his sleeping pillows for the night. He was over at the refrigerator, leaning in and searching.

"What are you doing?" I asked, startling him.

Nicholas lifted his head, connecting with the top of the fridge with a loud thud. "Fuck," he mumbled, rubbing at the top of his head. I pressed my lips together, trying not to giggle.

"I was just getting a drink that wasn't water, since my father forgets I'm twenty-three and not—" he started, but let the words just fall away when he turned around and saw me. His eyes didn't remain on my face too long. They skated down from my face to my sweat-shirt-covered body to the hem that hit right at mid-thigh. His mouth dropped open a bit and he stared so hard, it was as if he wanted to burn a hole through my legs.

"Not what?"

"What?" He blinked up to my face again, confusion in his eyes.

"You started a sentence and didn't finish it."

Nicholas blinked a few more times and then looked down at the beer in his hand, as if he hadn't even realized he'd removed it from the fridge. "Yeah...uh...I wanted a real drink now that the old man has gone to sleep."

"You rebel," I joked, padding over to the couch, making myself comfortable in front of the fireplace.

"Ha ha," he replied sarcastically. It was odd, but I felt him hesitate for a few moments before asking, "do you want one?"

I swung my arm over the back of the couch and turned my eyes on him. I wrinkled my nose at the idea of beer but conceded. "Sure."

"Don't tell me you have more exquisite alcohol in Purgatory." I watched as he rummaged through the fridge, picking out another beer and closing the door with his shoeless foot. He rounded the couch and reached out to hand me the bottle of dark liquid. He leaned down towards the coffee table, picking up a bottle opener sitting on top. He popped his cap off and tossed the opener over to me.

"Of course not, but beer has never been my top choice. I'm not picky about much, but this is one of those things." He shrugged and took a swig of his drink as I popped the top from my own bottle. "Besides, how can I refuse when someone as pretty as you offers it to me?"

He leveled me with his eyes over the top of his beer bottle, saying nothing. The next thing out of his mouth was not what I expected. "You said that those things didn't even know themselves anymore."

I tapped my nail on the bottle, taking a small sip that I make me wince. "Hmm?"

"Back at The Skies, you made a comment that they didn't even know who they were anymore. What does that even mean?”

“It doesn’t mean anything.”

“You are going to act coy now? Of all the times to open your mouth, you choose now to be coy.”

I rolled my eyes. “Stop whining. I’m not being coy. I really don’t know that much.”

“But you know enough to make an ominous comment like that.” He settled back in his corner of the couch and scanned me from head to toe again, this time making a point to not linger on my legs tucked under my thighs.

“If I tell you what little I know, will you shut up about it?”

“One of those things sliced through my side today. I’m not making that fucking promise.”

Annoyed, I took a long, disgusting pull of the beer. “Demons have souls or an essence, Nicholas. They aren’t as pretty or as pure as you angels, but they’re there. It keeps us in a type of homeostasis. Without them...” I trailed off, trying to find the right words.

He nodded, as if he had some type of understanding. “These shadow demons that ambushed us don’t have a soul?”

I point my bottle at him. “Correct. I only overheard talk about it once between a few demons. You know Lilith can take souls like I can, but I always just kill them outright because it’s the simpler choice. Other times, I do take the soul, but I can’t keep them soulless. I have to remove them from existence completely, because when you have that sort of thing removed from you, you become...lost.”

One of his eyebrows perked up, but he didn’t speak. I continued. “I heard them talking about Lilith experimenting with removing souls but just leaving the demons as they are. You’re vulnerable without that sort of balance, susceptible to suggestion, as it were. You don’t remember much of anything about yourself, you just see dark and...nothing.”

He placed his beer down on the coffee table and perched his elbow on the back of the couch. “Is that what you were talking about in the Divine Library? You know, when you talked about losing your soul and being...what was the word you used? Voided?”

I tilted my beer bottle back and forth. “Sort of. I wasn’t speaking about someone ripping my soul out, just that one day after every-thing I've done, maybe I'll reap what I sow." I laughed at myself and shook my head, looking down at my exposed knees. "No one really knows what true darkness is like until you're trapped in it with only a voice to guide your lonely thoughts. Lilith could mold them if she wanted, since they have nothing else going for them without their souls. She makes them ultimately submit, or I assume that's how it would go."

Nicholas ran a hand through his hair, making it stick up. "Well, that's a scary fucking thought."

I lifted my eyes in a *well, yeah* gesture. "These demons give off the vibe that that's exactly what she's doing. Lilith sent them there to bombard us, clearly tasked to attack, kill, attack."

"And?" Nicholas reached for his beer, his shirt lifting a bit, revealing a sliver of his abs and parts of the gauze covering his wound.

"Well, it's just so stupidly simple for Lilith. I've spent enough time with her to know she isn't stupid, and she isn't simple. What if those demons were just like Cullen? Sent as a test through the portal."

Nicholas let out a hum against the top of his beer bottle, the sound of his breath against the top making a low whistle. "Then what happened with the demon before the ambush? The one Markus ended up finding."

I pursed my lips and squinted, trying to think, the sound of the rain making it easier for me to gather my thoughts. "I don't know about that one. Maybe it slipped through the cracks. If voided demons aren't strong enough to maintain a bond with the host, the host being Lilith, then they can go rogue."

Nicholas took a drink from his bottle, then another, and another. "Okay."

"Okay?"

The crackle of the fireplace was loud from the way the silence enveloped the room. His answer was so simple, as if every new piece of information he got was just so much that he could only respond in monosyllables. He scratched the back of his neck and nodded. "Yup."

"You aren't going to interrogate me anymore?"

"That was hardly an interrogation."

"I would know, wouldn't I?" I said, sticking my tongue out between my teeth.

"I don't think you have anything to worry about," he said, looking towards the fireplace and gazing into the dancing flames. His face was illuminated, making his brown eyes brighter.

"What are you talking about?"

"About losing your soul or losing yourself. I honestly don't see that happening. Elise, possibly. I'm not totally convinced she isn't already consumed by the darkness."

I chuckled, tilting my head to the side mischievously. "Nicholas, is that your version of saying something nice about me?"

"Think whatever you want."

I fingered my hand through my hair. "Just because you fucked me doesn't mean you have to say or do nice things." He had pulled me out of that group of demons as if it was his mission to help me. I felt something tug at me the moment he had grabbed my hand and pulled me out. Gratitude? Happiness? Who the fuck knows.

Nicholas practically coughed up his swig of beer, pressing his hand to his throat to stop from coughing up a lung. "Dani...I already told you..."

"Yeah, yeah, it was a mistake. Whatever you have to say to make yourself feel better when you jerk off to the memory of my pussy in the middle of the night."

He had his beer slightly tilted to his lips as I said this, causing him to scrub a hand down his face and place the beer on the coffee table. "Fuck. You have absolutely no filter, do you?"

"With you? Not a chance."

He narrowed his eyes. "You know, I say nice things and do nice things because I'm a nice person. Sex is not the reason."

I narrowed my eyes right back at him. "It is *a* reason, though."

"No."

"Yes."

"No. God, can you just let it go?" His expression was exasperated. He looked over his shoulder towards where his father slept.

"I will. You must admit one thing, though."

"Alright, what?"

I let a devilish grin creep to my lips. I leaned forward, rising a bit so the sweatshirt pulled upward and showed a bit more of my thigh. My hands crawled across the middle cushion that separated us and remained just shy of his knee. "You liked it."

He pressed his lips together, as I watched his Adam's apple bob harshly. He snuck a look at my legs and then to my hands. His eyes closed for a minute but then popped open, boring right into mine as if challenging my words. "I liked it."

I scrunched my nose at him, reaching my hand up to caress his jaw. "Wasn't that easy?"

He didn't try to remove my hand when he spoke. "I'm surprised you don't want to talk about this more."

"Nah, you find me intriguing, and I find you intriguing. You wanted to fuck and so did I. We are two beings who wanted to get off and we did. It's quite simple when you break it down."

Nicholas let out a disgruntled sigh. "I didn't *want* to fuck, Dani. You make me sound like I was dying for it, like I had no self-control."

"If the wings fit, Nicholas, you demanding thing." I tapped my index finger on his lips, letting the pad of my fingertip linger over how soft they were before I let my hand fall away.

He pressed his hand to his chest. "Alright, alright, my bad. I should have asked permission."

I vigorously shook my head, my curls bouncing in all directions. "Oh god, no, you handsome ethereal creature you. I liked what you did. Granted, I was waiting for you to make a move I never thought would come, but well, next thing I know, my leggings are off and you are pulling sounds out of me I didn't know existed..." I started to barrel on, but he rushed over and placed a hand to my mouth. His leg was touching my knees and his face was inches from mine. I could smell the beer on his breath, and I drank it in.

"Can you not?" he asked in a pleading tone, but there was some amusement to his voice. "We get it. You liked what we did and.... I liked what we did, but that's it. It was a thing that happened that could likely be a very funny story in a few centuries."

He was finished, but he didn't move away from me. I lifted my mouth and wrapped my lips around the top of his hand, baring my teeth. I bit down on the flesh right near his thumb and laughed as he pulled away, waving his hand in the air. "You like me," I stated.

"Hmph, debatable," he mumbled, picking up his beer and draining it. I watched his hand wrap around the bottle and remembered what his hands felt like wrapped around my thighs as he lifted me up and away from the wall. I stood up abruptly, making my way around the coffee table and over to the mantle.

Nicholas followed me with his gaze as I walked over, his eyes glued to the hem of the sweatshirt, almost magically trying to see what was underneath...or what wasn't.

I started to scan the photos one by one. The first few that decorated the mantle were of Nicholas as a toddler, the same dark head of hair and playful smile on his face, like he knew something you didn't but would probably tell you at some point if you played your cards right.

"So, Markus asked about me?" I asked, not looking at him.

I heard him sniff behind me and move around on the couch, as if he was readjusting his posture. "I didn't say he asked about you."

"Look who's playing coy now."

I practically felt his eye roll at my back. "Executives ask about weapons brought into our realm all the time; it's nothing special."

I looked over my shoulder and gave him a face that told him that I wasn't going to accept his story. "We both know you don't believe a word you're saying."

"It really was nothing. It was quick and to the point. I said no and moved on."

I let out a hmm, which made him raise both his eyebrows, as if to ask *what*. "You said no."

"Didn't I just say that?"

"I know. You said no, which means you had an inkling shit wasn't right."

He leaned over and grabbed my beer from where I had abandoned it on the coffee table. "No, I said no because I would rather not have my ass chewed out by Markus Seraph."

I chewed on the inside of my cheek. "You are really fucking adorable when you don't want to admit the truth. What would they really have done to you? Smacked your hand and said, 'bad boy, don't do it again?'" I tried to mimic Markus's tone.

"He just gave me a weird vibe, that's all. I'm allowed to make judgment calls."

I looked back towards the photos. "That you are, and you probably made a good one, because we don't know what any of those fuckers are capable of...at least not officially."

I heard movement behind me and feet shuffling. His presence next to me was like a powerful cloud I could stand in for hours. He was calmer right now than I had ever seen him, but it was more than his relaxed clothing or the way he casually stood near me. It was the way his body seemed to be less overwhelmed with the circumstances we found ourselves in. He was home, in a place where he always knew he would be forever safe, and I envied him. Fuck, did I envy him.

I started scanning the photos again, watching as Nicholas grew up and gazing at the way his father grew up right along with him. Maurice Cassial was certainly the kind of man who aged like fine wine. There was a photo of him holding his son over his shoulders and you could just tell that Nicholas would end up looking just like his father. Their smiles made my lips perk up. "Your dad is hot."

Nicholas groaned against the lip of his bottle.

"I'm sure you've had to deal with girls throwing their pussies at you dad your whole life," I giggled.

"Gross. Okay, the main rule for staying here is you can't use pussy and my dad in the same sentence. *Please.*"

I waved my hand at him, focusing on the row of pictures again. I stopped at one that had him and his dad, but also a woman who hadn't shown up in the photos until now. I quickly looked down to the other photos and saw she was in three or four, but that was it. The rest were of Nicholas alone or included his dad or Reese or other people involved in his life. I plucked the photo from the mantle and traced my fingers along the glass frame. The woman had her arms wrapped around Nicholas from the back, laying her head on his shoulder. Her strawberry blonde hair flowed around her face in waves and cascaded down his tiny shoulders. They looked as if they had been giggling right before the photo was taken. She had happiness in her eyes and the way she hugged him was so loving and protective. "Is this your mother?"

Nicholas pushed his tongue out to swipe at his bottom lip. He nodded.

"She's beautiful."

He took the photo from me and stared at it, like he was trying to burn a hole through the frame, the glass, the photo itself. I thought back to our first meeting with Natalia, the way Nicholas seemed to tense but then dismissed any acknowledgement of his mother.

"What happened to her?"

He pressed his lips together for a moment as if thinking of what to say, but he didn't have an answer, so he just blew out a breath. "I don't know."

"Does your father?"

"He doesn't love talking about her and I don't push. She left when I was little, so that's all I know and all I need to know."

I watched him look at the photo one more time before he placed it back on the mantle. I clucked my tongue. "I assume you don't know why she left?" I glanced back over to the photo. She looked way too happy with her son to have any reason to leave.

"Nope."

"Is she the reason why your dad left The Skies?"

Nicholas looked down at me, his tall frame hovering over me. The lightning that lit up the dark night outside the window behind him sent a temporary glow around his body. "No, he had already left before they got married and had me." He gave me skeptical look. "How did you know he left The Skies?"

I shrugged before leaning in closer. "I have a feeling you got your fighting skills from your dad, so he must have been great. Why isn't he still there, swinging a sword around? Ariel, Jonah, and the rest of them are still there. Unless your father left with your mom or something. Logical reasoning."

Nicholas pulled his eyebrows down as if considering this.

"Hmph, well, I don't know. He just always told me he left for his own reasons. You may come to learn that you don't push someone like my father because it will get you nowhere and you'll just end up exhausted."

"Does Jonah have anything to do with her?" I pressed, nodding towards the photo of his mother.

"You are full of questions tonight. Maybe it's time we both go to bed," Nicholas said, draining the beer and leaning down to place it on the coffee table.

"You literally aired your dirty laundry in that meeting before shit went down."

"I absolutely did not." His biceps flexed as he crossed his arms over his chest.

"Oh, come on, you asked Jonah if any of this had to do with your mom. Maybe your father should know about that."

"Maybe you should stop talking about things you know nothing about." He said it so matter of factly, I looked directly at him. This was actually something he didn't want to banter about. I moved my weight to each of my feet, trying to find something to say.

He pressed his palm to the back of his neck, sliding it back and forth. "Sorry. This is just a lot for one day. Not to mention the fact that I have no idea if my best friend is still hanging in there after spending almost a whole day in close proximity with Elise." He tilted his head to the side and smiled at me.

I playfully shoved his shoulder and shook my head. "She isn't as bad as you think."

He nudged one shoulder up to say *whatever*. The silence surrounded us like a massive blanket, almost suffocating. I didn't want to leave for bed like this. I had let our time together in the training room slide because I wasn't the sentimental sex type. I believed that, male or female, anyone should be able to fuck and fuck without consequences, but this—whatever this was— was begging to be poked like a sleeping bear. I took a step towards him and then another. I saw the hairs on his arms begin to stand up a bit and the pulse in his neck pushed out harder. "You really don't have to sleep on the couch, you know. I feel bad."

His shoulders moved as he chuckled. "No, you don't." His breath hit my face and I tried to plant my feet harder to the ground when all I wanted to do was get on my toes and breathe him in.

"You aren't going to get lonely out here?" I asked, perking one of my eyebrows up as I tilted my head to look at him. His eyes searched mine and he shook his head silently. His eyes looked at my mouth and his teeth came out to bite his bottom lip. I wanted to end this night on a note that would make him feel better than this day had started.

I brought my hand up to his chin and took his bottom lip with my thumb, pulling it free of his teeth. Leaning up, I noticed that his breath hitched and his eyes darkened, seeming so heavily focused on me, I felt a tiny bit unsteady. So quickly, so swiftly, I pressed my lips to his, noticing his eyes closing when I was just seconds away from his face. His hands and long fingers traveled to my waist and held on. I didn't want the kiss to linger, so I pulled away, smugly looking at the way his eyes opened in a kind of trance.

I snuck a look down and noticed a perfectly distinct presence making an appearance in his sweatpants and smiled mischievously. He followed my gaze, noticing the same thing as me. He was getting hard and I wanted to see it, to put my hand down his pants and feel it, but I didn't. I did, however, place my flat palm against it and started to rub slowly, the fire next to us practically overheating me.

He let out a small, simple, low groan and I took my hand away. I looked over his face and leaned in, as if I was going to kiss him again. His eyes starting to flutter closed, waiting for me. I stopped right at his mouth, letting my breath tangle around with his. A crash of thunder hit, along with sheets of rain assaulting the windows, as if it was trying to break in. He swallowed and I watched his throat move, watching the smooth way his neck curved to meet his collarbones.

I licked his lips with my tongue. "You really fucking like me."

I pulled back and sashayed around him as I walked towards his room, leaving him and his hard cock to think about me the entire night. It was better than thinking about everything else, wasn't it?

I was a fucking saint.

CHAPTER SIXTEEN

DANI

I closed the door behind me, looking down at the crack right underneath the wood, watching as the light that flooded in from the living room grew dark. I let out a sigh and decided I wasn't tired enough to go to bed. I had exploring to do while I had the chance. I looked to the right, seeing a queen-sized bed still perfectly made. The sheets were crisp and had the perfect lines of folds along them. The comforter was a royal blue color and plush, like I could settle into it and feel as if I was along the clouds. The room was much bigger than I thought, but it didn't have much furniture, so that might have made it feel bigger than it was.

A light gray large dresser faced the bed and a large-scale window behind it. The curtains were closed slightly, but a sliver of the night sky peeked through, allowing me to see bits of the moon through the rain. To the left of the bed was a desk with a simple lamp and a few picture frames decorating the top of it. I leaned down, placing my hands on my knees as I looked at the photos. There was one of Nicholas and his father, holding swords above their heads and smiling, while another one was of him and Reese. Reese had Nicholas cradled in his arms, as if he was about to carry him over a threshold. I shook my head as I laughed but admired the way these memories were encapsulated forever.

The wooden desk had two drawers to the right and my curiosity got the better of me. I opened the top drawer, finding a few pens and empty notebooks, letting out a small huff of disappointment. I opened the second drawer to find it empty, except for a single photo. Just one. It sat in the middle of the drawer, and I plucked it from its resting place. I brought it up to my eyes and saw the same woman from the photo on the mantle. Her hair was a bit shorter in this photo, but not by much. She had a smile on her face that I'm sure Nicholas's father fell immediately in love with.

He may not want to talk much about his mother, but Nicholas cared about her, even if it was with just the smallest piece of his heart. Why was his father so vague about her? They both spoke about Jonah like his father had some issue with him that went beyond the dealings with Nicholas...so what was it? I looked more deeply at the photo, wishing this woman could somehow speak to me and tell me what I wanted to know. I placed the photo back in the drawer and closed it. I padded to the closet in the far-left corner and cut the light on. There weren't many clothes, but I had been expecting that. There were a good number of jackets and some nicer clothes for special occasions, various sets of shoes scattered along the floor, and I raised my head to look at the top shelf above the hanging clothes.

A large box with a lock attached to it was nestled there. It was long and rectangular, a thin layer of dust was on it, telling me it hadn't been touched in some time. I wanted to bring it down to see what was inside, but that couldn't happen. I wouldn't be able to get it open since I had no idea what the code was, and it was too high up for me to reach without some type of step ladder. Fuck Nicholas and his tree-like frame. I rolled my eyes and left the closet door cracked behind me after I cut the light. There wasn't much else in here for me to find. The walls were a creamy beige and a few medals hung from hooks, trophies placed on random floating shelves, but there was nothing spectacular about it. I had at least hoped to find a box full of sex toys I could tease him about. Even his side tables were empty, except for a lamp and the pictures. He wasn't making discovering anything about him easy.

I walked over to the light switch by the door and switched it off, deciding that snuggling into his bed was my only option now. I slithered under the sheets, soft and welcoming. The pillows were firm but seemed to mold around my head perfectly. I felt caressed from head to toe. I turned over onto my side and listened to the rain hit the window, letting it numb my mind and drift me off to sleep.

I didn't know how long I had been asleep when I heard a noise coming from behind me. It was a creaking sound, slow and deliberate, as if someone was trying to not make much noise and utterly failing. My back was turned to the door, so I didn't know who it was, but it didn't take a genius to figure it out. My eyes stared at the darkness against the opposite wall and listened as feet lightly padded across the carpet. I had never been a heavy sleeper in Purgatory, since there were high pitched screams of pain or pleasure always surrounding me. I had eventually been able to tune them out, but this was different. I hadn't encountered someone authentically *trying* to be quiet around me, so it piqued my curiosity.

I lifted my head up slightly, peeking over my shoulder, trying to see into the darkness. The closet door opened slightly as a figure walked in. I saw a small hint of light, a glow. It was the same type of glow Nicholas used to light our way in the tunnel to the Divine Library. I arched my eyebrow and started to shuffle my way out of the covers. I did it slowly and evenly, making sure to not ruffle the sheets or make the bed creak.

Once I was at the edge, I slid off and placed my feet on the carpet. The glowing light bobbed in the closet, not so bright as to blind anyone, but expelling enough light so that the person needing it could see. I tiptoed over to the closet and placed my back against the wall near the door, taking in a breath. I heard rustling and some movement of clothes, but then eventually, the glow was snuffed out. I waited a few seconds and then the figure appeared at the door.

"Well, hello there," I said.

The figure jumped back a little bit, catching their footing a few seconds after. "Ah, fuck!" His voice came out in a hoarse whisper.

Nicholas placed his hands on his thighs before straightening up again. He opened his palm to let the glowing light out again so that I could see all the angles of his face. The shocking exasperation on his features was still there.

"What are you doing here?" I questioned.

"I needed something."

"Right. In the middle of the night?"

He rolled his eyes. "Don't make it weird. I keep a few extra pillows in here and needed another one."

"Do you not have a separate place where you keep additional pillows?"

I noticed him chewing the inside of his cheek. "Yes, in a little hall closet, but there weren't any in there and I keep the good pillows in my room. It seems my father has figured that out, though. The old man needs to sleep with like, a thousand pillows."

"Aw, you poor baby. Your daddy stole all your plushy princess pillows."

"You're annoying," he said, shaking his head. "I didn't mean to wake you."

I pulled the sleeves of his sweatshirt down my arms so that my fingers could cup the material. "It's fine, I'm more amused than angry."

He considered this and gave me a nonchalant expression. He released his palm from under the glowing light and it settled in mid-air.

I looked more closely at his eyes; he looked sleepy, but not exhausted. "Were you uncomfortable from your lack of pillows or are you just *now* going to sleep and realized that you needed more?"

He gave me a shrug. "I couldn't sleep. Unfortunately, I probably won't be able to due to the pillow problem. You're picky about beer, and I'm picky about my lack of pillows. We all have our things."

"I told you to take your bed if you wanted."

He cleared his throat. "No, Dani. It's...it's not that."

"Then what?" I pressed.

"Just let it go." He placed his hands in his sweatpants pockets.

I pushed off the wall and stepped closer to him. He stepped back

297

a little, the glowing light following his every move. "Let me guess: you were thinking about me?"

He ran a hand through his hair in a nervous way, then stuck it back in his pocket. "No."

"Are you sure?" I asked.

"Absolutely."

"The way I left you wasn't very nice," I admitted playfully, pouting.

He chuckled softly. "No, but it didn't surprise me at all."

I bit down on my lower lip, peeking up at him through my lashes as I stepped closer. "Would you like me to make up for it?"

He took in a breath but when he tried to blow it out, it came out like a cough, as if his faux calmness was breaking down. "No. Nope. Bad idea."

I stepped closer again, but this time, I grabbed pieces of his shirt to keep him in place. He looked down at where I held him and cleared his throat, catching a glance at the door. He was probably deciding if he should make a run for it. The thought of him bolting for the door almost made me laugh.

"Bad idea because you don't want it?" I tightened my hold on his shirt, twisting it in my fists. "I mean, I won't make fun of you if you admit you want to make a second mistake," I joked.

Nicholas let out a small groan and wrapped his hands around my arms, sliding them down my forearms as if he was going to try to peel my hands off his shirt. "Dani, right now is not the best time for any of this, regardless of what I want."

I took my final step forward so that we were toe to toe and my chest could press against his. I leaned up a little, mimicking my previous move in the living room, letting his breath mingle with mine. I laughed against his mouth, our lips brushing a tiny bit. Fuck, he was tall. I could reach his mouth, but he had to angle himself down just a little to meet me. "Nicholas, we both know with every-thing going on, it's never going to be a good time." I released his shirt right as he released my forearms. I brought my hands underneath his shirt, skimming my fingertips over his skin, his abs, the gauze that lay over his wound.

"Does it still hurt?" I asked, actual concern in my voice.

He squinted at me, the light looming around him. "Not anymore."

I moved my hands up, his shirt following along, lifting the further my hands went. I wanted to feel him, all of him. I wanted to feel his warm skin and his breath on my overheated body. I wanted his fingers to touch me and explore me in all the ways he hadn't before. He moved his hands to my waist, pressing his fingers into my sides as if holding himself back.

"Maybe this is the last chance you'll get to have some actual fun. Don't you want that?" I questioned, grazing my fingernails over his abs to the waistband of his sweatpants. I knew he wanted this, and I sure as shit knew I wanted this. My only problem moving forward was I needed him to be as in it as he was the first time. I didn't want him to think about his decision for one minute; I wanted him to go full speed ahead. "Nicholas."

He was watching me fiddle with his waistband. "Mhmm?"

"Get out of your head for tonight."

I moved my hands away from him and walked towards the side of his bed. My back was turned, and I tapped my bare foot on the carpet. I saw the glowing light come closer to me as he followed behind, stopping a few inches away. "That's difficult and you know it."

"It seemed really easy for you before," I accused.

"What are you talking about?"

"The first time. You just went headfirst into it, no thought, no slowing down. I liked it. It wasn't just the rough, relentless part about it that I liked -- it was the way you didn't overthink."

He sighed and whispered. "You know that's not how I am. This entire time, you've known me I've never dived headfirst into anything. The training room was...I don't know."

"What made that time so different?" I wasn't frustrated, even if my tone seemed like I was. I wasn't begging for him to have sex with me. If he left and decided against it, that would be fine, but it would be a fucking solid decision.

He didn't say anything. I just heard his steady breathing. In, out, in, out. His glowing light went out suddenly and lightning struck, making a line of light inside the room, letting me see his shadow behind me. He had gotten closer, but not so close as to touch me yet.

His voice was soft when he spoke next. "It was a lot, Dani. It was a lot of adrenaline, and you were so close to me. I didn't know how you would react, and like I said, I never intended for us to have sex. I already admitted I liked it, so what else do you want?"

I balled my hands into fists and swiftly turned around, not realizing that he had gotten even closer. My chest hit his and he caught me, his hands on my hips. "I want you to tell me you don't want me. You liked it but it was a weird phase that you're over and done with, or some shit like that. I can be a plaything, Nicholas, but I won't play with someone who can't make up their fucking mind. It can make for really exhausting pillow talk," I whispered, letting my words push against him.

I felt his breath on my face when I looked up at him. The lightning would cast light here and there so I could see his face. He slid his hands back and forth on my hips. "Dani, I can't—"

I scoffed, trying to release myself from his hold, but he pressed on my hips tighter.

"Let me finish," he said in a stern voice as I settled back in front of him, waiting. "I can't because I don't want to be with you like we were before.... not right now."

"What does that even mean?" I noticed the breathy way he said the last few words. His hands were starting to bunch the sweatshirt up, lifting it up along my thighs so the fabric breezed slowly by my skin.

"It means—" he started, pulling the sweatshirt up a little higher, using one of his hands to hold it in place while his other skimmed the outside of my thigh, circling it with his finger, moving it to the inside and up, up, up to where the material of my panties met his fingertips. "I'm allowed to want to take my time."

I blinked up at the shadow of him in the darkness. "I've never been a slow-moving kind of demon."

He laughed, leaning down to tease my lips. "You'd be surprised how much you might like it."

Well, fuck. Nicholas Cassial had a seductive side I didn't know existed until now. I had told him there likely wasn't going to be another good time to take what we both wanted and right now, he was showing me that he not only agreed with me, but that he could make use of the time we had for as long as we had it.

Fuck. Fuck. Fuck. How did I end up losing all the power?

His knuckle hit the center of my panties and I felt my breath catch. He rocked his finger back and forth, letting his knuckle rub me in all the best ways. I felt the pull and heat in my stomach start to pool itself between my legs, and I brought my hand up to reach for his forearm to steady myself. He pressed a little bit more, never losing his rhythm. I bit down a moan from creeping out of my throat right as he bent his forehead to mine.

He removed his knuckle and brought two fingers right to the center of my panties and started to mimic his knuckle, applying more pressure. His smile pressed against my mouth when he finally kissed me, slow and artful. His lips were soft but not pushy. He didn't try to shove me against a wall and press against me. He just kissed me, rubbing between my legs with his long fingers. I let a small moan leave my lips and he swallowed it down. His fingers traced a line along the curve of my panties before he dipped his hand inside, touching me where I was the most wet and sensitive. I moaned into his mouth with each pass of his fingers.

I bit his lower lip as he brought his finger around to gather up my wetness and glided his fingers to my clit. He circled around my tight bundle of nerves slowly. He was almost lazy about the rotation of his fingers. It was a confident laziness, though, and it was severely turning me on. He kept kissing me, even when I brought my hand to the front of his sweatpants and found his cock. *Fuck* was it hard. I rubbed my hand up and down, leaning up to kiss him deeper, wanting to press my body against his. I wanted so much more friction than he was giving me now.

He pulled back from my mouth a bit. "Calm down, needy one."

His fingers circled my clit again and then dipped back down, collecting more wetness to circle it again. "Would you rather I beg?" I said softly.

He just laughed before he took his hands away, leaving me feeling empty and still very, very wet. I reached for his pants, wanting to pull them down so I could hop into his arms, allowing him to fuck me against his bedroom wall, but he playfully slapped my hands away. "Get on the bed, Dani."

I narrowed my eyes at his dark frame but did what he wanted. I felt hollow between my legs, like he had built something up just to leave it until he was ready to start again. I sat on top of the comforter, my knees pressing into the soft material. I felt him watching me as he followed my lead and sat on his knees in front of me. He stuck his hand out and tucked stray pieces of hair behind my ear. The move was gentle and calming, telling me he had no intention of moving fast and unbated. He leaned his head down and kissed me again, but this kiss was quick as he moved away from my mouth to kiss my cheek, my jaw, then my neck, before pulling back to look at me. Lightning flashed again and I caught a glimpse at the need in his eyes, but there was something else there, too.

Was that patience?

He seemed to have enough of that for the both of us.

I cupped his cock through his pants again, hearing the strangled way he groaned. He grabbed my hand and moved it away...again. I was getting annoyed with him. No matter how slow we were going to go, he could touch me, but I wasn't allowed to touch him...that was ridiculous. I huffed out an impatient sound and he snickered deviously, as if he knew I would be upset. "Nicholas—"

He cut me off when he placed his hands on my thighs, dragging them up and under the sweatshirt. He leaned into me, towards my ear. "You are going to have to be quiet, alright?" I brought my tongue out and licked my lips. He moved his lips away from my ear and back to my mouth, saying his next words against my parted, wet lips. "Lay back."

I leaned back and felt my head hit the pillow. I relaxed my body right as he grabbed my panties from underneath the sweatshirt and pulled them down my legs. The outside air swept between my legs, causing me to shiver, the cool air a reminder of just how *needy* I actually was. He tossed my soaked underwear to the floor, the smell of my arousal so thick in the air, I could have choked on it. He crawled over my body, letting his hand drift between my legs again, dusting his fingers over where I wanted him most, and smiled against my neck when I arched my back with every flick of his fingers.

"Are you going to fuck me at some point?" I asked, my fervent impatience hot on my breath.

"So needy," he chuckled against my neck. "Maybe. But not right now."

He gave my neck one kiss before sliding down my body and lifting the sweatshirt up, kissing my stomach, down to both my hip bones and pelvis. He kissed the insides of both my thighs, letting his breath hit between my legs teasingly. I looked down my body and saw that his shadowed figure was nestled between my thighs. I felt a wave of heat roll through me.

"I've been wondering what you taste like," he said desperately, right against my pussy. I immediately felt my body arch towards him. He wrapped his hands around my thighs, sliding them to my pelvis and placing one hand flat against me, keeping me in place.

He gave my waiting pussy a tentative lick, as if he were testing, as if he wanted to hear every single sound I made and feel every single twitch of my thighs, of my stomach and hips. I tried to bring myself closer, thrust my pelvis when he used his tongue again. This time, he licked me entirely, then again, again, again. Nicholas used his tongue on me like he had been starving for this, like he could sit between my legs and lap at me for hours. He buried his face so deep into my pussy, I was surprised he had enough oxygen to continue. I reached around and grabbed the pillow behind my head, wrapping my fist around the material to try and release some of the pleasurable tension building. All the moans I wanted to let out I had to lodge in my throat, and it was burning me.

"You taste just as sweet as I thought you would," Nicholas said against my clit, flicking it with his tongue a few times before taking it into his mouth and sucking. He released it, creating a leisurely circle around it with his tongue, and then sucked it back into his mouth again. I moved my head to the side and burrowed my face into the pillow, stifling my cry. I felt like my heart was going to rip out of my chest and I could feel small beads of sweat start on my forehead. My heels dug into the comforter and my thighs burned from the tension.

He moaned slightly against my pussy and stuck his tongue inside of me, then pulled out. He explored my entrance with his mouth, making sure I didn't wiggle too much as he licked me fully and fucked me with his tongue. This angelic creature was positively devouring me with his tongue, and I was about to beg for him to make me come, but then Nicholas pulled his hands away and brought them to the insides of my thighs, pulling back to use his fingers to spread me open. He flicked the tip of his skillful tongue against my clit, and I fisted the sheets at my side. The moonlight lit the back of his head enough to where his dark hair stuck up so much, I knew he had been repeatedly running his hands through it earlier. He continued to assault my clit with his tongue while he used one of his fingers to stroke my entrance.

After what felt like forever, he pushed one finger inside of me, probing and exploring. He did it slowly, as if he was waiting for my reaction before he pressed in a second. It didn't take much for him to slide all the way in. He curled his fingers upward, massaging the spot that made my eyes flutter closed and my head tilt back. I felt his smile ghost against me as he continued to fuck me with his long, skilled fingers and lick at me like he couldn't get enough of my taste.

There was a boiling in my stomach, hot and needy, ready to explode. I could feel the back of my neck, sticky with sweat, and I lifted one of my hands to run it through his hair, earning a low growl. I yanked him closer to me, as if he could even get any closer than he already was. Fuck, he was good at this. He pumped his fingers faster, matching the movements of his tongue, the sound of how wet I was softly echoing as his fingers went to work. I had to practically bite my own tongue when I felt everything push through me at once. I felt my legs tense and my stomach hollow out, stars sparkling behind my eyes.

"That's it," he coaxed as he lapped at my clit. "Come for me."

His intoxicating words sent a flood of arousal straight through me. He slowed his fingers as my trembling thighs started to settle.

My legs relaxed finally, and he kissed me gently between my legs. He slid his fingers against my slit and gave the tiniest satisfied laugh.

I tilted my head up, trying to catch my breath. He was climbing over me and settled his body between my legs before he hovered over my face, his erection hitting me where I was still sensitive. His breath was a bit ragged, but it was steady. He had his arm extended next to my head, while his other hand brought my chin towards him. He kissed me, letting me taste myself on his lips. "Was that so bad?" he whispered as he released my mouth, running his hand down my face to my neck, tracing his thumb along my pulse point.

"It was alright," I lied.

He grazed his nose against mine. "I think you already gave yourself away." He pressed his cock against me, and I let out a soft moan. "No need for lying now."

He leaned up and reached behind him, pulling his shirt off in one quick movement. The moon decorated him from behind, showing every cut of his frame, every ab, every muscle, every hair that stood up on his arms. He inched his hands under my sweatshirt, his fingers caressing my skin as he removed it. Once it was over my head, he tossed it to the floor with my panties and his shirt, and I leaned back and got more comfortable underneath him. I heard him blow out a breath as he fingered my sides and cupped his hands around my breasts, flicking and tugging gently on my nipples.

"Fuck. You are beautiful," he whispered, almost to himself. It was like, even though we weren't flooded in light, he could see what he always suspected. It was like he needed to say it out loud to make sure it was real, like the words weren't legitimate without it. I didn't know what to say. I didn't even know if he wanted me to respond, but I did.

"Thank you."

I could almost hear the way he collected himself. He cleared his throat and leaned down to kiss my neck, my collarbone, my shoulder, traveling down to one of my breasts before bringing one of my nipples into his mouth and swirling his tongue around the bud. This man was quite literally trying to kill me, and I was more than okay with it. He moved to my other breast and did the same thing, grazing his teeth along my nipples.

He jerked away from me and tucked his fingers into his waist-band, pulling down his sweatpants and underwear. His cock jutted out between us, and it was all I could do to not let my mouth fall open. In the training room, everything had happened so fast. I hadn't gotten a good look at what he had to offer. I had caught a glimpse, but most of my time was spent with my back to the floor and my face to the ceiling. Even now, it was difficult because it was dark, but yet again, the moon was my savior. He was big, but not so big that I wanted to shy away from him. Not that I would have said no to him, no matter what his size turned out to be. I had a feeling my hand wouldn't wrap all the way around him if I tried...and I wanted to try.

I propped up on my elbow and reached out to grab him, letting my fingers glide over his length. This time, he didn't try to stop me. He was letting me touch and explore him, and I was grateful for it. He hissed through his teeth, watching me touch him. I stroked back and forth, letting my hand slip over the tip and then back to his base. I started to get up on my knees to return the favor, wanting his cock in my mouth so much that my thighs were starting to shake from antic-ipation. Instead, Nicholas pulled my hand away from his cock and gently pushed me to lay on my back again. He made sure my legs were propped up and bent, leaning down over me.

He removed his sweatpants completely before positioning himself between my legs. The weight and heat of him consumed me as I arched up to connect with his body more. He reached between us and took hold of his cock, using the tip to slide along the wetness between my legs. I lifted my neck up to meet his lips with my own. He let me kiss him, let my tongue slip into his mouth and taste him. He pulled away just the slightest to say, "Remember, quiet, Dani." I nodded in understanding, then remembering that there were few lights and he likely couldn't see my response, so I verbally confirmed. Neither one of us wanted his father knocking or coming in and finding us in a compromising position. I would laugh it off and deal with the consequences, but Nicholas would feel much differently about the whole ordeal.

His lips captured mine again and he slowly pushed his cock inside of me, inch by inch until he was fully seated. I felt stretched, but I was begging for more. Nicholas paused, as if he was letting himself feel all the things I was feeling. He propped himself up on his forearms and I scooted my legs up so I could feel him deeper. I felt him start to move, each thrust meticulous and so fucking slow. I could feel each time he pulled back, each time he pushed back in. Every inch was accounted for, and I was going fucking crazy feeling it all. Maybe I could be a glutton for this slow and passionate nonsense.

"*Fuck*," I heard him whisper into my neck. I brought my hands up and around to his back, pressing my fingertips into his skin, feeling his hips flex as he pushed into me.

"I don't think I ever really got to appreciate how big you are," I said, a sharp moan leaving my lips that I tried to muffle down.

I felt my chest vibrate with his laughter as he kept moving, never quickening his pace, but never missing a mark on his rhythm. "Fuck, you really can't say things like that right now." His voice was low and breathy, with a seductive warning to it.

I wrapped my legs around his lower back, anchoring myself to him, as if he was going to somehow disappear. He lifted his face from my neck, and I felt his forehead rest against mine. His skin was licked with sweat, but I didn't mind. I just met his lips and kissed him again. He kissed me back, more desperate this time, like he was trying to reach something just out of his grasp. His hips sped up a bit and I raised my legs higher, widening them.

He placed his weight on his right arm as he brought his left up to his mouth, wetting two of his fingers before slipping them between us and circling around my clit. There were small sounds of his skin hitting mine, but not loud enough to rattle the walls and not loud enough where the rain, wind, and thunder from outside couldn't shut us out. His fingers pressed into my sensitive bundle of nerves, and I heaved in breath after breath, trying so fucking hard not to be loud.

"Fuck, fuck, fuck," I repeated softly as I felt that same feeling building. It was like a shot of vodka burning through my veins. My breathing became sharper, and I took his sides in my hands, kneading my fingers into him, needing something to hold onto before I went over the edge. He could feel it, I knew he could, because right before I went off, he dipped down to kiss me, as if he wanted all my sounds. He fucked me through my climax, not slowing down even when I pressed my hands to his shoulders to release his mouth. He brought his hand back to my face, right as a shot of lightning hurled out of the sky and light blossomed on his face for a moment, letting me see the way he was losing his resolve. I tightened my legs around him, pushing him to take that leap and fall over the delicious edge with me.

I leaned up and licked his ear lobe, biting down on the tender skin, feeling him shudder around me. He thrusted into me a few more times until he finally let go, pumping his hips erratically as his face scrubbed over mine. I felt his cock twitch inside of me, releasing everything he was holding back. His chest was heaving as if he had run a mile when he was done, when he was spent. He let out a heavy breath before I felt his body leave mine and slowly pull out of me, settling onto the bed next to me. He bent one of his knees up, while his other leg lay flat on the comforter. I closed my legs and turned on my side to face him.

"Well, well, Mr. Cassial," I joked, bending my elbow and placing my head in my upturned palm.

He ran a hand down his face. "What?"

"You really *really* fucking like me." I ruffled my hair with my fingers. "You don't even let a wound slow you down." I pointed to his side, still perfectly covered by the gauze.

"You're annoying," he said, but I heard the smile in his words. That must be his favorite way to describe me, and I felt giddy every time he said it. He absentmindedly placed a hand on his covered wound and pressed, making a small face but then relaxing, letting me know that he was fine.

I turned over and swung my legs over the side of the bed. I felt him shift, making the bed move. "Where are you going?" he asked.

"Bathroom," I answered. "Don't worry, I won't leave you here like some cheap whore." I knelt to the floor to feel for his sweatshirt and tugged it over my head.

Nicholas was still laying in his bed when I came back from the bathroom. I hopped up and scooted over to where he sat, propped up against the headboard. I sat on my knees and placed my hands on my thighs.

"You're still here?"

"It is my room, you know," he answered in a monotone voice.

"Well, of course, I'll just head to the couch, then. Thanks for the sex," I said sarcastically as I started to shuffle off the bed, but he caught my wrist.

"That's not what I meant. I just don't feel like leaving yet, okay?"

I chewed on my lower lip, thinking about my next words. "Alright then, but if you are going to stay, can we use your angelic night light for a little bit?"

He chuckled as it settled between us and bobbed back and forth, allowing me to appreciate him more than before. His hair was sticking up, his cheeks had a pink hue to them that was slowly fading, and the muscle in his neck ticked every so often.

"That's better," I said, satisfied, watching as he flattened his unruly hair a little and brought the comforter around his lap to cover his cock. He snapped his fingers in front of my face, forcing me to look up at him and away from anything below his waist.

"My eyes are up here," he joked, giving me a knowing side smile.

I groaned and mirrored the way he was positioned. I glanced at him from the corner of my eye and noticed he was checking me out, focusing on the sweatshirt covering my body now. God, he was cute. "Are you upset that I put it back on?"

He licked his lips and shook his head. "You can do whatever you want, Dani. You look fine with or without it on." He said this as if it wasn't just minutes ago that he was peeling it off me and toying with my breasts, delighted with what he found.

"There you go with your compliments."

"I would think women like when men say nice things about them when they're naked. Especially after they've had sex."

"We do, but I don't know if your compliments are genuine. Are you just saying nice things because you think I need to hear it?"

He gave me a confused expression. "Why the hell would I do that?"

I looked over at him, stunned he was acting so oblivious. "We both know you think I'm some sad demon who's only family has just thrown her under the bus to create a realm-shattering catastrophe. You're thinking, *"she could use a good compliment or two."*" I laughed at myself, but I stopped when I realized he wasn't laughing. He was just looking at me, his eyes narrowed and darting along my face, as if he was searching for something.

"I already said it: I can say and do nice things because I'm just a nice guy," Nicholas said, his tone serious, making me link my eyes with his. "If I say I don't think you have to worry about your soul, I mean it. When I say I think you're beautiful while you're naked underneath me, I think you're fucking beautiful. It's simple." He let out an irritated sigh.

"Alright, alright. I get it. Sorry," I apologized, fiddling my fingers together. Compliments had never made me uncomfortable before, but coming from him, I felt a little undeserving.

"Don't be sorry. I know it probably can't be the easiest waking up in Purgatory and then getting thrown into this fucking mess still not really knowing how you fit," he said, his forehead wrinkling.

"You're one to talk," I shot back, leaning my head back against the headboard. "You have a whole team of underhanded executives to expose."

He let out an exhaustive sigh. "Don't remind me. That's tomorrow's problem."

The light Nicholas had provided let me see the small wisps of dark hair on his chest, the light freckles decorating his skin. I stuck my hand out and traced a line from his jaw to his shoulder and down his arm, before resting my fingers against the top of his hand.

"Do you regret it?"

He arched an eyebrow casually at me.

I motioned towards the bed, silently commenting on everything that just happened.

He scrunched his mouth to one side, contemplating this. "Do I think it was avoidable? Yes. Do I regret it?" His brown eyes scanned my face and then looked down at my covered body, as if he was replaying the scene in his head. "No."

"Good, because you have a very skilled tongue. From my two orgasms, it seems like you have mastered everything," I complimented, earning an eye roll from him in the process. Nicholas wasn't shy in the way of being insecure or nervous, but I had a feeling he never played all his cards. This whole thing with me was rattling him. I also had the feeling he hadn't slept with many women before, but the ones he had slept with were lucky to have gotten to experience his slow, patient side in bed.

I wanted to know more about him, pick his brain while I had him and his mind within my grasp. "Has your dad ever told you about his time at The Skies?" I tucked my legs under the covers and huddled further into the soft sheets. If he was going to stay here tonight -- and it looked like he might be -- then I was getting comfortable.

"A little," Nicholas answered, seeming to settle himself into his bed as well. He tucked the one foot he had on top of the comforter underneath and reached behind him to prop one of his pillows under his back.

"Ah, so no dirty details or anything?"

"Nah, nothing like that. He likes to talk about it to a point, and then the story kind of just trails off. He changes the subject or just gives me a look that tells me we're done, so I just let it be."

"So, what does he tell you?"

He sighed. "Just things like how getting into The Skies was different then, and who your family was mattered a hell of a lot more than it does now. That's probably one of the only things he talks about that sheds any good light on Jonah."

I snuggle further into the pillow under my head. "Were they ever actually civil?"

Nicholas nods. "Yeah, once upon a time. They were like best friends or something. A lot can happen, I guess. People grow apart."

"I don't know. It sounds more like personal hostility, which is a far cry from growing apart."

Nicholas raised one of his arms and threw it behind his neck, resting on it. "I'm well aware."

"Maurice Cassial: mysterious and a total babe." He closed his eyes, using his other hand to pinch the bridge of his nose, clearly annoyed. I giggled, bringing the sheet up to cover part of my face. "Oops, that's probably not what you want to hear after we've had sex, huh?"

He shook his head at me. "Um, no, not exactly."

"Doesn't mean it's not true."

He grabbed more of the sheets and started pulling them over my face, covering me completely in gray cotton. He patted where my body was laying a few times to make sure I was tightly packed in my cocoon.

"Your dad seems like a great dad, though. All jokes aside," I said through my layers of fabric.

"He is. I mean, he has his moments, but I wouldn't be who I am now without him."

I started to maneuver myself out of the mess of sheets. "Was he some kind of master swordsman?"

"He was one of the best. In the most non-cocky way, he always says," Nicholas stated sarcastically.

"And somehow, you turned out alright, but your best friend grew up to have the biggest head?" I asked, poking him in the ribs, making him squirm, inching away from me.

"Reese has *always* had a big head. I probably wouldn't have made a lot of decisions in my life without him constantly nagging in my ear to do it. Granted, not all those decisions are ones I would like to relive, but hey, bonding." He poked me back, right in my cheek, but then he slid his finger from my cheek and laced it around different curls of my hair.

I watched his fingers and bit my bottom lip. I didn't want him to stop talking, so I decided to move to a new topic. "So, I did some snooping."

"Snooping?" He sounded hesitant, dropping his hand.

"Mhmm, before I went to bed. I found...err...I found a picture of your mom."

312

He looked over to the window behind his dresser. "Did you?" The thunder outside was just a low rumble, but the rain was still coming down.

"Yup. Not many people would keep a photo of someone they have no interest in ever trying to figure out," I pointed out.

"You never just let shit go, do you?"

"Not my style."

He sighed, tilting his head down. "She is still my mom, Dani. Just because I don't want to talk about her or I don't seem to show any interest doesn't mean I don't care." He gave me a sad smile. "I've just learned to take information where I can get it but not ever really ask for it, because that has never gotten me anywhere with anyone. It honestly just makes it worse for me."

"Your dad really loved her, didn't he?"

Nicholas bit his bottom lip and nodded. "From what I can tell...yeah."

I turned back over on my side as he continued talking. "They were all friends, apparently. Jonah, his wife, my parents. There is this whole blank space between when they were friends and now." He sounded frustrated and with everything else going on, I would be too.

I snorted. "Literally the only two people you can ask aren't willing to talk about it."

He banged his head against the headboard. "Yup." He rubbed his neck with his hand, then placed both his hands in his lap. "I don't know why I'm telling you all of this."

"Because I'm a phenomenal listener." I looked down at his hands on top of the comforter. I had a feeling if I kept looking at his face, I would be tempted to climb on top of him and ride him until he forgot his own name, but it was late, and he wanted to confide in me. I liked being seen as a confidante. It wasn't what I was always known for, what I was labeled as.

"How about you tell me something?" he said, genuine curiosity peeking.

"Something like what?" I asked. The light between us made me feel like we were in our own little bubble, as if whatever the fuck was going on right now was so far away, it wasn't concerning to either of us.

He stroked his chin, as if he was in deep thought. "Do you remember your life before Purgatory?"

That was the same question Natalia had asked me on our little excursion to Oculus. "Nope. I don't remember my death either, so let's just go ahead and skip that question."

"You make it sound like you're just like the rest of them down there, the ones she turns into demonic savages."

I laughed. "Not all of them are demonic savages. Some are just as useless down there as they probably were when they were alive. She just likes having the bodies around to do her bidding, that's all."

"And you are so special because?"

"I'm not."

Nicholas turned his head to look at me and fuck if I didn't want to kiss him, the way his lips were pouting with skepticism. "Dani, the woman gave you a specialized dagger and pretty much gave you special treatment your entire time down there, grooming you to be..." He moved his eyes over me. "This. Let's not forget that she has an entire plan that somehow revolves around you being here, in Heaven's Gate, right now, at this time."

"Well, when you say it like that, I do sound *super* special."

He lifted his eyes up, staring at the ceiling. I groaned, getting up a little and moving closer to him. He didn't look at me when he said, "Lilith had to start from somewhere."

I pulled myself all the way back up to sit and rested my chin on his shoulder. "And let me guess -- you think that has something to do with my death? My life before all this?"

He shrugged causing my head to bob. "Maybe."

"Unfortunately, Nicholas, we don't have a time machine to figure that out. We only have the present. What Lilith has planned is just her *plan*, it's not fate. It's not a certified ending." I kissed his cheek lightly and watched as he tilted his head down, letting his eyes fall away from the ceiling and onto my face. "I'm not being an optimist; I'm just being a realist."

"All that time in Purgatory, and you just..." he started to say, his mouth opening and closing as he attempted to find the right words. "You just don't give off the vibe I thought you would."

I couldn't dig deeper into my past because the only memory that came up is opening my eyes in that cell in Purgatory. That was the beginning of my story, and I never asked any questions. "What kind of vibe do I give off, huh?"

"I don't know, but there's something off that personally, I don't think has anything to do with the dark magic inside of you."

I sunk back down into the pillows next to him, my head now at his bicep. A bicep I wanted to wrap my hands around, or at least attempt to, because it was definitely bigger than my hand. "I only really become the darkest part of myself when I want to, or if I'm severely bated. Don't worry, you haven't pissed me off enough for you to feel its wrath."

Like I did with Cullen. He had pushed me, taunted me, played with the emotions I thought I had trapped down. He lifted them to the surface just to show me that I had that kind of killer instinct if the right words were spat at me. That if I was shown enough malicious disdain, I would see nothing but the task at hand. Maybe he was right. Maybe that was Lilith's intent all along. That soon, I would be pushed to be nothing more than what people like Ariel deemed me to be.

"Your dagger comes into that as well, right?"

"Well, my dagger is connected to me. Compulsion is just a way for us to be connected, but it doesn't *make* me who I am. It needs me more than I need it when it comes down to it. When I gain a lot of dark power, it does as well, making me a very dangerous little female."

He started to shift his hand over to where mine was sitting on top of the comforter. "I can't say that doesn't alarm me."

"But it turns you on, just a little bit." I moved my fingers, so that there was a small space between my index finger and thumb.

"Hmph," he answered, moving his much larger hand over mine. "Once we're back at The Skies, we'll get your dagger, alright?"

"And fall right back into all the bullshit."

He squeezed my hand and ran his other through his hair in an anxious gesture. "Right back into all the bullshit."

"What time is it?" I asked, looking around for anything that could tell me the time.

"Last time I checked, it was like eleven," he said, letting out a sigh.

I sunk my body even further into the covers. "If you don't mind, could we possibly continue this delightful conversation in a few hours?" If I—we—were going to face anything tomorrow, we couldn't do it with anything less than complete alertness. I could see when I looked up at Nicholas that his shoulders weren't as tense and his eyes were a little heavy, like if he chose to close them, he would be asleep in minutes.

"Right," he nodded, starting to remove the covers and making his way out of the bed.

"What are you doing?"

"Going back to the couch."

"Why would you do that?"

He scrunched up his face, as if trying to figure out a good answer. He was only halfway out of the covers and his cock was still hidden beneath them, but the sheets had slipped low enough for me to see the dark hair that traveled towards his pelvis and the v shape that was practically a neon sign to his crotch.

I patted the space next to me. "Don't worry, I'm not going to molest you in your sleep, Nicholas. Unless you ask nicely," I taunted him.

"Are you sure?" I watched as he hesitated.

"I'm more than sure. Don't be ashamed that you gave in to what you wanted. What happened was satisfying to all parties involved, and I think we got everything out of our systems. I don't think sleeping next to each other would really rock the boat anymore. The boat has capsized, my little angelic sex toy." I turned over and faced the wall, laughing to myself.

I felt the bed dip and the covers shift so he had enough on his side. Our legs touched briefly, and I felt instant goosebumps creep onto his legs before he pulled them away.

"Well.... since the boat has capsized and we are just sinking into the fucking abyss—" he started, reaching his hand underneath the covers and tugging at the sweatshirt I wore, the fabric moving against my skin.

I pressed my cheek harder into the pillow. "Do you want me to take the sweatshirt off, Nicholas?"

"I mean, you don't have to."

I giggled, rolling onto my other side so I could face him. His face had grown a slight shade of red, which I assumed was from embarrassment. "That's not what I asked."

"Never mind." He started to roll away from me, but I caught his arm, keeping him in place.

"No, you want something, so ask for it."

"Dani."

"Do you want me to take the sweatshirt off or not?"

He closed his eyes and opened them to my waiting face. "Yes."

I quickly pushed away from the mattress and tugged the sweatshirt over my head. I noticed the way he watched my movements with an eager eye. He knew tonight was just one night full of no fighting, no darkness, no issues. So, he let himself take in my face, my arms, my breasts, my stomach; he took in all of it. To my surprise, he gave me a satisfied smirk when I settled back into the bed. It was like he just wanted to know I was naked, in his bed, and that alone was enough for him to drift off to sleep.

"Happy?" I asked.

"For now," he said, grabbing the glowing light above our heads and snuffing it out. When the dark consumed us again, we were both silent. I turned back over and slid one of my hands underneath my cheek, trying to fall asleep to the sound of the rain.

His breathing started to become a steady, sleep-driven sound, and I knew that was my cue to sleep as well. My head was quiet now. It was quiet before, but right now, my head was a peaceful quiet. That light warmth, the voice that always seemed to be banging on a sealed door in my head, wanting to come out, seemed to be napping like a baby, as if it was content. The dark part of me that lurked in all corners of my being was dormant. It didn't need to come out anyway, but even when I searched for it, it was gone, as if it was locked away somewhere for the time being. I felt lighter.

Nicholas had mentioned believing in the light. Maybe I could believe in it knowing what contentment felt like. That contentment would be taken away, though, so what was the point of reaching for something I didn't deserve? The voice in my head started to stir, as if it was annoyed with me. I buried my head further into the pillow and just stopped thinking. Then finally...I fell asleep.

I woke up a little startled. It was still dark outside, but I had a feeling that in the next few hours, the sun would be up, and our problems would be the center of attention again. I didn't have time to think about what the rest of the day would bring, because I felt a hand on my waist. The hand tightened against my skin, and then I felt a leg brush against the back of mine. The hand moved up my stomach, fingers splaying over my skin and grabbing onto my breast. I bit my lower lip and felt fingers trap my nipple and slide over it, playing with it.

I let out a little moan, letting it blow past my lips. I heard a groan as my body was turned over so I was facing the other side. The morning light hadn't peeked through the horizon, so the darkness was shadowing most of his face, but Nicholas told me everything he needed with the way he used his body. I felt his arms wrap around my waist, pulling me closer to him. I felt the warmth of his breath and let the searing heat of his fingers linger for as long as it wanted. Nicholas didn't kiss me immediately, but he did dip his head down and kiss my neck. They were small but deliberate kisses, as if he was trying to plant small fires on every spot his lips touched.

My hand moved to his shoulder and down to his bicep, squeezing, feeling the way he flexed every time I moved myself against him. I let out a moan when he brought his hands against my lower back and tugged me flush against him. I was suddenly molten lava. He pressed that rigid part of himself against me, rocking into my skin, as if showing me what he wanted, that what I did to him was better than any verbal confirmation could ever be.

He removed his face from my neck, and I could slightly make out that his eyes were this hooded sort of desperation, like he didn't know what to do with himself at the moment, like all he knew was being as close as possible to me was the only solution. I pressed my lips to his in what seemed like a frantic move, but he met my lips with so much fire and need, I almost considered the idea that kissing him would be enough, that his soft but persistent lips would be enough for me. He ground his cock into my skin again and the wet pool growing between my legs told me I was not going to be satisfied with simple kissing.

He groaned against my mouth and took my bottom lip between his teeth, biting down enough to make me wince. I opened my legs a bit and let his cock slide against the slickness between my thighs. He let go of my lip and let out a small and shaken *fuck* at the feel of himself between my legs again. He pressed his hand to the back of my head, tangling his fingers into my hair, keeping my head in place as he pressed his cock over my pussy. He slid back and forth easily, making a point to slide right over my clit every time. I looked down and watched as he grabbed my leg up and over his hip, using his cock to tease me but bring me so much closer, closer, closer to the edge. I could feel it. I could feel it start to vibrate around me. It was a kind of high that I never wanted to come down from.

I felt my orgasm tearing through me and he grabbed my face to kiss me, *hard*. He grabbed my ass and pushed against me, rubbing over me again with so much force, I practically screamed into his throat. When I started to ease back down and regain my breath, he slowed, his mouth easing off mine as he gave me a small peck right at the edge of my lips. I let out a long, slow breath, blinking back my sanity. He pulled back from me, but I wrapped my hand around his shoulder, forcing him to look at me with a questionable glint in his eyes. I gave him a small smile, letting my tongue peek out between my lips.

"Is that all?" I asked, nuzzling my head into my pillow, teasing.

He leaned back into me. "What do you want?" A hint of amusement and eagerness glazed his words.

"What does it feel like I want?" I grabbed his hand and slid it between my breasts, down my stomach, between my legs, where I was incredibly wet and wanting, my pussy vibrating from my orgasm. I wanted more.

He let out a low groan but didn't move his hand away. He played with me, letting his fingers explore, running them over my clit but never lingering there long. I was slowly panting, wanting those fingertips back each time he took them away. He smoothly pushed two fingers inside of me and my breath hitched. He let his fingers curve and massage, all while I knew he was looking at my face, watching me. I almost whimpered when he removed them after a few minutes. He didn't flip me to my back and slide into me like I wanted him to. He did something I didn't expect, although with Nicholas, I had already decided assumptions weren't a good thing.

He pushed himself up from the bed, but before I could lift myself to be face to face with him, he grabbed my waist and flipped me around so that I was facing the pillows. My knees pressed into the mattress and my hair fell around my shoulders. I looked behind me as he wrapped his hand around his cock, giving it two long pulls. My lips pressed together, heat developing low in my stomach again, making me impatient. His cock was something I was starting to crave, and it completely unnerved me. I looked back towards the headboard as I felt that skin-warming heat again. His hand raked down my back and over the curve of my ass, as if he was just simply appreciating me. He moved his hand down the side of my ass and down my thigh. One of his fingers traced up my slit; I was so fucking wet, I was almost embarrassed. I heard him groan, as if he was thoroughly satisfied with what he felt.

I snuck a peek over my shoulder, letting my hair hide part of my face as his eyes roamed over me, his mouth slightly open, his breathing solid and patient, as if he could go all night admiring, but then he held his erection out and pressed the tip against me, between my shaking legs. He seemed to glow from above me, his muscled arms tightening with every slide over my pussy. He slid the head of his cock over my pussy over, over, over again, bracing one of his hands on my hip, pulling me back to meet his pelvis.

He leaned down, pressing his weight at my back. He was sweaty and smelled like me. His dark hair tickled at my shoulder just as he pressed his lips to my quivering shoulder blade. He didn't let up on his teasing and continued to rub his cock against me, the wetness between my legs intensifying to the point where the wet sound of him sliding echoed in my ear. He kept a hand on my hip but used his free hand to brush my hair from my face, letting his lips move over the shell of my ear. I heard him swallow hard, as if this was too much for both of us, but he had no plan of stopping or leaving us both needy and pleading.

"Do you want me to take my time?" Nicholas asked, his voice hoarse and rough. He wanted me to decide how he would handle me. I had seen both sides of him, the eager, frantic man and the passionate, deliberate one. I found myself liking both, to my surprise.

I found myself *craving* only one of them now.

"No," I whispered, side glancing the best I could to see his face before he removed himself from my back and positioned himself behind me.

I only had a chance to blink before he pushed into me, easily slipping all the way inside, bottoming out. He had both hands at my hips, digging his fingertips into my flesh. I let out gasp after gasp, prepared to keep my breathing as steady as possible, but then he started to move. And *fuck* was he moving. He pumped into me with such a fast rhythm, I almost cried out. He gave no warning, no preamble, and I reveled in it. He was relentless in the way he rode me, pulling my hips back against him with each piston of his own hips.

I couldn't keep as quiet as he wanted, but I tried. I started to lean down and press my face into the pillow, stifling my sounds. He ran the heels of his hands into my hips, leaning over a bit to hit a deeper spot.

"Shit, your pussy feels good around my cock," Nicholas groaned, bracing his hand on one of my shoulders.

As I buried my face into the cotton pillowcase, biting at the material, I pushed back to meet his thrust, not missing the way he squeezed my shoulder each time my skin collided with his.

I pressed my eyes shut as I practically suffocated myself to stay quiet, but it was way too much. Nicholas lifted his hand from my shoulder and grabbed my hair, wrapping the deep brown curls around his fingers. I brought my head up and attempted to tamp down all the noise I wanted to make, but the way he felt inside of me would surely be our mutual destruction. He pounded into me with so much force and so much fucking need, every single murmured *fuck* and *yes* that came from his mouth sent more wetness pooling between my legs.

"You take my cock so fucking well," he mumbled between his groans.

I forced my sounds into garbled moans, low pants, sighs, but I couldn't do it. He ruined any sense of control I was holding onto, and I was holding on by the thinnest of threads. He released my hair and brought his hand between my thighs to play with my clit.

A strained but satisfied scream left my lips. "Yes, yes, yes!"

Just as quickly as the words left my lips, he unclasped his hand from my hip and clapped it over my mouth, never stopping his movements inside of me. His face was back in my peripheral vision, his hot breath enveloping me, and I could hear the smile playing at his lips as he shushed me at the shell of my ear. He continued his assault on my clit, rubbing and pressing his fingers over it as he groaned into my neck. I was practically crying into his hand, the feeling too fucking good. He was doing all the right things, so many right things, hitting me so fucking deep, it felt like too much. I was sweating, practically overheated, but he kept moving faster and quicker, never letting his hand leave my mouth.

He pressed his palms hard against my lips. I was rounding my shoulders with the way he hovered over me, his chest warm and hot at my back.

My orgasm was at its peak now and it was beginning to blind me, sending a white-hot light behind my eyes. "Oh, my fucking god," I said, muffling the words against his hand.

Nicholas whispered in my ear as my pussy started to clinch around him. "That's a good fucking girl."

I grabbed onto the pillow underneath me, clenching it into my fist as I came hard, pushing back against him, grinding my ass up. A few sounds I made escaped out of the open spots between his fingers, but most of them were captured by his silencing hand. My heart was beating so hard, it hurt my chest. My knees were throbbing against the mattress and my thighs felt like I had just run a marathon, but it was a delicious kind of pain. He released my clit from his skilled touch and grabbed my hip again, steading me. He grunted and took his hand away from my mouth, squeezing my ass so hard, I knew he would leave bruises.

"Fuck," his rough, deep voice whispered out in the dark, confined room, making me shiver with the way it echoed along my skin.

He rocked his hips into me over and over, not fast but in quick, long strokes, before I felt him shudder above me as he came. I had to throw my face into the soft pillowcase again to suffocate my own sounds at the feeling of him. His hands started to massage where they had held me too tight as his breathing remained harsh and ragged. His cock twitched inside of me, and I circled my ass in response.

Nicholas gave my ass a tiny, playful smack and let out a soft chuckle before pulling out of me. He leaned over, kissing down my back, his cock ghosting over the place between my legs. He wrapped his arms around my waist and pulled me down with him so we were spooning. Freeing one of his arms, he rallied up the covers and blanketed them around us.

His arm folded over my waist while his face nuzzled into my hair. He let out a sigh that could have meant one of two things: content or exhaustion. Either one was something I could understand. His body felt so nice so close to me. His legs were tangled in mine, and I scooted back a little to bask in his warmth.

"Hmm," I released a hum from my lips. He sighed again, but this time, his sigh gave off apprehension.

"Say whatever it is you are going to say," Nicholas pressed.

"You are just surprising is all."

He leaned his head down and placed his lips to my shoulder. "What does that mean?"

"It means you're surprising to me. I am surprised," I reiterated.

He laughed against my skin. "Dani, you can't just let me bend you over and fuck you, then just say I'm surprising."

"Well, I just did. Deal with it." I snorted, laughing against the pillow as he dug his face further into my neck, his kisses tickling me. I used my hands to bat him away, turning my face back over my shoulder so that our faces were so close, he could have kissed me. "The total truth is that you may be angelic, but you fuck like a demon."

He was calculating and persistent in the way he moved his hips. It was like he knew everything without having to ask. When it came to sex, especially sex in Purgatory, body language was key, and Nicholas seemed to understand that all too well. He may not have a chest full of sex toys, but I was almost positive he had tricks up his sleeve.

"Should I take that as a compliment?" The question was laced with sarcasm.

"I think so. I know a few ladies down in Purgatory who would probably ride you so hard, your dick would fall off."

Nicholas groaned. "Alright, can we not talk about my dick falling off?"

I laughed again. "Sorry. Are you always this much of a cuddler after sex?"

He reached his hand up and started to draw lazy lines along my arm. "Oh, I'm sorry I want the girls I take to bed to not think I'm a total fuck boy. I actually like the girls I fuck. I even let them come before I do."

"Ah, I do recall you doing that," I said, letting out a little cry when he pinched me. "Can you count how many girls you've slept with on one hand?" I asked, curious.

He made a humming sound near my ear. "Yes."

"Interesting. That right there is *not* surprising."

"Unlike Reese, I didn't see the need to stick my dick in anything with a pretty face and spreadable legs." He traced his hand down my arm. "I'm going to assume that you've been a lot more *active* during your time in Purgatory?"

I bit my tongue, trying to figure out how to express what I wanted to say. "Let's just say they all served their purpose, man or woman, and I enjoyed myself. Case closed."

"Case closed then," he said with a tightness in his voice. Not in a way that he was judging me, but like he wanted to know who all these other people I'd taken to bed were. It really wasn't worth it. I wasn't thinking of any of them right now.

His cock was pressed to my back, right near my ass, and every small movement he made had me very aware that he was so close to where I would have happily taken him again.

"Good thing I can't get pregnant, because you might be fucked by now," I said after a moment of silence. He stiffened next to me, lifting his face up from my neck. It was like all the oxygen left the room and I was holding it hostage. I had said the truth, but I had forgotten he didn't know.

"Dani, I...fuck."

I stifled a small giggle. "So even when you were going all slow and sexy on me, you didn't think 'hmm, I should probably get some protection'?"

He moved his arm around and snuggled me closer to his body. "I just wasn't thinking."

"It doesn't matter anyway, Nicholas."

He lifted his body a bit and started to move my hair away from my neck and face. "None of you can have kids?"

I shook my head. "Nope. No kids, no aging, no nothing."

He started skimming my collarbone with his fingertip. "No aging?"

"Oh, come on, you can't tell me you don't know all this already?"

He was silent, as if telling me he had no idea. Well, shit.

"Lilith made it that way a long fucking time ago, so that no demons can procreate or grow old as long you belong to her. We live for eternity in this permanent state of being, never able to bring someone else into the world. Too much of a hassle. We're at our prime when Lilith picks you to come to Purgatory. She doesn't need you growing old just for her to replace us. She wants to *add* to what she already has." I let out a few breaths and then continued. "We aren't immortal. She has made that crystal clear with some of the things she's done to us.

"If Lilith wants you in her inner circle, I guess it's not super shitty. Special privilege and all that. You should see the demons she uses as errand boys or sends to Lucifer to use as puppets."

I let my voice trail off when I realized I was just rambling. It felt good to release it, but he didn't need to look inside and see all the fucked-up stuff that happens in a place he was never going to see. A place I was going to have to return to.

Nicholas nuzzled his nose against the line of my jaw, his cheek leaning against mine. "I'm sorry." Two words. Two simple words that said so much.

I blinked towards the wall. I never liked to go down the rabbit hole of the forever I was going to spend in Purgatory. I couldn't, because that would only make my time there after this was done unbearable. The wheels in his head were racing now; I could hear them cranking and collecting information, just to be more enthralled and confused the more I told him. I reached up and grabbed his hand. "Don't let it rattle your brain."

He grabbed my ass from under the sheets and squeezed, making me yelp. "Fine, but I'm sure once this is all over, we could try to reverse it."

I leaned back into him. "Reverse it?"

He shrugged. "Yeah, I mean, we have Natalia on our side and probably other Enchanters she can get to come along, so I wouldn't say it's impossible."

I turned and maneuvered myself so that I was face to face with him. His tall frame made that a little bit difficult, but I made it work. "One thing at a time, alright? Stop overloading yourself. You are going to make all this fucking we've done pointless if you start winding yourself up again."

Nicholas groaned, the sound sending a heat wave through my body. "That is not the reason this happened."

"Oh, so you're telling me that you just pounded me from behind because you felt like it? I call bullshit." I punched him in the shoulder, watching as he rubbed where I hit him as if it actually hurt.

"You were naked next to me, and I was..."

"Horny?"

"You are so fucking annoying," he muttered, burying his face in his pillow, peeking out at me with just one of his eyes. I tangled my fingers in his hair and pulled his face up to look at me completely.

"I'm not complaining, so take that as a good thing."

"I'll keep that in mind." He leaned forward and kissed me. He let his lips linger a moment before fully opening his mouth and kissing me the way I liked. I let my tongue out and found he was already in search of mine.

My eyes were closed tight, and my hand was tightening in his hair when I pulled him back. I could feel his cock starting to stir, and as much as I wanted to let him fuck me into forgetting my name, there was something I wanted to tell him.

"Nicholas, if I tell you something, will you promise not to spiral?"

"Spiral?"

I rolled my eyes. "You know, overthink. Consider all the options."

"I'll certainly try, but it's what I do. I spiral," he joked, eyeing me skeptically. The light was starting to break through the window, the rain just a light pattering now. I didn't know what storms were like in Heaven's Gate, so I was interested in knowing what the damage outside was.

I chewed the inside of my cheek. I needed to let someone else know what was going on in my head. "I have a voice in my head – well, I think its voice. It's more like a feeling of being lighter I guess, but like something is trying to speak to me or make me see something."

Nicholas leaned back to examine my face. I think he was trying to figure out if I was done explaining, or if I was just taking a moment to collect my thoughts. He only said, "a voice?"

I nodded. I pushed my hair out of my face. "It doesn't talk much and when it does, it's like muffled, but it feels warm and inviting. It's always in my head, but lately, it's been making more of an appearance."

"Was this voice uh…. frequent when you first got to Purgatory? Like when was the first time you ever heard it or umm…felt it?" He was trying to figure out his words. He didn't understand; I mean, I didn't even understand, and it was actually happening to me.

I thought back to my beginnings. "Sort of. It would come and go more frequently, especially when I was first getting my bearings. It was loud then, almost deafening, like it was trying to make sure I always knew it was there. It would almost burn with how warm it was. I kept it to myself, besides telling Elise, and she would tell me to ignore it, so I did."

Nicholas scratched his jaw. "Then it just went dormant?"

"Kind of. I just kept silencing it. Every time I would focus on what Lilith had to teach me or who I was becoming, it would just get quieter and quieter until eventually, I could ignore it. It just sat there, like it was waiting patiently, like it was watching me."

"It all of sudden appeared again in The Skies?"

"Yup. It feels like it's trying to pull me in this other direction. It's tempting. I don't know, it's almost like I can't breathe thinking about it." I blew out a breath. "This next part is going to sound weird, but just let me say it."

Nicholas chuckled. "All of this sounds weird, but okay."

"I find myself missing it sometimes. As much as I shove it down, ignore it, let my darkness stomp it to the back of my mind, I miss the lightness. I miss the warmth that comes with it. I felt like it kept sticking out a hand for me to take and I couldn't, or I wouldn't."

Nicholas tucked his fingers under my chin and lifted it so I would look at him. "I've never heard of something like this, but have you ever considered that maybe I was right?"

"About?"

"I mentioned your reasoning for being a part of all this might have started at the beginning of your relationship with Lilith. The first time it appeared was during your start in Purgatory. That's hardly a coincidence, Dani."

I grazed my fingers over his gauze-covered wound. "Spiraling..."

"Okay, okay, I'm sorry."

I snuggled up closer to him, wrapping my leg over his hip. "I forgive you."

He rested his nose against mine. "You heard this mysterious, intoxicatingly warm voice while you were in bed with me?"

I nodded, rubbing my nose against his. "Don't get cocky."

He gave me a small smile. "This is the last time I'll bring it up, but maybe you hear them for a reason?"

I considered this, pressing my lips together. I stuck my tongue out to wet them. "Possibly. In the beginning, it would come like a punch to my head, as if it was trying to break through a titanium wall, like it was just as confused and stuck as I was. Now, it's like it's taking a different approach, smoother. I almost want to invite it, but there's just something holding me back." I kissed him lightly. "It's like it knows something I don't."

Nicholas kissed me back and then kissed my cheek, my jaw, then my lips again. "Okay, well, I'll personally just spiral with this alone in my own head, but I don't want to cause you to spiral, so how about we put this to bed for now?"

"I like putting things to bed," I said in a low voice. That voice, that warmth; it was almost like a part of me I'd forgotten.

He rubbed my arms and wrapped his hands around my waist, feeling up my back and then down to grab my ass and pull me into him. "You are a special one, Dani. There's something about you that I can't put my finger on." He was starting to sound like Natalia. She'd said that she didn't think I was deserving of a demonic soul, even though I had one.

Nicholas believed my soul wasn't in danger of disintegrating. What did they see that I didn't?

"Is that a good or bad thing?"

"How about you ask me when all this shit is over?"

He rolled us over so that I was on my back, and he pressed into me. His cock was stiff and settled between my legs. I opened my legs wider, so he had more room to feel comfortable. His hair fell over his face in a boyish way that made him both incredibly sexy and still so young -- I almost felt like I was corrupting him. Both his hands braced on either side of my face, trapping me in. I felt extremely at ease here, with him.

"Dani, do one thing for me." I arched one of my eyebrows in question."Call me Nick, alright?"

I wrapped my arms around his neck, running my nails along his skin. "Why?"

He answered with a shrug. "Nicholas is so formal, and we haven't been formal for a while now. I want you to call me Nick, just because I want you to."

I looked at his face, at the sincerity there. "Can I still call you Nicholas sometimes?"

He chuckled. "Sure, but..." He dipped down and kissed my neck, licking at my skin. He brought his mouth up to my ear and his breath against my lobe had me arching up into him. "When I have you moaning my name, that's all I want to hear."

I felt nothing but molten, animalistic need. He captured my lips, and I eagerly kissed him back. We had a few more hours to do this, be this.... whatever *this* was. A few more hours with just the two of us. By the way he slid his hand down my body, he was thinking the exact same thing.

CHAPTER SEVENTEEN

NICK

I let the bathroom door close behind me and walked over to the sink, placing my hands on the porcelain rim. The cold press of it caused a much-needed wave of relaxation through my over-heated body. I looked at myself in the mirror and studied my reflection. Everything about me looked the same: same hair, same eyes, same scar underneath my eye from when Reese and I had gotten into a fight.

I tried to find anything that would make all the feelings in my stomach make sense. I looked up to my left, above the shower, and saw the rays of sunlight through the narrow window. It was already early morning, probably around eight, and I felt both alert and exhausted. I looked back at myself in the mirror and tried again.

Ah, there it was.

My hair looked like it had been tousled relentlessly, and not from a restless night of sleep. My lips looked a bit puffy, as if they never stopped kissing the softest lips they'd ever made contact with. My eyes traveled to my shirtless chest and noticed the bite marks along my collarbone, and a small purple mark that looked so much like a fucking hickey. Because it *fucking* was. I traveled down further to my abs and saw the remnants of scratch marks. The marks didn't break skin, but they were red and raised. I touched my fingers to the gauze that adorned my side, noticing how the marks deliberately moved around it.

Last night had really happened. Last night that had not ended last night. It had continued into the morning and literally ended maybe an hour or two ago when she had finally, *finally* settled into a dead sleep. Not that I had complained when every time we finished, no more than thirty minutes later, she would be completely ready for more. I probably should have called a time out, because fuck was I sore, but I found myself not wanting to say no to that face. I couldn't say no to her slender neck, her sexy collarbones, her perfect fucking breasts and ass.

I pressed my tongue to my cheek when I thought back to how sore *her* body must be, seeing as she had let me contort her into every position I could ever imagine. She did so with an eagerness in her eyes that had me impatient to be inside her. I pressed my fingertips to my lips, remembering how she tasted when I finally decided on what I wanted last night. Fuck, she had tasted so good, every bit as intoxicating as I knew she would. I could have happily had my face between her thighs for hours and hours, but I would do that at another time.

If we had another time.

I scrubbed my hand down my face and closed my eyes. I thought about it after I told her to start calling me Nick. I had gotten used to her using my full name, but it wasn't something I wanted to hear when she was orgasming. I realized that I have never heard my name so many times in my entire life in a single night, and the thought made a smile creep across my lips.

I pressed my hand over my mouth to try to stop it, but the smile was happening, and it was one of those smiles that was going to make my fucking cheeks hurt. Her calling me Nick meant we were getting somewhere, somewhere that didn't quite have a destination yet, and that made me a bit uneasy.

I remember trying to settle into a cuddling sleep, but a few minutes after, she had turned over, straddled my waist, and started to grind her tight, small body against my cock.

My response was just to kiss her, lift her up, and watch as she grabbed my cock and slowly let her soaking wet pussy take it all in until she was seated at my pelvis. I gripped the sink tightly, feeling the tension in my fingers as I remembered the way she rocked back and forth, pressing her fingers into my chest, scraping her nails down, creating the defined red lines that were now decorating my chest and stomach. She had bitten her bottom lip, her hair falling around her shoulders as she moved, and all I could do was graze my hands up her sides and arms, down her chest, flicking and playing with her nipples and down her stomach, where I pressed my thumb against her clit.

I was starting to understand the things she liked, the way her body responded to me, how to make her release all the sounds I wanted out of her. It was a power trip. She had started to move her hips faster, letting out little hiccups, arching up every now and then to bounce on top of me, which sent my eyes rolling back into my head. She had come with a moan that sounded like she wanted to scream, but she didn't have the chance. I had propped my body up and kissed her, pressing my hand against the back of her head. Dani had pulled back and rubbed her nose against mine, but then she had pushed me back down and told me she was feeling generous.

I had watched her lift off my cock and scoot down until her face was mere inches away from my dick. She arched her back so the top curve of her ass was in my view, taking me into her mouth with so much commitment that...fuck. I felt my cock twitch in my sweat-pants at the memory.

I let go of the sink, realizing I was breathing hard.

We had gotten it all out of our systems. Throughout the night, we woke desperate, needy, and wanting, tangled limbs and sweaty bodies colliding, silently begging each other for more, more, more.

She had moaned into the mattress for me to keep fucking her harder when I bent her over again, but this time, dragging her to the side of the bed so her feet could meet the carpet. Another time, she sat on my face, coming on my tongue as she moaned against my hand over her mouth. I played with her perfect breasts and nipples, and eventually, I couldn't take it anymore and ended up rolling us over, pushing inside of her, and fucking her with her legs spread as far as they would go. At some point, I had lifted her up into my arms and fucked her against the wall, both of us watching as my cock repeatedly disappeared inside of her, feeling how her pussy clenched around me when she came yet again.

We had ended with me inside of her, my front to her back. It wasn't rushed or frantic. I just shifted her leg over my own and I settled behind her as we lay on our sides back-to-back and I fucked her slowly, buried my face in her hair, smelling that same scent I always did when she was around. She smelled like cinnamon, and it was becoming the most enticing scent that ever existed. I didn't even like fucking cinnamon, but on her, I couldn't help it. Her sounds were soft, as if she didn't have any real breath, but she could muster enough small moans against the pillow for me to know she liked whatever I was doing.

When she came the last time, it was nearly silent, and I squeezed my hand tightly around her hip when I felt her contract around me and shudder against my body. I had leaned down to kiss her neck, but she looked over her shoulder and caught my mouth, kissing me fully. I opened my mouth, welcoming her soft lips as I continued to push into her, and I felt my own release barreling through me. Finally pulling out of her, she easily molded herself into my mattress and fell asleep, all those curls spilling around her and tickling my chest. I'd turned over onto my back and stared up at my ceiling, allowing myself to take a few moments to attempt to collect my thoughts. I'd glanced over at her small body curled next to me. The sun had let enough light into my room to cast a glow on her warm brown skin, and I found myself simply staring at her.

I looked at myself in the mirror again and mentally gave myself a pep talk about what needed to happen now. I had no idea what needed to happen now, but my brain wanted some sort of plan in place, even if it was just the *idea* that a plan was going to exist at some point. I did have one thing I planned to do today that didn't involve Dani at all—thank fuck— because being alone with her again wasn't something my head or my cock could deal with. What she had told me about that voice or feeling she had, it didn't sound familiar, and she had told me not to spiral. In all honesty, spiraling was what I did best. I did know someone who might be helpful, and if she could tell me what it is or its origin, then maybe we all would have somewhere to start when it came to Dani's role and who was helping Lilith. Whatever the outcome might be, it was worth a shot.

I froze the moment I heard my father's door open and footsteps outside the bathroom door, walking away towards the living room. My breathing stopped. I listened more intently and heard him scramble around in the kitchen, the refrigerator door opening and closing.

My father was a decently heavy sleeper, but sometimes, little sounds would wake him up in the middle of the night. It was rare, but it happened. His room had its own bathroom, so I wasn't concerned he would have come out of his room and heard us. Any real noises would have been muffled out by the thunderstorm, so why was I worrying?

Everything was fine. I was fine. We were fine. Totally fine.

I placed both my hands on my face and stepped away from the sink, suddenly feeling clothing underneath my feet. I looked down to see Dani's clothes from yesterday scattered on the floor. I knelt and looked over her red shorts and black t-shirt. I narrowed my eyes and reached out to pluck her bra from the ground, slowly closing my eyes and letting out a sigh when it fell from my fingers. Before I stood back up, I noticed the sweatpants I had offered her resting on the toilet seat, still folded. I groaned, remembering seeing her come out with just my sweatshirt on.

I peeked down at my sweatpants and silently cursed at the hard shape my cock made. I had to go out to face my father with a clear head and probably not a hard on, so I would have to remain in the bathroom until the traitorous appendage in my pants went down. I moved my sweatpants from the toilet seat to the back of the toilet itself and perched myself on the lid. I would eventually have to leave the bathroom at some point, but for now, I just needed a place to breathe where I wasn't cloaked in a sex haze.

How would I show my face at The Skies again? No...*when* would I show my face at The Skies again? When I traveled to Oculus, would

Natalia be able to tell me anything new? Was Jonah alright after the attack? Would he be able to *actually* answer my fucking questions or at least give me answers that didn't make me think I was going insane? I ran my hands through my hair roughly, feeling the sting in my scalp.

How in fucking heaven did my life become this?

The entirety of Heaven's Gate seemed to be hanging on by the most mediocre of threads and I had no idea why I felt like I had to be the one to fix it. I placed my hands on the back of my neck, threading my fingers together. I pressed against my neck, trying to release the tension knots when I heard the doorknob turn. My eyebrows rose as the door shifted forward and opened, revealing the current reason I was hidden in my bathroom.

Dani closed the door behind her and leaned against the wood, her hands behind her back. She tilted her head to the side and looked at me, a curious glint in her eyes. Her hair was moved to one of her shoulders and she had put my sweatshirt back on. I tried not to stare at the hem, where it met right at her thighs, but that was proving just as difficult as it was the first time. She cleared her throat, which quickly retracted all thoughts of what was underneath that sweatshirt from my mind. We spoke at the same time.

"Are you hiding in here?" Her.

"What are you doing in here?" Me.

She laughed a little. "When I woke up, you were gone, and your house isn't big enough for there to be many places for you to go."

"Oh well, yeah, I...uh..." I started, but I was finding it hard to think of something that made more sense than *oh, I was trying to find a place to not have to smell your cinnamon scent and probably start another sex marathon.* I could have said that, and she would have liked it, which was precisely the dilemma. "I'm not hiding."

"Looks like you're hiding, from where I'm standing."

"Well, I'm not. I just needed a minute, that's all." I got up and walked towards her. "Did you see my dad?"

She shook her head. "Nope, but I heard him banging around in the kitchen, so that must mean there is a delicious meal in my future." She rocked on her feet, shrugging her shoulders.

336

I blew out a breath at how cute she could be. I could feel an adoring expression start to show on my face, so I traded it for a more serious one. "He can't know what happened."

Dani leaned her head back against the door, exposing her neck to me. All I wanted to do was put my mouth on it again. "Of course, of course. I don't plan to go out there and just reveal to your father that you basically broke my vagina."

I placed my hands on my hips and stared up at the ceiling of the bathroom. "Jesus, Dani."

"Lighten up. You and I both know you'll give us away way before I will. You need to just relax and be happy we didn't break your bed. The way you fuck, I'm actually kind of surprised." She blinked innocently at me as I slowly looked away from the ceiling and straight at her face.

"You're annoying." That was a phrase I had stored away in my brain, locked in a safe I had labeled as Dani references. I couldn't think of anything else that embodied everything about her anytime she opened her mouth.

"Well aware, but we both know you enjoy it," she said, amusement in her tone. I was inches from her now. I towered over her, but she stood her ground, as if she was meeting my 6'2 frame perfectly instead of being just as intimidating in her simple, 5'2 stature. I watched as her stance faltered a bit as she officially took in my shirtless chest, the scratch lines on my stomach, and of course, my cock, which had been starting to go down, but...

She tilted her chin up at me. "You know your dad is going to be more suspicious about us both coming out of the bathroom at the same time if we don't decide what we're doing."

I pressed my tongue behind my top row of teeth. "Right. I'll let you take a shower first." I reached around her to grasp the doorknob when she got onto the tips of her toes and kissed the hickey she left on my collarbone. She kissed further inward, kissing my neck, stretching even further to kiss my jaw. I cocked my head away from her and smirked at the way she pouted.

"You just said that we both can't be in here right now. I'm trying to be smart and leave." I practically said the words through my teeth because fuck, she was drawing circles with her fingertips along my abs, dipping down and sliding her nail along the waistband of my sweatpants, then back up again. My cock was very, very interested in what she was doing.

She hummed. "I know what I said. That doesn't mean I can't mess with you in the process, *Nicholas*."

I leaned in towards her and reached my hand up to cup her chin, forcing her to look at me. "Nicholas?"

"You did say I could still call you that."

I started to say something, but she cut me off. "Unless this is one of those moments where you prefer I didn't...." Her voice got low and seductive as she trailed off.

I ghosted my lips over hers. "It can't be one of those moments."

She pulled a deep groan from my throat when she reached her hand inside my sweatpants and gripped my cock, stroking it. "Oh, why not?" She had a mocking tone to her words. "Your cock thinks differently."

I released her chin and pressed my palm against the door, right near her head. My stomach muscles contracted with the way she handled me, my hips flexing, wanting to fuck into her grip. She wrapped her hand at my base and slowly stroked to the tip, flicking her thumb at the head and then back down again. She repeated her motions over and over, causing the decently cool bathroom to start to feel like a sauna.

"Do you ever truly get tired?" I asked through hitched breaths.

She peeked at me through her lashes. "You really *haven't* been with a demon before, have you?"

I was exhausted from all the sex we'd had, but right now, I could have convinced myself to go again.

"You could always take a shower with me," she offered, running her free hand through my hair.

Fuck.

Was she sure that she was *just* a demon? Because right now, she felt like the devil, the supreme being of bad decisions. I had to go out there and face my father, pretend like everything was fine. I had to make my plan for when I used my portal key to get to Oculus. I needed to do a lot of things, and one of the things that I *didn't* need to do was slide my hand up her bare thigh and find that she had left my room without panties on. I could feel the heat of her before I even reached her pussy. But here I was, doing it.

Double fuck.

"You'd like that, wouldn't you?" I said, my voice low and only for her.

I placed two of my fingers against her as she nodded and instantly bit my tongue when I was met with how fucking wet she already was. She leaned further back into the wood of the door, and I slid two of my fingers easily inside her, pressing the heel of my hand against her clit. She continued to stroke my cock, which she had released from my pants. I had figured out that Dani made different sounds during different points of sex. She had these short little moans she made right at the beginning, like when something intrigued her or when something felt good and she was feeling it out. In the middle, she would make hiccuping breaths and her moans would get throatier, as if she officially liked whatever I was doing. It was my indication to keep going. Lastly, a few moments before she was about to come, she would usually bite her lip and whimper a little, and the moans or screams would come from her chest and vibrate around the room...or at least, they probably could have if I would have let them last night.

We were at the beginning stages of her sounds, and I let her moan against my cheek. She looked as if she wanted me to kiss her, but I didn't. I simply curled my fingers inside of her and watched as she started moving against my hand. Her legs spread automatically as she ground herself closer to her climax.

I let the tip of my tongue lick against her lips. "Are you always this needy? Or is this just for me?"

She muffled out a moan, respecting that we still had to be quiet. She rocked against my hand, and I moved with her, looking down at where she still had me in her fist.

"Nicholas..." she stated, letting the *'s'* at the end of my name linger a bit.

I pushed my fingers up into her and placed my forehead against hers. Her forehead was starting to dampen, and she was grazing her teeth over her bottom lip, not quite biting it.

"Try again," I pressed, testing her a bit at her use of my full name. She rocked harder, practically fucking my hand. I dipped my head down to her ear. "Say it right and I'll make you come."

She massaged the tip of my cock and then stroked back down to my base, frantically moving her hand up and down my length. I groaned low at the feel of her fingers tightening around me. She used her other hand to grip my bicep. My short nails were digging into the wood of the door, and I had to muster everything I had in me not to kiss her, because the minute I kissed her, it would be all over. Her breathing was becoming shallow, and I noticed the way her mouth was starting to form the start of my name.

"Fuck, please," she begged in a small voice, followed by a tug of my cock. Then she said it. She said it so smoothly and without hesitation that I could have come from that alone if I was an impatient kind of guy. "Please, Nick, make me come."

My eyes would have rolled back into my head if I wasn't so determined to watch her fall apart. I pressed the heel of my hand harder against her clit and rubbed. My curved fingers massaged that spot inside of her so hard, her legs started shaking. I would kiss her the minute she started to come on my hand, so hard that her sounds would go nowhere else, and they would be mine. I pumped my fingers, kneading her clit, and watched her squirm until her teeth started to bite into her lip, her eyes piercing into mine and burning through my very core. I set myself up to taste her lips. She was right there, right at the fucking edge of the cliff when...

"Nick!" a voice shouted from beyond the door.

I paused immediately, my hand making no movements, Dani immobile with me pinning her against the door. This was a literal nightmare.

"Nick!" my father shouted again as I heard him opening a cabinet. Then the pop and sizzle of bacon on a skillet rattled through my eardrums. If I didn't answer him, he would come looking for me, and if he went into my room, he would find my discarded shirt and Dani's panties. I quickly rallied.

340

"Yeah, Dad?" I answered, releasing my hand from the door, and pulling my other hand from where it was still inside my now wide-eyed demon, who was literally on the verge of laughter. I may have stopped touching her, but she still had her fist wrapped tightly around my aching cock.

"I'm making breakfast. Get Dani up and both of you can get something to eat."

Clearly, I wasn't on the couch when he came into the kitchen, so he must have seen that the bathroom light was on or just made an educated guess that I was still in the house. "Yup, I'll get right on that."

Dani smiled at me, showing all her perfectly white teeth. "I think what your dad meant is get Dani *off*, not up." She jerked my cock.

I stifled a groan and, with quite possibly all the strength I had, I grabbed her wrist and liberated my cock from her grasp. I felt empty without her touch, but I had to put some distance between us, which is why I took a few steps back, tucking myself back into my pants, even though my cock was very, very upset with my choices.

"It was a joke, Nick. Calm down."

I leaned down and yanked her clothes from the floor, putting them on the back of the toilet with my folded sweatpants. "Take a shower, Dani. I need to go talk to him." I nodded my head towards where my dad was beyond the door. I went over to the sink and quickly washed the scent of her off my fingers.

She scrunched her mouth to the side, sizing me up. "Alright." She strode past me, brushing her arm with mine. "Just know the shower would be better if you were in here with me. Since you want to be the good guy, I'll just think of you while I'm in here." She said this with such a nonchalant tone, I had to blink a few times to make sure I heard her right.

The shower *would* probably be better with me in it. It would be longer, the bathroom full of fucking steam, and if my father had no idea what had happened between us, he would surely know when he heard the slapping of water and the sound of her screaming my name. I wasn't going to risk it, no matter how tempting it was to fuck her so hard, she didn't think about anyone else, *ever*.

Woah, where the fuck did that come from?

I scrubbed the back of my head and headed towards the bathroom door, right as she turned on the water to the shower. Right before I opened the door, I looked back and saw her remove the sweatshirt, giving me a perfect view of her curves, smooth brown skin that didn't seem to have a flaw anywhere in sight, the delicious way her ass looked, perched high and round, as if it was just asking for my hand to grab it. Now I was remembering all the times I *had* grabbed it, the moments when I let my teeth sink into it. She snuck a look over her shoulder and squinted at me suspiciously, as if she knew every single thought running through my head. I rolled my eyes and snuck out the door, making sure my father was nowhere in sight, then made a beeline for my room.

I had quickly decided a shower was out of the question now, so I got my shit together and put on jeans and a new t-shirt, slipping my feet into a pair of high tops. I was just coming out of my room when I heard a voice that wasn't my father's from the kitchen. I guess I was too wrapped up in my own head to have heard somebody come into the house. I listened closer as I took cautious steps towards the living room. It was a female voice, not one I'd heard before, but then again, I wasn't the expert on women my dad was friendly with.

I rounded the corner slowly, leaning near the fireplace mantle, but stopped when they both came into view. They were near the kitchen counter, their bodies angled away from me. My father was telling her something and leaning in close, so I couldn't make out what he said. She let out a soft laugh, almost flirty, and placed a hand on his forearm. She had long dark hair that was tied into a braid, long enough to reach her lower back. She finally angled her face enough to make out some of her features. She was pretty, that was obvious. She was Indian, her skin an olive tone with a hint of a golden hue, her eyebrows dark and angled perfectly, as if she took the time out of her day to make sure they were sheer perfection. She had a gold hoop nose ring that caught a small bit of light each time she moved her head. She was tall, but not tall enough to compare with my father or me.

The mystery woman let out another laugh, placing her coffee

mug down. I scratched the back of my neck and stepped out from near the mantle, clearing my throat. They both looked at me expectantly. I looked back at them, waiting for someone to say something, but my father just looked at the woman next to him, opened his mouth, and then closed it. That was strange, but I was taught to have some sort of manners, so I crossed the room and stuck my hand out to her.

"Hey, I'm Nick." The woman smiled at me, probably one of the warmest smiles I had ever seen, and took my hand. Her eyes were a whiskey color that made me feel a smooth comfort within my veins. She had nails painted red with little silver sparkles on them. She looked a little younger than my father, but not by much.

"It's wonderful to finally meet you, Nicholas. Your father has told me a lot about you." She gave my hand a squeeze before she released it. She placed her hand on her chest. "I'm Daya Varma."

I looked over her shoulder to my father. "Well, I wish I could say the same thing about you." I had meant it to come out like a joke, but I could tell my father didn't see it that way with how he held his coffee mug tighter.

Daya just laughed and shook her head. "Don't be mad at him; it's my fault really."

I arched an eyebrow. "Oh?"

"Well, you see, your father wanted to tell you about..." Before she could continue, my dad came up behind her and placed his hands on her shoulders.

"Daya has brought Dani some other clothes. No need for her to be walking around in clothes from yesterday's disaster." He nodded towards the neatly folded clothes on the arm of the couch.

"She has?" I asked, lifting one of the corners of a folded shirt.

Daya nodded. "I have a daughter, Alex. She's around your age and she likes to design and create clothing, so I thought I would bring some of the extra pieces she had lying around."

I nodded back at her with understanding. I heard the shower water shut off, telling me Dani was done. "That's nice. It seems like she's out of the shower now if you want to catch her before she puts on her old clothes."

My dad had his hands still placed over Daya's shoulders and it looked like he was using his thumbs to massage her shoulder blades. She reached up and patted one of his hands, but then grabbed onto his fingers for a small moment and gave them a small squeeze.

Daya grabbed the clothes and held them in her palms, as if she was a waitress handling a plate of food. "I'll go see if she wants them." She gave me another smile, her nose ring sparkling in the morning sun as she walked past me towards the bathroom.

I let my eyes roam to my father to find his eyes had followed her, like he was in a trance. It was like he had forgotten I was there for a moment. His eyes looked the same as Reese's when he first saw Jules Fox on our first day of training. She had red hair that she had placed in two buns on each side of her head and a birthmark the size of my hand on her neck. Reese had taken one look at her and instantly, I saw the change in his face. He had the same eyes my father had now.

Puppy dog eyes.

I fast forwarded to when Reese asked her out, she said yes, but after a few weeks went by, she ended up catching him fucking around with her roommate. I always knew he wasn't the instant love type, which is why I didn't stop him when he'd told me he planned to ask Jules out to lunch with hearts for eyes. I wasn't with my father all the time like I was with Reese. I didn't know anything about Daya. I wasn't aware of the conversations they had been having, or how much she even knew about this situation at all. I just knew at that moment that he was downright smitten.

"You have a girlfriend?" I asked, plainly.

He blinked and then blinked again. His eyes finally looked at me with a more familiar shine. He furrowed his brow, as if he was taking in what I had asked.

"Huh?" my father asked, sounding dumbfounded. He turned towards the kitchen counter, setting his mug down and opening the cabinets to gather some plates.

"I asked if she was your girlfriend, Dad," I answered in the most obvious 'you aren't fooling anyone' tone I could muster. "Girlfriend, main squeeze, other half, ball and chain, any of those titles will do."

He closed the cabinet and started laying the plates out. "Girlfriend makes me sound like I'm twenty again. It's complicated. She didn't know how you would feel about the whole thing, so she was fine with just keeping things between us."

I scrunched up the side of my mouth. "Doesn't seem so complicated to me. Just so you know, I can't reprimand you for having a lady friend, Dad." He rolled his eyes. I walked over and leaned back against the kitchen counter. "Did you know her from before?"

He started to turn down the stove dials, bringing the eggs and bacon to a low heat. "Yes, but we didn't speak much. Plus, she practiced as a guardian angel, so we didn't really run in the same circles."

I nodded, knowing that back then, depending on where you were allocated in training pretty much determined the people you crossed paths with. You were what you were back then and that was all. If you didn't like it...well then, you were welcome to leave. Nowadays, you could fraternize with whoever you wished. You could even cross train if you so wished.

"A guardian? That's impressive." I placed my hands behind me and braced them on the counter. "And she has a daughter? Also at The Skies?"

My dad shook his head. "No, that wasn't something her daughter wanted to do, so she didn't push. I told her that *you* would never shut up about The Skies and how I wished you were more subtle about your interest."

"I wanted to make sure you got the message."

He chuckled but didn't say anything back. He just started to pile the food onto the plates one by one. I rolled my eyes at how nervous he looked.

"How long have you two been...?"

"A few months," he cut me off, exasperated.

"Dad, why didn't you tell me about her?"

"There is nothing to tell. We're just hanging out."

"I blatantly saw you two flirting. Hanging out sounds like you two sit around and discuss your latest hobbies and what kind of seasoning they had in the market this week. We both know you guys probably do exactly that but add in kissing."

He looked over at me with a pointed expression. "We talk now and then, alright? She comes over sometimes and we have dinner."

I narrowed my eyes. "So...like dates? Which can involve kissing?"

"Nicholas." He sounded irritated, but all I wanted to do was laugh.

"She seems nice, okay. It's odd to see you start to settle with someone, that's all."

After learning my mother left, my father always made himself available to me for whatever I needed. He was never *not* there. He wasn't a hovering parent, but he always made sure I was looked after. Dani didn't have to point out that my father was a good-looking man; that was always a fact growing up. There was never a time women didn't give him a second look while we walked through the village. When I got a bit older, I started to really notice it, but less like a boy and more like a full-blown teenager going through puberty.

Once I hit twenty, I realized he never actually went for any of them. Women would blatantly lean over counters in front of him or brush his arm with theirs, or even laugh at his not funny jokes with a breathy laugh. He would fall for none of it. He would always be home with me and smile as Reese and I would go about our lives as newly grown adult men, free to make our own mistakes and live our own lives. Daya didn't peg me as the type to flash the swell of her breasts for attention, which is why I think their coming together was more natural, probably a run in at the store. Something cute.

"How did you two meet, anyway?" I asked, wanting to confirm my own suspicions.

"Nothing fancy, I was coming home from my weekly stroll in the woods, and I noticed her carrying a bunch of grocery bags. I gave her a hand, that's all."

My father had a love for the outdoors that I never quite understood, so bad that he would train out there as a teenager, camp out in the woods regardless of the temperature, and sometimes just stand out in the rain, as if nothing else mattered. I hoped Daya loved the outdoors just as much as he did.

346

I smiled to myself at the idea. "That sounds literally perfect, Dad."

My dad looked up at me from where he was plating eggs and gave me a small smile. "Thank you. I think it was."

"I'm just happy you have someone when I'm not around."

He patted the kitchen counter absently with his fingertips and nodded, more to himself, as if to say, *'me too.'* I bit the inside of my cheek, trying to figure something out. "Dad, how much does she know?"

"About?" He was starting to pick up the plates and bring them to the table.

I grabbed his arm, halting him. He sat the ceramic plate down and faced me. "Oh, I don't know, Dad. *Everything.*"

My father placed his hand over mine and slowly dragged my fingers off his skin. "She knows enough to understand. She doesn't know all the minute details, but she does know about..." He nodded over to where Daya had walked down the hallway.

My eyebrows disappeared into my hairline. "You told her about Dani?" I brought my voice down a bit so that I wasn't yelling.

"I told her enough, like I said. Daya isn't judgmental, Nicholas. Yes, she was a little skeptical of Dani being a demon, but she trusts me, and she knows I trust you. She believes the same things I do."

"And that would be?"

My father let out a huff. "Not all demons are the culprits. The bad guys. We have both seen bad things happen to innocent people by the very people we believed to be the good guys, so to say our views on good and bad are skewed would be an understatement."

I pressed my lips together in defeat. My father was around when the attack on Oculus happened. I had never really asked him about his part in it. There were multiple sides to that story, and my father was one of those people who was willing to see all of them, but the time for that seemed to be long past. The whole attack was so hush, hush at The Skies, it was almost as if the only people who talked about it anymore was the new generation.

I raised my hands up in front of me and he just waved his hand at me, as if to say it didn't matter but to stop asking stupid questions.

347

Dani was safe in Daya's presence. I could breathe easier; not that I was worried for her or anything. Nope. I was just being cautious.

I rolled my neck, walking over to the counter and bringing the other plates with me. I went to get cups from the cabinet above the sink and take the orange juice out from the fridge. After a few moments of easy silence, he spoke.

"Nicholas, I wanted to ask you how you slept last night?" my dad had his back to me, but I could see the easy way his shoulder moved as he arranged the plates and napkins on the table. I was hunched over in the refrigerator, frozen in place. If I didn't say something for too long, he would know something was up. It was a simple question, a question anyone who clearly slept alone would be able to answer.

I grabbed the orange juice and straightened up, closing the door with my knee. "Perfect. Like a baby."

My father turned around and faced me, his arms crossed over his chest. "Is that so?"

I placed the orange juice next to the cups and started unscrewing the cap. "Yup."

My father clucked his tongue. "Funny. I'm pretty sure we both agreed that that is the worst couch to sleep on. As a matter of fact, I remember you telling me you would never get a good night's sleep on that couch, and you would be better off on the floor."

"Your point?"

"My point, son, is that there is no way in hell you slept on this couch all night and can honestly tell me you had a good night's sleep." He tilted his head to the side, waiting. When I opened my mouth, he started again. "Also, none of those sheets look like you attempted to sleep."

I rolled my eyes. "You ever think maybe I don't need sheets? Maybe I learned to sleep through the incredible back pain the couch provides."

My father stalked over to me with a suspiciously humored smile. "Or you spent the night in your room." He placed a large hand on my shoulder. "Listen, I don't care that she's a demon. I don't care that you slept in your room with her. I don't even care that you think you

348

can lie to me about it." He squeezed my shoulder. "What I do care about is my son thinking it's okay to have sex in my house. It wasn't okay when you were sixteen, and it's not okay now."

I closed my eyes so tight, I'm pretty sure I heard a blood vessel pop. This was where the floor sucked me in, and I was never seen again. All I felt right now was pure embarrassment. How in the hell did I think I was going to walk away from last night with no battle scars, no wounds? I kept my eyes shut when I asked, "You didn't uh... hear anything, did you?"

"Oh heavens, no. Good thing, too, because you would have felt very awkward last night if you had woken me up and forced me to come into your room and shut you both up."

"Ugh. How are you so sure if you didn't hear anything?"

"Nicholas, I may be old, but I'm still your father. The way you looked at that girl last night, there was a fifty-fifty chance that something was going to happen. This morning, when I found everything still folded and no sign of you even attempting to sleep there, I put it together; you decided to have a not so sleepover."

I placed both my hands on either side of my head and walked over to the arm of the couch. I sat down and placed my elbows on my thighs. "I'm sorry, Dad. I should have been more...considerate."

"Like I said I didn't hear anything. I mean there was a storm out there, so you two picked a great night to do it."

"Ew, Dad, stop. It's not like we planned for this ahead of time."

"Nicholas, I know." He shot his hip out and placed it against the back of the couch. "You like her?"

"I don't know. I think so. Maybe. Is this where you tell me I shouldn't have had sex with her if I was unsure how I felt about her?"

He shook his head. "No, not at all. If I said that, I would be the world's biggest hypocrite."

I sighed in relief. "Good, because that ship has sailed. It's not like this was the first time..." I trailed off, realizing all the words I was spewing. Of course, right now I would become a babbling idiot.

Fuck.

His eyes widened as I looked up at him from where I sat. Usually, we could look eye to eye, but right now, I was shorter than him and

349

he was towering over me. His eyes didn't look surprised, though; they almost danced, amusement lighting up the small wrinkles at the corners of his eyes. "Oh, you have it bad, son."

I tried to shrug in a noncommittal fashion. "What if it's just sex?" This is not a conversation for almost nine in the morning, but there was no turning back now.

"Nicholas, you are the string attached type of man, and I respect that. I hate to break it to you, poor boy, but you like this girl enough to have all night, in your room, while your dad sleeps five feet away sex with her."

I gaped at him, my mouth open and everything. "What makes you think I—we— were up all night? Presumptuous much."

My father held onto his stomach as he laughed, not because I had told a joke, but because he actually thought what I said was hilarious. "As much as you try to hide it, you look like you've been up all night," he said with a smirk, which made me want to vomit, but not before I heard laughter coming from down the hall.

We looked up as the two women came around the corner. Dani had abandoned her clothes from yesterday and was now wearing a gray and white crop top and black leggings. Her hair was still wet, but she had braided it and let it sit on one of her shoulders. I tried my hardest to avert my eyes, but they kept tracing the lines of her waist, the curve of her ass in those leggings, and my hands ached to touch the small sliver of smooth brown skin that revealed itself when her top rode up a bit. I had to ball my hands into fists to try to restrain myself. She turned slightly so she could tell Daya something, and then both women laughed again.

"What's so funny?" my dad asked, pointing between the two of them.

Daya waved her hand at him. "Oh, just girl things. Nothing you need to worry your pretty head about."

"Damn, Dad. I like her," I laughed, causing my father to run his hand over my shoulder and laugh as well, his laugh a little darker, like he was about to make me regret my comment.

He nodded over to Dani. "Alright then. Well Dani, how did you sleep?"

Dani placed her eyes directly on mine, but before I could really let my eyes bore into hers, she looked away and focused on my father. The glint in her eyes had me feeling like they were both conspiring against me. "Really good." I didn't realize I had been holding my breath until she stopped speaking, and I opened my mouth to let it out. I was going to mention us going to the table to eat when she continued. "Yeah, I was able to get a really good, *deep* sleep. Extremely *satisfying*." She smirked, and I could feel my heart crashing and my brain malfunctioning.

I felt my dad's hand hitting my back when I started coughing uncontrollably. Daya started to come over, but I put my hand up to stop her. She looked over to my father, who gave her a small smile and shook his head. She raised one of her eyebrows but walked to her coffee mug instead.

"Well, that's great, sweetheart. Nick was just telling me how he had a good night sleeping on the couch. All by himself, of course. He was very adamant about that part." I heard the sarcastic tone in my father's voice, and I have never wanted to punch my own father in the face as much as I wanted to right now.

Dani cocked her head to the side, letting her tongue quickly trace her bottom lip. "Are you sure, Mr. Cassial, because he looks a little tired. He looks like he might have expelled a lot of energy last night. No, no, not expelled, hmm... maybe *ejaculated* a lot of energy?"

Daya was now the one who started coughing, right as she lifted her mug to her lips. My father let out a deep belly laugh, and I sat there, lowering my face into my hands. I glanced up from my hands after a moment and noticed Dani as she walked—no, she sauntered —over to me, her hips swaying. "What on earth did you do last night to make you so tired, Nicholas?" She said my name with such a sharp tone.

"I feel like I'm missing something," Daya said, looking at each of us suspiciously.

My father came up next to her, grabbing his coffee mug. "I'll explain it to you later. For now, let's eat before the food gets cold. You both have a long day ahead, that's for sure." He and Daya placed their mugs on the table and went to go grab the orange juice cups I'd left on the counter.

Dani reached out and trailed her fingertips along my neck and up to my jaw when they turned away from us. She brought her fingers to the center of my chin and placed her thumb at my bottom lip, pulling it down. She sank her teeth into her lower lip and let my trapped lip go. "You smell like good sex," she said in the softest and most breathy tone I have ever heard. It came out neutral, as if the soft part was meant just for me.

She started to turn away from me and walk towards the table, but I followed behind her, letting my hand brush along hers as I passed her. "You smell like *great* sex."

BREAKFAST WENT ON AS IF EVERYTHING WAS NORMAL IN THE WORLD, AS IF WE could just forget that beyond this house and the extending tree line, something was happening that none of us could really pin down with a solid answer. My mind had wandered during their conversations, and I went down my never-ending spiraling path that led to even more questions and even fewer answers. I tried to shake it off as best I could, and for the most part, no one seemed to notice when I would drift off.

Daya answered any and all questions I had for her, which weren't as many as I think my dad thought it would be. I learned that her daughter, Alex, was two years younger than me and highly interested in fashion. She had been adamant at a young age that any part of The Skies was not for her, and she was happy in the village, pursuing her dreams. Her husband had died from a heart attack five years ago and when she talked about it, my father reached out his hand and clasped it around hers. Her husband had also been a guardian angel during her time at The Skies and she was happy with the years they had together. I could see she kept the happy memories close to her heart – she smiled when she spoke about her late husband.

She admitted to me that she was nervous, rightfully so, about me being so closely involved with demons, then coming in this morning to the information my father gave her about everything that had happened. It was a lot, but she believed my father when he told her I was a smart kid who knew what I was doing. Boy, did he have a shit ton of faith in me, because my faith in myself was wearing thin. Daya laughed at her own words when she finally admitted Dani was the most un-demon-like demon she had ever come across. Granted, that was before the war, before things got so fucking complicated for everyone, and she reevaluated the things she thought she knew.

Dani smiled over at her at the mention of her name and then snuck a glance over at me from across the table. Dani asked questions when the conversation would grow silent, ranging from my early life before The Skies all the way to the Animus Seeking, which she had seen from her window when she and Elise were stuck in their room. Her eyes lit up when I spoke about going to the human world. She listened like she was plainly intrigued, hanging onto every word I said. I had to restart a few of my sentences because the brazenly unapologetic demon decided to trail her foot along my leg and up towards my knee. I practically jumped out of my seat at the contact and had to immediately act like I was readjusting my position. I shook my head at her and watched as she took another bite of food to hold her laugh in, but then she did it again a few moments later, causing me to just get up from the table and put my plate away. She gave me a fake pout as I passed her, but I just rolled my eyes and adjusted my stirring dick in my pants.

After everyone put their dishes away, I went to my room for a jacket and walked back into the living room towards my sword, still leaning against the wall. I picked it up, feeling the weight in my hand and loving the way it felt just right. I sheathed it behind my back, fingering the leather strap of my baldric.

"Where are you headed?" my father asked, stepping up to me. I looked around him at Dani and Daya on the couch, talking and laughing as if they had known each other for years.

I focused back on my dad. "Oculus."

"Ah, for Reese and Elise."

I scratched the side of my head. "Yeah…"

"And something else?" he pressed, leaning in towards me.

"It's nothing. Just something I need to talk to Natalia about."

My father stroked his chin. "I assume that Dani isn't going with you?"

"I'm not going to be gone long, but there is something I need her input on that Dani can't be a part of, not yet. She'll be safer here with you guys."

He looked over his shoulder at her and sighed. "Keeping secrets is no way to start a relationship, Nicholas."

I ran my hand through my hair, frustratingly. "Relationship? Dad, please don't make whatever there is between me and her a thing. It's not a thing. It can't be."

"Because she's a demon?"

"It's not just that, but yeah, that is a big factor."

He chuckled, rocking back on his heels. "You are an adult, so you can make your own decisions, but I will tell you that if you like her, explore that for as long as it takes. Demon or not, you feel something." I opened my mouth to protest, but he cut me off. "You like her, Nicholas. There is no law saying you can't be with her. I'm not getting in your way. That is all you, son."

I let out a huff that sounded like defeat and my father patted my cheek. I pushed his hand away, so he decided to pat my other cheek. My mouth broke into a smile as he continued to go back and forth, slapping lightly at my cheeks. Once a small, annoyed laugh creeped out of my throat, he finally stopped. We both laughed, causing the girls to turn around and look at us. I caught Dani's eyes and noticed the minute she took in my expression and the sword strapped to my back. She was up and off the couch in a matter of minutes. She saddled up to my father, who raised his eyebrows at me before stepping back and walking over to his girlfriend.

Dani tilted her head to the side and placed her hands on her hips. Her hair had dried, causing her curls to spring from her braid. I was so fucking tempted to wrap my finger around the spirals, but I didn't.

She licked her lips before she spoke. "Where are you going?'

"Oculus." This conversation was literal déjà vu.

"Okay, let me go say bye to Daya…"

I waved my hand to stop her. "No, you can stay here."

She pressed her lips together, her brows furrowing. "You want to go alone?"

"I'm just going to check on the others and get intel from Natalia, that's all." She would either be pissed that I let what she said affect me so much, or she would want to come with me, and I needed some space from her. Not in a bad way, but with everything that had happened in less than twenty-four hours, I just needed to clear my head.

"Without me…" She said it like she was trying on the words for size. She was tasting them along her tongue, and she wasn't a fan.

"I don't know what beyond this village looks like for you right now, so staying here would be your best bet. I'll be back, don't worry."

"I'm not worried, I'm just curious what you're keeping from me."

"I'm not keeping anything from you."

She rolled her eyes. "You're a terrible liar."

I caught my father's eye from across the room and quickly looked away. He was giving me that *'just tell her what's on your mind'* look, and I wasn't in the mood. "Dani, I promise if I find anything useful, I'll come back and tell you. I don't know if people are looking for you, so I would rather you just stay here."

She tapped her fingers on her exposed skin under her crop top. "Sounds like you care about me."

I shrugged. "Maybe." I turned away from her and towards the backdoor. I would open the portal towards the woods and walk straight into Oculus. Sounded simple enough. When I swung the door open, I heard my father yell, "be careful, Nicholas," right as Daya yelled, "come back safely." They worried too much; or maybe I wasn't worried enough.

I pulled the tiger's eye crystal from my shirt. The chain felt cool on my neck. I didn't really know how this worked, since the last time I used my key to portal, I was in a panicked state and bleeding out of my side. I held the tip of the crystal and pointed it out in front of me, but before I could make a move, I heard a door close. I felt her presence before she said anything.

"You still aren't coming, Dani," I said sternly.

She let out a tired grunt and grabbed my arm, turning me around. I looked down at her and watched as she looked up at me with the determined expression I admired. "You really aren't going to tell me the *real* reason why you are leaving for Oculus without me?"

I had something in the back of my mind telling me that what Dani had been feeling and hearing had something to do with why she's so special. I didn't want whatever news I got, if I got any at all, to completely cast her into the dark place I found her in with that demon. I didn't even know if Natalia could help me out, but she was the only chance I had. I was doing this for her safety. I would not put it past Ariel to send sentries to look for her, strike her down immediately, so staying put would have to suffice for now.

"No, Dani. There is no *real* reason." Lies. Lies. Lies.

"I swear, if you are telling me you're going to Oculus, but you are really going to The Skies to get my dagger, I will kill you myself when you get back."

I widen my eyes. "Fuck, no. I don't plan to go back there until we are all together. Oculus is the truth, Dani. Just take my word for what it is."

She looked down at the ground, rustling dirt up from the ground with her boot. As if an idea sparked in her mind, she shot her head up. "Are you going to talk to Natalia because of what I told you last night?"

Fuck, she was good.

"You told me not to spiral with that, so I'm not." Lie.

"Right."

"Dani, our friends are there waiting to hear that we're fine, so I'm going to do just that. I'll speak with Natalia about next steps and maybe how this all might end. That is all."

She nodded, but in a way that told me she didn't believe me.

"I will come right back and tell you anything and everything. Then, we can portal to Oculus together, since I'll know what's going on from that side. Alright?"

She lifted her hands up. "Alright. Just know I think you're a giant dick for leaving me."

"It's not like I want to," I mumbled under my breath, but she heard me. The corners of her mouth twitch upward.

She punched my shoulder, opening her hand and letting it slide down to my bicep, squeezing. "I'll be here when you get back. You leave no detail out, got it?"

"Yes ma'am." I gave her a salute, which she laughed at.

She caught my hand before I could completely turn around. I looked down at where our fingers connected. The spike of electricity was back, and all I wanted was to pull her into me and kiss her.

"Where do angels go when they die?" she asked, as if it was the most normal question in the world. Her expression had morphed into one of slight sincerity, as if this question had played on her mind for some time.

I brought my head back to look at her – that was an odd question. It is an understandable one, but just odd. "Um, why do you want to know?"

She shrugged, as if it was just something that popped into her head. "I wanted to ask you last night, but it kept slipping my mind. I was a bit distracted." She winked up at me, smirking. "You saw what happens to demons who don't have a strong enough hold on themselves. They just disintegrate as if they are nothing when they die. The rest of us will rot away if we die and become part of the framework that makes up Purgatory. I know about those human souls that you extract when they die, taking them to Heaven and all, but where do you guys go?"

I took my hand from hers and rubbed my palms together, thinking of the right way to explain it to her. "Well, I've been told that their souls remain in Heaven's Gate, looking over all of us, over those in Heaven, and they are just at peace. Sometimes, there is a special ceremony, depending on the angel. All our angelic powers are threaded within our souls, so once angels die, their powers get embedded into the lands and the body becomes pretty much mundane. The only exceptions are angels like Jonah and those before him."

She mulled this over. "What happens if you are a shitty angel?"

I chuckled. "From what my father used to tell me, the bad people who claim to be good can't hide anywhere when the end finally comes. They end up where they belong."

"You believe that?" Dani asked, her eyebrow arched.

I bit my lower lip, thinking. "I actually do."

"Jonah?"

"What about Jonah?"

She narrowed her brown eyes at me, crossing her arms over her chest. She looked up at the trees as they swayed back and forth with the wind. It was a relatively warm morning, but the air still smelled like rain. "From what I could tell in that meeting, he seemed a little hurt by your accusations. I'm not saying I trust the guy and I'm not saying I don't think he is public enemy number one, but if he isn't the mastermind of all this, then he is still hiding something. Something that has to do with you."

"What's your point?"

"My point, Nicholas, is that if Jonah isn't the bad guy, but he's done some bad things, do you think he deserves to have his soul floating around with the good guys when the end comes?"

I leaned my weight on each of my feet. "I don't know. We all have made mistakes, Dani, but that doesn't mean we can't try to fix them in the hopes that we can find some sort of peace."

Her eyes roamed around my face, scanning every inch of my features before settling on my eyes. "That's pretty much what I'd thought you'd say."

"Why do I feel like I passed some sort of test?"

She pushed up on her toes and placed a kiss right on my lips before backing off. I didn't have the time to try and kiss her back, but she didn't seem to do it for the make out session. It was chaste and quick, likely just for her. I gave a small nod before turning and holding the crystal again.

I drew a circle with it, watching as the portal opened and a wave of light came through. All I had to think about was Oculus—calmly — and maybe I wouldn't land on my ass. I started to walk through the portal, but then I stopped. I scrunched my mouth to the side, debating my next words.

I looked over my shoulder at where she still stood, watching me. She watched me so easily, as if she could do it all day and never get tired. I felt the same about her. "Don't worry about your soul."

She cocked her head to the side in confusion.

I explained further. "Despite what you are, you deserve answers and peace, just like the rest of us."

She blinked. Once. Twice. Then, she gave me a half smile and I watched her cheeks turn red, as if she was blushing.

Well, that was a first.

I stepped through the portal with the look on her face ingrained in my memory.

When she asked me about Jonah, she was really asking about herself. To do all the things she'd done, but still not be so spiteful or so lost in her own darkness is something I never understood. Elise was every bit the demon I had imagined, but Dani...Dani was something else. It wasn't about the sex, even though that had been wildly amazing. I felt a connection with her that went beyond anything I expected.

Dani wasn't inherently bad. I didn't know anything about her life before Purgatory, but with everything she'd done while there, I could see how someone could think their only ending would be dark and tormented. I never believed that where you started dictated where you ended. With Dani, though, how she started could be the answer to all of this.

How she started could decide how it all ended.

CHAPTER EIGHTEEN

DANI

I looked out the window and watched as Mr. Cassial watered his flowerbeds. He would look over his shoulder occasionally and wave at people who passed by, but then he would go back to tending to his colorful collection of flowering plants. It was cute watching him make sure each section was thoroughly nourished. It made me laugh seeing such a tall, brawny man caring for something so delicate. I lifted the mug filled with steaming hot coffee to my lips.

I had finally simmered down a bit after Nicholas left for Oculus, but the memory of his words and the short kiss we shared before he left still had my mind reeling. Last night had been fun, explorative, *acrobatic*, then again, it had also been many things I couldn't quite comprehend. I liked him, but he was kind of hard not to like, even through the stubborn, hard-shelled surface. That armor he'd built up around himself was shattering, and I didn't know if it was because of all the things going on around us or if it was me. I also didn't know if I even wanted it to be me, because if I did, then what did that mean for myself or...us? What even *was* an us?

I wasn't stupid and I knew he was going to Oculus to question Natalia about what I told him the night before, but me pleading with him not to be an overthinking ass wouldn't have done any good. When Nicholas put his mind to something, that was it. That something could be professional like a mission...or that something could be getting you to come more times than you think is possible. He is just *that* determined.

Very capable. More capable than I wanted to admit.

My vision started to blur a little when I thought about how each time he shifted from passionate, heartfelt, let you feel every inch of my cock slowly Nick to the heated, fevered, let me press your face into a pillow while I rail you out and thoroughly obliterate your pussy Nick. Both were appreciated, and both had my cheeks warming thinking about them.

"He is quite cute, isn't he?" Daya, Mr. Cassial's girlfriend, said from behind me. I tensed a bit from her sudden appearance, but she didn't seem to notice. I counted to three, willing my current thoughts to fuck off. I looked over at her as she looked out the window, her face showing something that could only be called adoration. "He always makes sure those flowers are tended to, like clockwork." Her eyes watched as Nick's dad pulled weeds from the ground.

"It's good to have hobbies," I answered, taking one last look out the window and turning so that I could walk back towards the couch.

Daya tucked pieces of her dark hair behind her ear. "Yes, but I think it's more that he has something else to take care of."

I settled onto the couch, tapping my mug with my fingernails. "Because Nick isn't around?"

She nodded, taking a seat next to me. She kicked off her shoes and tucked her feet underneath her thighs. "He'll never admit it fully, but he misses having him around. It's just a parent thing. You want them to live their life and be an adult, but a part of you misses the routine of them being present."

I didn't say anything to that, since I didn't know how that felt. I wasn't a parent, nor did I ever remember having them. To be loved so unconditionally that someone just missed your very presence, that almost took my breath away.

Daya must have noticed how awkwardly silent I had gotten when she changed the subject. "You and Nick make quite the pair."

My response wavered a bit. "We aren't."

She narrowed her eyes at me, the whiskey color of them seeming to glow against the sunlight. "Oh, well, you two just seemed so cozy, that's all."

"Cozy? Right." I laughed.

"Maurice just told me this morning that Nick seemed more at ease. I mean, he has told me his son was always stubborn, but I guess he seemed...less like himself. In the best way."

I took a sip of my drink, letting it simmer on my tongue. "I think Nick would claim I'm corrupting him."

She giggled. "Perhaps, but I don't hear him complaining."

I nodded in agreement, smiling over my coffee mug.

Daya eyed me now, pressing her lips together. "The Soul Seether, huh?'

Not what I thought the first real topic of conversation would be about. Granted, the first time we ever spoke, she was knocking on the bathroom door, offering me clothes, and telling me I had a very eager angel waiting in the living room for me. That had made me laugh. I had made her laugh in return by saying that the leggings she gave me would probably give him a heart attack and proceeded to snatch them away from her.

"That's what they call me."

"That must put you under a lot of pressure." She sounded concerned.

"Sort of. I mean, it's the only thing I've ever known."

She hummed. "Lilith is a special kind of evil, isn't she?" This was poised more like her own opinion than a question.

I shrugged, taking a sip of my coffee. "Yeah, I mean she was alright in the beginning, but then things just changed...."

Daya remained quiet, letting me finish my thought.

"I don't know how to explain it, but I started to resent her, that's all. She would dote on me all the time, but then she started to pull away from me. It was so odd. It wasn't like she found another demon

362

or something, but she just got so busy, I guess. Now, that all makes sense."

"What do you mean?" Daya asked, placing her hand delicately on her knee.

"Lilith masterminding all of this shit. She must have hit the start button, which was why she started to appear to me less and less. I always had Elise, so it wasn't so bad all the time."

"Elise is your friend in Oculus, right now?"

I had forgotten how much Daya knew and how much I had said at breakfast this morning. She had listened easily and never had a trace of judgment on her face, even when we brought up my dagger, how the powers in it were tethered to me, and when we talked about my use of it in the Ethereal Bastille. Judgement never reared its ugly head. She had a motherly way about her expressions that I wasn't used to. She never asked for more than I was willing to give, and I thought about how much I appreciated that.

"She is in Oculus, yes. Friend? Umm, you would have to ask her. She has this weird way of not being my friend but having friendly tendencies. It's better if you don't try to figure it out."

Daya laughed, angling her elbow towards the back of the couch, and leaning her head against her hand. "Maybe she's afraid of hurting you."

"Hurting me?" That caught me off guard. The one thing Elise was good at was hurting people, physically and mentally. The last thing she would be afraid of was causing pain.

"I'm sure in Purgatory, any sort of emotion that makes you vulnerable comes highly unwanted. Elise probably doesn't want to show you any friendliness so that you can, I don't know, keep up your appearance," Daya explained, as if it were the simplest conclusion.

She had a point. Demons were friendly with each other, but at the drop of a hat, if Lilith were to suggest a match to the death between two friends, that friendship would be completely dissolved right on the spot. It's happened on more than one occasion for her pure entertainment. Those were in my earlier days, when I liked to think she was showing me everything Purgatory had to offer, letting me see all the bloodshed from a front row seat. She even had me pull out a few of their souls before they died, once she had presented me with my dagger. She would take their souls in her hand when I was done yanking it out of their chest and crush it within her long fingers. It would turn to dust, the fine granules leaving her palm as she let it fall to the ground.

"Did you ever come in contact with her?" I drained the last of my coffee and placed the mug on the coffee table.

Daya yanked a pillow from behind her and placed it in her lap. "Who?"

"Lilith."

She looked down at the rectangular pillow, tracing her fingers along the geometric pattern that covered it. "No, I never did, but I did come across her demons plenty of times when I was in the human world. They never really spoke much, nor did I speak to them, but they always looked on edge as I was watching over my humans."

"They never knew you were around, the humans?"

She laughed light-heartedly. "Oh, no. That is the one thing we learned in training. You were never seen and only watched, giving silent guidance, procuring safety. The key to being a good guardian."

I smiled at this, wondering if I had someone like that when I was a human, still alive and able to make choices at a whim without dire consequences. "You were around during the war though?"

"Of course, but I wasn't asked to fight. They left that up to the sentries. I was happy to be left out, though; I never believed in it. I would have never chosen to fight against Moira when everything was peaceful before. It just didn't make sense."

She shook her head, letting that memory fade and conjuring up another one. "I never quite understood Isaac's reasoning, but that man was never in his right mind, if you ask me."

"Isaac?"

"Jonah's father. He was nice enough, but he was power hungry. There could be peace amongst all of us and he was still unhappy."

I almost scoffed. It didn't surprise me at all that Jonah's father wasn't some delicate do-gooder who had no idea the kind of power he held. No one down in Purgatory asked Lilith about the war and her place in it. Everyone there just let it go and allowed her to continue with her secrets and ruthless dictating. If I was being really honest, the magic that kept her in Purgatory didn't faze her one bit; it was almost as if she really didn't care.

Maybe she didn't. Maybe she was just biding her time.

I pulled at the end of my braid. "There is something I don't understand."

Daya placed her hands together on top of the pillow and looked at me expectedly, as if to say, *go on.*

"Why would Jonah's father be so concerned with Enchanters? I mean, as the highest executive, he has some pretty big powers, right? I understand that Enchanters siding with Lilith is one thing, but just completely trying to slaughter them because they made a choice? I mean, why not just go to the source? Go for Lilith instead."

Daya chewed on her lower lip and looked over her shoulder at the window. Mr. Cassial was nowhere in sight now. She turned back to me and let out a breath. "Dani, you are asking the question that many have asked for quite some time now. Isaac did have the highest angelic power, Moira had the highest Enchanter power, and Lilith was the most powerful demon. They all had their respective places and roles, but sometimes, that's just not enough for people. I believe he simply did it as a lesson. I'm pretty sure siding with Lilith was just another thing that pissed him off."

"What are you getting at?" I pressed, leaning forward slightly. "Was there something else he was mad about?"

She tilted her head to the side, as if considering something. She pulled at her bottom lip with her teeth, her anxious energy radiating off her in waves. She readjusted herself on the couch. "Dani, do you know why I was slightly apprehensive about you?"

I pointed towards my head. "Well, I'm a demon, so that comes with the territory."

"Okay, true." She looked down, but then peeked up at me through her incredibly long eyelashes. "My family has a history with demons, one that causes me to have a different view on the past entirely." She started picking at a loose thread on the fabric of the pillow. "It's why I decided to be a guardian." She paused and then shook her head. "Decided isn't right. I was *told* I was going to be a guardian by my mother. I would have to pass demons, but I wouldn't have to fight like a sentry or be tasked with going to Purgatory like a messenger. My mother was quite adamant about keeping me from it."

"Why come to The Skies at all?"

She waved a hand at me dismissively. "I always wanted to go, but there were stipulations if I did, and that was at the very top. I wasn't picky. At the time, Isaac was someone we all looked up to; he seemed to keep the peace. At least, up front he did. To most angels, he kept the peace through and through until the day he died. Lilith wasn't a threat yet. She kept to herself and her demons, only leaving Purgatory if her demons got out of hand. All parties had somewhat of a truce, if you will. Oculus was the hub of interactions between all three of our kinds." She sighed. "Maybe that was Moira's first mistake, being so open to practically everyone." A piece of her hair escaped her braid, and she tucked it behind her ear.

I tugged more at the end of my braid, feeling the pressure in my scalp. "Wait, how did your family have an issue with demons when the war and all of that wouldn't have started until after you started at The Skies?" The war couldn't have been what made her family so hateful against demons, at least not yet. I knew she was holding something back from me, and maybe it wasn't my place to ask, but I had time to kill while Nick was off doing who the fuck knows what. Daya seemed like she wanted to tell me, but it was the classic how much information is too much.

She stroked the top of the pillow, as if to smooth down the plush bumps. The house made small creaking sounds around us. "My cousin fell in love with a demon and my family, they...it was just a lot. I always saw it as being fine. He was nice enough, but her mother and, well, my mother, ugh, they were furious. I was seventeen at the time, so what did I know?"

I didn't even know demons had any interaction whatsoever with anyone other than our own kind, particularly romantically. I tried to picture a world where no one was waiting for the other shoe to drop, a world where angels, demons, and Enchanters walked right by each other and said some sort of common greeting. Maybe it wasn't as sunshine and rainbows as I was making it out to be, but it was surely better than what it was right now.

I had to know more, I needed her to tell me as much as she could. "So, your mother didn't want you having anything to do with being near demons? So being a guardian was the best option? She hoped you wouldn't fall head over heels for a demon as well?"

She nodded, swallowing deeply, as if the thought of her family drama was difficult for her. "Layla told me she had met someone a few times, but never anything about him. They tried to keep it a secret, but her mother eventually found out and tried to forbid it. Layla just didn't care. Moira gave them a place near the outskirts of Oculus so they could live without ridicule. She even tried to speak with my family, but they wouldn't hear of a demon being a part of our family. I wasn't allowed to visit them, and eventually, it was like I didn't have a cousin anymore."

I reached over and placed my hand on her knee. "Daya, I'm sorry. That's terrible."

"It seems that way, but it gets worse, I'm afraid."

I squeezed her knee and let my hand settle there while she continued.

"A year went by, and everything was good, but one day, I came home to my mother crying and telling me that Layla was pregnant. I thought this was joyous news. A baby, you know? Something that would be full of love and bring us together again, but my thoughts were wrong."

I winced. This was before Lilith put the barren curse on demons. Daya was speaking of a time when demons were free to live for years, growing old in the process, and were able to grow families. She took in a long breath and let it out.

"I didn't understand. When the news spread, everyone was so happy about it, at least everyone I was aware of. There were, of course, angels who thought it was odd and demons who would curl their lips in disgust, but overall, the outpouring of love was beautiful. I thought it was so ridiculous of me to listen to my mother, so I went over and saw my cousin. I saw her pregnant and happy...and...the way he looked at her, that demon man she loved..." Daya trailed off, looking towards the fireplace. I couldn't be sure, but it looked as if she had a few tears coming from her eyes. I hadn't meant to push her to tell this story.

I racked my brain for any stories on a baby between a demon and an angel that I would have heard of. No one talked about it in Purgatory. Those two kinds having a baby would have been something that was talked about for years, right?

"Daya..." I started, but she wiped whatever tears she had on her cheeks with the back of her hand and looked over at me. Her eyes were tinted with small hints of red and still had the remaining glassiness of crying.

"Back then, the Divine Library had records of everything. That was the first place I went after I visited. I wanted to know more, and that was the one place I thought I would get my answers. A baby between an angel and a demon was something people just didn't understand, and I have always been the type to put people at ease with information and facts. So, I went to the library and looked through everything I could find. In older texts, they were called amalgams, while nowadays, hybrids and halflings would be the better term."

She shifted so that her feet were on the floor and her back was resting against the couch. "Everything I read mentioned them being feared centuries ago, only because they had angelic and demonic blood. There hadn't been one for ages, due to their unstable nature. People actively avoided producing that kind of...problem. The energy in the hybrids was always fighting with itself, never knowing which one was more in charge, so when it was time for their powers to release, it could be a massacre. They could be powerful beings. That kind of power had to be nurtured and disciplined."

Powerful enough for a high angel to be jealous or for a demon queen to be vengeful, I thought silently to myself.

Daya placed her hands in her lap, overlapping them on top of each other. "One look at that baby and none of it mattered. The baby was as normal as they come, with my cousin's eyes and its father's nose and mouth. Her mother did come to see her, one time. She even held the baby, but they didn't speak anymore after that day. My aunt always regretted that. She never admitted it, but I knew she did."

Her eyes darkened a bit. I tilted my head to the side and pushed her further. "What happened?"

Daya rubbed her forehead. "This is where things get confusing. A few months after the baby was born, my mother came to me at The Skies, and she told me that...." She blew out two long slow breaths, trying to regain her composure.

I placed my hand over my mouth, my brain automatically attempting to finish her story before she was ready.

She cleared her throat. "My mother came to tell me that the baby had passed. She told me that there were whispers an Enchanter had played a role in its death. She herself was adamant a demon was the culprit, which put an even worse strain on my family." Daya shook her head. "You should have seen the love the people in Oculus showed my cousin. It just didn't make sense to me, but she had told me Isaac had a source and he was taking action immediately. I had gone back to my room to pack to stay with my parents when I over-heard other angels say that they were dead set on blaming the demons, even going so far as blaming the baby's father. Everyone was taking sides and pointing fingers. I wanted to go to my cousin and be with her, but under my mother's gaze, I was a coward.

"Then, I was hearing different things, like Jonah's father knew that the Enchanters had more power than they needed, that they were likely working with the demons. He couldn't risk them using their powers on anyone else. If they could hurt an innocent baby, what would stop them from hurting everyone else? I'd never seen The Skies so unhinged before. Sentries were dispatched all around me, guardians were being called back to Heaven's Gate...it was madness."

I tapped my chin, thinking. "So, Jonah's dad just made a decision. Just like that?"

"If you had known Isaac, that would not have been surprising. I think he didn't like the fact that his own people were listening and confiding in Moira for years more than their own leader. I don't think Isaac needed much to make his choice. He wanted them powerless, literally. He always had a dislike for Enchanters, hated their differing powers, but in reality, he was just threatened by them."

"That's what started this war? The death of your cousin's baby?"

She gave me a sad smile. "Yes and no. There was peace in the realms, but there was always tension. I think people believed that this baby would somehow unite the two worlds of angels and demons. Not everyone would want that, but no one thought someone would rid the world of it. This baby could have shown what a world united looked like. Enchanters couldn't trust angels anymore, so I think they turned to the next best thing, hence siding with Lilith, since she "embraced" their gifts." She air-quoted, as if she didn't believe a word of it. "Which clearly didn't look good in Isaac's eyes."

"You went home during all this? You weren't there to help them?" I didn't want to sound accusatory, but I would have gone stir crazy if I was just left in the dark.

She sighed, turning her head slightly. "I regret it, not fighting. My mother would have been so upset with the side I chose to fight on." She got up from the couch, taking both our coffee mugs with her.

I slid to the edge of the couch and tapped my fingers along the front end. I was rattling my brain with all of this. I bit at my top lip until it was painful.

"Moira locked Lilith in Purgatory with all those Enchanters who took her side..." I started, looking over my shoulder as Daya placed the mugs in the sink. She turned to me and arched a curious eyebrow. "Under the orders of Jonah's father."

Daya scrunched her face, as if my words didn't make sense.

"What?"

"Moira put the lock on Purgatory in the midst of the war. Isaac was slaughtering her people and you want me to believe she just did as he asked? Just like that?" She folded her arms over her chest.

"From what Natalia said, that's what happened. That lock was put up at the request of Jonah's father. Then I guess Moira placed the glamor over Oculus to shield her land once the angels had left all the carnage."

Daya turned back to the sink, shaking her head. "Dani, I only met

370

Moira a handful of times, and the one thing I can say is that she would have only done what Isaac wanted her to if she was fearing for her life and the life of her people. It wouldn't have been some casual agreement."

I walked around the couch and over to the sink. I leaned my hip against the counter and watched her clean. She looked determined to do dishes, but I wasn't having it. I reached my hand out and cut the water off. She let out a breath and smirked.

"So, Isaac threatened Moira into putting up that lock, locking her own people inside of Purgatory," I said.

Daya nodded. "She must have told Natalia something that wouldn't sound so harrowing to a child."

I slammed both my hands on the edge of the counter, leaning the front of my body against it. "Where the hell was Jonah?"

Daya shook her head, her braid dancing back and forth behind her back. "He was a teenager, Dani. His father wanted him to take over one day. I never spoke to Jonah much in those days, but I knew through some other guardians that he didn't want to be his father. He had no real power then, so whatever Isaac said was the end of it." She leaned her back against the sink. "Every time I did see Jonah, he was almost always with Maurice, and he was so different from his father. Where Isaac was stoic and calculating, Jonah was always laughing and a little studious. He was just...different. When he ascended after his father died, he tried to make things better, but Moira was already weak, and he would have to start over with Natalia."

I nodded more to myself than to her. She thought Jonah was a good person. Despite how Nick's father felt about Jonah, Daya was allowed to have her own views and opinions. "And Nick's dad? He left The Skies, so is that the reason?"

Daya tilted her head to the side and tilted one corner of her mouth up. "That is something for Maurice to explain to you himself. Telling you about my life and my view on the war is one thing, but that isn't my place to speak on."

I rolled my eyes at her mysterious tone. I backed off that subject respectfully, though. I liked Mr. Cassial, so if he was wanting to keep his past to himself, then who was I to stop him? I pulled the rubber band out of the end of my hair, starting to undo the braid. "Daya, at the time, who do you think did it?"

I asked it like a casual question. I asked it like I didn't really care about her answer, but I did. I felt like it was important, whatever she had to say. She pushed off the counter and moved so that she was in front of me as I turned to place my back against the counter. "I haven't really considered it. There wasn't a lot of time for me to consider it, I guess."

"But you considered it enough to know that Enchanters wouldn't have done it," I volleyed back, wanting more.

"Enchanters wouldn't have had anything to gain from removing that baby from the equation. It wasn't a threat to them. Its power would have rivaled Moira's, but she wouldn't have seen it like that." She answered like she wanted that to be the final word on the matter, but I pushed on.

I rolled my neck. "So, you think Jonah's father masterminded it and did it himself? He orchestrated it, made up that whole source, and used it all to go against Moira?" I was starting to ramble now.

Daya shook her head vigorously. "Dani, stop. That is not at all what I think. I don't know what I think."

The sound of her words hit me like a punch to the face. She had revisited an entirely bad memory just to tell me a story. A story I didn't know was even relevant to today's situation. "Sorry, it's just..." I began, but she lifted her hand to stop me.

"It's alright, Dani. I would be eager to know the answers as well. So many lives were lost on all sides. I lost my cousin and that demon she loved and I...I just wish I knew the answers, but I don't. I was so relieved when Alex didn't want to step foot in The Skies."

I felt something in my chest, something that made me walk over to her and grab her by the arms, pulling her into me. She tensed a little, not from fear, but as if she was stunned. Hugging wasn't something unheard of to me, but to say I did it frequently would be a lie. She relaxed and wrapped her own slim arms around me. There was a warmth flooding my veins and it felt familiar and friendly.

"Lilith and Isaac would have both been threatened by the potential power that baby could have grown into. It could have ruined them if Layla had wanted it to, but my cousin, she wouldn't have wanted that, not for her child. She would have raised that baby with so much love." She muffled against me, squeezing me.

She pushed back, placed her hands on my shoulders, and looked at me. "I never got far enough in my investigation of it and eventually, I just gave up. It's a piece of history Heaven's Gate tries to forget, but some people just don't. Isaac did try, though. He started with blocks on portaling and after some time, angels just stopped creating their own portals all together. He removed all the items from the Divine Library, to erase all traces of Enchanters so that we could go back to a type of normalcy, but a normalcy he could dictate. Jonah tried to fix it, but fixing something *that* broken isn't easy."

I nodded, stepping back from her. "What happened to all those items?" My mind tried to wrap around what she had said. Lilith and Isaac would have been threatened but was Isaac the type to go through so much work to get what he wanted? Daya had mentioned him being power hungry, but would he have caused all this turmoil for one baby, for one baby whose future hadn't even been pieced together yet? As much as I wanted to ring Jonah's father's already rotting neck, I knew the answers to my questions.

"Oh, I'm not sure. Burned maybe. Sent back to Oculus, perhaps. There wasn't contact with Oculus, at least from The Skies, until Jonah took up his place." I licked my lips, deep in my own thoughts as I tried to listen to her. Silence overtook the moment, and she suddenly clapped her hands together, as if willing away the quiet. "I'm sorry for probably ruining your entire day, sweetheart. You should know that you really aren't the things Lilith makes you think you are." She let out a soft laugh with a smile that met her eyes.

I realized that, just like Nicholas's father, she had her way of ending the conversation without having to say it was over. The time for asking anymore questions would have to wait. Lilith had put that barren curse on Purgatory for some reason, and maybe this was it. She didn't want someone overthrowing her, battling her for dominance. She didn't like what she couldn't control.

Lilith fucked up a family to get rid of a baby who *could* have been her undoing. How did this fit into anything else? She just sat in her depraved prison waiting and then poof, she found me and made me a pawn in her game? She had played the long game and now, right now, she was seeing the fruits of her labors.

Not *her* labors though. She didn't do manual work, which makes her infant killing hard to fucking process. The one time she gets her hands dirty, it's to do *that*. Her endgame was still so unclear. I knew it wasn't so simple to just claim that she wanted to break down the portals and take over Heaven's Gate. Whoever was working with her had a stake in this as well, and something told me that the war had been their push over the edge, which would be ideal since Lilith loved manipulating the hurt and vengeful.

I felt my heartbeat pulse louder and my hands start to shake a bit with rage. I looked down at my feet, dark smoke starting to puff out. Soon, it would be a cloud of black around my ankles. I curled my hands into fists at my side, breathing in and out. Then I heard a rustling outside and almost immediately, there was twinge in my chest that slowly leveled my heart rate. I noticed the black smoke inching back into my skin. My rage was settling back into its steel confinement. That familiar warmth was starting to creep into me.

"Nick's back," Mr. Cassial announced. He must have come in while I was having my mental breakdown. I looked over at him and watched as Daya picked a tiny green leaf off his mustache. She kissed the corners of his mouth and went back to doing dishes.

He smiled over at me, walking past and patting me on the shoulder.

I rushed, probably a bit too eagerly, towards him, cutting him off as he tried to go down the hallway. "Mr. Cassial, can I ask you something?"

He slid his index finger across his mustache. "Sure thing."

I rocked from one foot to the other. "Do you regret it?" I lowered my voice a little so that Daya wouldn't hear, even though the running sink water should have drowned me out.

"Regret what?" He cocked his head to one side.

"Leaving The Skies."

He raised both his eyebrows, realization dawning on him. Then, he furrowed those dark brows and chuckled. He answered me in the sincerest way possible. "No, Dani. I don't. There are probably a lot of things I regret during that time in my life, but that was not one of them. I don't look back on that decision and think I should have chosen differently."

This made me smile. He was the kind of person you wanted to be around just because he was unapologetically himself. I moved to the side so that he could continue down the hall. I waited for him to ask me why I was asking, but he didn't. I had a feeling he wouldn't ever bring it up.

"Call me Maurice," he said over his shoulder before retreating towards his bedroom.

I opened my mouth to say something witty, to say anything back, but nothing came out. I looked towards the back door and watched as the door swung open and my raven-haired angel stepped over the threshold. He looked unharmed, just like when he left. I let my eyes rise to his face and my breath caught. His face looked like he had seen a ghost. He looked tired and a bit on edge. He hadn't seen me yet and I looked over to Daya, who started to greet him but noticed the same look on his face. I took a step forward, which caused one of the floorboards to creak, and he whipped his head to me.

I stopped as he gazed at my face. He took in my hair falling down my shoulders in waves, giving me a different look than my normal mess of curls. He raked his gaze down my body, not in a sensual way, but like he was searching for something. He scrubbed a hand down his face, closing the door behind him. Nick gave Daya a nod before walking over to me.

He grabbed my arms and looked down at me, causing me to lift one of my eyebrows in a silent question. He let out a long, low breath. "Hi."

A laugh caught in my throat. "Hi."

He cleared his throat but didn't move away from me. His face was starting to return to normal, as if he was mentally willing it to retreat to his normal Nick features. "Can we talk in my room?"

I shrugged and let him pull me towards his bedroom. He turned the knob to open the door, letting me go ahead as he trailed behind me. I walked halfway inside before I turned around, watching him look over his shoulder before he closed the door behind him. He ripped the strap that held his sword over his head and threw it against the wall. He leaned back, resting against the door as he closed his eyes.

"Are you alright?" I asked, lifting my hand to ruffle through my hair.

He opened his eyes towards the carpeted floor and slowly, so slowly, peeked up at me. His chest rose and fell with his breaths, and I noticed his shoulders were tense.

"Nick?" He let a small, almost shy smile form, some of that tension defrosting a bit.

"I...uh...fuck." He leaned his head back against the door with a thud. I sauntered over to him, getting so close, I crowded him into the door.

He peered down at me, but he kept his hands at his sides, sliding them into his pockets.

"Is everyone okay?" I meant Elise and Reese.

"Yeah, they're fine."

"Natalia?"

"She's fine."

I hummed. "But you aren't fine?"

His eyes widened. "Dani, I'm totally fine." His voice was shaky.

I snorted. "Very convincing."

"Dani..."

"Did something happen when you were there? You told me you would tell me everything."

He rolled his eyes up to the ceiling. "I know. I know I did."

"Do I need to give you motivation?" I asked, letting my tongue dart out between my teeth. I moved further into him, letting my hands dip under his shirt to explore his abs and chest.

He let out a soft moan, his eyes starting to get a little hooded. I got up on my toes and let my lips drag along his, feeling him open his mouth in a kiss. My tongue darted out to probe inside his mouth, and he met it with his own. He removed his hands from his pockets and grabbed my waist, letting his fingers touch the exposed skin my crop top allowed. I felt him squeeze me and then I was being pushed away. I teetered on my feet a little but blinked at him, confused.

"What?" I asked, annoyed. "Don't tell me you are back to "we can't do this" territory?"

He shook his head. "No. No...that's not it at all."

I placed my hands on my hips. "Then what? What has you all—" I waved my hand up and down his body. "Like this all of sudden, huh?"

He opened his mouth to speak, those lips of his moving, but nothing came out. He let out a long groan, placing both his hands to the back of his head and pushing upward, making his hair stick up in the back.

"Dani, you...I...ugh, fuck!" he yelled, but not loud enough for his dad or Daya to hear. I flinched, realizing this was a new side of him I was seeing. Something happened while he was in Oculus, something that caused him to lose his words. I didn't like this.

"Whatever it is, it can't be that bad, right? I've likely heard worse."

His face looked pained when I said this, and now, I was more confused than ever. He took one slow step at a time towards me as he crossed one of his arms over his chest, looking more anxious than he had before. His eyes drilled into my own, as if he wanted to pin me to this spot for eternity. He slid his tongue over his lips, letting out an unsteady breath, nervous energy radiating off him.

"I found out something."

I blinked once, waiting.

He squinted, as if his next words were ones he didn't want to say. "About you."

CHAPTER NINETEEN

NICK

Earlier

F*uck.*
    I figured using a portal in a calmer matter would make this shit easier but no, it did not. I landed in Oculus right on my feet, which caused the sharpest and most excruciating pain to shoot up my calves to my knees. I let out a groan and fell forward onto said throbbing knees, placing my hands out in front of me and pressing my palms to the dirt. I closed my eyes, mentally running through what I had to do while I patiently—*impatiently*—tried to let the pain subside.

I let out slow breaths and thought back to how I left Dani. Left her in the hands of my father and his new girlfriend. I didn't want to think about what was going on there right now; I just wanted her safe. I never thought she was the problem in all of this. Hell, I never thought much about her at all in the beginning. She so elegantly inserted herself into my thoughts like a sexy parasite and I, the stupidly willing host, let her. I surprisingly didn't have an ounce of regret. I was here, in Oculus, *for her.*

Scratch that—I was here in Oculus *because* of her. I was here for our friends...well, my friend and her sort of friend with the most incredible resting bitch face I had ever seen. If Natalia had no idea what was going on, then I was back to square one. There was something in my gut that really hoped the High Priestess could tell me something.

I pushed up from the ground and stretched my back, blinking. Then I blinked again. I blinked a few more times, willing my eyes to comprehend what they were seeing. The trees were taller and did the leaves look...greener? I looked down and ran my hand over the dirt, which looked fresh, like it had just been lain. I scanned the terrain; there were flowering plants everywhere, in all colors. Rose bushes were scattered to my right and a patch of sunflowers grew to my left. I wrinkled my nose at the smell of honey and some type of herb I couldn't place. The sky above me was a brighter blue, as if there was no longer a film over it.

Suddenly, I felt a hand grip my shoulder, and the tightness of their hold told me that they weren't letting me go anytime soon. I hadn't realized that someone had stepped up behind me. I felt magic surround me, slapping my hands to my sides, like an invisible rope was wrapped around my torso.

"State your business," the male voice attached to the strong hand commanded.

"I'm here to see Natalia," I answered, knowing honesty was the best policy right now.

The man scoffed, as if he didn't believe me. "Is she expecting you?"

I tried to move my shoulders, hoping to relieve the tension from his grip. "Probably."

A female voice chimed in on my left. I was able to turn my head—thank fuck—to look at her. She had silver hair cut short, the ends meeting just above her ears, bronze colored skin that made her cobalt blue eyes pop. "Do you want me to ask Her Highness?" She peeked a glance over to me, her eyes large and round.

The man let out a gruff laugh. "Of course not. No need to bother her with trivial matters. She told us to keep the perimeter clear." He squeezed my shoulder again, but this time, he pulled me up by it.

I licked my lips and tried again. "She *will* be expecting me, I promise you."

The female came up next to me. At my full height, she was shorter than me, but in this situation, she was no less intimidating. "Who would you be?"

The male Enchanter pushed on my shoulder, as if telling me to answer, even though she had literally *just* asked the fucking question.

"I'm Nicholas." I hoped that meant something. I snuck a glance at the female, and she arched a delicate eyebrow at me.

I felt weight on my back, and I realized the male Enchanter was now so close to me, I could feel his breath. "Her Highness told us to remain on the lookout since that catastrophe at The Skies. We are here to stop anyone from intruding."

I swallowed. "I'm not. I know her. She knows me. You can bring her here if you don't want me going any further."

The female Enchanter tilted her head. "She did mention someone by this name should be seen through." She sounded sure, but not sure enough to remove the stern tone the male had.

"She also said he would meet her in central Oculus." He went to grab my other shoulder, pressing just as hard. "This is the outskirts. If you were here to see her, then you should have landed where she said you would."

"She did say she was also waiting on someone. Maybe we should speak to her first," the female enchanter argued, stepping forward to try and separate us. He pushed her back, startling her as she regained her footing.

"I..." I only got one word out before I felt something around my throat. I reached my hands up towards my neck, feeling nothing. I felt absolutely nothing constricting my breathing, but my throat felt like it was closing in.

"I don't want your reasoning or excuses. I haven't been fond of angels for quite some time, and I don't think I'll be fond of you. My job is to keep Her Highness safe, just like I did her mother," he huffed out, throwing me back to the ground.

I tried to cough, but I couldn't. It felt like a truck was placed right at my throat, and there was no use trying to get it off. I saw small crackles of blue light from underneath my chin. Magic was around my neck, and magic was slowly blurring my vision. I felt cold dirt under my knees as I clawed uselessly at my throat. I heard the female Enchanter take in a sharp breath, and then I heard a voice, one with musical regality, one I recognized.

"Zane! Stop it!" Natalia hurried over to us. The dark circle closing in on my vision was starting to grow. "Let him go!"

The male Enchanter eased up a small bit, allowing me to cough and suck in air, air that burned going down but felt so fucking good.

"He is an intruder, Your Highness. I am disposing of what isn't wanted."

Natalia was standing over me now, flicking her hand up as I watched the blue flecks of magic around my throat disappear. A ghost of whatever was wrapped around my neck licked at my skin, but for the most part, it was gone. I looked at her feet, covered in her closed toed sandals as the hem of a plum-colored skirt swayed around her ankles. I peeked up at her through my lashes and saw she was giving me a thoughtful half-smile.

"I told you I was expecting someone, did I not? I told you to come get me." She was looking at the male Enchanter, Zane.

I looked over my shoulder at him. I recognized him. He was the very tall, very large enchanter that barreled towards us the first time we had come here. The one who was highly upset over the wellbeing of the High Priestess. His biceps were about the size of my head and pulsed with muscles. He wore only a vest and nothing underneath, showing off his olive skin and various tattoos. Swirls of black ink decorated his chest and arms. He wore black pants that were wide at the ankles, collecting pieces of dirt as he walked along the ground. His hair was loose, curls falling down his back.

"You did, Your Highness, but my priority is your safety. With everything going on, I don't trust anyone."

Natalia leaned down and grasped my hand, pulling me up. I stretched my neck and readjusted my sword at my back. Natalia patted my shoulder and looked at Zane.

"I appreciate that, Zane, but my orders were to come get me when Nicholas arrived. That is a direct quote from my mouth."

The female Enchanter stepped forward. "We are sorry, but you only gave us a first name. There could be many Nicholases, so we weren't sure."

Natalia casually glanced over to her. "That is when you come to retrieve me to get my final say. You do not take matters into your own hands when someone does not pose a threat against me."

The female Enchanter gave Zane the most death inducing side-eye I'd ever seen.

Zane scoffed. "Your Highness, he..." he started, but she cut him off, lifting her finger and instantly making him close his mouth. He let out muffled noises, but the magic from Natalia's fingertips told me she had temporarily sealed his lips shut.

"Did he threaten you or me in any way? Show any signs of malicious intent? Draw his weapon?" she asked, her voice still light but authoritative.

All Zane could do was shake his head.

Natalia nodded. "I want us to work together, Zane. I admire you wanting to keep me safe, and I will be eternally grateful for it." She reached out and placed a hand along his bicep. "My mother wanted you to take care of me, but disobey me again and I will no longer be needing your assistance, is that understood?"

He parted his lips a small bit, affirming she had released his lips from the spell. He glanced over her shoulder at me, narrowing his eyes. "Yes, I understand."

"Wonderful. Happy we got that settled. You and Anya can go back to your posts." She did the most graceful turn and walked back over to me. She placed her hands on my arms to turn me around, right as I watched Anya and Zane make their way further into the forest, their shoes crunching against fallen leaves.

Natalia walked in front of me, and I started to follow behind her when I heard Zane call out to me. "What is your whole name, so I won't forget you and I can tell the others?" He sounded slightly apologetic, but more likely, he didn't want to make another mistake.

I paused for a moment but twisted my body towards him ever so slightly. "Nicholas Cassial."

His eyebrows shot up to his hairline. "Cassial?"

I nodded.

"As in Maurice Cassial?"

"That's my father, yeah. Do you know him?" I asked, placing my hand around the leather strap across my chest.

Zane furrowed his thick brows, as if he was contemplating his answer. "Yes, actually. He was one of the few angels I ever really liked, one of the few I trusted." He opened his mouth to say more, as if there was something else at the tip of his tongue, but he didn't let it out. He just started to walk backwards. "I am sorry for the mistake, Nicholas." He turned his back to me.

I squinted at his body as it moved further away, feeling Natalia pull at my forearm. She hooked her arm through mine and led me through the pathway towards wherever she came from. I noticed more of my surroundings and my brain wasn't processing the changes very well. The weeping willows were still present, but they looked freshly watered and thriving. I heard rustles to my left and noticed a fucking squirrel leaping out of a bush and climbing up a tree.

I leaned down towards my companion. "What the hell is going on?"

"Hmm?" Natalia answered, staring straight ahead.

I pointed around me, not really knowing where to start. "All of this. What the hell happened?"

She squeezed my arm and sighed. "What do you think, Nicholas?"

I blinked over to her but answered anyway as we kept walking. "It looks like you removed the glamour, but you wouldn't do that... right?" I let my voice lift at the end, like a legitimate question.

She glanced over at the flowering plants and the moss that covered rock formations. "I would."

I stopped walking, causing her to stumble for a moment and release herself from my arm. I looked up at the trees bowing above our heads. "You removed it? Why? When?"

She dipped her hands into her skirt pockets and shrugged, laughing. "Calm down, Nicholas. I did it yesterday. It's not needed anymore. It served its purpose for many years, but I made the decision, along with the okay from everyone, to remove it. Easy. I refuse to hide anymore and after everything that went on yesterday, neither does anyone else here."

I raked my hand across the back of my neck. "Is it even safe to be doing this now?"

She pulled her hand out of her pocket and waved it between us. "Don't worry--there are barriers around us to keep us safe. I don't exactly know all the details of what we are up against, so what I have in place will have to do. You have nothing to fear."

"I'm not fearful," I muttered.

"Of course not," she taunted. "If we are going to work together against whatever kind of threat this is, I want you all to see what I see. What you've seen so far has been our weak spots, us at our lowest moments, but now, you can see Oculus isn't what it seems."

I looked around us some more, taking the things not available to me previously. My eyes drank it all in. "It's beautiful."

She gave me a full beaming smile, one that could light up any room on the darkest night.

"How did you know to find me, by the way?" She turned to start walking again and I followed.

"I saw your portal light." She said it as if the answer was obvious.

"Portal light?"

She crossed her arms as we walked. "The magic from the portal radiates a soft light that, as the creator, I can see. I had a feeling it was you."

"I didn't get choked out by a mountain man. Hallelujah."

She chuckled, her laugh almost like wind chimes. "Zane is a good man, he just...I don't know. He's seen a lot. Been through a lot. I was just a child when we were attacked, but he was right there, witnessing it all."

"Ah, so that's how he knows my dad."

"Most likely. Angels frequented Oculus quite a bit back then. I am sorry about that back there, though. I should have been more forth-coming with who you were. I, well..." she trailed off.

"You what?" I asked, seeing the center of Oculus come into view.

She stopped, halting me with one of her small hands. "I did tell you when we first met that my mother spoke about yours fondly, as if they had a true friendship. My mother did speak about your father in some small pieces, not enough for me to bring it up to you at the time. I just didn't know what revealing your last name would have done, how others would react. I didn't know how much your parents interacted here. I didn't want to make things more difficult, I suppose."

I stepped closer to her. "I hate that I was the experiment for his loyalty, but at least I know he won't try to kill me again." I was almost certain about that. *Almost.* I scratched behind my ear, trying to rally my thoughts. "Listen, it's probably too late to say this, but I'm sorry."

She narrowed her honey eyes at me in question. "Whatever for?"

"For what happened when we first met or fought, whatever. I'm sure that didn't make them any more amenable to angels." I didn't know why I was bringing this up right now, but I knew I wanted to be on an honorable footing with Natalia. I didn't know what explaining Dani's situation would bring, so I wanted to clear the air before anything else.

She laughed. "Oh that. I can't say the people have forgotten about it, but that is what good, quality healers are for. Everyone here is prepared to fight and die, just like you. With everything going on, I think you are the last thing on their mind, so I wouldn't fret too much. You'll have their help when or if you need it."

I simply nodded and started to walk ahead, letting her loop her arm through mine again. Every step closer to central Oculus was a step closer to something I wasn't prepared for. Once we stepped past the threshold of scattered grass and rocks of the outskirts, it was like a whole new environment. The houses that were once shattered and broken down were standing tall and on a solid foundation. The roofs were polished and crisp, the windows clean with not a hint of dirt on them. Vines lined the tops of the buildings and ivy threaded the sides of others.

None of what I was looking at made any sense. I had been told that Oculus was full of beautiful Enchanters once upon a time, but was now inhabited by the decrepit, misguided ones. After the war, everyone and everything just became these hardened, misshapen shells of what they used to be.

That's what I was *always* told.

The war was the same, Natalia had already certified that, but everything I grew up learning from others, since my father didn't speak much about it, seemed to be misconstrued. My father only spoke about Oculus in the most general sense. He never tried to create a more interesting story, but I think if I asked him about it now, he might be more open to trusting me. My thoughts were halted when the smell of chocolate hit my nostrils. I sniffed the air, thinking that I was losing my mind.

"Yes, Nicholas, that's chocolate you smell," Natalia answered with a cheeky grin on her face as she broke away from me. "Luna, the chef, uses magic winds to push the smell to everyone. It's quite impressive."

I opened my mouth to respond but was cut off by a voice that gave me instant relief.

"Nick!" Reese shouted as he walked out of a door to a shop on my left. The door swung back and forth behind him as he jogged over to me, the sounds of shouting and glasses clinking following him. His blonde hair was hanging freely, whipping behind him. He grabbed me by the shoulders, pulling me into a hug. "Shit, I thought you died."

"Let's not be dramatic," I muffled into his shoulder as I hugged him back.

He huffed out a breath as he let me go. His eyes traveled behind me to where Natalia stood, watching us. "Does he have all his pieces?"

She rolled her eyes. "Yes, he is in one piece. Just as perfect as he was before."

"Not too perfect." I reached my hand to the hem of my shirt and lifted it up, revealing the gauze covering my cut.

Reese tapped it lightly with the back of his hand. "Can't believe those fuckers got you. You alright?"

I nodded, letting my shirt fall back into place. "How's everything here?"

Reese widened his eyes. "Have you looked around, Nick? If shit wasn't going on back home, I would stay here forever. This is mind blowing. Everything here is fucking fantastic, except for one small, parasitic problem."

I cocked my head to the side and watched as Elise crept up, clearly trying to keep her presence a surprise. "What would you know about this place? Your ass hasn't left that pub since you realized it actually *was* a pub."

"Jesus, fuck. Can you warn me when you're about to appear?" Reese flinched at her sudden appearance, taking a few steps away from her.

"Not a chance. I like when you jump like a scared little rabbit."

I could see the way Reese was biting his tongue, trying not to explode. Natalia cleared her throat behind me, motioning for me to join her. I took a few steps back, to be next to her.

"I'll leave you all to catch up. I do have some matters to attend to." She squeezed my hand, giving me a sincere smile.

I needed to talk to her, though. "Wait, there's something I wanted to speak with you about. It's about, err...it's about..." I looked over to where Reese and Elise stood. My eyes traveled back to Natalia, where her own eyes waited patiently, but she finished my sentence for me.

"About *her*?" Natalia's keen observations were one of my favorite things about her, but it clearly meant that keeping a secret was a difficult task.

I raised an eyebrow slightly, waiting for her to spill other things she might know about Dani and me. Well, of course not, because there wasn't a Dani and me. That sounded like we had put some sort of label on what we were. Nope.

She squeezed my hand tighter and let go. "I won't be far. Come get me when you're done; we can speak then. I'll be in the apothecary. Just ask one of the shops keeps and they'll give you directions." She gave me curt nod and started to walk away, her dress flowing behind her with every step she took. The crown tattoo on her shoulder blade beamed.

I let out a sigh and made my way back over to the others.

"Dani isn't with you?" Elise asked the minute I was standing in front of her.

"It's great to see you too," I deadpanned.

She rolled her eyes. "My question."

"She's fine. My dad is looking after her."

My best friend's eyebrows shot up quickly. "You went home? You used your fucking portal key to take you home?" His laugh came out quickly and lasted for a while. He put his hand on his chest to catch his breath. He pulled on the gray t-shirt he wore and started to fan himself.

I pinched the bridge of my nose. "Yeah, it wasn't my finest moment."

"How did your dad react to you landing on his doorstep with a demon in tow and you bleeding?" He pointed towards my stomach.

"Surprisingly well. Except for the whole bleeding thing, he was concerned about that. That was a nice little moment between us." The sarcasm was thick in my voice. "As for Dani, I think he's starting to like her more than me."

Reese shrugged and shook his head. "Maurice is better than me." He ran a finger over his chin. "That means she slept at your house. That had to have been fucking weird."

I tried to not let my eyes bug out of my head and let out a subtle, but not so subtle, cough. "It was fine. Completely uneventful; sorry to disappoint." I punched his shoulder to avoid him seeing my hands shaking. I couldn't tell him what happened.

I was still processing what happened. I was processing the fact that I wanted it to happen again, and I shouldn't. Reese would lose his shit. He seemed to be settled with the fact that we had to work with them, but he would practically combust knowing I'd had an all-night fuck fest with one of them. I'd always known he didn't like demons; I'd always thought it was just being raised to hate them, but there were times when I thought it was something else. I knew his parents weren't fans, but then again, he wasn't a fan of his parents.

I would add that to the *long* fucking list of shit I didn't understand.

"Any news about what's going on back at The Skies?" I questioned, hoping that some update had made its way here.

Elise shook her head. "Nope. Natalia has kept this place on a lockdown since we got here. She sent out some of her minions to do a scope, but they've all come back with nothing. It's way too silent over there." Her face morphed into a scowl.

"Maybe they have shit under control," Reese said, clearly on the defense.

"You're back to defending Jonah?" Elise retorted.

"I'm not totally for anyone, I just don't think jumping to conclusions and thinking silence equals problems is the answer."

Elise snorted. "Okay Mr. I jump to conclusions as if I'm on a damn trampoline."

Reese nearly blew steam out of his ears. "No one wants your opinion, little one." He looked her up and down, clearly referring to their significant height difference.

She lifted her hand up and smacked him on the back of the head, causing him to wobble forward, clutching his head. Before he could make a move towards her, I stepped between them.

"Alright you guys, calm down. We were all doing so well until now." I sounded like a parental figure.

Reese shook his shoulders. "When do you want to head back there? You know, to deal with all the shit waiting for us?"

I fiddled with the leather strap across my chest, making part of my sword hit the back of my neck. "Soon."

"How ominous," Elise taunted. "Are you planning on leaving and bringing Dani back with you?"

I nodded. "Yeah. Once I talk to Natalia, I should have a better understanding of how we want to do things. None of us knows what's out there, and I think she would be better off staying in one place for now."

"How caring of you," Elise said, her voice uncomfortably suspicious. I ignored it. She stretched her arms up and over her head, her black tank top riding up.

I arched an eyebrow at her, refusing to reveal anything. I needed something to change the conversation away from my thoughts of the demon who was waiting for me to return.

"My dad has a girlfriend now," I quickly said to Reese, who was leaning forward and touching his toes. He shot straight up.

"No shit!" he exclaimed, rattling off questions to me about my dad's mysterious lady friend. The hairs on the back of my neck pricked up, as if someone was staring at me. Reese was telling me something when I flicked my eyes over to Elise, who had her gray eyes in a skeptical squint. Her thick bangs fluttered in the wind, but her eyes never left me. She looked as if she was simmering; not in an angry way, but in a way that said she knew something I didn't.

Reese pointed his thumb at Elise. "This one caused a scene the minute we got here."

Elise shot her piercing glare at him. "Fuck off. When I get whisked away from a fight, wherever I land next is going to feel my fucking wrath."

"You scared the poor kids." He tilted his lips down in a fake pout.

"No, I'm pretty sure you did that with your face."

I snapped my fingers between them. "What the fuck happened?"

Elise groaned. "Once we landed here, I might have let out some magic and caused a tree to fall on a building. It was unoccupied and no one got *hurt*." She looked at Reese with a snarky glance. "I call that a win in my book. Some kids got scared because they saw I had red and black smoke leaking out of my hands and my eyes were probably all black. They call it scary; I call it expressing myself."

"Elise..." I exhaled the breath I had lodged in my throat.

"I said I was sorry, alright. I almost threw up apologizing."

Reese nodded, confirming. "She was gagging the entire way." He snickered.

She let out a fake laugh, lifting her foot and slamming it down hard on top of his. Reese shimmed his foot from underneath hers and hopped back and forth. "Fuck! Fuck! Fuck!"

"Somehow you made it through without killing each other, so there's that." I acknowledged when he calmed down.

Elise crossed her arms over her chest, the strap of her tank top coming down over her shoulder. "He was either with Natalia or drinking his last brain cell away. I did some exploring when it got quiet, enough."

"Natalia wanted to spend time with me," Reese said matter of factly. He bundled his hair in his hands and tied it in a low bun near his neck with the hair tie around his wrist. "She actually offered to enhance my bow."

"Enhance your bow?" I asked.

"Make it less shitty," Elise answered.

Reese grabbed her shoulder and shoved her farther away from him. "She saw when that shadow thing took hold of it and turned my arrow on me, so she wants to shield my weapon from others' magic. Yours too, actually. I told her that was totally fine."

"She didn't really give you a choice, Blondie. Actually, you just nodded and silently handed it to her because I'm pretty sure you were just staring at her tits," Elise said, boredom lacing her words.

Reese rolled his shoulders, his hazel eyes glinting in the sun. "It's not my fault we have a connection. You wouldn't understand."

Elise muffled a laugh behind her hand. "A *connection*, right." She let her tongue drag along her top teeth. "That would make sense if she was actually into men..." She tucked a piece of her hair behind her ear. "Or idiots."

Reese and I both stopped breathing for a minute and stared at her. She blinked at us, a smug expression on her face. "Oh god. You guys are ridiculous. You think that girl is straight?"

"Well..." I said while Reese answered, "yeah. Of course, she is."

Elise claps her hands together once and brought her joined digits around to the back of her head. "If you never trust me about anything ever again, trust me when I tell you that your High Priestess prefers the company of pussy and not cock. Sorry." She wasn't sorry at all.

I looked over to my best friend, who seemed to be trying to come

391

up with something to say back. "She could be bisexual." He said this with so much conviction, I wanted to laugh.

Elise scrunched up her mouth, as if she was attempting to think. "I'm bisexual and I don't get a '*shared love of both sexes*' vibe from her. Don't believe me? Shoot your shot and see what happens, Blondie. I would love a good laugh."

"I will shoot my shot, you little shit," Reese spat back, starting to make his way past me.

I grabbed his arm, pulling him back. I personally needed to speak to Natalia, so his love life would have to wait. He gave me a look and I shook my head. "Not right now, my friend. I need to talk to Natalia about something. Can you hold your flirting in?"

Reese grunted, but nodded, looking over at Elise and narrowing his hazel eyes at her. I expected to find her staring him down, but she was actually looking at me again. She had that expression on her face, one that made me feel like I was stark naked in front of her.

I raised an eyebrow at her expectedly and she mirrored my action. I didn't have time for her silent riddles, so I patted Reese on the side of his head and started to make my way to one of the shops to ask where the apothecary was.

"So, nothing happened between you two?" Elise was standing behind me, tapping her foot against the dirt.

I slowly turned around and looked down at her. "No."

"You sure?"

"What the fuck are you asking?"

She took a long sniff into the air. "Ah, the smell of false innocence." She angled her head to the side, studying me. "You may have stumped your blonde fool back there, but some of us already know the truth." Her gray eyes shined mischievously.

Oh fuck.

"Don't worry, she didn't tell me. I'm just not stupid." She leaned in towards my chest and sniffed again. A smile climbed up her cheeks. "Oh, Nicholas. You smell deliciously *satisfied*."

I opened my mouth to deny it, but my mouth was too dry. A small sound came out, but nothing resembling the words I was trying to say. She brought her shoulders to her ears and dropped them with a loud sigh. "Hopefully, your little detour to sexual bliss was worth it, because whatever Lilith has planned is happening. They struck in your realm; not just a demon here and there, but a swarm. Like I said, it's too quiet. Whoever is helping her is waiting." She pushed her index finger into my chest. "You need to be ready to fight whoever that may be, even if it's your precious Jonah. I was there when you stood up to him, but something inside of you still thinks he's good. It's kind of disgusting, but I see it."

"Seems like you've given this a lot of thought," I answered.

She pointed towards a path laced with cypress trees, ignoring me. "Apothecary is that way. It's a large building with a black roof and white steam coming out of the chimney."

She lifted onto her toes and ran her hand through my hair, gripping my dark locks in her slim but strong fingers. She whispered in a low voice. "You have her scent all over you. It's comical. Just make sure she's back in one piece." She let go of my hair and whipped around, strutting back to where she left Reese.

"How caring of you," I said to her back, mirroring her earlier words. She didn't turn around, but I noticed her shoulders tense up a bit, the muscles in her back stiffening as she continued to walk.

I started walking in the direction she pointed me towards. As I walked, I discreetly lifted my shirt to my nose and inhaled.

Fuck. I did smell like her.

THE ENTICING SMELL OF FOOD STARTED TO DISSIPATE AND WAS SOON replaced with the smell of herbs and other earthy smells that had me wrinkling my nose, but not enough for me to turn around. The dirt path was lined with perfectly sculpted rocks that seemed to sparkle in the light. The way I was walking brought me closer to one of the riverbanks, and the smell of water and wet grass filled my nose.

Elise was correct when she had said black roof and white smoke coming from the chimney. The smoke was billowing out, as if the fire underneath it was thick and wild. The building looked around two stories tall, covered in glossy white stones. The oval windows were tinted over, so I couldn't see much of what was inside. As I rounded up the stairs towards the front door, I turned my head to see Natalia sticking her head out and smiling at me.

"The door is open, come on inside." She ducked back into the apothecary.

I took the black doorknob in my hand and twisted, hearing the small creak it made as I entered. I let the door close softly behind me as I took in the space. It was larger than I had imagined, but it only seemed smaller due to the amount of stuff in stock around me.

It smelled like oak and eucalyptus. Lavender weaved its way into my nostrils, followed by coffee. I scanned the area to my left, forest green, glass-fronted cabinets hanging on the walls, filled with small, labeled bottles. A table was overloaded with tall bottles filled with a dark liquid and wide, short bottles of powders. Papers were scattered on the top of the table, everything written in a language I didn't understand.

I heard footsteps and saw Natalia come around the stairs. She looked pristine, but her face had the look of frustration.

"Are you okay?" I asked.

She waved me off, planting a smile back on her face. "Of course. It was just a mishap with a healing ointment."

"Healing ointment? Don't some of you have healing *powers*?" I looked around the room, as if something in here would back me up.

She laughed that lyrical laugh of hers. "Well, yes, but some people like the physical stuff. I don't ask questions; it's magic, all the same. All the flowers and plants around here have some kind of magical property. It's good to have both under your belt." She scrunched her mouth to one side, wiping her hands on her dress.

I cleared my throat, obviously not knowing how to bring my questions up.

"Ah, you wanted to talk to me about something, right?"

I swallowed and nodded. "Is there somewhere more private we can go?"

Her eyes twinkled a bit. "Sure. Right upstairs, there's a room where we can talk." She motioned for me to follow her, but once she turned around and started walking, she ran straight into a pretty, short-haired blonde. Her hair was a golden color that almost matched the sun. She wore cream linen pants and a flowing green top, her wrists decorated in golden bracelets.

They both giggled, and the blonde looked over Natalia's shoulder at me. She cocked her head to the side and squinted her piercing blue eyes at me. "Who's this?"

Natalia turned on her heels to face me again. "Oh, Isabel, this is Nicholas." She placed her hand on Isabel's lower back. "Nicholas, this is Isabel, my girlfriend."

I raised my eyebrows. Internally, I was laughing hard at the fact that Reese would be severely disappointed. I stuck my hand out for her to take. "Nice to meet you."

She shook my hand and gave me a glowing smile. "You as well. Natalia did say we should be expecting a Nicholas soon. I hope you settle everything in Heaven's Gate." She started to look around, as if she was searching for something. "Did you bring your friend along?"

I looked over my shoulder at the window. "Reese? I left him by that pub in the main area." Was she talking about Elise?

Isabel pulled her eyebrows together. "Reese is the blonde one, yes? No, not him, the other one. The cute one with the curly hair."

Dani? How would she know Dani?

I let out a small, huffed laugh and snuck a glance over at Natalia, whose eyes were wide. I noticed her arm was still on Isabel's lower back. Isabel suddenly let out a small gasp, but she collected herself quickly, like she'd been pinched.

"You've met Dani?" I asked.

Isabel started to fidget around with her pants pockets, collecting her thoughts. "Natalia must have told me about her, that's all." A small reddish hue was creeping its way onto her chest. "I was actually on my way out, so I'll see you in a little bit."

She leaned in and gave Natalia a quick peck on the lips and scurried past me. Over her shoulder, she yelled, "It was nice meeting you!"

I was still staring at Natalia and watching her stick her tongue out, licking her lower lip. She closed her eyes for what felt like an entire minute and then looked up at me. "Shall we go upstairs?"

"Natalia, has Dani been to Oculus without me?"

She pushed her hair off her shoulder in a flourish, as if to tell me she didn't have to answer. Instead, she started walking towards the stairs.

"Natalia." I stood my ground.

"Whatever I tell you won't change the situation we are currently in, so I suggest you stop fretting over something irrelevant to the here and now," she answered, continuing to walk towards the stairs.

I let out an exasperated sigh and followed her. My long legs had me at her side in a matter of seconds and we took the wide steps up the staircase one by one. Once we got to the second floor, I noticed there was a significant difference between this floor and the first. The first floor had more of a shop feel, whereas the second floor had various doors and little end tables with brass lamps. There was a massive lobby area, a wide rug with silver tassels on the floor.

Doors trailed the sides of the building, coming around to make a kind of U shaped towards the back, windows in between.

"There is a lot going on in the rooms downstairs, so I think it's best if we talk up here." She traveled towards the middle of the room to one of the doors near the back. "This one should be empty."

She turned the brass knob on the door and walked inside. I followed behind her and noticed that the room had a couch bed in one corner and a table near the center. There was a lamp on top of it right now that made me think that it was being used as a desk. Natalia leaned against the desk and looked at me as I closed the door behind me.

"What would you like to speak about?" she asked sincerely.

I bit my bottom lip, not knowing how to start. "I'm going to ask you something, but I need you to let me finish before you ask anything."

"Alright, go ahead."

I pressed my back against the door and sighed. "Last night, Dani

396

told me something that I guess I just...I don't understand." I peeked up at her to see she was just staring at me, listening.

"Um, she told me she hears a sort of voice in her head. She feels a warmth or like a light feeling at times. She said it was with her when she first got to Purgatory, that eventually it went away or dormant, but that it's been coming back in bits and pieces since she's been in Heaven's Gate." I sighed again, this time with more breath so I felt it in my chest. "I've never even heard of something like this, let alone from a demon."

Natalia tilted her head to the side expectantly.

"I don't have anyone else to ask about this, and I don't know, it just sounds like straight magic. You're the only person I trust who I could ask who may know something." I ran my hand through my hair and slumped my shoulders.

"Are you finished?" she asked patiently.

"Yeah."

She hummed and fiddled with one of her earrings. "It sounds like you *want* me to know what you're talking about."

"Maybe I do."

"I'm about to heavily disappoint you, because I'm not versed in demonic behavior or the complete opposite of demonic behavior. Just like you, I haven't heard of anything like this. It doesn't sound like magic, at least not any I know of. I don't know of anyone who would want to put what sounds like light magic inside a demon. I don't even know if that's possible. What purpose would that possibly serve?" She looked as if she was actually thinking hard. She was trying to take this as seriously as I was.

"Why are you even asking? Besides the fact that it's an intriguing discovery."

I cleared my throat. "I think it might have to do with everything else."

"Like the attack on The Skies?"

"Yes, maybe. I don't know. Lilith has had this mysterious plan for a while now, and I think it all starts with her beginning."

"You mean when Lilith took her from Earth and brought her to Purgatory?"

I walked over to the couch bed, removed my sword, placing it on the floor as I sat down. "Dani told me it started the minute she woke up in Purgatory, so it has to have something to do with that. I just have a feeling that if we can find out what's so significant about when Lilith got her, then maybe *something* will start to make sense."

"Perhaps you're right."

"Dani did also say she wasn't afraid of it. She wanted to lean on it, go to it, but it was like she was holding herself back, or *something* was causing her to rethink."

Natalia folded her arms over her chest and stared at the floor. "I can't tell you what this means, Nicholas. I'm sorry."

I raised my eyes to the yellow ceiling. "I figured, but you were my best bet."

"But...I might be able to help you *see* what happened." She said each word slowly, as if convincing herself it was a good idea.

"Excuse me?"

She pushed off the table and came to sit on the couch next to me. "You want to know about her start with Lilith, to maybe give you some insight, right?"

"Mhmm."

"I can help you with that."

I raised one of my eyebrows. "I'm lost."

"Ugh, Nicholas. There's a way for me to send you into the past and glimpse at her beginning. It may be grainy, and the sound might be a little off, but you'll be there as if you were always there in the first place."

I placed my hands on my thighs. "That makes sense, I guess. One thing, though. How in the hell do you plan to send me to a past moment in Dani's head? She doesn't even remember it. She doesn't remember anything before she woke up in Purgatory."

Natalia quirked up one side of her mouth in a sly smile. "Just because we can't actively remember something doesn't mean that the memory doesn't exist."

I considered this. "Alright, again, that makes sense, but how do you plan to get in her head without her here? Isn't that kind of a requirement when you're trying to pick someone's brain?"

Natalia pursued her full lips and scooted towards the edge of the bed. "Yes and no. If it was between you and a stranger, then yes, they would need to be here, but with Dani, no. You should be fine to see inside her head."

My face must have made her laugh, because that's exactly what she did. "What? It's not going to hurt. Not much. Maybe like a little pinch. I've only done it a few times, but it's completely safe, I promise."

I waved my hand at her, trying to get her to stop talking. "No, no, go back. You said that Dani doesn't need to be here because I already have a connection with her?"

"Oh, that. Yes, it's really quite simple."

"Simple?"

Natalia rolled her eyes. She legitimately rolled her eyes, as if I was an idiot for even asking. "Nicholas, you don't have to explain what happened with you and Dani while we were separated, but you can't tell me you two didn't become closer. You came all the way here to ask me about something she told you, when we both know she told you because she trusted you with the information. She doesn't seem like the type to reveal this about herself to just anyone. As much as you probably don't want to admit it, you have a connection with her, Nicholas."

I placed my face in my hands, knowing my voice would sound muffled in my palms. "I think we have different ideas of *connection*."

I felt her get off the bed, standing right in front of me, hovering. "Nicholas, I'm not stupid. I'm well aware that you were physical with each other."

Ha. Physical. My abs are still sore from tensing up every single time I thrusted inside of her. I didn't say anything back, though.

"A physical connection is great and I'm not making assumptions, but we both know you aren't just here for the sake of Jonah. You are here for her, because you care, Nicholas. You may not want to admit it, but you don't want anything bad to happen to her. Because. You. Care."

I groaned into my hands. "You think that will help me get into her head?" I lifted my head. In the bright sun, she barely looked real.

"It will."

I pressed my tongue inside my cheek, contemplating. "I do...care. I care about her. I don't know what it means, but I do care, alright? But I'm mainly doing this for Heaven's Gate." Somehow adding that last part made my former admission seem less important.

Natalia turned away from me and walked towards the door. Where was she going?

"I'm glad you can admit that, Nicholas. We will use the connection you have with her, but with help from a lock of her hair." She started to open the door, but I shot up from the couch, causing her to look over at me quickly.

"A lock of her hair? I thought you could use my connection with her."

She let out a light laugh. "I can. I was truthful about that, and I have done something like this on connection alone, but you'll get a much more accurate picture if we use the lock of hair. Like you said, she doesn't remember it enough to even give you small pieces, so I need something stronger to tether you to her."

I shook my head in shock, walking over to her. "Wait, so did you just want me to say I cared about her?"

She shrugged. "Maybe."

"Wow, alright, how in the hell did you even get a lock of her hair?"

Natalia pressed her palm to my cheek and patted it twice. "I'm going to help you Nicholas, so just be grateful, okay?"

"Did you bring Dani here without us?" I asked, ignoring her request and already knowing the answer. How else would she have gotten a lock of her hair? Then again, Natalia had her ways, so she could have done it any time. Hell, she could have a lock of all our hair hidden somewhere.

She let her hand fall away from my face and winked at me. "I'll be right back." She closed the door in my stunned face.

How had I surrounded myself with the world's most stubborn women?

CHAPTER TWENTY

NICK

My patience was starting to wear thin when Natalia appeared again, closing the door behind her. She was holding a tiny bottle with a cork pushed into the top. The clear liquid sloshed on the inside as she dangled it between her fingers. I had settled myself on the couch bed and was resting my head against the wall, but I sat up straighter when she held the bottle out to me. She hadn't been gone long, but it had been long enough for me to almost fall asleep once or twice.

"What's this?"

"It's what you'll need to get the answers you want."

"And her hair?" I don't know why I almost felt my stomach turn thinking about what her hair would be used for. I took the bottle from her hands and examined it.

Natalia grabbed my feet and swung them off the couch so that she could take their place. "It's in there, compounded with some rosemary to increase the effects."

I popped out the cork and sniffed the liquid. A potent citrus scent flowed into my nostrils. I pulled back, wrinkling my nose. "And the smell?"

"Lemon balm. I thought it might go down better if you tasted something other than a plant. With the rosemary, when I put you to sleep, it will help you relax a bit so you aren't so stressed."

"I'm not stressed. I'm just...anxious."

She rolled her eyes. "Sounds like the same thing to me."

I lightly moved the bottle back and forth as I watched the liquid slosh from one side to the other. "What's going to happen, exactly? How long will I be under?"

Natalia bit her bottom lip. "Everyone is different, Nicholas, and I can only tell you what I know. You'll drink this and start to get sleepy. I'll secure you into your trance and you'll find yourself in somewhat of a blank space. I'm not inside your mind, so you have to guide yourself where you want to go. The lock of her hair is what physically connects you to her, so you'll need to focus on that, on her. Focusing is your main goal. If you can't focus, you will end up in a place you don't want to be. You know what you want to find, so find it. You want to know about her start, so focus on that."

I absentmindedly nodded.

"As for how long you're under, I'll leave you be for however long you want, but I can pull you out if I need to. If I see you struggling in any way, I will pull you out. Safety is something I deem highly important." She gave me a small smile, as if hoping that would reassure me.

"Okay."

"Nicholas?" I looked up at her. "What are you going to do, if the answer isn't what you're expecting? Will this have still been worth it?"

I couldn't think about that right now. I wanted this to go smoothly. It had to. "I think so. I don't know. I'll figure it out." I sounded like an idiot.

She gingerly nodded her head and pointed to the little bottle. "Drink up and get comfortable."

I took one deep breath in and one out. I brought the bottle to my lips and downed it. It felt like a slight burning sensation in my lungs. I coughed, as if it had gone down the wrong pipe. I regained my composure, swallowing until the burning began to subside. I tasted the lemon instantly, but the hints of rosemary stained my taste buds.

Everything happened so quickly. My shoulders slumped a bit, my limbs hanging down heavy and useless as I tried to move them. My heartbeat was starting to slow to a relaxing pace while my head was swimming with the need to fog over. My eyelids felt like they had a heavy weight on them, demanding to be closed. I felt Natalia's hand on my head, and then a tingling sensation along my neck and ears. Sparks of blue and purple caught in my periphery, and I knew she was doing her part in putting me under.

"I hope you find what you're looking for," I heard her say as my body went numb right as my head hit a pillow. The fog enveloped my head and my eyes shut.

It was dark, wherever I was, and my eyes felt like lead weights. My mind was slowly adjusting itself from the fog, and I shook my head several times until I started to feel like myself again. I was cautious to take any steps since I couldn't see a fucking thing. Even though there was nothing around me, I felt like everything was moving slowly. My eyes were starting to adjust to the dark, and I looked to my left and right, hoping something would give me a sign.

Natalia's words rang inside my head. *You know what you want to find, so find it. You want to know about her start, so focus on that.*

I knew what I wanted to find, and I knew I wanted to help Dani figure her shit out, even if she didn't care to do it herself. It was like an itch I needed to scratch, and it wasn't even my problem. Not fully, at least. I closed my eyes and thought about what I wanted to know. I focused on her face, her hair, her eyes, the way she bit her lip whenever she was being playful or annoying. I focused on the way she spoke to me, how she sounded like she was intrigued by the light but never felt good enough to embrace it.

I just focused on Dani, on helping her. Helping her meant understanding her relationship with Lilith, which in turn made me think about her and Lilith.

I felt the ground underneath me shift as I focused all my attention on that one thought. The way I was moving was like a conveyor belt in a certain direction. All of sudden, instead of moving slowly, I was thrust forward, as if I was being sucked by harsh winds. The dark around me started to fade and morph into something I was familiar with. It faded into less of the stark black and more of the darkness of a night sky. My whole body was brought to a stop, and I slammed into a tree.

My shoulder connected with the trunk, the stinging sensation rattled throughout my body. I groaned, grabbing my right shoulder and rolling it around, making sure I didn't dislocate anything. When I was pretty sure I was fine, I took in my surroundings. I was in a set of woods in the human world. I noticed the thick fog that surrounded my waist, almost as if I could wade through it if I wanted to. I looked behind me, trying to survey where I should be walking. The fog shadowed over the moon, so the light was dim at best.

A sound alerted me to look forward. Lights flashed through the trees, lights I recognized. Blue and red. I decided that walking wasn't enough for me and decided to jog over to the scene. As I got closer, I saw an opening through some of the trees. I slowed my steps as I got closer and closer. A car was wrapped around a tree near the beginning of the woods, and there were pieces of it scattered throughout the street. Police officers were spread out, speaking quickly to one another, the sound of an ambulance in the distance. I moved around the humans, looking for her.

This must be where it happened. This is where she died and Lilith took her, but where was she? Why did I...why did I have an overwhelming feeling of deja vu?

I had seen so many variations of death while doing my duty, but there were ones you just didn't forget. I tried to look for something to throw me off, to shake off this feeling that something about this was familiar. I scrubbed a hand down my face as I leaned against one of the cars. Maybe I hadn't done this right–I was shit with portals and now I was shit with sleep-inducing, memory-invading magic. I veered my eyes towards the totaled car and caught sight of something I knew all too well.

It was a white light, one I had been trained to detect. My first instinct was to go towards it, which is what my feet were already doing. Once I was next to the totaled car, I knelt down to the shattered window and saw a girl leaning back on the seat, her head facing me as she fluttered her eyes open and closed. She was barely alive, so she couldn't quite see me yet, or whoever was coming for her. She obviously wasn't Dani, and I moved out of the way as the ambulance got closer.

I was starting to get confused as to why I was in this moment when she wasn't even here. Maybe I had sent myself back to a memory of my own making, since something about this scene was so recognizable to me. Glass was everywhere, so I shifted around the pieces I could. I didn't know how this kind of magic worked, so I was being as cautious as possible. I went into this blind, on the notion that we needed answers. Dani deserved to know this about herself. She deserved to know Lilith's need for her, her importance. Clearly, yanking out souls with a dark magic dagger wasn't the only use she had.

I was determined to make this work.

With that one thought, I heard a crackle of leaves. I circled around the car and moved further into the woods again. Another crackle and then a soft sigh of pain. The fog was starting to dissipate just a little, but not enough for me to see with complete clarity. I stepped closer, closer, closer. I reached out to hug a tree, pressing my chest against the damp wood. I peeked my head out around it and waited to hear the crackle again. This time, I heard various crackling noises, as if multiple bodies had arrived.

"You couldn't have picked any other night for this?" I heard someone say. A male.

"I can't see shit," another one said. A female, but her voice sounded muffled.

"I will tear both of your throats out if you don't shut your fucking mouths," a female voice rang out, clearly the one in charge. "Do something about this, so you can stop complaining."

The fog thinned as if on cue. Slowly, the moon revealed itself to me inch by inch. It started to shed a light on the scene in front of me —and my breath caught in my throat.

I couldn't breathe. If I'd had a reason to speak right now, I couldn't. My heart started to hammer in my chest when I saw it. Fuck, I saw *it*. I saw *her*.

Dani was crouched down against a tree, looking as if she had been thrown from the car. There was blood coming from the side of her face, up near her hairline, soaking into her dark brown curls as it dripped down her chin. Blood was pouring from her leg, where a piece of metal lodged itself into her calf. Her shirt was ripped up and there were so many cuts and bruises, I didn't know where to look. Her shoulder looked like it had been dislocated, and there was a huge cut leaking blood on her side. She was practically sitting in her own blood. I wanted to go to her and fix her, but that wasn't an option.

The sight of her made my chest start to constrict, but it wasn't just her who caused me to want to hyperventilate. It's what was underneath her. I leaned my head against the tree and closed my eyes, opening them and wanting a different outcome. I didn't get my wish.

A white glow. A ring of light. The thing that led us angels to our appropriate souls was settled beneath her, as if it was always meant to be there. I could feel a headache coming on from the intense confusion. What in the fuck was going on?

I looked up at the three people standing before her. I recognized the man, the same demon she tortured in the Ethereal Bastille. I looked at the shorter girl with a cloak that covered her face, standing as if she was waiting for instructions. My eyes focused on the woman in the middle. She had blonde, almost white, hair that flowed over shoulders and down her spine. In the light of the moon, her eyes were almost black, with high cheekbones and a thin frame. I let out a shiver and a sense of dark dread came over me when I looked at her.

Was this Lilith? It had to be. I had never been told what she looked like or how she sounded. Most angels guessed. She took long, slow steps towards Dani's body, tilting her head downwards, examining her.

"Does it hurt, pretty girl?" Her voice was almost soothing. Trusting. Dani just let out another groan and she tried to lift herself up. "Would you like me to make it better for you? Ease your pain?"

The man, Cullen, chuckled from behind her.

Dani took a few shallow breaths and looked past me towards where the accident had happened. She looked back at the blonde woman and nodded. I noticed flashlights starting to shine in their direction.

A smile took over this woman's face that made my skin crawl. She reached out to caress Dani's cheek. "I want to help you, but you have to help me first."

Dani let out a small sharp cry and whispered, "please."

"Your friend over there doesn't have long and frankly, neither do you." She looked to the horrific accident. "Your friend could live if you'd like her to. My friend here can do away with those horrific injuries of hers." She nodded towards the girl with the cloak around her body. " I can make it so you never feel this pain again. Unfortunately, you'll have to give up your time here on Earth and come with me, where pain won't be a problem...for you."

Dani stopped moving and stared up at Lilith, as if she didn't quite understand.

"I think there is something over here," I heard one of the officers say. They were getting closer.

Dani took tiny hiccuping breaths as she spoke. Blood started to seep from her mouth. "I have to die for her to live?"

Lilith let out a humming sound. "You will die regardless, but I'm giving you the option to do something meaningful with your death. All you have to do is take my hand and give me your complete trust." She reached out her slim hand.

"You should make your decision quickly, before they get here," Cullen said, cracking his neck.

"I can take on a few police," the cloaked girl retorted. "Make them turn the other way for a moment."

Cullen clucked his tongue. "I don't mean them. I mean the ones with the pretty wings."

"They won't be an issue." What did that even mean?

Lilith shot both of them what I assume was a warning "shut the fuck up" look over her shoulder, and they both instantly tensed. She looked back over to Dani and waited. "I give you my promise that your friend will be fine, and you will be well compensated for your sacrifice." Lilith wiggled her fingers. "Take my hand."

Dani weakly reached out and slid her hand into Lilith's waiting one. Red coils wrapped around both their hands and Lilith seemed to breathe in deeply, intensely satisfied with what she had just done. The light underneath Dani's body dimmed and flickered.

Cullen watched as the light became less prominent and smiled.

The girl in the cloak walked away towards the totaled vehicle. The sound of the EMTs hit my ears. It would be too late.

Even though I wasn't there in real time, I felt the pull of that light around her. I felt an urge to help her. Dani had a light, which meant she was...my stomach did a somersault.

Dani was an angel. Or, at least she was supposed to be.

Fuck. Fuck. Fuckkity. Fuck.

Her light went out. That light that would have let me find her—it was gone.

Dani took one shallow breath after another until she didn't, until there was nothing left for her to do but be still. I blinked and Lilith had pulled away from her, letting Dani's hand drop limply. She turned to Cullen. "She should be in the cell. Make sure you're there when she wakes up."

Cullen nodded and let dark mist surround him as he stepped backwards. The girl in the cloak walked back over to Lilith. "We should go. I can only keep you here for so long. Any longer and the angels will get suspicious."

The officers made their way over to Dani's body and started to call others over. Everything was happening at once and I hardly had a moment to think.

Lilith ignored her words. "We go back. I have a very good feeling about this one. You are still in contact with him, yes?"

Him?

The cloaked girl nodded.

"Keep me updated when you can, and I'll rally my Enchanters when the time comes. He knows what to do, so once he sets it in motion, you'll know what you need to do. I trust you, so don't make me regret choosing you."

"You won't."

"We will get what we want in the end, I promise." She massaged the girl's arm, and I watched as the girl in the cloak created a portal with her fingers. I overheard the officers saying something about the girl in the car. "Are you sure you're alright?" and "we almost thought you wouldn't make it."

I didn't understand any of this. I started to walk over to Dani's body, her eyes closed, but despite the circumstances and setting, she looked the same as the girl I knew. I watched as the paramedics made their way over to her and shook their heads, sullen looks on their faces.

She was gone.

I started walking backwards, pulling at my hair. What did this mean for her? Why did Lilith do this? Why was this accident, this night, so familiar...

"What happened back there wasn't my fault." I heard Reese's voice.

"Then whose fault was it?" I flinched, as if someone had hit me, when I heard my own voice.

"Fuck if I know, but we're here now," Reese responded, sounding exhausted.

I was waiting for an angel to come and take Dani away, but the angel I was waiting on....was me. My heartbeat thumped painfully, as I tried to remember this night. Eventually, I went back far enough that it was clear. The portal Reese and I had gone through to get here had somehow malfunctioned, keeping us in some kind of portal limbo. I watched us walk to the scene of the accident and knew what the looks on our faces would be.

We would see that one of our angelic pick-ups didn't need us anymore. Reese would say that maybe it was a glitch, and I would say something along the lines of glitches don't happen. He would ignore me. I remembered all of this. I remembered the moment happening right in front of me. I watched as my past self stepped near me and looked down at Dani's body.

"Another one?" Reese asked, standing behind my back.

"I guess?" I said, the skepticism in my voice apparent.

Reese let out a huff. "Maybe it's just a bad night."

I watched as my past self scratched the back of my neck, unconvinced. I knew I felt the light. I knew it was supposed to be here. *She* was supposed to be here.

"Nick, let's go. We still have other ones to get." Reese stuck his thumb out over his shoulder. I followed after both of them, staring at my back. We passed by the totaled car again and I almost ran into my own back. I watched as I tilted my head up and sniffed the air. Reese was walking ahead, but I had stopped right next to the car window, leaning down to peek inside.

My stomach started to churn when I realized what I was smelling. My head started to pound, giving me a sense of vertigo. I knew I would look inside that car and see a cinnamon scented air freshener hanging from the rearview mirror. *Cinnamon.*

I wanted to throw up. I wanted to scream. I wanted to hit someone.

Everything started to close in on me and I couldn't stop it.

The world was tilting left and right and I knew I was fucking up my own thoughts.

Suddenly, I felt my whole body shake, not making the nausea any better. My head was vibrating, and a resounding ring pulsed through my ears. I closed my eyes, wanting it to stop. I needed it to stop.

I sucked in a breath, counted to five, and then blew it out, opening my eyes.

I blinked a few times before a room I recognized came into view. The light from the sun beamed down and I had to squint so my eyes could adjust.

"Nicholas. Are you alright?" Natalia had her hands on my shoulders, looking right at me.

I opened my mouth to speak but I couldn't form words. I had no words for what I saw, for what I knew. "Her light. It's...it's...fuck."

Natalia waited as I gathered myself. I took a couple of breaths to regain my senses. She grabbed a glass of water from the table and handed it to me. I gulped it down in a matter of seconds, some of it missing my mouth and dripping down the sides of my lips.

"She's an angel," I said plainly.

Natalia retained her neutral expression. "I beg your pardon?"

"Dani. She's an angel, or at least, she was supposed to be." I was still trying to understand it myself.

"But that's....that can't happen." Natalia pushed up from the bed and walked to the table.

I sighed. "It can. It shouldn't, but it can. We learned about it briefly. There has never been a reason for it to happen. I don't know why it happened, why Lilith did it."

"So, Lilith made Dani a demon and took away the choice for her to be an angel? You angels have a great deal of power when you wish to yield it. That kind of power, that kind of light, it doesn't just go away." Natalia was saying this more to herself than to me.

"That voice she heard in the beginning, when she got to Purgatory: that was it. The light she feels, the warmth, her angelic soul isn't totally gone. It's just being subdued by the dark."

Natalia lifted her eyebrows. "Lilith can't fully take it away, not unless she outright kills her. She clearly needs her around, but she replaced what Dani was supposed to be with what she wanted her to be. Now Dani believes it; she's grown accustomed to it."

"I have to go." I jumped up abruptly. My legs felt a bit like jelly, but I didn't let it get to me. I grabbed my sword, hoping to steady myself.

"Nicholas, you can't just tell her all this. You still have no idea *why* Lilith did any of it."

I continued to make my way to the door. "Right now, that part isn't the priority. She needs to know."

She grabbed my arm and spun me around. "What is that going to do, huh? Confuse her more? You don't even know what it means."

"I'm telling her, Natalia, and that's that," I said firmly. I grasped the doorknob, swinging it open to see Elise leaning against the door frame. She slyly looked up at me, pushing her hip out to one side. I heard Natalia behind me. How much had Elise heard?

"What were you two doing?" She pushed up on her toes to try to look around me.

I ignored her question. "I'm headed back home."

Elise pushed past me into the room. She looked Natalia up and down before spinning around to face us. I didn't have time for this.

"Natalia is right. You shouldn't tell her, not immediately."

I furrowed my brows. "Tell her...?"

Elise laughed. "Don't be stupid. Secrets don't stay secrets for long, you know."

I chewed on the inside of my cheek. "How much did you hear?"

Elise rolled her eyes, her hands on her hips. "All of it, but I didn't need to hear it."

Natalia looked over to me and crossed her arms. I stepped closer to Elise, needing to show her I didn't care if she was attempting to act coy and intimidate me. "What do you mean?"

Elise let her shoulders drop and shook her head, the switch-blades tattoo pulsing on her neck as she swallowed. She blew out a breath and looked up at me, her gray eyes, for once, totally clear and possibly honest. She almost looked relieved, but that quickly went away, replaced with disinterest. "I didn't need to hear it because I already know Dani was meant to be an angel." She narrowed her eyes and stepped closer to me. "I've always known."

CHAPTER TWENTY-ONE

NICK

"What did you just say?" I attempted to hold my voice at a steady level, but right now, that was proving to be extremely difficult.

"I think my words came out really fucking clear," Elise stated, making herself comfortable on the couch bed. She settled back on it, as if she didn't have a care in the world.

I dropped my sword to the ground and felt like my world was shifting, the nausea from being in a magic trance coming back with a vengeance. I rubbed soothingly at my temples. "You knew."

"That's what I just said, isn't it?" She rolled her eyes.

"For how long?"

She pretended to pick a piece of dust off her top. "A while. I don't know how you figured it out, but then again, I don't actually care."

"You didn't think to tell her any of this?" This came from Natalia, who I noticed hadn't left her spot, her arms still crossed. She had a quizzical look on her face, as if she wasn't angry but curious for answers.

Elise tilted her head to one side. "Nope." She popped the 'p' when she said it, and it irritated the ever living shit out of me.

"This is fucked up. You know that, right?" I asked.

She looked back at me with indifference in her eyes. "I'm well aware. What can you do though, you know?"

I stalked over to her, my long legs getting me there in just a few steps. "There is a fucking lot you can do, and number one would have been to tell her. You've literally let her go on and be something she isn't. That's fucked up, Elise."

Elise didn't look alarmed at how close I was. I was practically hovering over her, radiating with fury. I wasn't just mad for Dani; I was mad at the whole situation. All of this might have ended up differently if Elise would have just opened her mouth.

I pointed my finger at her, an inch away from her face. "You could have helped her and you fucking didn't. You've been lying to her. What have you gained from telling no one?' I leaned down and got in her face. "Are you working with Lilith? Do you plan to just fuck us all over when it's time to fight?"

Her nonchalant expression morphed into something of irritation and spite. Her gray eyes were starting to cloud over with a kind of darkness I hadn't seen before. She reached up with a quickness I wasn't prepared for and grabbed my wrist, pushing me back. "You have no idea what the fuck you're talking about." The pain from her hold radiated through my arm. I looked down to see black lines starting to trace my veins. "You don't know me or the things I've done. I don't have to explain myself to you or anyone else. Just because you and Dani decided to play house for a night doesn't mean you have miraculously gained access to information that isn't owed to you. I owe you *nothing*."

There was rhythmic pulsing in my arm, and it was starting to travel towards my chest. The dark shadows in my veins felt like inky venom, making my arm turn a hue of red that I knew wasn't normal. I tried to not think about the pain. "You owe it to her." I bit back a groan.

I pressed my lips together as the pulsing started to increase and I felt those black lines travel to my throat. It felt like when Zane was constricting my breathing, but this was worse. This was slow and agonizing.

Elise started to twist my wrist in the most uncomfortable position and used her other hand to grab my index finger. "Don't speak about things you know nothing about. You angels have this nauseating hero complex when in reality, you've only read the first few pages of the story and just skimmed the rest, never really understanding if you are actually needed. You don't know anything!" She continued to crank my wrist. I tried to pull back the tiniest bit, but she held onto me and pulled back my index finger further, causing a resounding snap throughout the room. She'd literally broken my fucking finger. I couldn't resist it anymore; I fell forward and landed on my knees, practically seething through my teeth. Elise leaned down and I looked at her as the tattoo on her neck vibrated. "Stop trying to be her hero, Nicholas. She doesn't need saving." Her voice cracked a bit, as if that hurt.

"Elise, stop this!" I heard Natalia shout, right as a bright yellow bolt of crackling light hit Elise in the face. She let go of my wrist and stumbled back until she hit the wall, grabbing at her face.

I could hardly flex my wrist, the dark venom still lingering in my bones. I tried not to think about my broken finger, using my other hand to graze along my chest and neck as I got up from the floor. I backed up to where Natalia stood, her hand out, palm facing up as she held a ball of light in her hands, shooting out like a starburst.

Elise huffed, practically growling as the light left her face and dispersed. Her chest rose and fell with hard, short breaths. Her cheek was red and sizzling, as if Natalia had burned her.

"Fuck! Was that necessary?" Elise said, the color in her eyes turning back to normal.

"You are allowed to be upset, but you aren't allowed to take your anger out on the people who want to help and understand," Natalia explained, concealing her magic as she closed her palm.

"Allowed?" Elise barked out a laugh. "You don't tell me what to do, witch." She narrowed her eyes at Natalia until they were tiny slits.

"Then who does, huh? Lilith?" I asked, walking up to her again but still maintaining a safe distance. I was clutching my hand over my mistreated finger.

"You are making me want to kill you slowly with your questions." Elise looked up at me.

"You could make things go so much smoother if you just answer me. All of this bullshit wouldn't even be necessary."

"But this game is just so much fun."

I sighed. "Elise, just answer the fucking question."

She looked at Natalia and then to me. "It's not like you'd believe me anyway. You will always think what you want, all the way up until the very end."

I raised an eyebrow at her, refusing to give in to her stalling. She shook her head, blowing out a breath, pointing to me and Natalia. "You've made a mistake putting yourself in the middle of all this shit."

She wasn't intending on answering me at all. " I'm supposed to believe that you *willingly* placed yourself in the middle of this shit?"

She lifted up one side of her mouth. "Sure. If that's what you want to think."

I groaned loudly. "Elise, for fucks sake, can you tell me anything worth knowing?"

"Yeah." She walked around me and headed for the door. "You can't be her savior, pretty boy. No matter what you think she should have been, she is what she is now. You can't *fix* her. Lilith has plans for her, and you can't undo them, as much as your pathetic little heart would like to try." I know she meant to say the last part in a mean tone, but I could have sworn I caught something else. Her eyes were looking past me, over my shoulder, like she was trying to focus on something other than my face.

Her eyes flicked to mine, and I saw it for just a moment.

Elise cared about Dani. She still lied to her and just like she said, it was hard for me to believe it was for a good reason. Elise was so good at pretending to be cool and uncaring about everyone but herself, with no fucks to give until you pissed her off, but maybe there was something I was missing. I don't know why I thought breaking her down would be an easy task.

"I'm guessing you aren't going to tell me if you know what those plans are?" It was a rhetorical question, we both knew that.

She wrinkled her nose, looking at Natalia and nodding over to me. "He catches on quick."

Natalia pushed her hair over her shoulder. "I can't have a traitor in my lands, so you need to tell us something of merit or I will have you removed." She had so much authority in that light, smooth voice of hers, and it stunned me every time.

Elise didn't even shudder. "Remove me, then. Just know that I've wanted all of you dead at least once since I got to this fucking realm and yet here you all stand...*alive*. Believe me, I have proved myself." She let out a *hmph*, turned on her heels, and opened the door. Elise stopped as she crossed the threshold and looked back at me. Her midnight hair made her look so ghostly with her pale skin, like a porcelain doll, if a porcelain doll had anger issues and a knack for evading questions. "I know you'll tell her when you get back, because you don't fucking listen, but try not to tell her how you'll figure shit out and make it all better like I know you want to. You'll be lying to her. I might be a bitch, Nicholas, but even I think that would be downright cruel."

She slammed the door.

I stared at it for what felt like hours, my mouth slightly open and an expression on my face that I knew said the only thing that made sense right now.

"What the fuck just happened?"

Natalia walked over to the closed door and leaned her back against it. "It will hurt terribly but I can always have Zane find her so she's forced to tell us something."

I shook my head, curious as to how her brand of torture worked. "No, that wouldn't do any good. She would probably enjoy the pain."

Natalia chuckled. "What are you thinking then?"

"I don't know. Talking to her again won't do any good. She seems dead set on keeping her secrets." Unfortunately, I didn't know if that was a good or bad thing at the moment.

"Is she right though? Do you still intend to tell Dani what you know?" Natalia walked over to me and placed her hand on my forearm. She gently grabbed my hand with the broken finger and examined it.

"I have to. Nothing either of you say is going to change that."

She nodded thoughtfully, as if she was expecting that answer. She wrapped her hand around my index finger, and I watched as small sparks of pink light flew around it. The pain I felt subsided quickly and my finger felt brand new in a matter of minutes. She withdrew her hand, and I flexed my fingers, making sure everything was as it should be. "Thanks."

She waved me off. "Did you see anything else while you were in the past?"

I placed both my hands in my pockets and shifted back and forth on my feet. "I saw myself."

"Yourself?"

I nodded. "You know about the Animus Seeking, right?"

"What about it?"

I looked up at the ceiling, almost wanting to laugh with the absurdity of it all. "It was supposed to be me, Natalia."

She lifted her perfect eyebrows at me quizzically. "What do you mean, you?"

"As in *I* was the one who was supposed to get to her. *I* was supposed to be there for her. *I* wasn't there all because someone fucked with the portal that was meant to take us there."

Natalia placed her hand on my back when I noticed my breathing was becoming ragged and irritated. I told her everything that happened, from start to finish. Natalia inhaled deeply and rubbed her forehead with two of her fingers.

"Nicholas, I hope you aren't blaming yourself for any of this. It's not like you knew she was going to be there."

I walked over to the door and placed my forehead against the cool wood. "I know, I know. It's just hard not to think about it like that."

"I'm going to retreat back to my earlier question, which is why would Lilith do this in the first place? She clearly didn't need Dani to breach the portal, so why has she been harboring her and making her into this soul ripping weapon? What does one have to do with the other?"

I let out a groan. "I have a really bad feeling we're going to find out."

Natalia remained silent, as if willing me to speak plainly.

I didn't turn around to face her. "She told me that whatever she was feeling, whatever she was hearing, was like she wanted to go towards it, but thought otherwise. She pushed away her own angelic power over and over again, even when it was battling for dominance." I finally turned around but stared at the ground. "Natalia, what if all that light magic she has goes out at some point?"

Natalia shook her head. "Like I said before, that power doesn't go away. She can't take away the light unless she completely destroys the host. Lilith needs her for something she obviously can't do herself."

"Dani has never been the bad guy in all this."

"Lilith has definitely tried her best to turn her into one." Natalia placed her hands together in front of her. "Nicholas, maybe Elise is right."

I fully lifted my head up to meet her waiting eyes. "What?"

She closed her eyes for a moment and then opened them. "Do you think that by telling her, it'll somehow rewrite the present and future?"

"Well, no..."

She cut me off. "I can tell you that it won't. You tell her and then what? She knows and now she's confused and upset. You want to apologize for not being there in time, but you'll likely say something that resembles wanting to find a way to help her. What happens if she doesn't want help?"

She made sense, but my frustration still loomed. "I knew there was something off about her. I just couldn't put my finger on it. It's killing me knowing this, imagining being her and not knowing, living a lie."

"You care about her, Nicholas, anyone can see that, but you're looking at this through the lenses of someone who wants a happily ever after. That's not fair. She is going to want the full story, and you don't have that. Not without Elise."

I wanted to fight against her words -- they were wrong. I didn't want a happily ever after with Dani, but maybe this information did pique my interest in what this could mean for...us. Even if it were to get out, she would never be openly accepted in Heaven's Gate, even with her hidden angelic powers. She had a backlog of torture and death miles long, and Heaven's Gate didn't think very highly of that. She wouldn't be given any special treatment.

I wondered if this new discovery made me want to be closer to her. That night in my bed, I forgot for a moment that she was anything but herself. Labels could've fucked off. Now, those labels were staring me in the face, and I was at a loss for words. Maybe I was wrong when I told her she didn't need to worry about her soul. Her soul was clearly already in danger. I still wanted her, that was apparent, but did I want her enough to fight for us?

I reached down to pick up my sword. I placed it into its holder at my back and ran my hand through my hair. "I'll leave Elise out of it. I'll tell her what I know because that's fair to her. Dani is a big girl, Natalia. She isn't a fragile flower. I know she probably won't like what she hears, but she deserves to know." I grabbed her hand, squeezing it. "If she falls apart, then, well, I guess I'll just have to be there for her."

Natalia squinted at me, but not as if she was skeptical of my words. No, it was like she was finally starting to understand me. "I still don't think it's a good idea, but I can't tell you what to do. Choose your words carefully, Nicholas. You may think you are trying to help, but you might cause more harm than good."

"Fully aware." I winked at her before turning around and heading towards the door.

"Nicholas!" she called from behind me.

"Yeah?"

She cleared her throat, fiddling her fingers together. "There is something I need to tell you before you go." I turned back to her, waiting. "Usually, when I'm pushing magic into someone's mind, there is going to be obvious resistance. It's something foreign bleeding into your cranium; I expect to struggle and get some push back, but usually, that's the only issue." She pulled her bottom lip between her teeth. "With you...there was resistance, but when I got through, there was something..." She flexed her hands out, as if she was trying to find the right words.

I stared at her. "Something what?"

"Missing."

"Missing? From my head?"

She reached her right arm over her chest to caress her other arm. "Sort of. There were missing spots here and there, blank patches. I tried to peek closer at them, but there was nothing there, just small remnants of magic, like someone removed something. The magic is faint, so I can't tell you much else, but it doesn't really seem to be affecting you. For now, I wouldn't worry about it."

"You want me to *not* worry about missing pieces of my *mind*?" I laughed in a non-joking manner, as if to ask if she was legitimately serious.

"I told you because I thought you should know, not because I think you should worry. You think you should tell Dani what *you* know, and I thought I should tell you what *I* know. Now, it all depends on what you want to do with the information. Like I said, though, don't ponder on it too much. We can look into it more when this is all over."

I placed my hands in my back pockets. "You don't know me too well, then, because I will probably spiral with that information."

"I had a feeling, but there isn't much either of us can do about it now."

"You're pretty optimistic about the way all of this will turn out."

She smiled that sparkling, white smile. "It's a trait I got from my mother. Maybe I just believe in you."

I gave her a small smile and a two-finger salute as I turned around to leave.

"I'll see you when you get back, Nicholas. Don't forget to focus on where you want to go in your portal this time. Stay focused."

I huffed out some form of okay, which made her chuckle, and left the room. I jogged down the steps and towards the door to the apothecary. Opening the door, I let the music of wind chimes fill my ears. I needed to tell Reese I was heading out, so I headed towards the last place I knew him to be. He was standing outside of the pub when I walked up.

"Are you leaving?" he asked the minute I stood in front of him.

"Yup, but I'll be back. Don't miss me too much, alright?"

Reese placed his hand over his heart, as if he was thoroughly gutted. "I miss you already."

I looked him up and down. "Did Natalia give you both new clothes?"

He nodded, dusting off the shoulder of his jean jacket. "I guess she didn't want us walking around in our old ones. I personally think she wanted to get my clothes off." He waggled his eyebrows.

I held in my laugh as I gave him a tight-lipped smile. "I bet. You're pretty hard to resist."

He punched me in the shoulder and crossed his arms over his chest. "Get back in one piece, alright? Meet back here later today and we'll head for The Skies."

"Correct. See you then." I ruffled his long blonde hair free of its hair tie, causing him to jerk back and away from me. I wanted to tell him what I knew, but I found myself deciding against it.

I started walking to the opening Natalia and I had come from when I caught sight of Elise through the trees, relaxing in a hammock. She had her head to the side, staring at me. Her face was expressionless, like she knew exactly what I was going to do—she had literally called me out on it— and didn't seem to care at this point. I raised my eyebrows at her in a silent question, maybe hoping she would take it as one more chance to open up, but she just looked away and up towards the trees.

Alright then.

I walked about halfway down the path and heard rustling. I stopped dead in my tracks and felt the muscles in my arms wanting to reach for my sword, but before I could obey, Zane came out from the brush. His long waves were pulled back in a low ponytail, which put his wide, broad shoulders on full display.

"Are you headed back?" he asked, his voice that gruff deep rumble.

I nodded.

He looked directly at me, as if he really wanted me to hear him. "You look just like him. Your father, I mean."

"I get that a lot," I said after a minute.

He started walking away from me, as if that was it and he was done with this exchange. "Get home safe."

"Thanks," I said quietly, more to myself, in the most confused tone I could muster. I'd add that to the list of things I should probably ask my dad about.

Right now, I had one thing to do, and I would be lying if I said I wasn't nervous about it. Natalia and Elise were probably right, and I should just let things play out how they are, make it easier on myself. If I was being honest, though, things with Dani were never easy, so why should I start now?

CHAPTER TWENTY-TWO

DANI

Present

"Something about me?" I asked him, watching as his eyes started to change from determined to hesitant.

"Mhmm." His lips pressed tightly together.

I knew he went to Oculus partially for me, because of what I told him. I had told him not to worry about it, but Nicholas seemed like the type to bite off more than he could chew. Based on the way he looked, whatever he had to tell me wouldn't be something I'd want to hear. I could just feel it. I narrowed my eyes, trying to somehow figure him out without hearing what he had to say.

He inhaled deeply and exhaled a long breath. "I went to Oculus to see Natalia about what you told me."

"I figured." I crossed my arms over my chest.

He gestured towards his bed. "You might want to sit down."

I moved my eyes to his unmade bed and our night together flashed through my memory, a warm feeling flooding my entire body. "I'm fine standing. Just spit it out."

He raised those deep brown eyes to the ceiling, as if he was thinking how to tell me whatever was on the tip of his tongue. He ran a shaking hand through his hair, pulling at the back of his head. "I told you I'd probably continue to think about what you told me and I did...and I wanted a second opinion."

"So, you went to Natalia for help? Without letting me in on what you were doing?"

"It sounds bad, I know."

I cocked my head to the side, my hair moving along my back. "I mean, you went to someone about an issue that has nothing to do with you, so I would say it's a little weird. How about you just tell me what you know? That would be a fantastic fucking place to start."

"That feeling you get, that sense of light or warmth you feel...it's a lot more complicated than you think."

An impatient feeling grew inside my chest.

Nicholas took the one long step he needed to be so close to me, I could see the pulse in his neck vibrating. "I was right about you. Natalia and I were both right."

I looked directly into his eyes and made sure my face was displaying the highest level of annoyance. "Nick, if you don't tell me what the fuck is going on, I will literally fly to Oculus myself. Stop dancing around the issue and just say it."

He backed away from me until the back of his knees hit his bed, causing him to sit down. He placed his head in his hands, the words coming out muffled. "You're an angel."

I scoffed. "Thanks, I like to think I'm quite nice when I choose to be, but what does that have to do with whatever you found?"

He peeked up at me, confusion in his eyes. He shook his head. "What? No, Dani. That's not what I mean." He gave me a pointed look, which caused my shoulders to stiffen. "You *are* an angel."

"Excuse me?"

He rubbed his hands down his pants. "You were supposed to be, but Lilith fucked things up. You've been living a lie. I still don't know what that means for you, but it's something you should know. So, here I am telling you, because I think you deserve some answers to whatever is going on inside of you. I told you something was off, that you didn't give off a demon vibe. I told you it had to do with how you started out and it does, Dani, it does." He sucked in a breath, as if it had taken a lot out of him.

I suddenly felt like my entire body was made out of concrete. I couldn't move any of my limbs and my head started to feel heavy on my neck. Everything felt too heavy, everything was too much. None of it made sense, no matter how many times I replayed his explanation in my head.

"You're joking," I stated, not even bothering to make it sound like a question.

He gave me a look of pure confusion. "Why would I joke about something like this?"

"Because frankly, that's the most ridiculous thing I've ever heard."

He gave me a heavy sigh, as if he was conceding. "I understand it's hard to comprehend, but it's true."

I massaged my temples, trying to stave off the impending headache. "It's hard to comprehend because it's crazy. You *sound* crazy trying to make me believe any of this. You are trying to find an answer that isn't there." I ran a hand through my hair, pulling at the curly ends. "How about you tell me what you actually found, and we can both just put this sad excuse for a joke behind us?"

Nicholas groaned, pushing the sleeves of his jacket up. "Dani, it's not a fucking joke. It's true. I wouldn't just make this shit up and I think you know that. I wouldn't come back from Oculus just to tell you a fucking lie. That's not me." He got up and walked towards me again, this time taking my forearms in his hands and squeezing. "You were supposed to be an angel and that's what's been inside of you this entire time. As much as I'd like to sugar coat it...I can't."

"You sound insane. It doesn't make sense—"

I let his hands continue to hold me as I looked up at him, ready to make another quick remark, but his face had me closing my mouth. His eyebrows were turned inward, his eyes were soft and almost pleading, and his voice was steady and slightly demanding. I'd seen Nicholas joke before, and this wasn't one. He wasn't lying.

I heard myself speak, but it sounded like a whisper. "The feeling... the voice, it's because I'm supposed to be a—" I couldn't make myself say it, but I let the realization trail off with all the unspoken words.

"Natalia said that angelic power doesn't go away, so when Lilith made you a demon, she just kind of placed darkness on top of it. Then I guess you kind of kept pushing it further and further down until you couldn't recognize it anymore."

I licked my bottom lip, realizing how dry my mouth was. "When I first got to Purgatory, it was so strong, it would give me these intense headaches. It was so loud and almost raging—"

"It was scared and it didn't know where it was, just like you," Nicholas said. "Angels have a connection to their powers; once we start developing them, it becomes like a friendship. It grows over time, once you start understanding it and using it, but you, Dani, you never really got to know your own power, which makes sense as to why you couldn't understand it. You couldn't connect with it.

"It hasn't let you go, though, and it never will. I think it just started to back off from you when it realized you were leaning another way. Now, with you being here, you're starting to feel it more. I think it knows that it's home." He blinked down at me, his lips twitching as if a ghost of a smile wanted to play along his lips.

I wanted to smile at that thought with him. It sounded nice. *Home.* Purgatory had seemed off to me, ever since I woke up, thrust into a life I assumed I deserved. I had fulfilled everything Lilith had asked of me, and I had made allies and maybe a few enemies down there; it had been a sort of home to me. Every time I went to bed, though, it was as if I could imagine myself somewhere else, somewhere I dreamt of. Maybe I was wrong. Maybe, the place and the life I had thought about in my dreams were real. That voice I would hear trying to pull me out of my darkness wasn't a trick at all/ maybe that was me, trying to fight to get to where I actually belonged.

Wait.

I leaned back a bit, pulling my arms out of his grasp. "How do you know all of this?"

His eyes darted back and forth between my eyes. "I told you how."

427

"No. You told me that Natalia helped you find out. You didn't tell me *how*."

He opened his mouth and closed it again. Opened it and closed it. I could hear pieces of a sentence beginning, but then he would stop and reevaluate. I reached my hand up and grabbed his chin, forcing him to look at me. "Speak."

He swallowed and I watched out of the corner of my eye as his Adam's apple bobbed. "I went into the past. Into your mind."

I felt my hand tense, watching him flinch at the tension. "You went into my head? How would you even do that? I have no memory of anything before Purgatory."

Through clenched teeth, he was able to grit his answer out. "Magic. Natalia used magic."

I released his face and placed my hand at my hip. "Well, that's fucking obvious. What I don't understand is how you were able to figure out what time to go to, where to go. Fill in the blanks, Nicholas."

He rubbed his jaw, then placed his palms together and tapped his index fingers together. "Yeah...about that. I wondered how I was going to do that as well. Natalia said that that memory isn't gone from your head, so we were able to access it. I had to drink this weird potion with parts of your hair in it, but it's not like I tasted hair, so I guess that's a good thing. That gave me a deeper connection to you—"

My eyes practically ripped out of their sockets. "My *fucking* hair?" He closed his mouth immediately. "She had a piece of my fucking hair?" I heard my voice grow louder, but I didn't care.

Nick put a finger to my lips, and I could feel his breath wash over my face. I would have felt the urge to kiss him if I wasn't so fucking flustered. "Yes, okay. Yes, it was fucking weird. No, I don't know how she got it, but I assume it's when you went to Oculus without my knowledge, but that part isn't important right now, so can you please keep it down?"

I wiped his finger away from my lips and lowered my voice. "I'll speak to her myself about how much of a fucking violation that is. My fucking hair, Nick."

He seemed to physically relax the minute I stopped calling him Nicholas, as if he didn't want me to be mad at him in any way. I was caught off guard -- I thought, at any moment, I'd wake up in Purgatory and this would have all been a dream. But every time I blinked, nothing had changed. I was still standing in front of a raven-haired angel who had just told me I was meant to have big white wings and live in this picturesque *heaven*. I could sense he was on edge, like he didn't want to say the wrong thing and upset me. Lucky for him, I was too busy trying to understand the past years of my fucking life to be upset at him.

"Can you sit down so I can explain it to you?" He motioned towards his bed again. I watched as his chest rose and fell as he eyed me patiently.

I rolled my eyes and walked over to the bed, sitting down right at the edge. He followed my movements and sat down next to me, our thighs almost touching. He told me the entire story, every single detail.

I chewed on the inside of my cheek as I mulled over his words. Lilith had made me a demon and taken me away from what I was meant to be. Cullen was there, so he knew. He knew the entire time. I knew there were never any real feelings, but he knew everything from the very fucking beginning. He knew it when he flirted with me, and he knew it all when he was fucking me. I had always thought he was around Lilith so much because he was fucking her as well, which still could have been very true. He was a part of all this, and he had willingly died without telling me. His commitment to Lilith was astonishing, but we demons don't turn away from a challenge.

We. We? We demons? Am I even allowed to claim that anymore?

"You don't know who this other girl was? The one Lilith seemed to trust?" I asked, positioning myself more comfortably on the bed.

He shook his head. "Nope, nothing. She seemed adamant about doing whatever Lilith said. She definitely had magic, since I'm sure she's the one who fucked with our portals."

I choked on my breath at his words. I watched him do the same as his eyes widened as the look on my face turned from contemplation to clear bewilderment. "Your portals?"

Nicholas closed his eyes and scrunched up his mouth, as if he was mentally trying to rewind the last five seconds. "The Animus Seeking. You remember me explaining that to you?"

"Yeah?"

He rubbed his forehead, pressing down on his eyebrows. "When I got to the time I needed, it all looked familiar. It felt like I'd been there before and then...I realized I had."

I swallowed the thick lump that had developed in my throat. "What does this have to do with me?"

"As I watched Lilith do everything she did...when it was over, I saw..." He let out a long, intense sigh. "I saw myself."

"I don't understand." Really, though, I did.

"Dani, I was supposed to be there. I was supposed to find you and see your light. Whoever that girl was, she stopped me from helping you." His voice was shaky, as if it hurt him to say each word. He tentatively reached for my hand, and I let him hold it, squeeze it. I didn't squeeze back, not because I didn't want to or because I didn't sympathize with his feelings, but because this was complete bullshit. None of this made sense and as much as I wanted to know what Lilith's plan was, I didn't think it would be any of this shit.

Lilith had been experimenting with demons in Purgatory this whole time. The ambush at The Skies barreled through my memory like a bolt of lightning. She had done that to them. She had given them pure tunnel vision to do her bidding just because she could. That was something so small for her, yet it caused so much havoc. She plucked me from my death to turn me into a weapon, into her pet project to take down her enemies.

"Dani?" Nicholas asked, but it sounded so far away.

I blinked over to him, then down at where his hand wrapped over mine. "Don't beat yourself up. You couldn't have prevented it."

"I know. I just hate it."

"Always trying to be the hero. None of this is your fault, so we can just skip the whole 'you feel bad because you should have done something' bit, alright?" I raised an eyebrow at him. "We both know you have no idea how to fix any of this, but we also know you want to try."

Nick smirked softly. "You think you know me already."

"I'm surprised you didn't tell your precious leaders about your sudden lack of souls to bring back."

He shrugged and rolled his shoulders. He tapped his fingers on the top of my hand. "We can't really linger too long, so Reese wanted us to get a move on. No one had mentioned anything when we came back, and no one mentioned anything long after it happened. I was going to, because I remember thinking that shit like that just didn't happen, but the Animus Seeking takes a lot out of you. I just went to sleep and didn't think about it. Yes, I know that sounds like a load of shit."

"I wasn't going to say it sounded like a load of shit, but I mean, what exactly would have happened? A new war breaks out over two measly souls? It just sounds like a quick way to make a mess."

Nicholas bit his bottom lip. "Well, I didn't say anything and another kind of war is breaking out anyway, so in the end, I guess it didn't really matter." He threaded his fingers through mine casually. I found myself liking this side of him, even though it was slightly sad and a little unforgiving in a situation that wasn't his fault.

"Fair enough."

Nicholas squinted at me suspiciously. "You seem to be taking this way too well."

"How would you like me to take it? I could be freaked out, which I am. I could be shocked, which I am. I could even act unsurprised, which...I am. Lilith does a lot of weird shit and I'm sure Natalia told you there isn't anything you can do to fix it."

Nicholas hummed next to me. "What she did was fucked up for sure, but an angelic-demon hybrid isn't unheard of. There hasn't been one in forever, like a really long time, so long that I'm a little unsure if it's actually just a myth. They were super powerful..." His voice trailed off as I took in what he said. His words started to muddle together and suddenly, his voice became Daya's voice. Her words started to bleed through his own and then, all I heard was her story. A demon and an angel created a child, a natural born symbiotic being of the two creatures, and it died because of what it could have been.

I had already summed up that Lilith was the culprit of it all. Jonah's father wanted power, but as much as they wanted to believe it, I don't think he would have gone to those depths to remain on his throne of angelic hypocrisy. From the way Daya put it, Jonah's father's real issue was with Moira, while Moira simply tried to maintain the peace. That child would have been the connection between angels and demons, and Lilith would have had to deal with the two worlds colliding in a way she wasn't comfortable with. It would be a world she couldn't control, so she took matters into her own hands and created the chaos she practically orgasmed over. Who would want to be working with her now?

My chest started to heat as I thought about it. If I was Lilith, I would be boiling over at the idea of a child who could be more powerful than me. Lilith had time to sit and plan, when Oculus was shattered and demons and angels were at each other's throats. She had time to encourage those Enchanters to want out of the confines that Natalia's mother was forced to put them in. She had plenty of time to realize the same thing I was realizing now.

Could a created hybrid be the same as a born one? Maybe the idea of one wouldn't be so maddening if it was her own.

Along with that thought came the idea that she suppressed my angelic side of myself. How in the hell was she planning to get me to regain my hold over it?

I was right to say I was a dangerous pawn. I just didn't know how dangerous.

"Sorry, am I boring you?" Nicholas snapped his fingers in front of my face. I rapidly blinked a few times and almost opened my mouth, but all the stuff about Daya's family just seemed too personal for me to share. Nicholas reached his hand up and slowly ran his knuckles over my jaw.

"No, not boring. It's just...Nick." I grabbed his hand so it was away from my face and I could breathe again. "I'm gonna be honest and say I've always thought something was off about myself, but aside from that, being a demon has felt okay. I'm good at it."

He gave me a puzzled expression, the scar under his eye standing out even more. "Yeah, because Lilith wanted you to be."

432

"Yeah, but being a demon isn't the worst thing in the world. It may not be the best home in the entire world, but I had a life there...I *have* a life there. It's hard to picture life anywhere else. Yeah, I mean, I had ideas that something bigger was meant for me, but I had people who grounded me."

He slid his tongue over his top row of teeth, looking down at his comforter, his legs, and then up to my face. "You have no idea what being an angel is like; you could love it."

"You say that like I would be welcomed here with open arms. That's laughable. This is one thing we both know will end with me going back to Purgatory and you being here, doing whatever the hell you do."

Nicholas let out an exasperated sigh. "You don't know that."

I snorted. "Oh, but you do. Again, the hero act is very hot, but it won't work this time." I reached up to slide my fingers through his dark hair. "Telling me was super noble, but the situation is still the same. Knowing this doesn't change how we approach anything, unless Natalia has some way to understand *this*." I waved my hand over my body.

He lifted his eyes to watch my hand move. "Natalia is a lot smarter than we think."

I stuck my tongue between my teeth. "Your optimism is cute."

He tugged my hand away, but kept it clasped in his own warm one and tugged me

a little bit closer to him. "A little optimism of your own would be great, you know. It's like you actually want to go back to that place."

I let out a small laugh that wasn't reciprocated. My laugh bounced off his exterior, which was as serious and unreadable as a brick wall. "That was always the plan. You are aware of that, right?"

"Yes, Dani. I was always aware, but..."

I squeezed his hand. "This changes nothing." He was trying to insert himself in a situation that didn't involve him. "What it sounds like is that you are trying to make up for something that isn't your fault. It's really shitty you weren't able to stop her but sitting here and trying to make it seem like I'm so much better than that *place* is useless, so save your breath."

"Alright. It was just fucking awful seeing you like that. Seeing her take advantage, I just...I fucking hated it. You haven't had a choice. You might not be able to stay forever, but I'm sure I could get them to let you stick around, sort shit out and whatever."

I smacked my lips together and gave him a smirk. "You just mean that you want me to stick around because you want to keep fucking around, right?"

"Uh, no. That's the last thing I'm thinking about."

"So you're saying that if I stayed, you wouldn't be interested in continuing to have sex?" I questioned, letting go of his hand and leaning back.

He opened his mouth and his eyes darted around the room, as if something in here would magically come to life and save him.

"Yup that's what I thought," I said, reaching up and patting his cheek. "As much fun as fucking you has been, that can't be my reason for staying. I don't even know why you're talking about a future that might not even happen."

He pulled his eyebrows together in skepticism.

"Lilith might win. You have to take that into consideration. I'm all for optimism, but Lilith is one of the best, so I wouldn't be too eager to think we have this in the bag."

"I guess I'm just super optimistic for *everyone*."

I ran my thumb over his lips. "Maybe."

He reached up and quickly traced the spot. Silence stretched between us. Neither of us knew what to do and I knew he wanted to have all the answers.

I could see why he was sad at watching my light flicker out. I didn't know what I would do if I was in his shoes, but in classic Nick fashion, he wasn't taking it well. I was never the type of creature who wanted to be saved. It wasn't that I thought I didn't deserve it, but I didn't have much time to consider if I even needed saving at all. When I'd woken up in Purgatory, my past was lost to me and I could only focus on what was in front of me. I would be lying if I said I hadn't almost shit my pants wanting to get out of my cell and be... well, saved.

After all the noise in my head settled, when I kept telling it to shut up and leave me alone, I had let Cullen pull me out of my cell and help me discover my new self, in my new environment. Then I had met Elise and instead of wanting to be saved, I felt stronger, destructive, powerful. Every kill, every soul... each time would fuel me, but each time, I would feel a little sad, as if some place inside the heart I hardly knew would break a little. How ironic is that?

I would have delved deeper into my own head if I hadn't felt a shadow over me and the softest lips kissing my own. He had his palm on my cheek, his kisses slow and searching, as if he was trying to get me to understand his feelings. Feelings for the situation? Feelings for me? That part was all still a little hazy.

He couldn't have feelings for me.

What happened last night was raw and real, and it was something I would take with me once I left this place, but it couldn't mean anything more on a deeper level. It couldn't, right? I'd had plenty of one-night stands with demons and I'd walked away satisfied and indifferent. I was never as harsh as Elise when it came to my noncommittal feelings, but I made sure no one was confused about what was happening.

With Nick, I was satisfied—*very* satisfied—-but I couldn't say my indifference came from the same place as all the others. I would be lying if I said I didn't want to keep sleeping with him, but I would also be lying if I said staying here was a good idea *because* I wanted to keep sleeping with him. I liked him, but did I like him enough to take his statements about staying seriously? Friends with benefits didn't seem like his vibe, so my mind rattled from what exactly he would gain. He would get my body but knowing what I knew about him...I don't think that would be enough.

Was that enough for me? Fuck. This is what his mouth did to me. This is what happens when our lips touched and, fuck me, I was starting to give into thoughts about us without this dark cloud of an ominous future looming. That dark cloud was because of me, and he didn't need that. He didn't deserve it. He deserved the life he had right here, not a life trying to make others see me how I was *meant* to be seen. Why was I threatening to give into something that would ultimately just fuck up his life? He was a solid fuck with probably the most perfect cock I had ever seen, an all-around good guy, but it would be selfish for me to keep him to myself. Fuck, I wanted to keep him to myself.

Fuck, fuck, fuck.

I needed him to understand, fully, where this would end up. He couldn't rely on me to stay. He had Reese. He would find some girl who would take up his time, an angelic masterpiece, not a girl damaged by the vicious agenda of a malevolent woman.

I pulled back, just as he started to graze his hand up my thigh.

"When this is all over, I'll end up with what I had when I came here. That's my dignity and Elise," I said, a bit breathless.

Nicholas licked his bottom lip and gave me a questioning expression. "Elise."

"Yes, Elise. As much as Reese may not like her and as much as you fiddle with disinterest towards her, she is one of the few people I can trust."

"Trust?" The one word came out like a loud, harsh bark as he cocked his head back.

"Do you have anything else to say other than one-word replies?"

He placed his palm face down on his comforter. "Not at the moment, no." I could see how he was clenching his teeth, as if he was holding back something physically hurting him.

I breathed out a weary sigh. "Nick, as much as I like you, I'm going back. I guess I'll learn to live with what I know about myself."

"You don't have to do that, though. Yes, there might not be a place in Heaven's Gate for you, but come on, Dani. You really want to go back to that hellhole with *Elise* and keep pretending you're something you aren't? That's quite possibly the most ridiculous thing I've heard you say."

I gaped at him. "This is what I *am*, Nick. You can tell me truths about myself all day long, but at the end of the day, I am still a demon, right here, right now. No amount of fucking information is going to change that. You really seem like you want to fucking change that. I've already told you no."

He gave me an incredulous look, as if what I said was an obvious statement. "Of course, I want to *change* that. I want you to be what you were meant to be. It's only right. It's only fair." He sounded sincere, he really did, but something in his voice gave me the impression that he wanted those things for me, but he didn't want it *just* for me. It sounded like he wanted it for himself as well: the way his eyes softened the minute he gazed at my face, the way his fingers twitched a bit as if he was eager to touch me but thought better of it.

I crossed my arms over my chest. It wasn't cold in his room, but I felt myself shaking. "You're right. It's not fair that Lilith took that away from me." I gave him a pointed stare that had me burning my eyes straight into his. He was handsome in a way that almost took my breath away. I wasn't going to lie and say that I didn't like the way he looked at me. I knew he didn't pity me, but I was highly aware he now placed me in the angelic category, which I didn't really like. He wanted me to forget who I was, what I've always been, wanted me to be something else. I really listened to the things he had to say and something about it made me just a tiny bit...angry.

"Nick, let me ask you something." I tilted my head to the side. "Let's say I entertain you and decide to stay here. I live in Oculus, free of the *hellhole*." I paused, his eyes glued to my lips as I spoke. "What happens if I can't grasp that angelic power inside of myself? What if I can't expel this dark energy and I just have to remain what I am? This soul ripping demon everyone knows me as?"

Nick flicked his eyes from my mouth to my eyes, narrowed and waiting. "What the fuck are you talking about?"

"It's a solid possibility. You make it seem like there's a way to fix everything and wrap it up in a tight little bow. You think you live in a world where everything works in your favor, but sometimes it doesn't. Honestly, I don't think you could handle that..."

"Dani—"

"Not when it comes to me." I pushed myself up off the bed and maneuvered my body so I was in front of him. I leaned down and placed my hands on his knees and parted his legs. I wiggled my body between them and watched as his eyes never left my face. He looked a bit unbalanced at my movements, but his eyes started to melt into that dark brown molten heat. In my periphery, I could see him place his hands at his sides and noticed him grasping the edge of the bed while his knuckles turned a pale white.

I brought my face down to him, which wasn't too far since he was so fucking tall, and let our noses graze one another's.

"Tell me something, Nick..." I let my breath hit his mouth and my voice drop to a sultry, slow tone. "If I stayed and got a handle on being an angel of some sort...if Natalia could somehow fix me, if we figure this all out, would you want a future with me? All that mushy, together forever, unconditional nonsense?" I licked at his lips with my tongue and felt his head lean towards mine. I slipped my hands up his thighs and tightened my grip on his legs.

"I don't know," he answered, but each word came out close together, as if he was trying to get everything out in one breath.

I squeezed harder on his thighs, sliding them up again, letting my fingers graze his inner thighs. "Yes. You. Do."

He pulled his hands away from the bed and wrapped them around the backs of my thighs. "Possibly."

"Hmm.." I moved one of my hands, sliding it up his chest and around his neck, letting my thumb play along his Adam's apple. "You'd make me your pretty little girlfriend, so prim and proper like the others, I'm sure. I'd probably start shitting rainbows out of my ass."

He didn't speak against that; he just looked at me. His eyes were still filled with lust as his hand traveled further up my legs to skim underneath my ass.

I pulled his face closer to mine, but I slid my face around the side of his cheek and let my lips dance along his ear. "What if that doesn't happen? What if I stay just like this, keeping that angelic power tucked away? A demon straight from Purgatory with a long list of blood and torture following her." He gulped and I felt it right against my palm. "Could you handle that? Would you still want me? Would your best friend still see you the same way when you're with me? Are you prepared for all the skeptical looks and whispers behind your back when you walk across that pristine lawn of The Skies?" I licked his earlobe, noticing the way he shuddered and pulled back. I cupped his chin and forced him to look at me. "No, Nick, I don't think you are."

He narrowed his eyes at me. He looked like he wanted to argue with me, but then something in his face softened, as if he was taking in my words. He was finally seeing everything I laid out. I loosened my grip on his face when he started to speak. "You love to assume things, don't you." It was a rhetorical question, I knew that much.

"It's not an assumption. It's a fact. That pretty angelic heart of yours wants to make it better. You want to make *me* better, and that's fucking noble, but I will never be exactly what you want. I will choose one over the other." I pushed his face back and shimmied myself away from his body. "I've spent too long down there to forget it all. Despite how I felt sometimes, I reveled in what I was doing. I was thrilled for every soul, every scream in my direction, every single cry for help. If that makes me a monster, then so be it, but I won't fucking apologize. As fucked up as it sounds, it helped me get out of my head when I was terrified. People feared me, but they also fucking loved me, and that will never go away, no matter what you do!"

He let out a loud groan of annoyance. "I'm not going to accept that because it's not what you are!"

"Fuck! It is!" I practically screamed. "It is. I can't just say *fuck off* to everything I've ever known. The fact that you will never understand is a damn shame."

"I'm not going to apologize for wanting a better life for you!"

I shook my head, placing my hands on my hips. "That's sweet as always, but you want to know what I've learned from this whole conversation?"

He tilted his head to the side, expectantly.

"That you haven't had to consider what me staying here could mean. I was always going to be a good little demon and go back to where I belong. You got your rocks off and enjoyed yourself, but a little fun was all it was. You liked me just fine, maybe decided it might be nice to talk and get to know me a little bit, but now, now that there is a beacon of hope for me...now you want to reevaluate, allow me your attention outside of your bedroom. You want to think about life beyond this whole fucked up mess we're in. You can deny it all you want, but there's a small inkling in the back of your head that is wondering what would happen if this," I gestured between the two of us, "wasn't temporary."

He opened his mouth to protest, but I extended my arm out in front of me and pushed my index finger up, telling him to be quiet. "You would want me to forget about this dark side of myself because *you* think I'm something better now, something that will just erase everything I've ever done, something worthy of your time and affection. I can't see myself wanting that, so that changes things for you. You erase all thoughts of a future when you consider me staying like *this*, when you consider my past, when you think about last night becoming a regular thing for your people to poke and prod at."

"You are putting words in my fucking mouth!"

"Admit it! You think because I have a fucking chance to live what you claim is a better life that I am somehow worthy. Did you just decide to give into the demon fetish you were harboring every time you fucked me? You were slumming it with me last night, but now you have to buckle down and hold yourself to a higher standard?"

He started to walk over to me, but I stepped away. "Dani, The Skies, Heaven's Gate, they all have a standard that I have to live by. I'm just trying to make this easier. I'm not the villain in this." He spoke the last part with what sounded like gravel in his tone.

I pull my lips into a hard line. "No, you aren't, but there is a piece of you that, beyond all the sex and jokes, thinks I actually might be the villain, that I might just go rogue. It's a small piece, but it's there, despite *trusting* me. I get it, I do, but now you see an opening, you want to make me detach myself from the darkness in hopes that I make myself better, when in reality, you are just making yourself feel better." I licked my lips and laughed; it was short and almost came out like a bark. "Even if I was going to cling to my angelic powers and stay here for a while, it wouldn't change the fact that there is demonic darkness within me. You and I both know that Natalia can't just rip it out. Lilith couldn't remove the angel in me, so let's not pretend that Natalia could be any different."

"I'm just trying to help because I care. I care about my life here and my friends and I care about you. I went to Natalia because I *care*, and yes, I found out something but...I mean..." He closed his eyes, as if he didn't know what to say next, how to help himself in this conversation. "You know that if I went to Purgatory with you, you would get looks and mocking tones and side eyes and that would piss you off." He was trying to make his point known, trying to solidify what I already understood. He was trying to hold onto whatever this is–was–with the thinnest shred of hope.

"I wouldn't give a fuck about anyone else. All those things are true, but I wouldn't care because I would be happy. I wouldn't change you to fit what everyone else thinks works. It's actually pretty simple, letting someone be exactly who they are despite everyone else."

He looked down at the floor, obviously not expecting my words. I meant them. I didn't know what I wanted from Nick, but I knew how I always handled myself: with a no fucks given attitude. That was something Elise practically ingrained in me. I don't even know if I wanted to see where things went with Nick, but even if I did, I would always feel like I was molding myself to be what he wanted, just to make him happy, and then lose myself in the process.

I crossed my arms over my chest, heaving out a loud breath. "I can't say the same for you, though. You will always think something is wrong with me; you'll always know I could have been *more*. You'll pity me for not making the choice to change and be a more 'superior' being. The way I see it, I wouldn't want to be with you at all, because you're wanting to choose me for what I *could be*, not what I *am*, right now."

"You make me sound like a dick."

"If the wing fits."

"Dani..."

"Tell me I'm wrong then!"

He ran both hands through his hair. "Dani, I...fuck, I don't know, but yes, I care about you, I like you, and I want to explore things, but I...can't. I want to believe we can win this thing against Lilith and that you'll be alright in the end. When it's over and things about you catch on, they'll want you to decide. You'll likely have more than Natalia on your side when it comes to figuring out how to help, but they will also be in favor of letting your angel out to play." He fluttered his long lashes and took a deep breath. "I'm not telling you what to do, but I have to keep my ties. So unless you choose to see things the way I see them, then I guess you're right." He had a sullen look on his face, as if the words were ones he wished never needed to be said. There they were, out and floating around us in the thick air of want and regret.

Acceptance was something I'd always wanted in the demons I'd met in Purgatory and over time, I got it. Granted, that acceptance came with an ounce of alarm and panic, or a pinch of unadulterated lust, but it was there, and I prospered because of it. I hadn't realized how much I wanted to be accepted by the man in front of me until the opportunity for him to prove it arose. And he failed.

"I'll always be a demon, Nick, no matter what happens. *Always.* You only want to accept the part of me that seems right to you, to make things easier for you. I can't deal with that, so I'll go back when this is done. When Lilith is dealt with, I'll go back to my life, and you can go find someone worthy of this life you love so much. So, let's go to Oculus and figure the rest of this shit out."

I turned around to the door when I heard him let out a laugh that almost sounded like a cough, like he didn't want to laugh but it came out anyway. "With Elise?"

I swiveled my head a tiny bit to look over my shoulder at him. "Of course. What's your deal with Elise right now?" I remembered the tone he had when he mentioned her before. He sounded baffled then and he sounded the same right now. I didn't understand.

He shrugged, scrunching his lips up. "Oh, nothing. It's just funny, that's all."

I ruffled the back of my hair, turning my face away from him and facing the door. "Well now you're being fucking weird, but whatever. When I get back to Purgatory, I'll let Elise in on what's going on and we'll figure something out. I'm sorry you won't be in the loop anymore." I started to walk towards the door again. "Can we please just go now?"

"You can't let Elise in on something she already fucking knows," he said roughly, as if he wanted the words to hurt. He sucked in a sharp breath in the next second.

I halted my steps, letting my hand slip away from the doorknob. I peered straight at the solid brown wood, my breath bouncing back at me as soon as it made contact with the door. My breathing was calm and determined a few seconds ago; now, it was hitched and rapid. My spine went ramrod straight and my shoulders tensed so hard, it hurt. The pain was almost soothing as my brain rattled with all the thoughts that ran through my head. The only one that mattered, the only one my mouth would speak aloud, was probably the most logical thing I could have said.

"What the *fuck* did you just say?" I slowly turned around on my heels, placing my now-shaking hands at my sides. I felt my neck heat up, and I wanted to tear out all my fucking hair just to cool down. Those words jolted more of a rage in me than hearing I should have been an angel, more than learning this gorgeous angel in front of me couldn't want me for who I was. No...this was something else, a feeling that I hadn't felt before.

Nicholas looked stunned now. I don't know if it was at my face, at the expression I had, or if it was the words he just let fly. He wiped his hand over his mouth, as if collecting himself.

"Dani, that didn't—I meant that..."

I cocked my head to the side. "You meant *what*? What did you mean, *Nicholas*?"

I practically heard him swallow, his eyes flickering a bit at my tone. "I just meant that...Elise...she, fuck." He ran his hand through his hair, causing small pieces to stick out.

I stalked over to him, the anger I felt distorting the colors in the room. All I saw was red. I grabbed him by his shirt, fisting the material. "Elise *what*? What does Elise know?"

I pulled the shirt tighter, and he grabbed at my fist, pressing his fingers between my own to try to break my hold, but it was no use. I could feel myself wanting to cool off just at his touch, but then the overwhelming surge of anger hit me, and I pushed it aside. In my periphery, I could see black smoke coming from my ankles and sliding up my calves. Nicholas looked down and saw it as well, letting out a heavy breath.

"She knows everything. She knows about you, about what Lilith did. She's known this whole time. Dani, calm down." If he thought admitting it to me was going to calm me or make me see some sort of reason, he could fuck right off. The smoke was wrapping around my thighs. It was dark, but translucent. If you didn't know what you were looking at, it would seem harmless, but in reality, it was anything but.

"And you just left that part out?" I pulled him closer to me, tilting his body down.

"I didn't see a point in telling you. She seemed pretty keen on keeping the information to herself. It doesn't matter, Dani, just let it go."

I raised my eyebrows at him. I felt the black smoke curl around my arms and slither over to his shoulders, around his neck and up his face. He looked from side to side, trying to keep an eye on my darkness. He was slowly starting to panic, but underneath his obvious fear, there was a hint of concern. *For me.*

"You want me to let it go? You don't let go of betrayal, Nicholas." I could feel that familiar darkness started to claw its way through my skin and bones. I knew the minute my eyes started to fade over to their muted black. I could see it in his face. I used the lightest push to fling him to the other side of the room, watching as he hit the wall with a thud. Nick's eyes remained closed for a minute as he regained his bearings. He looked behind him and noticed a small dent in his wall. He rubbed at the back of his head, quickly trying to get his words out.

"Dani, we have to focus on the plan. I shouldn't have told you, I'm sorry, I just...you were upset with *me* over..."

I put my hand up to stop him, black flaming ribbons peeking from each of my fingertips. Oh no, this was not going away, and I knew how to relieve myself of this feeling. "I don't care why, and I don't care about your apologies. *You* didn't betray me Nick, you just chose your blind loyalty over me. This?" I laughed like a crazy person.

"This is something entirely different. I suggest you don't get in my way."

I turned away from him and flung open the door, hearing the resounding bang as it hit the wall. I saw Daya in the living room and she stumbled back a bit when she took in what I assumed was a demon in full rage mode. As I walked, clouds of smoke followed me, dispersing with every step I took. The smoke bounced off my shoulders and even threaded into my hair. Maurice was standing in front of the couch as if he had heard the commotion, his coffee mug abandoned on the coffee table. He made no move to cause me harm, but he gave me a look like he wanted me to take a few breaths and sit on the couch, spill my feelings.

It sounded nice, but in reality, fuck that. Right now, I wanted to spill blood, and I knew whose.

Nick came stumbling out of his room as I made my way to the door to the backyard.

"Nicholas—" his dad said, his voice wary.

"Dad, it's fine, we're fine." He didn't sound reassuring, as much as I knew he would like to be. "We'll be back, I promise."

Daya rushed over to Maurice, tugging on his shirt to try to get him to do something.

"Nicholas, what the hell is going on?" his father said, following us as I grabbed hold of the doorknob.

"Nothing, Dad. Just leave it, okay?"

I looked over my shoulder; I could see clear colors, which meant that my eyes weren't black holes anymore, but still I radiated dark energy, thick in the air. I could taste my need for screams and agony. Maurice looked at me, his mustache shaven nicely and his hair slicked back, and then he looked at his son, the spitting image of him but twenty years younger. He went back and forth for a minute, and I didn't have fucking time for this.

"What did you say to her, son?" Nick gaped at his father, his mouth dropping open.

"Me?" he practically shouted. I let out an obnoxious cackling laugh as I flung the door open and stomped outside, not waiting for either of them.

I listened as the wet dirt from yesterday's rain mushed underneath my boots. I cracked my neck and pushed my wings out from my back. I didn't know the exact way to Oculus, but fuck it, I would figure it out. The door banged open behind me, and a discontented Nicholas was at my back. I turned and watched as he readjusted his sword that I guess he had grabbed before he left his room. He took in my wings, as if committing every line, every arch, every skin ripping talon tip to memory.

"You can't fly there."

"You wanna bet?"

"Dani, I know you're upset, but think about this before you do anything."

I cocked my head to the side, more annoyed than I've ever felt. "*Upset?* That's what you think? You think I'm fucking *upset?*"

He held up his hands in surrender, looking me right in the eyes.

"I'm *livid.*" I pulled my wings in tight. A flash of distorted color glazed over my vision, but then everything returned to normal. I was losing control of myself, and standing here talking to him would end up badly for everyone if I didn't get to Elise. I pulled my hands into fists and dug my nails into my palms.

"I shouldn't have said anything, I'm sorry." He was practically pleading now. He wanted to stick with his plan, to finish this. I had wanted to stay the course as well, but that was no longer my priority. Getting revenge and getting even are very thin lines to demons, and the only thing I wanted was her blood on my hands.

I smirked. "You planned to keep that from me, just like she kept something from me. You were gonna continue to let her keep up this charade for my fucking benefit." I stepped up to him, our noses almost touching. His eyes instinctively looked straight at my mouth. "I don't need coddling, Nicholas. I need the fucking truth. I've gotten more truth than I wanted from you today, so now it's time I got it from someone else." I ran my hands through his hair. I grabbed a handful of his dark locks and pulled, watching his face morph into sharp pain.

"Dani, what I said back there—" he started, but I cut him off by pulling his hair harder.

446

"You don't want me to fly to Oculus, then fine. Take me there yourself."

I watched him swallow, his neck exposed fully. He gave me a muffled okay through gritted teeth and eyed my wings as I retracted them. He pulled the portal key from inside his shirt and stepped around me, pointing it towards the trees in front of us.

I could feel Maurice and Daya watching us from the window, but I didn't turn around to look. Nick had a good home here, with his manicured backyard and blooming flower beds. I should focus on ending this and getting back to whatever life I'll have when Lilith is taken care of, but my clenched fists, tense shoulders, and rhythmic heartbeat said otherwise. Those things seek bones to crack for the betrayal I felt.

Jonah and Lilith would have to wait.

The light from the portal Nick made had me squinting my eyes and I huffed out a breath. I pushed past him, noticing the way the smoke misted around him, as if inviting him in. Fucking darkness, always wanting more than it needed. I felt him grab my hand before I barreled through the portal. I bit my bottom lip so hard, I could taste blood.

"You are wrong, you know." I shot a look at him over my shoulder. "What you said to me in there," he continued. "There is no part of me that thinks you're the villain, but there *is* a part of me that thinks *you* might think you are."

I ripped my hand away from his and shook it, as if I could remove the way his skin felt against mine. "Thanks for your input, but you can stop caring about me. You won't have to do it once this is all over, so please, spare us both."

I heard him sigh behind me, but I was staring straight ahead now. My fingers were itching to be wrapped around my dagger, making her cry with every slice and cut it made. My precious weapon was out of reach, but that didn't mean I was weak and useless. Elise was one of few who taught me how to use my powers and skills without a weapon, so it's only fair I show her each and everything I'd learned.

I let the portal engulf me and this time, I was steady as I walked forward. I knew Nick was right at my heels once the portal closed, and within seconds, I blinked and an entirely new Oculus was right in front of me. I recognized some of the things, but it was brighter, buildings more put together, flowers blooming everywhere. The smell of chocolate hit my nose instantly and the sound of wind chimes fluttered around my ears.

"Thank god, I did it right this time," Nick muttered behind me. I didn't know what he was talking about, but I noticed we'd landed right in the middle of everything. Enchanters stopped what they were doing and looked straight at me, taking in my smoking exterior. I narrowed my eyes at each of them, searching. I could feel my blood pulsing in my ears, my anger so fucking loud.

My ears perked up when I heard the familiar voice I was waiting for.

"Back so soon, hero?" Elise said, coming up on my right.

"Elise—" Nick started to say, but he stopped talking as soon as I walked the few steps to Elise and grabbed her by the throat. I felt my fingers squeeze her skin, the thought of cracking her esophagus running through my mind.

"What the hell?" I heard Reese behind me, his feet hitting the cobblestone as he ran.

Elise placed her hands over mine, trying to get me to let go, but I wouldn't. "You have some explaining to do," I gritted out, bringing her closer to my face.

She darted her gray eyes behind me and narrowed them before they bugged out from me gripping her throat harder. She was beginning to say something else, but I threw her back, watching as she landed into a tree trunk. She sunk down, bark cracking and flying off as she made contact.

"Fuck, Dani," Nick said.

Resounding screams and shouts sounded around me, but I didn't care. I was going to make this a fucking show, and I didn't care if the people watching me approved of it or not.

"Get up!" I yelled, stalking over to her. Each of my steps were slow as I watched her get her bearings, using the tree trunk for leverage as she got to her feet.

Elise shook her head, her bangs swinging back and forth. She heaved in a breath and let it out slowly, keeping her eyes trained on me. I thought she would come charging at me, but instead, she smirked and let out a small laugh. "I knew he wouldn't keep his fucking mouth shut."

The dark smoke trailed down my arm and circled around my fingers, growing bolder and darker as a silver flame enveloped my hand. I lifted my hand, watching as the flames danced, seeming to grow larger and fuller.

Elise watched my hand with no sense of urgency, but I noticed red and black ribbons of dark power slithering down her arms.

"Why did you keep it from me?" My voice was leveled and demanding.

In typical Elise fashion, hers was leveled and mocking. "You ask like you expect me to give you an answer."

Distorted colors cloaked my vision. I was done with her games. My whole body was vibrating. We weren't friends in the sense that we braided each other's hair and told each other our biggest fears, but I had trusted her, relied on her. All of that just seemed so...pointless now. Stupid. I was so stupid.

"You will tell me everything, even if I have to make you." I took quicker strides toward her as she lifted her hand up, her own dark flame growing larger.

"I'd love to see you try." She shot her flame out towards me, and I shifted to the left, dodging it.

She shot out another flame, but this one was a rope meant to catch my arm and tug me towards her. I grabbed it and watched as her red tipped little fires morphed into my own silver tipped ones. I yanked it towards me, pulling her forward onto her face.

I rushed over to her right as she was scrambling to get up and grabbed her by the neck. I lifted her face and slammed it back into the ground. I pulled her back up, about to ask her again, hoping she would relent.

Elise reached out her arm furthest from me and grabbed my arm. Inky black lines invaded my veins and I felt a burning sensation reaching up to my neck. My skin was on fire; I let her go, reaching for my sizzling arm.

"You want to play, Dani?" She pushed off the ground and before I knew it, she had let her wings out and grabbed me by the neck. "We'll play." I didn't have a moment to fight back before she dragged me off the ground and into the air. She was fast, and the trees of Oculus were disappearing quickly. I struggled to get out of her grip, pulling at her fingers, but she was relentless.

"Let me down!" I screamed. I kicked at her legs and thrashed my arms. She was letting those black streaks of pain move over my body, my legs tensing with pain and discomfort. They were on fire, tight as if I had pulled a muscle I could never stretch.

"You are so fucking ungrateful," Elise said, raising us higher and higher.

I whipped my head to her. "Ungrateful? You're a fucking liar! Put me down!" I was able to reach my hand out and scratch her face, and she let out a low grunt from my nails digging into the side of her face. Blood was starting to drip from the gouges, and I felt a joyous ringing in my bones.

Her eyes blazed and her tattoo pulsed, as if it was about to rip right off her skin. "Fine! With pleasure!"

The burning pain at my neck was instantly gone, and her hold on my throat vanished as she let go of me. She fucking dropped me. Trees flashed by me as I fell. The pain she let mix into my veins had made its way to my back, and I couldn't push out my wings. Every time I tried, pain would slam into my head, it was as if her magic hindered my own. The wind whipped upward, and my hair flew around my face as I tried to get hold of something, anything, to keep me from slamming into the ground at full force.

I tried again with my wings. Again, again, and again.

She would pay for this.

Even though the pain felt as if all the bones in my back were on fire, I pushed through it. The excruciating pain hit again and again as my wings attempted to manifest.

Finally, I felt tears sting the corners of my eyes. I strained one more time and my wings expanded.

CHAPTER TWENTY-THREE

DANI

I felt the bottom tips of my wings brush the dirt and dust off the ground as I corrected myself so I was pushing up and back towards Elise. She would have let me fall and hit the ground, likely breaking more bones than I would have liked. Bones would break, hers and mine, but I didn't want it all to happen so quickly. I looked down to see more Enchanters had started to gather, but I couldn't make out their faces. I could have guessed that everyone had about an ounce of fear in their eyes.

I didn't blame them.

Elise came into my view, her smug face completely collected. I caught a glimpse of her widened gray eyes right as I was making my way up to her. She clearly hadn't expected me to rally so quickly. Her mistake.

Before she could make any move against me, I propelled my arm up and extended a rope of solid black, hooking it around her ankle. The rope knotted itself around her and I didn't hesitate to pull my arm back and drag her toward the ground beneath us. I flung her down so fast, she didn't have time to think about her wings, or anything else for that matter. I heard the thud of her small frame,

451

and a shudder went through me, making me smile. I rapidly descended so that I was hovering over her splayed body.

I looked down at the back of her head and watched as she slowly placed her palms on the ground, grinding her fingers into the dirt and gravel. Her face was still concealed and she seemed to be taking her sweet time getting back up. I raised an eyebrow when her shoulders started shaking and a small knowing sound of a laugh came from her. Her laugh came out more clearly as she shook her head and looked up at me, her face cut along her forehead and cheeks, matted dirt caught up in pieces of her hair.

"You really love putting on a show, don't you?" Right as I was about to make my next move, she quickly came off the ground to swing her legs around and knock me on my ass. She grabbed my ankle and yanked me over to her with so much force, I felt the tiny rocks and broken tree branches scratch along my back through my shirt. She straddled my waist and wrapped her hand around my throat. Elise jerked me up towards her by my neck and then slammed me back into the ground, the back of my head creating a resounding thud.

"What is even happening right now?" I heard Reese say from behind us. I heard the chatter of more people, the shrieks and cries from scared Enchanters, the disgruntled muffles of ones who had probably had enough of this shit.

I felt Elise grab my neck again, preparing to force me down, but I felt her signature up-close move. Her midnight black venom burned and poisoned you from the inside out. It was slow and methodical, torturing. It paralyzed you and burned you at the same time, but if ever she stopped, the sensation would linger, so the longer she did it, the more you had to wait for it to wear off. If she did it long enough, you more than likely wouldn't survive. She would make sure of it.

I felt it travel towards my collarbones and up to my jaw. "Oh, Dani. You should really focus on what's happening now and stop fucking around with what you can't fix. It's beneath you." She sounded so condescending, I wanted to punch her in the throat.

I flexed my fingers, confirming I had movement in my hands, so that's exactly what I did. I brought my fist up and back, then throttled it towards her slender neck. She let go of me, letting out a few rough coughs. I felt my hand vibrate with rage and I slammed my palm against her chest, causing her to fly backwards into the tree. Black smoke seeped from my hand as she sailed away from me. The branches shook and rattled, leaves cascading down towards the ground. I huffed out a few harsh breaths, shoving myself off the ground. I stalked over to her as she was shaking leaves out of her hair and cracking her neck.

"Dani, stop!" I heard a familiar deep voice plead.

"Nick, shut up. We should really let this play out," Reese joked, letting out a small chuckle.

Nick let out an exasperated sigh. "Dani, look at me, please!"

I tightened my fists at my sides and looked over my shoulder. His brown eyes were so wide, they were saucers, and his cheeks had hints of pink that I knew wasn't from simple blushing. I kept a side eye on Elise, who was standing with her head tilted, waiting for Nick to say whatever he needed to say.

"Whatever you say won't change anything," I stated, narrowing my eyes at him.

He pressed his lips together. "I get you're angry, but this won't change anything either. Everything will still be the same when this fight between you two is over. Elise can answer for shit later, so can you please stop so we can focus?"

Elise let out the loudest laugh in the silence that surrounded us. I tilted my head up to the sky, truly considering letting this go. That consideration lasted all of a fucking minute. "I don't do later, Nick. I prefer instant gratification." I turned my head fully towards Elise, who had finally righted herself from when she had doubled over laughing. "Unless Elise would like to stop being a withholding bitch."

"There has to be a better way than this," Nick said.

"Wait, wait, you know what's going on with them?" Reese asked.

"Nick, you should really fucking go," I said, my voice steady.

Elise let out a *tsk* and shot her eyes behind me to where the boys stood. "You *really* should let demons be demons and not get in the middle of something that doesn't involve you." She picked dirt out from her hair. "You involved yourself, Nicholas. So do me the honor of watching me beat the shit out of your girlfriend."

"Elise—" Nick started, but before he could say whatever he wanted, I saw what caught his words in his throat. Elise's eyes formed whirls of reddish black, the tips of her hair casting the same colors but in a transparent smoky form. None of that had me apprehensive, but it was what was spooling from her lower back that grabbed my attention.

It was black and from this distance, looked as if it was textured in velvet. It wasn't too thick, but I knew that it carried some weight. Dark smoke clouded around every inch of it. The tip was spiked with orange-yellow points that somehow reflected the sunlight and made the sharp tips look even more menacing.

"Woah, what the fuck. She had a fucking tail this whole time?" Reese shouted.

"Reese, we have to go!"

I heard shuffling around me as people started to move even further back. I quickly looked around, noticing that right after that comment, Reese and Nick were running towards the buildings and disappeared. A few of the Enchanters were following them. I assumed they went for shelter, since Elise wanted to play ugly. Her tail meant she was on the cusp of unleashing everything she had on someone. I was edging at her restraint lines. Maybe it wasn't restraint, maybe she just didn't care and actually just considered this playtime.

"You make things so fucking hard for no reason, when you can just be honest with me and explain yourself." I was trying, but I knew it would do nothing. I had teased her with violence, and she'd been wanting some good old fashioned fighting like she used to do back in Purgatory. She wasn't about to back down now.

The reddish colors in her eyes grew bigger. "It won't matter what I say, because you'll never really understand. I'll be the bad guy for not telling you regardless, but hey, I'm fine with being bad. You on the other hand–" She curled the end of her tail, "you always knew something was off, but you wanted to please the creatures around you. You molded to what Lilith wanted, to what I taught you, and then you come here and you listen to pretty words from an even prettier angel. Telling you would have been a waste because you will always be what you've always been since the day you got to Purgatory..." She whipped her tail around my waist and jolted me over to her. "A pathetic little bitch."

My face scrunched up in discontent when suddenly, I felt a whip at my face from the spikes at the end. Stinging from the open wound tingled against my cheek. I felt myself being lifted and then thrown upward, just to be grabbed again and thrown into the side of one of the buildings. My back vibrated with pain when it connected with the brick, and I let out a grunt of pain. Elise shot up into the sky, her wings extending, the sun making the red at the bottom of them look even redder than normal. She came down at a diagonal with her right foot out and shoved me in the chest, causing my back to yet again collide with the brick exterior. She slapped me across the other cheek with the end of her tail, creating another open gash.

When she stepped over to me, close enough for me to reach her, I grabbed her face with my open palm, pushing out heavy dark mists as I shoved her back. She clawed at her face when I put most of my weight on my right foot and thrust my left foot out, kicking her straight in the stomach, watching her double over. I quickly went to grab her shoulders as she hunched over and brought my knee up to her face, hearing the crunch of a broken nose. "I'm pathetic for trusting you!"

I moved to do it again but felt the velvet texture of her tail wrap around my foot, whipping me to the other side of our makeshift arena. I skidded across the ground, creating an indention with my body in the dirt. My leggings were ripped, and my elbows were raw and bruised. I heard a ringing in my ears and touched my index finger to my earlobe, puffing out an annoyed breath when I noticed blood on my finger as I pulled it back.

I watched Elise crack her neck, while blood spilled down to her lips from where I'd broken her nose. She licked at the blood and seemed to savor it in her mouth. "You really are an ungrateful little shit, aren't you?" Yet again, she wasn't looking for my response. I squinted at her, confused by her words.

My legs felt wobbly, but I pushed off the ground and stood, eyeing her as she let her magic tail swing back and forth behind her. I let my wings out and started to ascend towards the sky, wanting to get a better advantage. Elise snapped her tail upward and wrapped it around my wings, letting venom leak into them. I felt them shudder at my back, recoil. She brought her tail down and I plunged back down, causing my teeth to clamp together. I could taste the blood in my mouth, and it made me want to ruin her all the more.

"I think I like you better on the ground, in pain and so weak." Elise wiped at her bloody nose and uncoiled her tail from my wings, allowing them to disappear. "I tried to make you into something worthy when you got to Purgatory. I tried to teach you things and mold you after Lilith practically threw you at my feet." She walked slowly towards me as I looked up at the trees and tried to settle my breathing, I tried to muster up all my anger, hurt, and vengeance. Her voice and words were like gasoline on an already lit fire.

She looked me up and down, making a face like what she was seeing was not worth her time. "You really should be thanking me for everything I've done. Like I said, completely ungrateful!" Elise let the inky venom seep out of the spikes at the end of her tail and the reddish whirls in her eyes pulsed. She was going to scratch me with that thing and watch me suffer. My back was throbbing from my wings being fucked with, but pain wasn't my enemy here.

She was. She was my concern. Elise slid her tail up my leg and I winced. I clamped my teeth together. I was seething with anger, my pores oozing with hate and betrayal and rage. I closed my eyes and felt my arms and legs tense up, but not in a painful way. They were tensing with the feeling of power gliding through them. I could feel my hands vibrate and my body start to feel warm. Even behind my closed lids, I could sense the darkness I was letting out start to envelop me. I felt that tiny tug and heard that lithe voice I had heard so many times before.

I wanted so much to move in that direction, but I just didn't care right now. Despite all the idealistic words that came from Nick's pretty mouth, it was still so unfamiliar to me, and I couldn't see myself just abandoning this feeling of power for the unknown. He had made it clear that what I wanted for myself right now was a deal breaker, and I personally couldn't waste my time waiting for him to decide otherwise. I wanted this familiar feeling of heady darkness, and it wanted me just the same. The light would have to wait.

The darkness sealed itself into my skin and bones. I could feel it even in the smallest places in my body. I pressed my palm flat on the ground, letting the grainy dirt and flecks of grass graze my palm. Elise and I didn't have the same kind of dark magic, but I could feel hers the same as she felt mine, so without opening my eyes, I knew she was seeing what was happening. I knew when she started to snicker and gave a quick sigh, before I felt her lift her tail up, ready to strike me.

She brought her tail down, the black ink dripping down on my hand, causing a small sting. I opened my eyes right as I caught her tail. The smoke from the larger half of her tail whipped and thrashed itself around my fingers, but I started to squeeze, pressing my fingers around it harder. Elise narrowed her eyes at me and started to pull away. When that didn't work, she started to cast a red-tinted flame in her palm. When I looked at her, things were contorted, colors muted, everything dulled so that I wasn't distracted and could focus my energy on what I wanted to do. What I would rip my own heart out to do.

I let my own magic flow into her tail, and it buzzed and undulated under my touch. She tried to pull away from me again, but I wouldn't let her. "I'm pathetic?"

I curled my fingers tighter around the tail and I tugged roughly. It was effortless. She let out a shriek, a sound I'd never heard her make, as I ripped her stupid fucking tail right off of her. There was no blood since her tail was a manifestation of her own powers, but it was still a part of her. Our powers flowed through our veins and would display themselves however we wished, but they can still be harmed. It was a thing I never quite understood when I had first gotten to Purgatory, especially when I had first expressed my wings. They were a part of me, but they didn't come from cords and tendons in my shoulders. Yet that didn't mean I couldn't feel when venom like Elise's sunk into them and made them weak.

The shadowy tail and its spiked end thrashed on the ground and recoiled in on itself like a dying snail. She staggered back, her palm still out and flaming with her power, but it was like she was in shock. I swiftly got to my feet, not feeling an ounce of the pain I'd felt a few minutes ago. I circled my neck, hearing the small cracks it made. "I am so far from pathetic. You made sure of that."

I shot out a black rope that wrapped around her flaming hand, snuffing out the flame at the same time. She started to create a flame in her other hand, but I expelled my wings and shot into the air, dragging her up with me. I watched as the branches and leaves scratched at her arms and face. I gave her a taste of her own medicine and let her go, raising an eyebrow as she fell. I wasn't going to let her get her wings out and continue this. That would be no good. I descended towards where she was falling and grabbed her, then turned to the right and slammed her body into a tree. The trunk vibrated and all I saw was her and the fact that I hadn't made her bleed enough. Whoever was still watching this unfold needed to see what I could do to her. Their feelings of fear would taste just as good as the celebration from the lesser demons in Purgatory.

Elise tried to push back, but I placed my hand on the tree, the bark rough against my skin. Ribbons of silvery black escaped from the open holes in the trunk and snaked themselves around her wrists, pulling her arms behind her and forcing her upright. I forced the ribbons to hold her wrists so tightly, the circulation would slow. I had the ribbons do the same with her ankles, securing them so tightly, I knew the magic would leave an imprint. I leaned into her body as she breathed heavily, pulling against the restraints. I could see the ribbons pulsing and tints of silver slither from ribbon to ribbon. My magic wasn't menacing like hers, although I suppose it could be, but I had never gotten that far. I liked my prey indisposed, not totally useless.

My ribbons were constricting her movements so much, I could tell that her magic was coming out in puffs and spurts. I wanted to double over at the way she looked right now, but I just leaned into her, feeling her breath and getting a front row view of her pissed off furrowed brow. I brought my hand up to her eyebrow. I curled my fingers, placing the tips of my nails to her skin and pushing in, dragging them down her face. Once I was at her cheek, I brought my other hand up and did the same thing to the other side.

"Tell me why you lied, Elise. Tell me why you felt the need to keep this from me and then have the fucking audacity to call me ungrateful? Ungrateful for what? For you pushing me to be this *thing*, but always keeping a little secret from me?" I felt the darkness drip out of me, folding and contorting itself into the form of my dagger. I was so fucking stupid for letting Nick keep it....so fucking stupid.

I wrapped my hand around the hilt of it, feeling how foreign it felt. It clearly wasn't the leather of my dagger, and the weight wasn't there, but it would do what it needed to do. Elise's gray eyes followed the way the smoke wrapped around itself to keep its shape. The point of the hooked tip glinted against the sun, as if to make a point that it was just as sharp as any physical weapon.

"You don't need to show off for me, Dani. Lilith might have brought you into our world, but I made you. Do your worst."

I didn't let her say another word and plunged my smoking dagger into the side of her thigh. I heard bones crunch as I shoved it in further, her leg buckling with the pressure and pain. Elise let out a groan so loud, her throat contracted. I pulled the dagger out and plunged it right back into the same spot, my heart thrumming at the sight, the darkness joyously spreading throughout my body. Elise struggled against my restraints, but I only told them to hold her tighter. I cocked my head to the side as I pulled out my dagger, the wisps of smoke coiling around the blood that clung to it. I lifted my empty hand and watched a gleaming black and silver ribbon of magic weave itself out of my palm like a hypnotic snake. I flicked my wrist and the ribbon secured itself around her throat, covering her switchblade tattoo, tight and unmoving.

"You should be so proud of how much you've taught me. Am I worthy of your honesty yet, *friend*?" I said, looking right in her gray eyes. I could see myself reflected in them. I could see my black eyes, no colored iris to break up the dark. I could see the smoke and fluttered flames of darkness stenciled around me. It looked as if it was protecting me, but I knew it was just holding me, egging me on, and I was letting it. I was feeding it. Elise's eyes told me she was unafraid as always, but there was a twitch in her eye that told me she could be moved to speak. How long until she cracked was something I didn't have the answer to.

I brought the dagger up to her stomach, letting the tip touch the slither of exposed skin. The blood from her thigh gushed down her leg, creating a pool at her feet. Our faces were so close, I could feel her staggered breath. "I will ask you one more time." I noticed her wings trying to push themselves out, so I shoved her back into the tree, watching as they retreated in their version of a whimper. "Why did you lie?"

Elise narrowed her eyes and tipped her eyes down to where I was prepared to push into her skin. Her bloody lips turned up in a small smirk as she leaned in as much as she could. "I should have let Lilith kill you." Elise swallowed, just to carefully open her mouth, spitting blood directly in my face. I growled, making a sound that came from somewhere I didn't know existed. I shoved the dagger forward, the tip driving into her stomach. I pushed it further, further...

My hand had stopped moving and started vibrating. Then came the pain, the electrocuting pain of what felt like pure lightning in my wrist, up my forearm, towards my bicep. The air around me thinned and I felt like my lungs couldn't expand enough to breathe. I let go of the dagger and staggered back. It dissolved into a puff of mist and my vision started cracking, the darkness surrounding me screeching and screaming from the pain of the jolts. My head was thundering from the lack of air. I couldn't think, I couldn't collect my anger in heaps anymore. It started to dissipate. The pain wasn't enough to completely debilitate me, but it *was* enough to create a separation between me and my lethal darker half. I whirled around, trying to find the source of my pain.

Enchanters backed up and eyed me with alarm and panic. I skipped over each and every one of them as my knees started to buckle. The darkness within me searched the crowd, slithered and scanned until it found its target.

Natalia.

She looked as prim and authoritative as usual. She didn't look wary of my appearance, but she did look determined as yellow sparks danced around her fingertips. They flashed, causing me to blink as I felt the electricity in my feet and ankles. She wasn't so far away that I couldn't make out her facial features, and the look in her eye told me she didn't want to hurt me, but as her eyes darted to what surrounded me, it told me what I wanted to know. She was trying to practically exorcize this darkness away from me and that darkness was giving her a fight.

"Dani!" a deep voice I knew too well yelled. With that voice came a lithe ringing in my ears, a musical warmth, a song that lulled my frantic heart. The light I had discarded pulsed against my heart, right as I felt a presence at my back as I caught sight of Nick standing next to Natalia, Reese at his side.

I turned around, just to be pummeled to the ground by Elise, who, in my weak moment, had ripped herself out of her restraints. She placed her palm on my chest and thick leeches of venom ran across my body. I screamed out so loud, I practically lost my voice. Then she was off me, blown back by a gust of wind that also sent me skidding across the ground. The trees rattled, the shingles shook on the adjacent buildings and mounds of dust rose around us. I coughed and held my hand up to my chest, raking my nails over where I still felt the remnants of her venom.

The colors in my vision were starting to return and that light warmth, that musical voice, was still there, humming against my heart, but the darkness loomed. It wanted back in, and they were both tugging at me as I climbed up to my knees and pushed off the ground.

"Dani!" I heard his voice again and heard scurrying feet. I felt his warm hand on my shoulder at the same moment I felt that light peek out behind its hiding place. I looked up at him as he started to open his mouth, but a vengeful Elise flung her hand out, sending a red pulsing flame our way. I started to stand, but Nick reached up to his sword with speed I didn't know he possessed and blocked her advance, sending the flame back towards her. Elise twisted around, letting the flame past her arm.

"Oh, this one's quick!"

"Elise, stop!" Nick pleaded, holding his sword out, his expression that of a man who didn't want to fight.

"How cute," Elise said, shooting flame after flame of red magic at him. Each time, he blocked them. His blade moved at different angles to volley them back at her. Enchanters dodged them as they bounced around. He lunged towards her, just to have her catch his sword in her hand. She pressed against the blade, digging the sharp edges into her fingers and shoving him back hard. Elise grunted and lassoed a dark red rope around his sword as he thrusted it at her and ripped it out of his hands, throwing it to the side. "Maybe I don't need to hurt her; maybe hurting you will do the trick."

I pushed back the light I felt, shoving back into its hiding spot, and pulled whatever darkness I still had out, letting loose a surge of dark magic right at her abdomen, the darkness in me starting up again like it wasn't just electrocuted, right as she opened her palm to let that fucking toxic venom out to play. An arrow shot from the sky and landed right through her shoulder, causing her to stumble back, my magic missing her and barreling through one of the shops. I looked up to see Reese hovering above us, his large, narrow white wings flapping.

Elise ripped the arrow out of her shoulder in one movement and threw it on the ground. Her eyes flamed and she hurled towards us. I stood, stalking past Nick and launching myself towards her, but then the ground rumbled beneath us, the feeling of an earthquake beneath our feet. The grass and dirt started to crack underneath us, pebbles and shards of rock flying around us. I felt something rough slide around my ankles as I tried to swat the pieces of rubble away. I tried to take a step but couldn't. Elise had stopped as well, trying to take another step forward, but she was halted. I looked down at my feet and noticed branches were cuffed around my ankles. I was lifted up and then everything turned upside down as I was hung by my ankles, the blood starting to rush to my head immediately. I looked over at where Elise was strung up as well. The branches scratched at my skin and my shirt started to fold down, exposing my stomach.

Natalia walked casually towards the center of where our entire fight had taken place. She pressed her lips together, clearly thinking of what to say.

"You think hanging me with a tree is going to stop me, you witch?" Elise shouted, flicking her fingers and making a noise of pain as she rolled her wounded shoulder. Blood seeped out of the wound from Reese's arrow. She tried again, but nothing came out and another searing sound of pain left her lips. "What the fuck is going on?"

Natalia clucked her tongue, holding up both her hands, palms up. Cuff-like yellow circlets were wrapped around our wrists. "You will stop this now, or *I* will finish this fight for you. I suggest you get your situation figured out before we meet what is waiting for us, because with you both acting like children, you might as well be as good as dead!" She sauntered over to Elise, and I watched as best I could from my inverted perspective as her tattoo pulsed and glowed. "You will want to get that looked at if you don't want to expire sooner than you'd like." Elise nearly seethed with anger, but then made a face when it looked like steam was coming from her shoulder wound.

I caught Nick's eye, and he almost looked apologetic, if not a little unnerved.

"Just let me go!" Elise cried, making herself sway back and forth as she tried wiggling out from the branches.

"Are you going to behave?" Natalia asked.

"I don't know, ask her. She started it," Elise said, nodding over to me.

Natalia glanced up at me, raising a perfectly arched eyebrow.

"I'll behave," I answered. The colors that had vacated my vision returned to their normal state, the smoke around me having left just as quickly as it came. The warmth and light in my body peeked out again, almost sighing when it noticed everything was alright.

We both fell to the ground with a thud without warning. Elise started to get up and make a move towards me, but she collapsed again, the steam from her wound becoming more apparent. Natalia's honey eyes gave her a once over. "Behave and let the healers fix it."

"What is it?" Elise said through her gritted teeth.

"Angelic magic infused in the bow. Fun fact, little one: most angel weapons are infused with light magic," Reese said, landing on the ground with a soft thud. He pulled his wings in until they disappeared behind him. He knelt down beside her. "It's disrupting your freaky darkness, basically causing your ass to malfunction. How does it feel to be so weak?"

"Reese, lay off, alright?" Nick said, pulling his best friend up and away from her.

Enchanters with white collars around their burgundy tunics hustled over to Elise and cautiously reached down to help her up. I walked over to where Nick and Natalia stood, glancing at Reese, who had a self-satisfied smile on his face. I glanced around at the mess we had made. The cracked tree trunks, a destroyed building, and the ground was cracked and scattered with indentations from our bodies. The main crowd of Enchanters had gone, but others stayed to start picking up bricks and debris, all while giving me exhausted looks.

"I'm sorry," I muffled out, hoping that only Natalia would hear it.

"As long as you've reeled it in, that's all that matters. I would ask that you don't use my home for your revenge again." She wiped her hands down her long skirt but refused to look at me. I knew she meant my overwhelming darkness, and as I searched my body, it was there, but it was dormant. I was back to my regular self. I could feel the lingering power trip still in my veins but nothing resembling what was there before. The healers came to me to help but I waved them off. "We should prepare to leave, when your, umm...when she is done being looked after." Natalia fluttered her fingers towards her left side, and I watched as she brought Nick's sword back over to him, placing it in his waiting hands. They nodded towards each other as if they had a mutual understanding.

"She would have killed you!" We all turned to see Elise struggling in the arms of the healers. "She would have killed you if I had just let you do whatever the *fuck* you wanted!" She shoved away from the Enchanters, who made little effort to get her back. Elise stalked over to me, but made no move to harm me, at least not with her magic or her fists.

I stood in front of Nick and looked her over. "What are you talking about?"

Elise blinked rapidly, her long lashes hitting the tops of her cheeks. She pointed at my chest. "That little thing inside of you, that stupid fucking angelic light, it was never going to go away. Lilith knew that when she brought you there, but I had no idea *what* you really were. All I knew was that she told me to make you lethal, make you tough, make you feared and revered." She squinted her eyes at me. "And that's what I did. You were pathetically simple when I met you, but you took to fighting and torture so quickly. You kept questioning things, like something was holding you back, and I couldn't take it, so I asked Lilith what your deal was."

I tried to settle my heart as she spoke. She articulated every word and never took her eyes off me. "She confided in me what you were and that you were to be kept on track. If you defected, if you let that little light of yours take over, if you became something I couldn't keep in line, if I couldn't shove that demonic energy down your throat so your angelic light would be nothing more than a memory, she would rip your fucking throat out! She would kill the light and the dark. She gave you that dagger to feed your darkness. She didn't want something she couldn't control, and she has been controlling you, Dani, with little things here and there this whole time, her *pathetic* little pawn. Her fearless little Soul Seether. Whether Nicholas told you or I did, it doesn't matter; telling you wouldn't have changed a fucking thing. I *don't* know what her end goal really is, I *don't* know who she's working with, and frankly, you don't have time to figure yourself out, despite how much *someone* would like you to." She cut her eyes to Nick. I heard his quick intake of breath, and I stuck my tongue in my cheek.

I furrowed my brow as I watched her sway in front of me. Her wound was starting to fester. "If you are so over all of this, if you are so over me and my bullshit, then why did you come with me to begin with? When Ariel summoned me, why did you come?"

She winced a little from her pain and licked her lips. She looked over my shoulder at Reese, then darted her eyes to Nick, the words tumbling out of her mouth faster than I could stop them. "You should have known better than to *fuck* a demon and think you wouldn't catch feelings, Nicholas. Heroes don't always win, and they don't always get the girl." The healers came up behind her as she started to fall. They hooked her arms around their shoulders and began to carry her away.

"Do you need us to call for Zane?" One of the enchanters, a woman with shoulder length white hair and a snub nose, asked.

Natalia shook her head. "No, I spoke to him earlier about maintaining his patrols." The female Enchanter nodded and continued walking behind the others. The High Priestess looked at me with her lips pressed together, and I felt Nick stiffen behind me. It was like I could damn near feel the way his shoulders were made of ice and his spine was unmovable.

"What the fuck is she talking about?" Reese asked, his hazel eyes bouncing from Nick to myself.

Nick took a shaky breath and cleared his throat. "It's nothing."

"Nothing? I don't believe half the shit that comes out of her mouth, but why the fuck would she say something about you two sleeping together if it's just nothing?" Reese's tone was accusing and sharp. His cut jaw ticked as he waited for a response.

"Reese, really, that's nothing important right now. It's hardly the priority."

"Priority? Oh! So you're telling me you guys did fuck, but it's not on the top of *your* list of important stuff?"

Nick rubbed the back of his neck, looking incredibly uncomfortable. This was the first time in a long time that I felt like I was intruding on something.

"We can talk about this any other time, but right now just isn't it."

"Oh okay! Well, if that's the case, then maybe we can fucking talk about this one having an angelic light, or is that not important right now either?" Reese stuck a long finger out at me.

Nick looked in my direction, but quickly looked back at his friend. "She does have an angelic light. It's been pushed pretty far down from her time in Purgatory, but it's there. I don't have time to explain all of it, but Lilith manipulated her soul into being demonic when it was supposed to be angelic."

Reese looked like his eyes were about to pop out of his head. "What in the demonic fuckery?"

"And Elise knew," I added, my voice laced with annoyance.

"Let me guess, you knew when you were racing out of here when you went to talk to Natalia earlier?" Reese asked, directing his question to Nick.

Nick simply nodded.

"You didn't think telling your best friend about this little piece of information, just, you know, to keep him in the loop…" Nick opened his mouth, but Reese cut him off. "Oh no, you just left me here with the demon who was keeping stuff from all of us. Actually, I'll do you one better: you let me get pushed into a portal with a crazy demon while you went and took a visit to pound-town with a hybrid who has literally everything to do with the problems we're facing."

"Reese, just listen–"

"No, no! I went along with all of this because you're my best friend, my brother, but all this is *bullshit*. I don't care if it was a few minutes after you found out about Dani, you should have fucking told me. If I'm gonna back you up, you need to let me know things."

"Oh, come on, we both know how you would have acted if I would have told you. Irrational and hot tempered, big fucking surprise." Nick sounded tired, but there was an edge to his voice.

Reese came right up to his face, almost touching noses. "I would have had a right to feel those things, but of course, you think you know everything. You think you know what will work for everyone to make things easier for *you*. Fuck everyone else, right? Nicholas Cassial has it all figured out." Reese backed off; his bow slung over his back rose and fell as he rolled his shoulders.

Makes things easier for you. I'd practically said the same thing to him earlier. It was interesting, and also a little sad, to see that others had the same views as me. I knew that Nick came from a good place, but sometimes, that just wasn't enough when the damage it dealt was anything but good.

"Now that you know, nothing has changed, so stop acting like I lied to you!"

"Lying, omitting, it's all the same! You and I both know you were just gonna let me find all this out on my own without it coming from your mouth, which is fucked up. This whole ending right now, the ending with Lilith, it affects all of us, even the mentally insane one with the healers right now."

I saw Nick's mouth move, but no words came out, because Reese was right. Nick closed his eyes tightly and ran a hand through his hair in what looked like defeat. A part of me wanted to comfort him, but a part of me understood where Reese was coming from. I hadn't known Nick as long as Reese, but I had to agree that Nick would have likely withheld information from his friend until it was totally necessary. It was a strategy I was clearly not fond of, but I also liked the idea that he wanted to tell me first before anyone else. There was another part of me that, despite my quarrel with Elise, knew that if I had had information like that, I would have likely told her first before everyone else.

Reese let out a sharp *hmph* and rolled his eyes. "Maybe, if you wouldn't have taken it upon yourself to go running off to your fuck buddy and tell her everything, you and I could have figured out something. We could have brought Natalia in earlier, we could have both questioned Elise, we could have managed the situation with what we both knew, but no. You had to bring her here angry and in fight mode. Thank the stars they didn't destroy this place." Reese turned around and started stomping off in the other direction. Enchanters helping pick up shards of wood and tree branches made a path for him to walk through. Natalia watched as he left and tucked her hand in her skirt pockets. She was keeping out of this, knowing there was nothing she could say to help these two friends. They would have to fix it themselves.

"Reese!" Nick shouted after him, but his friend didn't respond. Then, in the next moment, he shouted over his shoulder, directing his next words right at the dark-haired angel next to me.

"You want us to be a team, Nick? Then stop trying to be the *only* hero. Doing that won't save anybody."

I DIDN'T HAVE AN ACTUAL GAME PLAN FOR MY NEXT MOVE, BUT I FELT THE way Nick's shoulders deflated as he watched his best friend walk away from him. It was a blow up that I didn't want to happen, but it would have happened in some shape or form. Right now was incredibly shitty timing. We were tearing apart piece by piece, and the ironic thing about it was that we were never really a united front in the first place. It was another one of Nick's ideals that we could be something we weren't if we all had a common enemy. Logical thinking, but the execution was fucked. Elise clearly admitted to keeping me alive by keeping me oblivious. That was a lot to unpack, and Nick and Reese had an unannounced cat fight that I was having a hard time choosing sides for.

"Fuck," Nick mumbled, shoving his sword behind his back.

"Fuck, indeed," I echoed, looking up at him.

He looked back at me with a kind of solace in his eyes that made me a little sad. He reached out and rubbed his thumb over my cheek, causing me to hiss at the sensation of his skin grazing the open gash at my cheek. It was a caring touch, a touch I would have loved hours ago, but he had named his price when it came to moments like this. For me, the price was too high. I grabbed his wrist and pulled it away, placing it back at his side.

"No more of that, alright?" I said, squaring my shoulders back.

He raised his eyebrows slightly, but then quickly lowered them in understanding. "Sure."

I looked to where Reese had wandered off to and against my better judgment, I started moving toward that direction.

"Where are you going?" I heard Nick ask from behind me. I ruffled my hair around the top, moving most of it to the other side of my head. I passed Natalia, who simply gave me a small smile but didn't say anything more than that.

"Taking a walk."

It didn't take long for me to find the blonde angel. He was settled on a large rock near the water that I remembered well enough, his bow was placed next to him. Natalia had found me at this very spot when she brought Elise and I here. The rippling water smelled refreshing, and the smell of sweet whiskey was in the air, as if the pub I had noticed on my way down here had opened its doors, flooding the sky with its finest drinks. Foxgloves grew around the trees in a multitude of colors, and Reese had taken a red stalk of the flower in his hand, pulling at the petals and flicking them into the water, watching as the delicate piece floated away from him. He was angled away from me, but I could feel his tension and his upset. I could practically taste it.

"I know you're there," he finally said after a moment or two of me standing like a fucking creep.

I walked up next to him, taking a seat on a similarly large rock diagonal from his. I had tried to come up with various ways to start a conversation on my way over here, but nothing of merit seemed to come up. The dirt under my boots was a little mushy from where the water must have lapped over it, and I pressed the tip of my shoe into the earth. The silence between us was thick and hard to break through. I had never tried to get someone to talk to me, at least not like this, where there was no real place to start and everything I wanted to say sounded stupid or unhelpful.

I heard him take in a breath, stuttering my thoughts as I waited for him to speak. He plucked another petal from the flowering plant. "You look like shit."

I scrunched up my face. "I'm sure you aren't wrong."

He clucked his tongue, taking a piece of his hair that had escaped his bun and placing it behind his ear. "I don't want to talk about my feelings, Dani, so if that's why you're here, feel free to fuck off."

"What makes you think I want to hear about your feelings? You made yourself very clear back there."

"Good. Glad someone was listening."

I rolled my eyes. "Which part are you more upset about?"

He was mid-pluck when he looked over at me, his eyebrows pulling together. "Huh?"

"Are you more upset that Nick and I had sex, or are you more upset he didn't tell you about what Lilith did to me?"

He blinked, as if this was the first time he was separating them into two different entities. "I don't know. They both kind of suck."

I chuckled. "Are you kidding me? You are actually mad that your best friend got laid."

He threw the foxglove down and placed his hands on his knees, squeezing, clenching and unclenching his fingers. "Nick can get laid whenever he wants. Fuck, I have been begging him to stick his dick in something for a really long time, I just wasn't expecting him to..."

"Fuck a demon?" I finished for him. I wasn't offended; I was actually curious.

"Ah, but no, Nicholas had to go and one up himself and fuck a halfling," Reese sarcastically spat out, finishing it with a halfhearted laugh.

"It's not like he was aware."

He waved a hand in my direction. "Doesn't really matter. He knew you were at least a demon before that and he did it anyway. Male urges and all that, right?"

I tilted my head from side to side. "Okay, fine, but you can't honestly tell me that you don't feel more upset that he completely left you out?"

"Didn't I say something about *not* wanting to talk about my fucking feelings?"

I let out an exasperated sigh. "Fine! I'll express your feelings for you. You and Nick were each other's right-hand men, until all of this shit happened and we show up and ruin your weird little dynamic. You can live with that at first, but Nick starts wanting us to work together and you don't understand it, but you run with it because he's your best friend. Then Nick has a few lapses of judgment with me and stumbles upon some golden information and suddenly, I'm the first person he tells. Despite the fact that the information is *about* me, but I digress. Now, your friend doesn't see why you would be upset over something like this and you're over here contemplating if your friendship really meant anything to him at all." I hold my hand over my heart, really emphasizing the last line. "Did I get it right?"

He narrowed his hazel eyes at me, swallowing slowly. His throat bobbed with the movement and his chest rose and fell with his steady breathing. "Nick has always been the type to follow the rules. It's laughable that he chose now to go off book. He got veered off course by a demon...hybrid."

"I don't make Nick's decisions for him. If he didn't tell you something or if he decided to choose a different path, that was his choice to make. He's a big boy."

"You want me to believe that you had *nothing* to do with his decisions, seriously? When you had him in bed, whispering in his ear?"

My eyes widened in irritation. "I'm not the enemy here, Reese. It sounds like someone has been whispering in *your* ear falsehoods about demons. It seems like they've been doing it your entire life." His jaw ticked. "Why is it that Nick can have a rational thought when it comes to demons and everything associated with them, but you explode, jump to conclusions, and have assumptions leaking out your ass?"

Reese reached up and scratched the back of his head. "I don't get along with my parents super well, but during the times we did speak, they told me stories about your kind, and they didn't paint you in a pretty light. That kind of shit sticks with you, especially when you're told it almost every fucking day."

I wanted to know about his parents and everything they'd told him. I wanted to ask him about his childhood and why he seemed so guarded. It was a complete contrast to Nick's loving father, and I wanted to know more. Reese was a hot-tempered asshole, but despite that, he came off as if he was up for anything, always down for a laugh. With the way he spoke about his upbringing and poison about demons, I would think he would have ended up dark and moody. I wondered if Nick and their friendship had a direct effect on who he was today.

"People mold stories into whatever they want, Reese. Tell their own narrative. Your parents aren't an exception. That war fucked with a lot of people."

He was quiet then, reaching behind him to pull another foxglove from the ground. It was yellow this time. "Maybe."

"Listen, Reese, I didn't want this, okay? I really don't think I would've chosen to live in Purgatory if I had been given a proper choice, but I wasn't. I've done a lot of fucked up things I'm not sorry for, but in my short time here, I have never once thought about hurting any of you. I haven't given you a reason to dislike me, except for your own biased views." I could just about see his molars grinding together through his clenched jaw. "I got a distorted after-life, and you got a distorted look at reality, both from people who claimed to have our best interest at heart. Hate to break it to you, but we might have a few things in common."

Reese ran his hand through the foxglove, some of the petals breaking off as he glided his fingers over it. "Is this supposed to make me like you?"

I snorted. "Nope, but you don't have to like me to give me a tiny piece of your trust."

He laid the foxglove on the ground between his feet and stretched his arms above his head. His shirt rode up, revealing a sliver of a solid stomach and small wisps of blonde hair. "I just don't like it, the whole situation. You and your connection to Lilith gives me a black hole kind of pit in my stomach. This whole thing about her manipulating your soul doesn't make things any better." He cleared his throat, placing his elbows on his knees and weaving his fingers together to sit his chin on top of his hands. "I just don't want to get fucked over if somehow, your connection with Lilith becomes something more than you can handle and none of us know how to fix it."

"You say it like I actually understand it."

"Your lack of knowing is why I'm on edge."

I shrugged. "Trust, Reese. That's what it comes down to. When you have that, nothing else really matters."

He puffed out a breath. "Fine, I'll give you that." He looked out at the water, his eyes moving as it rippled down its path. He closed his eyes and took a few small breaths. He shook his head, rubbing his index finger over his eyebrow. "I'm not actually pissed off about the sex. It's fucking weird and I don't even know if I'll ever get used to the two of you together—"

473

I let out a sharp laugh as I started to pick dirt and leaves from my hair. "We aren't together."

Reese scratched at his cheek. "I'm surprised and unsurprised at the same time."

"I'm surprised you aren't jumping for joy over the news."

"Eh, Nick isn't the type who just has random sex with no feelings. Then again, Nick is also the type who likes to follow the rules, and relationships when it comes to your kind isn't in any rule book, so if I know Nick like I think I do, he's internally combusting from lack of structure."

I bit the inside of my cheek, thinking back to my conversation with my raven-haired angel. This entire revelation had thrown everything off kilter, and maybe he was trying to right everything by offering me an option to be what I was meant to be. I understood that. If he simply wanted it because he thought it would make me happy and improve my life, I might have given it a second thought, but Nick didn't *just* want that. He wanted me to hand myself over to the light, to carve out my darkness all because it would fit into his orderly life. He was gorgeous and had a mouth made for sin, but he wasn't enough to make me change myself.

"Nick has a lot of things to figure out and I'm not one of those things anymore," I said, pressing my mouth into a hard line. "Like I told him, when this is over, I'll go back to Purgatory and he can go back to his organized little life, without all the chaos I'd bring."

"If I'm being honest, there was bound to be chaos with or without you." I could see the strain in his voice as he spoke his next words. "I guess you're just easier to blame. I see the fucking cracks in Heaven's Gate, and I know there is a lot more behind it than just demons and angels. It's just difficult to give up an ideal so easily."

"I get that. It's time to start seeing things how they are, though. That means bringing some of that Reese I saw at that meeting with Jonah to the forefront. Hopefully, things will feel less like a big secret is looming once Lilith is dealt with."

"I know, I know, alright. I'm already starting to understand that. Don't worry, I know how to separate my feelings in a fight. " Reese looked over his shoulder. "Are you planning to take the tiny lethal one with you?"

"Most likely."

Reese chuckled, low and mostly from his stomach. "You gonna kick her ass some more when you're back there?"

"Oh, for sure. Nice shot back there, by the way." I nodded.

"Hm...another thing we have in common. We both would like to punch our friends in the face." He picked up the foxglove at his feet.

I wiped at my cheek, dried blood crusting on my fingers. I wiped my hands against one another and stood, brushing my palms down the front of my leggings. "I don't think what Nick did was as bad as Elise, but I do think he owes you an apology. But, if you want to punch him, I'm not going to stop you."

I walked over to him as he looked up at me. I extended my hand out to help him up, but he waved me off, stating he was going to stay there for a little while. I took back my hand and started to make my way up the tiny hill and back to the main square.

"This doesn't make us friends, you know," he called over his shoulder.

I twisted my body so I could see him. "Well, we weren't friends when we fought those shadow demons together. All I'm asking is that you give a repeat performance."

"Now that, I can do."

CHAPTER TWENTY-FOUR

NICK

This is the legit opposite of what I wanted when I left. I don't regret telling Dani something that she had every right to know, but I can honestly admit that maybe I went about it for reasons not completely unselfish. This turned into a giant cluster-fuck of unnecessary violence and yeah, sure, I could blame Elise for not being more forthcoming, but maybe Reese was right and this whole situation could have been dealt with better. Dealt with better on *my* end.

I hated watching her walk away from me and I especially hated the way she moved my hand away, as if that was the absolute last thing she wanted. It probably *was* the last thing she wanted, and I would do what she asked and take a step back. That didn't mean I had to like it. I hated what had transpired within the last hour, but what had just happened within the last few minutes had my stomach in knots. It hurt in a way that creeped up from my stomach towards that beating organ in my chest.

I severely fucked up. I knew that. Reese's words settled uncomfortably in my mind as I started walking.

Makes things easier for you. It reminded me a lot of what Dani had said to me earlier when I somehow couldn't find the words to make myself clear.

Was that what I was really like? Was that how I came off?

I had started all of this with an order from a higher up, and now it was starting to unfold into something I didn't know how to navigate. The people I wanted to trust were rubbing me the wrong way and the people I couldn't trust were somehow becoming my allies. I was good at structure and order, commands and duty, but this...whatever the fuck was going on wasn't something I could easily figure out. It was like everything I had ever known was now molding and shifting into something unrecognizable, yet I still wanted to take hold of it and decipher it. I never went into things *wanting* to be a hero, I always just was. I was always the one to get Reese out of his messes, the one who trainees came to with questions, I was always the one with the fucking plan.

The credit was usually given to me and maybe...that was where I went wrong. This wasn't about credit or glory or the thanks given to me by a beautiful demon.

I thought telling Dani was me being a good person, but thinking back on it now, maybe my reasonings weren't just for her benefit. I wanted to tell her because that's just what good people do and she deserved to know, but maybe she was right. My persistence on who she could become was unwarranted. She deserved what she was owed, but this little piece of information gave her a way into a different life. Maybe that night of talking and incredibly mind-blowing sex had me thinking that a different life would include both of us.

Me telling her she was an angel didn't instantly change her, and knowledge that maybe, if she wanted, she could have one life over the other hadn't changed her either, so I don't know why I thought it would. She thought I fucked her as some sort of need to check off sleeping with a demon from my list. All sleeping with her did was make me want to know more about her, breathe her in , hold her...

I would settle for holding her fucking hand.

I realized I hadn't been paying attention to where I was walking and ran straight into the thin body of the High Priestess. She looked at me as if she was undisturbed by our bodies colliding. She gracefully took hold of my forearms and gave me a considerate look.

"Are you alright?"

I chewed on the inside of my lip before I answered. "I'm alright. I just..."

She raised a delicate eyebrow. "Don't know where to start." There was no inflection at the end of her words, which told me she was simply just finishing my statement instead of asking the question.

"Pretty much. I didn't want this, you know. I thought telling her quickly would be a good plan. I knew she would be upset and then the whole thing with Elise just came out and I just didn't think after she spoke about leaving." I could feel my disdain for the whole thing in my voice, my heartbeat starting to pace faster.

Natalia nodded softly. "You don't have to explain to me. Although, I will remind you that I did say telling her would not be beneficial in this moment. What's done is done. Whether you meant to cause damage or not, the damage has been dealt, so all you can do is figure out a way to fix it; quickly, if I might add."

I let my eyes close for a moment and then opened them, taking a long breath in and out. "Do you agree with them?"

Natalia tilted her head to the side confused. "Agree with what?"

"That I make decisions to make things easier on myself. Reese and Dani literally said the same thing to me in less than twenty-four hours." I let out a half-hearted chuckle.

The High Priestess stuck her tongue in her cheek and her eyebrows furrowed slightly. Her elegant voice brought me out of my head. "Nicholas, I don't think you have done anything in your life to hurt anyone intentionally. I think you make decisions with others' best interest at heart." She pointed her finger to my chest, but then tapped her fingernail against me. Her honey-colored eyes narrowed a bit, telling me that the compliments were coming to an end. "But, and correct me if I'm wrong you don't always consider the bigger picture when making these decisions. You wonder why no one is thanking you for your plan or simply just going along with it. Well, that's simple. When you have a team, Nicholas, everyone has a say, a role, everyone's interests are accounted for, their ideas are accepted with open arms, everyone is in the *loop*." She raised her hand to my chin. "You have an idea of a team, what you want from these people around you, yet you are still trying to be the *only* leader, the only hero, as your friend says. Lilith will beat all of us if you cannot learn to take a step back and realize what you're doing."

I swallowed hard, taking in each and every one of her words. Each syllable hit me like a punch to the gut.

"As for your very vocal blonde friend, I think it's mostly pride, but regardless, just apologize. He holds your friendship much closer than you think he does. It was easy when it was always just the two of you but now..." She looked over in the direction that Dani had walked and then over her shoulder where the healers had taken Elise. "Well, now things are different. Whatever is going on with you and Dani will take time."

I rubbed the back of my neck. "Yeah, I'm well aware of that."

"I don't know what you said to her or what's really going on." She gestured her hand towards where the fight broke out. "But I do know you care about her, and I have a strong feeling you might have put your foot in your mouth."

I looked up then to see a small smile forming on her pink lips. I rolled my eyes and huffed. "Alright, alright. You sound like my father, you know that?"

Natalia laughed, a laugh that almost twinkled. "To raise a son like you, he would have to be a great father, *that* I am completely sure of. Just go talk to them."

"I think Dani wants her space. You're right. I did put my foot in my mouth. It's not like what I said wasn't the truth, but I wasn't really listening to her. I wanted things...easier for myself." I said the last part on a low breath, as if speaking the words again finally made more sense. "For myself, for us maybe. There isn't even an us even before all this. Fuck, I don't know, Natalia. This is very much out of my scope of knowledge."

She tucked a wavy strand of hair behind her ear. "Hmm, well, maybe it's time to stop relying on just *yourself*, huh?"

I squinted at her, realizing she had brought the point she was trying to make back. Of course she did -- she had a way of understanding what you needed to hear even when you didn't. "You should really charge people for the advice you give."

"I should, shouldn't I?"

I folded my hand over her bicep and gave her a reassuring squeeze. I moved around her and started to make my way past the wooded area to the water, letting my feet take me further down the line of shops and businesses.

"Where are you going?" Natalia called after me, curiosity in her voice.

I turned around and started walking backwards, answering her. "If I'm going to try to make us a real team, I'll have to start with public enemy number one."

Natalia nodded. "The building has a sign near the front lawn, with a shimmering cross on it. It neighbors the apothecary. Good luck, Nicholas. Please, keep your foot as far away from your mouth as possible."

THE SAME LOOKS GIVEN TO ME WHEN I HAD MADE MY WAY TO THE apothecary earlier today were thrown my way again. I paid them no mind this time though, because I was on a mission and that mission included a very aggressive demon who I had a feeling had a lot more layers than she would like to admit. I rounded a corner and saw the apothecary come into view, smoke billowing out the top and the window to the first floor wide open, letting out heavy fumes of lavender. I looked next to it and saw what Natalia was talking about. There was a building about the same size as the apothecary, but its second floor had a wraparound balcony that overlooked the ground below, covered in daisies and clovers.

I peered over the wordless sign that just held a shimmering cross and confirmed I was in the right place. A few healers hustled around as they went in and out the doors of the balcony space. The looks on their faces were determined, if not just a bit anxious. Some of them looked down at me with interest, while others shook their heads and returned to their duties. I ran a hand through my hair, trying to mentally prepare for this conversation, which I knew was stupid since Elise was going to be an outlier in this no matter what. I shuddered at the memory of my finger bending unnaturally and the snapping sound it made.

The sound of clattering and shouting took me out of my thoughts immediately. Another loud banging noise sounded. I took a few steps towards the building and quickly jolted up the stairs, pushing open the door without any sort of normal greeting. I collided with one of the healers, who raised her hands up in frustration and moved past me the moment I mumbled out a rushed 'sorry'.

"That shit fucking burns!" a very harsh and venomous voice rang out down the hall from where I stood. I turned to one of the enchanters who was settled behind a pull out table that came from the wall. She was folding what looked like towels on top of it.

I bit my bottom lip. "Where is she?"

She was an older woman, crinkles around her eyes and veins protruding from her hands. Her eyes were wide, but those eyes weren't innocent, especially not when they narrowed and her eyebrows knitted furiously. "The loud one?"

"Yeah," I said apologetically.

A tall man with a buzz cut and decorated designs shaved into the side of his head stepped up beside me. "We need more amethyst, the dose we had wasn't strong enough, love." He had an Australian accent that caught me off guard.

Another loud clang vibrated throughout the room. "Fuck! Whatever you have isn't working. Just leave me the *fuck* alone!"

The man next to me pressed his lips together and raised both his eyebrows. He then noticed me as if he was just realizing I was next to him. His eyes were teal and offset his skin, which was a rich brown color. He had gold studs in his earlobes that bounced small flicks of light across the room. "Is she one of yours?"

"One of mine?" I asked, confused.

He waggled his eyebrows and pointed behind me towards where

a threatening growl vibrated towards us. "The vicious little demon back there."

I shook my head rapidly, understanding. "She isn't one of *mine*. I mean I know her, but like we aren't like friends. I am here to talk to her though."

His shoulders started shaking in laughter, as he pointed at himself. "Names Xander and you should just follow the screaming I suppose. I'd check my reflexes if I were you. She's already managed to throw a few glass jars."

I started to turn and walk in the direction towards the hallway but I caught myself, turning back to them. "Do you happen to have that amethyst you were asking about?"

Xander looked to the woman for the answer. She grumbled something I couldn't hear and turned her back to us and searched one of the medicine cabinets."Unfortunately, we're all out."

"What is it supposed to do exactly?"

"It has healing properties that we as healers do not possess in our own natural bodies. For your little friend, it would be used more like a mini tranquilizer," Xander explained. "It's also known to banish anger and rage, but I'm pretty sure she has way too much of that and just burns right through what we've tried to give her, hence the need for a stronger dose. Whatever your cute blonde friend had in that arrow fucked with her on the inside so for now it's just going to have to retreat the normal way. It can be painful, but trying to *help* her is painful to everyone else. If she would just calm down, a little bit would go a long way."

I rubbed my temple with my index finger, thanking them and making my way down the hall.

Cute blonde friend? I'd have to make sure to tell Reese about that little compliment later. I heard a pounding sound, as if someone was running their fist into a table, and I looked at a wooden door right as a girl in the healer's uniform came out in a waterfall of tears. My mouth fell open just as she rushed past me. *Fucking Elise.* I walked the direct path the girl came from and set my fingers against the swinging door.

"Elise?" I asked, tentatively.

A grunt sounded from inside the room and then a relieved sigh. "Ah, if it isn't the angel with the big fucking mouth."

I stepped into the room and was overwhelmed with the settling scent of peppermint. It was enough to cause me to take another whiff and let the tension in my shoulders start to release. I heard a breath catch behind me and I looked over my shoulder to see two healers slowing as they passed the door. I was about to tell them I was handling it when Elise decided to speak instead.

"There is nothing to fucking see here! If you are going to stand there, can you please get someone to spray this room? It smells like shit in here!"

I closed my eyes the minute the young healers scurried away and took a long inhale in and a long exhale out. "I happen to think it smells just fine."

I caught her mid eye roll when I opened my eyes. "You would. Smells so fucking minty in here, I want to vomit."

"Maybe that's because you aren't letting yourself actually relax. You ever consider that? It's a healing building for a reason." I took in the room. There was a plush bed in the corner and a little table to eat near the middle. A light fixture made of tree vines adorned the ceiling, creating light. A few metal bits and pieces of glass were all over the floor and scattered along the top of the table. The two windows in the room were slightly cracked, and I didn't know if that was from Elise or had always been there.

Elise snorted. "Right. These people wouldn't know how to heal someone if it bit them in the ass." She sat in one of the velvet armchairs against the wall across from the door. Elise adjusted herself and then winced, grabbing at her shoulder.

I walked further into the room and shut the door behind me. "It wouldn't bother you so much if you just let them help you."

She rolled her gray eyes. "I let them patch up my leg and make the scars on my face disappear, but whatever Blondie did to my shoulder is clearly too much for their pea brains."

I looked at where Dani had stabbed her thigh, the blood and the scabbed wound, and then moved up to her face, where her pale cheeks were ripped from Dani's nails. Now, her face was just as

483

porcelain as it once was. That wound on her shoulder though…that festering and bubbling I'd seen had gone away, but it was still red.

"I can practically taste the magic from that fucking arrow. It tastes like pure fire. A demon gets hit by enough of those things and they would probably explode. I would actually love to fucking see that." Elise tried to roll her shoulder, but it was no good.

"Just let them put that shit on your shoulder so we can go," I said, trying to make my voice as authoritative as possible.

Elise peered up at me from where I stood in front of her. She placed her arms on top of the chair's armrests and dug her nails into the fabric. Her eyes were dancing in a playful manner, as if I was amusing. "Oh, Nicholas, you forget that I'm not Dani, so this whole dominating tone of yours really does nothing for me. Now, if you want to get on your knees and ask me nicely, then I might consider it."

I pulled my sword from its holster along my back and laid it gently on the small dining table. I turned around, leaning back against the table, placing my hands behind me on the edge to brace myself against it. "You *really* like to make shit difficult, don't you?"

She rolled her eyes at me. "Keeps things interesting, don't you think?"

"No, not really."

"Well, that's because you are no fun, Nicholas."

I let out a soft sigh and lifted myself up onto the table, shoving my sword back. "Why did you let her do that to you?"

Elise tapped the top of her shoulder wound with her index finger, scrunching up her face at each small touch. "What do you mean?"

"You could have just told her everything before she had you pinned to a tree and plunging a shadowy dagger into your thigh, but you didn't. You let her do all that, for what?"

"You just love to pry open doors you have no business opening, don't you?"

"I only do it when it pertains to the situation." Her eyes were practically burning a hole into the side of my face when I turned to look at her. "Did you really mean it?"

"You are going to have to be more specific."

"When you said that you should have just let Lilith kill her? Did you mean it? Is everything you said true? Lilith threatening to kill her if she didn't fall in line?"

Elise relaxed back into the chair and closed her eyes. "I don't know, I like feeling like a frustrating mystery."

"Elise, fucking come on! You can't say something like that and then just treat it like some big joke. It's not a mystery, it's stalling, and I'm done with it! We all are." I sighed loudly and then snuck a peek at her, her eyes closed. She was blatantly ignoring me, and it was irritating, to say the least. With her eyes closed, it gave me a moment to really look at her and think. I thought back to everything she had said to Dani before the healers had taken her away. I thought about everything from the very moment I met her. She had come with Dani all on her own and if I was thinking differently, I would believe that she did that for Lilith's sake, to be in her favor. Now I knew that was wrong. Elise said that Lilith wanted Dani to comply and become a host for so much darkness, that her light was covered by it and if she didn't, she'd get rid of her. Elise had done her job and she had done it well, but it wasn't about doing it for Lilith.

Elise didn't want Dani to die by Lilith's hand. She didn't do any of this for Lilith's sake. She did it for—

"Dani."

She hummed as she tapped her fingernails against the velvet armrests.

A small smile ticked at the corner of my mouth. "You care about her."

I saw her fingers tighten around the smooth curves of the armrest, her eyes flicking open, fire burning in them. She flinched for a moment as she bounded off the chair. She was eye level to me as I hunched my shoulders. I wasn't shocked by her unbridled emotion; I was expecting it. It honestly looked like it hurt, the way her chest was heaving. She grabbed my shirt with her good arm and twisted the fabric into her fingers. She pulled me forward as I watched the red glints of fire dance in her eyes.

"You don't know a fucking thing." The crossing switchblade tattoo on her neck pulsed.

"It's alright to admit you care, Elise."

"Jokes on you because I don't fucking care. It's actually hilarious that you think so. Don't project your angelic emotions onto me; it's disgusting."

I leaned in a bit, slightly amused at how right I was. "I'm not buying it. I can't believe I didn't see it sooner."

"There is nothing to see, you annoying prick," she snarled at me.

"You came here to protect her."

"Shut up."

"You came here because you had no idea what was going on, but you wanted to make sure she was alright."

"Fuck off."

"You didn't want Lilith to hurt her, so you pushed her. You pushed her to keep her alive."

"Tread carefully, pretty boy." She tightened her hold on my shirt.

I pressed my lips together, trying not to laugh. "You want to know why you did that, Elise?"

Her eyes were tiny slits now as she waited. She stayed silent, almost daring me to let the next words pass my lips.

"Because you fucking *care*."

Her eyes widened and she held onto my shirt as she pulled me towards her and whirled me around before I could say anything else. Mid turn, she grabbed the back of my neck and slammed me down onto the table, pressing my cheek to the wood surface. I felt a sharp twinge of pain, realizing I had accidentally bitten my tongue. My shoulders tensed up, but I could see a defensive move a mile away. Elise leaned down as she pressed her fingers into the side of my neck.

"You are starting to irritate me more than your friend," she said against my ear, her hair brushing the skin at the top.

I swallowed, trying to find my words, which was difficult when half my face was smashed. "You are only irritated because you know I'm right."

She huffed against my ear. "Stop making me sound like a fucking pussy, Nicholas. I'm not. The decisions I made have nothing to do with your little girlfriend, so just fucking stop."

I tried to raise my head up, but she pushed me back down. I could feel my teeth rub aggressively against the inside of my cheek. I shouldn't push my luck, but with Elise, I couldn't beat around the bush. I just had to give everything to her straight. "Every decision you've made has been because of her. I think if you didn't let your fucking pride get in the way, you would have just been honest, but no, you couldn't do that. You had to keep her at arm's length, like I'm sure you do everyone."

She let out one loud grunt and released my neck, pulling away from me and stomping across the room. I remained bent over the table for a few moments, waiting. I pushed myself up, placing the palms of my hands against the table, reaching up to rub the side of my face. My skin felt flattened from the wood and cool to the touch. I slowly turned around to look at her, staring at me from across the room as if waiting for me to collect myself. The wound in her shoulder was pulsing and looked as if it needed that amethyst stuff sooner rather than later.

She shook her head, her dark full bangs fanning back and forth. "You make everything sound so fucking simple, you know. It makes me want to throw up, how simple you think everything is."

"I never said it had to be simple. I just said it would have been easier. This could have made a difference," I argued.

"Easier how, huh? Ever since I met her, I knew something was off but I didn't think about it. I just did what I was told, but then when Lilith told me, yeah, I thought it was fucked up, but you learn to just not ask questions down there." Elise licked her lips, pausing for a moment. She let out a light chuckle that sounded almost a little defeated. "I don't do friendships because they require a bond I can't commit to. There is always something that is going to fuck them up, and it's a real waste of time to try and hope for the best."

"Dani wanted your friendship, didn't she?"

"Of course, she fucking did. Even if I wanted to, if I didn't keep her demon brimming at the surface..." She trailed off, biting her lower lip.

"Elise, it's okay that you—" I started but she waved her hand before I could finish and started speaking again. "I made sure Lilith didn't kill her, alright? That doesn't make us friends, but it also doesn't make me a monster. I just didn't want all my hard work to go to waste if she decided to defect and Lilith ripped her heart out."

"It's okay to admit you didn't want her to die because you started to like her," I coaxed, wanting something other than sarcasm to leave her mouth.

She twisted the side of her mouth as if she were scrutinizing my words. "I will likely never admit that."

"Okay, will you admit that you came to Heaven's Gate with her to keep an eye on her, because you care about her and her wellbeing?"

She thought about this again. "No, probably not."

I raised my eyes to the light yellow ceiling. "What will you admit?"

Elise placed her hand on her hip and tapped each finger against her slice of exposed skin under her black tank top. "I'll admit, Dani is probably one of *the* most annoying demons I have ever met."

I chuckled, nodding. "I'll agree with you there."

"But that doesn't mean she deserved to die just because a small piece of familiar light successfully seduced her into what she was meant to be," she added nonchalantly. "That doesn't mean I care and that doesn't mean I'm protective, that just means regardless of how much I love blood and torture, I still have a moral compass. As depraved as it may be."

"Somehow, that doesn't surprise me."

She let out a 'hmm' right as she hissed and looked at the wound in her shoulder. I looked around and noticed a few jars cluttering a long entry table. I walked over and grabbed each jar, reading the label on the front. I stopped when I got to the label with the exact thing I needed. There was a little bit left inside of the jar, but it would be enough. It wasn't a powder, but it sparkled like it used to be. I held the jar in my hand and turned towards the now scowling demon.

"What are you doing?" Elise asked, each word coming out slowly.

"Like you said, you're a demon with a moral compass, as fucked up as it may be. You don't want whatever Lilith has coming and despite what you say, I know you care what happens to Dani, so let me put this weird pink shit on your shoulder so we can go and you can be your murderous self, alright?"

Elise walked over to me and then past me, jumping up and sitting on the table. I followed her movements with my eyes and smirked as she looked at me expectantly, as if to say *come the fuck on, dumbass.* I unscrewed the jar and placed it on the table. It didn't have a scent, but it was thick when I stuck my fingers in and scooped a small amount out. I hovered my fingers over her wound and lightly pressed the pads of my finger down onto it, just to hear her hiss out in pain. I rubbed it in along the edges and then dabbed it where the gash was the worst. The redness surrounding it seemed to slowly lessen, and the paste started to mold around the edges of her wound to create a healing scab.

Sweat prickled on her neck as the amethyst worked its magic. The paste bubbled as it seemed to eat away at her pain, equally causing a slight bit of pain in return.

"A tail, huh? That's new."

"She wanted a fight. I gave her one. Done and done," Elise said matter of factly.

"But a tail? I mean, will it grow back or manifest back or however you came to have one?" I was pulling at straws here.

"Yes, Nicholas, I can get it back, just not instantly. Our powers are quite literally a part of us, so it felt like she ripped off an actual part of my fucking body. Just imagine if someone cut off one of your wings...shit would hurt like a motherfucker."

My stomach churned at the thought of my wings being chopped off, and I instantly understood her words. I moved the conversation along. "You know, I think you kind of enjoy Dani being annoying. She even keeps *you* on your toes."

She clucked her tongue and scoffed. "Then I guess we actually have something in common, now don't we, Nicholas?"

"Do tell," I asked, smoothing the paste into her wound and giving it one last pat down before I left it alone.

Elise scrunched her nose up and shivered, as if the paste was leaking a stream of cold water down her back. "She's gotten to you, hasn't she?"

"I don't know what you mean."

"One night with her and you are just head over heels."

I remained silent, which was probably a mistake. She continued. "She's got the damsel in distress thing going on now, which I'm sure just gets your dick hard thinking about saving the day and wrapping her in your strangely defined arms."

I screwed the top back on the jar and walked over to the entry table, placing it down with a thud. I brushed crusted paste off my fingers, feeling it tingle a bit at the tips. I didn't turn back around. Elise laughed. "I saw the way you ran to her side when I was literally going to destroy her. You want to push me into caring about her? Well, I can push back."

"I already admitted to caring about her, though, so it's not the same." I remained facing away from her.

"True. Let me guess: the minute you found out about her, the thoughts of her as an angel ran through your head. Futuristic thoughts."

I closed my eyes, curling my hands around the edge of the wood table in front of me.

"She isn't innocent, Nicholas."

I slammed my hand on the entryway table and turned around, almost making myself dizzy with the sudden movement. "Don't you think I know that?"

Elise moved her shoulder up and down and reached her opposite hand up to touch her scabbed over wound. She rolled her shoulder without flinching and then shot up from the table, planting her feet on the wooden floor. "I know you say you do, but why do I get the feeling that you think her being a demon is something she can just remove, that she's a snake shedding her old skin? Demonic power, especially Dani's, isn't something you want to give up, no matter how good of a person you are. Even if she *could* give it up, she wouldn't."

"She made that clear, okay? I already know all of this."

"Mmhmm, yet you still hope she'll want to rid herself of the darkness and be your angelic sweetheart."

I ran my hand down my face in frustration. "I know it's complicated. Yes, I should have thought about all this before I slept with a demon. Granted, I didn't know all the other details, but I won't apologize for wanting her to explore another side of life."

Elise pushed her bangs out of her face. She walked over to me and patted my chest with her palm. "Wanting her to explore *your* side of life is almost like putting her in a box, you idiot. She is so much more than that now, and what you're asking will only ever get you half of her."

I opened my mouth to argue but she pressed her finger to my lips and shook her head. "Dani is never going to choose what you want. She is always going to choose herself, which I honestly applaud. That doesn't make her selfish, but *you*, wanting her to choose at all, now that does make *you* selfish."

I decided to let the subject rest before Elise could stop trying to rip my heart out. As much as she didn't want to admit it, she was protective of Dani in what seemed like all aspects. As much as she didn't want them to be friends, she seemed to know her "friend" on a much deeper level than she would ever admit. As much as I hated to admit it, but she might actually be right.

She grabbed my sword off the table and grazed her hand along the hilt. Elise with my sword was unsettling to say the least. "I mean come on, think about it you could have her pussy all the time if you just let her be." She tossed my sword at me which I caught swiftly. A laugh rumbled out of me, which she just rolled her eyes at as she reached for the door.

Elise pulled it open to meet the eyes of the two healers from earlier, plus Isabel. The Enchanter gave me a warm smile then cast her smile on Elise, who raised a distinct eyebrow at her.

"Nicholas, I didn't know you'd be here."

I shrugged, nodding towards Elise. "I just came to get the town menace."

Isabel gave a small laugh, which Elise wrinkled her nose at. "I help maintain this building and the apothecary. I was told there were some err...issues." She peeked over at Elise.

"Umm, yeah. It's taken care of. We are just heading out now."

"You help run the apothecary as well?" Elise asked, suddenly interested in the conversation.

"Yes, Natalia let me oversee things two or three years ago."

Elise raised both her dark eyebrows now. "That's why you look familiar. I saw you when I went to see Nicholas there with Natalia."

I looked at Elise confused. "Before you showed up and eaves-dropped?"

Elise rolled her eyes. "I saw her by the door; she had her hand on it like..."

"Oh that! I do that with every room both over there and here. It's an Enchanter's blessing. It's a calming spell for each room," Isabel explained articulately. The bracelets she wore on her wrist jingled as she rubbed her palms together. "The mint aroma can only do so much."

"Ah! So you're the reason it smells like shit." Elise craned her neck up to look at me. "I'm guessing there wasn't that fucking smell in your room when you found out Dani—."

"Okay, Elise, we don't need to bore her with all your blunt thoughts and emotions." I kept my voice light but clipped. Despite Isabel being so close with Natalia, I didn't need everyone knowing about Dani. It just made things more complicated.

"Ugh whatever, I'm bored now anyway. Can we go?"

I swiped my tongue over the front of my teeth, the awkwardness settling in.

"Ah, alright, I'll have the ladies just clean up if you've resolved the issue."

I hummed. "I think we have an understanding." I looked at Elise, who gave me a very fake, very large, closed mouth smile. "We can stay and help if you need."

Elise let out a choking sound of disgust. "You can stay. I'm going so we can make some heads roll."

Isabel blinked from me to Elise and then waved her hands. "Don't worry about it. Go on ladies." She ushered the healers into the room as they carried brooms and dustpans inside. "I heard what happened; is everyone alright?"

"Just some hurt pride, I'm sure, but nothing serious," I assured her.

"Natalia is doing a lot to make sure this all gets finished with as few lives lost as possible. She's told me whatever is happening seems to be contained at The Skies, but I just worry about her, you know?" Isabel's eyes brimmed with tears, but she held them back. She shook her head, hoping to regain her composure.

I grabbed her hand and squeezed. "We'll get to the bottom of this, and I'll make sure she comes back alright. I didn't know for sure that she was coming with us."

She sniffed and nodded. "Of course, she is. She feels a bit responsible since the portals were of her making in the first place."

"It's nobody's fault. Lilith has help, so there was really only so much she could do."

Elise smacked her lips. " I'll personally make sure those shit faces working with her get my fist up their asses. Later." Elise moved past Isabel and started down the hall.

I sighed and let Isabel's hand drop. She tucked both her hands into her pockets as she watched Elise stroll down the hallway. "She's a firecracker, isn't she? Quite confident."

"Yeah, well, for this situation, the more confidence the better, right?"

She placed a lock of her golden blonde hair behind her ear. Her stark blue eyes crinkled up so that her whole face was smiling. "You'd be right."

We said our goodbyes and I jogged down the hall to catch up with Elise. Healers carrying crates of bottles with various liquids and powders stopped to look at her while others just moved out of the way as she passed.

"You could have been nicer" I said when I fell into step next to her.

"That's asking too much."

The man from earlier caught my eye and gave me a quick wave. Elise caught the gesture and snickered. "He's cute. If things don't work out with Dani, maybe he's your type."

"I think his type is Reese."

Elise snuck a glance back over to the Enchanter, eyeing him up and down before saying, "yeah, Blondie doesn't have a chance with him."

I laughed and pushed open the doors to the outside. "Yeah, and he doesn't have a chance with Natalia either."

Elise stopped short on the first step on the porch, while I trotted down all of them to the grassy ground. "Excuse me?"

The sun was at its highest point now and I had to shield my eyes from it as I looked at her. "Natalia is very much into the ladies."

"I'm never wrong about these things," she confirmed.

"You just met her girlfriend."

Elise bounded down the stairs, right as another scowl crept up to her facial features. "That woman is her girlfriend?"

We started down the path, the smell of water and cedar filling my nose. "Yeah."

"Hmph."

"What's that sound for?"

"Nothing. I don't like her."

I scoffed. "Do you like anybody?"

"Fair point. You do know how I feel about blondes."

We hustled further down the path and caught sight of Natalia, her wavy dark hair blowing in the slight breeze. The glitter on her shoulders and cheeks sparkled as she turned to us. The wreckage from earlier was gone, aside from the mangled tree trunks. As Natalia gave us a small smile, I noticed Dani behind her. She was directly in front of the sunlight, and it illuminated her skin. I had to mentally slap myself when I considered reaching out to run my hand down her arm and feel how soft her skin was. I wanted to put my face in her hair and breathe in that cinnamon scent. I wanted my face so obnoxiously close to hers that the only thing left for her to do was to kiss me. I wanted Dani, that was a fact; my cock started to strain in my jeans just by fucking looking at her. She gave me a tight-lipped smile as we approached. I had made her believe her not making a choice was it for me. Maybe it wasn't. I *wanted* her. I realized that when I looked at her the morning after our adventurous night. I wasn't thinking about her being a demon when those thoughts crossed my mind; I was just simply thinking about her just as she was, without all the extra. I needed us to fix this so I could at least have a small fraction of time to articulate my thoughts and feelings.

Dani slid her eyes slowly to Elise and started to open her frustratingly perfect mouth, but I held my hand up. "No more fighting, bickering, nothing." I looked at Elise, whose eyes were transfixed on Dani. "There is some shit you both need to talk about, but just believe me when I say you are *both* on the same team here."

"I'll believe it when she tells me the whole truth." Dani flicked her mass of curls over her shoulder.

Elise let out a sigh and looked at the ground. This was as vulnerable as she was going to get for now.

"Now we're a team?" I turned my head to see Reese come from the woods. He pushed a tree branch out of his way, ducking underneath it. His bow bounced on his back.

I placed my hands in my jacket pockets. "Yes, we are. Listen, about what I said or well, didn't say. It wasn't meant to intentionally leave you out or I don't know, make you feel like I didn't care."

Reese pulled his eyebrows in. He placed both his hands on his hips. "Nick, I don't think anyone thinks you do this shit intentionally."

"I'm sorry I kept you out of the loop."

He pulled his arm back and punched me in the shoulder. "It's okay, as long as you learned your lesson like a good boy."

I grabbed my shoulder, trying to pretend like it hurt. "If you honestly want me to run through the full explanation of everything, I can."

Reese shook his head vigorously. "Oh, fuck no. My brain can only take so much, and I think I got the gist of things. As long as you know that from now on, all information you receive, we *all* receive." He pointed his index finger and made a circle with it, enveloping all of us. He then pointed his finger at Elise. "How's that shoulder, little one? Done keeping secrets?"

Elise gave him both her middle fingers, gave Dani one last look, and then stomped away from all of us.

Reese's lips turned up into a smile as he turned to me. "I'm so ready to make some fuckers bleed."

I narrowed my eyes at him. "You and Elise are surprisingly a lot alike."

He took a step back from me. "You take that back."

Dani let out a small laugh, which caught my attention. Her smile fell when she noticed me looking and that tight facial expression was back. "We should go. I'm starting to get antsy."

Natalia nodded her agreement. "Yes, we should. I'll portal us to the grounds, get a sense of the surroundings before we head inside." We all nodded and followed her towards the path Elise took.

"I was telling Isabel that I'm surprised you're coming with us. She's a little worried," I said, speaking so that she heard me as she walked ahead of me. Natalia had long legs just like me, but somehow, she was much faster.

Natalia flattened her palms over her skirt. "She worries too much, and frankly, so does Zane. That man tends to forget that I tell him what to do and not the other way around. He'll be monitoring the walls I've put up just in case anything leaves the perimeter of The Skies." She chuckled to herself as she walked over to Dani, whose ass I had to force myself not to stare at while I walked behind her.

Reese slapped his hand down on my shoulder, startling me out of my thoughts. "Listen, if it's any consolation, I don't care that you guys had sex. I mean, it's strange and I don't want to know anything about it, but if you want to continue, I'm not going to keep you from what makes your dick happy."

I opened my mouth to speak but nothing came out – only a weird strangled noise. Finally, I found words. "Thanks. I'll, uh, keep that in mind. What did you guys talk about anyway?" The fact that I had my best friend's blessing to continue to fool around with the girl who currently did not want to fool around with me anymore was laughable if the circumstances weren't what they were.

Reese shrugged, pulling his hair tie out and letting his long hair flow. "Nothing important, just came to an understanding."

I let that relief wash over me. Everyone was on even ground now. We were either on neutral territory or back to normal. It seemed like a great way to fall into whatever was waiting for us. I had demolished the hope that everything was alright at The Skies, but the fact that nothing had extended past the building itself, meaning the outlining villages, was odd. I wanted my father and Daya to be safe, but the fact that everything seemed so contained had a shudder running up my spine. It all felt so calculated.

"Are you guys ready?" Natalia asked, giving each of us a pointed look.

Elise cocked her head to the side. "Born ready."

"Let's get this party started," Reese said.

Small curls started to fall into her eyes, but Dani let them stay as she looked at me with her intense brown eyes. We were about to go into something we likely weren't prepared for and the last time I'd kissed her was right before everything went to shit. "I asked you a while ago to figure out where your loyalties lie. Have you, Nicholas?" She said my name, every syllable a sharp cut.

She was asking me to think about what I was getting into. She was asking me if I had to make the choice to run my sword through Jonah or any one of the executives, could I? She was asking would I defend these people in front of me against the people I had listened to during my formative years. I'm pretty sure I would do all that for *her*.

Fuck, what was happening to me?

"Actions speak louder than words, right?" I volleyed back.

Her lips twitched for a moment, as if she wanted to give me one of the smiles I so desperately wanted to see. She didn't. We all watched as Natalia whipped her hand around to create a circle, the light from within it glowing bright. I severely hoped Elise and Dani could keep their shit together to get this done. I hoped Dani could believe I did want the best for her. *For her.* Not for me.

I stepped up to the light as I watched Dani disappear. Natalia gave me one last solid nod before stepping through.

I looked behind me at the lush green hedges and trees, at the flowers that constantly seemed to sprout out of nowhere, but were beautiful, nonetheless. I watched the Enchanters for a moment, living their lives as if today was the only day that mattered. I wondered if it was like this before the war. A little girl running back and forth playing hide and seek with her friends stopped to look at me and waved.

I waved back.

I could see myself spending much more time here if given the chance. No, not just myself, not *by myself*. That beating organ in my chest faltered and stuttered as I stepped through the portal thinking that I wanted to spend time here with...*her*.

CHAPTER TWENTY-FIVE

UNKNOWN

"Have you found it?" I asked one of the sentries.

The blonde boy shook his head, magically closing the lock on one of the doors to the rooms in the Ethereal Bastille. The sentries had been working diligently to bring all the useless angels down here after they were put into a slumber of sorts. I hated being this messy, but as long as they didn't get in the way, then I was fine with lumping them all together down here until it was over.

"Then keep looking; it has to be somewhere," I commanded, sneering at him. He nodded once and moved past me.

I let out a huffed sigh. This was meant to be easy. Lilith had told me that this demon was tough, but that she would fall right into our hands and it seemed like everything was falling into place. Except for this. *This* was proving difficult.

"Sir?" a voice said from behind me. I turned around to see a sentry waiting to speak.

"What is it?" I asked, clearly frustrated.

"The others are headed this way; we just got word."

Fuck. I breathed a long breath in as the sentry waited patiently for my next words. "What did she tell you to do?"

The angel cleared her throat. "She told us to be ready and prepared. Do not harm the Soul Seether, but all others are of no concern."

I thought this over. "That's fine. Be prepared to keep them alive, but do as you're told." I waved her off, needing to think. None of this would mean anything if I couldn't find what we needed. Lilith only told us so much, but I wanted this. I wanted this so much, I had killed an innocent of my own kind for this. I believed in proving my loyalty, and if she wanted it in exchange for giving me a piece of what I wanted, then so be it. That Finley boy didn't deserve it but we do what we must, I supposed. I couldn't risk exposing myself so, desperate times, desperate measures.

His portal key was heavy in my pockets every time I walked. I couldn't leave it lying around. Moira's offspring hadn't found me out, but she was smart and quick with her powers just like her mother. Lilith had expected that and made her own moves against her.

Who knew so many Enchanters down in Purgatory would be so willing to bestow their powers to another? I wasn't *that* surprised, actually. My heart stuttered as I thought about them down there, wanting out and finally seeing a way to get what they wanted.

I rubbed my temple with my index and middle finger. I thought I would need to just get to the Soul Seether after all that, but things had now gotten complicated.I didn't like that one bit. The Cassial boy and everyone else had gotten in the way.

I walked down the hall of the Ethereal Bastille and heard a commotion coming from one of the rooms. I stomped further down the hall and looked into one of the open doorways. I smirked as I came eye to eye with Jonah Zuriel. He was tied to a chair, straining against his restraints. Pieces of his clothes were torn, his face scratched and dirty. He narrowed his eyes at me and curled his lip.

"I will not stand for this! I will make you regret it all..."

I shook my head laughing as he started to create light in his hands, trying to conjure his executive magic.

"Ah, but you won't. You have an odd liking for that boy and I would hate for him to become a casualty so quickly because you decide you want to make things difficult."

Jonah halted his magic, his hands stiffening. The white flutters near his fingertips that had started to trail down his hand stopped and started to disappear. He immediately ceased all means of wanting to fight. I didn't understand it, but if the Cassial boy was what I had to dangle in front of him, then I would. "What is it that you want?" he asked, sounding exhausted.

"All in due time. You will pay for the sins of your father." I waved my hand at the sentries at his side. "Keep him alive but have your fun." I walked out of the room and listened as Jonah made a loud groan, the chair he had been tied to sounding like it hit the ground hard. I chuckled to myself as I made my way out of the Ethereal Bastille.

"Sir! Sir!" An out of breath sentry ran up to me and I placed a hand out to stop them.

I raised a brow expectedly.

"We found it." The sentry held up what I had been looking for, what Lilith had promised would be here when she arrived.

"Thank you," I said, the sentry handing it over to me. I let my chest puff out in pride. I would finally have the peace I wanted. Now, all we had to do was wait for them to come to us. I placed my hand firmly on the angel's shoulder. "Now, we wait for them to make their move."

Lilith would have what she wanted, and so would I.

CHAPTER TWENTY-SIX

NICK

It wasn't as bright as it should have been when I stepped out of the portal. The sun was high and beaming in Oculus, but peering up at The Skies, the clouds made their presence known and it felt much later in the day. It was as if the entire sun had disappeared because it too was scared of what was happening. There were no unfamiliar scents lurking around and everything *looked* like it was in place, as if nothing had really changed.

Something was missing, though.

The Skies was a place I had come to know as continuously moving. Even if you thought it was quiet, there was always someone off in the distance training, or you could hear laughing, or even the flutter of wings along the treetops. Right now, I heard absolutely nothing. A shudder went down my spine as I realized that hearing nothing was worse than seeing pools of blood or unmoving bodies. I had no idea what I was walking into, what to expect.

I took a short look around, taking into account all the people in front of me. Elise had her eyebrows turned down as she scanned the perimeter. Reese and Natalia were eyeing the looming front gates of the tall, castle-like building. Dani, I hadn't realized, was saddled up next to me, casting her gaze up at my face.

"Not what you expected?" she asked, no teasing or sarcasm laced into the words.

I shrugged, answering honestly. "Not at all."

"That makes one of us, then."

I lifted my brow at her. "You expected it to be this quiet?"

Dani smirked at me before starting to walk ahead. "Yeah, Lilith hates messes and always has someone clean them up. She likes to make things hurt and bleed, but she likes to confine her mess."

I opened my mouth, but Reese's voice cut me off. "I'm going to fly up and check the other side."

"You really think that's a good idea?" I asked, feeling like something was coming but having no clue when and what.

Reese chuckled. "I'm a big boy, my friend. I got this." He raised his hand and wiggled his fingers.

I rolled my eyes and clasped my hand with his, squeezing. He shot out his wings and pushed off the ground, darting towards the sky above. Natalia stepped up to me, narrowing her eyes.

"I don't feel anything off and I usually would right about now, unless someone is *making* it feel like this."

Gusts of wind whipped through the trees and rustled the leaves. Clumps of them moved and danced in circles before gracefully hitting the ground. There was a pit in my stomach I couldn't get rid of.

"Whatever it is must be messing with your magic, because it feels like ominous death to me," Elise stated, looking up at the darkened windows of the towers. "You live down in Purgatory long enough, that feeling is second nature to you. It couldn't hide if it tried."

"It has to be the same person who messed with the portals," Natalia said.

Elise hummed. "Sounds about right." She looked over at Dani, who was looking at something in the distance. "This is all about you, so what do you want us to do?"

Dani eyed her up and down, but then focused back where she was looking.

Elise scoffed. "Of course, you're still being a fucking brat."

"Shut up," Dani hissed.

I had my own issues with Dani, and I didn't want to get in the middle of their complicated friendship...again. A thorough perimeter check took a few minutes, but Reese was normally quick about those kinds of things and helping him over there sounded much better than being here right now.

"It's a simple question: do we wait out here for them to properly greet us or do you want to go in there and tear some heads off? You should be happy I'm even fucking asking you," Elise spat out.

"Oh, I probably should be happy you're fucking including me in things, since you didn't want to do it before." Dani's words came out seething and angry.

Natalia stood between them. "Now is not really the time for the two of you to be fighting again. Do everyone a favor and focus this... energy on something that can actually help us."

I pointed to where Reese had gone off to. "I'm going to make sure everything is okay with him over there, alright?" I wasn't really asking a question, but I assumed just ascending off into the sky would have been rude.

I was about to release my wings when I heard a crack, a tree branch. It would have been normal to hear those kinds of noises if the circumstances were different, but right now, it made the air thicker and the wind stopped in its tracks. I had my back turned to the noise, and I saw Dani look around my arm. Another crack came from my left side, causing Natalia to whip around, but when I turned my head, nothing was there. Dani was still peeking around my arm when her nose scrunched up, as if she was confused and on edge at the same time.

"Friend of yours?" Elise asked, causing me to tilt my head to the side in confusion.

A familiar voice rang out now, calling my name. "Nick?"

I turned around on my heels, reaching for the hilt of my sword strictly out of habit. "Ollie?"

The tall sentry raised a hand as he came over, his short dark hair perfectly combed, as if he had somewhere nice to be later today. Ollie had started his journey to be a sentry at the same time as Reese and me. I wouldn't have called us friends, but we'd had enough conversations for us to be friendly. We were close enough for me to be happy he was okay. The last time I remember seeing him was at my last Animus Seeking. The glossy brown leather of his sword hilt peeked over his shoulder and his long legs took quick strides towards us.

Ollie stretched his hands out in front of him. "Where have you been, man?"

"Uh, I've been around. What about you? Have you been here the whole time?"

I could feel the hesitation from the three females around me. I didn't have to look to see that their shoulders were tense, their breaths steady as if they didn't want to show how uneasy they might be.

Ollie nodded. "That whole ambush with the demons was a hot fucking mess, but we rallied and got it handled. Lost a few good guys, but it happens. Jonah and them have it all confined inside." He nodded up to the building behind us. "He didn't want anything reaching out to the other villages, you know?" His eyes darted to Natalia, then to Elise, and lastly, they landed on Dani, where they lingered for a bit before returning to me.

"Makes sense." I subtly looked behind him for signs of anyone else. *Where the fuck is Reese?*

"New friends, Nick?" Ollie asked, giving me a small smile, one side of his mouth tipping upward. His gaze yet again lingered on Dani, and it made me uncomfortable.

There was a small growl that came behind me, and I didn't have to even look to know that it was Elise. "Something like that."

"Ah, well, we should probably get inside. Jonah will be really happy you're alright." Ollie sounded so nonchalant, so easy going. He sounded like himself, but then again, he didn't. He started to walk past us, causing his shoulder to run into Natalia's as she turned around to follow him. Her breath caught and her eyes widened, but then settled back into their normal state. She glanced over at me, her brow furrowing, and she gave her head a small shake, as if she was telling me no, this didn't feel right.

"Where is everybody else?" I asked. He stopped walking and slowly turned around.

"Some of us are watching the borderline of the woods and others are inside. We saw the portal and I was told to check it out. How did you even get a key? I don't remember you ever having one." He quickly looked at Natalia, as if he knew the answer but wanted me to say it. How did he even know I had a key? I ignored his question all together. Another small growl came from Elise as she swiped her eyes along the woods, as if she was searching for something I wasn't aware of.

Ollie waited for a beat and then said, "it's whatever, come on." He cocked his head towards the entrance.

I didn't like this, and by the looks of the people around, neither did they. Ollie was a good guy, but right now, the guy I knew was a blur and the one standing in front of me seemed to want to give off friendly vibes, but the vibes were distorted and unfamiliar. "I think I'm gonna wait for Reese."

He combed his fingers through his hair. "Reese is fine, Nick. There are plenty of us around the grounds, so one of us had to have seen him and probably brought him inside."

"Reese wouldn't have just let you take him inside without letting us know he's fine." That I knew for an absolute fact.

Ollie let out a small breath, patient and steady. Elise took a few steps forward. "I don't particularly like Blondie, but I'd have to agree that he wouldn't have just left without an explanation." Elise was obnoxiously short compared to Ollie, but she stood as if she was as tall as a redwood tree. I could see black veins pulsing in the back of her arms.

"Why doesn't Jonah just come out to see us and bring us inside?" Natalia suggested, the musical lightness of her voice and the High Priestess regality pushing through. Her amber eyes scanned him, searching for something.

Ollie's dark eyes shot over to her. "He's busy. I'm going to bring you to him. I don't know why you are making this difficult." His voice sounded deeper, as if something inside of him was getting angry.

"It's not difficult, Ollie. If Jonah wants to see us, he can meet us out here. It's actually pretty simple," I said. "While he's at it, he can bring Reese out with him since he's fine, right?"

Ollie cracked his neck. "Have you always been this stubborn?"

"Yeah, but I also don't *trust* you."

The already thick air grew thicker. I could taste something on my tongue, but I couldn't make out what it was. Ollie bore his eyes into mine, as if he was trying to penetrate my very soul. "You think I'm lying?"

I didn't look away from him as I clenched and unclenched my fist, aching to get my hand around my sword. Something inside of me was screaming that I would have to use it. "I do."

Something flashed across his eyes that caused me to take a step back. It was misty and dark, that friendly demeanor disintegrating before my eyes. The darkness in his eyes had a glassy haze over it, as if his vision was misshapen. "I never really understood why Jonah took such a liking to you."

Even though I couldn't see it, I knew the thick air around us was caused by him and everyone else here. They weren't protecting the border of the woods around the The Skies; they were here, in the shadows. We were always taught to hide, track, and be stealthy in our training, but magic was never a part of that. There was something else here, something else motivating them. I heard a loud groan and the clashing of weapons where Reese had flown off to.

Elise darted her tongue out as if she was licking the air and smacked her lips together. "Oh, I know that taste. Compulsion is so heady."

"It's almost as strong as mine," Dani said under her breath.

Ollie's nostrils flared. "You want to be difficult? Fine." He reached towards the hilt of his sword. "You could have been left out of this. Protecting her, choosing them, will be the worst decision you've ever made." He said the words directly at me before he drew his sword but decided to elbow Elise hard into the side of her shoulder, sending her flying. He twirled the sword in his hand, the dark mist in his eyes deepening. The trees rustled, but not from the wind this time: from other angels. Large wings fluttered and footsteps sounded all around us.

I noticed silver tips of dark flames in my periphery and saw that both of Dani's arms were completely engulfed in dark magic. Wings flapped hard above us and feet hitting the ground to scuffling on the grass surrounded us. This was an ambush of a different kind. I recognized different faces and felt a pit in my stomach with what I was being made to do. I wasn't going to go quietly.

The angels drew their weapons as they charged towards us. Ollie swung out, causing me to jump back and snap into focus. I drew my own sword, slicing it back at him. Dani shot out rope after rope of black magic and Natalia wrapped a bright yellow electric ribbon around one sentry, closing her fist to tighten her hold, and used him as a weapon, throttling him into different angels back and forth.

They all seemed hellbent on getting to us, not letting the crack of their own bones stop them. They were like the shadow demons from before, but these were faces I knew.

Ollie's face was menacing and irritating. He swung back and forth, each turn of his sword harsher than the last. He wanted me to bleed, to feel pain. I brought my weapon down at an angle, slicing his arm. He hissed and I swiped down at the other arm, but before I could connect my blade with his skin, our weapons clashed. Under this compulsion, he felt stronger than me, but I knew our skills were the same, our training exactly the same. He shoved me back and I collected my footing before he barreled at me. I blocked his sword with my own, bringing one of my legs back for extra stability as I bent my other knee. He was using all his weight to push against me, and I was starting to sweat from pushing back at him.

I saw angels fly back from the violent blast Elise had thrown at them. She hopped up on one of their backs and brought her hands around the female angel's neck, twisting it in a grossly disturbing angle until the angel was lifeless. Elise unfurled her healed tail, picked up the body with her shadowy appendage, and chucked it towards a horde of sentries.

Dani was on the ground face down with a sentry's boot on her back. I watched as she spread her hand along the grassy surface and tendrils of black, dancing like snakes popped up from the dirt. The tendrils wrapped around the sentry's legs and throat. The black coils searched for more victims, tightening around random necks and gripping so hard, their faces turned purple. Her eyes had turned midnight black, telling me her darker half had been let out to play.

I was so fixated on watching her work that Ollie had seen his opening and kicked his leg out, and I fell forward as he moved out of the way. My sword fell out of my grip and instead of picking it up, I used my hands to block Ollie's foot from landing on my throat. I grabbed the bottom of his shoe and shoved him back. I jumped up and before he could catch his footing, I shot my left foot out and kicked him in the stomach. He stumbled back into a tree trunk. I reached down for my sword and turned back to see him gripping his own so tightly, his knuckles were white.

A bolt of green light hit a tree near us. The tree shook and trembled, but then it cracked, breaking in half and falling over, crushing the sentries in its path. I fought back and forth with Ollie as he thrusted his sword at me. He was fast on his feet, and I felt a slice of burning pain when he cut my thigh, and when I thought he was going to cut again, a blast hit my back, causing me to topple over. I fumbled to keep my sword in my grip, but it was no use; it tumbled out of my hand, but not out of reach. All the breath had left my body, making me feel as if my head had been shoved under water for too long. I saw sparks of gold light around me; I looked over my shoulder to see another angel with those same sparks bouncing around their fingers.

Ollie kicked me over so that he could plant his feet on either side of my shoulders. His arm was leaking blood from where I struck him. We had trained to do the same job, but all those hours of training had led to this. "I can't believe Jonah actually thought you were one of the best." He lifted his sword, threatening to plunge it into my throat when I saw the distinct line of an arrow behind him. That same arrow sunk into the back of the sentry who had hit me with his magic and then pushed through the front of his stomach and straight into Ollie's back. The tip of the arrow was silver, and the point gleamed even though the sun was nowhere to be found.

I would know those arrows anywhere.

I heard a rapid flutter of wings when I saw Reese hit the ground.

He had blood on his face, and it decorated his hands and forearms, splotches marking his tan skin. He swung his bow at his side, his quiver securely attached to his back. He pushed the sentry over with the pad of his finger, the angel hitting the ground hard. Ollie looked down at his stomach, right as Reese pulled the arrow out, blood spurting out and hitting my face. I reached out my arm, grabbing my blade. I hadn't wanted it to come to this, but this wasn't a moment to think. I gave Ollie a meaningful look before pushing my sword so far into his chest that the hilt hit his sternum. Blood rushed out of his mouth, but it wasn't all red as it should be: black was infused along with it. As his knees hit the ground, his eyes returned to their normal color and he looked lost, sad. I pulled my sword from him and watched as his body slumped over, unmoving.

Reese stepped between the bodies and leaned forward a bit, extending his arm out towards me. I gratefully grasped his hand and let him haul me up. We gave each a quick hug, then Reese swallowed hard before looking at the two bodies at our feet as the sound of shrieks, growls, and grunts filled the grounds of The Skies.

"What the fuck is going on?" Reese asked, exasperation in his voice. "One minute I'm scanning the exterior, the next minute that one girl I dated a year ago— Emma something— comes barreling at me with a fucking spear. I didn't even know we used spears!" There was a tear in his shirt, the torn edges soaked in blood. I narrowed my eyes at it, trying to make out how bad it was.

Reese waved me off, pushing his hair out of his face. "Don't worry, it's not deep. I dodged out of the way before she could do any real damage. Fucking ambushes, man; luckily, most of this blood isn't mine. There were four of them, but I guess I lucked out better than you guys." He looked over his shoulder at the carnage. I looked along with him as Natalia placed her hand out and shot magic at the ground, causing the dirt and grass to rise up like a makeshift hill and barrel towards a group of sentries. Dani caught arrows released at her, one by one, turning them to dust. She kept one and it became less like a common weapon, suddenly covered in shadow and silver. Angels charged towards her, and she used that one arrow to gut them.

"They've been manipulated into killing us, apparently. Dani is who they want; we're just casualties. Just like the demons at the meeting."

Elise was high in the sky fighting airborne angels, using her tail to whip them to the ground or using her magic to lasso them around the neck and bring them to her so she could punch through their chest.

"If this is what's going on out here, what the fuck is going on inside?" Reese wondered.

"That's what I'd like to know as well."

Reese took one long look at Elise in the sky, a smile on her face as she released her venom from her hand and pressed it to an angel's throat. He let out a long, solid breath before looking back at me. "I'll head back up there. Let's hope she doesn't mistake me for one of them." Reese punched me in the shoulder and shot up towards the sky.

I twirled my sword in my hand, having to step to the side as a bolt of glittering light nearly hit me in the face. Even though I knew this fight wouldn't be easy and it would get even harder the moment we got inside, my focus was clearer now. I quickened my steps as I lunged forward, slicing my sword in front of me, watching as it shredded flesh and blood spewed onto the grass. I made quick foot-work of getting around attacks and dodging weapons. An arrow came down and pierced my shoulder, causing me to turn around and raise my sword, deflecting another. Reese came behind my attacker, knocking him out with one end of his bow, giving me a thumbs up afterwards. His wings billowed around him, a stark white in the cloudy sky. I mimicked the gesture, suddenly having to block a blade threatening to come down on me.

I hadn't thought about how many sentries there were here and how many more would be coming. They were coming out of the woods and seemed to be multiplying as we went. They were like the demons from before but they still had their souls intact, just being blinded. It would have taken so much magic to gather all these angels and manipulate their minds. Every time I looked over at Dani, they were never trying to kill her; rough her up a bit, yeah, but kill her? No. My shoulder ached from the arrow I ripped out, but my adrenaline raced.

"Natalia! Can you...." I started, wanting to scream to Natalia to try to nullify this in any way, but then I heard a low, raspy groan from above me. I watched as one of Elise's wings was sliced from top to bottom. The leather membrane of it shuddered and she faltered. She tried to release magic from her hand but keeping herself upright and steady in the sky was proving more of a priority. A sentry came up behind her, grabbed her other wing, and threw her down towards the ground.

At that moment, we all lost our focus. The fight in front of us mattered, but as Elise sailed to the ground, I blocked one blow from a sentry at my side, slicing across her neck as I watched Natalia follow Elise's falling body. She looked unfocused, and a broad sentry quickly took advantage, knocking the end of his dagger at the back of her head. Elise landed on the ground with a thud, the back of her head hitting a thin rock.

My eyes instinctively closed, but I opened them right as Reese shot two arrows, one for an angel near him and another for one below him. A female sentry hurriedly came up behind him, wrapping her own bow around his neck. Reese tried to knock her out with his own bow, but the sudden takeover caused another angel to tear his hands from his beloved weapon and thrust the bow at his stomach. Reese was never good when it came to his own angelic magic. He had never found a need to learn more about it, since he could rely so heavily on the things he was good at. I could tell he was regretting that now. The female behind him was strong enough to press her bow hard against his throat. I saw the moment he was out and they let him drop, hitting the ground just as hard as Elise.

I started to run over to him, to try to regain the momentum we had, but I was stopped dead in my tracks by the tip of a blade and an unfamiliar face. I may not have known the angel in front of me, but the malice on her face was the same as Ollie's had been. She was there, but she wasn't. The dark magic that loomed in her body, the thing telling her to kill, eliminate, obey, was just too strong for her to fight off. I raised my sword, knowing I had to steel myself. I stepped back, only to feel the tip of another blade at my back.

I sought out Dani, who was flinging sentries away from her left and right. She was oozing shadowy magic and her eyes were even darker than I had realized. She shot back one sentry and turned around to roundhouse kick another, but this one caught her leg and yanked her to the ground. He swiftly picked her up by her throat as magic escaped his hand.

Steam pulsed out continuously as he held her up, and she let out the most gut turning scream I'd ever heard. The scream pulled at my heart, tugged on all sides of what beat in my chest. Angelic magic could be beautiful, but it could also be highly dangerous. Even if Dani's internal angelic magic recognized the one harming her, it would be afraid of the level of aggression this man was aiming at her.

"I think you've had enough fun for now," the female sentry said as I looked away from Dani. I tried to bring my sword up again, still willing to fight, but the angel behind me brought the end of their foot to my back and hit me hard. I fell to my knees, pain in my thighs, but the angel in front of me stopped me from falling over. She pressed her fingers into the wound at my shoulder, and I let out a closed mouth scream. She looked over my shoulder at the sentry behind me, and I felt a sharp blade stab into the back of my other shoulder. My eyes widened and I bit down on my tongue, tasting blood. The sentry swiftly pulled their sword out, and I bit harder.

I was sweating and my vision was blurry from the pain. I looked over at where the sentry had Dani held up by her throat, but another angel came up to him and exchanged a few quick words. Angels were dragging Reese and Elise along the ground towards the entrance. Another had placed Natalia over his shoulder and followed them.

Dani blinked her eyes open, looking drunk and tired. The angel holding her nodded at his counterpart, then head butted her so that she slumped over, knocking her out.

I felt the blood leaking from my shoulders and every time I tried to keep my eyes open, it was like it hurt worse than the first time. The world around me swayed but I saw a figure coming towards us.

They looked familiar, almost like I recognized her...him...everything was fucking blurry. They walked over to where the sentry had Dani in his arms.

"If you damaged her, she will have your fucking head. Not to mention, you've made a fucking mess. *He* won't like it."

It was a woman, but I couldn't make out her voice, where I knew it from. The ringing in my ears was making it impossible to hear much. I saw her look over to me and then to my assailants, nodding. She sashayed away as if she didn't have a care in the world.

I would be going inside, but not in the way I wanted.

None of this was what I wanted.

The large sentry carried Dani away, his figure becoming smaller the further he walked. I wanted to help her, I wanted to help all of them, but I was just so fucking tired. I saw the shadow of an arm above my head and I watched as it came down right at the side of my head. Pain took over as the blunt end of a sword hilt connected with my skull.

Everything went black.

MY HEAD WAS KILLING ME. THE THROBBING PAIN WAS TOO MUCH. I FELT LIKE my skull was going to rip out of my head. This sort of pain was foreign to me, the kind that caused your eyes to stay shut but also made you want to vomit. I tasted blood in my mouth and tried to press my lips together, feeling how dry they were. My head throbbed again, reverberating through every tiny pocket of my fucking brain. I tried to lift my arms and apply pressure to my skull with my hands, but I couldn't.

I couldn't move my hands, my arms staying still. I tried again and realized my hands were tied behind my back. I felt the throbbing return with every ounce of strength I tried to use to release my hands. My wrists cried out in pain from my useless attempt. Magic bound my wrists but I didn't know what kind. I forced my eyes open, my vision blurry and fogged. I lowered my eyelids and took a slow breath in and out, trying again. I took my time, letting my eyes open a small bit at a time.

The room came into view, furniture and colors slowly coming together. I gently moved my head, noticing I was on the floor, sitting on my knees. A large table sat in front of me, and I could hear voices scattered throughout the room. None of the voices were easily recognizable. The room itself was starting to become clear to me, though.

We were in a briefing room.

This was the same room we had been in when the ambush happened.

There were darkened marks on the table and the window was still stained with remnants of blood. All of that seemed so long ago, but every moment of it was so fresh in my mind. I heard a groan next to me and looked to my left, noticing Elise and Reese both in the same position as me, hands behind their back, sitting on their knees. Elise had her head slumped forward, but she let out groans of pain, letting me know she was eventually going to wake up and she wouldn't be happy when she did. Dark red, almost black liquid was coming down the back of her neck, while some of it had already hardened. I saw the slight glow of the magic dampening handcuffs around her wrists, but they didn't just shine a golden light this time. The light had an undertone of other colors, proving to me that other magic was at play here.

Reese looked like he was starting to blink but I couldn't tell. I tried to get a better look, but then a hand came down on my shoulder, intentionally pressing into my open wound.

"Ah, looks like this one is awake." I peered up at them. It was the same angel who had stopped me in my tracks. She wasn't looking at me when she was talking, though. I followed her line of sight, seeing another sentry coming towards her. Her voice was harsh when she spoke again. "Is she awake yet?"

Another female sentry shook her head. "Not yet. He said she would come to eventually." She snuck a glance over to me and nodded her head in my direction. "What are we doing with them?"

The first shrugged, still grasping onto my shoulder. "We were supposed to be waiting for them to wake up, but now–" She squeezed my shoulder, causing me to let out a grunt. "I'll have to let them know they are starting to come to." She shoved me away from her and walked alongside the other as they made their way across the room.

I darted my eyes around, searching every part of the room that I could see from my vantage point. I caught sight of black hair, long and wavy, from the top of one of the chairs at the table. The head it was attached to moved slightly back and forth, until those honey eyes locked onto mine. I widened my eyes at Natalia, who had her hands firmly planted face down on the table. I wondered why she wasn't doing more, causing some sort of scene. Her forearms were prone and I noticed the muscles ticking in her arms. She was trying to move her hands but something was keeping her in place. Something told me that dampening magic was also in place to keep any mental magic she had in check.

I was on the floor behind the chair at the end of the long table, but Natalia caught my eye again, tilting her head to the other side of the table. With some pain, I shuffled to the right, trying to see around the chair. My heart pulled in my chest, my breathing stunted in my throat. That cascading heap of curls were slumped over Dani's shoulders and her head was tilted to the side. Despite the situation, she looked peaceful and fuck...she was beautiful. Even with the lengthy burn scars on her neck and the blood that caked her hands, she was someone I couldn't take my eyes off of.

Both her hands were cuffed to the chair, gold magic dampening cuffs with the colorful streams of magic curling around them, and a few sentries were watching her like hawks. I pulled at my wrists again, but yet again, I felt a sting of pain, as if the more I tried to release myself the tighter they got. I sucked in a breath, looking back at Natalia, who simply pressed her lips together, giving me a sorrowful look. She was at a loss for what to do.

A snort-like groan came from beside me, sliding my eyes over to the demon opening her eyes. Those gray eyes shot around the room, and she tried to move her arms, but they weren't budging. She shuffled from knee to knee, trying to wiggle her way out, but all she got in return was more agitation. The sentries around us started to notice her movements and most of them smirked at her attempts to break free.

"What the fuck is going on?" Elise barked, teetering on her knees again.

A male sentry grabbed her by her neck, stilling her. His eyes had the same lost, blackened look as the others, his auburn hair falling in front of his face. "How about you stay still before I make you?"

Elise made her eyes into tiny slits, curving her mouth into one of disgust. "How about you get out of my face, before I bite the flesh off yours?"

The sentry scoffed and pushed her back, letting go of her neck. He cracked his neck and made his way over to Reese, who was just now starting to open one of his eyes. He peered over at me and Elise, and then took in the rest of the room. The male sentry stood right in front of Reese, looking down at him with a smirk. "You finally awake, princess?"

Reese raised an eyebrow at him but said nothing. The male sentry bent slightly at the knees. "I asked you a question; it's only polite to answer." He grabbed Reese's face, placing his fingers near his cheeks and squishing his mouth together. Reese's eyebrows scrunched together as he tried to get out of the man's hold. The sentry let him go, but not without landing a hard slap on the side of his face.

"You all are so pathetic you couldn't even kill us?" Elise sneered.

Reese moved his jaw from side to side. "You really want to know why they didn't kill us?"

Elise licked her lips and ignored him, looking straight at her target.

The male sentry leaned against the chair at the head of the table, looking bored and unimpressed by her. "Change of plans."

I cleared my throat, taking one short look at Dani and then looking away. "Where are the others?"

The sentry looked at me, his dark, misty eyes unnerving. "Others?"

"The other angels. I would hardly think it would make any sense to just murder everyone."

A female sentry spoke up. "A chunk of them are in the Ethereal Bastille; others are having a nice little slumber in their rooms thanks to a healthy dose of sleeping magic."

"For that many people, you would need strong magic to project that kind of dormancy magic," Natalia said, pressing her fingertips into the table.

Another sentry chuckled. "Aw, are you jealous that you aren't the most powerful Enchanter, your Highness?" The sentry plucked a strand of Natalia's hair and twirled it around her finger, tugging so that the High Priestess winced from the pain. "Don't worry, once little miss Soul Seether over there wakes up, everything will go as planned."

At that moment, Dani made a soft noise that caught everyone's attention. It was like she was trying to swallow, but it just came out like short breaths. Her chest rose and fell in short bursts, but then she was awake, as if someone had jolted her with a bolt of lightning. She frantically looked around the room. Her hair fell into her face, sweat beaded on her forehead and neck, her hands clenched and unclenched. Her eyes found mine almost instantly, and I didn't know what to say when she looked at me like that. I had never witnessed that look on her face. The look of unknowing, it was so different from the look she had when I had taken her away from Cullen's body. I wanted to tell her that everything was going to be okay, but I didn't know if that was true. If I said that, I would be lying to both of us.

The doors on the opposite side of the room opened with a screech. The sound of wood on stone resounded through the room. I heard stomping feet and the sound of someone hauled along with them. A sentry pulled out one of the empty chairs and slid it to one side of the room, so all of us could see it.

My mind was scrambling for answers when I saw who the sentries were carrying in. They dragged him along, since he could hardly walk on his own to the chair. He looked almost relieved to be able to sit, even if the situation was dire. They threw him in the chair, and he tried to straighten in the armchair, but his body wouldn't let him, so slumping against one of the armrests would have to do. He took in shallow breaths as he gazed along the room, but when he got to me, it was like he was seeing a ghost.

"Jonah," I said, the words leaving my lips in as much confusion as I could muster.

He wasn't the bad guy, unless he was taking this whole thing to an entirely new level. I glanced at Natalia, whose eyes started to glass over a bit as if she could cry at any minute, but like the regal figure she was, she held them in.

Jonah opened his mouth to speak but nothing came out. He took in more breaths that looked like they hurt. There were scratches on his face and burn marks on his hands. His clothes looked like they had been ripped, and there were patches of blood in various places. He was alive. That's what mattered.

Jonah wasn't the problem. It looked like someone had a problem *with* Jonah.

"What does she want from me?" Dani yelled, looking around the room.

No one answered her. They all seemed to be waiting for something. Someone.

A male sentry with a buzzcut, the one who burned her neck, came up from behind her chair and yanked her head back by her hair. "Just wait and see, pretty girl."

My blood boiled, and I didn't know if it was the way he was touching her, how he talked to her, or what. She shook her head to get out of his grasp and he just pulled her hair harder. He leaned down to her ear but whispered loud enough for us to hear. "You cooperate and I won't have to burn that pretty neck of yours again." He shoved her head forward and stepped back. I could see the movements in Dani's jaw, telling me she was grinding her teeth together.

"Maybe she'll even let your friends live," the sentry who had slapped Reese in the face added, patting Elise on the head. She growled and snapped her teeth at him. "But I doubt it."

"None of us understand any of this. Are we meant to just be a part of this without any understanding?" Natalia asked, squaring her shoulders. Even from here, I could see her crown tattoo trying to glow, trying to regain its strength.

Click, click, click.

The sound of heels on the stone floor had us all looking in the direction of the distinct noise. I caught Reese's hazel eyes side-eyeing me, and I mirrored the look back. Jonah narrowed his eyes at the doorway and wrapped his fingers around the chair's armrest, as if he knew what he would be anticipating. My heart beat in an unsteady rhythm as I waited.

Click, click, click.

"Oh, but sweetheart, the mystery is the best part," a female voice rang out through the stone. I knew that voice. I'd heard it before.

Natalia stiffened as the *click, click* of heels got closer. She started to shake her head as if she needed to get the voice out but it wouldn't let her go. "No."

I racked my mind, the throbbing thankfully subsiding.

I heard it today before I got knocked out.

I heard it when I went back in time, that female with the cloak who had fucked with our portal to the human world.

I heard it...

In Oculus.

Isabel

Blonde hair swished as she entered the room, leaning against the threshold. She placed her hands in the pockets of her pants and smiled. It was a lazy smile, but confidence and deceit hid behind it. She narrowed her eyes at Natalia and that lazy smile turned into one of mischief. "Aw, why so sad, sweetheart? Are you upset you couldn't figure it out?" Her tone was mocking and sarcastic.

"I knew I didn't fucking like her," Elise barked.

Isabel cut her eyes to Elise. "I'm not very fond of you either, I can assure you."

"Who are you?" Reese asked, huffing in a breath.

"Natalia's traitorous fucking girlfriend," Elise snapped. "Told you you were shit out of luck with her."

Reese opened his mouth, but nothing came out. When he started to speak, Natalia beat him to it.

"Why?" Natalia asked in a small voice.

Isabel walked towards Natalia and perched herself on the wooden table next to her girlfriend's chair. She reached her hand out, cupping Natalia's chin. "All in due time." Natalia tried to pull away from her grasp, but the traitorous Enchanter just held on tighter. "Oh, don't be like that. Maybe if you didn't make it so easy to earn your trust, you could have prevented all of this. Poor little queen so desperate for someone to love you."

"Just leave her alone!" Dani yelled from across the table. Isabel swung her head in her direction.

She smirked. "Don't worry, Soul Seether. She isn't the one we want, but you know that. Beautiful Natalia here was just a means to an end." Isabel hopped off the table and sauntered over to me, the angels parting a way for her. "You're all collateral. I wouldn't have cared if you died out there, but he thought it would be better to keep you alive—for now." She looked down at where I was on the ground, her eyebrows raised.

She clapped her hands together. "Oh, this came together so wonderfully!" She patted the top of my head. "You get to see your little girlfriend do what she does best. Exciting, isn't it, Nicholas?"

I let out a grunt. "Just let us go, Isabel, or tell us what's going on."

She pushed her pink lips out into a pout. "Now that would ruin all the fun, wouldn't it? I will tell you one thing, though." Isabel cocked her head to the side, her blonde hair moving with her. "It's amazing what the power of so many willing Enchanters can do for you. It's overwhelming, but it was a necessary evil. Seducing a queen is easy, but breaking through their power, now that—, she brought her hand up and colorful magic crackled from her

fingertips, growing larger. Her eyes shifted with the various colors that bounced around her hand. "That is something that takes much more strength."

"You bitch," Natalia spat out.

Isabel slightly turned and pointed her index finger at Natalia, a small spark of blue shooting out from her fingertip and right at the High Priestess's mouth. Natalia instantly closed her mouth and tried to open it again but couldn't. She made muffled noises from behind her lips, and Isabel gave a *tsk*, wiggling her index finger. "No need for name calling, my love."

Isabel moved past Jonah like he wasn't even there, but he followed her movements.

She walked around, stopping at Elise and swatting her hand across the side of her face before moving onto Reese and simply rolling her eyes before moving towards Dani. Dani stiffened as she got close, her dark eyes darting to Reese and then to Elise, who was seething next to me. Isabel twirled one of Dani's curls around her finger. "You would have made an interesting angel."

She was taunting all of us. She was a bitch, that was for sure. Dani twitched at the way Isabel was pulling her hair.

"Fuck you," Dani said. She was angry. She had every right to be. "Fuck you and whatever plan Lilith has. Whatever she wants, I'm not doing it."

Isabel grabbed under her chin, bringing her face up. Magic moved from her fingers to Dani's chin, and I heard Dani groan as Isabel's magic seeped down her neck. "Oh, you'll do it. You have a very handsome reason to do everything we say, now don't you, Soul Seether?" She tilted Dani's head to look at me. Dani looked like she was lost, like she had no sure-fire way out of this. She didn't.

None of us did.

"Now, now, Isabel, let's not tarnish our prized possessions," a voice echoed through the room. It sounded as if it was coming from beyond the door.

I watched as Jonah closed his eyes and started to get up, as if he was ready to fight, but two sentries pressed down on his shoulders, keeping him in place. He looked at me, as if pleading for me to do something. I didn't know what he wanted *me* to do. I wanted to help him, and I wanted to help the demon that my heart rapidly decided to beat for, but as I tried to pull on my restraints, it was still no use.

Isabel let Dani go with a bratty sigh and crossed her arms over her chest.

Footsteps echoed as they got closer and closer. A small smile crept up on Isabel's face as she waited. Elise kept her eyes on the entrance to the room, while Reese gave me another confused look, which I volleyed back. The voice sounded familiar, but it was different. This voice sounded dark and demanding.

"You are quite the little liar, Nicholas." The footsteps got closer and closer.

I furrowed my brow in confusion.

I heard a zip through the room, like the sound of an arrow sailing through the air. A thud sounded and then cracking wood reverberated around the room. We all stared at what looked like a blade now stuck in the middle of the long table. The blade was angled into the wood as if it was hooked at the end. The hilt was leather, rich and brown. The middle had razor slits that looked sharp, even from where I was on the floor.

Isabel's eyes flashed with magic as she stared at it.

Dani zeroed in on the weapon in the middle of the table, her eyes glued to it.

I didn't have to look at the etchings carved into the silver to know what it said. I knew exactly what it said. It was her dagger, and it was out of my room and right in front of us.

I noticed Elise had stunted her breathing, her eyes on the weapon as well.

My eyes were pulled from the dagger when a figure walked into the room.

"Oh my god," Reese said, eyes fixed on the man who had entered the room. I looked at him and realized his eyes were locked on mine. A knowing look was written all over his face.

I was so stupid.

"A bad liar at that." He cocked his head to the dagger, running a hand through the side of his gray hair.

I pressed my lips together and took a breath, trying to steel myself for whatever came next. "Why are you doing this, Markus?"

CHAPTER TWENTY-SEVEN

DANI

The golden cuffs bit into my wrists but the pain wasn't what had me scowling. I was scowling at the man who had finally let us see what he really was. Markus was free of his lies and deceit, but that just meant we all had to suffer for it. Despite the dampening powers of the handcuffs, I could feel the magic seeping off my dagger lodged in the table. I blinked away from it and up at Natalia, who had her own scowl on her face. Her scowl was aimed at Isabel, who was smiling slyly over at Markus.

I just didn't understand what any of this was about.

Markus walked into the room as if he didn't have a care in the world. The possessed sentries seemed to follow his every move. Every single step he took was accounted for.

"Why are you doing this, Markus?" Nick said from the floor, anger and confusion lacing his words.

Markus just chuckled, swiping at the lapels of his blue suit. "Hiding that beautiful weapon from me was a valiant effort." His gray hair was slicked back now, as if he took the time to look his best just for this occasion. He sauntered over to the chair at the head of the table, pulling it back and taking a seat. He raised a hand, curling one of his fingers in a *come here* motion. Three sentries stood in front of Nick, Elise, and Reese, grabbing them by their forearms, yanking them up.

Elise tried to shake her way out of their hold, but it was useless. They practically dragged her closer to Markus. Isabel raised her eyebrows at her as she passed. Nick and Reese both looked like they were surveying the surroundings, attempting to seek a way out. The sentries stopped when they deemed themselves close enough to Markus and he turned his head to Nick.

"You know, you really do remind me of your father. Always wanting to be the best, fix things, but really having no idea how to do it." He shook his head. "I really didn't want it to come to this, Nicholas, I swear."

"You don't know anything about my father."

Markus gave a curious smile. "I know enough."

"So, you're working with Lilith?" Reese cut in.

Markus waved his hand dismissively. "Working for, working with. Depends how you look at it. The goal is the same, so it honestly doesn't matter. She isn't all that bad, you know."

Elise snorted. "Right. Let's not continue with all these fucking lies."

"I wouldn't be such a smartass. *She* isn't so happy with you," Isabel stated, leaning against the wooden table. She brushed the back of her hand along my cheek. "You let this one have too much free reign, but that's no matter. She's *not* all that surprised you were a stow away on this little adventure."

Elise blinked her gray eyes over to me before she looked back at Isabel. The blonde Enchanter smirked at her. "Who knew you were such a softie?" Elise tried to shuffle out of the sentry's hold, but he placed his hand on the back of her neck, pulsing out magic to choke her. She gargled out sounds between labored breaths. Isabel giggled next to me.

"Enough of that. You all had your fun on the lawn, alright?" Markus nodded towards the dagger stuck in the table. "Bring it to me."

One of the sentries at the far end of the room hustled over, ripping it from the wood and presented it to him. Markus stroked the smooth side of the blade, letting his fingers move over the grooves. "This all could have been so simple, Jonah. If you would have just listened to me, heard me out, I wouldn't have had to go to these lengths. Now look at us, at odds with one another. You even made me lock up poor Ariel, annoying prick that he is. " He pointed the dagger at Jonah, who had two sentries at his side, their hands on his shoulders. "You should have seen the look on his face when I turned against them."

"Jonah, Isabel, Lilith, my dagger, me–what the fuck do you want?" I spat out from my seat. I was frustrated and more than slightly exhausted at beating around the bush. All the secrets, all the lies; it was bullshit.

Markus gave me a small smile as he placed the tip of the blade on the table and twirled it. "You, precious one, you were living your perfect human life when this all started. You want to blame me for all of this? The man who started all of this is long dead." He lazily glanced at Jonah. "Your father would be so disappointed in you."

Nick furrowed his brow, trying to keep up with everything he was hearing.

Markus cleared his throat, letting the dagger lay flat against the wooden table. "We all used to live in peace. *All* of us. There was always some strain when it came to demons and angels, but everyone knew their place. Oculus; Oculus was the place where you could run into anybody." He tapped the hilt of the dagger, leaning back in his chair. "Your mother was so adamant on making everyone feel welcome. Every. Single. Person." He locked his eyes on Natalia, who swallowed hard.

Markus raised his eyebrows. "Isaac Zuriel was selfish and a beast of a leader. He hated your mother, hated that she was so well liked, so powerful, so accepting. Angels would rather have spent time in Oculus than training here at The Skies. That was a fact; I was one of them." His hands wrapped around the ends of the armrests.

"I was never on his side, Markus!" Jonah yelled, wincing.

Markus let out a joyless laugh. "You didn't do anything about it, though, now did you?"

"I was a child!"

"You were a grown man! You could have stood up to him, but you didn't!" Markus pushed the chair back sharply, the skidding sound sharp in my ears.

"What do you want with my dagger?" I shouted, anger bubbling through my body.

Isabel yanked my head back by my hair, causing me to yelp. I noticed Nick shifting in the sentries' arms, as if he wanted to rush over to me. "It's terribly rude to interrupt, Soul Seether. Wait your turn." She shoved my head forward, blowing a kiss towards Natalia, who just narrowed her honey eyes.

Markus wiped his hands down the front of his jacket and quickly swiped a hand through his hair, collecting himself. He sidled up next to Nick before he continued. "Intimacy between our kinds was always bound to happen, but it hadn't between an angel and a demon in a very long time. If it did, no one knows about it, or they never bore any children. Too many unknowns and past myths and legends about what they could create, until Moira decided to house a demon- angel couple who were pregnant."

His eyes went sad, and I knew how this story would play out. I'd heard it before, straight from Daya's mouth. The story was the same, but hearing from Markus seemed different.

"You see, Nicholas, halflings can be dangerous if not given the proper attention and training. It never ended happily. Their powers can be so volatile, they kill everyone around them. It's true they can favor one parent's powers over the other, but as they grow, they would surpass the highest executive, the Queen of Hell, and even Moira herself."

Lilith didn't want that. She didn't want something stronger than her, even an infant. She was ruthless. Lilith could deal with Jonah's father and Natalia's mother, but this child was an unknown, an outlier. Lilith hated outliers."

Markus placed his hand on Nick's shoulder. Nick tried to flinch away but couldn't. "That child didn't even make it past its first year before being slaughtered. Now, you're probably wondering by whom?" Markus reached over for my dagger and tapped it against Nick's cheek. "And how is this relevant to why you're here?"

527

"All this started over a fucking baby?" Reese asked, sounding stunned.

"Oh, Mr. Diniel, wars have been started over less, I assure you," Markus answered. "The enchanters were outraged this had happened on their territory, angels and demons were beside themselves, it was a goddamn mess. I had always thought Lilith herself removed that child from existence, but that wasn't what made me angry, unlike everyone else."

I narrowed my eyes, considering all the facts. Where was he going with this?

"The cracks started to show." He traced the hooked tip of the blade along Nick's cheek. "Isaac seemed to have heard that Enchanters had killed it. Enchanters thought it was demons and the demons thought it was the angels. Isaac just needed one word from any source, and he saw red. He believed Enchanters had too much magic, too much power. He wanted Moira to give them up, make them rescind their powers, but she refused. She didn't think her people were capable of such a heinous crime in the first place."

Markus dropped his hand and lightly pushed Nick out of the way as he stalked over to Jonah. I watched as his hand flexed around the dagger's hilt. He stood in front of Jonah, his back to us, but his voice boomed around the room for us to hear. "Enchanters didn't trust demons, but your father was making it hard for them to trust *him*. He pushed them away, right into the waiting arms of the Queen of Darkness herself. She spoke of embracing their powers, while he spoke of ending them."

"And when the time to choose came. They apparently chose wrong, isn't that right, Jonah?" Isabel muttered, rounding the table and settling next to Natalia, tracing her finger over her sealed lips. I saw the sparks of magic and Natalia took in a large breath when she realized she could open and close her mouth again.

"My father never spoke to me about his plans. He told me after the decision was made. I wouldn't have been able to stop him; he didn't listen to me! I never wanted him to do anything like that. I was great friends with Moira and Enchanters alike. I never wanted any of that!"

"My mother wouldn't have let him get away with that," Natalia countered.

Markus let out a soft chuckle. "She was fiercely strong, your mother, but not enough."

I ground my teeth together so hard, I felt a pain in my jaw. "Your storytelling is fucking wonderful, but what does any of that have to do with you or anything you have against Jonah?"

Markus didn't turn to her. He just cocked his head to the side as if he was examining Jonah. "Your father brought all those sentries to scare them into submission but ended up doing what he always wanted. He slaughtered all those people. More innocents died that day. *She* died that day, Jonah!"

My ears perked up at his infliction, at the way he leaned into the word *she*. His voice was heavy and earnest.

"You lost someone in that fight," I said, almost to myself, but Markus slowly turned around and eyed me. Isabel stared at me from over her shoulder as she traced lazy lines up and down Natalia's forearm.

Markus hummed, smoothing one side of his gray hair down. "Yes. I loved her, and Isaac had no remorse for any of those lost."

Isabel turned around and leaned against the table. "We both lost someone. Someone we both held dear." She eyed me with a malicious glint in her blue eyes. "My *mother*."

Reese let out a choking noise and a sentry shoved his back to shush him. "You had a thing with her mom? I almost got impaled with a spear because you want to avenge your dead girlfriend?"

Isabel shot her eyes to him, glowing with a rainbow of color. Reese started wheezing, as if his airway was closing. "You will not speak about my mother. Ever." She blinked and he coughed, taking in one harsh breath after another.

"Why didn't you try to prevent it your fucking self?" I said, the cuffs on my wrist starting to cut. The magic they exuded was burning into them.

"I was a mere peasant to Isaac. We all were, unless we were the absolute best. I thought perhaps his son could stop him, but he was useless and weak, trying to make amends with the people he let live in hiding for so long." Markus sneered as the words came out of his mouth.

"And me? Why am I so important to Lilith? To any of you?" I said, my mouth curling up in annoyance. I peeked a glance over at Nick, who was surveying Jonah, but I could tell this part of the conversation highly interested him.

Markus walked over to the table, my dagger still gripped in his hand. "Ah, the looming question, I'm sure. You see, after Moira created that barrier blocking Lilith and the Enchanters from getting out, I was furious with the whole ordeal, and young Isabel here was forced to be without a mother. Those Enchanters didn't deserve that, and even though I didn't particularly like Lilith, I hated Isaac even more. Isaac turned this place into a militia and wanted to bleed it onto his son, so I decided I couldn't do it anymore, even if that meant defecting.

"Angels were actively avoiding Purgatory. Of course, I had other ideas, portal monitoring and portal keys a thing of the future, so I took young Isabel with me and sought out Lilith. We were found quite quickly and brought to her, probably assuming she would end my life. I made my plea, telling her my story, speaking of Isabel and how I wished to change things. She regarded me with interest, looked Isabel over, and simply told me she had no place for me there." Markus placed the dagger on the table and flicked the hilt, watching as it spun in a circle. I looked over at Elise, who had an eyebrow raised.

"She did have other ideas," Markus continued. "She confided her plans to me. That baby had set her off wondering what a halfling of her own could do. She would have to make sure the soul was strong enough and willing, even if unknowingly. She had plans that had to be harbored and nourished until they were ready to bloom and be executed. Lilith wanted me to muster up my feelings and remain here, watching as Isaac died and Jonah took power. She carved out a piece of my soul so I could hear her, know when she called me, when she needed me."

I flinched at the idea of that, at Lilith planning all of this fucked up mess so long ago. Biding her time. Waiting. "And you?" I glanced at Isabel, who practically broke out in a beaming grin as she answered.

"Markus went back. I remained in Purgatory, cared for by fellow Enchanters and Lilith herself. You see, if I just started fumbling around with Moira's barrier, that would have caused issues and ruined our plans. I unfortunately don't have enough power to remove it completely, but I could breach the portal a small bit to let her through now and again. She would find angelic souls and they would reject her help, or she would bring them back and they would be disappointments. But...you, oh *you* were everything she imagined." Isabel placed her hands together in front of her chest. "Once she had you, Lilith wanted me in Oculus, since Moira had passed. Natalia was a bit lost, relying on Jonah, and it was the perfect time for me to swoop in and turn on the charm, get the new High Priestess to trust me so I could tell her all about your excursions and comings and goings." She grazed her fingernail underneath Natalia's chin.

"Once Nicholas learned of your origin, it was time to get this party started." She leaned down and got close to the High Priestess' face before she opened her mouth and snapped her teeth together. Natalia flinched, trying to pull herself backwards, her hands magically forced against the table, preventing her from moving.

"So you *were* listening to their conversation when I saw you in the apothecary. You've been a fucking creep this whole time," Elise barked.

"That Finley boy was a test of my loyalty, but of course, you know all about how that ended," Markus said with a grossly sly smile. "He was so eager to think Jonah thought so highly of him."

"Oh fuck, you needed his key to get him in Purgatory to kill him, because using your own would have given you away. You got her to cast a haze on you so we wouldn't know it was you who had his key." Reese nodded his head to Isabel, pieces of his hair framing his face. Pieces of dirt and dust were scattered along the blond strands.

"Hmm, breaking that stupid portal this pretty thing created for the demons to come through..." He side-eyed Natalia. "It was difficult, but angelic magic and the force of fed-up Enchanters can do wonders. I have to say, one demon breaking through happened earlier than I wanted, but we made do. Of course, Nicholas, you just had to try to dig deep and poke holes in certain plans, running to Jonah every chance you got, but it all worked out." Markus waggled a finger at Nick, as if reprimanding him for getting in the way of this plan.

"The demons at the ambush, you opened it so they could come through," Elise said.

Markus swiped a hand on the shoulder of his suit. "The demons at that meeting -- that was astonishing. Talk about perfect timing."

Angelic magic and the force of fed-up Enchanters.

"It takes one to make it and two to destroy it," I muttered under my breath. Isabel wrinkled her nose at me and I stared back at her. "You think my dagger is going to help you get revenge? Get everything you want, destroy this place?"

Markus picked up my dagger and moved it back and forth like a pendulum. "I want to destroy it and build from scratch. We knew that sacrifices had to be made. Lilith believes in what I want, and I will give her what she wants in return."

Elise scoffed. "You're working with the Queen of Hell. You honestly think she gives a flying fuck about what you want?"

"What does she want in return?" Nick asked, his voice low and meaningful. His skin was a little paler than normal, likely from the blood loss, but his unwavering look of determination had my heart hurting. I was still upset with how our conversation in his bedroom had gone, but that didn't mean I couldn't still feel a certain way about him.

"Now's the fun part." Isabel clapped her hands together twice and snapped her fingers, a spark of yellow magic flaring to life. The sentries keeping Jonah in place picked up the chair he was in, bringing it closer to the table. Jonah let out a huff as the chair slammed to the ground, unsettling him in his seat. There was dried blood on his face, and he looked tired, but also nervous, as if he was waiting with bated breath just like the rest of us.

I wondered why he wasn't trying to fight back, use magic of his own to save himself. Despite this man *not* being the bad guy, he was still such a mystery.

Markus rounded the table and came up to me. He leaned down so that his face was level with mine. "You are a very skilled demon. So much untapped dark magic still inside you, but you have that angelic magic begging to be free as well." He used the hooked part of my dagger to brush back a piece of my hair. "Lilith wants out of her prison, to play among the rest of us. Free the Enchanters. You are the key. She just needs you to get a little stronger." The metal from the blade grazed my temple and then my cheek, nicking my skin.

"You'd be strong enough to break Moira's magic," Isabel said, practically skipping over to Jonah, sliding her fingers along the back of his chair.

"How do you expect me to free this angelic part of myself, huh?"

Markus huffed, annoyed. "Lilith figured I could have what I wanted at the same time she got what she wanted. Isabel and I could both get what we wanted. You have a decent amount of darkness consuming you. I mean, look at what you did to poor Cullen. We needed to make sure that part of you was still strong. Now, we need to give it some light to really give you the boost you need. What better way to obtain that kind of power than taking it from someone else?" He gave me a crooked grin before slowly looking over at Jonah.

I noticed Nick widened his eyes as realization sunk in. Reese and Elise looked from each other to me and then to Jonah. Natalia flexed her fingers, trying with all the power I knew she had to get out of her magical restraints, but it was no use.

"What exactly are you asking me to do?" My voice was shaky.

"Oh, what you do best, my dear. Angelic magic is in the soul. It's still in yours. You are simply going to do what you were programmed to do. Take his soul and draw it into yourself. The highest executive's magic should be more than enough to jump start your powers. Light will call to light and all that. You'll be a force, flowing with so much power." He placed my dagger on the table and slid it over to me.

"Taking souls is one thing; consuming them is something entirely different. Only hell born demons can do that," Elise stated, her neck tattoo pulsing.

Isabel snickered. "You think so? I think you doubt how powerful your pretty High Priestess is. It seems you didn't read far enough into that book you found in your quaint little library."

Isabel knew so much because Natalia had confided in her. She had thought they had the kind of trust where what she said was sacred. That had all been a cruel lie.

"I won't do it," Natalia answered.

The blonde Enchanter just blew out a breath of annoyance. "You will. If you don't, I'll go to Oculus and snap the necks of all your beloved people. How does that sound, sweetheart?"

Natalia swallowed hard, pressing her lips together. The glitter on her shoulders and cheeks seemed to dim at Isabel's words.

"Can you really do that?" Nick asked, eyes locked on Natalia. I could smell the sweat coming off her body, the fear and anguish. I could also smell the way she tried to push that aside and be strong, even though that strength was fading with every moment we were here.

She licked her lips. "I can, but it's magic I don't like touching. My mother never used that sort of magic, so I didn't either. It takes a lot to place one soul into another; it's quite draining. Demons do it in hell, where they can feed off the magic already present."

"All I'm hearing is that you know how to do it." Isabel clucked her tongue.

I closed my eyes, feeling the dagger's pull to me as it laid in front of my eyes. "If I don't?"

Markus let out a dark laugh, as if my question was ill-advised. "You will. Look at the collateral damage your refusal would cause." He pointed at Elise, then Reese, and he made a point to turn my head so I would look right at Nick. "I don't like a mess, Soul Seether, so do us all a favor and act accordingly. You will enjoy it, I promise. You will be part of a whole new beginning."

I parted my lips to let out a solitary breath. Markus tapped the hilt of my dagger and stood up straight. I didn't know what to do. He was asking me to rip Jonah's soul out and take his angelic power for myself. He would be a shell, likely to want to die without it. He wanted me to use my enormous new hybrid powers to unlock the portal that held Lilith in place, giving her the free reign she wanted.

He wanted to tear down The Skies and rebuild it, into what, I wasn't sure. Peace wouldn't be known after that; he was blind in ever thinking that.

What about Maurice and Daya? What would happen to all those villages? Would he bring them into his chaos as well? Would Lilith send her soulless demons on them? Nick gave me a sullen look as I met his eyes. His brown irises bore into mine, and that kind of intense staring would cause a lesser creature to look away, but I couldn't. He looked at my dagger and then quickly went back to me. His face started to morph into one of contemplation, his brow furrowing. Then his eyebrows rose and his eyes flicked down to my dagger intensely. I followed them, and then he was looking at me again, as if he was trying to make me understand. I shook my head slightly, but then stopped. I understood. I understood perfectly. He was saying so much without saying anything at all.

I cleared my throat, letting the energy from my dagger fill my nostrils and trace around my neck, humming in my ears. It wanted so badly to be with me.

"I'll do it."

CHAPTER TWENTY-EIGHT

DANI

I listened to the gleeful hum of Markus hovering over me as I clenched my fingers around the end of the armrest. Isabel raised one of her eyebrows curiously but didn't say anything further. I then heard the all too familiar snarl of Elise at my left.

"What the hell? Dani, what the actual fuck?" Elise yelled, whipping her body around to try to get to me, to no avail.

"I'm actually with Elise on this, what the fuck?" Reese added, giving me one long stare, and then looking over to Nick, who remained quiet, just looking at the floor instead of meeting his best friend's eyes.

Isabel giggled, practically dancing over to my companions. "Oh, don't be mad just because she made the right choice." She patted Reese's cheek before moving along, making her way around the table to me.

Natalia's ever-knowing gaze was like looking into the sun when I made eye contact with her. It wasn't an accusing stare but one of contemplation, as if she was trying to piece together my motive and reasons. She cocked her head to the side as her eyes shifted from me to Isabel. Natalia's flawless face morphed into a scowl as she laid eyes on her former lover.

Isabel looked over my head to Markus, who simply nodded at her. The blonde leaned down so her face was parallel to my cheek. "You better not fuck this up, Soul Seether. Your friends are counting on your good behavior." She pressed a quick kiss to my cheek, snickering. Her hand hovered over my wrist and her fingertips pulsed out colorful magic that wrapped around my cuffs, sending tiny electric sparks into my skin. The magic jumped and dove into the cuff on my other wrist.

I heard a small clink as the handcuffs broke, nearly shattering as they released my wrists. The magic from my dagger could be felt immediately, and my hands were itching to be around it, consumed by it. I reached my hand out but stopped right above the leather hilt of my weapon. It spoke to me like a song that I knew all the words to. I wrapped my fingers slowly around the leather and breathed a sigh of relief. There was a welcomed warmth that flooded into my skin, sending a contrasting shiver down my spine.

Markus pulled my chair out for me as I stood up, moving each of my wrists in a circle. Everyone in the room watched me as if they were spectators at a show. It reminded me of where I came from, of what I did. I thought back to the lesser demons who would come and watch me torture and humiliate the well-deserving fuckers who came to me, the way the smell of fire would seem to unknowingly push me further into my crazed manner. This wasn't anything like Purgatory, but I didn't need the brimstone and demonic patrons to settle my need to be the best at what I did. They already knew that.

That was why I was *here*.

I swished my hips left and right as I made my way over to where Jonah sat. His eyes widened as he watched me stop in front of him, blinking and then looking away. I tilted my head to the side, my curls cascading over my shoulder. I extended my arm out, pressing the blade of my dagger underneath his chin and tilting his face up. I looked into his eyes and could practically taste the sadness and the apology. His eyes didn't look scared, which surprised me most of all. They did, however, look over my shoulder at my raven-haired angel, who had snuck a peek in our direction but turned away the moment eye contact was made.

"Make it slow, sweetheart. I want to watch him suffer," Markus said, his voice relaxed but eager.

I closed my eyes and let out a small smile before a sigh left my lips.

"Just do it," Jonah said, closing his eyes, as if he was waiting for what I was supposed to do. I felt power circulating in my toes and ankles, inching along my calves and thighs, the smell of dark magic heady and intoxicating. It enveloped my body like it had missed me, wrapping itself around my dagger, wisps of it wafting around Jonah's chin.

"Look at me," I said, my voice low and commanding.

He didn't respond and his eyes remained closed.

"*Look. At. Me.*" I made sure every word was precise. Jonah pressed his lips together and opened his eyes, accepting my command. I could see a reflection of myself in his eyes.

My pupils were nonexistent, an inky black taking over. The dark smoke was seeping off me as if my hair had gotten caught up in some type of dark fire. This transformation happens so quickly, I'm never fully aware of it. When it's out, it rages. I wanted to take, take, take, but I yanked myself back from what the darkness wanted. I thought about what I wanted, right now. I heard the tapping of Isabel's fingernails on the wooden table without having to look back at her.

"You know what I think is so *funny*, Markus?" I asked, sliding my dagger along Jonah's cheeks. The traitorous angel didn't speak, so I continued. "Is that you think that I give a fuck about what Lilith wants." I nearly felt his shoulders stiffen. "That woman stole a chance from me, and you think I will do her bidding just like that? I'm not so blinded by my revenge like you to not think of the aftermath. Lilith will get rid of you when this is through, like the trash that you are." I held the hilt of my dagger tighter, giving Jonah a small smirk as his face contorted into a dawning realization.

I turned sharply around on my heels. Markus and Isabel were staring at me, Isabel with her magic at the ready, but I didn't care. The sentries were starting to make moves to their weapons. I walked slowly, releasing dark magic near the ground in ropes. They were too focused on me to notice it. I stopped at Natalia's side, quickly looking down at her as she shifted her eyes to the space between her hands and back up at me. "I don't answer to Lilith." I twirled the dagger in between my fingers. "I don't answer to *anyone*."

I flipped the dagger so the hooked point was aimed downward. I had a death grip on it.

"Seize her!" Markus shouted, pointing in my direction.

Isabel furrowed her brow, looking annoyed and angry. "No need, I've got it." She lifted her hand quickly, the colorful shocks of light illuminating her hand. The ball of magic was growing as she started to thrust it at me, but I was quicker. I brought my dagger down in between Natalia's hands. The sound of shattering glass filled the room as opal shards clattered along the wood. The High Priestess was up on her feet in seconds, giving Isabel a cool, collected smile.

"You forget this dagger was forged straight from Hell, so that would make it more powerful than any pathetic holding spell," I mocked.

"I will kill every single one of your followers for this!" Isabel expelled that waiting ball of magic from her hand, causing Natalia to shoot out her own magic, stopping Isabel's in its tracks and sending her flying back towards the wall.

"What are you useless shits doing? Kill them! Leave the Soul Seether to me!" Markus yelled to the sentries around us, his voice cracking.

Natalia huffed out a breath, then quickly let out three bright pink darts in the direction of the others, releasing their restraints. The resounding sound of shattering magic filled my ears, but my vision was still hazy and gray. Markus still wanted me alive; he would see this through no matter the cost.

"I will make you watch all your friends die, Soul Seether. You will have nothing left."

The minute the restraints holding them were gone, the others sprang into action. The sentries around me had started to make moves towards us, but they landed on their faces and asses from my slithering ropes around their ankles to give us a better start.

"Thank fuck," Elise said as she turned around and hoisted her knee up, landing her hit right between the male sentry's legs. She kneed him in the face multiple times, relishing in the blood that spewed from his face.

I turned around and whipped my dagger out of my hand, watching it fly through the air and land into the neck of a sentry next to Jonah. He grabbed at his neck as my dagger made the wound worse, turning and twisting. Another sentry ran to my side, the redhead from earlier, her sword ready to strike. I swiveled out of the way right as she nearly sliced my side. I reached down and grabbed the sword by its shiny blade, cutting my palm. I squeezed it into my palm, feeling it slice into my flesh. The metal began to turn dark and hard, like crusted lava. It crumbled and broke apart as each piece grew black and rock-like. The sentry looked down in shock, but I took the few steps to get to her and grabbed her neck, holding out my other hand, summoning my dagger.

The weapon ripped itself out of the previous sentry's neck and sailed right into my hand. I wasted no time plunging the hooked end into her neck, lifting it at an angle as the hook ripped her skin apart. Blood spurted from her neck as her body went limp and I shoved her to the side, letting her body drop with a thud to the ground. Reese had a dark-haired sentry's head between his arms, his forearms underneath his neck as he kicked at the back of his knee, the sentry collapsing to the ground. Reese yanked the bow off his back and gathered the arrows he had.

I started to make my way to Jonah, hoping to get to the other sentry blocking him, but Nick got to him first, clearly having snagged a sword off one of the dead sentries scattered on the ground. They were putting up a fight and I was eager to end it. I narrowed my eyes at a furious Markus. Two sentries came up on either side of me, but I hopped up a few centimeters off the ground and elbowed the one at my right in the throat and kicked out my left leg, sending the one to my left flying backwards. "Did you really think I was ever going to side with you?"

The sentries from before tried to charge at me again and brought others with them, but I let darkness and fuming agitation guide my magic as I let thick onyx ribbons hook around their necks. The ribbons slithered their way up their jaws and forced their way into their throats. I could feel them suffocating, gasping for air. Their eyes were begging for mercy that would never come. I wouldn't allow it.

I jumped up onto the wooden table and stomped over to Markus, who had his fists balled up next to his sides. Before I could hop down to the other side of the table, a shot of light hit me right at the side of my face, causing me to stumble backwards off the table to the ground. I blinked my eyes open as green-ish yellow sparks bounded against the ground until they disappeared.

Fucking Isabel.

She looked menacingly crazy as she rounded the wooden table, not giving me a chance to catch her as she sent an electrical shock through my entire body, my heart feeling like it was beating rapidly, way too fast for its own good.

"Isabel, we need her!" Markus shouted.

"There will be others, I'm sure," Isabel said, her blue eyes lighting up in a colorful hue as I started to convulse, a high-pitched moan of agony leaving my throat. My darkness felt like it was being jolted and burned every time it tried to lunge at her. Suddenly, it was gone, a piercing scream in its place that wasn't my own. I looked down my body to see Elise slicing down Isabel's neck with her venomous shadowy tail. Her eyes were fire, a bright red. Isabel held her neck, slinking back, almost tripping over the bodies that littered the ground.

I noticed Nick and Jonah fighting side by side. Jonah himself had picked up a sword and held it as if it was an old friend. The way he moved with it was similar to Nick, but I could tell he had his own style. He was a bit slower, as if the wounds drained him of what would usually be quite impressive magic. He cut down two sentries, turning on his heels to dodge one blow, just to cast one himself. Nick pushed back one angel after another, suddenly busting out his wings to join Reese in the sky. Sentries filtered through the doorway, ready to fight, but this was different than out on the lawn. We weren't trying to figure out the enemy; we weren't blind to the issues.

Elise extended her hand out to me, and I took it as she hauled me up. She had a look that said *'you'll thank me for this later'*. Deep down, I was grateful for her, despite everything.

"I should have let you all fucking die when I had the chance!" Isabel screamed, her hands smeared in the black that was Elise's venom. She had clearly started to heal her neck wound as she trudged towards us.

"I think this is between you and me," Natalia said from behind the blonde, her voice back to the regal, musical tone I was used to. She wrapped her magic around Isabel's throat and mid-section, tightening as Isabel let out a huff. Natalia yanked her up and threw her over to the windows. Her body made a splat as it collided with the glass. The High Priestess didn't let her go, though; she brought Isabel back over and slammed her against the table.

Natalia created a mist around Isabel's face that floated into her eyes, her stark blue irises were no longer their original color. They were clouded and glazed, as if she was blind. Natalia forced Isabel to extend her arm on the table, palm facing up.

"Give me my sight back, you fucking bitch," Isabel spat harshly.

Natalia pressed a finger to Isabel's lips and the Enchanter couldn't move her mouth any longer. "Language, darling."

Elise rushed past me when I hadn't noticed a sentry charging my way, kicking his sword from his hands and punching him underneath his jaw. I swore I saw teeth fly out from the impact. A rumbling sound landed in my ears as I looked over at Natalia, who was now manipulating the table underneath Isabel's hand to become sharp and spiked. She flattened her hand and a jagged piece of wood shot up from the table and through her former girlfriend's hand.

I just smirked and looked around the room, locking my sights on Markus. He was dodging behind sentries, using his own people as shields. What a piece of shit. I felt bad for him, for his story. Losing someone you cared deeply for would have taken a toll on anyone, but to harbor that kind of hate for so long had to be agonizing. I hated Lilith for what she did, and we would have words soon, but decades from now, I'm sure I'd have moved on. Markus was using Jonah as a means to an end, just like Lilith was using me.

I conjured my own wings, rising towards the ceiling. I tossed my dagger up in the air, knowing it would be waiting for me when I needed it, the shadow of my wings gracing the floor below me. I dove towards Markus, who I could tell was on the verge of using his own wings when I grabbed him by the lapels of his suit jacket and brought him up with me. I used my magic to keep him steady and curl around him, constricting his airway. I heard an arrow zoom past my head, then I felt the sharp upward wind of someone falling fast. I quickly looked over my shoulder to see Reese wink at me as he collided with another angel.

I faced Markus again and snapped my fingers. My dagger was in my hand in seconds, and I had the tip hooked around his ear as I looked deep into his eyes. Before I ended him, before I finished this, there was something I needed to know. He had told us everything on his end, but there was something I just didn't quite understand.

"Why is Lilith ripping out the souls of demons?" Markus shifted his eyes around my face and smacked his lips together, as if he was fighting the words. My compulsion was too sweet to pass up. You work hard against it, but it hurts and burns. I figured sending soul-less demons after us was a way to get rid of us until we came back, but she had been doing it for a while now. It couldn't have all been for that one moment.

Markus finally spoke, the words coming out fast. "I don't know. One of those little freaks came early and I had to get rid of it, but some of the trainees found it. I had to get Isabel to erase their minds. Lilith never told us plans that didn't involve what was going on now."

He was lying. Omitting how much, I didn't know.

"You know more than that," I pressed, puncturing part of his ear and bringing the blade down. Dark red liquid oozed from the back of his ear, and he winced.

He sputtered before answering. "I did ask her about it once. She told me it was a contingency plan. She told me not to mind what she was doing and focus on the goal, that the demons she experimented with were weak anyway, so it didn't matter. She would have what she wanted from you, whether you willingly gave it or she forced it from you."

I narrowed my eyes in confusion at his words. A contingency plan? I was about to open my mouth to ask him something else when I heard a yelp from below. I looked down, taken out of my thoughts as I watched a large sentry haul Natalia back. Elise created a reddened flame in her hand and thrusted it at the sentry, who let go of Natalia as he tried to bat it away. The flame leaked into his clothes, dissolving into black liquid that caused him to let out a cry of pain.

I watched as Isabel haphazardly created a portal for herself and disappeared, the blood from her wounded hand still splattered on the wood. Natalia turned around, looking for Isabel and finding her nowhere.

"I don't know why I thought this would be easy," I heard Markus say. "Maybe all this wasn't worth it. This place is riddled with lies and tyranny." He sounded like he was mumbling nonsense.

He muttered, "I will never know his fascination with that boy." I realized I had lost my hold on him then, but right as I looked at him to get it back, he extended his arm and shot out a stream of light. I tried to cut them off, but they burned my arm, causing me to hiss out in pain. I followed them as they hit a distracted Nick right in the back as he flew up ahead. He had his sword up to strike, but the streams of light stopped him.

"Nick!" I heard Reese yell, right as a sentry tried to pierce his back. He grabbed one of his arrows and slammed it into the sentry's chest.

Nick let out a shout of pain, his back arching as if it had stunned him, before he started to fall to the ground. Jonah flew to catch him before he hit the floor.

I might not have had the best relationship with that stubborn angel at the moment, but that didn't mean I wanted to see him in pain. I cast my dagger in shadows, not needing it at the moment, and grabbed Markus by his jacket, throwing him down onto the table, causing the wood to crack and break. I landed on the table next to him and looked over to where Jonah held Nick. I tucked my wings inward so as not to completely put them away. Reese and Elise were still fighting but simultaneously looked over. Natalia had her hand pressed to a tall sentry's throat as he started to cough up blood and convulse.

I could see that Nick was breathing and his eyes flickered ever so slightly.

"The boy has done nothing to you!" Jonah shouted. I could hear a falter in his voice, as if he could have started crying.

Markus coughed as Nick blinked his eyes open, taking in deep breaths as he brought his hands out in front of him, as if trying to focus on something he could control. The top of his jacket was burnt and charred, but he wasn't bleeding severely, except for the slashes and cuts from the fight. It was as if Markus only wanted to hurt him to get a rise out of Jonah. The highest executive helped Nick sit up, placing a hand to the side of his face tenderly. It was a gesture that told me Jonah did care about him, despite keeping secrets, secrets that from what I could remember about our Divine Library visit, Markus wasn't even aware of.

I stepped on Markus' chest with my foot as he heaved out a breath. "Do what you must to me, Soul Seether. I'm about to get everything I wanted. Lilith will have what she wants with or without my involvement." He said it with so much vigor, as much as someone could when their airway was constricting. Markus tilted his head towards Jonah and Nick, letting two words slip out of his mouth.

"Kill him."

My breathing stuttered as I heard those stark words leave his lips. I pressed harder on his chest as he whooshed out air from his lungs. I could feel my boot digging into his skin, wanting to make a permanent indentation. Two sentries above us flapped their wings and headed towards the two men in front of me.

"No!" I heard myself shout. It was a foreign sound, almost strained. I bent down and grabbed Markus' head, bringing his face to mine. "Call it off!"

Markus just smiled, a smile of someone happy with his choices in the most disgusting way. I slammed his head against the wood, watching as his teeth slammed together and blood gushed from the inside of his ears. Cracks in the once pristine wood table started to develop behind his head. A sentry charged towards me, the same sentry who had burned the fuck out of my neck. He was threatening to do the same thing to the rest of my body, his hands lit up with gold and white magic as he threw light at me. I threw out my own dark magic, watching that light crumble to pieces. Tendrils of darkness quickly curled around his neck, charring his skin. The sizzling sound of the sweet karma I gave him filtered through the room.

"Watch out!" Reese yelled from above, readying his arrow in seconds as he shot down one of the sentries headed for Nick and Jonah. One of the angels was hit while the other ducked out of the way, the arrow nearly missing him. Natalia threw out her own magic, but the angel dodged it as well, determined to meet its mark. They were close, so fucking close.

Markus just laughed under me as I rallied up a burst of dark magic in my palm and was set to throw it in the angel's direction, knowing I wouldn't miss. In the last second, a sword shot upward and diagonal, stopping the angel in his tracks. Nick huffed out a breath as he barreled his sword through the angel's chest, blood coating the front of his shirt.

He looked at me as the sentry fell to the ground. His eyes moved to my hand, still covered in my own dark magic, and I could see the small sliver of a smile in his eyes, knowing I would have saved him if it had come to that. He looked a little weak but not completely down for the count.

Nick turned to look at Jonah and within seconds of our triumph, Jonah's breath stiffened. He looked down at his stomach and I watched as Nick followed the movement. The end of a long metal sword was protruding out. The sentry swiftly pulled the blade out, and Jonah sucked in a sharp breath as blood pulsed out of his open wound. Natalia blasted the sentry who had struck him with her own powerful magic, practically turning him to dust on the spot. She rushed over to Jonah as Nick stood still, watching as one of the few men he looked up to hit the ground on his knees and stagger forwards.

I placed a hand over my mouth, unable to form words.

I grabbed Markus's head and hit it against the wooden table so many times, I lost count. "You fucking piece of stupid shit! Does that make you feel better?" I screamed as the smile on his face never left, as if he was happy to die at my hands, regardless of anything else.

Jonah was his goal and he completed it. Living in the world he wanted hadn't happened, but that was not what his heart truly desired. I manifested my dagger into my hands, watching the fight around us. I needed the sentries to stop.

I pulled him up by his lapels. "How do I make them stop?" I stabbed him in the chest, curving the hook inside. He would be in pain, but he would not die just yet. He coughed, blood spilling from his mouth and splattering along his chin. He was fighting against me yet again.

"You got what you wanted; now, tell me how to make them stop! It isn't like you will live to see what happens next." I curved the dagger further, feeling the tug of his soul against the tip.

Markus spit out more blood as he tried to move his hands to put up some resistance, but I readjusted my position so that the bottom of my boots were pressing down onto his hands. He groaned in agony and my blood boiled from the enjoyment of watching it.

"Isabel, s-she c-cast a spell to contain the manipulation, just as Natalia put up a ward to cast anyone out of Oculus except an opening for you. You were a-able to come through unaffected." He took in a breath. "Break the ward and they'll stop."

I twisted the dagger more. I leaned into him, hoping he would seethe at my words. "I hope you enjoy the confines of Hell. If you thought death would bring your loved one back to you, I wouldn't count on it." I yanked the dagger out, watching as the shadowy white ball of magic hung from the tip, writhing around like a fish out of water. I gripped it in my hand, ripping it away from my weapon and looking Markus right in the eye.

I took his soul in both my hands and began to rip it in half. Souls felt like clouds, if clouds had membranes and emotions. It was everything you were, and without it, with it ripped it and torn to shreds, the reason to live was nonexistent. Markus convulsed on the ground as he strained for breath and contorted his body, as if I was doing the very action of ripping him in two. I crushed the soul in my hands and watched as his eyes glassed over, a look of vacancy taking hold. He was breathing but unmoving. I plunged my dagger into his heart, watching as he writhed for a few moments before eventually settling into his much-needed death.

I was sweating and panting, but the sweet, sweet adrenaline was the only thing I could taste. My darkness craved more of it, and it ached to do this again and again. I felt my heart pull in a different direction, a direction right in front of me. Natalia and Nick were over Jonah's slow-breathing body. I flicked my eyes up to Reese and Elise, watching as they fought seamlessly. Natalia was making sure every sentry was pushed back, turned to dust, or writhing in pain. I pushed my wings back out and flew over to Natalia, hauling her up from the ground.

I placed my hands on her upper arms, causing her to look at me, a bit stunned. "You are the only one who can stop this." Natalia looked confused, her delicate eyebrows furrowing.

"Break her barriers and this will stop."

Natalia's eyes cleared with understanding, looking around quickly and pulling her bottom lip between her teeth. Then, she nodded. "Watch my back." I dipped my head in confirmation. She placed her hands out, as if she was trying to extend them to reach all sides of the room. I didn't feel anything; I actually had no idea what the fuck she was even doing to break the wards or how that happened.

The air pulled from the room suddenly, like the walls were caving in. The fighting slowed as everyone tried to catch their breath. I looked over to Nick, who had Jonah's head on his lap, and he caught my eye. The room started to shake and the trees outside swayed and thrashed, as if they wanted out of their confines as well.

The glass from the windows were pulsing and branches from the violent trees outside were crashing into it. Natalia's whole body was glowing every hue one could imagine. Her fingertips were sparking, and the sound of glass breaking resounded against the walls, but the breaking sound was not from here -- it was from the wards destroyed out there. The air in the room was back and the feeling of heaviness on my chest was gone. A crack and then an explosive shattering boomed around us. The windows shattered, and glass blew around us, making us cover our heads.

Then, there was stillness. Not the kind of stillness of before where the eerie feeling of something bad was upon us, but the stillness of a quiet you didn't know existed. I peeked around the room and watched as Natalia seemed to sway on her feet, almost ready to fall over. I instinctively ran to her, helping her rest against my side.

The sound of swords and choice words were gone. Glass littered the ground and the cloudy murkiness of the sky peeled back to reveal dim sunlight. The smell of blood was thick, despite the copious amount of fresh air now filtering in from the broken windows.

I watched as every sentry still standing shook their heads and blinked rapidly. They looked around, trying to make sense of everything.

Natalia had done it.

CHAPTER TWENTY-NINE

NICK

The shocked look on every angel's face had me wanting to question them, have them explain to me what they remembered, or at least try to help in some way. I watched as Natalia created magic so powerful, it shook the room. Blood dripped down from my cheek where small shards of glass had struck me. As I knelt on the ground, Jonah's body in my lap, I watched as Dani hooked her arm around the High Priestess's body and started walking over to where I sat. She gracefully placed Natalia on the ground, hovering over me.

"Is he going to be alright?" Dani asked. She sounded hesitant, as if she didn't know if that was a dumb question.

I heard feet land on the ground around me as angels who were once fighting against us in the air were now remembering themselves. "I don't know," I answered as I listened to Jonah's shallow breaths and watched as his wound leaked more and more blood. I had tried to apply pressure to it with my hand, trying to stop the bleeding, but it was too deep. This place was too chaotic to try to get him to the infirmary, and who knew what the fuck the rest of this place even looked like since Markus and Isabel's take over?

Elise and Reese saddled up next to Natalia, who was just starting to catch her breath. The question was on my tongue. She caught my eye before I could ask it, answering me without me having to open my mouth. "Healing a wound this deep would take much out of me, but I will try, if that is what you want." She looked tired and her hands were shaking.

I looked up to my best friend, whose eyes were wide with worry and shock. He shoved a hand roughly through his hair but remained silent. Elise crossed her arms over her chest and just stared down at Jonah.

"Is that Jonah?"

"What the hell happened?"

"Fuck, my head!"

I felt the bodies of different angels coming closer or seeking information from each other. This was about to be a shit show of uncertainty, and I wasn't in the right mindset for it.

"Yo, Cassial, what the fuck is going on!?" An angel I knew, Ryan I think his name was, asked from behind me, his voice demanding answers. "What happened to Jonah? What happened period?"

Before I could spin around to put him in his place, a harsh voice did it for me. More specifically, a sharp-tongued demon. "Hey, kid, back off!" Elise snarled, stepping around me, causing the sentry to take a few steps back.

"Woah, woah, you're a demon."

"Nice of you to notice; there's a lot for you to catch up on," Elise mocked, looking around the room. Ryan looked from Elise to Dani, flicking his eyes back and forth to each of them. Reese pushed Elise back, causing her to practically hiss at him.

"Long story, but as for right now..." He clasped his hands around his mouth in a circle. "Everyone, follow me to the Ethereal Bastille. We have some shit to take care of! Everything will be explained on the way!" Reese looked down at me and nodded once before slowly gathering the lost angels, who seemed to follow him as if he had all the answers, which, in hindsight, he did. I was happy to hand the reins over to him and mentally decided I should do it more often. I can't always be the one in charge. It seemed I didn't need to be.

Dani sat down next to me and laid her hand on Jonah's arm.

"Do it," I told Natalia. Jonah's face was getting paler, his chest was rising and falling a little less frequently. His skin was damp and clammy.

Natalia sucked in a breath and let it out in one smooth movement. The glitter on her cheeks had returned and sparked to life every second, as if the sparkle was recharging itself. She reached her arm out, starting to place her hand on Jonah's wound when he caught her wrist. She stopped abruptly, her honey eyes widening in surprise.

Jonah released her wrist and glided his hand around her own, gracefully holding her hand. "You turned into a beautiful young woman; your mother would be so proud of you," he said between shallow breaths. Natalia smiled and squeezed his hand. "Save your strength. This fight is not over."

I screwed my face up in confusion. "What are you doing?"

Jonah looked up at me with the same look he'd given me so many times, a look that said he was in awe of me but was concerned for me at the same time. I was never one who condoned favorites, but I came to the understanding that I was clearly one of his. I never understood why. I always considered it was because I was just *that* good at what I did. I worked hard enough for it, but maybe it was more than that.

"Just let her help you," I said, frustration in my voice.

Jonah let out a strangled chuckle. "It's alright, Nicholas." He reached his arm up and squeezed my forearm. "Markus was right. I shouldn't have been so afraid of my father all those years. I should have done more. I'll have to live with that." He looked over at Natalia, who nodded her understanding, but the look on her face said he didn't need to apologize.

He closed his eyes for a moment, then opened them, his eyelids hooded. His amber eyes looked into my dark brown ones, his look stern. "Tell your father I did what he asked, I tried my best, and I hope it was good enough. That I'm sorry." I raised my eyebrows. "Tell him that–" his words trailed off a bit as he caught his breath, his eyes closing ever so slightly. "She deserved so much better."

I watched as the last words left his lips and he shut his eyes, looking as if he was going to sleep, but I knew he was gone. Gold light filtered around him, but light illuminated around us, almost blinding me as wisps of gold bounced off him. It swirled above him and dispersed, as if it was never there. When executives died, they tended to replace them like any other job, your magic just elevating with you, but high executives were an entirely different story. Jonah had his position bestowed by his father, his magic going to him when his father died, so without an heir, his magic would go...where?

I was stunned at his death and whatever came with it, but also stunned at his words. I didn't understand them whatsoever.

She deserved so much better.

I felt a hand brush my shoulder. The smell of cinnamon filled my nostrils through all the sweat, blood, and utter fucking depression that covered this place. "Do you know what he was talking about?" Dani asked.

I shook my head. I didn't know shit.

"Fuck, that burns," I said through my teeth as Natalia rubbed a healing salt along the back of my bicep. When she lifted my shirt sleeve a few moments ago, raised reddened skin caught her attention. She told a few of the healers from Oculus to bring her what she needed. Other healers had turned our infirmary into nonstop chaos.

Natalia had given Jonah one last sullen look before she told us she would portal to Oculus and bring us what we needed. The infirmary attendants here would be out cold with the rest of the angels and asking them to take over and fix our wounds would be asking too much. Soon after she left, the High Priestess returned with ample help and a furious looking Zane at her side.

"I told you going alone was dangerous, but did you listen to me?"

Zane rambled on as Natalia tuned him out. She swiftly turned around, placing her palm up against his chest, causing him to halt.

"I was just involved in a very thorough fight and found out my relationship was a complete and utter lie. Not to mention, she got away. So can you please just do as I say? Leave your '*I told you so's*' for another time." Zane let his large chest puff out, as if he wanted to argue but didn't, following behind her as she turned around to continue out of the room.

Everything had been a blur as we helped the angels from the Ethereal Bastille gain their footing again, retelling the story as best we could while trying to understand it ourselves. I took Natalia to our infirmary as she gave orders to her people. Powders, salts, and liquids in various colors and smells filtered in as they saw every one of us. Elise grumbled about not needing help from useless witches the entire time. Reese gave me a confused look as he got a wink from the Enchanter with the piercing blue eyes I had met when I'd found Elise, but he'd followed him to an empty room anyway. Then there was Dani, who let the healers guide her to her own room, but everything about her told me she was thinking, calculating, trying to figure something out.

Ariel sauntered into the room moments after Natalia finished rubbing the burning salt into my skin and had me tell him the story. He looked dirty and dazed, his haughty attitude never changing as he talked about how stupid Markus had been to think that plan of his would have succeeded. That if he had known what was going on, he could have stopped him. I had to hold in my smirk at the idea of this ass-wipe doing anything but pleading for his life. Natalia let out a hushed giggle behind me as she re-examined my coverings.

"I've already told them to take Jonah's body to a separate room and clean him up until we can have a proper ceremony." I looked him in his eyes then, but my mouth didn't form any words, so I just pressed my lips together and nodded. Natalia squeezed my shoulder, careful not to disrupt my healing wraps.

I heard footsteps thundering down the hallway and a voice I recognized all too well, a voice I had heard my entire life.

"For the love of all that's ethereal, Nicholas!" my father shouted as he stopped at the door and saw me. I knew I looked like shit and probably smelled even worse, but he jogged over to me and pulled me into the tightest hug I've ever gotten. When he pulled back, his eyes were glassy, but he held it back enough to be able to speak. "You're alright?" He looked up and down my body, as if making triple sure I had all my limbs.

I gripped my dad's arms, looking him in the eyes. "Yes, I'm fine. A little beat up, but I'll live."

Ariel cleared his throat and we both looked at him. He only looked at me, though. "I'll speak to you once we have retained some order." He gave my father a once over and sneered, turning away and out the door in seconds.

My father huffed. "He's still jealous, even now."

"Figures."

"I heard about Jonah," my father said in a low voice. Natalia seemed to make herself busy on the other side of the room.

I licked my lips. "Yeah, Ariel just told me we're going to have a proper ceremony for him when things start cleaning up."

My father looked a little pained at the mention of a ceremony, but not like he didn't want to have one. It was like it hurt him to think about having one in the first place. I had grown up with this man my entire life, but he always seemed to throw curve balls about his past at every turn. After everything that had happened, things my father still won't tell me, he still looks sullen over the death of his...friend.

"Dad, he told me to tell you he did what you asked, that he hoped it was good enough. He said he was sorry. What does any of that mean?" I was practically pleading for answers.

He furrowed his thick eyebrows as he ran his index finger over his mustache. "I told Jonah a long time ago to look after you, that's all. I told him to give you the chances you deserved but to keep you close."

"Keep me close? Dad, what does that..." I cut myself off, pushing those thoughts aside and bringing up something more interesting to me. "Dad, he said she deserved better."

The color from my father's face drained and his eyes narrowed.

He moved his eyes over to Natalia, who was keeping busy, but I knew she was listening. "Nicholas, people say a lot of things when their time is ending, things that don't make sense..."

"Maurice, did you find him?" Daya rounded the threshold and sighed in relief. A girl who could be her twin popped up behind her. She had long, dark, glossy hair pulled into a high ponytail, randomly placed purple streaks throughout it. Her skin was the same golden complexion; her eyes glowed with the same whiskey coloring. She had a septum piercing in her nose that glinted with white jewels.

Daya took the few steps it took to reach me and wrapped her arms around me. I hugged her back, my eyes lingering on the waiting girl at the door. She pulled back, giving me the same once over my dad had already given me, and stepped back. She followed my eyes, looking over her shoulder. "Oh, Nicholas, this is Alex, my daughter. She was visiting when the news started to explode. We tried to get here as fast as we could, but your father didn't want to fly without me. I haven't used my wings in so long, so I had to dig up my old portaling skills to get us all here."

Old portaling skills? Well, that was something to ask about later.

Alex could have been a spitting image of her mother's younger years. Daya was taller than her daughter, but not by much. Where Daya was lean with a narrow waist, Alex was curvy with rounded hips. She wore a ripped jean jacket and black v-neck that put her generous chest on display, which I looked away from with speed I didn't know I had.

"Hey," I said. This whole situation was probably not what she had envisioned as the backdrop for her first meeting with me.

"Hey," she echoed back, giving me a genuine smile, her full lips tilting up completely as she gave me a wave, walking over to her mom.

"Your room is all set up for you to come home and rest," my dad said, leaning against the table I was sitting on.

"I am really fucking happy I decided not to come here, I can tell you that much," Alex scoffed, tilting her head to the side and giving me a cheeky smile. Daya scolded her daughter and shook her head.

Natalia walked back over to us, standing next to me on my other side. "I think that would be good. I think we all need some time away from this place. Restoration in a time of healing, I know it well." She tucked a hair behind her ear.

"What about..." I started but she cut me off, knowing what I was going to say before I said it.

"They can stay in Oculus with me until we make our next move." She leaned into my ear so that only I could hear her. "She'll be safe there."

A knock came at the door, and we all looked in the direction of the sound. I found my heart beating, no, thumping in my chest as I locked my eyes on her. "Am I interrupting?" She had pulled her hair into a low ponytail that rested on her shoulder.

My father looked from me to Dani and back to me, clearing his throat. "Ah, no, dear, we'll go check on Reese and be back."

I grabbed my father's jacket sleeve. "What about what Jonah said, dad?"

"Nicholas, please, I've already almost lost you once. Don't give those things too much thought. Just focus on healing and getting better." I let go of his sleeve as he walked out after Daya and Alex. For now, I had to let it go.

Didn't mean I couldn't spiral, as per usual.

Dani walked further into the room, turning around and leaning against the table. I let my legs swing as I readjusted myself on the uncomfortable examination table. Natalia patted Dani's shoulder as she passed us, moving towards the door. "I'll leave you to talk. Just call for me or Zane when you're done; there are a few more wounds I need to look over, but you should be good for now." She turned towards Dani. "Have you been all cleared by the healers?"

Dani raised an eyebrow. "Sure. They gave me some stuff that smelled like shit for the burns, but other than that I can see, hear, and walk straight, so, all good."

Natalia nodded, as if that was a sufficient enough answer, and walked out, shutting the door behind her.

There was an uncomfortable silence after she left. I started to move my lips to say something, but every time I tried to form a sentence or even a syllable, nothing would come out. I had nothing to say that seemed like a perfect start to a conversation.

"Are you okay?" she asked in a concerned voice. When I looked at her, her brown eyes were trained on my face.

"Yeah." *Was I okay though?* The answer came out easily enough, but even I didn't actually believe it.

Dani squinted. "Yeah, okay, try again."

"I'm alright, really."

"Okay, so you want me to just believe that over two hours ago, you found out that one of your fearless leaders helped orchestrate this whole thing and the one leader you thought might have been the bad guy died right in front of you, and you want me to believe that you are just alright?" I opened my mouth, but she pressed on. "Not to mention the fact that you just had to fight and kill a chunk of your own people? Oh, yeah, totally alright." She shrugged in mocking, nonchalant fashion.

I shook my head, realizing I almost wanted to laugh at her words. "Why do you care?"

Dani scrubbed a hand down her face. "Nick, just because we aren't going to have this obnoxiously epic but incredibly corny love story doesn't mean I can't be a little concerned."

I pressed my lips together, not completely liking what she was saying. "How very...undemon of you?"

She poked me in my bicep. "Not just a demon." There was no laughter in her voice when she said it, like she knew it was a fact about herself, but she had no idea what to do with this new knowledge. It was inevitable, though, and it wasn't something she could hide from.

I pushed off the table and walked over to the bed at the other side of the room, retrieving my jacket. I slipped my arms through the sleeves. "I'm okay, actually. A little bit confused and shaken, but I'll be fine. I kind of have to be. This isn't over."

She let out a long breath and a joyless chuckle. "I'm well aware. Isabel got the fuck out of there and Lilith, well, she's just putting her next plan in motion. Setbacks frustrate her, but they don't stop her. It's admirable, to say the least."

"Admirable is a word for it."

She pressed her index finger to her lips, and it took everything in me to not walk over to her and replace her finger with my mouth, but she didn't want that from me. *It's because she thinks you don't want anything to do with her.* "With Jonah gone, how does that work? I mean, I saw it with my own eyes, his magic leaving him, but I mean... what now? Who do you guys bow down to now?"

I placed my hands in my pockets, shrugging. "To be determined. This hasn't happened before. I think there's something in his office that will hold his magic, like a magical urn, until we find a rightful leader. Don't quote me on any of that. Ideally, no one is worried about that right now. It's about getting this place in working condition again, getting angels ready to fight whenever it's time. Be more prepared."

Dani smirked. "Still such a good soldier. You could probably whip demons into shape if given the chance."

I rubbed the back of my neck. "I'll pass, but thanks." I hated to ask it but I had to, given everything that had happened; I had to know. "Did you ever consider it?"

"Consider what?"

"What Markus told you to do? With Jonah and your dagger?"

She was quiet for a moment. For a single moment, she looked the most innocent she had ever looked in all the time I'd known her. She truly contemplated my question, thought back to her exact feelings before she gave me an answer. "Yes."

I wasn't shocked. "Why didn't you?"

She huffed, slowly circling the examination table. "Forgetting all the parts about Lilith taking away my angelic right, if you asked me a year ago if I wanted the equal powers of both an angel and a demon, I would have first questioned if it was possible, then stopped you mid explanation and just said hell yes. Now, knowing all that power wouldn't be for me, that it would be used for someone else to do unknowingly shitty things with, I just couldn't allow that." She drummed her fingernails on the table. "I thought about having that power, knowing that Jonah sacrificed himself to help me beat Lilith, but if I did what she wanted, I don't *know* how to be both, use both sets of powers, without burning the realm down around me. I assume that's what she wanted, so in the end, I still would have lost. It was better to fight and never give myself the option. Markus was a fool and Isabel? She is just a scared little girl filled with bloodlust."

I watched as she twirled her hand in the air as dark shadows manifested and her dagger slid out from nowhere. She held onto it as if it was a part of her -- maybe it was. "It's a connection to Lilith I wish I didn't have, but there aren't too many hell-made weapons anymore, so as much as I wanted to shred this into a million pieces, I can't. It has more to do."

"You're allowed to say you aren't okay either." I volley back her words.

She lifted one side of her mouth into a small smile. "Your concern is cute, but I'm peachy. Just your everyday identity crisis. I'm not the one having angels rummage through my stuff to find contraband and then having a high executive tell me ominous things before he passes on in my lap." She pointed the hooked tip of her dagger at me.

"Ominous is an understatement." *She deserved better.*

"Any leads on what it means?"

"Well, I tried asking my dad and that went about as well as it always goes." I rolled my eyes.

"I mean, I love a man of mystery, but as hot as your dad may be, he might have a little too much mystery for me. I would say just let it be, but we both know you won't."

I ran both my hands through my hair, pulling at the strands. "This is a fucking lot for one day."

She quickly walked over to me, shooing her dagger away and placing her hands on my shoulders, careful to watch her finger placement so she didn't mess with my healing wraps. "A lot of people say things in death, whether it's nonsense or facts. I know because I've heard it all." She looked up at me from where she stood. She was so small and confident, as if she knew without a doubt that she had my full attention. "I'm going to admit, I think you are kind of adorable when you spiral, but this isn't the time for it. I know you want to go on this epic mind fuck of a journey for this information but focus on what's in front of you. You said it yourself, what happened here today isn't the end. You need to be here and focused to get all these angels ready for whatever comes." Her face was so close to mine, I could feel small wisps of her breath. She let her voice descend into a low whisper. "Because if you leave it in the hands of your best friend, every last one of you is fucked."

I snorted out a laugh as she let me go but stayed in front of me, barking out her own laughter. Our laughter held up for a moment until we went silent again.

"So, you're staying in Oculus?" I asked as she fiddled with a piece of her hair.

"Yeah, it should be nice. Plot the next steps and all that. It's not like waltzing right back into Purgatory blindly would be ideal."

I rubbed my palms together. "I'm sure Lilith is pretty furious with you. Well, both you and Elise."

She hummed. "Yeah...Elise."

"Talk to her, Dani. You might understand the situation more if you just hear her out."

She waved her hand at me, as if what I said was inconsequential. She would never stop frustrating me. "I should let you see Natalia again or your dad. I just wanted to...you know..." She waved her hand in my general direction.

"Make sure I wasn't curled up in the fetal position?"

"Yes that."

I chuckled and smirked at her. "How incredibly corny of you."

She crossed her arms over her chest and tilted her head at me, her curls bouncing and a few escaping around her face. "Don't look too deep into it. If we're on the same *team*, I'm allowed to care about a member of my *team*. When this is all over, you will have a well-rounded story about how you teamed up with a hybrid, a living legend, and defeated the big bad monster. That will make your future angelic wife give you starry eyes -- it's quite impressive." Her expression never changed as she attempted to spell out my future. "But don't worry, you can leave out the part about us fucking."

I looked at her with my mouth slightly parted, letting her words sink in. She wasn't wrong that maybe I'd had thoughts that in the future, that would be the story I would tell people. How I got paired with a demon from Purgatory and we set off on this mysterious journey of twists and turns, but ultimately defeated the enemy. It would be a story that they would tell around The Skies for as long as I was able to hear it. Now, I didn't know if that was the official story I wanted. I wanted us to win, I wanted to defeat the bad guys, but maybe–maybe–I still wanted her here when those stories were being told.

"Dani," I said, just her name singularly, but it spoke volumes to her, and she stopped me abruptly.

She shook her head. "Don't act like you don't want that kind of happily ever after ending."

"Well, I mean, sure, who doesn't? But Dani, I wanted to talk to you about all this, when I told you the truth about yourself, what I said..."

She rushed over to me, pressing her palm over my mouth, shushing me. "Today has been a lot and like I said, there are more important things to think about." She pulled her head back a small bit, stunned. "Fuck, I sound like you when I first met you; it's really fucking weird." Her hand smelled like lavender, and it was sending a relaxing wave through my senses. "What you said, how you feel, it's expected, I guess. You have standards and rules here, so my little rule follower must obey." She looked a little sad, even though I knew she was trying to be sassy. She removed her hand and I licked my lips, realizing they had gone dry.

I had told her I wanted her to choose, not so much those words, but that's what came out of my mouth. I had acted like it was the only way, but maybe I was being selfish. Every angel thinks about their life ending with a perfect partner, by the book and angelic in every way, but now, that idea rubbed me the wrong way. Purity doesn't really matter, so long as they look the part, but now, I thought back to how no one actually told me that that was how things went. I just assumed. I had never laughed or been more at ease with a female than when I was in my bed that night with her. That had to mean something.

She didn't want to change me, so why was I trying to change her?

The darkness was scary, but I had never lived in it, bared witness to its features and called it home like she had. I had only heard rumors and stories, same as with Oculus, and that turned out to be an entirely different narrative altogether. She could have torn this building down if she had taken Jonah's magic and infused it with her own. I would have been scared of her at first, most likely, but did I think she would have figured out a way to handle it, take control of it, simmer it down just so we could win?

Yes, I absolutely fucking did.

"Hmm," I answered, leaning down closer to her face. Her shoulders stiffened, as if she wasn't expecting this. "You're right. There are more important things to think about."

She blinked up at me, her eyelashes fanning over her cheeks each time.

"You should know, though, *you* are one of those important things."

"Nick, I swear to fuck if you make me sleep on that uncomfortable-ass couch again, I will run an arrow through your dick."

I walked out from my room and right into the chest of a very angry Reese. I rolled my eyes, crossing my arms over my chest.

"How about you go to sleep at *your* house then?"

He scoffed. "Yeah, my parents think I'm all tainted now that I fought beside a demon, forgetting the fact that Markus abducted us all and we almost died, but whatever."

I patted his shoulder. "Then the couch is your bed until further notice. Ariel said they're still fixing things up. He's working with Natalia for wards around the building, so it's your house, your room at The Skies with Ariel breathing down your neck, or staying here. Choose wisely."

Reese threw his hands up right as my father hustled from upstairs, giving us both a swift good morning.

"Maurice, tell your son he needs to stop being selfish and give me his bed for a few nights." My dad just laughed and shook his head, heading straight for the refrigerator. Reese grew even more frustrated. "Ugh, fine, then tell him to stop being a hog and share the good pillows."

My father slammed the fridge door and waggled his finger at Reese. His hair was still messy from waking up, but it looked like he had tried to fix it with his fingers. "Stop whining and come in here and settle down."

My father had made sure we both remained well-rested and doted on while we recovered. For all of a month, he was our in-house nurse, doing exactly what Natalia and the healers had instructed. He had me recite every single fucking thing that happened while never returning to my question from when we were in the infirmary. He only brought up Jonah when it was about the upcoming ceremony and nothing more. Jonah's last words were like a tattoo etched in my brain, but I left it at that, ready to come back to it when there were less-pressing matters. It was never far from my mind, though.

I did mention Zane, which sent him into a surprising story about the brawny Enchanter. My dad was so open about some things and so closed off about others. Daya was the same. There was no sneaking to her and gathering information, because she always said it wasn't someone's place to tell another person's story. I admired her for it, but that didn't mean I didn't huff in annoyance when she'd pat my shoulder, shaking her head.

I thought about Dani a lot, more than I liked to admit. Natalia had sent Reese and I home with drinkable pain subsiders and they luckily tasted tolerable, so once I settled into bed, my mind drifted to important things. She was important and maybe she was kind of, sort of, important to me. I was just trying to figure out how much. The pain subsiders also made me drowsy, which I was thankful for, so my mind wouldn't start drifting to thoughts about Dani that were less than honorable.

I knew she was safe in Oculus, but I still...cared.

Daya walked in through the front door, putting her hand up in a hello, while Alex shuffled in behind her, her hair changed from purple stripes to electric blue ones, grabbing a bagel from my dad's hand as she passed. She greeted Reese and I with a mouthful and sat down at the table. This had been my new normal this month, seeing Daya at my house almost every day and Alex at least three times a week. I may be twenty-three but seeing my dad cuddle and kiss his girlfriend was still gross. I was happy for him, but I didn't want to see him make out with anyone.

Things were changing around here.

There was a light outside that caught my attention and I tapped Reese on the shoulder, pointing to the window near the backdoor. He followed my gaze as the light grew brighter and then faded. A knock sounded at the door, and I hustled over to it before anyone could make a move. I pulled it open and saw Natalia looking back at me, a multicolored sparkle on her cheeks, two gold bands wrapped around her right bicep.

"Good morning, Nicholas and...family," she said, looking over my shoulder at probably a bunch of wide-eyed expressions. "Can we come in?"

Elise and Dani flanked her sides, waiting. I nodded, stepping aside and making room.

Natalia walked inside, Elise following her, her black combat boots stomping inside as she looked around. "Well, isn't this cute."

Dani slowly came in last, giving me the coolest smile I've ever seen. I had never wanted to push somebody up against a wall and feel the heat of their body more than I did right then. Maybe I just wanted to take her face between my hands and look at her. Honestly, it could have gone either way.

I had told my father and Daya about Dani, about how I found out and the aftermath. Daya had seemed unsurprised at my words, as if that made sense to her. My father wasn't exactly happy with me when I had told him about how I basically told her that I couldn't be with her or even try because of her refusal to choose. He was a little shocked when I told him I knew I was an idiot.

Daya had checked my wounds and gave me a small smile as I

rested my head against my headboard. My dad had waited for her to leave before he wrapped his knuckles on my end table. "Don't let your pride get in the way of something you want, Nicholas. Demon or angel, that girl made the choice to rally with you in the end, and that speaks volumes. Life is much more fun if you find a girl who keeps you on your toes." He chuckled to himself as he looked at me to make sure I heard him. I bit the inside of my cheek as I nodded, watching him walk out of my room.

Dani gave Daya and my father a small wave as Elise raised her middle finger proudly at Reese, who narrowed his eyes at her. Alex, being the only one besides myself to see the gesture, stifled a laugh as she broke away pieces of her food.

Natalia cleared her throat as we all focused on her.

"To what do we owe the pleasure?" my father said finally. I had overheard him and Natalia speaking about her mother when Reese and I settled into our rooms earlier this month. The conversation was long and filled with laughter and few quiet moments. They had both, along with an annoying Ariel, gone around explaining the whole ordeal to the surrounding villages and filling in parents on the fates of their children.

"We have a plan, but it's likely not one you'll be eager to assist with," Natalia answered, clasping her hands together.

"Of course, it won't be," Reese said sarcastically.

"If you're scared, just say so, Blondie," Elise said, leaning back as she sat down.

"Lilith is the main source of the problem and likely she is where Isabel has sought her refuge." Natalia's voice was disdainful as she said her ex-girlfriend's name.

"Okay, that tracks, but what does that mean for your plan?" I asked, looking from Natalia to Dani.

Dani sat on the edge of the couch, one of her long legs crossed over the other. She wore shorts that showed off the miles of brown skin I was itching to touch. She looked at me with calmness in her eyes, but calmness embedded with determination. "The plan is to go to Purgatory."

"What!?" Reese, my dad, Daya, Alex, and myself all shouted at the same time.

Natalia held up her hands. "I know, I said the same thing, but from what they tell me, not all demons are followers of Lilith. Some just want to live their lives as it is, so help could be gained. They may know things to help stop her."

"Lilith isn't coming here and waiting for her to try again is fucking torture, so I say we go straight to the source. I even know a place we can stay while we're there." Elise shrugged, as if this plan was the simplest in the world, as if the Queen of Hell wasn't angry with her.

"You want them to go to Purgatory?" my father asked, his meal planning forgotten.

Natalia turned around from her place on the couch to face my father, who had his hands braced on the back. "Yes. We have all details; everything has been thoroughly thought over. I will help in any way I can, I have people in Oculus who are as hurt by all of this as you are."

"You think this will be simple? Just go to Purgatory and save the day?" Reese said.

Elise laughed. "No one said it would be easy. I honestly don't think your angelic asses are ready for Purgatory."

"Lilith won't just kill you all on sight once you step foot down there? Angels casually in Purgatory; I can't see that going well," Alex asked, picking at pieces of her bagel.

"Potentially, but something tells me she has something planned. An instant kill isn't what she's after," Dani answered. She rubbed her hands along her thighs. "Angels or no angels, trouble is going to be found. Like Natalia said, we know people on our side, so we know where to go and where to avoid for now."

I swallowed, Daya catching my attention. "You don't even have your weapons. I'd want special ones forged at the blacksmith if you plan to carry out this crazy idea."

I winced as Reese made a groaning noise in annoyance. He hadn't been happy when they'd disposed of all the weapons found on the lawn. He had practically cried over his bow; it was hilariously heart-breaking.

"Are you open to this?" my dad asked, his eyes widened at his girlfriend.

"Come on, Maurice. Let's not pretend you wouldn't have jumped at the chance at his age."

My father scratched along his mustache and looked over at me from behind the couch. "You're a grown man, Nicholas. You've seen what a fight can do to you. It's your call. If it's what you want, if you feel confident, then so be it. I'll be a nervous wreck, but I'll back you."

This man owed me so many explanations, but they would come eventually. I hoped.

Elise clucked her tongue. "Oh, we love a supportive dad moment."

Natalia smoothed down her hair. "We're telling you this because we want your help, but you don't have to come if you don't want to." She gave me a reassuring nod.

I placed my hands in my pockets and rocked back on my heels. "What do you think?" I looked at my best friend. His hair was in waves around his face, his lips scrunched in contemplation. His face relaxed when he realized I was asking him instead of just deciding.

He let out a long groan. "Fine. I can't have you doing this shit alone."

I felt all eyes on me then, like it was now up to me. *Fuck.* Dani's eyes were the only ones I wanted contact with, so that's exactly what I did. Her eyes were waiting for me when I found them. She looked expectant as she cocked her head to one side, that cheeky smile of hers playing at the corner of her lips.

"So, *Nicholas*, what will it be?" She was pushing me in the way only she could.

Dani was the type who liked action; she wanted me to do what I felt. Words to her were pretty, but they were fleeting. I could spiral and say I needed to think about it, calculate the options, but they had a plan, and it was their turn to lead. I didn't know what it was like in this darkness, but I could find out. She was handing it to me, wanting to bring me along.

I would take it. That thing in my chest beat too hard and rapidly for me not to.

I walked over to her, looking down at where she sat and leaned over, that cinnamon scent wrapping around me. I inhaled slightly and narrowed my eyes at her, watching as her brown eyes dilated. There was still a small fire in her eyes for me, as much as she tried to subdue it. I could work with that.

She had stepped into my world, so I would do the same.

"I'm in."

EPILOGUE

LILITH

My sweet Soul Seether thinks she can simply defy my plan and nothing will happen. *Pity*. It's precious to see how settled she's become. The stories Markus would let me in on; oh, she was seeing a whole new world.

That man was a fool. He was a means to an end, and he got his ending, I suppose. Pure revenge is never the way to go. I looked over to Isabel, her hand wrapped in a bandage.

She was always my favorite.

She arrived at my feet, broken and blinded by magic. Moira's daughter was a surprising creature. She would be no bother, though.

Dani, my Soul Seether. She let the darkness take over and she killed that fool as my heart grew with pride. Isabel had looked at me as if I'd grown a third eye. I had stroked her hair and simply told her the truth.

"Sacrifices have to be made, but sweet girl, do you think I thrive off one plan alone?" Isabel beamed with confidence.

Dani and her newfound team will come for Isabel and for me, and I'll be waiting. I'll wait for her. My Soul Seether has a mind of her own, but that darkness is strong in her.

Her angelic side will continue to pull at her but will cower at every turn.

Elise was good for something, I suppose.

A mind of her own

That independent nature of hers will crumble. I'll let her think she's close. I'll let her

think she can win. Just because she refused my plans this time doesn't mean she can refuse them again.

She has something worth losing now.

Plans change. Maybe I'd been going about it all wrong when another plan formulated in my mind as Markus' revenge plot was seemingly coming together. Contingency plans are a must. Isabel simply smiled when I sent her to heal after telling her what I had in store.

Dani will be the ruin I desire for everyone around her, whether she likes it or not.

THE END

ACKNOWLEDGMENTS

Firstly, of course, the husband, who already got a spot in my dedication, but oh well, here he is again. You are my sunshine and the most annoying man I've ever met, but I honestly wouldn't have it any other way. You pushed me to finish this book and I did. Your undying support and ACTUALLY helpful ideas (I know crazy, right?) made this book a real life piece of work and I am eternally grateful for you, my love. I love you, David, forever and always.

To my mom, I love you more than the moon, the sun and the stars...to infinity and beyond.

To Brittany, Kaylah, Amanda, and Claudia...you guys are my entire bookish hearts and social media is a true mastermind for bringing us together. Each of you knows what you mean to me individually and how much you have done for this book. I never had a doubt in my mind that I had your support. Keep spamming my phone with "Have you edited today?" messages...they aren't *that* annoying.

To all the artists I've come to love along the way. You brought my babies to life and I could never truly express what that did for my motivation.

Thank you to the indie authors who helped me and advised me. Nikki St Crowe, Jenika Snow, Ashley Bennett & Marae Good, you get a virtual hug. There is so much room in the indie author community for everyone to shine, so thank you for helping me shine brighter than ever.

Lastly, to my editor, Alexa, my amazing cover designer AJ, and my formatter Deanna...you guys ROCK. Now that I know you, you can't get rid of me.

About the Author

Allie Shante was born and raised in Georgia and graduated from Georgia State University with a biology degree. While science was fun, books have always been a part of her heart and writing right up there with it. After writing and never finishing any of the books she started, she buckled down years later to finish a novel she never actually expected to write, let alone finish.

When she's not reading and writing confident females and stubborn men, she enjoys being an overprotective dog mom and crushing escape rooms with her husband.

Check her out at: www.authorallieshante.com
Follow Allie on Instagram: @allieshantewrites
Follow Allie on Tik Tok: @allieshanteauthor

Printed in Great Britain
by Amazon

32694345R00330